DATE DUE

HEAVEN'S WAGER

HEAVEN'S WAGER

TED DEKKER

WORD PUBLISHING

NASHVILLE

A Thomas Nelson Company

ISBN: 0-7394-1240-X

Printed in the United States of America

For LeeAnn, my wife,
without whose love I
would be only a shadow
of myself. I will never
forget the day you saw heaven.

1

An overhead fan swished through the afternoon heat above Padre Francis Cadione's head, squeaking once every rotation, but otherwise not a sound disturbed the silence in the small, dimly lit room. A strong smell of lemon oil mixed with pipe smoke lingered in the air. The windows on either side of the ancient desk reached tall and narrow to the ceiling and cast an amber light across the oak floor.

Some described the furnishings as gothic. Cadione preferred to think of his office as merely atmospheric. Which was fitting. He was a man of the church, and the church was all about atmosphere.

But the visitor sitting with folded hands in the burgundy guest chair had brought his own atmosphere with him. It spread like an aura of heavy perfume that dispensed with the nostrils and made straight for the spine. The man had been sitting there for less than a minute now, smiling like a banshee as though he alone knew some great secret, and already Padre Cadione felt oddly out of balance. One of the visitor's legs swung over the other like a hypnotizing pendulum. His blue eyes held their gaze on the priest's, refusing to release the connection.

The padre shifted his eyes, reached for his black pipe, and clicked its stem gently along his teeth. The small gesture of habit brought a familiar easiness. A thin tendril of tobacco smoke rose lazily past his bushy eyebrows before meeting wafts of fan-air and then scattering. He crossed his legs and realized the moment he had done so that he'd inadvertently matched the visitor's posture.

Relax, Francis. You're seeing things now. He's just a man sitting there. A man not as easily impressed as others, perhaps, but a mere man nonetheless.

"So then, my friend. You seem to be in good spirits."

"Good spirits? And what do you mean by good spirits, Padre?"

The man's gentle voice seemed to carry that strange aura with it—the one that had tingled the padre's spine. It was as though their roles had become confused. Spun around by that old ceiling fan whacking away up there.

Padre Cadione drew at the pipe and released the smoke through his lips. He spoke through the haze. Atmosphere. It was all about atmosphere.

"I only meant you seem to be pretty happy with life, despite your . . . adversity. Nothing more."

"Adversity?" The man's left brow arched. The smile below his blue eyes broadened slightly. "Adversity is a relative term, isn't it? It seems to me that if someone is *happy*, as you say, his circumstances cannot be adequately described as *adverse*. No?"

Cadione wasn't sure if the man actually wanted an answer. The question felt more like a reprimand—as if this man had risen above mere happiness and now schooled those foolish mortals who still struggled with the simple pursuit of it.

"But you are right. I am in very good spirits," the man said.

Cadione cleared his throat and smiled. "Yes, I can see that."

Thing of it was, this man was not just happy. He literally seemed thrilled with whatever had gotten under his skin. Not drugs—surely not.

The visitor sat there cross-legged, staring at him with those deep blue eyes, wearing an inviting smile. Daring him, it seemed. *Come on, Padre, do your thing. Tell me about God. Tell me about goodness and happiness and about how nothing really matters but knowing God. Tell me, tell me, tell me, baby. Tell me.*

The priest felt a small, nervous grin cross his face. That was the other thing about this man's brand of happiness. It seemed infectious, if a tad presumptuous.

Either way, the man was waiting, and Cadione could not just sit there forever contemplating matters. He owed this man something. He was, after all, a man of God, employed to shed light. Or at least to point the way to the light switch.

"Being certain of one's place in life does indeed bring one happiness," Cadione said.

"I knew you could understand, Padre! You have no idea how good it is to speak to someone who really understands. Sometimes I feel like I'm ready to burst and no one around me understands. You do understand, don't you?"

"Yes." Cadione nodded instinctively, grinning, still surprised by the man's passion.

"Exactly! People like you and I may have all the wealth in the world, but it's this other thing that is really the magic of life."

"Yes."

"Nothing compares. Nothing at all. Am I right?"

"Yes." A small chuckle escaped Cadione's lips. Goodness, he was starting to feel as though he were being led into a trap with this long string of *yeses*. There could be no doubting the man's sincerity. Or his passion, for that matter. On the other hand, the man might very well have lost his reason. Become eccentric, even senile. Cadione had seen it happen to plenty of people in the man's social strata.

The visitor leaned forward with a sparkle in his eyes. He spoke in a hushed voice now. "Have you ever seen it, Padre?"

"Seen what?" He knew he sounded far too much like a young boy sitting wide eyed at the instruction of a wise father, but Cadione was powerless to stop himself.

"The great reality behind all things." The man lifted his eyes past Cadione to a painting of God's hand reaching out to a man's on the wall behind. "The hand of God." He nodded at the painting, and the priest twisted in his seat.

"God's hand? Yes, I see it every day. Everywhere I look."

"Yes, of course. But I mean really *see*, Padre? Have you actually seen him *do* things? Not something you believe he *might* have done. Like, *Lookie there, I do believe God has opened up a parking spot near the door for us, Honey.* But have you really seen God do something before your eyes?"

The man's exuberance reignited the tingle in Cadione's spine. If the man had lost his sensibilities, perhaps he had found something better. Of course, even if God did have his fingers down here on Earth stirring the pot, people couldn't just open their eyes and *see* it. He pictured a large thumb and forefinger picking up a car and moving it to allow a van easy parking.

"Actually, I can't say that I have."

"Well, I know someone who has. I know someone who *does*."

A silence settled. The visitor stared at him with those piercing baby blues. But the eyes were not the eyes of a madman. Padre Cadione drew on the pipe, but it had lost its fire and he was rewarded with nothing but stale air.

"You do, huh?"

"I do." The man leaned back again, smiling softly. "And I have seen. Would you like to see, Padre?"

There was a magic in the man's words. A mystery that spoke of truth. He swallowed and leaned back, once again matching the visitor's posture. It occurred to him that he had not actually responded to the man's question.

"It might change your world," the man said.

"Yes. I'm sorry, I was . . . uh . . ."

"Well then." The man drew a deep breath and crossed his legs once again. "Open your mind, my friend. Wide open. Can you do that?"

"Yes . . . Yes, I suppose."

"Good. I have a story for you."

The visitor took another deep breath, thoroughly satisfied with himself, it seemed, and he began.

2

The city was Littleton, a suburb of Denver. The neighborhood was best known as Belaire, an upper-middle-class spread of homes carefully spaced along black streets that snaked between bright green lawns. The street was named Kiowa after the Indians who'd long ago called the plains their own. The home, a two-story stucco topped with a red ceramic tile roof—affectionately called the Windsor by the developer—was the most luxurious model offered in the subdivision. The man standing at the front door was Kent Anthony, the holder of the hefty mortgage on this little corner of the American dream.

In his left hand, a dozen fresh-cut red roses moved to a gentle breeze, starkly accenting the black, double-breasted suit that hung from his narrow shoulders. He stood a lanky six feet, maybe six-two with shoes. Blond hair covered his head, close cropped above the collar. His eyes sparkled blue above a sharp nose; his smooth complexion cast the illusion that he was ten years younger than his true age. Any woman might see him and think he looked like a million bucks.

But today was different. Today Kent was *feeling* like a million bucks because today Kent had actually *earned* a million bucks. Or maybe several million bucks.

The corners of his mouth lifted, and he pressed the illuminated doorbell. His heart began to race, standing right there on his front porch waiting for the large colonial door to swing open. The magnitude of his accomplishment once again rolled through his mind and sent a shudder through his bones. He, Kent Anthony, had managed what only one in ten thousand managed to achieve, according to the good people in the census bureau.

And he had done it by age thirty-six, coming from perhaps the most unlikely beginnings imaginable, starting at absolute zero. The skinny, poverty-stricken child from Botany Street who had promised his father that he would make it, no matter what the cost, had just made good on that promise. He had stretched his boundaries to the snapping point a thousand times in the last twenty years and now . . . Well, now he would stand tall and proud in the family annals. And to be truthful, he could hardly stand the pleasure of it all.

The door suddenly swung in and Kent started. Gloria stood there, her mouth parted in surprise, her hazel eyes wide. A yellow summer dress with small blue flowers settled graciously over her slender figure. A queen fit for a prince. That would be him.

"Kent!"

He spread his arms and smiled wide. Her eyes shifted to the hand holding the roses, and she caught her breath. The breeze swept past him and lifted her hair, as if invited by that gasp.

"Oh, Honey!"

He proudly offered her the bouquet and bowed slightly. In that moment, watching her strain with delight, the breeze lifting blonde strands of hair away from her slender neck, Kent felt as though his heart might burst. He did not wait for her to speak again but stepped through the threshold and embraced her. He wrapped his long arms around her waist and lifted her to meet his kiss. She returned the affection passionately and then squealed with laughter, steadying the roses behind him.

"Am I a man who keeps his word, or am I not?"

"Careful, dear! The roses. What on Earth has possessed you? It's the middle of the day!"

"*You* have possessed me," Kent growled. He set her down and pecked her cheek once more for good measure. He spun from her and bowed in mock chivalry.

She lifted the roses and studied them with sparkling eyes. "They're beautiful! Really, what's the occasion?"

Kent peeled off his coat and tossed it over the stair banister. "The occasion is you. The occasion is us. Where's Spencer? I want him to hear this."

Gloria grinned and called down the hall. "Spencer! Someone's here to see you."

A voice called from the hallway. "Who?" Spencer slid around the corner in his stocking feet. His eyes popped wide. "Dad?" The boy ran up to him.

"Hi, Tiger." Kent bent and swept Spencer from his feet in a great bear hug. "You good?"

"Sure."

Spencer wrapped his arms around his father's neck and squeezed tight. Kent set the ten-year-old down and faced them both. They stood there, picture perfect, mother and child, five-three and four-three, his flesh and blood. Behind them a dozen family pictures and as many portraits graced the entryway wall. Snapshots of the last twelve years: Spencer as a baby in powder blue; Gloria holding Spencer in front of the first apartment, lovely lime-green walls surrounded by wilting flowers; the three of them in dwelling number two's living room—a real house this time—grinning ear to ear as if the old brown sofa on which they sat was really the latest style instead of a ten-dollar afterthought purchased at some stranger's garage sale. Then the largest picture, taken two years earlier, just after they had purchased this home—house number three if you counted the apartment.

Kent saw them all in a glance, and he immediately thought a new picture would go up now. But on a different wall. A different home. A much bigger home. He glanced at Gloria and winked. Her eyes grew as if she'd guessed something.

He leaned down to his son. "Spencer, I have some very important news. Something very good has just happened to us. Do you know what it is?"

Spencer glanced at his mother with questioning eyes. He nimbly swept blond bangs from his forehead and stared up at Kent. For a moment they stood, silent.

Then his son spoke in a thin voice. "You finished?"

"And what is *finished* supposed to mean? Finished what, boy?"

"The program?"

Kent shot Gloria a wink. "Smart boy we have here. And what does that mean, Spencer?"

"Money?"

"You actually finished?" Gloria asked, stunned. "It passed?"

Kent released his son's shoulder and pumped a fist through the air. "You bet it did! This morning."

He stood tall and feigned an official announcement. "My friends, the Advanced Funds Processing System, the brainchild of one Kent Anthony, has passed all tests with flying colors. The Advanced Funds Processing System not only works, it works perfectly!"

Spencer grinned wide and whooped.

Gloria glowed proudly, reached up on her tippytoes, and kissed Kent on his chin. "Splendid job, Sir Anthony."

Kent bowed and then leapt for the living room. A catwalk spanned the two-story ceiling above; he ran under it toward the cream leather furniture. He cleared the sofa in a single bound and dropped to one knee, pumping that arm again as if he'd just caught a touchdown pass. "Yes! Yes, yes, *yes!*"

The Spanish-style interior lay immaculate about him, the way Gloria insisted it remain. Large ceramic tile ran past a breakfast bar and into the kitchen to his right. A potted palm draped over the entertainment center to his left. Directly before him, above a fireplace not yet used, stood a tall painting of Christ supporting a sagging, forsaken man holding a hammer and spikes. *Forgiven,* it was called.

He whirled to them. "Do you have any idea what this means? Let me tell you what this means."

Spencer squealed around the sofa and jumped on his knee, nearly knocking Kent to his back. Gloria vaulted the same cream leather sofa, barefooted, her yellow dress flying. She ended on her knees in the cushions, smiling wide, waiting, winking at Spencer, who had watched her make the leap.

Kent felt a fresh surge of affection seize his heart. Boy, he loved her! "This means that your father has just changed the way banks process funds." He paused, thinking about that. "Let me put it another way. Your father has just saved Niponbank millions of dollars in operating costs." He thrust a finger into the air and popped his eyes wide. "No, wait! Did I say millions of dollars? No, that would be in one year. Over the long haul, *hundreds* of millions of dollars! And do you know what big banks do for people who save them hundreds of millions of dollars?"

He stared into his son's bright eyes and answered his own question quickly before Spencer beat him to it. "They give them a few of those millions, that's what they do!"

"They've approved the bonus?" Gloria asked.

"Borst put the paperwork through this morning." He turned to the side and pumped his arm again. "Yes! Yes, yes, yes!"

Spencer slid off his knee, flopped backward on the couch, and kicked his legs into the air. "Yahoo! Does this mean we get to go to Disneyland?"

They laughed. Kent stood and stepped toward Gloria. "You bet it does." He plucked one of the roses still gripped in her hand and held it out at arm's length. "It also means we will celebrate tonight." He winked at his wife again and began to dance with the rose extended, as if it were his partner. "Wine . . ." He closed his eyes and lifted his chin. "Music . . ." He spread his arms wide and twirled once on his toes. "Exquisite food . . ."

"Lobster!" Spencer said.

"The biggest lobster you can imagine. From the tank," Kent returned and kissed the rose. Gloria laughed and wiped her eyes.

"Of course, this does mean a few small changes in our plans," Kent said, still holding up the red bud. "I have to fly to Miami this weekend. Borst wants me to make the announcement to the board at the annual meeting. It seems that my career as a celebrity has already begun."

"This weekend?" Gloria lifted an eyebrow.

"Yes, I know. Our anniversary. But not to worry, my queen. Your prince will be leaving Friday and returning Saturday. And then we will celebrate our twelfth like we have never dreamt of celebrating."

His eyes sparkled mischievously, and he turned to Spencer. "Excuse me, sire. But would Sunday or Monday suit you best for a ride on the Matterhorn?"

His son's eyes bulged. "The Matterhorn?" He gasped. "Disneyland?"

Gloria giggled. "And just how are we supposed to get to California by Sunday if you're going to Miami?"

Kent looked at Spencer, sucking a quick breath, feigning shock. "Your mother's right. It will have to be Monday, sire. Because I do fear there is no carriage that will take us to Paris in time for Sunday's games."

He let the statement stand. For a moment only the breeze sounded, flipping the kitchen curtains.

Then it came. "Paris?" Gloria's voice wavered slightly.

Kent turned his head toward her and winked. "But of course, my queen. It is, after all, the city of love. And I hear Mickey has set up shop to boot."

"You are taking us to *Paris?*" Gloria demanded, still unbelieving. The giggle had fled, chased away by true shock. "Paris, France? Can can we *do* that?"

Kent smiled. "My dear, we can do anything now." He lifted a fist of victory into the air.

"Paris!"

Then the Anthonys let restraint fly out the window, and pandemonium broke out in the living room. Spencer hooted and unsuccessfully attempted to vault the couch as his parents had. He sprawled to a tumble. Gloria rushed Kent and shrieked, not so much in shock, but because shrieking fit the mood just now. Kent hugged his wife around the waist and swung her in circles.

It was a good day. A very good day.

3

They sat there, the three of them, Gloria, Helen, and Spencer, in Helen's living room, on overstuffed green chairs, the way they sat every Thursday morning, preparing to begin their knocking. Gloria's right leg draped over her left, swinging lightly. She held folded hands on her lap and watched grandmother and grandson engage each other with sparkling eyes.

The fact that Spencer could join them came as one of the small blessings of homeschooling. She had questioned whether a boy Spencer's age would find a prayer meeting engaging, but Helen had insisted. "Children have better spiritual vision than you might think," she'd said. It only took one meeting with Helen for Spencer to agree.

At age sixty-four, Gloria's mother, Helen Crane, possessed one of the most sensitive spirits harbored in the souls of mankind. But, then, knowing her story of the years before Gloria's birth, even the most dimwitted soul would at least suspect why. She'd been to hell and back, Gloria thought, in ways very few could imagine, much less actually experience. Helen's was a story that could fill an entire volume. Suffice it to say that it had deposited her here with a crystal-clear wit and a damaged body, neither of which was noticeable at first glance. It was when she spoke that one would first hear her wit. And it was when she walked, with her limp, that others might wonder what she had endured to weaken those legs so.

Gloria's father had died when she was very young, leaving Mother alone to find solace with God. And nothing seemed to bring her that solace like the hours she spent shuffling about the house, hounding heaven, drawing near to the throne. The shuffling used to be pacing, an insistent pacing that actually began many years ago while Gloria was still a child. Gloria would often kneel on the sofa, combing the knots from her doll's hair, watching her mother step across worn carpet with lifted hands, smiling to the sky.

"I am an intercessor," Helen told her young daughter. "I speak with God."

And God spoke to her, Gloria thought. More so lately, it seemed.

Helen sat flat footed, rocking slowly in the overstuffed green rocker, her hands resting on the chair's worn arms. A perpetual smile bunched soft cheeks. Her hazel eyes glistened like jewels set in her face, which was lightly dusted with powder but otherwise free of makeup. Her silver hair curled to her ears and down to her neck. She was not as thin as she had been in her early years, but she carried the additional fifteen pounds well. The dresses her mother wore were partly responsible. She could not remember ever seeing her mother wear slacks. Today the dress was a white summer shirtwaist sprinkled with light blue roses that flowed in soft pleats to her knees.

Gloria glanced at her son, who sat with his legs crossed under him the way he always sat, Indian style. He was telling his grandmother about the upcoming trip to Disneyland with wide eyes, stumbling over his words. She smiled. They had finalized the plans last evening at Antonio's while dining on steak and lobster. Kent would leave for Miami Friday morning and return Saturday in time to catch a 6 P.M. flight to Paris. The short-notice tickets had cost the world, but the fact had only put a broader smile on her husband's face. They would arrive in France on Monday, check into some classy hotel called the Lapier, catch their breath while feasting on impossibly expensive foods, and rest for the next day's adventure. Kent was finally about to live his childhood dream, and he was setting about it with a vengeance.

Of course, Kent's success did not come without its price. It required focus, and something was bound to give in favor of that focus. In Kent's case it was his faith in God, which had never been his strong suit anyway. Within three years of their marriage, Kent's faith left him. Entirely. There was no longer room in his heart for a faith in the unseen. He was too busy chasing things he *could* see. It wasn't just an apathy—Kent did not do apathy. He either did or he did not do. It was either all out or not at all. And God became not at all.

Four years ago, just after Spencer had turned six, Helen had come to Gloria, nearly frantic. "We need to begin," she'd said.

"Begin what?" Gloria had asked.

"Begin the knocking."

"Knocking?"

"Yes, knocking—on heaven's door. For Kent's soul."

For Helen it was always either knocking or hounding.

So they had begun their Thursday morning knocking sessions then. The door to Kent's heart had not opened yet, but through it all Gloria and Spencer had peeked into heaven with Helen. What they saw had them scrambling out of bed every Thursday morning, without fail, to go to Grandma's.

And now here they were again.

"Delightful!" Helen said, flashing a smile at Gloria. "That sounds positively wonderful. I had no idea there was more than one Disneyland."

"Heavens, Mother," Gloria said. "There's been more than one Disney park for years now. You really need to get out more."

"No, thank you. No, no. I get out quite enough, thank you." She said it with a grin, but her tone rang with sincerity. "My being a stranger in that world out there is just fine by me."

"I'm sure it is. But you don't have to sequester yourself."

"Who said I was sequestering myself? I don't even know what sequestering means, for goodness' sake. And what does this have to do with my not knowing about a Disneyland in Paris, anyway?"

"Nothing. You were the one who brought up being a stranger. I'm just balancing things out a bit, that's all." God knew Helen could use a little balance in her life.

Her mother's eyes sparkled. She grinned softly, taking up the challenge. "Balance? Things are already out of balance, Honey. Upside down out of balance. You take one hundred pounds of Christian meat, and I guarantee you that ninety-eight of those pounds are sucking up to the world. It's tipping the scale right over, love." She reached up and pulled at the wrinkly skin on her neck. Nasty habit.

"Maybe, but you really don't have to use words like *sucking* to describe it. That's what I'm talking about. And how many times have I told you not to pull on your neck like that?"

Dramatics aside, Helen was right, of course, and Gloria took no offense. If anything, she warmed to her mother's indictments of society.

"It's just flesh, Gloria. See?" Helen pinched the loose skin on her arms and pulled, sampling several patches. "See, just skin. Flesh for the fire. It's what's tipping the scales the wrong way."

"Yes, but as long as you live in this world, there's no need to walk around pulling your skin in public. People don't like it." If she didn't know better, she would guess her mother senile at times.

"Well, this isn't public, for one thing, dear." Helen turned to Spencer, who sat watching the discussion with an amused smile. "It's family. Isn't that right, Spencer?"

She turned back to Gloria. "And for another thing, maybe if Christians went around pulling their skin or some such thing, people would actually know they were Christians. God knows you can't tell now. Maybe we should change our name to the Skinpullers and walk around yanking on our skin in public. That would set us apart."

Silence settled around the preposterous suggestion.

Spencer was the first to laugh, as if a dam had broken in his chest. Then Gloria, shaking her head at the ridiculous image, and finally Mother, after glancing back and forth, obviously trying to understand what was so funny. Gloria could not tell if Helen's laughter was motivated by her own skin-pulling or by their infectious cackling. Either way, the three of them had a good, long hoot.

Helen brought them back to a semblance of control, still smiling. "Well, there's more to my suggestion than what you might guess, Gloria. We laugh now, but in the end it will not seem so strange. It's this ridiculous walking around pretending not to be different that will seem crazy. I suspect a lot of heads will be banging the walls of hell in regret someday."

Gloria nodded and wiped her eyes. "Yes, you're probably right, Mother. But you do have a way with images."

Helen turned to Spencer. "Yes, now where were we when your mother so delicately diverted our discussion, Spencer?"

"Disneyland. We're going to Euro Disney in Paris," Spencer answered with a smile and a sideways glance at Gloria.

"Of course. Disneyland. Now Spencer, what do you suppose would be more fun for a day, Euro Disney or heaven?"

The sincerity descended like a heavy wool blanket.

It was perhaps the way Helen said *heaven*. As if it were a cake you could eat. That's how it was with Helen. A few words, and the hush would fall. Gloria could feel her heart tighten with anticipation. Sometimes it would begin with just a look, or a lifted finger, as if to say, Okay, let us begin. Well, now it had begun again, and Gloria sighed.

Spencer's mouth drifted into a smile. "Heaven!"

Helen lifted an eyebrow. "Why heaven?"

Most children would stutter at such a question, maybe answer with repeated words learned from their parents or Sunday school teachers. Basically meaningless words for a child, like, "To worship God." Or, "'Cause Jesus died on the cross." But not Spencer.

"In heaven . . . I think we'll be able to do . . . anything," he said.

"I think we will too," Helen said, perfectly serious. She sighed. "Well, we'll see soon enough. Today it will have to be Paris and Disneyland. Tomorrow maybe heaven. If we're so fortunate."

The room fell silent, and Helen closed her eyes slowly. Another sign.

The sound of her own breathing rose and fell in Gloria's ears. She closed her eyes and saw pinpricks in a sea of black. Her mind climbed to another consciousness. *Oh, God. Hear my son's cry. Open our eyes. Draw our hearts. Bring us into your presence.*

For a few minutes Gloria sat in the silence, displacing small thoughts and drawing her mind to the unseen. A tear gently ripped opened in heaven for her then, like a thin fracture in a wall, allowing shafts of light to filter through. In her mind's eye, she stepped into the light and let it wash warm over her chest.

The knocking started with a prayer from Helen. Gloria opened her eyes and saw that her mother had lifted her hands toward the ceiling. Her chin was raised, and her lips moved around a smile. She was asking God for Kent's soul.

For thirty minutes they prayed like that, taking turns calling on God to hear their cry, show his mercy, send word.

Near the end, Helen rose and fetched herself a glass of lemonade. She got hot, praying to heaven, she said. Being up there with all those creatures of light made her warm all over. So she invariably broke for the lemonade or ice tea at some point.

Sometimes Gloria joined her, but today she did not want to break. Today the presence was very strong, as if that crack had frozen open and continued to pour light into her chest. Which was rather unusual, because usually the tear opened and closed, allowing only bursts of light through. A thoughtful consideration by the gatekeepers, she had once decided. So as not to overwhelm the mortals with too much at once.

Thoughts of Paris had long fled, and now Gloria basked in thoughts of the unseen. Thoughts of floating, like Spencer had said. Like the pinpricks of light in the dark of her eyes. Or maybe like a bird, but in outer space, streaking through a red nebula, wide mouthed and laughing. She would give her life for it, in a heartbeat. Thinking of it now, her pulse thickened. Sweat began to bead on her forehead. Raw desire began to well up within her, as it often did. To touch *him*, to see the Creator. Watch him create. Be loved with that same power.

Helen once told her that touching God might be like touching a thick shaft of lightning, but one filled with pleasure. It might very well kill you, she said, but at least you'd die with a smile on your face. She'd chuckled and shook her head.

Her mother seated herself, slurped the lemonade for a few seconds, and set the clinking glass beside her chair. Helen sighed, and Gloria closed her eyes, thinking, *Now, where was I?*

It was then, in that moment of regularity, that the tear in heaven gaped wide, opening as it never had. They had prayed together every Thursday, every week, every month, every year for five years, and never before had Gloria even come close to feeling and seeing and hearing what she did then.

She would later think that it is when contemplating inexplicable times such as these that men say, *He is sovereign. He will do as he wills. He will come through a virgin; he will speak from a bush; he will wrestle with a man. He is God. Who can know the mind of the Lord? Amen.* And it is the end of the matter.

But it is not the end of the matter if *you* are the virgin Mary, or if *you* hear him from a bush like Moses, or if *you* wrestle with God as did Jacob. Then it is only the beginning.

It happened suddenly, without the slightest warning. As if a dam holding the light back had broken, sending volumes of the stuff cascading down in torrents. One second trickles of power, feathering just so, like lapping waves, and the next a flood that seemed to pound into the small living room and blow away the walls.

Gloria gasped and jerked upright. Two other audible heaves filled the room, and she knew that Spencer and Helen saw it as well.

The buzzing started in her feet and ran through her bones, as if her heels had been plugged into a socket and the juice cranked up. It swept up her spine, right into her skull, and hummed. She gripped the chair's padded arms to keep her hands still from their trembling.

Oh, God! she cried, only she didn't actually cry it, because her mouth had frozen wide. Her throat had seized. A soft moan came out. "Uhhhh . . ." And in that moment, with the light pouring into her skull, rattling her bones, she knew that nothing—absolutely nothing—could ever compare to this feeling.

Her heart slammed in her chest, thumping loudly in the silence, threatening to tear itself free. Tears spilled from her eyes in small rivulets before she even had time to cry. It was that kind of power.

Then Gloria began to sob. She didn't know why exactly—only that she was weeping and shaking. Terrified, yet desperate for more at once. As if her body craved more but could not contain this much pleasure in one shot. Undone.

Far away, laughter echoed. Gloria caught her breath, drawn to the sound. It came from the light, and it grew—the sound of a child's laughter. Long strings of giggles, relentlessly robbing the breath from the child. Suddenly Gloria ached to be with the child, laughing. Because there in the light, captured in a singular union of raw power and a child's unrestrained giggles, lay eternal bliss. Ecstasy. Maybe the very fabric from which energy was first conceived.

Heaven.

She knew it all in a flash.

The light vanished suddenly. Like a tractor beam pulled back into itself.

Gloria sat arched for a brief moment and then collapsed into the chair's soft cushions, her mind spinning through a lingering buzz. *Oh, God, oh, God, oh, God, I love you! Please.* She could not say the appropriate words. Perhaps there were no appropriate words. She moaned softly and went limp.

No one spoke for several long minutes. It was not until then that Gloria even remembered Helen and Spencer. When she did, it took another minute to reorient herself and begin seeing things again.

Helen sat with her face tilted to the ceiling, her hands pressed to her temples.

Gloria turned to her son. Spencer was shaking. His eyes were still closed, his hands lay on his lap, palms up, and he shook like a leaf. Giggling. With his mouth spread wide and his cheeks bunched and his face red. Giggling like that child in the light. The sight was perhaps the most perfect image she had ever witnessed.

"Jesus," her mother's soft voice groaned. "Oh, dear Jesus!"

Gloria squeezed the chair just to make sure she was not floating, because for a moment she wondered if she'd actually been taken from the chair and set on a cloud.

She looked at her mother again. Helen had clenched shut her eyes and lifted her chin so that the skin on her neck stretched taught. Her face rose ashen to the ceiling and Gloria saw then that her mother was crying. Not crying and smiling like Spencer. But crying with a face painted in horror.

"Mom?" she asked, suddenly worried.

"Oh, God! Oh, God, please. Please, no!" Helen's fingers dug deep into the chair arms. Her face grimaced as though she were enduring the extracting of a bullet without an anesthetic.

"Mother! What's wrong?" Gloria sat straight, memories of the incredible laughter dimmed by this sight before her. "Stop it, Mother!"

Helen's muscles seemed to tense at the command. She did not stop it. "Oh, please God, no! Not now. Please, please, please . . ."

From her vantage, Gloria could see the roof of her mother's mouth, surrounded by white dentures, like a pink canyon bordered by towering pearl cliffs. A groan broke from Helen's throat like moaning wind from a deep, black cavern. A chill descended Gloria's neck. She could not mistake the expression worn by Helen now—it was the face of agony.

"Nooooo!" The sound reminded Gloria of a woman in childbirth. "Noooo . . ."

"Mother! Stop it right now! You're frightening me!" She jumped up from the chair and rushed over to Helen. Up close she saw that her mother's whole face held a slight tremor. She dropped to her knee and grabbed her mother's arm.

"Mother!"

Helen's eyes snapped open, staring at the ceiling. The moan ran out of air. Her eyes skipped over the white plaster above. She mumbled softly. "What have you shown me? What have you shown me?"

She must have found herself then, because she suddenly clamped her mouth shut and dropped her head.

For a moment they stared at each other with wide eyes.

"Mom, are you okay?"

Helen swallowed and looked over to Spencer, who was now watching intently. "Yes. Yes, I am. Sit down, my dear." She shooed Gloria back to her seat. "Go sit down. You're making me nervous." Helen was obviously scrambling for reorientation, and the words came out with less than her usual authority.

Gloria stood, stunned. "Well, you scared the living daylights out of me." She retreated to her chair, trembling slightly.

When she faced Helen again, her mother was crying, her head buried in her hands. "What *is* it, Mother?"

Helen shook her head, sniffed loudly, and straightened. "Nothing, Honey. Nothing."

But it was not *nothing;* Gloria knew that.

Helen wiped her eyes and tried to smile. "Did you hear the laughter?"

Gloria glanced at her son, who was nodding already. "Yes. It was . . . it was incredible."

Spencer grinned at her. "Yeah. I heard the laughter."

They held stares, momentarily lost in the memory of that laughter, smiling silly again.

The contentment came back like a warm fog.

They sat silently for a while, numbed by what had happened. Then Helen joined them in their smiling, but she could not hide the shadows that crossed her face. Still, the laughter consumed Gloria.

At some point a small thought ran through her mind. The thought that they were leaving for Paris soon—to celebrate. But it seemed like a fleeting, inconsequential detail, like the memory that she'd brushed her teeth that morning. Too much was happening here to think of Paris.

4

Across town, Kent, light-footed and as carefree as he could remember feeling, walked up the broad steps leading to Denver's main branch of the multinational banking conglomerate Niponbank. It was an old, historic building with a face-lift of gigantic proportions. Although sections of the original wood-frame structure could still be seen on the back half of the bank, the front half appeared as grand and as modern as any contemporary building. It was the bank's way of compromising with elements in the city who did not want the building torn down. The stairway flared at street level and narrowed as it ascended, funneling patrons to three wide glass doors. Behind him eight lanes of Thursday morning's traffic bustled and blared obnoxiously, but the sound came as an anchor of familiarity, and today familiarity was good.

He smiled and smacked through the glass doors.

"Morning, Kent."

He nodded to Zak, the ever present security guard who meandered about the main lobby during business hours. "Morning, Zak. Beautiful day, isn't it?"

"Yes sir. It surely is."

Kent walked across the marble floor, nodding at several tellers who caught his eye. "Morning."

"Morning."

Mornings all around. The long row of tellers readied for business to his left. A dozen offices with picture windows now sat half-staffed on his right. Hushed tones carried through the lobby. High heels clacked along the floor to his right and he turned, half expecting to see Sidney Beech. But then, she'd already left with the others for the bank's annual conference in Miami, hadn't she? Instead it was Mary, a teller he'd met once or twice. She stepped by with a smile. Her perfume followed her in musty swirls, and Kent pulled the scent into his nostrils. Gardenia blossoms.

A dozen circular pedestals stood parallel to the long banking counter, each offering a variety of forms and golden pens to fill them out. A twenty-foot brass replica of a sailing yacht hovered five feet off the floor at the foyer's center. From a distance it appeared to be supported on a single, one-inch gold pipe under its hull. But closer inspection revealed the thin steel cables running to the ceiling. Nevertheless, the effect was stunning. Any lingering thoughts of the building's historic preservation evaporated with one look around the lobby. The architects had pretty much gutted this part of the building and started over. It was a masterpiece in design.

Kent stepped forward, toward the gaping hall opposite the entrance. There the marble floor ended, and a thick teal carpet ran into the administration wing. A large sea gull hung on the wall above the hall.

Today it all came to him like a welcoming balm. The sights, the smells, the sounds all said one word: *Success*. And today success was his.

He'd come a long way from the poor-white-trash suburbs of Kansas City. It had been the worst of all worlds—bland and boring. In most neighborhoods you either had the colors of wealth or the crimes of poverty, both of which at least introduced their own variety of spice to a boy's life. But not on Botany Street. Botany Street boasted nothing but boxy manufactured homes sporting brown lawns only occasionally greened by manual sprinklers. That was it. There were never any parades on Botany Street. There were never any fights or accidents or car chases. To a household, the neighbors along Botany Street owed their humble existence to the government. The neighborhood was a prison of sorts. Not one with bars and inmates, of course. But one to which you were sentenced with the drudgery of plowing through each day, burdened with the dogged knowledge that, even though you weren't running around stealing and killing, you were about as useful to society as those who did. Your worthless state of existence meant you would have to park your rear end here on Stupid Street and hook up to the government's mighty feeding tube. And everyone knew that those on the dole were a worthless lot.

Kent had often thought that the gangs across town had it better. Never mind that their purpose in life was to wreak as much havoc as possible without going to prison; at least they had a purpose, which was more than he could say about those on Botany Street. *Stupid Street.*

His candid observations had started during the third grade, when he'd made the decision that he was going to be Jesse Owens one day. Jesse Owens didn't need a basketball court or a big business or even a soccer ball to make the big bucks. All Jesse Owens needed were his two legs, and Kent had a pair of those. It was on his runs beyond Botany Street that Kent began to see the rest of the world. Within the year he had arrived at two conclusions. First, although he enjoyed running more than anything else in his little world, he was not cut out to be Jesse Owens. He could run long, but he could not run fast or jump far or any of the other things that Jesse Owens did.

The second thing he figured out was that he had to get off Botany Street. No matter what the cost, he and his family had to get out.

But then, as a first-generation immigrant whose parents had begged their passage to America during the Second World War, his father had never had the opportunity, much less the means to leave Botany Street.

Oh, he'd talked about it enough, all the time in fact. Sitting on the shredded brown lounger after a long day shoveling coal, in front of a black-and-white television that managed one fuzzy channel. On a good day he might have a generic beer on his lap. "I tell you, Buckwheat (his dad always called him Buckwheat), I swear I'll take us out of here one day. My folks didn't come two thousand miles on a boat to live like rabbits in someone's play box. No sir." And for a while Kent had believed him.

But his dad had never managed that journey beyond Botany Street. By the time Kent was in sixth grade he knew that if he ever wanted a life remotely similar to Jesse Owens's or even the average American's, for that matter, it would be solely up to him. And from what he could see there were only two ways to acquire a ticket for the train leaving their miserable station in life. The one ticket was pure, unsolicited fortune—winning the lottery, say, or finding a bag of cash—a prospect he quickly decided was preposterous. And the other ticket was high achievement. Super high achievement. The kind of achievement that landed people Super Bowl rings, or championship belts, or in his case, scholarships.

Beginning in grade seven he divided the sum total of his time between three pursuits. Surviving—that would be eating and sleeping and washing behind the ears now and then; running, which he still did every single day; and studying. For several hours each night he read everything he could get his spindly fingers on. In tenth grade he got a library card to the Kansas City Municipal Library, a building he figured had about every book ever written about anything. Never mind that it was a five-mile run from Botany Street; he enjoyed running anyway.

It all paid off for him one afternoon, three months after his father's death, in a single white envelope sticking out of their mail slot. He'd torn the letter out with trembling fingers, and there it was: a full academic scholarship to Colorado State University. He was leaving Stupid Street!

Some came to characterize him as a genius during his six years of higher education. In reality, his success was due much more to long hard hours with his nose in the books than to overactive gray matter.

The sweet smell of success. Yes indeed, and today, finally, success was his.

Kent walked into the hall. The back foyer was empty when he entered. Normally Norma would be sitting at the switchboard, punching buttons. Beyond her station the wide hall continued to a series of administrative divisions, each housing a suite of offices. At the hall's end, an elevator rose to three additional floors of the same. Floors four through twenty were serviced by a different elevator used by the tenants.

Kent's eyes fixed on the first door, ahead to his right, shadowed in the hall's fluorescent light. Bold, white antique letters labeled the division: Information Systems Division. Behind that door lay a small reception room and four offices. The spawning ground for Advanced Funds Processing System. His life. The division could have been placed anywhere—in a basement bunker, for all that mattered. It had little to do with the Denver branch specifically and was in fact only one of a dozen similar divisions hammering out the bank's software across the globe. Part of Niponbank's decentralization policy.

Kent walked quickly down the hall and opened the door.

His four coworkers stood in the small lobby outside of their offices, waiting for him.

"Kent! It's about time you joined us, boy!" Markus Borst beamed. His boss held a champagne glass brimming with amber liquid. A large, hooked nose gave him the appearance of a penguin. A bald penguin at that.

The redhead, Todd Brice, pushed his oversized torso from the sofa and grinned wide. "It's about time, Kent." The kid was a fool.

Betty, the department secretary, and Mary Quinn held champagne glasses they now raised to him. Red and yellow crepe paper hung in ribbons from the ceiling.

He dropped his case and laughed. He could not remember the last time the five of them had celebrated. There had been the occasional birthday cake, of course, but nothing deserving of champagne—especially not at nine o'clock in the morning.

Betty winked one of those fake black lashes. "Congratulations, Kent." Her white-blonde hair was piled a little higher than usual. She handed him a glass.

"Ladies and gentlemen," Borst announced, lifting his own glass. "Now that we are all here, I would like to propose a toast, if I may."

"Here, here," Mary chimed in.

"To AFPS, then. May she live long and prosper."

A chorus of "Here, here!s" rumbled, and together they sipped.

"And to Kent," Mary said, "who we all know made this happen!"

Another chorus of "Here, here!s," and another round of sips. Kent grinned and glanced at the light glaring off Borst's balding head.

"Gee, thanks, guys. But you know I couldn't have done it without you." It was a lie, but a good lie, he thought. In reality he could have done it easily without them. In half the time, possibly. "You guys are the best. Here's to success." He lifted his glass.

"Success," they agreed.

Borst downed the rest of his drink and set it on the coffee table with a satisfied sigh. "I say we close her down at noon today," he said. "We have a big weekend coming up. I'm not sure how much sleep we'll be getting in Miami."

Todd lifted his glass again. "To knocking off at noon," he said and threw back the balance of his drink.

Mary and Betty followed suit, mumbling agreement.

"Betty has all of your plane tickets to the Miami conference," Borst stated. "And for Pete's sake, try not to be late. If you miss the flight, you're on your own. Kent will be giving the address since he obviously knows the program as well as any of us, but I want each of you to be prepared to summarize the essentials. If things go as well as we expect, you may very well be mobbed with questions this weekend. And please, leave any mention of program bugs out of your comments for now. We don't really have any to speak of at this point, and we don't need to muddy the waters yet. Make sense?"

The man was handling himself with more authority than was customary. No one responded.

"Good, then. If you have any questions, I'll be in my office." Borst nodded theatrically and retreated to the first door on the right. Kent swallowed the last of his champagne. *That's it, Borst, go to your office and do what you always do. Nothing. Do absolutely nothing.*

"Kent." He lowered his empty glass and found Mary at his elbow, smiling brightly. Most would tag Mary as chunky, but she carried her weight well. Her brown hair was rather stringy, which did not help her image, but a clear complexion saved her from a much worse characterization. In any case, she could write basic code well enough, which was why Borst had hired her. Problem was, AFPS did not consist of much ordinary code.

"Morning, Mary."

"I just wanted to thank you for bringing us all here. I know how hard you've worked for this, and I think you deserve every bit of what you have coming."

Kent smiled. *Brown-nosing, are we, Mary?* He wouldn't put it past her, despite the innocent round eyes she now flashed up at him. She went with the flow, this one.

"Well, thanks, Mary." He patted the hand at his elbow. "You're too kind. Really."

Then Todd was there at his other elbow, as if the two had held a conference and decided that he would soon hold the keys to their futures. Time to switch their attention from the bald bossman to the rising star.

"Fantastic job, Kent!" Todd lifted his glass, which was empty, and threw it back anyway. By the looks of it, Todd had a few hidden vices.

Kent's mind flashed back to the two-year stint during graduate studies when he himself had taken to nipping at the bottle during late nights hovering over the keyboard. It was an absurd dichotomy, really. A top honors student who had found his brilliance through impeccable discipline, now slowly yielding to the lure of the bottle. A near drowning on one of his late-night runs had halted his slippery slide back to Stupid Street. It had been midwinter, and unable to muscle through a programming routine, he'd gone for a jog with half a bottle of tequila sloshing in his gut. He had misjudged a pier on the lake for a jogging path and run right off it into freezing waters. The paramedics told him if he'd not been in such good shape, he would have drowned. It was the last time he'd touched the stuff.

Kent blinked and smiled at Todd. "Thanks. Well, I've got some work to finish, so I'll see you guys tomorrow, right?"

"Bright 'n' early."

"Bright 'n' early." He nodded, and they stepped aside as though on strings. Kent walked past them to the first door on the left, across from the one through which Borst had disappeared.

This was going to be all right, he thought. Very much all right.

❦

Helen hobbled along beside her daughter in the park, eyeing the ducks waddling beside the pond, nearly as graceful as she. Walking was a thing mostly of the past for her wounded legs. Oh, she could manage about fifty yards without resting up for a while, but that was definitely it. Gloria had persuaded her to see an orthopedic doctor a year earlier, and the quack had recommended surgery. A knee replacement or some such ridiculous thing. They actually wanted to cut her open!

She'd managed a few hours of sleep last night, but otherwise it was mostly praying and wondering. Wondering about that little eye-opener God had decided to grace her with.

"It is lovely here, don't you think?" Helen asked casually. But she did not feel any loveliness at all just now.

"Yes, it is." Her daughter turned to the skating bowl in time to see Spencer fly above the concrete wall, make a grab for his skateboard in some insane inverted move, and streak back down, out of sight. She shook her head and looked back at the pond.

"I swear, that boy's gonna kill himself."

"Oh lighten up, Gloria. He's a boy, for goodness' sake. Let him live life while he's young. One day he'll wake up and find that his body doesn't fly as well as it used to. Until then, let him fly. Who knows? Maybe it brings him closer to heaven."

Gloria smiled and tossed a stick toward one of the ducks swaying its way in search of easy pickings. "You have the strangest way of putting things, Mom."

"Yes, and do you find me wrong?"

"No, not often. Although some of your analogies do stretch the mind." She reached an arm around her mother and squeezed, chuckling.

"You remember that time you suggested Pastor Madison take the cross off the church wall and carry it on his back for a week? Told him if the idea sounded silly it was only because he had not seen death up close and personal. Really, Mother! Poor fellow."

Helen smiled at the memory. Fact of it was, few Christians knew the cost of discipleship. It would have been a fine object lesson. "Yes, well, Bill's a fine pastor. He knows me now. And if he doesn't, he does a fine job pretending as though he does."

She guided her daughter by the elbow down the path. "So you leave tomorrow, then?"

"No, Saturday. We leave Saturday."

"Yes, Saturday. You leave Saturday." The air seemed to have grown stuffy, and Helen drew a deliberate breath. She stopped and looked around for a bench. The closest sat twenty yards away, surrounded by white ducks.

Gloria's voice spoke softly at her elbow. "You okay, Mother?"

Suddenly Helen was not okay. The vision strung through her mind, and she closed her eyes for a moment. Her chest felt stuffed with cotton. She swallowed hard and turned away from her daughter.

"Mother?" A cool hand encircled her biceps.

Helen fought back a flood of tears and narrowly succeeded. When she spoke, her voice warbled a bit. "You know that things are not what they seem, Gloria. You know that, don't you?"

"Yes. I know that."

"We look around here, and we see all sorts of drama unfolding about us— people marrying and divorcing and getting rich and running off to Paris."

"Mother . . ."

"And all along, the drama unfolding in the spirit world is hardly noticed but no less real. In fact, it is the real story. We just tend to forget that because we cannot see it."

"Yes."

"There are a lot of opposites in life, you know. The first will be last, and the last, first." Gloria knew this well, but Helen felt compelled to say it all, just the same. To speak like this to her only daughter. "A man finds the whole world but loses his soul. A man who loses his life finds it. A seed dies, and fruit is born. It is the way of God. You know that, don't you? I've taught you that."

"Yes, you have, and yes, I do know that. What's wrong, Mother? Why are you crying?"

"I am not crying, Honey." She faced Gloria for the first time and saw her raised eyebrows. "Do you see me weeping and wailing?" But her throat was aching terribly now, and she thought she might fall apart right here on the path.

She took a few steps into the grass and cleared her throat. "Death brings life. In many ways, you and I are already dead, Gloria. You know that, don't you?"

"Mother, you *are* crying." Her daughter turned her around as if she were a child. "You're trying not to, but I can hear it in your voice. What's wrong?"

"What would you think if I were to die, Gloria?"

Gloria's mouth parted to speak, but she said nothing. Her hazel eyes stared wide. When she did find her voice, the words came shaky.

"What do you mean?"

"Well, it's a simple enough question. If I were to pass on—die—and you buried me, what would you think?"

"That's ridiculous! How can you speak to me like that? You're nowhere near dying. You shouldn't think such thoughts."

The tension provided Helen with a wave of resolve that seemed to lighten her emotion for the moment. "No, but *if*, Gloria. If a truckdriver missed his brakes and knocked my head off my shoulders—what would you think?"

"That's terrible! I would feel terrible. How can you say such a thing? Goodness! How do you think I would feel?"

She looked directly at her daughter for a few seconds. "I didn't say *feel*, Honey. I said *think*. What would you suppose had happened?"

"I would suppose that a drunken truckdriver had killed my mother, that's what I'd think."

"Well, then you would think like a child, Gloria." She turned away and feigned a little disgust. "Humor me in my old age, dear. At least pretend that you believe what I've taught you."

Her daughter did not respond. Helen cast a sideways glance and saw that she had made the connection. "Mother, there is no end to you."

"No. No, I suppose there isn't, is there. But humor me. Please, darling."

Gloria sighed, but it was not a sigh of resignation—it was a sigh that comes when the truth has settled. "All right. I would think that you had been taken from this world. I would think that in your death, you had found life. Eternal life with God."

"Yes, and you would be right." Helen turned to face Gloria and nodded. "And what might that be like?"

Gloria blinked and turned to the pond, lost in a hazy stare. "It would be . . ." She paused, and a smile curved her lips ever so slowly. ". . . like what we saw yesterday. Laughing with God." Her eyes grew wide, and she faced Helen.

"So, then, would you want me to find that?"

Her daughter's eyebrows narrowed in question for a fleeting moment, and then she nodded slowly. "Yes. Yes, I suppose I would."

"Even if finding it meant losing this life?"

"Yes. I suppose so."

Helen smiled and drew a deep, satisfied breath. "Good."

She stepped close to Gloria, put her arms around her daughter's waist, and pulled her close. "I love you, Sweetheart," she said and rested her cheek on her daughter's shoulder.

"I love you too."

They held each other for a long moment.

"Mother?"

"Yes?"

"You're not going to die, are you?"

"Someday, I hope. The sooner the better. Either way, our worlds are about to change, Gloria. Everything is turning inside out."

5

Kent woke at 6 A.M. on Friday, instantly alert. His plane departed at nine, which gave them two hours to dress and make their way to the airport. He flung the sheets aside and swung his legs to the floor. Beside him, Gloria moaned softly and rolled over.

"Up and at 'em, Sweetheart. I've got a plane to catch."

Gloria grunted an acknowledgment and lay still, milking the waning seconds for the last of sleep, no doubt.

Kent walked under the arch into their spacious bathroom and doused his head under the tap. Fifteen minutes later he emerged, half dressed, expecting to make a trip to the kitchen to ask Gloria about his socks. But he was spared the jaunt downstairs—he would not find Gloria down there because she was still in bed with an arm draped over her face.

"Gloria? We have to leave, Sweetheart. I thought you were up."

She rolled toward him and sat up groggily. "Oh, goodness! I feel like a freight train hit me."

Her complexion looked rather peaked, at that. He sat beside her and ran a finger under her chin. "You look pale. Are you okay?"

She nodded. "Stomach's a bit upset."

"Maybe you have a touch of the flu," Kent offered. He rested a hand on her knee. "Why don't you take it easy. I can get to the airport alone."

"I wanted to take you."

"Don't worry about it. You rest up. We have a big trip tomorrow." He stood. "The twelve-hour flu has been making the rounds at the office. Who knows? Maybe I brought it home. Do you know where my navy silk socks are?"

Gloria motioned to the door. "In the dryer. Honestly, Honey, I'm fine. You sure you don't want me to take you?"

He turned and gave her a wink. "Yes, I'm sure. What's a trip to some lousy air-port? We have Paris to think about. Get some rest—I'll be fine." Kent bounded down the steps to the laundry room and rummaged around until he found the socks. He heard the clinking in the kitchen and knew then that Gloria had fol-lowed him down.

When he rounded the refrigerator, Gloria was scooping grounds into the cof-fee machine, her pink housecoat swishing at her ankles. He slid up behind her and slipped his arms around her waist. "Really, Honey. I have this handled."

She dismissed the comment with a flip of her wrist. "No. I'm feeling better already. It was probably that asparagus I ate last night. You want some coffee? The least I can do is send you away with a decent breakfast."

He kissed her on the neck. "I'd love some coffee and toast. Thank you, Sweetheart."

They ate together on the dinette set, Kent neatly dressed, Spencer rubbing sleep from his eyes, Gloria looking like she had risen from her coffin for the occa-sion. Coffee gurgled, porcelain clinked, forks clattered. Kent eyed Gloria, ignor-ing the concern that whispered through his skull.

"So, you have tennis today?"

She nodded. "One o'clock. I play Betsy Maher in the quarterfinals." She lifted a white cup to her lips and sipped. "Assuming I'm feeling better."

Kent smiled gently. "You'll be fine, Honey. I can't remember the last time you missed a match. In fact, I can't remember the last time you missed anything due to illness." Kent chuckled and bit into his toast. "Man, I remember the first time we played tennis. You remember that?"

His wife smiled. "How could I forget with your reminding me every few months."

Kent turned to Spencer. "You should've seen her, Spencer. Miss Hotshot with her tennis scholarship trying to take on a runner. She might have been able to place the ball where she wanted, but I ran her into the ground. She wouldn't stop. And I knew she was getting tired after the fourth set, because I could barely stand up and she was over there wobbling on her feet. I'd never seen anybody so competitive." He glanced at Gloria. Some color had come back into her face.

"Until she puked."

"Gross, Dad!"

"Don't look at me. Look at your mother."

Gloria just smiled. "Don't forget to tell him who won, dear."

"Yes, your mother did whip me good that day—before she puked, that is. I think I fell in love with her then, while she was bent over by the far net post."

"Gross!" Spencer giggled.

"Fell in love, ha! As I remember it, you were head over heels for some other thing in a skirt at the time."

"Perhaps. But it all began between us then."

"Well, it took you long enough to come around. We didn't even date until you were out of school."

"Yes, and look at where we are today, dear." He stood, slid his dish into the sink, and returned to kiss her on the cheek. Her skin was warm. "I think it was worth the wait, don't you?"

She smiled. "If you insist."

Twenty minutes later, Kent stood by the front door and saluted them, packed bags in hand. "Okay, you guys have the itinerary, right? I'll see you at five o'clock tomorrow night. We have a plane to catch at six. And remember to pack the camera, Honey. This is one trip that's going down in Anthony family history."

Gloria walked to him, still wrapped in her pink bathrobe. "You take care of yourself, my prince," she said and kissed him gently on the cheek. "I love you." For a moment he looked into those sparkling hazel eyes and smiled.

He bent and kissed her forehead. "And I love you. More than you could possibly know, Sweetheart."

"See you, Dad," Spencer said sheepishly. He walked over and put a flimsy arm around his father's waist.

Kent ruffled his hair. "See you, Chief. You take care of Mommy, you hear?" He kissed him on the forehead.

"I will."

He left them standing at the door, his son under his wife's arm. There was a connection between those two he could never entirely grasp. A knowing glint in their eyes that sapped his power, made him blink. It had been painfully obvious yesterday around the dinner table. But he had just made them rich; it was to be expected, he supposed. They kept exchanging glances, and when he'd finally asked them about it, they'd just shrugged.

Man, he loved them.

The flight from Denver International to Miami was an eventful one. At least for Kent Anthony it was eventful, if for no other reason than because every waking moment had become eventful. He had become a new man. And now in the DC-9 cabin, even his peers recognized him in a new light. Five others from Niponbank's Denver branch were making the belated trip to Florida for the conference. He'd meandered about the aisle, talking to all of them. And all of them had looked at him with a twinkle in their eyes. A glint of jealousy, perhaps. Or a spark of hope for their own careers. *Someday, if I'm so lucky, I will be in your shoes, Kent,* they would be thinking. Of course, there was always the possibility that the glint was actually light—a reflection from the oval windows lining the fuselage.

His boss, Markus Borst, sat three rows up with his shiny bald spot poking just above the seat like an island of sand in a black sea. Borst had worn a toupee over that bald spot all last year, discarding it only after the underhanded comments had driven him to hide for long days with a DO NOT DISTURB sign on his closed door. What the superior did behind that door, Kent could not fathom. He was certainly not breaking records for coordinating software design, as his title suggested. And when he did emerge from his cave, he did little but look over Kent's shoulder and wish he'd thought of this, or mumble about how he could have done that.

And now, within the week Borst could very well be working for him. Kent ran a finger under his collar and stretched his neck. The red tie had been a good choice. It accented the navy suit well, he thought. The perfect attire for meeting the real powerhouses in the bank's upper echelon. They would have heard about him by now, of course. Young man, firm grip, broad shoulders, brilliant mind. From the western United States. He's got the stuff.

An image of a podium facing a thousand executives around dinner tables formed in his mind. He was at the microphone. *Well, it wasn't so difficult once I constructed the advanced timing paradigm. Of course, it's all a matter of perspective. Brilliance is a function more of the destination than of the journey, and let me assure you, my friends, we have arrived at a destination never before imagined, much less traveled.* The conference hall would shake under thunderous applause. He would hold up his hand then, not emphatically but as a slight gesture. It did not take much to command.

Not so long ago, a man named Gates—Bill Gates—introduced an operating system that changed the world of computing. Today Niponbank is introducing the Advanced Funds Processing System, and it will change the world of banking. Now they would be standing, pounding their hands together. Of course, he wouldn't take direct responsibility for the work. But they would understand, just the same. At least those at the top would understand.

Beside him Will Thompson cleared his throat. "Hey, Kent. You ever wonder why some people move up the ladder so quickly and others stay put their whole careers? I mean people with the same basic skills?"

Kent looked at the forty-year-old loan manager, wondering again how the man had finagled his way on this trip. Will insisted that his boss, already in Miami, needed him to explain some innovative ideas they had been working on to some higher-ups. But Kent didn't know Will to have an innovative bone in his body. His colleague's black hair was speckled with gray, and a pair of gold-rimmed glasses sat on his nose. Yellow suspenders rode over a white shirt in good East Coast fashion. If he considered anyone at the bank a friend, it was Will.

"Hmm?"

"No, really. Look at us. I still remember the first day you skipped into the bank, what, seven years ago?" He chuckled and sipped at the martini on his tray. "You were as green as they come, man. Hair all slicked back, ready to set the office on fire. Not that I was any more experienced. I think I had a whole week on you. But we came in at the bottom, and now look at us. Making triple digits, and still climbing. And then you take someone like Tony Milkins. He came six months or so after you and he's what? A teller." Will chuckled again and sipped his drink.

Kent shrugged. "Some want it more. It all comes down to the price you're willing to pay. You and I put our dues in, worked long hours, got the right education. Shoot, if I were to sit down and calculate the time and energy I've put into making it this far, it would scare most college kids right out of school and into boot camp."

"No kidding." Will sipped again. "Then there's a few like Borst. You look at them and wonder how in God's name they ever sneaked in. You'd think his old man owned the bank."

Kent smiled and looked out the window, thinking he'd have to be careful what he said now. One day it would be him that people like Will talked about. True enough, Markus Borst was misplaced in his position, but even those well suited for their positions bore the brunt of professional criticism from the lower ranks.

"So, I guess you'll be moving up now," Will said. Kent glanced at him, noting a hint of jealousy there.

Will caught the look and laughed it off. "No, well done, my friend." He lifted a finger and raised his brows. "But watch your back. I'm right behind you."

"Sure," Kent returned with a smile.

But he was thinking that even Will knew that the notion of Will doing any such thing was an absurd little piece of nonsense. The loan manager could look forward to nothing but slipping into eventual obscurity, like a million other loan managers throughout the world. Loan managers simply did not become household names like Bill Gates or Steve Jobs. Not that it was Will's fault, really. Most people were not properly equipped; they simply did not know how to work hard enough. That was Will's problem.

It suddenly occurred to Kent that he'd just come full circle on the man. He thought of Will in the same way that Will thought of Tony Milkins. A slacker. A friendly enough slacker, but a dope nonetheless. And if Will was a slouch, then people like Tony Milkins were slugs. Ham-and-eggers. Good enough to collect a few bills here and there, but never cut out to spend them.

"Just watch your back too, Will," Kent said. "Because Tony Milkins is right there."

His friend laughed and Kent joined him, wondering if the man had caught his offhanded dig. Not yet, he guessed.

The plane touched down with a squeal of rubber, and Kent's pulse accelerated a notch. They deplaned, found their luggage, and caught two cabs to the Hyatt Regency in downtown Miami.

A porter dressed in maroon, with a tall captain's hat and a nametag that read "Pedro Gonzalas" quickly loaded their bags on a cart and led them through a spacious foyer toward the front desk. To their left, a large fountain splashed over marble mermaids in a blue pool. Palm trees grew in a perfect circle around the water, their leaves rustling in the conditioned air. Most of the guests walking about had come for the conference. Left their branches across the globe to gather in dark suits and gloat over how much money they were all making. A group of Asians laughed around a smoking table, and Kent guessed by their demeanor that they might be near the top. Important men. Or at the very least, thinking themselves important. Some of his future peers, perhaps. Like the short, white-haired one drawing most of the attention, sipping an amber drink. A man of power. Filthy rich. Two hundred and fifty dollars a night for a hotel like this would come out of his tip fund.

"Now *this* place is first class," Todd said beside him.

"That's Niponbank for you," Borst agreed. "Nothing but the best. I think they took the whole hotel. What do you think *that* cost?"

"Geez. Enough. You think we'll have open access to those little refrigerators in the rooms?"

Mary turned to Todd with a raised brow. "Of course we will. What, you think they lock them up for the programming staff? Keep their minds clear?"

"No. I know they'll be open. I mean free. You think we'll have to pay for what we take?"

Borst chuckled. "Don't be a moron, Todd. They cover the entire trip, and you're worried about free booze in little bottles. I'm sure there'll be plenty to drink at the reception. Besides, you need to keep your head clear, boy. We're not here for a party. Isn't that right, Kent?"

Kent wanted to step away from the group, disassociate himself from their small talk. They sounded more like a boy scout troop than programmers who had just changed history. He glanced around, suddenly embarrassed and hoping they had not been overheard.

"That's right," he offered and drifted a few feet to his left. If he was lucky, the onlookers wouldn't put him with this group of clowns.

They'd come to the long, cherrywood check-in counter, and Kent stepped up to a Hispanic dark-haired woman, who smiled cordially. "Welcome to the Hyatt," she said. "How may I help you?"

Well, I have just become rather important, you see, and I am wondering if you have a suite . . .

He terminated the thought. *Get a grip, man.* He smiled despite himself. "Yes, my name is Kent Anthony. I believe you have a reservation for me. I'm with the Niponbank group."

She nodded and punched a few keys. Kent leaned on the counter and looked back toward the men laughing in the lounge chairs. Several were shaking hands now, as if congratulating themselves on a job well done. *Excellent year, Mr. Bridges. Stunning profits. By the way, have you caught wind of the young man from Denver?*

The programmer? Isn't he here somewhere? Brilliant, I've heard.

"Excuse me, sir."

Kent blinked and turned back to the counter. It was the check-in clerk. The pretty dark-haired one. "Kent Anthony, correct?" she asked.

"Yes."

"We have a message for you, sir." She reached under the counter and pulled a red envelope out. Kent's pulse spiked. It was starting already then. Someone other than the bonehead troop under Borst's command had sent him a message. They had not sent it to Borst; they had addressed it to him.

"It's marked urgent," she said and handed it to him.

Kent took the envelope, flipped it open, and withdrew a slip of paper. He scanned the typed note.

At first the words did not create meaning in his mind. They just sat there in a long string. Then they made some sense, but he thought they had made a mistake. That they had given him the wrong message. That this was not *his* Gloria to which the note referred. Couldn't be.

His eyes were halfway through the note for the second time when the heat came, like a scalding liquid searing through his veins from the top of his head right down his spine. His jaw fell slack, and his hand began to quiver.

"Are you all right, sir?" a voice asked. Maybe the clerk's.

Kent read the note again.

Kent Anthony:

Your wife Gloria Anthony is in Denver Memorial hospital STOP
Complications of undiagnosed nature STOP
Condition deteriorating quickly STOP
Please return immediately STOP
End Message

Now that quiver had become a quake, and Kent felt panic edge up his throat. He whirled around to face Borst, who had missed the moment entirely. "Markus." His voice wavered.

The man turned, smiling at something Betty had just said. His lips flattened the moment he laid eyes on Kent. "What is it?"

Yes indeed! What was it? Leave these in power about him to their excesses before he'd had a chance to help them understand who he was? Leave the party in Borst's hands? Good grief! It was a preposterous notion!

Surely Gloria would be fine. Just fine.

Please return immediately, the message read. And this was Gloria.

"I have to go. I have to return to Denver." Even as he said it, he wanted to pull the words back. How could he leave now? This was the pinnacle. The men laughing over there by the fountain were about to change his life forever. He had just flown two thousand miles to meet them. He had just worked *five years* to meet them!

"I'm sorry. You'll have to take the meeting for me." He shoved the note at his boss and stumbled past him, suddenly furious at this stroke of fate.

"Great timing, Gloria," he muttered through clenched teeth, and immediately regretted the sentiment.

His bags were still on the cart, he realized, but then he didn't care where his bags were. Besides, he would be right back. By tomorrow morning, perhaps. No, tomorrow evening was the Paris trip. Maybe on the way to Paris then.

Okay, Buckwheat. Settle down. Nothing has happened here. Just a little glitch. A bug. She's only in the hospital.

Kent boarded a Yellow Cab and left the bustle at Miami's Hyatt Regency behind. Gloria would be okay. Had to be. She was in good hands. And what was one conference? A dread fell into Kent's gut, and he swallowed.

This had not been in the plans. Not at all.

6

The waiting room in Denver Memorial's ICU wing was decorated in a rust color, but in Helen's mind it was red and she wondered why they would choose the color of blood.

Helen gripped pastor Bill Madison's arm at the elbow and steered the much larger man toward the window. If anybody could understand, it would be the young, dark-haired Greek who had attracted her to the Community Church in the first place ten years earlier. He had been fresh out of seminary then—not a day over twenty-five and bubbling with love for God. Somewhere in there the church bureaucracy had tempered his passion. But Pastor Madison had never been confused about his beliefs.

He had arrived in the night sometime, but she could not remember precisely when because things were fuzzy now. They were all exhausted, that much was clear, and her knees throbbed with a dull pain. She had to sit. Behind them, Spencer sat like a lump on one of the blood-rust waiting chairs.

Helen knew her strained voice betrayed her anxiety, but given the circumstances, she hardly cared. "No. I'm not telling you I *think* I've seen this. I'm telling you I *did* see this." She squeezed hard, as if that might help him understand. "You hear me?"

Bill's dark eyes widened, but she didn't know if it came from her announcement or her squeezing. "What do you mean, you *saw* this?" he asked.

"I mean I *saw* this!" She stretched a shaking arm toward the swinging doors. "I saw my daughter in there, on that bed, that's what I saw." The anger came back as she recalled her vision, and she shook with it.

He eyed her with a raised brow, skeptical to the bone, she saw. "Come on, Helen. We all have impressions now and then. This is not a time to stretch perceptions."

"You are questioning my judgment then? You think I did not see what I say I saw?"

"I'm just saying that we shouldn't rush to conclusions at times like these. This is a time for caution, wouldn't you say? I know things are difficult, but—"

"Caution? What does caution have to do with the fact that my daughter is in there spread on the table? I saw it, I'm telling you! I don't know why I saw it or what God could possibly mean by showing it to me, but I saw it, Pastor. Every last detail."

He glanced about the room and steered her toward the window. "Okay, keep your voice down, Helen." A thin trail of sweat leaked past his temple. "When did you see this?"

"Two days ago."

"You saw all of this two days ago?"

"Isn't that what I just said?" she demanded.

"Yes." He turned from her and sat on the windowsill. His hands were shaking. Helen stood by the window.

"Look, Helen. I know you see things differently than most—"

"Don't even start, Pastor. I don't want to hear it. Not now. It would be insensitive."

"Well, I'm trying to be sensitive, Helen. And I'm thinking of the boy over there. No need to bury his mother just yet."

Helen looked toward Spencer, who sat, chin on palms, legs swinging under the chair. Dark circles looped under his bloodshot eyes. Through the night he'd slept a fitful hour, at most.

"I'm not *burying* my daughter, Bill. I am confiding in you. I saw this, and it terrifies me that it is precisely what I saw."

He did not respond to that.

She stared out the window and folded her hands. "The fact is I like it even less than you. It's gnawed at me like a cancer since that first moment. I can't seem to wrap my mind around this one, Bill." A lump rose to her throat. "I can't understand why God is doing this thing. And you would think *I* should know, of all people."

His hand reached out and rested on her shoulder. The gesture brought a sliver of comfort. "And how can you be certain it is God?"

"It doesn't matter. It is God by default. What he allows, he does."

"Maybe, but only if he is truly God. Omnipotent. All powerful. And if so, it is for him to decide why he would do such a thing."

"Yes, I *know* that, Bill! But it's my daughter in there hooked up to a machine!" She lowered her head, confused and angry at the emotions boiling up within her.

"I'm very sorry, Helen." Bill's voice sounded strained.

They remained silent for a few long moments, face to face with the impossibilities of the matter. Helen wasn't sure what she expected from him. Certainly not a pithy statement of inspiration. *Now, now there, Helen. Everything will be just fine. You'll see. Just trust in the Lord.* Heavens! She really ought to know. She'd been here before, facing the threat of death like this.

"So then, you saw more?" Bill was speaking. "Did you see her die?"

She shook her head. "No, I did not see her die."

She heard him swallow. "We should pray then," he said.

Helen tried to still her emotions. "I did not see her death, but I did see more, Bill."

He didn't answer right away. When he did, his voice came haltingly. "What . . . what did you see?"

She shook her head. "I can't say, really. I . . . I don't know."

"If you saw it, how could you not know?"

She closed her eyes, suddenly wishing she had said nothing to the man. She could hardly expect him to understand. "It was . . . hazy. Even when we see we don't always see crystal clear. Humanity has managed to dim our spiritual eyesight. But you already know that, don't you, Bill?"

He did not respond immediately, possibly offended at her condescension. "Yes," he finally offered in a weak voice.

"I'm sorry, Pastor. This is rather difficult for me. She is my daughter."

"Then let's pray, Helen. We will pray to our Father."

She nodded, and he began to pray. But her head was clogged with sorrow, and she barely heard his words.

⌒⌒⌒

Kent browsed through the trinkets in the airport gift shop, passing time, relaxing for the first time since he'd read that message eight hours earlier. He'd caught a connection to Chicago and now meandered through the concourse, waiting for the 3 A.M. redeye flight that would take him to Denver.

He bent over and wound up a toy monkey wielding small gold cymbals. The primate strutted noisily across the makeshift platform, banging its instrument and grinning obnoxiously. *Clang-ka-ching, clang-ka-ching.* Kent smiled despite the foolishness of it all. Spencer would get a kick out of the creature. For all of ten minutes possibly. Then it would end up on his closet floor, hidden under a thousand other ten-minute toys. Ten minutes for twenty dollars. It was skyway robbery.

On the other hand, it was Spencer's face grinning there for ten minutes, and the image of those lips curved in delight brought a small smile to his own.

And it was not like they didn't have the money. These were the kinds of things that were purchased by either totally irresponsible people, or people who did not bother with price. People like Tom Cruise or Kevin Costner. Or Bill Gates. He would have to get used to the idea. *You wanna live a part, you'd better start playing that part. Build it, and they will come.*

Kent tucked the monkey under his arm and sauntered over to the grown-up female trinkets neatly arranged against the wall beside racks of *I love Chicago* sweaters. Where Gloria had picked up her fascination with expensive crystal, he did not know. And now it would no longer matter, either. They were going to be rich.

He picked up a beveled cross, intricately carved with roses and bearing the words "In his death we have life." It would be perfect. He imagined her lying in some hospital bed, propped up, her green eyes beaming at the sight of the gift in his hand. *I love you, Honey.*

Kent made his way to the checkout counter and purchased the gifts.

He might as well make the best of the situation. He would call Borst the minute he got home—make sure Bonehead and his troop were not blowing things down there in Miami. Meanwhile he would stay by Gloria's side in her illness. It was his place.

And soon they would be on the plane to Paris anyway. Surely she would be able to travel. A sudden spike of panic ran up his spine. And what if the illness was more serious than just some severe case of food poisoning? They would have to cancel Paris.

But that had not happened, had it? He'd read once that 99 percent of people's fears never materialize. A man who internalized that truth could add ten years to his life.

Kent eased himself into a chair and glanced at the flight board. His plane left in two hours. Might as well catch some sleep. He sank deep and closed his eyes.

cて~◎

Spencer sat next to Helen, across from the pastor, trying to be brave. But his chest and throat and eyes were not cooperating. They kept aching and knotting and leaking. His mom had gone upstairs after seeing Dad off, saying something about lying down. Two hours and an exhaustive run through his computer games later, Spencer had called through the house only to hear her weak moan from the master bedroom. His mom was still in bed at ten o'clock. He'd knocked and entered without waiting for an answer. She lay on her side, curled into a ball like a roly-poly, groaning. Her face reminded him of a mummy on the Discovery Channel—all stretched and white.

Spencer had run for the phone and called Grandma. During the fifteen minutes it took her to reach their house he had knelt by his mother's bed, begging her to answer him. Then he had cried hard. But Mother was not answering in anything more than the occasional moan. She just lay there and held her stomach.

Grandma had arrived then, rambling on about food poisoning and ordering him around as if she knew exactly what had to be done in situations like this. But no matter how she tried to seem in control, Grandma had been a basket case.

They had literally dragged his mom to the car, and Grandma had driven her to the emergency room. Dark blue blotches spotted her skin, and he wondered how food poisoning could bring out spots the size of silver dollars. Then Spencer had overheard one of the nurses talking to an aide. She said the spots were from internal bleeding. The patient's organs were bleeding.

"I'm scared," he said in a thin, wobbly voice.

Helen took his hand and lifted it to her lips. "Don't be, Spencer. Be sad, but don't be afraid," she said, but she said it with mist in her eyes, and he knew that she was terrified too.

She pulled his head to her shoulder, and he cried there for a while. Dad was supposed to be here by now. He'd called from the airport at six o'clock and told the nurse he was catching a 9 P.M. flight with an impossible interminable layover in Chicago that wouldn't put him into Denver until 6 A.M. Well, now it was seven o'clock, and he had not arrived.

They had started putting in tubes and doing other things to Mom last night. That was when he first started thinking things were not just bad. They were terrible. When he asked Grandma why Mom was puffing up like that, she'd said that the doctors were flooding her body with antibiotics. They were trying to kill the bacteria.

"What bacteria?"

"Mommy has bacterial meningitis, Honey," Grandma had said.

A boulder had lodged in his throat then. 'Cause that sounded bad. "What does that mean? Will she die?"

"Do not think of death, Spencer," Grandma said gently. "Think of life. God will give Gloria more life than she's ever had. You will see that, I promise. Your mother will be fine. I know what happens here. It is painful now, but it will soon be better. Much better."

"So she will be okay?"

His grandmother looked off to the double swinging doors behind which the doctors attended his mom, and she started to cry again.

"We will pray that she will be, Spencer," Pastor Madison said.

Then the tears burst from Spencer's eyes, and he thought his throat might tear apart. He threw his arms around Grandma and buried his face in her shoulder. For an hour he could not stop. Just couldn't. Then he remembered that his mother was not dead, and that helped a little.

When he lifted his head he saw that Grandma was talking. Muttering with eyes closed and face strained. Her cheeks were wet and streaked. She was talking to God. Only she wasn't smiling like she usually did when she talked to him.

A door slammed, and Spencer started. He lifted his head. Dad was there, standing at the door, looking white and ragged, but here.

Spencer scrambled to his feet and ran for his father, feeling suddenly very heavy. He wanted to yell out to him, but his throat was clogged again, so he just collided with him and felt himself lifted into safe arms.

Then he began to cry again.

❧

The moment Kent slammed through the waiting room door he knew something was wrong. Very wrong.

It was in their posture, his son's and Helen's, bent over with red eyes. Spencer ran for him, and he snatched the boy to his chest.

"Everything will be all right, Spence," he muttered. But the boy's hot tears on his neck said differently, and he set him down with trembling hands.

Helen rose to her feet as he approached. "What's wrong?" he demanded.

"She has bacterial meningitis, Kent."

"Bacterial meningitis?" So that would mean what? Surgery? Or worse? Something like dialysis to grace each waking day. "How is she?" He swallowed, seeing more in those old wise eyes than he cared to see.

"Not good." She took his hand and smiled empathetically. A tear slipped down her cheek. "I'm sorry, Kent."

Now the warning bells went off—every one of them, all at once. He spun from her and ran for the swinging doors on numb legs. The sign above read "ICU." The ringing lodged in his ears, muting ordinary sounds.

Everything will be fine, Kent. Get a grip, man. His heart hammered in his ears. *Please, Gloria, please be all right. I'm here for you. I love you, Honey. Please be all right.*

He gazed around and saw white. White doors and white walls and white smocks. The smell of medicine flooded his nostrils. A penicillin-alcohol odor.

"May I help you?"

The voice came from his right, and he turned to see a figure standing behind a counter. The nurses station. She was dressed in white. His mind began to soothe his panic a bit. *See now, everything will be just fine. That's a nurse; this is a hospital. Just a hospital where they make people better. With enough technology to make your head spin.*

"May I help you?" the nurse asked again.

Kent blinked. "Yes, could you tell me where I can find Gloria Anthony? I'm her husband." He swallowed against the dryness of cotton balls seemingly stuffed in his throat.

The nurse came into better focus now, and he saw that her nametag read "Marie." She was blonde, like Gloria—about the same size. But she did not have Gloria's smile. In fact she was frowning, and Kent fought the sudden urge to reach over there and slap those lips up. *Listen lady! I'm here for my wife. Now quit looking at me like you're the Grim Reaper and take me to her!*

Marie's dark eyes looked across the hall. Kent followed the look. Two doctors bent over a hospital bed behind a large, reinforced viewing window. He made for the room without waiting for permission.

"Excuse me, sir! You cannot go in there! Sir—"

He shut her out then. Once Gloria saw him, once he looked into her beautiful hazel eyes, this madness would all end. Kent's heart rose. *Oh, Gloria . . . Sweetheart. Everything will be just fine. Please, Gloria, Honey.*

Four faces popped into his mind's eye, suddenly, simultaneously, with a brutality that made him catch himself, midstride, halfway to the room. The first was that of the wench back there with dark eyes. Grim Reaper's bride. The second was Spencer's. He saw that little face again, and it was not just worried. It was crushed. The third was Helen's sweet smiling face, but not smiling. Not at all. Wrinkled with lines of grief maybe, but not smiling. He wasn't sure he'd ever seen it that way.

One of the doctors had moved, and he saw the fourth face through the window, lying there on that bed. Only he did not recognize this face at first. It lay still, stark white under the bright lights overhead. A round, blue corrugated tube had been fed into the mouth, and an oxygen line hung from the nostrils. Purple blotches discolored the skin. The face was bloated like a pumpkin.

Kent blinked and set his foot down. But he did not move forward. Could not move forward.

Bile rose into his throat, and he swallowed hard. What this one face here could possibly have to do with the others he could not fathom. He did not know this face. Had never seen a face in such agony, so distorted in pain.

And then he did know this face. The simple truth tore through his mind like an ingot of lead crashing through his skull.

This was Gloria on the bed!

His heart was suddenly smashing against his rib cage, desperate to be out. His jaw fell slowly. A high-pitched screaming set off in his mind, denouncing this madness. Cursing this idiocy. This was no more Gloria than some body pulled from a mass grave in a war zone. How dare he be so sure? How dare he stand here frozen like some puppet when all the while everything was just fine? There had been a mistake, that was all. He should run over there and settle this.

Problem was, Kent could not move. Sweat leaked from his pores, and he began to breathe in ragged lurches. *No!* Spencer was out in the lobby, his ten-year-old boy who desperately needed Mommy. This could not be Gloria! He needed her! Sweet, innocent Gloria with a mouth that tasted of honey. Not . . . not this!

The doctor reached down and pulled the white sheet over the bloated face. And why? Why did that fool pull that sheet like that?

A grunt echoed down the hall—his grunt.

Then Kent began to move again. In four long bounds he was at the door. Someone yelled from behind, but it meant nothing to him. He gripped the silver knob and yanked hard.

The door would not budge. *Turn, then! Turn the fool thing!* He turned the knob and pulled. Now the door swung open to him, and he staggered back. In the same moment he saw the name on a chart beside the door.

Gloria Anthony.

Kent began to moan softly.

The bed was there, and he reached it in two steps. He shoved aside a white-coated doctor. People began to shout, but he could not make out their words. Now he only wanted one thing. To pull back that white sheet and prove they had the wrong woman.

A hand grabbed his wrist, and he snarled. He twisted angrily and smashed the man into the wall. "No!" he shouted. An IV pole toppled and crashed to the floor. An amber monitor spit sparks and blinked to black, but these details occurred in the distant, dark horizon of Kent's mind. He was fixated on the still, white form on the hospital bed.

Kent gripped the sheet and ripped it from the body.

A *whoosh!* sounded as the sheet floated free and then slowly settled to the ground. Kent froze. A naked, pale body laced with purple veins and blotches the size of apples lay lifeless before him. It was bloated, like a pumped-up doll, with tubes still forcing mouth and throat open.

It was Gloria.

Like a shaft of barbed iron the certainty pierced right through him. He staggered back one step, swooning badly.

The world faded from him then. He was faintly aware that he was spinning and then running. Smashing into the door, facefirst. He could not feel the pain, but he could hear the crunch when his nose broke on impact with the wooden door. He was dead, possibly. But he couldn't be dead because his heart was on fire, sending flames right up his throat.

Then he lurched past the door somehow, pelting for the swinging ICU entry, bleeding red down his shirt, suffocating. He banged through the doors, just as the first wail broke from his throat. A cry to the Supreme Being who might have had his hand in this.

"Oh, God! Oh, Gauwwwd!"

To his right, Spencer and Helen stood wide eyed, but he barely saw them. Warm blood ran over his lips, and it gave him a strange, fleeting comfort. The gutturals blared from his spread mouth, refusing to retreat. He could not stop to breathe. Back there his wife had just died.

"Oh, God! Oh, Gauwwwd!"

Kent fled through the halls, his face white and red, wailing in long deathly moans, turning every head as he ran.

A dozen startled onlookers stood aside when he broke into the parking lot, dripping blood and slobbering and gasping. The wails had run out of air, and he managed to smother them. Cars sat, fuzzy through tears, and he staggered for them.

Kent made it all the way to his silver Lexus before the futility of his flight struck him down. He slammed his fist against the hood, maybe breaking another bone there. Then he slid down the driver's door to the hot asphalt and pulled his knees to his chest.

He hugged his legs, devastated, sobbing, muttering. "Oh, God. Oh, God. Oh, God!"

But he did not feel God.

He just felt his chest exploding.

7

Kent Anthony held Spencer on his lap and gently stroked his arm. The fan whirled high above, and an old Celine Dion CD played softly, nudging the afternoon on. His son's breathing rose and fell with his own, creating a kind of cadence to help Celine in her crooning. He could not tell if Spencer was awake—they had hardly moved in over an hour. But this sitting and holding and just being alive had become the new Anthony home signature in the week or so since Gloria's sudden death.

The first day had been like a freight train smashing into his chest, over and over and over. After sobbing for some time by the Lexus he had suddenly realized that little Spencer needed him now. The poor boy would be devastated. His mother had just been snatched from him. Kent had stumbled back to the waiting room to find Helen and Spencer holding each other, crying. He'd joined them in their tears. An hour later they had driven from the hospital, dead silent and stunned.

Helen had left them in the living room and made sandwiches for lunch. The phone had rung off the hook. Gloria's church partners calling to give their condolences. None of the calls were from Kent's associates.

Kent blinked at the thought. He shifted Spencer's head so he could reach a glass of tea sitting by the couch. It was one good thing about the church, he supposed. Friends came easily. It was the *only* good thing about the church. That and their attending to the dead. Kent's mind drifted back to the funeral earlier that week. They had managed to mix some gladness into the event, and for that he was thankful, although the smiles of those around him never did spread to his own face. Still it made for a manageable ordeal. Otherwise he might have broken down, a wreck on that front pew. An image rolled through his mind: a slobbering man, dressed in black and writhing on the pew while a hundred stoic faces sang with raised hymnals. Might as well toss him in the hole as well.

A tear slipped from the corner of his right eye. They would not stop, these tears. He swallowed.

Helen and two of her old friends had sung something about the other side at the funeral. Now *there* was a religious case. Helen. After setting sandwiches before them that first day, she had excused herself and left. When she returned three hours later, she looked like a new woman. The smile had returned, her red eyes had whitened, and a buoyancy lightened her step. She had taken Spencer in her arms and hugged him dear. Then she had gripped Kent's arm and smiled warmly, knowingly. And that was it. If she experienced any more sorrow over her daughter's death, she hid it well. The fact had burned resentment into Kent's gut. Of course, he could not complain about the care she had shown them over the last ten days, busying herself with cooking and cleaning and handling the phone while Kent and Spencer floated around the house like two dead ghosts.

She was on her way to collect Spencer now. She had made the suggestion that the boy visit her for a few hours today. Kent had agreed, although the thought of being alone in the house for an afternoon brought a dread to his chest.

He ran his fingers through his son's blond hair. Now it would be him and Spencer, alone in a house that suddenly seemed too big. Too empty. Two weeks ago he had described their next house to Gloria while they dined on steak and lobster at Antonio's. The house would be twice the size of their current one, he'd told her. With gold faucets and an indoor tennis court. They could afford that now. "Imagine that, Gloria. Playing on your own air-conditioned court." His wife had smiled wide.

In his mind's eyes he saw her leaning into a forehand, her short white skirt swishing as she pivoted, and a lump rose in his throat.

He lay his head back and moaned softly. He felt trapped in an impossible nightmare. What madman had decided that it was time for his wife to die? If there was a God, he knew how to inflict pain exceptionally well. Tears blurred Kent's vision, but he held himself in check. He had to maintain some semblance of strength, for Spencer if not for himself. But it was all lunacy. How had he grown so dependent on her? Why was it that her passing had left him so dead inside?

The doctor had patiently explained bacterial meningitis to him a dozen times.

Evidently the beast lingered in over half of the population, hiding behind some cranial mucous membrane that held it at bay. Occasionally—very rarely—the stuff got past the membrane and into the bloodstream. If not caught immediately it tended to rampage its way through the body, eating up organs. In Gloria's case the disease had already set its claws into her by the time she got to the hospital. Eighteen hours later she had died.

He'd replayed that scene a thousand times. If he'd taken her to the hospital Friday morning instead of traipsing off for glory, she might be alive today.

The monkey and the cross he'd purchased as gifts still lay in his travel bag upstairs, absurd little trinkets that mocked him every time he remembered them. *"Lookie here, Spencer. Look what Daddy bought you!"*

"What is it?"

"It's a stupid monkey to help you remember Mommy's death. See, it's smiling and clapping 'cause Mom's in heaven." Gag!

And the crystal cross . . . He would smash it as soon as he built up the resolve to open that bag. The doorbell rang, and Spencer lifted his head. "Grandma?"

"Probably," Kent said, running the back of his wrist across his eyes. "Why don't you go check?"

Spencer hopped off his lap and loped for the front door. Kent shook his head and sniffed. *Get a grip, old boy. You've handled everything thrown your way for years. You can handle this.*

"Hello, Kent," Helen called, entering the room at Spencer's leading. She smiled. She was wearing a dress. A yellow dress that struck a chord of familiarity in Kent. It was the kind of dress Gloria might have worn. "How are we doing this afternoon?"

How do you think, you old kook? We've just lost our hearts, but otherwise we are just peachy. "Fine," he said.

"Yes, well I don't believe you, but it's good to see that you're making an attempt." She paused, seeing right through him, it seemed. He made no attempt to rise. Helen's eyes held his for a moment. "I'm praying for you, Kent. Things will begin to change now. In the end, they will be better. You will see."

He wanted to tell her that she could keep her prayers. That of course things would get better, because anything would be better than this. That she was an old, eccentric fossil and should keep her theories of how things would go to herself. Share them with some other cross-stitchers from the dark ages. But he hardly had the energy, much less the stomach, for the words.

"Yeah," he said. "You taking Spencer?" Of course she was. They both knew it. "Yes." She turned to the boy and laid a hand on his shoulder. "You ready?" Spencer glanced back at his father. "I'll see you soon, Dad. You okay?"

The question nearly had him blubbering. He did not want the boy to go. His heart swelled for his son, and he swallowed. "Sure, Spencer. I love you, son."

Spencer ran around the couch and hugged his neck. "It's okay, Dad. I'll be back soon. I promise."

"I know." He patted the boy's back. "Have fun."

A soft *clunk* signaled their departure through the front door. As if on cue, Celine ceased her crooning on the CD player.

Now it was just his breathing and the fan. He lifted the glass of ice tea, thankful for the tinkle of its ice.

He would sell the house now. Buy a new one, not so large. Scrap the tennis court. Put in a gym for Spencer instead.

The tall picture of Jesus holding a denim-clad man with blood on his hands stood to Kent's right. *Forgiven*, the artist had called it. They said that Jesus died for man. How could anyone follow a faith so obsessed with death? That was God, they said. Jesus was God, and he'd come to Earth to die. Then he'd asked his followers to climb on their crosses as well. So they'd made as their emblem a familiar symbol of execution, the cross, and in the beginning most of them died.

Today Jesus might have been put to death by lethal injection. An image of a needle reared in Kent's mind, and he cringed, thinking of all the needles Gloria must have endured. *Come die for me, Gloria.* It was insane.

And to think that Gloria had been so enraptured with Christianity, as if she actually expected to meet Christ someday. To climb up on that cross and float to the heavens with him. Well, now she had her chance, he supposed. Only she hadn't floated anywhere. She'd been lowered a good eight feet into red clay.

An empty hopelessness settled on Kent, and he sat there and let it hurt.

He would have to go back to work, of course. The office had sent him a bouquet of flowers, but they had made no other contact. He thought about the Miami meeting and the announcement of his program. Funny how something so important now seemed so distant. His pulse picked up at the thought. Why had they not called to tell him about the meeting?

Respect, he quickly decided. You don't just call a man who has lost his wife and segue into office talk. At least he had a bright career ahead of him. Although, without Gloria it hardly seemed bright. That would change with time.

Kent let the thoughts circle in his mind as they had endlessly for days now. Nothing seemed to fit. Everything felt loose. He could not latch on to anything offering that spark of hope that had propelled him so forcefully for years.

He leaned back and stared at the ceiling. For the moment his eyes were dry. Stinging dry.

〜〜〜

Spencer sat in his favorite green chair across from Grandma Helen with his legs crossed Indian style. He'd pulled on his white X-Games skateboard T-shirt and his beige cargo pants that morning because he loved skateboarding and he thought Mom would want him to keep doing the things he loved most. Although he hadn't actually hopped on the board yet. It had been a long time since he'd gone more than a week without taking to the street on a board.

Then again, things had changed a week ago, hadn't they? Changed forever. His dad had lost his way, it seemed. The house had become big and quiet. Their schedule had changed, or gone away, mostly. His heart hurt most of the time now.

Spencer ran his fingers through blond curls and rested his chin on his palms. This hadn't changed though. The room smelled of fresh-baked bread. The faint scent of roses drifted by—Grandma's perfume. The brown carpet lay beneath them exactly as it had two weeks ago; the overstuffed chairs had not been moved; sparkling china with little blue flowers still lined an antique-looking cabinet on the wall. A hundred knickknacks, mostly white porcelain painted with accents of blue and red and yellow, sat in groupings around the room and on the walls.

The large case Grandma called a hutch hugged the wall leading to the kitchen. Its engraved lead-glass doors rested closed, distorting his vision of its contents, but he could see well enough. A small crystal bottle, maybe five inches high, stood in the middle of the top shelf. The contents looked almost black to him. Maybe maroon or red, although he'd never been good with all those weird names of colors. Grandma had once told him that nothing in the hutch mattered to her much, except that one crystal bottle. It, she said, symbolized the greatest power on earth. The power of love. And a tear had come to her eye as she said it. When he had asked her what was in the bottle, she had just turned her head, all choked up.

The large picture of Jesus rested quietly on the wall to their right. The Son of God was spread on a cross, a crown of thorns responsible for the thin trails of red on his cheek. He stared directly at Spencer with sad blue eyes, and at the moment, Spencer didn't know what to think about that.

"Spencer."

He turned to face Grandma, sitting across from him, smiling gently. A knowing glint shone in those hazel eyes. She held a glass of ice tea in both hands comfortably.

"Are you okay, Honey?"

Spencer nodded, suddenly feeling strangely at home. Mom wasn't here, of course, but everything else was. "I think so."

Helen tilted her head and shook it slowly, empathy rich in her eyes. "Oh, my poor child. I'm so sorry." A tear slipped down her cheek, and she let it fall. She sniffed once.

"But this will pass, son. Sooner than you know."

"Yeah, that's what everybody says." A lump rose in his throat, and he swallowed. He didn't want to cry. Not now.

"I've wanted to talk to you ever since Gloria left us," Helen said, now with a hint of authority. She had something to say, and Spencer's heart suddenly felt lighter in anticipation. When Grandma had something to say, it was best to listen.

"You know when Lazarus died, Jesus wept. In fact, right now God is weeping." She looked off to the window opened bright to the afternoon clouds. "I hear it sometimes. I heard it on that first day, after Gloria died. It about killed me to hear him weeping like that, you know, but it also gave me comfort."

"I heard laughter," Spencer said.

"Yes, laughter. But weeping too, at once. Over the souls of men. Over the pain of man. Over loss. He lost his son, you know." She looked into his eyes. "And there weren't doctors clamoring to save him, either. There was a mob beating him and spitting in his face and . . ." She didn't finish the sentence.

Spencer imagined a red-faced man with bulging veins spraying spit into that face on the painting over there. Jesus' face. The image struck him as odd.

"People don't often realize it, but God suffers more in the span of each breath than any man or woman in the worst period of history," Helen said.

Surprisingly, the notion came to Spencer like a balm. Maybe because his own hurt seemed small in the face of it. "But can't God make all that go away?" he asked.

"Sure he could, and he is, as we speak. But he allows us to choose on our own between loving him and rejecting him. As long as he gives us that choice, he will be rejected by some. By most. And that brings him pain."

"That's funny. I've never imaged God as suffering. Or as hurting."

"Read the old prophets. Read Jeremiah or Ezekiel. Images of God wailing and weeping are commonplace. We just choose to ignore that part of reality in our churches today."

She smiled again, staring out of that window. "On the other hand, some will choose to love him of their own choosing. And that love, my child, is worth the greatest suffering imaginable to God. That is why he created us, for those few of us who would love him."

She paused and directed her gaze to him again. "Like your mother."

Now a mischievous glint lit his grandmother's face. She sipped at her tea, and he saw a tremble in her hand. She leaned forward slightly. "Now, that's a sight, Spencer," she said in hushed voice.

Spencer's palms began to sweat. "What is?"

"The other side." She was grinning now like a child unable to contain a secret.

"The other side of this pain and suffering. The realm of God." She let it drop without offering more. Spencer blinked, wanting her to continue, knowing that she would—had to.

Helen hesitated only a moment before dropping the question she had brought him here to ask. "Do you want to see, son?"

Spencer's heart jumped in his chest and his fingers tingled cold. *Want to see?* He swallowed. "See?" he asked, and his voice cracked.

She gripped the arms of her chair and leaned forward. "Do you want to see what it's like on the other side?" She spoke hushed, eagerly, quickly. "Do you want to know why death has its end? Why Jesus said, 'Let the dead bury the dead'? It will help, child."

Suddenly his chest felt thick again, and an ache rose through his throat. "Yes," he said. "Can I see that?"

Grandma Helen's mouth split into a broad smile. "Yes! Actually you would've been able to see it that first day, I think, but I had to wait until after the funeral, see? I had to let you mourn some. But for some reason things have changed, Spencer. He is allowing us to see."

The room was heavy with the unseen. Spencer could feel it, and goose flesh raised on his shoulders. A tear slipped from his eye, but it was a good tear. A strangely welcomed tear. Helen held his gaze for a moment and then took a quick sip of her tea.

She looked back at him. "Are you ready?"

He wasn't sure what *ready* was, but he nodded anyway, feeling desperate now. Eager.

"Close your eyes, Spencer."

He did.

It came immediately, like a rush of wind and light. A whirlwind in his mind, or maybe not just in his mind—he didn't know. His breath left him completely, but that didn't matter, because the wind filled his chest with enough oxygen to last a lifetime. Or so it felt.

The darkness behind his eyelids was suddenly full of lights. Souls. People. Angels. Streaking brightly across the horizon. Then hovering, then streaking and looping and twisting. He gasped and felt his mouth stretch open.

It struck him that the lights were not just shooting about randomly, but they flew in a perfect symmetry. Across the whole of space, as if they were putting on a show. Then he knew they *were* putting on a show. For him!

Like a million Blue Angels jets, streaking, hair-raising, perfect, like a billion ballerinas, leaping in stunning unison. But it was their sound that made little Spencer's heart feel like exploding. Because every single one of them—one billion souls strong—were screaming.

Screaming with laughter.

Long, ecstatic peals of barely controlled laughter. And above it all, one voice laughed—soft, yet loud and unmistakably clear. It was his mom's voice. Gloria was up there with them. Beside herself with joy in this display.

Then, in a flash, her whole face filled his mind, or maybe all of space. Her head tilted back slightly, and her mouth opened. She was laughing with delight, as he had never seen anyone laugh. Tears streamed over bunched cheeks, and her eyes sparkled bright. The sight did two things to Spencer at once, with crushing finality. It washed some of that joy and desire into his own chest, so that he burst into tears and laughter. And it made him want to be there. Like he had never wanted anything in his whole life. A desperate craving to be there.

The whole vision lasted maybe two seconds.

And then it was gone.

Spencer slumped in his chair like a blubbering, laughing, raggedy doll.

When Grandma Helen finally took him home two hours later, the world seemed like a strange new place to him. As if it were a dream world and the one he'd seen in Grandma's house was the real one. But he knew with settling certainty that this world, with trees and houses and his dad's Lexus parked in the driveway, was indeed very real.

It made him sad again, because in this world his mom was dead.

8

Kent punched the numbers again, hoping that this time, Borst would be in his office. In the last two weeks he'd left three messages for his supervisor, and the man had yet to return a call. He had called the first week and left word with Betty that he would be taking two or three weeks off to collect himself, put things in order.

"Of course," she'd said. "I'll pass it right on. Do what you need to do. I'm sure everyone will understand. Our hearts are with you."

"Thank you. And could you ask Borst to give me a call?"

"Sure."

That had been seventeen days ago. Goodness, it had not been *he* who'd passed on. The least they could do was return a call. His life was in enough disarray. It had taken all of two weeks for him to take the first steps back to reality. Back to the realization that aside from Spencer, and actually because of Spencer, his career was now everything.

And now Borst was avoiding him.

The phone rang three times before Betty's voice crackled in his ear. "Nipon-bank Information Systems; this is Betty."

"Betty. Hi. This is—"

"Kent! How are you?" She sounded normal enough. Her reaction came as a small wave of relief.

"Okay, actually. I'm doing better. Listen, I really need to speak with Borst. I know he must be busy, but do you think you could patch me through for a minute?" It was a lie, of course. He knew nothing of the kind. Borst had not had a busy day in his life.

She hesitated. "Uh, sure, Kent. Let me see if he's in." A butterfly took flight in his belly at her tone. Borst was always *in*. If not in his office then in the john, reading some Grisham novel. *Let me check?* Who did they think he was?

Betty came back on. "Just a minute, Kent. Let me put you through."

The line broke into Barry Manilow's "I Write the Songs." The music brought a cloud to Kent's heart. That was one of the problems with mourning; it came and left without regard for circumstances.

"Kent!" Borst's voice sounded forced. Kent imagined the man sitting behind that big screen in his office, overdressed in that navy three-piece he liked to wear. "How are you doing, Kent?"

"Fine."

"Good. We've been worried about you. I'm sorry about what happened. I had a niece who died once." Borst did not elaborate, possibly because he'd suddenly realized how stupid that sounded. *Don't forget your pet ferret, Monkey Brains. It died too, didn't it? Must've been devastating!*

"Yeah. It's tough," Kent said. "I'm sorry for taking so much time off here, but—"

"No, it's fine. Really. You take all the time you need. Not that we don't need you here, but we understand." He was speaking quickly. "Believe me, it's no problem."

"Thanks, but I think the best thing now is to get back to work. I'll be in on Monday." It was Friday. That gave him a weekend to set his mind in the right frame. "Besides, there are a few clarifications I need to make on the funds processing system." That should spark a comment on the Miami conference. Surely the reception to AFPS had been favorable. Why was Borst not slobbering about it?

"Sure," his supervisor said, rather anemically. "Yeah, Monday's good."

Kent could not contain his curiosity any longer. "So, what did they say to AFPS?" he asked as nonchalantly as possible.

"Oh, they loved it. It was a real smash, Kent. I wish you could have been there. It's everything we hoped for. Maybe more."

Of course! He'd known it all along. "So did the board make any mention of it?" Kent asked.

"Yes. Yes, they did. In fact, they've already implemented it. System wide."

The revelation brought Kent to his feet. His chair clattered to the floor behind him. "What? How? I should have been told. There are some things —"

"We didn't think it would be right to bother you. You know with the missis dying and all. But don't worry; it's been working exactly as we designed it to work."

We *nothing, Bucko. It was my program; you should have waited for me!* At least it was working. "So it was a big hit, huh?" He retrieved his chair and sat down.

"Very big. It was the buzz of the conference."

Kent squeezed his eyes and gripped his fist tight, exhilarated. Suddenly he wanted to be back. He imagined walking into the bank on Monday, a dozen suits thumping his back with congratulations.

"Good. Okay, I'll see you Monday, Markus. It'll be good to get back."

"Well, it'll be good to have you back too, Kent."

He thought about telling the man about the changes he'd made to the program before leaving for Miami but decided they could wait the weekend. Besides, he rather liked the idea of being the only man who really knew the inner workings of AFPS. A little power never hurt anybody.

Kent hung up, feeling decent for the first time since Gloria's death. It was settled, then. On Monday he would reenter his skyrocketing career. It would breathe new life into him.

გთხ

Monday morning came slow for Kent. He and Spencer had spent the weekend at the zoo and Elitch Gardens amusement park. Both the animals and the mobs of people served to distract them from their sorrow for a time. Helen had dragged them off to church on Sunday. Actually, Spencer had not needed dragging. In fact, it might be more accurate to say that *Spencer* had dragged him off to church—with Helen's full endorsement, of course. Pastor Bill Madison had lectured them on the power of God, which only served to annoy Kent immensely. Sitting in the pew, he'd thought about the power of death. And then his mind had drifted to the bank. Monday was on his mind.

And now Monday was here.

The arrangements had gone smoothly. Helen would watch Spencer at her place on Monday and Tuesday. Linda, one of Helen's buddies from church, would watch him Wednesday morning at the house. Spencer insisted he could finish off his homeschool curriculum on his own this year. Next year he might attend the public school.

Kent rose a full hour ahead of schedule, anxious and not knowing exactly why.

He showered, dressed in navy slacks and a starched white shirt, and changed ties three times before settling on a red silk Countess Mara. He then sat at the kitchen table, drinking coffee and watching the clock. The bank opened at eight, but he would walk in at ten after. Seemed appropriate. Make a statement, although he was not sure why he needed to make a statement. Or even what that statement would be. Possibly he relished the image of walking through the bank after everyone else had arrived, nodding to their smiles of consolation; acknowledging their words of congratulations. He dismissed the notion. If anything, he felt like sneaking in and avoiding the predictable shows of sympathy. Still, some form of congratulations would be in order.

A hundred scenarios ran through his mind, followed by a healthy dose of self-correction for letting the thoughts occupy him at all. In the end he blamed it all on his stressed mental state. Some psychiatrists suggested that men bent upon success became more attached to their work than to their spouses. Married to their jobs. He doubted he'd ever gone to such extremes, but the notion seemed somewhat attractive now. After all, Gloria was gone. So then, possibly he was having first-date jitters.

Kent scoffed at the idea and stood from the table. Enough blather. Time to go.

He climbed behind the wheel of the silver Lexus and drove to the bank. The butterflies rose in his stomach when the renovated office complex, now bearing the name Niponbank, loomed on the corner of Fifth and Grand. A thousand times he'd approached the old, red-brick building in the Lexus, barely aware of the downtown maze through which he drove. Hardly noticing his stopping and starting at lights as he closed in on the twenty-story structure, sitting there like an oversized fire station.

Now every movement became acute. A newsman ran on about inflation over the stereo. Cars streamed by, completely lost to the fact that he was reentering their world after a three-week absence. Pedestrians wandered in abstract directions with intent, but otherwise aimless. He wondered if any of them had lost someone recently. If so, no one would know. The world was moving ahead, full stride, with or without him.

The light just before the bank remained red for an inordinate period. Two full minutes, at least. In that time he watched eighteen people ascend or descend the sweeping steps leading to the bank's main floor. Probably tenants from the upper stories.

The car behind him honked, and he started. The light had turned. He motored across the intersection and swung the Lexus into the side parking lot. Familiar cars sat in their customary slots. With one last look in the mirror, his pulse now drumming steadily, Kent eased out of the sedan. He snatched his brief-case from the backseat and strode for the main entry.

Like walking up to a dream date on prom night. Good grief!

Long, polished, white steps rose like piano keys to the brass-framed glass doors. The year-old face-lift suited the building. He grabbed the brass handrail and clicked up the steps. With a final tingle at the base of his spine, he pushed through the entry.

The three-story lobby loomed spacious and plush, and Kent paused just inside the doors. The tall brass yacht hovered ahead, stately and magnificent, seemingly supported by that one thin shaft. Sidney Beech, the branch's assistant vice president, clacked along the marble floor, thirty feet from Kent. She saw him, gave him a friendly nod, and continued her walk toward the glass-enclosed offices along the right wall. Two personal bankers he recognized as Ted and Maurice talked idly by the president's office door. A dozen stuffed maroon guest chairs sat in small groupings, waiting in perfect symmetry for patrons who would descend on the bank at nine.

To Kent's left, the gray-flecked floor ran up to a long row of teller stations. During peak hours, fifteen tellers would be shuffling bills across the long, hunter-green counter. Now, seven busied themselves for the opening.

Kent stepped forward toward the gaping hall opposite him where the marble floor ended and the teal carpet ran into the administration wing. The large seagull that hung on the wall above the hall seemed to be eyeing him.

Zak, the white-haired security guard, stood idly to Kent's right, looking important and doing exactly what he had done for five years now: nothing. He had seen it all a thousand times, but coming in now, it struck him as though new. Like a déjà vu. *I've been here before, haven't I? Yes, of course.* At any moment a call would come. Someone would notice that Kent Anthony had just entered the building. The man responsible for the new processing system. The man whose wife had just died. Then they would all know he had arrived.

But the call did not come.

And that bothered him a little. He stepped onto the carpet and swallowed, thinking maybe they had not seen him. And, after all, these front-lobby workers were not as close to his world as the rest. Back in the administration sections they referred to those who worked out in the large foyer as the *handlers*. But it was them, the *processors*, who really made banking work—everyone knew that.

Kent breathed deeply once, walked straight down the hall, and opened the door to his little corner of the world.

Betty Smythe was there at her desk on the left—bleached, poofy-white hair and all. She had a tube of bright red lipstick cocked and ready to apply, one inch from pursed lips already too red for Kent's taste. Immediately her face went a shade whiter, and she blinked. Which was how he supposed some people might respond to a waking of the dead. Only it was not he who had died.

"Hi, Betty," he said.

"Kent!" Now she collected herself, jerked that red stick to her lap, and squirmed on the seat. "You're back."

"Yes, Betty. I'm back."

He'd always thought that Borst's decision to hire Betty had been motivated by the size of her bra rather than the size of her brain, and looking at her now he was sure of it. He glanced about the reception area. Beyond the blue armchairs the hall sat vacant. All four oak office doors were shut. A fleeting picture of the black nameplates flashed through his mind. Borst, Anthony, Brice, Quinn. It had been the same for three years now.

"So how are things going?" he asked absently.

"Fine," she said, fiddling with the latch on her purse. "I don't know what to say about your wife. I'm so sorry."

"Don't say anything." She had not mentioned AFPS yet. He turned and smiled at her. "Really, I'll be fine." So much for the blaring reception.

Kent walked to the first door on the left and entered his office. The overhead fluorescent stuttered white over his black workstation, tidy as he had left it. He closed the door and set the briefcase down.

Well now, here he was. At home once again. Three computer monitors rested on the corner station, each displaying the same exotic-fish screensaver in unison. His high-back leather chair butted up to the keyboard.

Kent reached for his neck and loosened his collar. He slid into his chair and touched the mouse. The screens jumped to life as one. A large three-dimensional insignia reading "Advanced Funds Processing System" rolled out on the screen like a carpet inviting entry. "Welcome to the bank," the last of it read. Indeed, with this little baby, an operator had access to the bank in ways many a criminal would only dream of through fitful sleep.

He dropped into his chair, punched in his customary access code, and dropped a finger on the ENTER key. The screen went black for a moment. Then large yellow letters suddenly popped up: ACCESS DENIED.

He grunted and keyed in the password again, sure he had not forgotten his own son's name: SPENCER.

ACCESS DENIED, the screen read again. Borst must have changed the code in his absence. Of course! They had integrated the program already. In doing so, they would need to set a primary access password, which would automatically delete the old.

Kent hesitated at the door to his office, thinking again that he had been in the office for a full five minutes now and not one word of congratulations. Borst's closed door was directly across the hall. He should walk in and let the man bring him up to speed. Or perhaps he should make an appearance in Todd's or Mary's office first. The two junior programmers would know what was up.

At the last moment he decided to check in on Will Thompson in the loan department instead. Will would know the buzz, and he was disconnected.

He found Will at his desk, one floor up, bent over his monitor, adjusting the focus.

"Need any help with that?" Kent asked, grinning.

Will looked up, surprised. "Kent! You're back!" He extended a quick hand. "When did you get back? Gee, I'm sorry."

"Ten minutes ago." Kent reached down and twisted a knob behind the monitor. The menu on the screen immediately jumped into clear view.

Will smirked and sat down. "Thanks man. I always could count on you. So, you okay? I wasn't sure I'd ever see you back here."

Kent sat in a guest chair and shrugged. "I'm hanging in there. It's good to be back to work. Keep me distracted, maybe."

The loan officer lifted an eyebrow. "So, you're okay with it all?"

Kent looked at his friend, not sure what he was asking. "It's not like I have a lot of choice in the matter, Will. What's done is done."

"Yeah. You're right. I just thought that on top of your wife's death and all, you might see things differently." The room suddenly seemed deathly quiet. It struck Kent then that something was amiss. And like Betty, Will had not congratulated him. A thin chill snaked down his spine.

"See what differently?" he asked.

Will stared at him. "You . . . you've talked to Borst, right?"

Kent shook his head. Yes indeed, something was very much amiss, and it wasn't sounding good. "No."

"You're kidding, right? You haven't heard a thing?"

"About what? What are you talking about?"

"Oh, Kent . . ." His friend winced. "I'm sorry, man. You've got to talk to Borst."

That did it. Kent stood abruptly and strode from the room, ignoring a call from Will. His gut turned in lazy circles down the elevator. He stepped into the computer wing and walked right past a wide-eyed Betty to the back offices where Todd and Mary would be diligently at work.

He smacked through Todd's door first.

"Hey, Todd."

The redhead started and shoved his chair back. "Kent! You're back!"

A stranger sat in a chair to the junior programmer's right, and the sight caught Kent off guard for a moment. The man rose with Todd and smiled. He stood as tall as Kent, he wore his hair short, and his eyes were the greenest Kent had ever seen. Like two emerald marbles. A starched white shirt rested, crisp, on broad shoulders. The man stuck his hand out, and Kent removed his eyes from him without taking it.

Todd stood slack-jawed. A button on his green shirt had popped open, revealing a hairy white belly. The programmer's eyes looked at him like black holes, filled to the brim with guilt.

"I'm back. So, tell me what's up, Todd. What's happening here that I don't know about?"

"Ah, Kent, this is Cliff Monroe. I'm showing him the ropes." He motioned to the man beside him. "He's new to our staff."

"Good for you, Cliff. Answer my question, Todd. What's changed?"

"What do you mean?" The junior programmer lifted his shoulders in an attempt to look casual. The motion widened the shirt's gap at his belly, and Kent dismissed the sudden impulse to reach in there and yank some hair.

Kent swallowed. "Nothing changed while I was out, then?"

"What do you mean?" Todd shrugged again, his eyes bugging.

Kent grunted in disgust, impatient with the spineless greenhorn. He turned and stepped across the hall to Mary's office. He pushed the door open. Mary sat at her desk with her phone pressed to her ear, facing away from the door, talking. She turned around slowly, her eyes round.

As if, Honey! You knew I was coming. Probably having an important discussion with a dial tone. Fitting partner.

Kent shut the door firmly and strode for Borst's door, his spine now tingling right up to his skull. The man sat stiffly in his chair, his three-piece suit tight, sweat beading his brow. His bald spot shone as if he'd oiled it. His large, hooked nose glistened like some shiny Christmas bulb. The superior made a magnanimous effort to show shock when Kent barged in.

"Kent! You made it back!"

Of course I made it back, you witless fool, he almost replied. Instead he said, "Yes," and plopped down in one of Borst's tweed guest chairs. "I called you on Friday, remember. So who's the new employee?"

"Cliff? Yes, he's a transfer from Dallas. An excellent programmer, from what I hear." The middle-aged man flicked his tongue across thick lips and ran a hand through what hair he had. "So. How's the missis?"

The room lapsed into silence. The missis? Gloria? Borst must have realized his blunder, because a stupid grin crossed his face, and he went red.

Kent spoke before the man could cover his error, hot with anger. "The missis is dead, remember, Markus? It's why I've been gone for three weeks. You see, there's an office across the hall that has my name on it. And for five years now, I've been working there. Or had you forgotten that as well?"

Borst turned beet red now, and not from embarrassment, Kent guessed. He continued before the man could recover. "So how did the AFPS presentation go, Markus?" He forced a smile. "Are we on top?" He meant, am *I* on top, but he was sure that Borst would catch the drift.

The phone rang shrilly on the desk. Borst glared at Kent for a moment and then snatched it up, listening.

"Yes . . . yes put him through."

Kent sat back and crossed his legs, aware that his heart was pounding. The other man straightened his tie and sat upright, attentive for whoever was about to address him on the phone. He turned from Kent and spoke. "Yes, Mr. Wong . . . Yes, thank you, sir."

Mr. Wong? Borst was thanking *the* Mr. Wong?

"I'd be delighted." He turned and faced Kent purposefully. "Yes, I'm tied up with a luncheon on the East Coast Wednesday, but I could fly to Tokyo on Thursday." Kent knew that something very awful was happening here. He was now sweating badly, despite the air conditioning.

"I'd be delighted," Borst said. "Yes, it did take a lot, but I had a good crew on it as well . . . Yes, thank you. Good-bye."

He dropped the phone in its cradle and stared at Kent for a long moment. When he finally spoke, it came out rehearsed. "Come on, Kent. Surely you didn't expect all of the glory on this, did you? It's my department."

Kent swallowed, suddenly fearing the worst. But that would be virtually impossible.

"What did you do?" His voice sounded scratchy.

"Nothing. I'm just implementing the program. That's all. It is *my* program."

Kent began to tremble slightly. "Okay, let's back up here. In Miami I was set to introduce AFPS to the convention. You remember that, right?" He was sounding condescending, but he could not help himself.

Borst nodded once and frowned.

"But I got called away, right? My wife was dying. You with me here?"

This time Borst did not acknowledge.

"So I asked you to wing it for me. And I'm assuming you did. Now, surely somewhere in there you mentioned my name, right? Gave credit where credit was due?"

Borst had frozen like ice.

Kent scooted forward on his seat, steaming. "Don't tell me you stole all the credit for AFPS, Markus. Just tell me you didn't!"

The division supervisor sat with an ashen face. "This is *my* division, Kent. That means that the work out of here is *my* responsibility. You work for me." He went red as he spoke. "Or did *you* forget *that* simple fact?"

"You put the paperwork through! This has always been my bonus! We've discussed it a thousand times! You left me out?!"

"No. You're in there. So is Todd, and so is Mary."

"Todd and Mary?" Kent blurted incredulously. "You put my name in small print along with Todd's and Mary's?" And he knew Borst had done exactly that.

He shoved an arm toward the door. "They're junior programmers, Markus! They write code that I give them to write. AFPS is *my* code!" He nearly shouted now, boring down on the supervisor with a straining neck.

"I designed it from scratch. Did you tell them that? It was *my* brainchild! I wrote 80 percent of the functioning code, for Pete's sake! You yourself wrote a measly 5 percent, most of which I trashed."

That last comment pushed Borst over the edge. The veins on his neck bulged. "You hold your tongue, mister! This is my department. I was responsible for the design and implementation of AFPS. I will hire and fire who I see fit. And for your information, I have been allotted a twenty-five-thousand-dollar spiff for the design engineer of my choice. I was going to give that to you, Kent. But you are rapidly changing my mind!"

Now something deep in Kent's mind snapped, and his vision swam. For the first time in his life he felt like killing someone. He breathed deeply twice to stabilize the tremor in his bones. When he spoke, he did so through clenched teeth.

"Twenty-five thousand dollars!" he ground out. "There was a performance spiff on that program, Markus. Ten percent of the savings to the company over ten years. It's worth millions!"

Borst blinked and sat back. He knew it, of course. They had discussed it on a dozen occasions. And now he meant to claim it all as his. The man did not respond.

The rage came like a boiling volcano, right up through Kent's chest and into his skull. Blind rage. He could still see, but things were suddenly fuzzy. He knew he was erupting, knew Borst could see it all—his red face, his trembling lips, his bulging eyes.

Gripping his hands into fists, Kent suddenly knew that he would fight Borst to his death. He had just lost his wife; he was not about to give up his own livelihood. He would use every means at his disposal to claim his due. And in the process he would bury this spineless pimp before him.

The thought brought a sterling cool to his bones, and he let it filter through his body for a moment. He stood, still glaring angrily. "You're a spineless worm, Borst. And you're stealing my work for your own."

They held stares for a full ten seconds. Borst refused to speak.

"What's the new code?" Kent demanded.

Borst pursed his lips, silent.

Kent spun from the man, exited the office with a bang, and stormed down to Todd's office. He shoved the door open.

"Todd!" The junior started. "What's the new AFPS access code?"

Todd seemed to shrink into his chair. "M-B-A-O-K," he said.

Kent left without thanking him.

He needed a rest. He needed to think. He grabbed his briefcase and walked angrily past Betty's desk without acknowledging her. This time one of the tellers called a greeting to him as he rushed through the towering lobby, but he ignored the distant call and slammed through the tall glass doors.

9

The madness of it all descended upon Kent one block from the bank. It was then that a burning realization of his loss sank into his gut. If Borst pulled this off—which, judging by the call from Wong, he was doing just splendidly—he would effectively strip Kent of everything. Millions of dollars. That hook-nosed imbecile in there was casually intercepting his life's work.

Kent's chest flushed with a wave of panic. It was impossible! He'd kill anybody who tried to steal what was his. Shove a gun in the guy's mouth and blow his brains out, maybe. Good grief! What was he thinking? He could hardly shoot a prairie dog, much less another man. On the other hand, maybe Borst had just given up his right to life.

And what of Spencer? They would be virtually broke. All the boasting of Euro Disney and yachts and beachfront homes would prove him a fool. An image of that grinning monkey from the Chicago airport clapped its cymbals through his mind. *Clang-ka-ching, clang-ka-ching.*

Kent snatched up his cell phone and punched seven digits. A receptionist answered after two rings. "Warren Law Offices."

"Hi. This is Kent Anthony." His voice wavered, and he cleared his throat. "Is Dennis in?"

"Just a minute. Let me see if he's available."

The line remained silent for a minute before his old college roommate's voice filled his ear. "Hello, Kent. Goodness, it's been awhile. How you doing, man?"

"Hey, Dennis. Actually, not so good. I've got some problems. I need a good attorney. You have some time?"

"You okay, buddy? You don't sound so good."

"Well, like I said, I've got some problems. Can I meet with you?"

"Sure. Absolutely. Let's see . . ." Kent heard the faint flip of paper through the receiver. "How about Thursday afternoon?"

"No, Dennis. I mean now. Today."

Dennis held his reply for a second. "Pretty short notice, buddy. I'm booked solid. It can't wait?"

Kent did not respond. A sudden surge of emotions had taken hold of his throat.

"Hold on. Let me see if I can reschedule my lunch." The phone clicked to hold music.

Two minutes later Dennis came back on. "Okay, buddy. You owe me for this. How about Pelicans at twelve sharp? I already have reservations."

"Good. Thanks, Dennis. It means a lot."

"You mind me asking what this is about?"

"It's employment related. I just got screwed out of a major bonus. I mean major, as in millions."

Static sounded. "Millions?" Dennis Warren's voice cracked. "What kind of bonus is worth millions? I didn't know you were in that kind of money, Kent."

"Yeah, well, I won't be if we don't act quick. I'll give you the whole story at lunch."

"Twelve o'clock then. And make sure you have your employment file with you. I'll need that."

Kent pulled back into traffic, feeling a small surge of confidence. This wasn't the first time he'd faced an obstacle. He glanced at the clock on the dash. Nine o'clock. He'd have to burn three hours. He could retrieve a copy of his employment agreement from the house—that would take an hour if he stretched things.

"God, help me," he muttered. But that was stupid, because he didn't believe in God. But maybe there was a Satan and his number had come up on Satan's big spinning wheel: *Time to go after Kent. After him, lads!*

Ridiculous.

༺

Pelicans Grill bustled with a lunch crowd willing to pay thirty bucks for the privilege of eyeing Denver's skyline while feasting. Kent sat by the picture window, overlooking Interstate 25, and stared at his plate, thinking he really should at least finish the veal. Apart from a dip from the mashed potatoes and a corner sawed off the meat, his lunch sat untouched. And that after an hour at the table.

Dennis sat dressed smartly in a black tailored suit, cut with care to hang just so on his well-muscled frame. The jet-black mustache and deep tan fit his Greek heritage. By the Rolex on his wrist and the large emerald ring on his right forefinger, Kent's college roomy had obviously done just fine for himself. He had listened to Kent's tale with complete rapture, biting at his steak aggressively and *humphing* at all the right junctures. The man had just heard of Gloria's death for the first time, and the announcement had brought his fork clattering to his plate. He stared at Kent, frozen, his mouth slightly agape.

"You're kidding?" he stammered, wide eyed. Of course he had known Gloria. Had met her at their wedding, three years after college, when they were both just getting started. "Oh, Kent, I'm so sorry."

"Yeah. It all happened so quickly, you know. I can barely believe it's happened half the time."

Dennis wiped his mouth and swallowed. "It's hard to believe." He shook his head. "If there's anything I can do, buddy. Anything at all."

"Just help me get my money, Dennis."

His friend shook his head. "It's incredible how these things can come out of nowhere. You heard about Lacy, right?"

Lacy? A bell clanged to life in Kent's mind. "Lacy?" he asked.

"Lacy Cartwright. You dated her for two years in college. Remember her?"

Of course he remembered Lacy. They had broken up three months before graduation. She was ready for marriage, and the thought had frightened him clean out of love. Last he'd heard she had married some guy from the East Coast the same year he and Gloria had married.

"Sure," he said.

"She lost her husband a couple years ago to cancer. It was quick from what I heard. Just like that. You didn't get the announcement? Last I heard she'd moved to Boulder."

"No." Kent shook his head. Not surprising, really. After the way he'd cut her off, Lacy wouldn't dream of reintroducing herself at *any* juncture, much less at her husband's funeral. She was as principled as they came.

"So what do you think about the case?" Kent asked, shifting the conversation back to the legal matter. Dennis crossed his legs and leaned back. "Well . . ." He sucked at his teeth and let his tongue wander about his mouth for a moment, thinking. "It really depends on the employment contract you signed. You brought it with you?"

Kent nodded, withdrew the document from his briefcase, and handed it to him.

Dennis flipped through the pages, scanning the paragraphs quickly, mumbling something about boilerplate jargon. "I'll have to read this more carefully at the office but . . . Here we go: Statement of Propriety."

He read quickly, and Kent nibbled on a cold pea.

The attorney flopped the document on the table. "Pretty standard agreement. They own everything, of course. But you do have recourse. Two ways to look at this." He held up two fingers. "One, you can fight these guys regardless of this agreement. Just take them to court and claim that you signed this document without full knowledge."

"Why? Is it a bad document?" Kent interrupted.

"Depends. For you, in your situation, yes. I'd say so. By signing it you basically agreed to forfeit all natural rights to proprietary property, regardless of how it materialized. You also specifically agreed to press no claims for compensation not specifically drawn under contract. Meaning, unless you have a contract that stipulates you are due 10 percent of the savings generated by this . . . what is it?"

"AFPS."

"AFPS . . . it's up to the company to decide if you are entitled to the money."

Kent's heart began to palpitate. "And who in the company decides these things?"

"That's what I was going to ask you. Immediately, it would be your superior."

"Borst?"

Dennis nodded. "You can go over his head, of course. Who above him knows of the work you put into this thing?" Kent sat back, feeling heavy. "Price Bentley. He's the branch president. I sat in a dozen meetings with him and Borst. He has to know that the man is about as bright as mud. Can't I bring in coworkers?"

"If you want to sue, sure. But by their reactions, it sounds to me like they might be more on Borst's side than yours. Sounds like the guy was doing some fast talking while you were out. Your best bet is probably to go straight to the bank president and appeal your case. Either way you're going to need strong support from the inside. If they all side with Borst, we're going to have to prove a conspiracy, and that, my friend, is near impossible."

Kent let the words soak in slowly. "So basically either I gain favor with one of Borst's superiors and work internally, or I'm screwed. That about it?"

"Well, like I said, I really need to read this thing through, but, barring any hidden clauses, I'd say that's the bottom line. Now, we can always sue. But without someone backing up your story, you might as well throw your money to the wind."

Kent smiled courageously. But his mind was already on Price Bentley's face. He cursed himself for not taking more time to befriend upper management. Then again, they'd hired him as a programmer, not as a court jester. And program he had, the best piece of software the banking industry had seen in ten years.

"So I go back there and start making friends," he said, looking out the picture window to the cars flowing below. From the corner of his eye he saw Dennis nod. He nodded with him. Surely old Price was smart enough to know who deserved credit for AFPS. But the idea that another man held the power to grant or deny his future sat like lead in his gut.

10

Kent walked straight to Price Bentley's office on Tuesday morning before bothering with Borst.

He'd spent Monday afternoon and evening chewing his fingernails, which was a problem because he had no fingernails to speak of. Spencer had wanted to eat chicken in the park for dinner, but Kent had no stomach for pretending to enjoy life on a park bench. "Go ahead, son. Just stay away from any strangers."

The night had proved fitful. A sickening dread had settled on him like a human-sized sticky flysheet, and no matter what twists and turns he put his mind through, he could not shake it free. To make matters worse, he'd awakened at three in the morning, breathless with panic and then furious as thoughts of Borst filtered into his waking mind. He'd spent an hour tossing and turning only to finally throw the covers across the room and swing from bed. The next few hours had been maddening.

By the time the first light filtered through the windows, he had dressed in his best suit and downed three cups of coffee. Helen had collected Spencer at seven and had given Kent a raised eyebrow. It might have been his palms, wet with sweat. Or the black under his eyes. But knowing her, she had probably seen right into his mind and picked through the mess there.

He had nearly hit a yellow Mustang at the red light just before the bank because his eyes were on those sweeping steps ahead and not on the traffic signal. His was the first car in the lot, and he decided to park on the far row in favor of being seen early. Finally, at eight sharp, he'd climbed from the Lexus, swept his damp, blond locks back into place, and headed for the wide doors.

He ran into Sidney Beech around the corner from the president's office. "Hi, Kent," she said. Her long face, accentuated by short brown hair, now looked even longer under raised brows. "I saw you yesterday. Are you okay? I'm so sorry about what happened."

He knew Sidney only casually, but her voice now came like warm milk to his cold tremoring bones. If his mission was to win friends and influence the smug suits, a favorable word with the assistant vice president couldn't hurt. He spread his mouth in a genuine smile.

"Thank you, Sidney." He reached for her hand and grasped it, wondering how much would be too much. "Thank you so much. Yes. Yes, I'm doing better. Thank you."

An odd glint in her eye made him blink, and he released her hand. Was she single? Yes, he thought she was single. The left corner of her lip lifted a hair. "That's good to hear, Kent. If there's anything I can do, just let me know."

"Yes, I will. Listen, do you know what Mr. Bentley's schedule is today? There's a rather important issue that I—"

"Actually, you might catch him now. I know he has an eight-thirty with the board, but I just saw him walk into his office."

Kent glanced in the direction of the president's office. "Great. Thank you, Sidney. You're so kind."

He left, thinking he had overdone it with her, maybe. But then, maybe not. Politics had never been his strong suit. Either way, the exchange had given him a sensibility that took the edge off the manic craziness that had gripped him all night.

True to Sidney's words, Price Bentley sat in his office alone, sorting through a stack of mail. Rumor had it that Price weighed his salary: 250. Only his salary came in thousands of U.S. dollars, not pounds. The large man sat in a gray pin-striped suit. Despite being partially obscured by a layer of thick flesh, his collar looked crisp, possibly supported by cardboard or plastic within its folds. The man's head looked like a plump tomato atop a can. He looked up at Kent and smiled. "Kent! Kent Anthony. Come on in. Sit down. To what do I owe this pleasure?" The president did not rise but continued flipping through the stack.

If the man knew of Gloria's passing, he was not going there. Kent stepped to an overstuffed blue guest chair and sat. The room seemed warm.

"Thank you, sir. Do you have a minute?"

"Sure." The bank president leaned back, crossed his legs, and propped his chin on a hand. "I have a few minutes. How can I help you?"

The man's eyes glistened round and gray. "Well, it's about AFPS," Kent started.
"Yes. Congratulations. Fine work you guys put together back there. I'm sorry you couldn't be at the conference, but it went over with quite a splash. Excellent job!"

Kent smiled and nodded. "That's what I heard. Thank you." He hesitated. How could he say this without sounding like a whiner? *But sir, his blue ribbon was bigger than my blue ribbon.* He hated whiners with a passion. Only this was not about blue ribbons, was it? Not even close.

"Sir, it seems there's been a mistake somewhere."

Bentley's brows scrunched. "Oh? How's that?" He seemed concerned. That was good. Kent picked up steam.

"The Advanced Funds Processing System was my brainchild, sir, five years ago. In fact, I showed you my rough diagrams once. Do you remember?"

"No, I can't say that I do. But that doesn't mean you didn't. I see a thousand submissions a year. And I'm aware that you had an awful lot to do with the system's development. Excellent job."

"Thank you." So far so good. "Actually, I wrote 90 percent of the code for the program." Kent leaned back for the first time. He settled into the chair. "I put a hundred hours a week into its development for over five years. Borst oversaw parts of the process, but for the most part he let me run it."

The president sat still, not catching Kent's drift yet. Unless he was choosing to ignore it. Kent gave him a second to offer a comment and then continued when none came.

"I worked those hours for all those years with my eye set on a goal, sir. And now it seems that Borst has decided that I do not deserve that goal." There. How could he be any clearer?

The president stared at him, unblinking, impossible to read. Heat rose through Kent's back. Everything now sat on those blind scales of justice, waiting for a verdict. Only these scales were not blind at all. They possessed flat gray eyes, screwed into that tomato head across the desk.

Silence settled thick. Kent thought he should continue—throw in some light-hearted political jargon, maybe shift the subject, now having planted his seed. But his mind had gone blank. He became aware that his palms were sweating.

Bentley suddenly spread his jowls in a grin, and he chuckled once with pursed lips. Still not sure what the man could possibly be thinking, Kent chuckled once with him. It seemed natural enough.

"The savings bonus?" the president asked, and he was either very condescending or genuinely surprised. Kent begged for the latter, but now the heat was sending little tingles over his skull.

"Yes," he answered, and cleared his throat.

Bentley chuckled again, and his jowls bounced over his collar with each chuckle. "You actually thought that you had a substantial bonus coming, didn't you?"

The breath left Kent as if he'd been gut-punched.

"Those saving spiffs are hardly for non-management personnel, Kent. Surely you realized that. Management, yes. And this one will be substantial indeed. I can see why you might be slobbering over it. But you have to pay your dues. You can't just expect to be handed a million dollars because you did most of the work."

Kent might have lost his judgment there, on the spot—reached over and slapped Fat-Boy's jowls. But waves of confusion fixed him rigid except for a blinking in his eyes. Niponbank had always boasted of its Savings Bonus Program, and everyone knew that it was aimed at the ordinary worker. A dozen documents clearly stated so. Last year a teller had come up with an idea that earned him a hundred thousand dollars.

"That's not how the employment manual lays the program out," Kent said, still too shocked to be angry. Surely the president didn't think he could get away with *this* line of argument. They would fry his behind in court!

Bentley's lips fell flat. "Now, you listen to me, Anthony. I don't give a rat's tushy what you think the employment manual says. In this branch, that bonus goes to the management. You work for Borst. Borst works for me." The words came out like bullets from a silenced pistol.

The president took one hard breath. "What work you did for the bank, you did on our time, at our request, and for it we paid you well over a hundred thousand dollars a year. That's it. You hear me? You even think about fighting this, and I promise you we will bury you." The large man said it, shaking.

Kent felt his mouth drop during the diatribe. This was impossible! "You can't do that!" he protested. "You can't just rip my bonus off because . . ." And suddenly Kent knew precisely what he was up against. Bentley was in on it. He stood to receive huge sums of money from the bonus. He and Borst were in on this together. Which made it a conspiracy of sorts.

The man was glaring at him, daring him to say more. So he did.

"Listen!" He bit the word off with as much intensity as Bentley had used. "You know as well as I do that if I had been in Miami, I would have made that presentation, and I would be receiving most if not all of the bonus." A lump of self-pity rose to join the bitterness, and he trembled. "But I wasn't, was I? Because I had to rush home to tend to my wife, who was dying. So instead, you and Borst put your slimy heads together and decided to steal my bonus! What was it?" Kent wagged his head, mocking. 'Oh, poor little Anthony. His wife is dying. But at least he'll be distracted while we stab him in the back and strip him naked!' Is that about it, Bentley?"

The bank president's reaction was immediate. His eyes widened, and he drew an unsteady breath. "You speak like that to me in my own office? One more word out of you, and I'll have you on the street by day's end!"

But Kent had lost his political good sense entirely. "You have no right to do any of this, Bentley! That is my bonus you are stealing. People go to jail for theft in this country. Or is that news to you, as well?"

"Out! Get out!"

"I'll take this to the top. You understand me? And if I go down, you're going down with me. So don't even think about trying to cut me out. Everyone knew that the programming was my code."

"You might be surprised what everyone knew," Bentley shot back. He had forsaken that professional sheen, and Kent felt a spike of satisfaction for it.

"Yes, of course. You will bribe them all, I suppose?" he sneered.

The room went quiet again. When Bentley spoke again, it was low and stern, but the tremor was unmistakable. "Get out of my office, Anthony. I have a meeting in a few minutes. If it's all right with you, I need to prepare a few notes."

Kent stared the man down for a moment. "Actually, nothing is okay with me just now, sir. But then, you already know that, don't you?" He stood and walked behind the chair before turning back.

"And if you try to take my job from me I will personally sue you to the highest heaven. Your bonus may be an internal matter, but there are state laws that deal with employment. Don't even think about stripping me of my income."

He turned to the door and left Bentley sitting with big jowls and squinty eyes, like Jabba the Hut.

It was not until he heard the door close behind him that Kent fully realized how badly it had just gone for him. Then it crashed on him like a block of concrete, and a sick droning obscured his thoughts. He struck for the public rest-rooms across the lobby.

What had he done? He had to call Dennis. All of his worst fears had just come to life. It was a prospect he could not stomach. *Would* not stomach. Walking across the lobby, he suddenly felt like he was pushing through a steam bath. More than anything he'd ever wanted, possibly even more than the money itself, Kent wanted out of this nightmare. Go back three weeks and check back into Miami's Hyatt Regency. This time when they handed him the note it would have a differ-ent name on it. *I'm sorry, you have the wrong party,* he'd say. *I am not Ken Blatherly. My name's Kent. Kent Anthony. And I'm here to become a millionaire.*

Ignoring a young man he recognized as one of the tellers, Kent bent over the sink and threw water on his flushed face. He stood, watched the water drip down his face, and strode for the public phone in the corner, not bothering to wipe his face. Water spotted his starched shirt, but he couldn't care less. Just let Dennis be in. Please let him be in.

The young teller walked out, his eyes wide.

Kent punched the number.

"Warren Law Offices," the female voice came.

"Dennis in?" Silence. "Is Dennis in?"

"Who's calling?"

"Kent."

"May I tell him what it is regarding?"

"Just tell him it's Kent. Kent Anthony."

"Please hold."

No new thoughts formed in the silence. His mind was dipping into numb-ness.

"Kent! How's it going?"

Kent told him. He said it all in a long run-on sentence that ended with, "Then he threw me out."

"What do you mean, threw you out?"

"Told me to get out."

Silence again.

"Okay, buddy. Listen to me, okay?" Those were sweet words because they came from a friend. A friend who had something to say. That would be good, wouldn't it?

"I know this may sound impossible right now, but this is not over, you hear me? What he did in there, what Bentley just did, changes things. I'm not saying it hands us the case, but it gives us some pretty decent ammo. Obviously the political approach is dead. You pretty much slaughtered that. But you also managed to give us a fairly strong case."

Kent felt like crying. Just sitting down and crying.

"But I need you to do something for me, buddy. Okay? I need you to walk back to your office, sit down at your desk, and work the day out as if nothing at all happened. If we're lucky, they will fire you. And if they fire you, we'll slap the biggest unlawful discharge suit on them the state has ever seen. But if they don't fire you, I need you to continue working in good faith. We can't give them cause to release you. They might consider your confrontation this morning as insubordination, but there were no witnesses, right?"

"Right."

"So then you work as if you did nothing but go to Bentley's office and deliver some paper clips. You hear me? Can you do that?"

Kent wasn't sure he could, actually. The thought of seeing Borst and company back there made him swallow. On the other hand, he had to keep his options open. He had a mortgage and a car payment and groceries to think about. And he had Spencer.

"Yes, I can do that," he replied. "You really think we have something here?"

"It may be messy and take awhile. But yes, I do."

"Okay. Okay. Thanks, Dennis. I owe you."

"Don't worry. There'll be a bill if things go our way."

Kent tried to chuckle with his friend. It came out like a cough.

He hung up, straightened himself in front of the mirror, and let his eyes clear. Ten minutes later, he left the restroom and strode for the administrative offices, clenching his jaw. He'd been through hell already. There could be nowhere but up from here.

Nowhere but straight up.

⌇⌇⌇

Helen shuffled over the groove a dozen years of pacing had worn in her bedroom carpet along the length of the double French doors leading to her second-story balcony. It was her prayer closet. Her prayer groove. The place from which she most often broke through to the heavens. In better days she would think nothing of staying on her feet, pacing for hours at a stretch. But now her worn legs limited her to a plodding twenty minutes, tops. Then she would be forced to retreat to her bed or to the rocker.

She wore a long, pink housecoat that swayed around her bare feet. Her hair rested in tangles; bags darkened her eyes; her mouth had found frowning acceptable these days. Despite her understanding of a few things, the fact that her daughter was now gone did not rest easily. It was one thing to peek into the heavens and hear the laughter there. It was another thing altogether to be stuck here, yearning for that laughter. Or even the sweet reprimanding voice of her dear Gloria, instructing her on the finer points of manners.

She pulled at her skin and smiled briefly. *Skinpullers.* Gloria was right, it was a ridiculous name.

It was most often the memories that brought floods of tears to her eyes. But in the end she supposed that it was all right, this weeping. After all, Jesus himself had wept.

Five feet to the right, her white-lace-canopy bed waited with sheets already pulled back. Beside it, a clay bowl filled with red potpourri sent wafts of cinnamon across the room. The ceiling fan clicked overhead, barely moving the air in its lazy circles. Helen reached the end of her groove and turned back, eyeing that bed. Now it was on her left.

But she was not headed there just yet, despite the midnight hour. Not until she broke through here, in her groove. She could feel it in her spirit—or more accurately, her spirit *wanted* to feel something. It wanted to be spoken to. Soothed by the balm from heaven. Which usually meant that heaven wanted to soothe her. Speak to her. It was how God drew mortals, she'd decided once. He spoke desire into willing hearts. Which actually came first, the desire or the willing, was sort of like the chicken or the egg scenario. In the end a rather ridiculous exercise best left to theologians.

In either case, Helen knew to trust her senses, and her senses suggested she intercede now—intercede until she found what peace her spirit sought. If for no other reason than she knew of no other way. The problem began when her eyes had been opened to that scene in the heavens before Gloria's death. She had seen her daughter lying on the hospital bed, and that had sent her over a cliff of sorts.

Oh, she had recovered quickly enough, but it was the rest of the vision that had plagued her night and day over the last few weeks.

Helen closed her eyes and paced by feel, ignoring the dull pain in her knees, subconsciously stepping off the seven paces from end to end. Her mind drifted back to the meeting with Pastor Madison earlier that afternoon. He had said nothing more about their conversation at the hospital. But when she walked into his office today and plopped down in the guest chair facing him, he'd stared her straight through. She knew then that he had not so easily shaken her claim at having seen more.

"How you doing, Bill?" she'd asked.

He did not bother answering. "So, what's happening, Helen?"

"I don't know, Pastor. That's what I came to find out. You tell me."

He smiled and nodded at her immediate response. "Come on, Helen. You are as much a pastor to me as I am to anybody here. You made some pretty strong statements at the hospital."

"Yes. Well, it hasn't gotten any better. And you are wrong if you think that I do not need you to pastor me. I am nearly lost on this one, Bill."

"And I am *completely* lost, Helen. We can't have the blind leading the blind, now, can we?"

"No. But you have been placed in your office with a gifting that comes from God. Use it. Pastor me. And don't pretend that you are a mere clergyman without supernatural guidance—we have enough of those to fill the world's graveyards as it is."

The large Greek smiled and folded his hands on his oak desk. He presented a perfectly stately image, sitting there all dressed in black with a red tie, surrounded by bookshelves stuffed with expensive-looking books.

"Okay, Helen. But you can't expect me to see the way you see. Tell me what you saw."

"I already told you what I saw."

"You told me that you saw Gloria lying in the hospital. That's all you told me. Except that you saw more. So what did you see?"

She sighed. "I was praying with Gloria and Spencer, and we were taken to a place. In our minds or our spirits—I don't know how these things actually work. But I was given a bird's-eye view of Gloria's hospital room two days before she died. I saw everything, right down to the green pen in the attending physician's coat."

She said it with a firm jaw, steeling herself against emotion. She'd had enough sorrow to finish the year out, she thought.

Pastor Madison shook his head slowly. "It just seems incredible. I mean . . . I've never heard of such vivid precognition."

"This was not *pre* anything. This was as real as if I were there."

"Yes, but it happened *before*. That would make it *pre*. A vision of what is to happen."

"God is not bound by time, young man. You should know that. I was there. Maybe in spirit only, but I was there. It is not my job to understand how I was there; I leave that to the more learned in the church. But understanding does not necessarily change an experience. It merely explains it."

"I don't mean to argue with you, Helen. I'm not the enemy here."

Helen closed her eyes for a moment. The pastor was right, of course. He might very well be her only ally in all of this. She would be wise to choose her words with more care.

"Yes. I'm sorry. It's just . . . maddening, you know." Memories of Gloria clogged her mind, and she cleared her throat. "I'm afraid I'm not entirely myself these days."

"But you are yourself, Helen." His deep voice came soothingly. A pastor's voice. "You are a woman who has lost her daughter. If you were not frustrated and angry, I might worry."

She looked up at him and smiled. Now he was indeed pastoring her, and it felt like it should—comforting. She should have come here a week ago.

"You said you saw something else, Helen. What was the rest?"

"I can't tell you, Bill. Not because I don't want to, but because I have only seen glimpses that make no sense. And I've felt things. It is the feelings mostly that bother me, and those are hard to explain. Like God is whispering to my heart but I can't see or hear his words. Not yet."

"I see. Then tell me how it feels."

She looked past his shoulder to a long string of green books with a German-looking name stamped in gold foil across each spine: knowledge.

"Questions? Step right up! We have the answers. Yes, ma'am. You in the yellow dress."

"Yes. Why does God kill the innocent?"

"Well, now. That depends on what you mean by kill. Or by innocent—"

"I mean kill! Dead. Head against the rocks. And innocent. Plain innocent!"

"Helen?"

She looked back at Bill. "Tell you how it feels? It feels like those whispers to the heart. Like you've just walked into a dark dungeon. You've just seen one skull, and the hair on your neck stands on end, and you know there must be more. But you see, that's where it all gets fuzzy. Because I don't know if it's God's dungeon or Satan's dungeon. I mean, you would think it was Satan's. Who ever would think of God having a dungeon. But there are others peering into this dark space, as well. Angels. God himself. And there is the sound of running feet—running away. But I know that the skull there on the black earth is Gloria's. I do know that. And I know it's all part of a plan. It's all part of the running feet. That's the thing. You see, my daughter was sacrificed."

Helen paused and drew her breath carefully, noting that it had grown short. "There are some more things, but they would not make any sense right now." She looked up at him with heavy eyes.

"And this does?"

She shrugged. "You asked for it."

Pastor Madison looked at her with wide eyes. "And I don't think you can be so sure that your daughter was sacrificed. God does not work like that."

"You don't think so? Well, it's one thing to read about how God butchered a thousand nasty Amalekites long ago, but when the object of his ax is your own daughter's neck, the blindfolds go on, do they?"

Bill sat back without removing his eyes from hers. His dark brows were pulled together, creating furrows above the bridge of his nose. He'd stopped shepherding, she thought. Not that she blamed him. She had stopped bleating.

"It's okay, Bill. I don't really understand it, either. Not yet. But I would like you to pray with me. Pray *for* me. I'm a part of this, and it's not yet finished; that much I do know. It is all just beginning. Now you're a part of it. I need you, Pastor."

"Yes," he said. "Of course I will. But I want you to at least consider the possibility that you are misreading these images." He held up his hand. "I know it's not in your nature to do so, Helen. But so far all that has happened is that your daughter has died. I'm not minimizing the trauma of her death, not at all. In fact that very trauma may be initiating all of this. Can you at least understand my line of thinking?" His eyebrows lifted hopefully.

She nodded and smiled, thinking he might very well be the one who was misunderstanding here; he appeared to have missed the point entirely. "Yes, I can. Any psychiatrist in his right mind would tell me the same." She stood then. "But you are wrong, Bill. Gloria's death is not the only thing that has happened. They are rather frantic in the heavens, I think. And there is more to come. It is *this* for which I need your prayers. That and possibly my sanity. But I assure you, young man. I have not lost it yet."

She had walked out then.

He had called two hours later and told her he was praying. It was a good thing, she thought. He was a good man, and she liked him.

Helen let the memory drift away and brought her mind back to the present. Lack of understanding seemed as valuable to God as understanding. It required man to dip into the black hole of faith. But dipping into the hole was pretty much like walking through the dungeon at times.

She tilted her head back and breathed to the ceiling. "Oh God, do not keep silent; be not quiet, oh God, be not still." She quoted the Psalms as she often did in prayer. It was a kind of praying that seemed to fit her new life. "I am worn out calling for help; my throat is parched. My eyes fail looking for my God."

Yes indeed. In its own way, God's silence was as powerful as his presence. If for no reason other than it nudged you toward that hole. Taking the plunge was another matter. That took faith. Believing God was present when he felt absent.

She closed her eyes and moaned at the ceiling. "God, where have you gone?"

I have gone nowhere.

The voice spoke quietly in her spirit, but loudly enough to make her stop halfway down her groove.

Pray, daughter. Pray until it is over.

Now Helen began to tremble slightly. She sidestepped to the bed and sat heavily. "Over?" she vocalized

Pray for him and trust me.

"But it is so difficult when I cannot see."

Then remember the times when you have seen. And pray for him.

"Yes, I will."

The voice fell silent.

A wave of warmth swept through Helen's bones. She stretched her arms for the ceiling and tilted her head back. How could she have ever doubted this? This being who breathed through her now? "Oh, God, forgive me!"

Her chest swelled, and tears spilled from her eyes, unchecked. She opened her mouth and groaned—begging forgiveness, uttering words of love, trying to contain the emotions burning in her throat.

Helen sank to the mattress twenty minutes later, thoroughly content, unable to rid her face of its broad smile. How could she have possibly questioned? She would have to tell the pastor in the morning. It was all painfully obvious now.

An hour later, all of that changed.

Because an hour later, half an hour after she'd fallen into the sweetest sleep she could imagine, God spoke to her again. Showed her something new. But this time it did not feel like a soothing breath sweeping though her bones. This time it felt like a bucket of molten lead poured down her neck.

A scream woke her, filling her mind like a blaring klaxon that jerked her from the dream. It was not until she'd bolted up in bed and sat rigid that she realized the scream was coming from her own mouth.

"God, noooooo! Noooo! Noo—"

She caught her breath mid-wail. God no *what?* Why was she drenched in sweat? Why was her heart racing like a runaway locomotive?

The vision came back to her like a flood.

Then she knew why she had awakened screaming. She moaned, suddenly terrified again.

Darkness crowded her, and she glanced around the room for references, for some sense to dash this madness. Her wardrobe materialized against the far wall. The French doors glowed with moonlight. Reality settled in. But with it, the stark vision she had just witnessed.

Helen dropped to her back and breathed again, pulling in long, desperate breaths. "God, why, God? You can't!"

But she knew he could. Knew he would.

It took her three full hours to find a fitful sleep again and then only after changing her pillowcase twice. She thought it might be the wetness from her tears that kept her from sleep. But in the end she knew it was just the terror.

God was dealing in terror.

11

Kent dragged himself to the bank Wednesday morning, gritting his teeth in a muddle of humiliation and anger. He'd managed his way back to his office yesterday after the Bentley fiasco—fortunately without encountering a soul. For two hours he'd tried to work—and failed miserably. At eleven he'd left, brushing past Betty, mumbling something about an appointment. He had not returned.

Today he entered through the front door, but only because of his attorney's insistence that he maintain normalcy—act like nothing under the sun was bothering him when actually he was falling apart inside. He hurried through the lobby with his head down, fiddling with his third button as if something about it required his full attention. One of the tellers called out his name, but he pretended not to hear it. The button was far too consuming.

He rested his hand on the door to the Information Systems suite and closed his eyes. *Okay, Kent. Just do what needs to be done.* He pushed his way in.

Betty stared at him uncomfortably. Oversized fake black lashes shielded her eyes from the fluorescents. He had an urge to pluck one of them off. Then when she batted her eyes, there would be only one lash fanning the reception room; the room was too small for two anyway.

He nodded. "Morning."

"Morning," she returned, and her voice cracked.

"Borst in?"

"He's in Phoenix today. He'll be back tomorrow."

Thank God for small favors.

Kent walked into his office and closed himself in. Ten minutes later he came to the grinding conclusion that he could not work. Just couldn't. He could pretend to work and play Dennis Warren's game if it would reward him with a fat settlement. But with the door closed, pretending felt absurd.

He punched up a game of solitaire and found it dreadfully boring after the second hand. He tried to call Dennis but learned from the little bimbo at the law offices' front desk that he was in court.

When the knock on the door sounded at ten, it came as a relief. A kind of put-me-out-of-my-misery relief. Kent punched the dormant solitaire game off his screen. "Come in," he called and adjusted his tie knot out of habit.

The new transfer walked in and shut the door. Cliff Monroe. All crisp and clean and charged to climb the ladder. He smiled wide and stuck out his hand—the same hand that Kent had ignored two days earlier.

"Hi, Kent. It's a pleasure to meet you. I've heard a lot about you." His pineapple-eating smile covered the full spectrum—a genuine ear-to-ear grin. "Sorry about the other day."

Kent took the hand and blushed at the memory of *the other day.* "Not your fault. I should apologize. Not the best first impression, I guess."

Cliff must have taken Kent's tone as an invitation to sit, because he grabbed a chair and plopped down. His eyes flashed a brilliant green. "No, it wasn't a problem, really. From what I've picked up between the lines, if you know what I mean, you had every reason to be upset."

Kent straightened. "You know what's going on?" Cliff was still wearing that grin. His teeth seemed inordinately white, like his shirt. "Let's put it this way, I know that Kent Anthony was primarily responsible for the creation of AFPS—I knew that while I was still in Dallas. That's where I transferred in from. I guess the boys upstairs decided that you could use another decent programmer. It's not permanent yet, but believe me, I hope it becomes permanent because I love this place. Even if I don't have my own office yet." Somewhere in that long preamble Cliff had lost his grin. He pressed on before Kent could refocus him. "Yes sir, I would absolutely love to move to the mountains here in Denver. I figure I can crack code during the week, make some decent dough, and the slopes will be mine on the weekends. Do you snowboard?"

The oversized kid was a piece of work. Kent just stared at the programmer for a moment. He'd heard of this type: all brain when it came to the keyboard, and all brawn when it came to the weekends. He smiled for the first time that day.

Cliff joined him with a face-splitting grin of his own, and Kent had an inkling that the kid knew exactly what he was doing.

"I've skied a day or two in my time," he said.

"Great, we can go sometime." The new transfer's face dropped long. "Sorry about what happened to your wife. I mean, I heard about that. It must be hard."

"Uh-huh. So what do you know besides the fact that I was responsible for AFPS?"

"I know that things got a bit topsy-turvy at the convention. Your name was somehow bypassed in all the fuss. Sounds like Borst grabbed all the glory." Cliff grinned again.

Kent blinked and decided not to join him. "Yeah, well you may think that's a cheesy let's-all-have-a-grin-about-it affair, but the fact is, Borst not only got the glory, he's getting all the money as well."

The kid nodded. "Yeah, I know."

That set Kent back. The kid knew that as well? "And you don't have a problem with that?"

"Sure I do. I also have a problem with the fact that the slopes are two hours away. I came to Denver thinking the resorts are out everybody's backdoor, you know. But unless we can find a way to move mountains, I think we're both kinda stuck."

Yes, indeed, Cliff was no dummy. Probably one of those kids who started punching up computer code while they were still in diapers. "We'll see."

"Well, if you need my help, just ask." Cliff shrugged. "I know I will."

"You will what?"

"Need help. From you. My responsibility is to dig into the code and look for weaknesses. I've found the first three already."

"Look for weaknesses, huh? And what makes you think there are any weaknesses? What three?"

"Todd, Mary, and Borst." That grin wrinkled the kid's face again.

Kent could hardly help himself this time. He chuckled. Cliff was looking more and more like an ally. Another small gift from God, possibly. He'd tell Dennis about this one.

He nodded. "You're all right, Cliff. But I wouldn't be saying that too loudly around here, if I were you. You know what they say about power. It corrupts. And by the sound of things, Borst has found himself a load of power lately."

Cliff winked. "Not to worry, Kent. I'm on it already. You got my vote."

"Thanks."

"Now seriously, I do have a few questions. Do you mind running me through a few routines?"

The kid was a walking paradox. At first glance, clean cut and ready to brown-nose the closest executive, but something entirely different under the starch. A snowboarder. Spencer would get a kick out of this.

"Sure. What do you want to know?"

They spent the rest of the morning and the first afternoon hour plowing through code. Kent's instincts proved correct: Cliff was a regular programming prodigy. Not as fluent or precise as Kent, but as close to him as anybody he'd met. And likable to boot. He'd set up shop down the hall in an office that had served as the suite's overflow room before his arrival. He retreated there shortly after one.

Kent stared at the door after Cliff's departure. What now? He picked up the phone and began to dial Dennis Warren's number. But then he remembered that the attorney was in court. He dropped the phone in its cradle. Maybe he should talk to Will Thompson upstairs. Recruit the loan officer's support on the matter of the missing bonus. That would mean walking past Betty again, of course, and he could hardly stand the thought. Unless she was taking a late lunch.

Kent shut his computer down, grabbed his briefcase, and headed out.

Unfortunately, Betty was back from lunch, unwittingly transferring blush from her well-oiled face to her phone's mouthpiece while gabbing with only heaven knew who. Some other lady who had absolutely no clue about banking. Her beautician perhaps.

Kent didn't bother reporting his plans. He found Will upstairs, banging on his monitor again. "You need some help there, young man?"

Will jerked up. "Kent!" He sat back and nodded in a bouncing motion.

"You still having problems with that monitor?"

"Every time you come by, it seems. The thing keeps winking off on me. I need to inadvertently push it off the desk and requisition a new one. Maybe a twenty-one incher."

"Yeah, that'll definitely push the loans right along. The bigger the better."

Will conducted a few more of his nods and smiled. "So I heard that you had a run-in with Bentley yesterday," he said.

Kent sat calmly in the guest chair facing Will, ignoring the heat suddenly washing over his shoulders. "And how did you know that?"

"This is a small city we work in, Kent. Complete with built-in, free-flowing lines of communication. Things get around."

Good night! Who else knew? If big-mouth here knew, the whole world would soon hear. Probably already had. Kent glanced around the room and caught a pair of eyes resting on him from the far side. He shifted his eyes back to Will.

"So what did you hear?"

"I heard that you walked in there and demanded to be named employee of the month for your part in the AFPS development. They said you were screaming about it."

The heat spread right down Kent's spine. *Employee of the month?* That lousy imbecile! I could . . ." He bit off the rest and closed his eyes. They weren't messing around, then. He had become their fool. The poor fellow in administration who wanted a bigger pat on the back.

"You didn't actually scream at—"

"You're darned right I screamed at that jerk!" Kent said. "But not about some lousy employee-of-the-month parking space." He breathed heavily and tried to calm his pulse. "People are actually buying that?"

"I don't buy it." Will sat back and glanced around. "Keep your voice down, man."

"What's everybody else saying?"

"I don't know. They're saying that anyone who screams at Bentley about employee-of-the-month status has got a screw loose, to be sure." A slight grin crossed the loan officer's face. "They're saying that if anybody should get employee of the month it should be the whole department because AFPS came from the department."

Something popped in Kent's mind, as if someone had tossed a depth charge in there and run for cover. *Kaboom!* He stood to his feet. At least he *wanted* to stand to his feet. His efforts resulted in more of a lurch. The room swam dizzily.

He had to get to Dennis! This was not good!

"I've got to go," he mumbled. "I'm late."

Will leaned forward. "Kent, sit down for heaven's sake! It's not a big deal. Everybody knows you were the real brains behind AFPS, man. Lighten up."

Kent bent for his case and strode deliberately from the desk. He only wanted one thing now. Out. Just out, out, out.

If there had been a fire escape in the hall, he might have taken it in favor of chancing a face-to-face encounter with another employee. But there was no fire escape. And there *was* another person in the elevator. She might have been Miss America, for all he knew, because he refused to make eye contact. He pressed into the corner, praying for the moments to pass quickly.

The backdoor released him to the alley, and tears blurred his vision before the latch slammed home. He bellowed angrily, instinctively. The roar echoed, and he spun his head, wondering if anyone had heard or seen this grown man carrying on. The alley lay dark and empty both ways. A large diesel engine growled nearby— an earthmover, perhaps, breaking ground on someone's dream.

Kent felt very small. Very, very, very small. Small enough to die.

⌁

While Kent was dying at work, Helen was doing her best to forget the images that had visited her the previous night. But she was not doing so good.

She stirred the pitcher of ice tea slowly, listening to Spencer hum "Jesus, Lover of My Soul" in the other room. All of their lives seemed to hinge on that song, she thought, remembering how Spencer's grandfather had loved to sing it in his mellow, baritone voice. From grandfather to grandson. Ice clinked in the tea, and she began to sing softly with him. "Jesus, Lover of my soul . . ."

If the boy only knew.

Well, today he would know a little more. Enough for things to brighten.

She hobbled past Spencer, who sat, as usual, cross-legged on the floor, then she eased into her worn green rocker. A small glass bottle sat in the hutch, ancient and red, glaring at her with its history. It held its secrets, that glass vile, secrets that brought a chill to her spine still. She swallowed and shifted her eyes. Now the picture of the cross with Jesus spread out, dying on its beams, stared directly at her, and she kept up with the boy in a wobbly soprano. ". . . Let me to thy bosom fly . . ." She would have to hold it together now—in front of the boy at least. She would have to trust as she had never trusted. As long as she could keep her eyes off the scales of justice that had found their way into her mind, she would do fine. As long as she could trust that God's scales were working, even though her own tipped, lopsided, in her mind, she would make it.

Funny how so many saw that cross as a bridge over the gulf between God and man—between heaven and earth—and yet how few took the time to cross it. No pun there, just a small nugget of truth. How many were busy looking for another way across? How many Christians avoided the death of God? Take up your cross daily, he'd said. Now, there was a paradox.

"Spencer."

"Yes, Grandma?" He looked up from the Legos that had held his attention for the last half-hour. He'd built a spaceship, she saw. Fitting.

She looked around the room, thinking of how best to tell him. "Did your father talk to you last night?"

Spencer nodded. "Sure."

"About his job?"

Spencer looked up at her curiously. "How did you know that?"

"I didn't know. That's why I asked. But I did know he was having . . . complications at work."

"Yeah, that's what he said. Did he tell you about it?"

"No. But I wanted to help you understand some things today about your father."

Spencer let the Lego pieces lie on the floor and sat up, interested. "He's having a hard time."

"Yes he is, isn't he?" She let silence settle for a few seconds. "Spencer, how long do you think we've been praying for your father to see the light?"

"A long time."

"Five years. Five years of beating on the brass heavens. Then they cracked. You remember that? Almost three weeks ago?"

The boy nodded, wide eyed now. "With Mom." Spencer scrambled to his feet and climbed into "his" chair opposite Grandma. The air suddenly felt charged.

"It seems that our prayers have caused quite a stir in the heavens. You should know, Spencer, that everything happening with your father is by design."

The boy tilted his head slightly, thinking that through. "Mom's death?"

The boy was not missing a beat here. "It has its purpose."

"What purpose could God have in letting Mom die?"

"Let me ask you, which is greater in regard to your mother's death? *Her* pleasure or your father's sorrow?" She suddenly wanted to throw her own grief on the scales and withdraw the question. But that was not her part here—she at least knew that.

He looked at her for a moment, thinking. The corner of his mouth twitched and then lifted to a small sheepish grin. "Mom's pleasure?" he said.

"By a long shot, Honey. You remember that. And no matter what else happens to your father, you remember that a hundred thousand eyes are peering down on him from the heavens, watching what he will do. Anything can happen at any time, and everything happens for a purpose. Can you understand that?"

Spencer nodded, his eyes round with eagerness.

"You ever hear of a man named C. S. Lewis? He once wrote, 'There is no neutral ground in the universe: every square inch, every split second, is claimed by God and counter claimed by Satan.' It's like that with your father, Spencer. Do you believe that?"

Spencer closed his mouth and swallowed. "Yes. Sometimes it's hard to know . . ."

"But you do believe it, don't you?"

"Yes. I believe it."

"And why do you believe it, Spencer?"

He looked at her, and his eyes shone like jewels. "Because I've seen heaven," he said. "And I know that things are not what people think they are."

Her feelings for the boy boiled to the surface, and she felt a lump rise in her throat. Such a tender face under those blue eyes. He had Gloria's face. *Oh, my God, my God. What could you possibly be thinking?* Her chest felt like it might explode with grief, looking at the boy.

She felt a tear slip from her eye. "Come here, Honey," she said.

The boy came and sat on the arm of her chair. She took his hand and kissed it gently then pulled him onto her lap. "I love you, my child. I love you so dearly."

He blushed and turned to kiss her forehead. "I love you too, Grandma."

She looked into his eyes. "You are blessed, Spencer. We have just begun, I think. And you have such a precious part to play. Savor it for me, will you?"

"I will, Grandma."

"Promise?"

"Promise."

For a long time, Helen held her grandson, rocking in the chair in silence. Remarkably, he let her—seemed to relish the embrace. Tears were soon flowing freely down her face and wetting her blouse. She did not want the boy to see her cry, but she could not stop herself. Her life was being shredded, for God's sake.

Quite literally.

12

Kent slumped into a dead sleep sometime past midnight Wednesday, with visions of vultures circling lazily through his dreams. He woke late and scrambled to dress for work. The thought of returning to the den of thieves made him sick just now, but he had not seen his way past Dennis Warren's suggestion that he at least maintain his status of employment with the bank. And he had not succeeded in making contact with the attorney the previous afternoon, despite a dozen attempts. His lawyer's bimbo was developing a dislike for him, he thought.

And now it was morning. Which meant it was time to go back to the bank. Back to hell. Maybe today he would wash Borst's feet. Give him a good rubdown, perhaps. Congratulate him for making employee of the month. *Jolly good, sir.* Good grief!

"Dad."

Kent looked up from the edge of the bed, where he'd just pulled on his last sock. Spencer stood in the bedroom doorway, fully dressed. His hair lay in a tangled web, but then the boy was going nowhere today.

"Hey, Spencer."

His son walked in and sat next to him. "You're up late," the boy observed.

"Yeah. I slept in."

Spencer suddenly put an arm over his shoulder and squeezed him gently. "I love you, Dad."

The show of affection brought a heaviness to Kent's chest. "I love you too, son."

They sat together, still and quiet for a moment.

"You know that Mom is okay, don't you?" Spencer looked up. "She's in heaven, Dad. With God. She's laughing up there."

Kent blinked at that. "Sure, son. But we're down here. There's no heaven down here."

"Sometimes there is," Spencer said.

Kent ruffled the boy's hair and smiled. "Heaven on earth. You're right. Sometimes there is." He stood and fed his tie around his collar. "Like when your mother and I got married. Now *there* was some heaven. Or like when I first bought the Lexus. You remember when I came home with the Lexus, Spencer?"

"I'm not talking about that kind of heaven."

Kent walked to the mirror on the wall, not wanting this conversation now. Now he wanted to tear Borst's throat out. He saw his eyebrows furrow in the mirror. Beyond, Spencer's reflection stared back at him. This was his boy on the bed, eyes round, legs hanging limp almost to the ground.

"C'mon, Spencer. You know I don't see things the way you do. I know you want what's best for Mom, but she's just gone. Now it's you and me, buddy. And we will find our own way."

"Yeah, I know."

That's right, son. Let it go.

"But maybe we should follow Mom's way."

Kent closed his eyes and clenched his jaw. Mom's way? And what was Mom's way? Mom's way was death. *Yeah, well, why don't we all just die and go to heaven?*

He pulled his tie tight and turned back to Spencer. "We don't live in a fantasy world; we live in a real world where people actually die, and when they die it's the end. Six feet under. Game's over. And there's no use pretending otherwise."

"What about God?"

The doorbell chimed in the foyer. That would be Linda, the sitter Helen had arranged for, coming to watch Spencer for the day. Kent turned for the door.

"Why don't you just believe in God?"

Kent stopped and turned back toward Spencer. "I do believe in God. I just have a broader concept, that's all."

"But God loves you, Dad. I think he's trying to get your attention."

Kent swung around, his gut suddenly churning. He wanted to say, *Don't be so simplistic, Spencer. Don't be so stupid!* Wanted to shout that. If what was happening in his life had anything at all to do with some white-bearded scribe in the sky, then God was getting senile in his old age. It was time for someone with a little more compassion to take over.

Kent turned back to the door without responding.

"He won't let you go, Dad. He loves you too much," Spencer said softly.

Kent whirled, suddenly furious. His words came before he could stop them. "I don't care about your God, Spencer! Just shut up!"

He spun around and steamed for the front door, knowing he had crossed a line. He pulled open the door and glared at the brunette baby-sitter who stood on the front steps.

She shoved out her hand. "Mr. Anthony?"

"Yes." Kent heard Spencer pad up behind him, and he wanted to turn to the boy and beg his forgiveness. Linda was staring at him with bright gray eyes, and he diverted his gaze past her to the street. *Spencer, my dear son, I love you so much. I could never hurt a hair on your head. Never. Never, never!*

He should turn now and hold the boy. Spencer was all he had left. Kent swallowed and stepped past her. "Take care of him," he instructed without shaking her hand. "He knows the rules."

Every bone in Kent's body ached to spin and run back to Spencer. Yet he trudged forward to the Lexus waiting in the driveway. He saw his son from the corner of his eye when he slammed the door shut. The boy stood in the doorway with limp arms.

Kent roared down the street, thinking he had just stooped as low as he had ever stooped. Might as well have licked some concrete while he was down there. Why the subject of God sent him into such a tailspin he could hardly fathom. Death usually seemed to bring people to their knees, begging the man upstairs for some understanding. But Gloria's death seemed to have planted a root of bitterness in his heart. Maybe because she had died so violently despite her faith. And his mother-in-law Helen's prayers had ended where all prayers end: in her own gray matter.

He arrived at the red-brick bank filled with foreboding from its first sighting, ten blocks earlier. He would call Dennis again today—find out how quickly they could get a suit filed. Maybe then he could leave.

Kent made his way to the alley behind the bank. There was no way he would step through those fancy swinging doors up front and risk running into fat-boy Bentley. The rear entrance would do just fine for the balance of his tenure, thank you. He stepped down the dingy alley.

White fingers of steam rose from a sewer grate halfway down the narrow passage.

Garbage lay strewn beside the dumpster, as if the whole cage had been tipped and then righted again. Some homeless vagrant too eager for his own good. Kent pulled a ring of keys from his pocket and found the silver one he'd been issued for the door a year earlier after complaining he needed longer access. Since then he'd come and gone as he pleased, often working late into the night. The memory sat in his mind now, mocking.

How many hours had he given to the bank? Thousands at least. Tens of thousands, all for Borst and Fat-Boy. If Spencer's God was somehow actually involved in the world, it was as a tormentor. *Let's see which of them we can get to scream the loudest today.* Kent pushed the key into the slot.

A whisper rasped on the wind behind him. "You ain't seen nothin' yet, you sicko." Kent whirled.

Nothing!

His heart pumped hard. The dumpster sat still; the alley gaped on either side, empty to the streets, white strands of steam lifted lazily from the grate. But he had heard it, clear as day. *You ain't seen nothin' yet, you sicko!*

The stress was getting to him. Kent turned to the gray-steel fire door and reinserted the key with an unsteady hand.

To his left, a movement caught his eyes, and he jerked his head that way. A man wearing a torn red Hawaiian shirt and filthy slacks that had possibly once been blue leaned against the dumpster, staring at him. The sight frightened Kent badly, and his hand froze on the key. Not three seconds ago, he would have sworn the alley was empty.

"Life sucks," the man said, and then lifted a brown bag to his lips and took a slug from a hidden bottle. He did not remove his eyes from Kent's. Scattered patches of scraggly hair hung off his neck. His lumpy nose shined red and big.

"Life really *sssssucksss!*" He grinned now, and his teeth were jagged yellow. He cackled and lifted the brown bag.

Kent watched the vagrant take another slug. He yanked on the door and stepped in quickly. Something was haunting him; his mind was bending. *Get a grip, Kent. You're losing your grip.*

The door swooshed shut, and suddenly the hall was pitch dark. He groped the wall, found the switch, and flipped it up. The long fluorescent tubes stuttered to white, illuminating the empty hall. Long and empty like the prospects facing his life now. Bleak, white, long, empty.

Life sucks.

Kent forced himself to the end and out to the main corridor. Somehow he had embarked on a roller coaster, swooping up and down and around sharp curves at breakneck speed, intent on throwing him to his death. Some thrill ride from hell, and he wasn't being allowed to disembark. Each hour was rolling into the next, each day full of new twists and turns. They say that when it rains, it pours. Yes, well, it was pouring all right. Fire and brimstone.

Betty was gone when he stepped into the Information Systems suites, probably to the john to apply yet another layer of mascara to her foot-long fake lashes. She'd always fancied herself to be half her age with twice the life. Kent slipped into his office and closed the door quietly. *Here we go then.* He sat and tried to still the buzzing in his head.

For a full minute Kent stared at the exotic fish making their predictable sweeps across the three monitors. It was not until then that it occurred to him that he still gripped his briefcase. He dropped it on the floor and picked up the phone.

It took five minutes for the cranky secretary at Dennis Warren's office to finally put him through, and then only after Kent's threat to call back repeatedly every three minutes if she didn't tell Dennis this very minute that he was on the phone.

Dennis came on. "Kent. How goes it, my friend? Go easy on my girls."

"She was giving me lip. Shouldn't give lip to customers, Dennis. Bad business."

"You're not a customer. Not yet, Kent." A chuckle. "When you get a bill, you'll be a customer. So what's up?"

Kent chose to ignore the jab. "Nothing. Unless you call sitting in an office doing nothing for eight hours while everybody around you has their ear to the wall, listening for your *nothing,* something. It's falling apart here, Dennis. The whole bank knows."

"Lighten up, buddy."

"We have to move forward, Dennis! I'm not sure how long I can do this."

A long silence filled his ear, which was rather uncharacteristic of his friend, who never seemed at a loss for words. Now Dennis was suddenly silent. Breathing, actually. Breathing heavily. When he spoke his voice sounded scratchy.

"We can move forward on this as soon as you are positive, Kent."

"Positive? About what? I *am* positive! They think I've lost my mind around here! Do you understand that? They think I'm off the deep end, for goodness' sake! We're going to bury these guys, if it's the last thing we do!" He let the statement settle, wondering if his voice had carried out to the hall. "Right?"

A chuckle crackled on the phone. "Oh, we'll be doing some burying, all right. But what about you, Kent?" Now Dennis was speaking around short breaths, pausing after each phrase to pull at the air. "Are you positive about where you stand?" A breath. "You can't go soft halfway through." A breath. Another breath. Kent scrunched his eyebrows.

The attorney continued. "It's not like God's going to reach down and hand you answers, you know. You decide to go one way, you go all the way that way. Right to the end, and screw them all if they need their crutch!" A series of breaths. "Right, Kent? Isn't that right?"

Kent furrowed his brow. "What are you talking about? Who's talking about going soft halfway? I'm saying we bury them, man! Screw 'em all to the wall." He let the comment about the crutch go. Something was confused there.

"That's right, Kent," the attorney's voice rasped. "You do whatever it takes. This is life and death. You win, it's life; you lose, it's death."

"I hear you, man. And what I'm saying here is that, by the looks of things, I'm already a dead man. We have to move now."

"You do things their way and you end up getting buried. Like some fool martyr." A ragged pause. "Look at Gloria."

Gloria? Kent felt his pulse rise in agreement with his attorney. He understood what Dennis was doing now. And it was brilliant. The man was reaching out to him; connecting with him emotionally; drawing the battle lines.

"Yes," he said. And Dennis was saying that the bank and God were on the same side. They both wanted to do some burying. Only God was really fate, and fate had already done its burying with Gloria. Now the bank was having its go. With him.

The hair lifted on the nape of his neck. "Yes. Well, they're not going to bury me, Dennis. Not unless they kill me first."

The phone sat unspeaking in his palm for a few seconds before Dennis came on again. "No. Killing is against the rules. But there are other ways."

"Well, I'm not actually suggesting killing anybody, Dennis. It's just a figure of speech. But I hear you. I hear you loud and clear. And I'm ready. When can we get this ball rolling?"

This time the phone went dead for a long time.

"Dennis? Hello?"

"No," Dennis returned. His voice was distant, like an echo on the phone now. "I don't think you are ready. I don't think you are ready at all, my fine friend. Perhaps this afternoon you will be ready."

The phone clicked. Kent held it to his ear, stunned. This afternoon? What in the world did this afternoon have to do with anything? A sudden panic rose to his throat. What was going on? What in—

The phone began burping loudly in his ear. An electronic voice came on and told him in a roundabout way that holding a dead phone to the ear was a rather unbrilliant thing to do.

He dropped the receiver in its cradle.

Yes indeed, the roller coaster from hell. *After him, lads! After him!*

Now what? What was he supposed to do in this cursed place? Sit and stare at fish while Borst sat across the hall, planning how to spend his forthcoming fortune?

Cliff poked his head in once and offered a "Good morning" around that pineapple-eating grin of his. Kent forced a small smile and mumbled the same.

"You keep your nose clean, now. You hear?" Cliff said.

"Always. Clean's my middle name," he returned. He tried to find some levity in his own irony, but he could not.

"Okay. Just hang in there. Things will look up if you hang in there."

When Kent looked up, Cliff had pulled out. The door clicked shut. Now what did *he* know? Like some father offering sound wisdom. *Hang in there, son. Here, come sit on my lap.*

He tried to imagine Cliff catching air on a snowboard. The image came hard. Now Spencer, there was someone who could catch air. Only it was on a skateboard.

Kent spent an hour running through e-mail and idiotic bank memoranda. Most of it went to the trash with a click. He expected that at any moment one of the others would pop in and say something, but no one did, and the fact began to wear on him. He heard their muffled voices on several occasions, but they seemed to be ignoring him wholesale. Maybe they didn't know he'd come in. Or more likely they were embarrassed for him. *Did you hear about Kent and Bentley? Yeah, he's really flipped, huh? Poor guy. Lost his wife—that's what did it. For sure.*

Several times he contemplated calling Dennis back—asking him what he'd meant about this afternoon. But the memory of the man's voice echoing in the receiver made him postpone the call.

He called up AFPS and entered the new password: MBAOK. The familiar icon ran across the screen, and he let it cycle through a few times before entering the system. A program like this would be worth millions to any large bank. He should just download the source code and take it on the road. It was his, after all.

But that was the problem. It was not his. At least, not legally.

Kent was startled by the sudden buzz of his phone. Dennis, possibly. Calling to apologize about that ludicrous exchange. He glanced at the caller ID.

It was Betty. And he was in no mood to discuss office business. He let the phone buzz annoyingly. It finally fell silent after a dozen persistent burps. What was her problem?

A fist pounded on his door, and he swung around. Betty stood in the door frame, stricken white. "You have a call," she said, and he thought she might be ill. "It's urgent. I'll put it through again."

She pulled the door closed. Kent stared after her.

The phone blared again. This time Kent whirled and snatched up the receiver. "Hello."

"Hello, Mr. Anthony?" It was a female voice. A soft, shaky female voice.

"Yes, this is Kent Anthony."

A pause. "Mr. Anthony, I'm afraid there's been an accident. Do you have a son named Spencer Anthony?"

Kent rose to his feet. His hands went cold on the receiver. "Yes."

"He was hit by a car, Mr. Anthony. He's at Denver Memorial. You should come quickly."

Adrenaline flooded Kent's bloodstream like boiling ice. Goose flesh prickled down his shoulders. "Is . . . Is he okay?"

"He's . . ." A sick pause. "I'm sorry. I can't . . ."

"Just tell me! Is my son okay?"

"He died in the ambulance, Mr. Anthony. I'm sorry . . ."

For a moment the world stood still. He didn't know if the woman said more. If she did, he did not hear it because a buzzing had erupted in his skull again.

The phone slipped from his grasp and thudded on the carpet. Spencer? His Spencer!? Dead?

He stood rooted to the floor, his right hand still up by his ear where the receiver had been, his mouth limp and gaping. The terror came in waves then, spreading down his arms and legs like fire.

Kent whirled to the door. It was shut. Wait a minute, this could have been one of those voices! He was going mad, wasn't he? And now the voices of madness had touched him where they knew he would be hurt most. Tried to yank his heart out.

He died in the ambulance, the voice had said. An image of Spencer's blond head lying cockeyed on an ambulance gurney flashed through his mind. His boy's arms jiggled as the medical van bounced over potholes.

He staggered for the door and pulled it open, barely conscious of his movements. Betty sat at her desk, still white. And then Kent knew that it had been a real voice.

Blackness washed through his mind, and he lost his sensibilities. The days leading up to this one had weakened them badly. Now they simply fell away, like windblown chaff.

He groaned, unabashed, oblivious to the doors suddenly cracking around him for a view of the commotion. A small part of his mind knew that he was lumbering through the hall, hands hanging limp, moaning like some retarded hunchback, but the realization hung like some tiny inconsequential detail on the black horizon. Everything else was just buzzing and black.

Kent stumbled through the hall door, on autopilot now. He was halfway to the main lobby when the cruelty of it all crashed into his brain and he began to gasp in ragged pulls like a stranded fish gulping on the rocks. Spencer's sweet, innocent face hung in his mind. Then Gloria's swollen body, still blotched and purple.

He lifted his hands to his temples and fell into an unsteady jog. He wanted to stop. Stop the groaning, stop the pain, stop the madness. Just stop.

But it all came like a flood now, and instead of stopping he began to sob. Like a man possessed, Kent ran straight through the main lobby, gripping the hair at his temples, wailing loudly.

For a moment, banking stopped cold.

Twelve tellers turned as one and stared, startled. Zak, the security guard, brought his hand to the butt of his shiny new .38, for the first time, possibly.

Kent burst through the swinging doors, leapt down the concrete steps, and tore around the corner. He slammed into the car, hardly knowing it was his.

Spencer! No, no, no! Please, not Spencer!

His son's face loomed tender and grinning in Kent's mind. His blond bangs hung before his blue eyes. The boy flipped his head back, and Kent felt a wave of dizziness at the ache in his own chest.

The door to his Lexus was not opening easily, and he frantically fumbled with a wad of keys, dropping them once and banging his head on the mirror as he retrieved them. But he did not feel any pain from the gash above his left eye. It bled warm blood down his cheek, and that felt strangely comforting.

Then he was in his car and somehow screaming through the streets with his horn blaring, wiping frantically at his eyes to clear his vision.

He felt barely conscious now. All he noticed were the pain and blackness that crashed through his mind. He wove in and out of traffic, banging on the wheel, trying to dislodge the pain. But when he squealed to a stop at the hospital and met a wide-eyed paramedic head on, bent on restraining him, uttering consolations, he knew it made little difference.

Spencer was dead.

Somewhere in the confusion, a well-meaning man in a white coat told him that his son, Spencer, had been struck by a car from behind. A hit-and-run. One of the neighbors found him sprawled on the sidewalk, halfway to the park, with a broken back. Spencer couldn't have known what hit him, he said. Kent screamed back at the man, told him he should try letting a car snap *his* spine at forty miles an hour and see how that felt.

He stumbled into the room where they had left Spencer's little body lying on a gurney. He was still in his shorts, bare chested and blond. They had worked with his body, but at first glance Kent saw that his son's torso rested at an odd angle to his hips. He imagined that body snapping in two, folding over, and he threw up on the gray linoleum floor. He lurched forward to the body, hazy now. Then he touched his son's white skin and rested his cheek on his still rib cage and wept.

It felt as though a white-hot iron had been pulled from the fires of hell and stamped on his mind. No one deserved this. *No one.* That was the tattoo.

The pain burned so strongly that Kent lost himself to it. They later told him that he'd ranted and raved and cursed—mostly cursed—for over an hour. But he could remember none of it. They gave him a sedative, they said, and he went to sleep. On the floor, in the corner, curled up like a fetus.

But that was not how he remembered things. He just remembered that most of him died that day. And he remembered that branding iron burning in his skull.

13

Helen Crane piloted the ancient, pale yellow Ford Pinto through a perfectly manicured suburbia, struck by the gross facade. Like a huge plastic Barbie-doll set carefully constructed on the ground to cover a reeking cesspool beneath. Made to cover these dungeons down here.

It felt strange driving through the world. Lonely. As if she were dreaming and the houses rising above green lawns were from another planet—because she knew what was really here, and it resembled something much closer to a sewer than this picture-perfect neighborhood.

That was the problem with holing yourself up in prayer for a week and having your eyes opened. You saw things with more clarity. And God was making her see things more clearly these days, just as he'd done with Elisha's servant. Drawing her into this huge drama unfolding behind the eyes of mortals. She played the intercessor—the one mortal allowed to glimpse both worlds so that she could pray. She knew that. And pray she had, nearly nonstop for ten days now.

But it was just the beginning. She knew that just as she would know the turning of the leaves signaled the coming of autumn. More was to follow. A whole season.

She was starting to accept God's judgment in the matter. Much like a housewife might accept her husband's leadership—with a plastic smile to avoid confrontation. Of course, this was God, not some man brimming with weaknesses. Still, she could not let him so easily off the hook for what he had done. Or at the very least, allowed—which, given his power, was the same thing. Her time seemed to be divided equally between two realities. The reality in which she cried pitifully, chastising God for this mad plan, begging for relief, and the reality in which she bowed and shook and wept, humbled to have heard God's voice at all.

Chastising God was foolishness, of course. Utter nonsense. Humans had no right to blame their difficulties on God, as if he knew precisely what he was doing when he breathed galaxies into existence but was slipping now in his dealings with the beings on planet Earth.

On the other hand, it was God himself, in all of his wisdom, who had created man with such a fickle mind. Believing one day, doubting the next; loving one moment, forgetting within the hour. Mankind.

"Oh God, deliver us from ourselves," she muttered and turned the corner leading toward Kent's.

She no longer struggled with the believing, as most did. But the loving . . . Sometimes she wondered about the loving. If human nature was a magnet, then self-gratification was steel, clinging stubbornly. And loving . . . loving was like wood, refusing to stick to the magnet no matter how much pressure was applied. Well, like it or not she was still human. Even after all she had been through before this mess. Yes indeed, Kent here was a *saint* compared to what she had been.

"Why are you taking us here, Father? Where does this road end? What have you not shown me?"

In the five weeks since she'd first seen the heavens open, together with Gloria and Spencer, she had seen a glimpse of the light every day. But only on three occasions had she seen specific visions of the business up there. That first one when she had learned of this whole mess. The second showing Spencer's death. And a third, a week ago, just after Spencer had joined his mother.

Each time she had been allowed to see a little more. She had seen Gloria laughing. And she had seen Spencer as well, laughing. She didn't know if they laughed all the time—it seemed the pleasure of it would wear thin. Then again, wearing thin would require time, and there was no time in heaven, was there? And actually it had not been one big laughter up there. Not every moment was filled with laughter, if indeed there even were such things as moments on the other side. Twice in the last vision she had seen both Spencer and Gloria lying still, neither laughing nor speaking but hanging limp and quivering, their eyes fixed on something she could not see. Wallowing in pleasure. Then the laughter came again, on the tail of the moment. A laughter of delight and ecstasy, not of humor. In fact, there was nothing funny about the business her daughter and grandson were up to in the heavens.

It was the business of raw pleasure. If she had not seen that, she might very well have gone mad.

Helen blinked and turned onto Kent's street. His two-story rose like a tomb, isolated against the bleak, gray sky.

In her last vision, Helen had caught a glimpse of this thing's magnitude, and it had left her stunned. She had seen it in the distance, beyond the space occupied by Gloria and Spencer, and for only a brief moment. A million, perhaps a billion creatures were gathered there. And where was *there?* There was the whole sky, although it seemed impossible. They had come together in two halves, as though on cosmic bleachers peering down on a single field. Or was it a dungeon? It was the only way Helen could translate the vision.

An endless sea of angelic creatures shone white on the right, clamoring for a view of the field below. They appeared in many forms, indescribable and unlike anything she had imagined.

On the left, pitch blackness created a void in space filled only with the red and yellow of countless flickering eyes. The potent stench of vomit had drifted from them, and she had blanched, right there, on the green chair in her living room.

Then she saw the object of their fixed attention. It was a man on the field below, running, pumping his arms full tilt, like some kind of gladiator fleeing from a lion. Only there was no lion. There was nothing. Then the heavens faded, and she saw that it was Kent and he was sprinting through a park, crying.

She had gone to him that afternoon and offered him comfort, which he'd promptly rejected. She had also asked him where he'd been at ten that morning, the time of her vision.

"I went for a run," he'd said.

Helen pulled into the drive and parked the Pinto.

Kent answered the door after the third buzz. By the rings under his eyes the man had not been sleeping. His hair lay in blond tangles, and his normally bright blue eyes peered through drooping lids, hazed over.

"Hello, Kent," Helen offered with a smile.

"Hello." He left the door open and headed for the living room. Helen let herself in and closed the door. When she walked under the catwalk he had already seated himself in the overstuffed beige rocker.

The odor of day-old dishrags hung in the air. Perhaps week-old dishrags. The same music he had played for days crooned melancholically through the darkened living room. Celine someone-or-other, he had told her. Dion. Celine Dion, and it wasn't a tape; it was a CD, like the initials of her name. CD.

She scanned the unkempt room. The miniblinds were closed, and she blinked to adjust her eyesight. A pile of dishes rose above the breakfast bar to her right. The television throbbed silently with colors to her left. Pizza boxes lay strewn on a coffee table cluttered with beer bottles. If he permitted, she would do some cleaning before she left.

Something else had changed in the main room. Her eyes rested on the mantel above the fireplace. The large framed picture called *Forgiven* was missing. It had been of Jesus, holding a denim-clad killer who held a hammer and nails in his hand that dripped with blood. A faint, white outline showed its vacancy.

She slid onto the couch. Kent was not being so easily wooed. *Father, open his eyes. Let him feel your love.*

Kent glanced at her as if he'd heard the thought. "So, what do you want, Helen?"

"I want you to be better, Kent. You doing okay?"

"Do I look like I'm doing okay, Helen?"

"No, actually you look like you just returned from hell." She smiled genuinely, feeling a sudden surge of empathy for the man. "I know there's little I can say to comfort you, Kent. But I thought you might like some company. Just someone to be here."

He eyed her with drooping eyes and sipped at a drink in his left hand. "Well, you think wrong, Helen. If I needed company, you think I'd be in here watching silent pictures on the tube?"

She nodded. "What people need to do and what they actually do are rarely even remotely similar, Kent. And yes, I do think that even if you did need company, you would be in here watching the tube and listening to that dreadful music."

He shifted his stare, ignoring her.

"But your situation is not so unique. Most people in your position would do the same thing."

"And what do *you* know about my position?" he said. "That's asinine! How many people do you know who've lost their wife and their son in the same month? Don't talk about what you do not know!"

Helen felt her lips flatten. She suddenly wanted very much to walk over there and slap his face. Give him a dose of her own history. How dare he spout off as if he were the sole bearer of pain!

She bit her tongue and swallowed.

On the other hand, he did have a point. Not in her being clueless to loss; God knew nothing could be further from the truth. But in his assertion that few suffered so much loss in such a short time. At least in this country. In another time, in another place, such loss would not be uncommon at all. But in America today, loss was hardly in vogue.

Father, give me grace. Give me patience. Give me love for him.

"You are right. I spoke too quickly," she said. "Do you mind if I do a little cleaning in the kitchen?"

He shrugged, and she took that as a *Help yourself.* So she did. "You have any other music?" she asked, rising. "Something upbeat?"

He just *humphed.*

Helen opened the blinds and dug into the dishes, praying as she worked. He rose momentarily and put on some contemporary pop music she could not identify. She let the music play and hummed with the tunes when the choruses repeated themselves.

It took her an hour to return the kitchen to the spotless condition in which Gloria had kept it. She replaced the dishrags responsible for the mildew odor with fresh ones, wondering how long they would remain clean. A day at most.

Helen returned to the living room, thinking she should say what she had come to say and leave. He was obviously not in the mood to receive any comfort. Certainly not from her.

She glanced at the ceiling and imagined the cosmic bleachers, crowded with eager onlookers, unrestrained by time. She stood behind the couch and studied the man like one of those heavenly creatures might study him. He sat dejected. No, not dejected. Dejected would be characterized by a pouting frown, perhaps. Not this vision of death sagging on the chair before her. He looked suicidal, devastated, unraveled like a hemp rope chewed by a dog.

"I cleaned the kitchen," she said. "You can at least move around in there without knocking things over now."

He looked at her, and his Adam's apple bobbed. Maybe her voice reminded him of Gloria—she hadn't considered that.

"Anyway. Is there anything else I can do for you while I'm here?"

Kent shook his head, barely.

She started then. "You know, Kent, you remind me of someone I know who lost his son. Much like you did, actually."

He ignored her.

She considered leaving without finishing. *Are you sure, Father? Perhaps it is too soon. The poor soul looks like a worm near death.*

God did not respond. She hadn't really expected him to.

"He was crazy about that boy, you know. They were inseparable, did everything together. But the boy was not so—what shall I say—becoming. Not the best looking. Of course, it meant nothing at all to his father." She dismissed the thought with a wave. "Nothing at all. But others began to ridicule him. Then not just ridicule, but flatly reject. They grew to hate him. And the more they hated him, the more his father loved him, if that was possible."

Helen smiled sweetly. Kent looked at her with mild interest now. She continued.

"The boy was murdered by some of his own peers. It about killed the father. Reminds me of you. Anyway, they caught the one who killed his son. Caught him red-handed with the weapon in his hand. He was homeless and uncaring—headed for a life behind bars. But the father did not press charges. Said one life had been taken already. His son's. Instead, he offered love for the one who'd killed his son."

She looked at Kent's eyes for a sign of recognition. They stared into her own, blank. "The unexpected affection nearly broke the young killer's heart. He went to the father and begged his forgiveness. And do you know what the father did?"

Kent did not respond.

"The father loved the killer as his own son. Adopted him." She paused. "Can you believe that?"

Kent's lip lifted in a snarl. "I'd kill the kid." He took a swig from that drink of his.

"Actually, the father had already lost one son. To crucifixion. He wasn't about to let another be crucified."

He sat there like a lump on a log, his eyes half closed and his lower lip sagging. If he understood the meaning behind her words, he did not show it.

"God the Father, God the Son. You know how that feels, don't you? And yet you have murdered him in your own heart. Murdered the son. In fact, the last time I was in here, there was a picture of you above the fireplace." She motioned to the whitewashed wall where the picture had hung. "You were the one holding the hammer and nails. Looks like you got tired of looking at yourself."

She grinned.

"Anyway. Now he wants to adopt you. He loves you. More than you could ever know. And he knows how this all feels. He's been here. Does that make sense to you?"

Kent still did not respond. He blinked and closed his mouth, but she wasn't about to start interpreting his gestures. She simply wanted to plant this seed and leave.

For a moment she thought that he might actually be feeling sorrow. But then she saw his jaw muscles knot up, and she knew better.

"Think about it, Kent. Open your heart." Helen turned from him and walked toward the door, wondering if that was it.

It was.

"Good-bye, Kent," she said, and walked out the door.

She suddenly felt exhilarated. She realized that her heart was pounding simply from the excitement of this message she had delivered.

Her Pinto sat on the driveway, dumb and yellow. She withdrew her keys and approached the car door. But she didn't want to drive.

She wanted to walk. Really walk. An absurd notion—she had been on her feet enough already, and her knees were sore.

The notion stopped her three feet from the car, jingling the keys in her hands. She could not walk, of course. Helen glanced back to the front door. It remained closed. The sky above hung blue in its arches. A beautiful day for a walk.

She wanted to walk.

Helen turned to her left and walked to the street. She would walk. Just to the end of the block. Granted, her knees were not what they once were, but they would hold her that far if she walked slowly. She hummed to herself and eased down the sidewalk.

⤛⤜

Kent saw the door swing shut, and its slam rang like a gong in his mind. He did not move except to swivel his head from the entry. But his eyes stayed wide open, and his fingers were trembling.

Desperation swept in like a thick wave, and on its face rose a wall of sorrow that took his breath away. His throat tightened to an impossible ache, and he grunted to release the tension in the muscles. The wave engulfed him, refusing to sweep by alone, carrying him in its folds.

Then Kent's shoulders began to shake, and the sobs came hard. The ache worked on his chest like a vise, and he was suddenly unsure if it was sorrow or desire now squeezing the breath out of him.

Spencer was right.

Oh, God! Spencer was right!

The admission erupted from his mind, and Kent felt his mouth yawning in a breathless cry. The words came out audibly, in a strained croak.

"Oh, God!" He clenched his eyes. Had to—they were burning. "Oh, God!"

The words brought a wash of comfort, like a soothing anesthetic to his heart. He said it again. "Oh, God."

Kent sat in the wave for a long time, strangely relishing each moment of its respite, aching for more and more. Losing himself there, in the deepest sorrow, and in the balm of comfort.

He recalled a scene that played on the walls of his mind like an old, eight-millimeter film. It was Gloria and Spencer, dancing in the living room, late one evening. They held hands and twirled in circles and sang about streets that were golden. His camera eye zoomed to their faces. They gazed at each other in rapture. He had discarded the moment with a chuckle then, but now it came like the sugar of life. And he knew that somewhere in that exchange lay the purpose of living.

The memory brought a new flood of tears.

When Kent finally stood and looked about the living room, it was dusk. Spent, he trudged into the kitchen and opened the refrigerator without bothering to turn on the lights. He pulled out a day-old pizza, slid onto a barstool, and nibbled on the soggy crust for a few minutes.

A mirror glared at him from the shadowed wall. It showed a man with sagging cheeks and red eyes, his hair disheveled, wearing the face of death. He stopped his chewing and stared, wondering if that could be him. But he knew immediately that it was. There was the new Kent—a broken, discarded fool.

He turned his back to the mirror and ate part of the cold pizza before tossing it and retiring before the television. Kent fell asleep two hours later to the monotones of some Spanish soccer commentator.

The alarm clock's green analog numbers read 11 A.M. when his eyes flickered open the following morning. By noon he had managed a shower and clean clothes. He had also managed a conclusion.

It was time to move on.

Only six days had passed since Spencer's death. Four weeks to the day since Gloria's passing. Their deaths had left him with no one. But that was just it—there was no one left to mourn with. Except Helen. And Helen was from another planet. That left only him, and he could not live with himself. Not just himself.

He would have to find death quickly, or go off and find some life.

Killing himself had a certain appeal—a kind of final justice to the madness. He had mulled over the idea for long hours in recent days. If he did kill himself, it would be with an overdose of some intoxicating drug; he'd already concluded that after discarding a hundred other options. Might as well go out flying high.

On the other hand, something else was brewing in his head, something set off by Helen's words. This God business. The memory lingered like a fog in his mind, present but muddled. The emotions had nearly destroyed him. A sort of high he could not remember having felt.

He remembered thinking, just before falling asleep the night before, that it might have been his love for Spencer that triggered the emotions. Yes, that would be it. Because he was desperate for his son. Would give anything—everything—to give him life. How incredible that one little life could mean so much. Six billion people crawling over the globe, and in the end, the death of one ten-year-old boy caused him to ache so badly.

Kent left the house, squinting in the bright sunlight.

It was time to move on.

Yes, that was the conclusion.

But it was really no conclusion at all, was it? Move on to *what?* Working at the bank carried as much appeal as a barefooted trek across the Sahara. He hadn't had contact with any of his coworkers for a week now. How could he possibly face Borst? Or worse, fat-boy Bentley? They no doubt carried on, soaking in acclamations of a superb job, reaping his rewards while he sat dead in the water, surrounded by two floating bodies. If he had even a single violent bone in his body he'd take that nine-millimeter pistol his uncle had given him for his thirtieth birthday and walk on down to that bank. Play postal worker for a day. Deliver some good will.

He could sue, of course—fire a few legal projectiles their way. But the thought of suing with Dennis Warren's assistance now brought a sickness to his gut. For one thing, Dennis had gone off to lala land that last day. His attorney's words still rumbled through his mind: *I don't think you are ready. I don't think you are ready at all, my fine friend. Perhaps this afternoon you will be ready.*

This afternoon? Then Spencer had died.

No, Dennis was out of the question, Kent concluded. If he did sue the bank, it would be with another attorney.

That left finding another job, a thought that sickened him even more than the notion of suing. But at least he would be able to continue paying the bills. A lawsuit might very well suck him dry.

Either way, he should probably talk to Helen again. Go back for some of the comfort she seemed to have a handle on. God. Maybe Spencer was right after all. Kent felt a knot rise to his throat, and he cursed under his breath. He wasn't sure he could stomach too many more of these emotional surges.

The day passed in a haze, divided between the park and the house, but at least Kent was thinking again. It was a start. Yes, it was time to move on.

14

The vision came to Kent that night in the early morning hours, like a shaft of black through the shadows of his mind.

Or maybe it wasn't a vision. Maybe he was actually there.

He stood in the alley behind the bank. Steam rose from the grate; the dumpster lay tipped on its side, reeking foul, and Kent was watching that vagrant slurping at his bagged bottle. Only now he wasn't tipping the bag back. He was sticking a long, pink tongue down the bottle's neck and using it like a straw. It was the kind of thing you might expect in a dream. So yes, it must have been a vision. A dream.

The vagrant no longer wore faded clothes but a black tuxedo with shiny shoes and a pressed shirt. Downright respectable. Except for the straggly hairs growing off his chin and neck. It appeared as though the man was attempting to cover up a dozen red warts, but the long strands of hair only emphasized them, and that certainly was not respectable. That and the tongue trick.

The vagrant-turned-respectable-citizen was rambling on about how lucky Kent was with his fancy car and big-time job. Kent interrupted the prattling with the most obvious of points.

"I'm no better off than you, old man."

"Old man?" The vagrant licked his lips wet with that long pink tongue. "You think I'm old? How old do I look to you, fella?"

"It's just an expression."

"Well, you are right. I am old. Quite old, actually. And I have learned a few things in my time." He grinned and snaked his tongue into the bottle again without removing his eyes from Kent.

Kent furrowed his brow. "How do you do that?" he asked.

The tongue pulled out quickly. "Do what?"

"Make your tongue do that?"

The vagrant chuckled and fingered one of the warts under his chin. "It's one of the things I've learned over the years, boy. Anybody can do it. You just have to stretch your tongue for a long time. See?" He did it again, and Kent shuddered.

The man pulled his tongue back into his mouth and spoke again. "You ever see those tribal people who stretch their necks a foot high? It's like that. You just stretch things."

A chill seemed to have descended into the alley. The white steam from the grate ran along the ground, and Kent was thinking he should get on in to work. Finish up some programming.

But that was just it. He didn't want to walk through that door. In fact, now that he thought about it, something very bad had happened in there. He just couldn't quite remember what.

"So what's keeping you, boy?" The man peered at the door. "Go on in. Take your millions."

"Huh? That's what you think?" Kent replied. "You think people like me make millions slaving away for some huge bank? Not even close, old man."

The grin left the vagrant's face, and his lips twitched. "You think I am stupid? You call me old man, and yet you talk as though I know nothing? You are a blathering idiot!"

Kent stepped back, surprised by the sudden show of anger. "Relax, man. I don't remember calling you a fool."

"Might as well have, you imbecile!"

"Look, I really didn't mean to offend you. I'm no better off than you, anyway. There's no need to be offended here."

"And if you think you're no better off than me, then you're really a fool. Furthermore, the fact that you're not yet even thinking of doing what I would do in your place proves you are a moronic idiot!"

Kent furrowed his brows, taken aback by the vagrant's audacity.

"Look. I don't know what you think you would do, but people like me just don't make that kind of money."

"People *like* you? Or *you?* How much have *you* made?"

"Well that's really none of your . . ."

"Just tell me, you fool," the man said. "How much money have you rightfully made in that cement box over there?"

"How much . . . rightfully?"

"Of course. How much?"

Kent paused, thinking about that word. *Rightfully.* Rightfully he had made the bonuses due from AFPS. Millions. But that hardly counted as income. And it was certainly no business of this weirdo, anyway.

A sly grin lifted the vagrant's lips. He tilted his head slightly and narrowed his eyes. "Come on, Kent. It's really not that difficult, is it?"

Kent blinked at the man. "How do you know my name?"

"Oh, I know things. I've been around, like I said. I'm not the fool you might think. I say you've made millions, boy. And I say you take your millions."

"Millions? It's not like I can just waltz into the vault and take a few million."

"No. But you have a key, now, don't you?"

"A key? Don't be stupid, man. A key to this door has nothing to do with the vault. Besides, you obviously know nothing about security. You don't just walk into a bank and steal a penny, much less a million."

"Stop calling me stupid, you spineless idiot! Stop it, stop it, stop it!"

Kent's heart slammed in his chest.

The vagrant barely moved now. He glared at Kent, and his voice growled low. "Not that key, you fool. The key in your head. The backdoor to that software. You have the only backdoor code. They don't even know it exists."

The alley grew still. Deadly still. It occurred to Kent that he had stopped breathing.

"I won't tell. I promise," the man said through his grin. He opened his mouth wide and began to cackle. The sound of his laughter bounced off the tall brick walls.

Kent jumped back, stunned.

That mouth widened, showing a black hole at the back of the vagrant's throat. His tongue snaked like a long road leading into the darkness. It grew like a vortex and swallowed the alley in echoing chuckles.

Kent bolted upright.

Silence crashed in on him. Darkness met his wide eyes. Wet sheets stuck to his stomach. His chest thumped like an Indian war drum.

He sat in bed, wide awake, paralyzed by the thought that had awakened him so rudely. The images of the vagrant quickly dwindled to oblivion, overshadowed by the singular concept he'd dropped in Kent's mind. Not a soul had known of the backdoor he'd programmed into AFPS that last week. He'd meant to tell Borst in Miami, complete documentation on it as soon as they returned. That was before.

ROOSTER.

That was the code he'd temporarily assigned to the security entry. With it, any authorized banking official could enter the system through an untraceable handle, tackle any security issue, and leave without affecting normal operations. Of course, not just any banking official would be authorized. Only one or two, perhaps. The president and vice president, who would have to guard the code in the strictest confidence. Under lock and key.

Kent swung his legs from the bed and stared into darkness. Outlines of the room's furniture began to take vague shape. The realization of ROOSTER's significance ballooned in his mind like a mushroom cloud. If the bank had not discovered the backdoor, then it would still be open to anyone with the code.

And he had the code. The vagrant's key.

ROOSTER.

What could an operator accomplish with ROOSTER? Anything. Anything at all with the right skills. Software engineering skills. The kind of skills that he himself possessed with perhaps greater mastery than anyone he knew. Certainly within the context of AFPS. He'd *written* the code, for heaven's sake!

Kent pushed himself from the bed, quaking. He glanced at the clock: 2 A.M. The bank would be deserted, of course. He had to know if they'd found ROOSTER during the program's initial implementation. Knowing Borst, they had not.

He went for the closet and stopped at the door. What was he thinking? He couldn't go down there now. The alarm company would have a record of his entry at two in the morning. How would that look? No. Out of the question.

Kent turned for the bathroom. He had to think this through. *Slow down, boy.* Halfway to the bathroom he spun back to the bedroom. He didn't need to use the bathroom. *Get a grip, man.*

On the bed again he began to think clearly for the first time. The fact of the matter was that if they had overlooked ROOSTER, he could enter AFPS and create a link with any bank on the federal reserve system. Of course, what he could do once he was there was another matter altogether.

He couldn't very well take anything. For starters, it was a federal crime. People grew old in prison for white-collar crime. And he was no criminal. Not to mention the simple fact that banks did not just let money walk without tracing it.

Each dollar was accounted for. Accounts were balanced, transactions verified.

Kent crossed his legs on the bed and hugged a pillow. On the other hand, in implementing AFPS prematurely, without his help, Borst not only had inadvertently opened his flank but he had left the barn door open on a billion accounts throughout the world. Kent felt a chill run through his veins. Niponbank's accounts alone numbered nearly one hundred million worldwide. Personal accounts, business accounts, federal accounts—and they were all there, accessible through ROOSTER.

He could waltz right into Borst's personal account if he so desired. Leave nasty messages on his bank statements. Scare the fool right into the arms of God. Ha! Kent smiled. A thin sheen of sweat covered his upper lip, and he drew an arm over his mouth.

He imagined Bentley's eyes when he opened a statement and, instead of that hundred-thousand-dollar bonus, found a notice of an overdraft. He would stiffen like a board. Maybe go purple and keel over dead.

Kent blinked and shook the thoughts from his head. Absurd. The whole notion was absurd.

Then again, everything in his life had become absurd. He had lost his resolve to live. Why not go for a piece of glory, pull off the crime of the century, steal a wad from the bank that had screwed him? It might give him a reason to live again. He'd lost a lot in the recent past. Taking a little back had a ring of justice.

Of course, doing it without getting caught would be nearly impossible. *Nearly* impossible. But it *could* be done—given enough planning. *Imagine!*

Kent did that. He imagined. Till dawn brought shape and color to his surroundings he imagined, wide eyed, with his legs bunched and a pillow under his chin. Sleep was out of the question. Because the more he thought about it, the more he realized that if ROOSTER still lived, he could be a wealthy man. Filthy rich. Start a new life. Make some of his own justice. Risk life in prison, to be sure, but life nonetheless. The alternative of plodding along the corporate trail again struck him more like a slow death. And he'd had enough of death.

It was Wednesday. Today he would go to the bank and casually find out if the ROOSTER still lived. If it did . . .

A chill ran right through Kent's bones. It was indeed time to move on. And what of Helen's little guilt trip? This God business? It would have to wait, of course. If the mighty red ROOSTER lived, he had himself a banquet to plan.

15

Kent drove past the bank at eight-thirty, parked on a side street, and walked briskly toward the back alley. It occurred to him that the vagrant might be there, hiding in the dim light. The thought spiked his pulse. He pulled up at the entrance and peered around the brick wall, blinking against an image of a long pink tongue poking through the neck of a bottle. But the alley appeared empty except for that dumpster, which had been emptied. Kent made straight for the rear door and slipped into the bank. He breathed once deeply, checked his tie, and strode for the Information Systems suite.

Betty's eyes popped when he opened the door and stepped in. He smiled and dipped his head, purposefully courteous. "Morning, Betty."

Her mouth opened, but no sound come out.

"What's the matter? Cat got your tongue? Borst in?"

She nodded. "Good morning. Yes."

"Good morning," he repeated and walked for Borst's office.

He tapped on the door and stepped in at the sound of a muffled call. Borst sat behind his desk, all dressed up in a new dark brown suit. The toupee had made a comeback, covering his bald spot with slick black hair. Jet black. Bright red suspenders rounded out the look.

Borst's eyes bulged out, and he bolted from his seat as though an electrode had juiced him there. The suspenders pulled his slacks snug into his crotch when he straightened. He looked like a clown.

"Good morning, Borst." This would have to go smoothly. Easy now. Step by step. "I'm back. I assume that I do still work here, right?"

The man blinked and licked pink lips. "Good night, Kent! You scared me. I had no idea you planned on coming in this morning. We didn't hear from you." His lips twitched to a grin. "Yes. Sure you still work here. Have a seat. How are you?"

"Actually, I'd like ten minutes to get situated. That okay?"

"Sure. I leave for Phoenix at noon." The man's eyebrows lifted. "You here to stay, then?"

Kent turned from the door. "Give me a few minutes. We'll talk then." He pulled the door closed and saw that Borst was already reaching for the phone. Reporting in to Bossman, no doubt. Kent's heart pounded.

Did they know?

Of course not. How could they know of a dream? He had done nothing yet.

Kent nodded at an oogle-eyed Betty and slid into his office. He locked the door. The exotic yellow fish still grazed placidly on his screen. His fingers trembled badly when he lowered them to the keyboard, and he squeezed them into fists.

Okay, settle down, man. All you're doing is checking on a piece of your own code. Nothing wrong with that.

The plan was simple. If ROOSTER remained intact, he would go in there and suck up to Borst. Buy himself some time to think this out. If they had closed ROOSTER down, he would resign.

A touch on the mouse made the fish wink off. A dozen icons hung suspended against a deep blue underwater oceanscape. Kent drew the mouse over the red-and-blue AFPS icon to an explorer icon. Entry into the system would be tracked—at least any entry through the doors of which they were aware. And if he was lucky they had not expanded their security measures to cut off his terminal completely.

His heart thumping loudly in the room's silence, Kent flew through the menus to a hidden folder requiring his own password for entry. He punched it in. The contents sprang to life. He scrolled down and scanned for the file in which he'd placed ROOSTER. The list ran by too quickly, and he repeated the scan, reading more methodically. *Come on, baby. You have to be here.*

And then it *was* there, throbbing in his vision: MISC. He dragged the mouse over the name and double-clicked.

The screen snapped to black. Kent caught his breath, aware that his legs trembled slightly now. He was on his toes under the desk, and he lowered his heels to settle the quaking. *Come on, baby.*

The monitor flashed white, riddled with black letters and symbols. Code. Kent exhaled loudly. ROOSTER's code! A living, viable, untraceable hook into the funds processing system, right here at his fingertips.

He stared at it without moving for a minute, awash with relief that he'd had the foresight to add this final whistle to the package. It wasn't pretty. No colors or boxes yet. Just raw code. But now another question: Would it still link to the system? Kent suddenly felt the heat of panic wash down his back. What if they had found it and left the code but removed its hook into the system?

He hit a key and entered a single word: RUN. A new line immediately appeared, asking for a password. He entered the name. R-O-O-S-T-E-R.

The screen darkened for a second and then popped up with the familiar blue menu he'd worked from for so many years. Kent blinked at the screen. He was in AFPS! Beyond security. From here he could do what he wished without the knowledge of another living soul.

In the right hands, it was a security measure in itself, designed to deal with sabotage and viruses. In the wrong hands it was a way into the bank's vaults. Or worse, a way into every account tied to the bank.

Kent backed out quickly, handling the mouse with a sweating palm. He watched the menus retrace their steps to the deep blue ocean scene, then he lowered his hands to his lap. Even now, short of dusting for prints, Borst could not discover that anyone had even touched this computer, much less peeked up the bank's skirt.

He breathed deeply and stood. It was insane. These crazy thoughts of stealing money would be the end of him. Preposterous. They would bury him. He thought suddenly of Spencer and lifted a hand to his brow. It was all madness.

Either way, he now had his answer.

A fist pounded on the door, and Kent bolted a full foot off the carpet. He spun to the computer and scanned the keyboard. No, there was no trace. Relax. *Relax, relax!*

"Who is it?" he called.

"Cliff."

Cliff. Better than Borst. Kent let him in. "Sorry, I didn't know it was locked," he lied.

"What are you doing in here, Kent?" The new recruit smiled. "Anything I should know about?" He nudged Kent as if they shared an understanding.

"Yeah, right." Kent willed his heart to settle. He sat and crossed his legs. "So what can I do for you?"

"Nothing. Betty just told me you were back. I figured you needed a welcome." The grin straightened. "I heard what happened. You know . . . to your son. I can hardly imagine. Are you okay?"

"Actually, I'm not sure what okay means anymore, but I'm ready to get back to work, if that's what you mean."

"I'm sure it'll take some time. Maybe getting your mind on work is the best way to pass it. And speaking of work, I've dug pretty deep since you were last here." He smiled again. "You'd be proud of me. I've found things I'm sure only you know about."

A chill broke over Kent's crown at the words. *ROOSTER?* "Yeah? Like what?"

"Like links to the Chinese banking codes that are still inactive. Now, that's what I call foresight, man."

"Well, it *is* a global system, Cliff. So what else have you dug up with that long snout of yours?"

"A few anecdotal notes buried in the code—things like that. *Borst has the brain of sausage.*" He grinned wide.

"Good night, you found *that?* That *was* buried. I should probably pull it out."

"No, leave it in. He'll never find it."

They nodded, smiling.

"Anything else?" Kent asked.

"That's it so far. Well, it's good to have you back." Cliff stood and walked to the door. "After you get settled I have some code to run by you. You up for that?"

"Sure."

The younger man slapped the wall and disappeared. Now, that was close. Or was it? Actually, the chances of Cliff or anybody finding ROOSTER would be akin to picking a particular grain of sand from a bucket full of the stuff. Either way, he'd have to keep an eye on the man.

Kent settled his nerves with a few long pulls of air and walked into Borst's office.

"Have a seat, Kent."

Kent sat.

"We weren't sure we'd see you again."

Yeah, I'll bet. You and your pal Bentley both. "Well to be honest, I wasn't so sure myself. So, how were things in my absence?" he asked, thinking the question stupid but unable to think of a better way to begin this sucking-up thing to which he had now committed himself.

"Fine, Kent. Just fine. Boy, you've been through hell, huh?"

Kent nodded. "Life can deal some pretty nasty blows." He suddenly despised being here. He should stand now and walk away from this foolishness.

"But I'm back. I need to work, Markus." *That's right, get personal with him. Appeal to his need for friendship.* "I need it bad. All I really have left is my career. I miss work here. Can you understand that?" His voice came soft and sensitive.

"Yes. Makes sense." The man had taken the bait. He paused and shifted his eyes. "Look, Kent. I'm sorry about the misunderstanding about AFPS. I just . . ."

"No. You don't need to say anything. These things happen. And I apologize for blowing up the way I did. It was totally uncalled-for." *Gag. If you only knew, you slimeball.*

Borst nodded, delighted behind that controlled smile, no doubt. "Well, we all got a bit off line, I think. Perhaps it's best we just put the incident behind us."

Kent crossed his legs. The sweat was drying cold on his neck. "You're right. Water under the bridge. So how is AFPS these days?"

Markus brightened. "In a word? Incredible. We put together a doozie, Kent. They're already saying that it will save a third of the manpower the old system used. Price has estimated the overall savings to the bank at over twenty million annually."

Price? First-name basis now. Partners in crime. Probably had dinner together every night. "Great. That's great. No bugs?"

"Sure. Plenty. But they're minor. Actually, you'd probably be best suited to start working on them." The Information Systems supervisor had honestly fooled himself into full ownership of the system, Kent thought.

The man shifted the conversation back to what was apparently his favorite topic these days: money. "Hey, I still haven't allocated that twenty-five-thousand-dollar bonus," he said with a glint in his eyes. "At least not all of it. I'm giving Betty, Todd, and Mary five thousand each. But that leaves ten thousand. You need any spare change these days, Kent?" He jerked his brows high a few times. "Hmm?"

Kent nearly lost the charade then. Came within a gnat's whisker of leaping over the cherrywood desk and strangling his boss. For a few seconds he could not respond. The other *three?* Betty was getting a five-thousand-dollar spiff too? But that was just fine, of course, because he, Kent Anthony, the creator of said program, was to get double that. Yes sir! A whopping ten grand. And Borst? What would bug-eyed Borst's cut be? Oh, well, Borst was the main man. He would get 10 percent of the savings for ten years. A mere fifteen, twenty million. Chump change.

Sounded like a good, round number. Twenty million.

"Sure," Kent said. "Who couldn't use ten thousand dollars? I could cut my Lexus payment in half." That last comment slipped out before he could reign it back. He hoped Borst did not catch his cynicism.

"Good. It's yours. I'll talk to Price this afternoon."

"I thought you were going to Phoenix today."

"Yes. We are. I'll talk to Price on the plane."

It was an unstoppable freight train with those two. Kent swallowed his anger. "Thank you." He stood. "Well, I guess I should get started. I want to talk to the others—you know, make sure there are no misunderstandings."

"Good. Splendid idea. It's good to have you back."

Kent turned at the door. "One more thing, Markus. I kind of blew it with Bentley the other day. You wouldn't mind putting in a word for me, would you? It was just a bad week." He swallowed deliberately and was surprised at the sudden emotion that accompanied it. They said the grief would last a year, gradually easing. Evidently he was still in the stage where it could be set off with a mere swallow.

"Sure, Kent. Consider it done. And don't worry. He and I are rather tight these days."

Yes, I'll bet you are, Kent thought. He left before the revulsion had him doing something silly, like throwing up on the man's carpet.

⌒⌒⌒

Pastor Bill Madison parked his gray Chevy on the street and strode up to Helen's door. She had sounded different on the phone. Almost excited. At least peachy. Like someone who had just been handed some very good news. Or like someone who had flipped their lid.

Given the last few weeks' events, he feared the latter. But then this was Helen, here. With Helen you could never know. The New Testament characterized followers of Christ as peculiar. Well, Helen was just that. One of very few he would consider peculiar in their faith. Which was in itself strange when he got right down and thought about it. Perhaps they should all be rather unusual; Christ certainly was.

She had asked him to pray, and he had indeed prayed. But not simply because of her request. Something was happening here. He might not have the spiritual eyes that Helen claimed to possess, but he could sense things. Discernment, some called it. A spiritual gift. The ability to look at a situation and sense its spiritual origins. Like, *This face sends chills up my spine; it must be evil.* Not that he always operated in the most accurate mode of discernment. He had once felt chills peck at his heart, looking at a strange, alien-looking face on the television screen. To him it looked downright demonic. Then his son had informed him that it was a closeup of a friendly little creature found in the Amazon. One of God's creatures.

That had confused him a little. But this thing with Helen—it was more than just a weird face on the boob tube. It was an aura that followed her around in much the same way he imagined an aura might have followed Elisha or Elijah around.

He rang the doorbell. The door swung in immediately, as if Helen had awaited his arrival with her hand on the knob.

"Come in, Pastor." She wore a yellow dress, tube socks, and running shoes, a ridiculous sight for one who had trouble walking even around the house.

"Thank you, Helen." Bill stepped in and closed the door, glancing at her legs. The musty scent of roses hung in the air. The old lady's perfume was everywhere. She left him for the living room, smiling.

"Is everything all right?" he asked, following.

She did not respond directly but walked across the carpet humming her anthem, "Jesus, Lover of My Soul." She had told him once that the song summed it all up. It made death worthwhile. Bill stopped behind her large, green easy chair, fixated on the sight of Helen walking. She was seemingly oblivious to him.

"Are you okay?"

"Shhhh." She hushed him and lifted both hands, still pacing back and forth. Her eyes rested closed. "You hear that, Bill?"

Bill cocked his head and listened, but he heard nothing. Except her faint humming. "Hear what?"

"The laughter. Do you hear that laughter?"

He tried to hear laughter, but he heard only her soprano hum. *Let me to Thy bosom fly* . . . And he smelled roses.

"You might have to open your heart a little, but it's there, Pastor—very faint, like the breeze blowing through trees."

He tried again, closing his eyes this time, feeling a little foolish. If one of the deacons knew he was over at Helen Crane's house listening for laughter with her, they might very well begin the search for a new shepherd. After hearing nothing but Helen for a few moments, he gave up and looked at her.

Helen suddenly stopped her pacing and opened her eyes. She giggled and lowered her hands. "It's okay, Pastor. I didn't really expect you to hear anything. It's like that around here. Some days it's silent. And then some days he opens up my ears to the laughter and I want to walk around the house kissing things. Just kissing everything. Like today. Would you like some tea?"

"Yes, that would be nice."

She shuffled toward the kitchen. She had her socks pulled up to midcalf. A red Reebok logo splashed across the heel of her shoes. Bill swallowed and eased around the chair. She might very well have lost it, he thought. He sat on the green chair.

Helen emerged from the kitchen holding two glasses of tea. "So, you're thinking that my elevator is no longer climbing to the top floor, am I right?" She smiled.

"Actually, I had given it some thought." He grinned and chuckled once. "But these days, it's hard to differentiate between strangeness and craziness." He lost the grin. "They thought Jesus was crazy."

"Yes, I know." She handed him the drink and sat. "And we would think the same today."

"Tell me," Bill said, "did you see Spencer's death in all of this?"

"Yes."

"When?"

"The night after we last talked, a week or so ago. When we talked, I knew there would be more skulls in the dungeon. I could feel it in my spine. But I never really expected it to be Spencer's skull lying there on the ground. It nearly killed me, you know."

"So this is really happening, then." He said it calmly, but he found himself trembling with the thought. "This whole thing is really happening. I mean . . . orchestrated."

"You have put two people in the dirt. You should know. Looked real enough to me."

"Fine, I'll grant you that. It's just hard to swallow this business about you knowing about their deaths beforehand. Maybe if I could see into the heavens like you can, it would be easier."

"It's not everybody's place to see things so clearly, Pastor. We all have our place. If the whole world saw things clearly our churches would be flooded. The nation would flock to the cross en masse. What faith would that require? We might as well be puppets."

"Yes, well, I'm not so sure having full churches would be so bad."

"And I'm not so sure the deaths of my daughter and grandson were so necessary. But when I hear their laughter, when I'm allowed to peek to the other side, it all makes sense. That's when I want to walk around and start kissing things."

He smiled at her expression. In many ways they were very similar, he and Helen. "So then . . ." He paused, collecting his thoughts.

"Yes?"

"In my office last week you told me you'd had a vision in which you heard the sound of running feet in a dungeon. To whom do the running feet in your dungeon belong?" He glanced at her feet, clad in those white Reeboks. "You?"

She laughed. "No." She suddenly tilted her head, thinking. "At least I had not considered it. But no, I don't think so. I think the running feet belong to Kent."

"Kent?"

"He's the player in this game. I mean, we're all players, but he is the runner."

"Kent's the runner. And where is Kent running?"

"Kent is running from God."

"This is all about Kent?"

She nodded. "And about you and me and Gloria and Spencer. Who knows? This might very well be about the whole world. I don't know everything. Sometimes I know nothing. That's why I called you over today. Today I know some things."

"I see." He looked at her feet absently. "And why are you wearing running shoes, Helen? You walking more these days?"

"With my knees?" She wiggled her feet on the carpet. "No, they just feel good. I've got this itching to be young again, I guess." She stared out the window behind Bill. "It seems to ease the pain in my heart, you know."

Helen sipped quietly at the glass, and then set it down. "I've been called to intercede for Kent, Pastor."

He did not respond. She was an intercessor. It made sense.

"Intercede without ceasing. Eight hours a day."

"You spend eight hours a day praying for Kent?"

"Yes. And I will do so until it is over."

"Until *what* is over, Helen?"

She looked at him directly. "Until this game is over."

He studied her, looking for any sign of insincerity. He could see none. "So now it's a game? I'm not sure God plays games."

She shrugged. "Choose your own words, then. I have been called to pray until it is over."

Bill shook his head with disbelief. "This is unbelievable. I feel like we've been transported back to some Old Testament story."

"You think? This is nothing. You should read Revelation. Things get really strange later."

The sense of her words struck at him. He'd never thought of history in those terms. There had always been biblical history, the time of burning bushes and talking donkeys and tongues of fire. And there was the present—the time of normalcy. What if Helen's peculiar view behind the scenes was really just an unusual peek at the way things really were? And what if he was being allowed to peek into this extraordinary "normalcy" for a change?

They sat and talked for a long while after that. But Helen did not manage to shed any more light on his questions. He concluded it was because she herself knew little more. She was seeing through a glass dimly. But she was indeed seeing.

And if she was right, this drama of hers—this game—It was indeed all just beginning.

16

Lacy Cartwright leaned back in the lounge chair on her balcony, drinking coffee, enjoying the cool morning breeze. It was ten o'clock. Having a day off midweek had its advantages, she thought, and one of them was the quiet, out here under a bright blue Boulder sky while everyone else worked. She glanced over her body, thankful for the warmth of sun on her skin. Just last week Jeff Duncan had called her petite. Heavens! She was thin, maybe, and not an inch over five-three, but petite? Her coworker at the bank had said it with a glint in his eye, and she had suspected then that the man had a crush on her. But it had been under two years since her husband's death. She was not ready to engage a man.

The breeze feathered her face, and she lifted a hand to sweep the blonde strands behind her ear. Her hair rested on her shoulders in lazy curls, framing hazel eyes that smiled. A thin sheen of suntan oil glistened on her pale belly between a white halter top and jean shorts. Some women seemed to relish baking in the sun—lived for it even. Goodness! A picture of a hot dog sizzling on a grill popped into her mind, and she let it hang there for a moment. Its red skin suddenly split, and the image fizzled.

Lacy turned her head and studied the distant clouds looming black toward the southeast. Denver had had its share of weather lately, and it appeared the area was in for a little more. Which was another reason she liked it up here in Boulder more than in the big city. In Denver, if you weren't dealing with weather, you were dealing with smog. Or at the very least, traffic, which was worse than either. She ought to know—she'd spent most of her life down there.

But not anymore. After John's death two years earlier she had upped and moved here. Started a new career as a teller and busied herself with the monumental task of ridding her chest of its ache. She'd done it all well, she thought. Now she could get on with the more substantive issues of starting over. Like lying out in the sun, waiting for the UV rays to split her skin like that hot dog. Goodness!

A high-pitched squeal jerked her mind from its reflections. She spun toward the sliding glass door and realized the awful sound was coming from her condo. As if a pig had gotten its snout caught in a door and was protesting. But of course there were no pigs in there, squealing or not. There was, however, a washing machine, and if she wasn't mistaken, the sound was actually coming from the laundry room, where she had started a load of whites fifteen minutes ago.

The sound suddenly jumped an octave and wailed like a siren. Lacy scrambled from the lounger and ran for the laundry room. It would be just her luck that old Mrs. Potters next door was jabbing at the oversized nine-one-one numbers on her trusty pink telephone at this very moment.

Lacy saw the soapy water before she reached the door, and her pulse spiked, midstride. Not that she'd never seen soapy water before—saw it all the time, but never bubbling under a door like some kind of monster foaming at its mouth. She felt the wet seep between her toes through the navy carpet a good five feet from the door. She let out a yelp and tiptoed to the door. This was not good.

The door swung in over an inch of gray water. The washing machine rocked madly, squealing, and Lacy dove for the control knob. Her palm smashed it in, which under normal conditions would have killed the thing right then. But evidently things were no longer normal in this room, because the boxy old machine just kept rocking and wailing.

The plug! She had to pull the plug. One of those big fat plugs behind the contraption. Water bubbled over the top of the washer and ran down to the floor in streams. Frantic now, Lacy flopped belly-down on the shaking appliance and dove for the back. The plug stuck stubbornly. She squirmed over the lid so that her feet dangled, all too aware of the water soaking her clothes. She put her full weight into the next tug. The plug came free, sending her flying backward, off the dying machine and to the floor like a fish spilled from a net.

She struggled from the floor, grateful for the ringing silence. In all the commotion her hair had attracted enough water to leave it dripping. She gazed about, and her stomach knotted at the sight. A pig stuck in the door might have been better.

Before John died this would all have been different. She would simply call the precinct and have him run by to take care of things. For her it would be a quick shower and then perhaps off to lunch.

But that was before. Before the cancer had ravaged his body and sent him to the grave exactly two months before he would have made sergeant. An image of her late husband all decked out in those navy blues and shiny brass buttons drifted through her mind. He was smiling, because he had always smiled. A good man. A perfect cop. The only man she could imagine herself with. Ever.

Lacy bent over her oak dinette table half an hour later, the phone book spread yellow before her, a paper towel protecting the phone from her blackened fingers. Her attempt at messing with gears under the machine had proved futile. A lazy voice filled her ear.

"Frank," it drawled. Frank was chewing gum by the sounds of his rhythmic smacking. He'd obviously slept through the etiquette portion of his plumber-school training.

"Hi, Frank. This is Lacy Cartwright. I'm guessing you're a certified Goldtech technician, right?"

"Yes, ma'am. What can I do for you?" *Smack, smack.* She swallowed.

"Well, I have a problem out here, Frank. The water pump on my washing machine somehow got stuck open and flooded the floor. I need it repaired."

"Stuck open, huh?" A hint of amusement rang in the man's voice. "And what model number are we talking about?"

"J-28," she said, ready for the question.

"Well, you see? Now there's a problem, because J-28s don't get stuck open. J-28s use pumps operated on a normally closed solenoid, and if anything, they get stuck closed. You hear any sounds when this machine went belly up?"

"It squealed."

"It squealed, huh? I'll bet it squealed." He chuckled. "Yes, ma'am, they sure know how to squeal, them Monroe pumps." The phone went silent. Lacy was wondering where they had found Frank. Seemed to know pumps, all right. But maybe his own pump was not reaching the wellhead.

When he did not offer any further comment, she spoke. "So what do I do?"

"Well, you need a new pump, Miss Cartwright."

Another short silence. "Can you install a new pump for me?"

"Sure, I can. It's not a question of *can*, ma'am. I've been putting in new pumps for ten years." An edge had come to his voice midsentence. She lifted her eyes and caught her reflection in the dining room mirror. Her blonde hair had dried in tangles.

"The problem is, we don't have any Monroe pumps in stock today. So you see, even if I wanted to come out there, which I couldn't do for three days anyway, I couldn't do it because I don't have anything to do it with." He chuckled again.

Lacy blinked. She suddenly wasn't sure she even *wanted* Frank to fix her washing machine. "Is it hard?"

"Is what hard?"

"Do you think I could replace the pump?"

"Any idiot could replace that pump, Miss." *Evidently.* "Three bolts and a few wires, and you're in and out before you know it. I could do it with a blindfold on. In fact, I *have* done it with a blindfold on." *Good for you, Frankie.* "But, like I said, Honey. We have no pumps."

"Where else can I get a pump?"

"Nowhere. At least nowhere in Boulder. You go to the manufacturer in Denver, they might sell you one."

Denver? She gazed out the window to those ominous clouds in the southeast. It would be an hour there, another hour in traffic regardless of where it was, and an hour back. It would blow her day completely. She glanced at the clock. Eleven. On the other hand, her day was already blown. And she couldn't very well wait a week for Frankie to come out and walk around her condo with a blindfold on while he did his thing.

"Well, lady, I can't sit here all day."

Lacy started. "I'm sorry. Yes, I think I'll try Monroe. Do you have the number?"

Thirty minutes later she was in the car, headed for the freeway, with the old J-28 pump in a box beside her. Frank had been right. Once she managed to tip the washer enough to prop it up with a footstool and slide under it, removing the little beast had not been so bad. She had even closed her eyes once while loosening a bolt, wondering what possessed a man to try such a thing.

Lacy pulled onto the freeway, struck by how easily the course of her day had changed. One minute lying in attempted bliss, the next diving into soapy gray water.

Goodness.

ఴఴఴ

The week had flown past, skipping across the peaks of Kent's nerves like a wind-surfer pushed by a gale-force wind. It was the wind of imagination, and it kept his eyes wide and burning. By the end of that first day Kent knew what he was going to do with a certainty that brought fire to his bones.

He was going to rob the bank blind.

Literally. He was going to take every penny he had coming. All twenty million of it. And the bank would remain as blind as a bat through it all. He sat there at his desk, exhilarated by the idea, his fingers frozen over the keyboard as his mind spun.

He tried in vain to concentrate on Cliff's questions about why he'd chosen this routine or where he could find that link. And that was a problem, because now more than ever, fitting back into the bank as Joe Smooth Employee took on significance. The way he saw it, he already had some ground to make up; some kissing up to do. Walking around the bank with a big red sign reading "Here walks the man who screamed at Bentley over employee of the month parking" would not do. He would have to concentrate on being normal again. On fitting in with the other fools who actually believed they were somehow important in this nine-to-five funny farm. There was the small matter of his having lost a wife and son, but he would just have to bite his tongue on that one, wouldn't he? Just try not to bleed all over the place. He would have to rein in his mind, control his thoughts. For the sake of ROOSTER.

But his thoughts kept sliding off to other things.

Things like what he would do with twenty million dollars. Things like how he could hide twenty million dollars. Things like how he could *steal* twenty million dollars. The details flew by, dizzying in his analytical mind. A hundred sordid details—each one spawning another hundred, it seemed.

First, he would have to decide from where to take the money. Using ROOSTER he could take it from almost anywhere. But, of course, *anywhere* would not do. It would have to come from a place where twenty million would not be quickly missed. No matter how untraceable the transaction itself might be, its net result would be nearly impossible to hide. Nearly.

Then he would have to decide where to put the money. He would never actually have the physical bills—the coin—but even a ledger balance of twenty million was enough to generate at least interest. And that kind of interest was not something he needed. If the money ever turned up missing, the FBI would be all over it like stink on sewer. He would have to find a way to lie at the bottom of that sewer.

He'd have to plan the actual execution of the theft very carefully, of course. Couldn't very well be caught downloading twenty million dollars. "What are those large balances on your screen, Kent?"

"Oh, nothing. Actually, that's my bonus from AFPS, if you must know. I'm just taking an early withdrawal."

He would also have to find a way to exit his current life. Couldn't be a millionaire and work for Borst. Had no ring of justice to him. And this whole thing was really about justice. Not just with his job but with life in general. He had climbed the ladder like a good boy for twenty years only to be dropped back on his tail in the space of thirty days. Back down to Stupid Street where the concrete was hard and the nights cold. Well, now that he had taken the time to think things through, being forced to climb that ladder again, rung by rung, made as much sense as setting up post on the local corner, bearing a sign that read "Will work for beer."

Not a chance. It took him thirty days to fall; if all went well it would take him no more than thirty to pop back on top.

The hardest part of this whole scheme might very well be the spending of the money. How could Kent Anthony, computer programmer, step into a life of wealth without raising eyebrows? He would have to divorce himself from his past somehow. Not a problem. His immediate past reeked of every imaginable offensive odor anyway. The notion of divorcing himself from that past brought a buzz to his lower spine. His past was tainted beyond redemption. He would put it as far behind him as possible. Wash it from his memory entirely. Begin a new life as a new man.

In fact, it was in this last stage of the entire plan that he would find himself again. The thought of it pushed him into the certainty that coursed through his bones like charged electrons. After weeks of empty dread, it came like a euphoric drug.

Kent looked over Cliff's shoulder at the wall—at the picture of the white yacht hanging in the shadows. An image of that same boat he'd plastered on the refrigerator at home sailed through his mind. His promise to Gloria. *I swear, Gloria, we will own that yacht one day.*

A lump rose to his throat. Not that she had cared much. She'd been too enamored with her mother's religion to appreciate the finer things. Kent had always hung on to the hope that it would change. That she would drop her silly obsessions and run after his dreams. But now she was gone.

For the first few days the thoughts whispered relentlessly, and he began to construct possible solutions to the challenges. Not too unlike debugging. A natural exercise for his mind. While Cliff busied himself with the code before them, Kent busied himself with another code altogether. This morning alone, he had apologized three times for his drifting mind. Cliff guessed it had to do with the loss of his wife and son. Kent nodded, feeling like a pimp for hiding behind the sentiment.

It was one o'clock before he shut down the Cliff machine. "Okay, Ace. I've got some errands to run over lunch. You should have enough to keep you busy for a couple of days anyway." He stood and stretched.

"I suppose you're right. Thanks for the time. I'll just keep digging. You never know what I'll come up with."

A thought crossed Kent's mind. "Actually, why don't you focus on debugging for a few days and leave the digging. I mean, be my guest, dig all you want, but wandering aimlessly through my code is not necessarily the best use for a mind like yours, pal." He shrugged. "Just my opinion, of course. But if you want to find something, just ask me. I'll save you a mountain of time."

Cliff smiled brightly. "Sure, if you're here. I think that was the concern. What happens if Kent Anthony disappears?"

"Well, a week ago that strategy made sense. But it's now obsolete. I'm here to stay. You tell that to whoever punches your buttons." Kent grinned to make the point stick.

Cliff saluted mockingly. "You got it, sir."

"Good then. Off you go, lad."

Cliff left grinning ear to ear. Kent honestly felt nearly jovial. The drug of his plotting had worked its way right through his veins. It felt as though he had stepped out of some nightmare and found himself at the gates of a new undiscovered world. And he fully intended to discover every corner of it.

He locked his office, made some comment to Betty about how much work there was, and hustled out the back. Normally he would have preferred the front doors, but now was not normally. Now he would have crawled through a trapdoor in the floor if there had been one.

He hurried down the alley to his car and slid onto the leather upholstery before considering his destination. The library. He had some books to check out. No. That would leave a trail. The bookstore, then. He had some books to purchase. With cash. The nearest Barnes and Noble was three miles down Sixth Avenue. He made a U-turn and entered the flow of traffic.

Kent was not one to stop and lend a hand to stranded vehicles. Road kill, he called them. If the morons didn't have the foresight to either have their cars properly serviced or sign up for AAA they surely didn't deserve his extended hand. The dead vehicles were usually old cars stuffed with people from Stupid Street anyway. As far as he was concerned, a little breakdown on the road in heavy traffic was a good indoctrination to responsibility, a rare commodity these days.

Which was why it struck him as strange that the white Acura sidelined ahead on the left-hand side of the divided thoroughfare even caught his attention. And even stranger was the simple fact that once it was in his eyesight, he could hardly remove his eyes from the vehicle. And no wonder. It sat like a beacon of light ahead, glowing white, as if a lightning bolt had lit it up. It suddenly occurred to him that the sky was indeed rather foreboding—in fact downright dark. But the Acura was actually glowing up there, and all the other cars just sped by as if it did not exist. Kent gripped the steering wheel, wooden.

A woman with blonde hair, dressed in jeans and a green shirt, was climbing out. She turned to face his approach, and Kent's heart bolted. He didn't know *why* his heart jumped like that, but it did. Something in her face, possibly. But that was just it; he could hardly *see* her face from this distance.

Then Kent was past the car, torn by indecision. If ever there was a soul who deserved assistance, it was this one. On the other hand, he didn't do roadkill. Thirty yards flew by before he jerked the wheel impulsively and slid to a stop, five inches from the guardrail, cars moaning by on the right.

The instant he stopped, he decided it had been a mistake. He thought about pulling back into traffic. Instead, he slid out of the seat and jogged the forty yards back to the Acura. If the glow that had surrounded the car had ever actually been there, it had taken leave. Someone had pulled the plug. The woman had lifted the hood so that it gaped, black-mouthed, at him like a steel alligator. She stood watching his approach, bouncing in his vision.

Kent was ten feet from the woman when recognition slammed into his mind like a sledge. He pulled up, stunned.

It was the same for her, he thought. Her jaw dropped to her chest, and her eyes grew wide. They stood fixed to the pavement like two deer caught in each other's headlights.

"Kent?"

"Lacy?"

They responded simultaneously. "Yes."

Her eyes were like saucers. "Kent Anthony! I can't believe it's actually you. My . . . my car died . . ."

He grinned, feeling oddly out of sorts. She was prettier than he remembered. Thinner perhaps. Her face was still rather ordinary, but those eyes. They shone like two beaming emeralds. No wonder he'd taken to her in college. And age was wearing well on her.

"Lacy Cartwright. How on Earth did you end up stranded on the side of the road?" *Her car broke down, you idiot. She told you that.*

She broke into a wide grin. "This is weird. I don't know what happened. It just stopped . . ." She chuckled. "So how in the world are you?"

"Good. Yeah, good," he said, thinking it both a downright lie and the honest truth.

He stood silent for a full ten seconds, just staring at her, at a loss for what to say next. But then she was doing the same, he thought. *Come on, man. Get a grip.*

Kent finally motioned to the car. "So, what happened?"

She gazed at the tangle of tubes under the hood. "It just died. I was lucky to pull over without hitting the rail."

The atmosphere was charged with expectancy. High above, a line of lightning crackled through black clouds. "Well, I'm not a mechanic, but why don't you get in and turn her over and I'll poke around a little."

"Good." She held his eyes for a moment as if trying to read any message there. He felt a strange tightness squeeze his chest.

Lacy jumped behind the wheel, eyeing him through the windshield. He dipped his head under the raised hood. Good grief! He was staring at a ghost from the past.

The engine turned over, and he jerked back, immediately hoping she had not seen his reaction. No sense coming off like a wuss.

The engine caught and rumbled to life.

Kent stood back, studied the running motor for a moment and, seeing nothing extraordinary, slammed the hood shut.

Lacy was out. "What did you do?"

He shrugged. "Nothing."

"You're kidding, right? This thing was dead, I swear."

"And I swear that I did nothing but breathe on it. Maybe I should've been an auto mechanic. I could fix cars by breathing on them." He grinned.

"Well, you always did have a lot of hot air." Lacy shot him a coy look and smiled slyly.

They chuckled, and Kent kicked at the pavement, suddenly shy again. He looked up. "Well, I guess you're fixed up. I heard you'd moved to Boulder."

"Yeah."

"Maybe we should get together."

The smile vanished from her face, and he wondered if she'd heard. "You heard about Gloria, right?" he asked.

"Gloria?"

"Yes. My wife died awhile back."

Her face registered shock. "I'm so sorry! I had no idea."

He nodded. "Yeah. Anyway, I should probably get going. I have to get back to work."

She nodded. "Yeah, I have to get back to Boulder. My washer broke down." She offered no further explanation.

He nodded again, feeling suddenly stranded. "Yeah." She was not moving.

"I'm really sorry about your wife, Kent. Maybe we should get some coffee and talk about it."

"I heard you lost your husband a couple years ago."

She nodded. They were nodding a lot. It was a good way to fill in the blanks after, what? Thirteen years?

"You have a card?" he asked. That sounded dumb. Sounded like he was hitting on her, and he had no intention of hitting on anyone. No desire at all.

"Sure." She reached through the window, withdrew her purse, and handed him a card. Rocky Mountain Bank and Trust. Customer Service.

"I didn't know you were in banking." He glanced up at her. "You know I'm in banking, right?"

"Someone said that. Information Systems, right?"

"Yeah. Good, I'll call you. We'll catch up."

"I'll look forward to it," she said, and he thought she meant it.

"Good." Lots of *goods* and *yeahs* and nodding. "Hope your car runs well," he said and dipped his head to her.

Then he was jogging back to his car. The horizon flashed crooked fingers of lightning, and thunder boomed. The rain was eager, he thought. When he reached his door, Lacy's white Acura sped by and honked. He waved and slipped behind the wheel. Go figure.

⌒⌒⌒

Lacy drove west through a hard pour with her gut twisted in knots. The chance meeting with Kent had thrown her completely off center. She sped down the blacktop, fixated on the *whap, whap* of the windshield wipers, slowly exiting the big city. But her heart was back there, on the roadside, gazing into those lost blue eyes.

Kent looked as though he'd stepped out of some lost corner of her mind, a carbon copy of the zany college student who'd managed to capture her heart. Her first love. It had been his sincerity, she'd mused a thousand times. A man as sincere and honest as he was ambitious. The unique blend of those traits had whipped up a potion that had her swooning for the first time in her life. Well, his blue eyes and blond hair had not exactly impeded her swooning, she supposed.

He had lost his wife. Didn't he have a son as well? Poor child.

And under that haunting facade hid a man aching for comfort yet repelled by it at once. She should know. She'd been there. "God, help him," she breathed, and she meant it. She meant not only that Kent would receive help, but that *God* would help him. Because Lacy believed in God. She had fallen to his feet just over a year ago while climbing out of her own despondency, learning that she did not have the world by its tail.

"Father, comfort him," she whispered. The wipers squeaked.

Lacy fought a sudden urge to pull off, whip the car around, and chase Kent down. Of course, that was ridiculous. Even if such a thing were possible, she had no business chasing after an old flame who'd just lost his wife. And since when had she become the chasing type, anyway? *Listen to me, even thinking in terms of chasing! Heavens! I don't mean chasing like some dog in heat, but chasing as in trying to . . . help the man.*

She glanced at the new water pump in the passenger seat and remembered the broken washing machine. Now, if that machine had not broken down precisely when it had, she would have missed him entirely. If the strange service tech had not been as accommodating on the phone, if he'd had a pump in stock, if she had not driven to Denver, if her car had not lost its spark for a moment when it did—any single fluctuation in this endless string of events, and she would not have met Kent.

And on top of it all, Kent had pulled over without knowing whom he would be helping. That much was evident by his shock when he recognized her.

On the other hand, every event that ever occurred did so only after a string of other events lined up perfectly.

Lacy glanced at a brown smudge on her right sleeve, a spot of smeared grease. Had he seen it? She returned to her line of thinking. Almost anything was statistically possible. But the pull in Lacy's heart suggested that today's string of events was not just a random occurrence. It had been somehow orchestrated. Had to be.

On the other hand, stranger things had happened.

Lacy ground her teeth and dismissed the mental volleys. But they did not go so easily; within the minute they were back, nipping at her mind.

In the end she decided that none of it mattered. Kent had her card. He would either call, or he would not call. And that had nothing to do with chance. It had everything to do with his choice. Her heart jumped at the thought.

An obscure memory from her early adolescent years flashed through her mind. She was all dressed up for the prom, clad in a pink dress with white frills and her hair pulled back in a cluster of curls. It had taken her and her mother a good three hours to make everything just so. It was her first date, and Daddy had told her how proud he was of her, looking so beautiful. She sat on the living room couch, holding a white carnation for her date. Peter. But Peter was late. Ten minutes, then half an hour, then an hour. And she just sat there swinging her legs, feeling all gooey inside and trying to be brave while her father stormed on the phone. But Peter never came, and his parents knew nothing about their son's whereabouts. Her father took her out for dessert, but she could not manage eye contact with anyone that night.

A lump filled her throat at the memory. Dating had never gone well for her. Even dating with Kent, who had dropped her on her seat at the slightest hint of commitment. She would do well to remember that.

What had she been thinking, *chasing* after him? She no more needed a relationship now than she needed a bout with lupus.

On the other hand, he might call.

17

Helen tossed and turned, and even in her sleep she could feel her eyes jerking behind closed lids. Slapping feet echoed through her head, sounding like a marathon runner who had taken a wrong turn and ended up running through a tunnel. A tunnel called Kent's life.

The feet beat on—*slap, slap, slap*—without pause. Heavy breathing chased the slapping. The runner pulled deliberately against the stale dark air. Maybe too deliberately, as if he or she were trying to believe that the breathing was all about flooding the lungs with air, when actually it was just as much about fighting off panic. Because steady sounds do that—they fight off uncertainty with their rhythm. But this runner seemed to be losing that battle with uncertainty. The deliberate breaths were sounding a little ragged around the edges.

The slapping feet had made frequent visits to her mind in the last week, and that bothered her because she knew they were saying something. She just hadn't been able to decipher their message. At least not all of it.

She knew they were Kent's feet. That Kent was running. Running from God. The running man. She'd heard of a movie called that once. *The Running Man.* Some gladiator type running for his life through a game show.

Pastor Madison didn't like her calling this a game, but here in her own mind she could call it whatever she wanted. And it felt like a serious game show to her. The stakes were death; the prize was life. But in a cosmic sort of way, that prize wasn't so different from winning a Kenmore refrigerator with built-in ice maker or a '64 Mustang convertible, now, was it?

She took a deep breath and tried to refocus her thoughts. *Lighten up, Helen. Goodness, you're going off the deep end. We're not playing* Wheel of Fortune *here.*

Her mind sank into the dungeon again and listened to those slapping feet.

How long could a person run like that? Another sound bounced around in the dark. A thumping sound. A pounding heart to go along with the heavy breathing and the slapping feet. Which made sense, because her heart would certainly be pounding if she ran.

She imagined herself running like that.

The thought came like a sharp jab to her solar plexus.

She caught her breath.

Now there were only two sounds in the tunnel: the beating feet—*slap, slap, slap*—and the pounding heart—*thump, thump, thump.* The breathing had stopped.

Helen bolted up in bed, suddenly awake, a single thought now whispering through her skull: *That breathing stopped when you stopped breathing, sister! That's you in there!*

She snatched her hands to her chest. Her heart pounded to the same cadence she had heard in her dream. In the tunnel. The only thing missing was the slapping feet. And no matter how weird things were getting, she knew that she certainly had not been running up and down her hall in her sleep.

Helen knew the point of it all, then, sitting in bed feeling her heart throb under her palm. If she was not actually in the game, she was *meant* to be. Her feet were *meant* to be slapping along the floor of that tunnel. This insane urge to walk was not just some senile thing; it was the pull of God on her spirit. *Walk, child, walk. Maybe even run. But at least walk.*

It might be Kent in there running for his life, but she was in there too, breathing down his neck! Praying for him. She was in the game too. And her part was the intercessor. That was it.

Helen threw the sheets off and stood beside her bed. It was 5 A.M. She should walk, maybe. The thought stopped her cold for a moment. She was not a walker, for heaven's sake. The doctor had wanted to put new knees in her legs less than a year ago! What on earth did she think she would do now? Hobble up and down the driveway until the neighbors called the police about the lunatic they saw out their windows? Walking back and forth on her plush carpet in running shoes was one thing. Taking a prayer trek through the streets like some prophet was another thing altogether.

And more important, why on God's green earth would he want her to walk at all? What did walking have to do with this craziness? God certainly did not need on old lady's walking to move his hand.

Then again, neither had he needed old Joshua and his cohorts traipsing around Jericho to tumble the wall, now, did he? And yet he had demanded that. This was not so different.

Well, yes, this *was* different. This was different because this was now and that was then and this was her and that was Joshua!

Helen grunted and made for the bathroom. She was up. She might as well get dressed. And there was another reason why this was different. This was different because this was mad! What would Pastor Madison say? Goodness!

She stopped midstride, halfway to the bathroom. *Yes, but what would God say? Was that God talking to you back there, telling you to walk?*

Yes.

Then walk.

Yes.

It was settled then, in that moment.

Twenty minutes later Helen stepped from her house wearing her white Reeboks and over-the-calf basketball socks below a swishing green dress with yellow sunflowers scattered in a pattern only the original designer could possible identify.

"Oh, God have mercy on my soul," she muttered and stepped from the landing to the sidewalk. She began to walk down the street with no destination in mind. She would just walk and see.

And she would pray.

卐

Kent rolled through the hours with all the constancy of a yo-yo those first two weeks. One moment consumed with the audacity of his ever-clarifying plot, the next blinking against memories of Spencer or Gloria. To say that he was unstable would have brought the textbook definition into clear focus.

The ideas came like weeds, sprouting in his mind as though some mad scientist had spilled super-growth formula on them. It didn't even occur to him until the end of the first week that the twisting and turning up there did not stop when he fell asleep. In fact, his best ideas seemed to sneak their way into his mind then, when he tossed in fitful sleep. In his dreams.

Just as the vagrant had flashed his tongue about and told Kent just what he thought of the situation, other voices seemed to be suggesting other opinions. He could never quite remember their precise words or even the overall context of their suggestions, but he seemed to wake each day with an eagerness to explore a vague notion. And regardless of why his mind seemed to favor the night, Kent did not complain. It was the stuff of genius, he thought.

The meeting with Lacy nagged at him occasionally, but the growing prospects of his new life overshadowed the strange encounter. Several times he pulled her card out, intending to call. But he found things confusing once he attempted to clarify his reason for contacting her. *Oh hi, Lacy. How about a nice romantic dinner tonight? Did I tell you that my wife and son just died? Because that's important. I'm a free man, Lacy.* Gag! He was certainly in no mood for a relationship.

On the other hand, he was starving for friendship. And friendship was relationship, so in that sense he was growing slowly desperate for a relationship. Maybe even someone to tell . . . Someone to share this growing secret with. But that would be insane. Secrecy was his friend here.

Life at the office began to take on its own rhythm, not so different from the one that had once marched him through the days before his world had turned upside down. And the nights. It was the night routine that Kent began to methodically add to his work regimen. He needed his coworkers to be thoroughly accustomed to his late nights at the office again. His whole plan depended on it.

It was impossible to lock or unlock the building without triggering a signal that notified the alarm company of the event. The entries were posted on the branch manager's monitors each morning. So Kent made a point of entering and leaving through the backdoor, creating a consistent record of his work habits, and then offhandedly reporting the progress he'd made the previous night to Borst.

What they could not know was that the debugging he accomplished in those late hours while they slept took only a fraction of the time indicated. He could produce more clean code in one hour than any of the others could in a day. He not only possessed twice the gray matter any of them did, but he was working on his own code.

Not his own code as in AFPS, but his own program as in refining ROOSTER and the way ROOSTER was going to wreak its havoc on the world.

Cliff made a habit of poking his head in each day, but Kent did his best to minimize their interaction. Which simply meant knowing at all times what the zany snowboarder was working on and staying clear of his routines.

"You seem awfully well adjusted for having just gone through such loss," Cliff stated at the end of Kent's first week back.

Kent scrambled for a plausible explanation. "Denial," he said, turning away. "That's what they say, anyway."

"Who says that?"

He had not been to a shrink. "The pastor," Kent lied.

"You're kidding! I had no idea you went to church. I do too!"

Kent began to regret his lie immediately.

"So how long have you been a Christian?"

"Well, actually I'm really not that well connected."

"Sure, I can understand that. They say 80 percent of churchgoers are disconnected beyond Sunday services. So I hear that your wife was a strong believer."

Kent looked up. "Really? And who told you that?"

"I just picked it up somewhere."

"Somewhere like where? I didn't know it was common knowledge around here."

Cliff shrugged uncomfortably. "Well, from Helen, actually."

"Helen? My mother-in-law's been talking to you?"

"No. Relax, Kent. We talked once when she called in."

"And you just happened to talk about me and my wife? Well that's real sweet of you— 'Poor Kent, let's gossip about his faith, why don't we? Or should we say, his lack thereof.'"

"We're Christians, Kent. Some things are not as sacred as others. Don't worry, it goes no further than me."

Kent turned away, angry without knowing exactly why. Helen had her rights. Gloria was, after all, her daughter. He began to avoid Cliff then, at the end of his first week back to work. Although getting away from the pineapple-eating grinner was easier said than done.

It took Borst most of two weeks to buy into Kent's reformed attitude. But a daily dose of soothing accolades administered by Kent greased the wheels to the man's mind easily enough. Kent had to hold his nose while smearing the stuff on, but even that became easier as the days passed.

Borst asked him about the schedule once after Kent had handed him the fix to a bug that Borst himself had attempted and failed to remedy. It had taken Kent exactly twenty-nine minutes the previous night to locate the misplaced modifier responsible.

"You got it, huh? Gotta hand it to you, Anthony. You sure can crank this stuff out." He lifted his greasy head. "You seem to work best at night these days, don't you?"

A flare hissed white-hot in Kent's mind. His heart flinched in his chest, and he hoped desperately that Borst was not catching any of his reaction. "I've always worked best at night, Markus." He'd discovered that Borst liked to be called Markus by his friends. He lowered his eyes. "But since the deaths, I'm not crazy about being alone at night with nothing to do, you know?"

"Yeah, sure. I understand." He waved the pages in the air. "You did all of this last night, huh?"

Kent nodded.

"What time you pull out of here?"

Kent shrugged. "I came back at, oh, maybe eight or so, and left at midnight."

Borst smiled. "Four hours? Like I said, you're good. You keep working like this, and the rest of us will run out of things to do." He chuckled. "Good work." He'd winked then, and Kent swallowed an urge to poke his eye out.

Instead he smiled. "Thank you, sir."

The *sir* brought a flare of pride to Borst's nostrils, and Kent left, determined to use the expression more frequently.

He resumed his friendship with Will Thompson within the first few days. As before, their shallow talk led to nothing of substance, which was fine by Kent.

"I just can't believe you're back after what they put you through," Will told him, walking to lunch the third day. Taking time for lunch sat rancid in Kent's gut, but he was on a mission to appear as ordinary as possible, and the occasional lunch would fit the image well.

"You know, if Spencer had not passed away, I don't think I would be here. But when you lose the ones you love the most, things change, Will. Your perspectives change. I just need to work now, that's all." He looked across the street to Antonio's Italian Cuisine. "Who knows? Maybe once things have settled I'll move on. But now I need stability."

Will nodded. "Makes sense."

Touché, Will. Indeed it makes sense. Everything needs to make sense. You remember that when they question you about me.

Betty Smythe became just another office fixture again, smacking her lips at the front desk, handling all of Borst's important calls and constantly scanning her little world with the peeled eyes of a hawk. It made little difference to Kent, who simply closed his door. But when the poop hit the fan, hers would be the most active mouth, flapping nonstop, no doubt. He wanted her gabbing to favor him, not cast suspicion his way. So he began the distasteful task of working his way into her corner.

A bouquet of roses, for all of her support, started him off on the right foot. The fact that she had not lifted a single finger in support of him didn't seem to temper her appreciation. Then again, judging by the amount of acrylic hanging off the end of her fingers, lifting them would be no easy task.

"Oh, Kent! You shouldn't have!"

He had always wondered if women who carried on with wide eyes about flowers really did find them as stimulating as they let on. He could see a cow slobbering over vegetation, but women were hardly cows. Well, most women weren't. Betty came pretty close, which probably explained why she had just rolled her eyes back as if she were dying and going to heaven over the red blossoms on this particular arrangement of vegetation.

"But I should have," he replied with as much sincerity as he could muster. "I just wanted you to know how much your support has helped me."

A quick flicker in her eyes made him wonder if he had gone too far. If so, she quickly adapted. "You're so kind. It was nothing, really. Anybody would have done the same." She smiled and smelled the roses.

Kent had no idea what she could possibly be referring to, but it no longer mattered. "Well, thank you again, Betty. I owe you." *Gag!*

"Thank you, Kent." Somehow one of the petals had loosed itself and stuck on her upper lip. It looked ridiculous. She didn't seem to notice. Kent didn't bother to tell her. He smiled genuinely and turned for his office.

Todd and Mary were like two peas in a pod—both eager to please Borst and fully cognitive of the fact that they needed Kent to do it. They both trotted in and out of his office like regular pack rats. "Kent, how would you do this?" Or, "Kent, I've done such and such but it's not working quite right." Not that he particularly minded. At times it even made him feel as though nothing had really changed— he had always been at the center of their world.

It was the way they straightened when Borst walked by that brought Kent back to earth. In the end, their allegiance was for Bossman.

Todd actually apologized for his behavior at one point. "I'm sorry for . . . well, you know." He sat in Kent's office and crossed his legs, suddenly a tinge redder in the face. He pushed up his black-rimmed glasses.

"For what, Todd?"

"You know, for the way I acted that first day."

Kent did not respond. Let the boy squirm a little.

"It's hard being caught in the middle of office politics, you know. And technically speaking, Borst *is* our boss, so we don't want to cross him. Besides, he was right. It's really his thing, you know?"

A dozen voices screamed foul in Kent's head. He wanted to launch out and turn this boy. Slap some sense into him. And he could've pulled it off, too. But he only bit his lip and nodded slowly.

"Yeah, you're probably right."

Todd grinned sheepishly. "It's okay, Kent. Borst promised to take care of us."

Todd obviously told Mary about the conversation, because the next time she sat her chunky self in his guest chair, she wore a grin that balled her cheeks. She dove right into a question without referring to the incident, but Kent knew they had talked. Knew it like he knew both she and Todd were, spineless, Twinkie-eating propeller-heads.

During his second week back, Kent began leaving for lunch through the front lobby. Despite his aversion to doing so, he'd done it before so he would do it now. He walked nonchalantly, avoiding eye contact but responding to the occasional call of greeting with as much enthusiasm as he could stomach.

They were all there, like windup dolls, playing their parts. The tellers whispered about their fanciful relationships and counted the money. Zak the security guard paced and nodded and occasionally swung his stick like he'd learned from some Hollywood movie. Twice Kent saw Sidney Beech, the assistant vice president, clicking across the floor when he entered the lobby, and each time he pretended not to see her. Once he saw Porky—that would be Price Bentley—walk across the marble floor, and he immediately cut for the bathrooms. If the bank president saw him, he did not indicate so. Kent chose to believe he had not.

By the end of the second week, the routines had been reestablished and Kent's most recent altercations with the bank all but forgotten. Or so he hoped. Everything settled into a comfortable rhythm, just like the old days.

Or so they thought.

In reality, with the passing of each day, Kent's nerves wound tighter and tighter, like one of those spring-operated toys in the hands of an overeager child. At any moment the spring would break and he would snap, berserk.

But the plan was taking shape, like a beautiful woman walking out of the fog. Step by step, curves began to define themselves, and flesh took on form. The emerging image was Kent's link to sanity. It kept him from going mad during the long hours of pretending. It gave him a lover to fondle in the dark creases of his mind. It became . . . everything.

He was setting them up for one major backstab.

He was going to rob them blind.

18

Dawn had come to Denver with a flare of red in the East. Bill Madison knew because he had watched the sun rise. From gray to red to just plain blue with a little smog thrown in to remind him where he lived.

Helen had called the previous evening and asked him to join her in the morning. They had talked twice on the phone since his last meeting with her, and each time Helen's words had rung in his mind for a good hour or two after the final click of the receiver. The prospect of seeing her again had brought a knot to his gut, but not a bad knot, he thought. More like the twisting you might expect just before the first big drop on a roller coaster.

"And why, precisely, am I joining you?" he'd asked good-naturedly.

"We've got some talking to do," she said. "Some walking and talking and praying. Bring your walking shoes. You won't be disappointed, Pastor." And he knew he wouldn't be. Although he doubted they would really be doing much walking. Not with her bad knees.

He stepped up to her porch at 6 A.M. feeling just a tad foolish with the tennis shoes on. Helen opened the door on his first ring and walked right past him and into the street without uttering a word.

Bill closed the door and scrambled after her. "Hold up, Helen. Good night! What's gotten into you?" He said it chuckling. If he didn't know her, he might guess she'd suddenly become a spring chicken by the way she moved her legs.

"Morning, Bill," she said. "Let's walk for a minute before we talk. I need to warm up."

"Sure."

That's what he said. *Sure.* As if this were just one more day in a long string of days in which they had climbed from bed in the dark to meet for an edge-of-dawn walk. But he wanted to ask her what on Earth she thought she was doing. Walking like some marathoner in a knee-length dress and socks hiked above her calves. It looked ridiculous. Which made him look ridiculous by association. And he had never seen her take such bold strides, certainly not without a noticeable limp

He shoved the thought from his mind and fell in. He was, after all, her pastor, and like she said, she needed shepherding. Although, at the moment, he was following more than shepherding. How could he be expected to feed the sheep if it was ten feet ahead of him?

Bill stumbled to catch up. Not a problem—she would begin to fade soon enough. Until then he would humor her.

They walked three blocks in silence before it began to occur to Bill that Miss Knee-Socks here was not fading. If there was any fading just now it was on his end of things. Too many hours behind the desk, too few in the gym.

"Where we going, Helen?" he asked.

"Oh, I don't know. We're just walking. Are you praying yet?"

"I didn't know I was supposed to be praying."

"I'm not sure you arc. But as long as I am, you might as well."

"Uh-huh," he said. Her Reeboks were no longer shiny and white like they had been a week earlier. In fact, they were not the same pair because these were well worn and the other had been almost new. Her calf muscles, flexing with each step, were mostly hidden by a thin layer of fat that jiggled beneath the socks, which encircled her legs with red stripes just below her knees. She reminded him of a basketball player from the seventies—minus the height, of course.

Her fingers hung by her side, swinging easily with each stride.

"You ever wonder why God used a donkey to speak, Bill? Can you even imagine a donkey speaking?"

"I suppose. It is rather strange, isn't it?"

"How about a whale swallowing Jonah? Can you imagine a man living in a fish for three days? I mean, forget the story—could you imagine that happening today?"

He dropped his eyes to the sidewalk and studied the expansion cracks appearing beneath them every few feet. "Hmm. I suppose. You have a reason for asking?"

"I'm just trying to nail down your orientation, Bill. Your real beliefs. 'Cause lots of Christians read those old stories in the Bible and pretend to believe them, but when it gets right down to it, they can barely imagine them, much less believe they actually happened. And they certainly would balk at such events happening today, don't you think?"

She strode along at a healthy pace, and he found himself having to work a bit to match her. Heavens! What had gotten into her?

"Oh, I don't know, Helen. I think people are pretty accepting of God's ability to persuade a whale to swallow Jonah or make a donkey talk."

"You do, do you? So you can imagine it, then?"

"Sure."

"What does it look like, Bill?"

"What does what look like?"

"What does a whale swallowing a full-grown man whole look like? We're not talking about chomping him up and gulping down the pieces—we're talking swallowing him whole. And then that man swimming around in a stomach full of steaming acids for a few days. You can see that, Bill?"

"I'm not sure I've ever actually pictured the details. I'm not even sure it's important to picture the details."

"No? So then what happens when people start imagining these details? You tell them the details aren't important? Pretty soon they toss those stories into a massive mental bin labeled 'Things that don't really happen.'"

"Come on, Helen! You don't just jump from a few details being unimportant to throwing out the faith. There are elements of our heritage we accept by faith. This doesn't necessarily diminish our belief in God's ability to do what he will—including opening the belly of a whale for a man."

"And yet you balked when I told you about my vision of Gloria's death. That was a simple opening of the *eyes*, not some whale's mouth for a man."

"And I did come around, didn't I?"

"Yes. Yes, you did."

She let it go with a slight smile, and he wondered at the exchange. Helen walked on, swinging her arms in a steady rhythm, humming faintly now. *Jesus, Lover of My Soul . . .* Her favorite hymn, evidently. "You do this every day, Helen?" he asked, knowing full well she did not. Something had changed here.

"Do what?"

"Walk? I've never known you to walk like this."

"Yes, well I picked it up recently."

"How far do you walk?"

She shrugged. "I don't know. How fast do you think we're walking?"

"Right now? Maybe three, four miles an hour."

She looked at him, surprised. "Really? Well then, what's three times eight?"

"What's eight?"

"No. What's three *times* eight?"

"Three times eight is twenty-four."

"Then I guess I walk twenty-four miles each day," Helen said and grinned satisfactorily.

Her words sounded misguided, like lost birds smashing into the windowpane of his mind, unable to gain access. "No, that's impossible. Maybe a mile a day. Or two."

"Oh, heavens! It's more than a mile or two, I know that much. Depends on how fast I'm walking, I suppose. But eight times three *is* twenty-four. You're right."

Her meaning caught up with Bill then. "You . . . you actually walk . . . eight hours?" Good heavens! that was impossible!

"Yes," she said.

He stopped dead in his tracks, his mouth gaping. "You walk *eight hours* a day like this?"

She answered without looking back. "Don't fall apart on me, Pastor. My walking is certainly easier to accept than Jonah and his whale."

Bill ran to catch up. "Helen! Slow down. Look, slow down for just a minute here. You're actually saying you walk like this for *eight hours* a day? That's over twenty miles a day! That's *impossible!*"

"Is it? Yes, it is, isn't it?"

He knew then that she was pulling no punches, and his head began to buzz. "How? How do you do it?"

"I don't, Bill. God does."

"You're saying that somehow God miraculously allows you to walk twenty miles a day on *your* legs?"

She turned and lifted an eyebrow. "I should hope I walk on my legs. I would hate to borrow yours for a day."

"That's not what I mean." He was not laughing. Bill looked at those calves again, bouncing like a stiff bowl of jelly with each step. Apart from the socks, they looked plain enough to him. And Helen was asserting that she was walking twenty-four miles a day on those damaged knees that, unless his memory had gone bad, just last week favored hobbling over walking. And now this?

"Do you doubt me?"

"No, I'm not saying I doubt you." He didn't know what he was saying. What he did know was that a hundred voices were crying foul in his mind. The voices from that bin labeled "Things that don't really happen," as Helen had put it.

"Then what are you saying?"

"I'm saying . . . Are you sure you walk a full eight hours?"

"Walk with me. We will see."

"I'm not sure I can walk eight hours."

"Well, then."

"Are you sure you don't take breaks . . ."

She lost it then, right on the sidewalk in front of Freddie's Milk Store on the corner of Kipling and Sixth. She pulled up suddenly and planted both hands on her hips. "Okay, look, mister. You're the man of God here! Your job is to lead me *to* him, not away from him. Now, forgive me if I'm wrong, but you're starting to sound as though you're not sure anymore. I'm walking, aren't I? And I've been walking for over a week—eight hours a day, three miles an hour. You don't like it, you can go ahead and put your blinders back on. Just make sure you look straight ahead when you see me coming."

He dropped his jaw at the outburst. Heat flared up his neck and burned behind his ears. It was at times like this that he should be prepared with a logical response. Problem was, this was not about the logical. This was about impossibilities, and he was staring one right in the face. Which made it a possibility. But in reality, he already knew that. His outer self was just throwing a fit, that's all.

"Helen . . ."

"Now, I also had some trouble with this at first, so I'm willing to cut you some slack. But when I give you simple facts, like *I walk eight hours a day,* I don't need you analyzing me like I'm loony tunes."

"I'm sorry, Helen. Really, I am. And for what it's worth, I believe you. It's just not every day this kind of thing happens." He immediately wondered if he did believe her. You don't just believe some old lady who claims to have found kryptonite and discovered that Superman was right all along—it does work! On the other hand, this was not just some old lady.

She studied him for a full five seconds without another word. Then she *humphed* and marched on deliberately.

Bill walked beside her in silence for a full minute, unnerved. A hundred questions coursed through his mind, but he thought it better to let things settle. Unless he had missed something here, Helen was claiming that God had empowered her with some kind of supernatural strength that allowed her to walk like a twenty-year-old. A strong twenty-year-old at that. And she was not just claiming it, she was showing him. She had insisted he come and see for himself. Well, he was seeing all right.

She strode by him, step for step, thrusting each foot out proudly like Moses strutting across the desert with cane in hand.

He glanced at her face and saw that her lips were moving. She was praying. Prayer walking. Like those mission teams that went overseas just to walk around a country and pray. Break the spiritual strongholds. Only in Helen's case, it was Kent who would presumably benefit.

This was happening. This was *really* happening! Never mind that he had never in his life even heard of, much less *seen*, such a thing, this was happening right before his eyes. Like a hundred Bible stories, but alive and well and here today.

Bill suddenly stopped on the sidewalk, aware that his mouth hung dumbly open. He closed it and swallowed.

Helen walked on, possibly not even aware he'd stopped. Her strides showed not a hint of weakness. It was as if her legs did their business beneath her without her full knowledge of why or how they operated. They just did. Her concern was praying for Kent, not understanding the physics of impossibilities. She was a walking miracle. Literally.

Doubt suddenly felt like a silly sentiment. How could you doubt what you saw?

Bill took after her again, his heart now surging with excitement. Goodness, how many men had seen something like *this?* And why was it so hard to accept? Why so far out? He was a pastor, for Pete's sake. She was right. It was his job to illuminate the truth, not doubt it.

He imagined his pews full of smiling church members. *And today, brothers and sisters, we want to remember sister Helen, who is marching around Jericho.*

His bones seemed to tingle. He skipped once to match stride with Helen, and she looked at him with a raised brow.

"You just pray while you're walking?" he asked, and then he immediately held out his hands in a defensive gesture. "I'm not doubting. I'm just asking."

She smiled and chuckled once. "Yes, I pray. I walk, and I pray."

"For Kent?"

"For this crazy duel over Kent's soul. I don't know all the whys and hows yet. I just know that Kent is running from God, and I'm walking behind him, breathing down his neck with my prayers. It's symbolic, I think. But sometimes I'm not even sure about that. Walk by faith, not by sight. Walk in the Spirit. They that wait upon the Lord shall renew their strength; they shall walk and not grow weary. It wasn't literal back then, but now it is. At least it is with me."

"Which suggests that the whole business about Kent is real as well, because now it's not just visions and things in the head but this walking," Bill said. "Do you know how unusual that is?"

"I'm not so sure it's unusual at all. I just think I'm unusual—you said so yourself. Maybe it takes a bit of unusualness for God to work the way he wants to work. And for your information, I knew it was real before this walking thing. I'm sorry to hear that you thought my visions were delusional."

"Now come on, Helen. Did I say that?" He frowned and turned sideways so she could see his expression.

"You didn't need to." She set her jaw and strode on.

"Can I touch them?" he asked.

She scrunched her brow. "Touch what? My legs? No, you can't touch my legs! Heavens, Bill!"

"Not *touch* touch them! Goodness!" He walked on, slightly embarrassed. "Are they warm or anything. I mean, can you feel anything different in them?"

"They buzz."

"Buzz, huh?" He looked at them again, wondering how God altered physics to allow for something like this. They should bring some scientists out here to prove a few things. But he knew she would never allow that.

"What do you mean by *duel*? You said this was about a crazy duel over Kent's soul. That's not exactly out of the textbooks."

"Sure it is. The books may use different words, but it all boils down to the same thing. It is war, Bill. We do not wage war against flesh and blood but against principalities and powers. We duel. And what greater prize than a man's soul?" She faced forward deliberately. "It's all there. Look it up."

Bill chuckled and shook his head. "I will. Just for you, Helen. Someone's got to make sure you don't walk right off the planet."

"So that's your idea of shepherding?" Her eyes twinkled above a smile.

"You asked for it. Like you said, it's my gift. And if God can transform your legs into bionic walkers, the least he can do for me is give me a little wisdom. To help you walk."

"That's right. Just make sure the wisdom is not your own, Pastor."

"I'll try. This is just incredible!"

"You should go back now, Bill." Helen strode forward, down the sidewalk, right down Kipling. "I've got some praying to do. Besides, we don't want to get you stranded out here, now, do we?"

"I shouldn't walk and pray with you?"

"Has God told you to walk and pray with me?"

"No."

"Then go be a pastor."

"Okay. Okay, I'll do that." Bill turned, feeling as though he should say something brilliant—something commemorative. But nothing came to mind, so he just turned and retraced his steps.

∽∾∾

They say that a split personality develops over years of dissociative behavior. Like a railroad track encountering large, gnarly roots that slowly but inevitably heave it up and split it into two wandering rails. But the development of Kent's double life was not such a gradual thing. It was more like two high-speed locomotives thundering in opposite directions with a rope tied to the tail end of each. Kent's mind was stretched there in that high-tension rope.

The persona he presented at the bank returned him to the appearance of normalcy. But during the hours on his own, away from the puppets at work, he was slipping into a new skin. Becoming a new man altogether.

The dreams strung through his mind every night, whispering their tales of brilliance, like some kind of alter ego who'd done this a thousand times and now mentored the child prodigy. *What of the body, Kent? Bodies are evidence. You realize that they will discover the cause of death once they examine that body. And you do need the body—you can't just sink it to the bottom of a lake like they do in idiotic movies, Kent. You're no idiot, Kent.*

Kent listened to the dreams, wide eyed and fast asleep.

He ingested a steady diet of ibuprofen for the pain that had latched on to his neck. And he began to settle himself with the occasional nightcap. Only they were not so occasional after the third day. They were nightly. And they were not just nightcaps. They were shots of tequila. His taste for the juice that had nearly killed him in college came back like a soothing drug. Not enough to push him into oblivion, of course. Just enough to calm his ragged edges.

When he wasn't at work, Kent was either poring over research or thinking. A lot of thinking. Mulling the same detail over in his mind a hundred times. Thinking of every possible angle and searching for any loophole he had not considered.

The Discovery Channel had a daily show called *Forensics*. A downtown library had seen fit to catalog fifty consecutive episodes. It was a show detailing actual cases in which the FBI slowly but methodically honed in on criminals using the very latest technology in forensics. Fingerprints, bootprints, hair samples, phone records, perfume, you name it. If a person had been in a room, the FBI experts could almost always find traces.

Almost always. Kent watched the shows unblinking, his analytical mind tracking all of their weaknesses. And then he would reconsider the smallest details of his plan.

For example. He had already determined that he would have to execute the theft *at* the bank—inside the building. Which meant he would have to get *to* the bank. Question: How? He couldn't very well have a cab drop him off. Cabs kept records, and any break from routine might lead to a raised eyebrow. He had to keep those eyebrows down. So he should drive his car, of course, the way he always got to the bank. Yes, possibly. On the other hand, cars represented physical evidence. They left tracks. They could be seen by passersby or vagrants, like that one he'd seen in the back alley. Then again, did it matter? What would he do with the car afterward? Drive it away? No, he definitely could not drive off. Cars could be tracked. Torch it? Now, there was a thought. He could leave a five-gallon container of gasoline in the trunk, as if it were meant for the lawn mower at home, and rig a loose wire to detonate the fuel. *Boom!* That was ridiculous, of course. Even a beat cop would suspect the torching of a car. Maybe send it over a cliff with a full tank. Watch it burst into flames on the rocks. Of course, cars rarely actually exploded on impact.

Then again, why rid himself of the car at all?

The car detail consumed hours of drifting thought over the days. And it was the least of his challenges. But slowly, hour by hour, the solutions presented themselves to him. And when they did, when he had tested them in his mind and stripped them of ambiguity, Kent found something he never would have suspected at such discoveries. He found exhilaration. Bone-trembling euphoria. The kind of feeling that makes you squeeze your fists and grit your teeth to keep from exploding. He would pump the air with his right arm, the way he had done not so long before, with Gloria and Spencer giggling at his exuberance over the completion of AFPS.

Without exception, these occasions called for a shot of tequila.

Rarely did he stop long enough to consider the madness of his plan. He had grown obsessed. The whole thing, stealing such an enormous sum of money and then vanishing—starting over—was laced with insanity. Who had ever done such a thing? In a line of a hundred thousand children, it would not be *him* but the one whose mother had mainlined heroin throughout her pregnancy who would be most likely to one day attempt such a feat.

Or the man who had lost his wife, his son, and his fortune in the space of a month. No, it was more, he thought. It was his savage thirst for what was due him. For a life. For revenge. But more than those things. As a simple matter of fact, there was nothing else that made sense any longer. The alternative of trudging along a new career path on his own sat like lead in his gut. In the end it was this thought that compelled him to throw back the last mouthful of tequila and discard any reservation.

Through it all, Kent maintained a plastic, white-collar grin at the bank, ignoring the knots of anxiety twisting through his gut and the anticipation bursting in his chest. Fortunately, he had never been one to sweat much. A nervous sweater in Kent's current state would walk through the days dripping on the carpet and changing identical shirts every half-hour in a futile attempt to appear relaxed and casual.

Helen, his religious whacko mother-in-law, saw fit in her eternal wisdom to leave him alone those first two weeks. Which was a small miracle in itself. Helen's God had performed his first miracle. She did call Kent once, asking if she could borrow some of Gloria's old tennis shoes. Seemed she had taken to exercise and didn't see the need to buy a brand-new pair of Reeboks for sixty bucks when Gloria's were just growing mold in the closet. Why she wanted all four pair, Kent had no clue. He just grunted agreement and told her to come by the next day. They would be on the front porch. When he returned from work, they were gone.

Happy walking, Helen. And if you don't mind, you may walk right off a cliff.

❧

Kent found his way past the confusion surrounding Lacy Cartwright on a Thursday night fifteen days after their strange meeting, almost three weeks after his decision to rob the bank.

It came at midnight during one of those exhilarating moments just after a key to the entire theft had erupted in his mind like a flare. He thought of Lacy, possibly because the solution igniting his mind's horizon brought his focus to the future. Post-theft. His new life. Not that Lacy would fit into any new life, heavens no. Still, once her image presented itself, he could not shake it free.

He dialed her listed number with an unsteady hand and sat back.

Lacy answered on the fifth ring, just as he was pulling the receiver from his ear. "Hello?"

"Lacy?"

"Who is this?" She was not sounding too pleased about being called at midnight by a stranger.

"Kent. I'm sorry. Is it too late?"

"Kent?" Her voice softened immediately. "No. I was just going to bed. Are you okay?"

"I'm fine. I just thought . . . I just needed someone to talk to." He paused, but she remained silent.

"Listen to me. Sounds stupid, I know—"

"Lighten up, Kent. I've been there, remember? You're no more *fine* than I am a porcupine."

He leaned back against the cushions on the sofa and cradled the cordless phone on his neck. "Actually, things are good. Surprisingly good. I've got no one in the world to talk to, but apart from that rather insignificant detail, I would say that I'm recuperating."

"Hmm. How long has it been?" Her voice sounded sweet and soft over the receiver.

"Couple months." Had he told her about Spencer? Suddenly it was a lump rising in his throat instead of a hard-beating heart. "My son was killed in a hit-and-run four weeks ago." He swallowed.

"Oh, Kent! I'm so sorry. That's terrible!" Her voice trembled with shock, and Kent blinked at that. She was right. It was terrible—mind numbing, really. And he was already forgetting the tragedy of it all. So quickly. That made him what? A monster? "How old was your son?"

"Ten." Maybe this was not such a good idea. She was bringing things back into clear focus.

"Kent, I'm . . . I'm so sorry."

"Yeah." His voice sounded unsteady—choked with emotion. Two thoughts slinked through his mind. The first was that this emotion was redemptive—he did care after all; he was not a monster. The second was that the emotion was actually more self-pity than mourning over loss—lamenting the notion that he was indeed a monster.

"I don't know what to say, Kent. I . . . I think I know how it feels. Have you had any counseling?"

"A therapist? No. But I have a mother-in-law, if that counts."

She chuckled nervously. "What about a pastor?"

"Religious counsel? There was plenty of that to go around at the funeral, believe me. Enough for a few hundred years, I would say." What if she was religious? "But no, not really."

The phone rested silently against his cheek. "Anyway," he continued. "Maybe we could talk sometime."

"We're talking now, Kent."

The comment caught him off guard. "Yes. We are." He felt out of control. She was stronger than he remembered. Maybe the comment about religious counsel had been misplaced.

"But we can talk more whenever you're ready," she said. "I couldn't very well turn down an old friend in need, now, could I?" Her voice was soft again. "Really, call me whenever you want to talk. I know the value of talking things through."

He waited a moment before replying. "Thank you, Lacy. I think I would like that."

They talked for another half-hour, mostly about incidentals—catching up stuff. When Kent hung up, he knew he would call again. Maybe the next day. She was right: Talking was important, and he had some things he wanted to talk about.

19

The first real bump in the road came the following Monday.

Kent sat hunched over a tiny table in the coffee lounge in Barnes and Noble Booksellers after leaving work early to run some "errands"—an activity he knew would quickly outlive its plausibility as a valid excuse for leaving the bank. After all, how many errands could a single man without a life run?

He'd scoured the shelves, found two books, and wanted to make certain they contained the data he was after before making the purchase. *The Vanishing Act* lay at an angle on the green-tiled tabletop before him. The other book, *Postmortem Forensics,* rested open between his hands, spread to a chapter on skeletal remains.

Within five minutes he knew the books were perfect. But he decided to read just a little further in one particular chapter. Like another article he'd gleaned off the Internet suggested, the editor here was confirming that a gunshot wound would not bleed after death. If the pump wasn't pumping—if the heart wasn't beating—the blood would not flow. But he already knew that. It was this bit about the effects of high heat to flesh and skeletal remains that had Kent's heart suddenly drumming steadily.

He flipped the page. Human flesh was rather unpredictable, sometimes flaming to a crisp and other times extinguishing itself midburn. Various accelerants assisted the burning of flesh, but most left a residue easily detected in postmortem forensics. Gasoline, for example, left a detectable residue, as did all petroleum products.

Kent scanned quickly down the page, tense now. What then? If he could be certain of the flesh burning . . . A sentence jumped out at him. "Magnesium is sometimes used by mortuaries to—"

"Excuse me, sir."

The voice startled Kent, and he snapped the book shut. A middle-aged man sat across from him, smiling past wire-framed glasses. His black hair was swept back neatly, glistening atop a small, pointy head. A pinhead. He was dressed not unlike Kent himself: tailored black suit, crisp white shirt, red tie held snugly by a gold tie bar.

But what had Kent's pulse spiking was the fact that the stranger now sat down at Kent's table, elbows down and smiling like he had been here first. That and the man's piercing green eyes. Like snowboarder Cliff's eyes. He sat, stunned, finding no words.

"Hello." The stranger grinned big. His voice seemed to echo low and softly, as if he'd spoken into a drum. "I couldn't help noticing that book. *Postmortem Forensics,* huh? Is that the kind of book that tells you how to carve someone up without getting caught?" He chuckled. Kent did not.

The man calmed himself. "Sorry. Actually, I've always been rather interested in what happens after death. You mind if I look at the book? I might want a copy myself." The man stretched out a big tanned hand.

Kent hesitated, taken back by the man's audacity. He held out the book. Was it possible this man was an agent, somehow on to him? *Relax, Kent. The crime is nowhere but in your mind.* He fixed his jaw and said nothing, hoping the man would catch his disinterest.

The stranger scanned through the book and stopped dead center. He flipped the book around and showed a centerfold of a spread-eagle corpse. "Now where do you suppose this man is?" he asked.

"He's dead," Kent answered, "in a grave somewhere."

"You think?" The man's eyebrow arched. "You think your son is in a grave somewhere as well, then?"

Kent blinked and stared at the man hard. "My son?" Now he was growing angry. "What do you know of my son?"

"I know that he was struck by a car a month ago. He say anything to you before he died? Something that morning before you left, perhaps?"

"Why?" Kent demanded. Then it hit him. "Are you a cop? Is this part of the investigation of my son's death?"

"In a matter of speaking, yes. Let's just say we are reviewing the implications of your son's death. I understand you were angry when you left him."

Linda! They had interviewed the baby-sitter. "I wouldn't say angry, no. Look, mister. I loved my boy more than you'll ever know. We had a disagreement, sure. But that's it." What was going on here? Kent felt his chest tighten. What was the man insinuating?

"Disagreement? Over what?"

The man's eyes stared like two green marbles with holes punched in them, dead center. It occurred to Kent that the eyes were not blinking. He blinked and wondered if the man had blinked in that split second while his own eyes flicked shut. But they did not look as if they'd blinked. They just stared, round and wet. Unless wet meant that he had indeed blinked, in which case maybe the man had blinked. If so, he was timing it pretty good.

The agent cleared his throat and repeated himself. "What was your disagreement over, Kent?"

"Why? Actually we really didn't have a disagreement. We just talked."

"Just talked, huh? So you felt pretty comfortable leaving him in the doorway like that?"

Kent flashed back. "How I felt is none of your business. I may have felt like throwing up, for all you should care. Maybe I'd just ingested a rotten apple and felt like puking on the street. Does that make me a murderer?"

The man smiled gently. His eyes were still not blinking. "Nobody called you a murderer, Kent. We just want to help you see some things."

"Do you mind if I see your credentials? What agency are you with, anyway?"

The man casually reached for his pocket. He found a wallet in his breast pocket and pulled it out.

Kent did not know where the man was headed. Didn't even know what he meant by what he'd said. He *was* aware, however, of the heat snaking up his neck and spreading over his skull. How dare this man sit here and question his motives? He had loved Spencer more than he loved life itself!

"Listen, sir, I don't know who you are, but I would die for my boy, you hear?" He didn't intend for it to come out trembly, but it did. Suddenly tears blurred his vision, but he stumbled forward. "I would lay down my life for that boy in a heartbeat, and I don't appreciate anybody questioning my love! You got that?"

The stranger pulled a card from his wallet and handed it to Kent without moving his eyes. He didn't seem affected by these emotions. "That's good, Kent."

Kent dropped his eyes to the card: "Jeremy Lawson, Seventh Precinct," it read in a gold foil. He looked up. The agent's wire glasses rode neatly on his nose above a smug smile.

"I'm just doing my job, you realize. Now, if you'd rather, I can haul you in and make this formal. Or you can answer a few questions here without coming apart at the seams on me." He shrugged. "Either way."

"No, here's just fine. But you just leave my son out of this. It takes a real sicko to even imagine that I had anything to do with his death." He trembled saying it, and for a moment he considered standing and leaving the cop.

"Fair enough, Kent. And to be straight with you, I believe that you did love your son." He offered no more but sat there, smiling at Kent, unblinking. And then he did blink, just once. Like camera shutters, snapping a shot.

"Then that's that," Kent said. "If you've done your homework, you'll know that I've been through enough these last few months as it is. So if you're finished, I really need to get back to work."

"Well, now, that's just it, Kent. Seems to me there just might be more here than meets the eye."

Kent flushed. "Meaning what?"

"Have you talked to anyone else about this?"

"Talked to anyone else about *what?*"

The agent grinned knowingly and licked his forefinger. He turned the page to the book and glanced at its contents. "Just answer the question, Kent. Have you talked to anyone else? A stranger, perhaps."

Kent felt his hands tremble, and he removed them from the table. "Look. You're speaking a foreign language here. Do you know what I'm saying? I don't have the slightest idea what you mean by any of this. You come in here haranguing me about my son—practically accuse me of killing him—and now you want to know if I've talked to any strangers lately? What on Earth does this have to do with me?"

The cop may very well have not even heard him by his response. "A vagrant, say. Or a homeless man in an alley? You haven't talked to anyone like that recently?"

The man pried his eyes from the book and stared at him, that ear-to-ear grin still splitting his jaw. Kent squinted, sincerely wondering if Mr. Cop here hadn't slipped over the edge. His own fear that this bizarre exchange led anywhere significant melted slightly. What could a vagrant possible have anything to do with . . . ?

Then it hit him, and he stiffened. The cop noticed, because his right eyebrow immediately arched curiously.

"Yes?"

The vagrant in the alley! They had talked to the spineless vagrant!

But that was impossible! That had been his mind playing with images!

"No," Kent said. "No, I haven't talked to any vagrant." Which was true enough. You did not actually talk in your dreams. Then again he *had* seen the vagrant in the alley prior to the dream, hadn't he? The man's summary of life whispered through Kent's mind. *Life sucksssss* . . . But he hadn't actually talked to that vagrant either.

"Why don't you ask me if I've had wine and cheese with the president's wife lately? I can answer that for you, as well."

"I think you did talk to a stranger in an alley, Kent. And I think he may have told you a few things. I want to know what he told you. That's all."

"Well, you're wrong. What? Some fool said he told me a few things, and that makes me a suspect in the crime of the century?" Kent almost choked on those last few words. *Control yourself, man!*

"Crime of the century? I didn't say anything about a crime, my friend."

"It was a figure of speech. The point is, you are groping for threads that simply do not exist. You are badgering me with questions about events that have nothing at all to do with me. I lost my wife and my son in the last few months. This does not automatically place me at the top of some most-wanted list, am I right? So then, unless you have questions that actually make sense, you should leave."

The man's smile left him. He blinked again. For a few seconds the agent held him in a thoughtful stare, as if that last volley had done the trick—shown Pinhead here who he was really up against.

"You are a bright one. I'll give you that. But we know more than you realize, Kent."

Kent shook his head. "Not possible. Unless you know more than I do about me, which is rather absurd, isn't it?"

The man smiled again. He shifted his seat back, preparing to leave. Thank goodness.

He dipped his head politely and offered Kent one last morsel to chew on. "I want you to consider something, Kent. I want you to remember that eventually everything will be found out. You are indeed a brilliant man, but we are not so slow ourselves. Watch your back. Be careful whose advice you take."

With that, the agent stood and strode away. He put his hands deep into his pockets, rounded a bookcase ten yards away, and vanished.

Kent sat for a long time, calming his heart, trying to make sense of the exchange. The man's words nagged him like a burrowed tick, digging at his skull. An image of the man, sitting there with his slicked hair and cheesy grin, swallowed his mind.

Ten minutes later he left the bookstore without buying the books he'd come for.

20

Kent sat in the big tan leather lounger facing the tube Monday night taking stock of things. The Forty Niners led the Broncos sixteen to ten, and Denver had the ball at the fifty yard line, but Kent barely knew it. The roar of the crowd provided little more than background static for the images roaring through his mind.

He was taking stock of things. Getting right down in the face of the facts and drawing conclusions that would stay with him until he croaked.

At least that's how his self-analysis session had started out, back when Denver led six to three. Back before he had gotten started early on his nightcap. Actually he had dispensed with the nightcap routine at the first quarter whistle and settled for the bottle instead. No use kidding around. These were serious matters here.

At the top of his list of deliberations was that cop who had interrupted his reading at Barnes and Noble. The pinhead was on the case. Granted, not *the* case, but the man was onto *him,* and he was the case. Kent took a nip of liquor. Tequila gold. It burned going down, and he sucked at his teeth.

Now what exactly did that mean, *on the case?* It meant that Kent would be a fool to go through with any robbery attempt while Detective Pinhead was around. That's what it meant. Kent took another small taste from the bottle in his hand. A roar blared through the room; someone had scored.

But then, how could anyone know anything about anything other than what had already happened? Not a soul could possibly know about his plans—he'd told no one. He had started the fine-tuning of ROOSTER, but no one else had access to the program. Certainly not some pinhead cop who probably didn't know computer code from alphabet soup.

"We know more than you think we do, Kent."

"We do? And who's we? Well I think you're wrong, Pinhead. I think you know zero.

170

And if you know ten times that much it's still a big fat whoppin' goose egg, isn't it?"

The simple fact was, unless Pinhead could read his mind or was employing some psychic who could read minds, he knew nothing about the planned robbery. He was bluffing. But why? Why would the cop even suspect enough to merit a bluff? Regardless of why or how, the notion of continuing, considering this latest development, rang of madness. Like a resounding gong. *Bong, bong, bong! Stupid, stupid, stupid! Get your butt back to Stupid Street, fool.*

But he could plan. And he should plan, because who was to say that Pinhead would hang around? For that matter, even with the man on the case, Kent's plan was foolproof, wasn't it? What difference would an investigation make? And there *would* be an investigation, regardless. Oh yeah, there would be one heck of an investigation, all right. You don't just kill someone and expect a round of applause. But that was just it. There would be an investigation, no matter what he did. Pinhead or no pinhead. So it really made no difference whether the cop stayed on the case or not.

An episode of *Forensics* Kent had watched on Saturday replayed through his mind. It featured a case in which some idiot had plotted the perfect murder but had one problem. He'd killed the wrong man. In the end he had attempted the murder again, this time on the right person. He had failed. He was rotting in some prison now.

That was the problem with having the cops already breathing down your neck; they would be more likely to stumble onto some misplaced tidbit that nailed you. To be done right, most crimes had to come out of the blue. Certainly not under the watchful nose of some pinhead who was stalking you.

But this was not most crimes. This was *the* perfect crime. The one all the shows could not showcase because no one knew it had even occurred.

Kent lifted the bottle and noted that it was half empty.

And the cop was not the only one breathing down his neck. Cliff, the mighty snowboarder-turned-programmer, was annoying Kent with his intrusive style of *Let's check your code, Kent.* What if Boy Wonder actually stumbled onto ROOSTER? It would be the end, of course. The whole plan rested squarely on the shoulders of ROOSTER's secrecy. If the security program was discovered, the plot would blow up. And if anybody could find it, Cliff could. Not as a result of his brilliance as much as his dogged tenacity. There was a single link buried in AFPS that led to ROOS-TER: an extra "m" in the word "extremmely," itself buried in a routine not yet active. If the "m" were deleted by some spelling-bee wizard intent on setting things straight, the link automatically shifted to the second "e" in the same word. Only someone with way too much time on their hands could possibly uncover the hook.

Someone like Cliff.

Kent went for a chug on the bottle and closed his eyes to the throat burn. The game was in its second half. He'd missed the big showdown at the end of the first. Didn't matter.

"Be real," he mumbled. "Nobody's gonna find no link. No way this side of Hades."

And he knew he was right.

An image of Lacy drifted through the fog in his mind. Now, *there* was a solution to this whole mess. He could discuss the fine points of committing a federal felony with Lacy. Cut her in. An anemic little chuckle escaped his lips at the thought. It sounded more like the burp that followed it.

Fact was, even if he wanted a relationship with a woman, it was simply not feasible. Not with mistress ROOSTER in his life. It wasn't that they wouldn't both share him. It was that they *couldn't*. Assuming they wanted to. Which was yet one more problem: He was thinking of ROOSTER as if it were a real person that possessed a will worth considering. ROOSTER was a link, for heaven's sake! A plan. A program.

Either way, he still could not cohabit with both ROOSTER and any living soul. Period. ROOSTER demanded it. The plan would fall apart.

So then, what on earth did he think he was doing with Lacy?

Good question. He should cut her off.

Cut her off from what? It wasn't as if he had a relationship with her. One freak roadside encounter with a stranger and a phone call hardly made a relationship.

On the other hand, Lacy was no stranger. She stood there by her car in Kent's mind, like a ghost stepping from the pages of his past.

Still, he had no desire for a relationship that could be characterized as anything but platonic. There was Gloria to think of—in the dirt nearly three months. That long? Goodness. And mistress ROOSTER.

Get a grip, Kent. You're losing it.

He lifted the bottle, sipped at the burning liquid, and scratched his chin. Sweat wet the skin beneath two days of stubble. He looked at his shirt. It was the same Super Bowl T-shirt he'd slept in for a week. Not a problem. Now that he was doing his own laundry, changing clothes had lost its appeal. Except for underwear, of course. But he could just throw the underwear in the machine once every other week and stuff them in a drawer without all the folding and sorting mess. Which reminded him; he needed another dozen. The machine could easily hold a month's worth. Once a month was clearly better than once every two weeks.

Kent looked at the tube. The game was nearing an end. Outside, the night was pitch black. He licked the bottle and thought about Pinhead again. A needle of anxiety pricked his skin. It was madness. *When you're ready, just call me,* she'd said in the voice echoing from the past. Lacy.

He made the decision then, impulsively, with two minutes to play and the Broncos now leading twenty-one to nineteen.

He climbed out of the lounger and picked up the phone, his heart suddenly stomping through his chest. Which was absurd because he certainly had no emotions for Lacy that would set off its pounding. Except that he did want to see her. That much he could not deny. The realization only added energy to his heart's antics as he dialed her number.

❧

Lacy had just slipped on her bathrobe when the phone began its ringing. The caller ID showed only that the call was "out of area," and she decided to pick it up on the remote chance it was a call she actually wanted to take.

"Hello."

"Hello. Lacy?"

Kent! Her heart leapt. She would know that voice anywhere.

"Yes?"

"Hi, Lacy. Is it too late?"

"And you are . . . ?"

"Oh, I'm sorry. It's Kent. Geez, I'm sorry. Pretty stupid, huh? Call up and ask if it's too late without introducing myself. I didn't mean to sound . . ."

"What do you want, Kent?"

The phone returned only silence for a few moments. Now why had she come off so curt? And why was her breathing tight? *God, help me.*

"Maybe I should call back at a better time," Kent said.

"No. No, I'm sorry. You just took me by surprise. It's only ten. You're fine."

He chuckled on the phone, and she thought he sounded like a boy. "Actually, I was wondering if I could talk to you," he said.

"Sure. Go ahead." Lacy settled onto a chair by the dinette.

"I mean come up there and talk to you."

Now her pulse spiked. "Up here? When?"

"Well . . . tonight."

Lacy rose to her feet. "Tonight!? You want to come up here tonight?"

"I know it's a bit late, but I really need someone to talk to right now."

It was her turn to freeze in silence.

"Lacy?"

What was she to say to this? *Come on up, Lover Boy.*

His voice came again, softer. "Okay, well, maybe it's not such a good idea . . ."

"No, it's okay." It was? It was nothing of the kind.

"You sure? Maybe we could meet at the Village Inn."

"Sure."

"In an hour?"

The sum of this matter began to spread through Lacy's mind like icy waters. Kent was coming to Boulder tonight. He wanted to talk to her.

"Sure," she said.

"Good. I'll see you in an hour, then."

"Sure."

Silence filled the receiver again, and Lacy suddenly felt like a high school girl being asked out by the captain of the football team. "So, what do you want to talk about?" she asked. It struck her that the question was at once both perfectly legitimate and absurd. On one hand, their relationship should remain strictly platonic, for obvious reasons. Reasons that droned through her head like World War II bombers threatening to unload at the first sign of flak. Reasons like, this man had dropped her once before and if it had hurt then, it might kill her now. Reasons like, he had just lost his wife. He was no doubt rebounding like the world's tight-est-wound super-ball.

On the other hand, since when did reasoning direct the heart?

"Nothing," he said.

It was the wrong answer, she thought. Because in matters of the heart, "noth-ing" was much more than "something."

"Okay, I'll see you there," she said and hung up the phone with a trembling hand.

∽∾∾

It took Lacy forty-five of the sixty minutes to prepare herself, which was in itself nonsense because other than changing clothes she had not yet *unprepared* herself from the day's preparedness, which had taken her less than fifteen minutes just this morning. Nevertheless, it took her forty-five, due in part to the fact that the blouse she thought would best suit the occasion needed ironing. Not that this was an occasion as such.

Kent was there, at the Village Inn, sitting in a corner booth nursing a cup of coffee when she arrived. He glanced up as she slid onto the bench opposite him. His eyes brightened, which was a good thing because they appeared a bit red and blurry, as if he'd been crying in the last hour. His breath smelled strongly of mints.

"Hi, Kent."

He smiled wide and extended a hand. "Hi."

She took it hesitantly. Goodness. What was he thinking? This was not a business deal that required a handshake.

Looking at him now under the lights Lacy saw that Kent had seen some abuse lately. Dark circles cupped his eyes, which were indeed rather lethargic looking. The lines defining his smile seemed to have deepened. His hair was as blond as it had been the day he'd told her to take a hike years ago, but now it was disheveled. It was Monday—surely he had not gone to work like this. Something had been pummeling him, she thought, but then she already knew that. He had walked through the valley of death. You always got pummeled in the valley of death.

They sipped at their coffees and talked small talk for half an hour—the weather, the new stadium, the Broncos—all in all, things that neither seemed to have any interest in. Without going into their past, they really didn't have much to talk about. But it hardly mattered; just sitting there across from each other after so many years held its own power, however awkward or halting it might be.

The thought of revisiting their past brought an edginess to her heart. They could always talk about death, of course. It was their common bridge now. Death. But Kent was not thinking death. Something else was running around behind those eyes.

"I met a cop today," he said out of the blue, staring at his coffee.

"A cop?"

"Yeah. I was just sitting there in the bookstore, and this cop sits down and starts giving me the third degree about Spencer. About my boy, Spencer." His face drifted into a snarl as he talked. He looked up, and his eyes were flashing. "Can you believe the audacity of that? I mean—" He glanced out the window and lifted a hand helplessly. "I was just sitting there, minding my own business, and this pinhead cop starts accusing me."

"Accusing you of what?"

"I don't even know. That was just it. He goes on as if I had something to do with . . ." He stopped and swallowed, his Adam's apple bobbing against the emotion boiling through his chest. "With Spencer's death," he finished.

"Come on, Kent! That's absurd!"

"I know. It *is* absurd. Then he just went on, as if he knew things, you know."

"What things?"

"I don't know." He was shaking his head. The poor man sat there like someone strung together by a few brittle strands of flesh. Surely he could not have had anything to do with his own son's death! Could he? Of course not!

"It was like a scene out of *The Twilight Zone.*"

"Well, I'm sure you have nothing to worry about. The authorities do things like that as a matter of routine. It's ridiculous. You'll never hear from the man again."

"And maybe you're wrong," he said. She blinked at his tone. "Maybe I have plenty to worry about. The last thing I need is some pinhead with a badge poking his greasy head into my life! I swear I could tear his head off!"

She stared at him, unsure how to respond. "Maybe you need to lighten up, Kent. You've got nothing to hide, right? Don't let it get to you."

"Yeah, easy for you to say. It's not your neck he's breathing down."

Now she felt her face flush. "And it's not yours, either. The police are just doing their job. They should be the least of your concerns. And just in case you're confused here, I'm not one of them. I work at a bank, remember?"

Kent looked at the ceiling and sighed. "I'm sorry. You're right." He collected himself, nodding as if slowly coming to agreement. Then he closed his eyes and shook his head, gritting his teeth in frustration.

Yes indeed, he had been pummeled lately. She wondered what had really happened to bring him to this strange state.

He was smiling at her, his blue eyes suddenly soft and bright at once, like she remembered them from their previous life. "You're right, Lacy. You see, that's what I needed to hear. You always did have a way with the simple truth, you know."

She gulped and hoped immediately that he had not noticed. It was not his words but the way he had said them that bothered her, as if at that moment he was dripping with admiration for her.

She chuckled nervously. "If I remember correctly, you were never too stupid yourself."

"Well, we had our times, didn't we?"

She had to look away this time. An image of Kent leaning over her as they lay under the great cottonwood behind her dormitory filled her mind. "I love you," he was whispering, and then he touched her lips with his own. She wanted to shake the image from her head, force her heart back to its normal rhythm, but she could only sit there, pretending nothing at all was happening in her chest.

"Yes, we did," she said.

Tension hung in the air as if someone had thrown a switch somewhere and filled the room with a thick cloud of charged particles. Lacy could feel his eyes on her cheek, and she finally turned to face him. She gave him a controlled grin. This was madness! He had lost his sensibilities! Two minutes ago he was ranting about some cop and how he would like to tear the poor fellow's head off, and now he was staring at her like some honeymooner.

Death does that to people, Lacy, she reasoned quickly. *It makes them lose their sensibilities. And you're reading way too much into that look. It's not as bad as it looks.*

And then bad went to terrible. Because then Lacy felt heat swallow her face despite her best efforts to stop it. Yes indeed, she was blushing. As red as a cooked lobster. And he could see it all. She knew that because he too was suddenly blushing.

Panic flashed through her mind, and she impulsively considered fleeing. Of course that would be about as sensible as Kent's tearing a cop's head off. Instead, she did the only thing she *could* do. She smiled. And that just made it worse, she thought.

"It's good to see you again, Lacy." He shook his head, diverted his eyes. "I kept telling myself that the last thing I needed was a relationship so soon after Gloria's death. It hasn't even been three months, you know. But I realize now that I was wrong. I think I do need a relationship. A good friendship, without all the baggage that comes with romance. No strings, you know. And I see now that you can give me that friendship."

He faced her. "Don't you think?"

To be honest, she didn't know what to think. Her head was still buzzing from that last heat wave. Was he saying he wanted nothing but a platonic relationship? Yes, and that was good. Wasn't it?

"Yes. It took me six months to get over John. Not *over*, over, of course. I don't think you ever get *over*, over. But to a point where I could see clearly. Some are faster healers. They're back on their feet in three or four months; some take a year. But all of us need someone to stand by. I don't think I could have made it if I hadn't found God."

If he had been eating a cherry tomato, he might have choked on it at the comment. He coughed.

She ignored him. "Ultimately his is the only relationship that brings peace. I guess sometimes it takes a death to understand that." Kent's eyes were following the rim of his coffee cup. "But, yes, Kent. You're right. It is good to have a friendship that is completely unpretentious."

He nodded.

They talked for another hour, telling for the first time their own stories of loss. Lacy's mind kept wandering back to that heat wave that had fallen over them, but in the end she settled herself with the reasoning that these things happened to people who had walked through the valley. They lost their sensibilities at times.

By the time they shook hands and bid each other a good night, the clock's fat hand was past the midnight hour. By the time Lacy finally fell asleep, it was nudging the second morning hour. Surely it was well after Kent had arrived home and fallen comfortably asleep in his big, empty house, she thought.

She was wrong.

21

Helen Crane lived roughly eight miles from Kent's Littleton suburban neighborhood. Depending on traffic the crosstown jaunt took anywhere between fifteen and twenty minutes in her old yellow Pinto. But today she wasn't in the Pinto. Today she was on Reeboks, and the walk stretched into a three-hour ordeal.

It was the first time her walking actually took her anywhere. The minute she'd stepped off her porch, with the sun starting to splash against the Rockies, she'd felt an urge to walk west. Just west. So she'd walked west for over an hour before realizing that Kent's house lay directly in her path.

The silent urge arose in her gut like steel drawn to a powerful magnet. If Pastor Madison had been correct, she figured her normal pace carried her along at an easy three miles per hour. But now she pushed it up to four. At least. And she felt no worse off for the wear, if indeed there was any wearing going on in these bones of hers. She certainly did not feel fatigue. Her legs tingled at times as if they were thinking of falling asleep or going numb, but they never actually slowed her down.

Three days earlier she had tried walking through her eight hours and she had finally fatigued at the ten-hour mark. The energy came like manna from heaven, daily and just enough. But she had never felt the energy directing her anywhere except along the streets of her own neighborhood.

Now she felt as a salmon must feel when it strikes out for the spawning ground. Her daughter's Reeboks fit perfectly. She had already tossed her own pair in the garbage and switched to a black pair that Gloria had favored. Now she strutted down the sidewalk sporting black shoes and white basketball socks. Once she had looked at herself in the full-length hall mirror and thought the getup looked ridiculous with a dress. But she didn't care—she was a dress person. Period. She would leave fashion statements to the fools who gave a rat's whisker about such matters.

Helen entered the street leading to Kent's home and brought her focus to the two-story house standing at the far end. Not so long ago she had referred to the home as Gloria's home. But now she knew better. Her daughter was skipping across the clouds up there, not hiding behind pulled drapes in that stack of lumber. No, that was *Kent's* house.

That's your house.

The thought made Helen miss a step. She turned her mind to praying, ignoring the little impulse.

Father, this man living in that house is a selfish, no-good hooligan when you get right down to it. The city is crawling with a hundred thousand people more worthy than this one. Why are you so bent on rescuing him?

He didn't answer. He usually didn't when she complained like that. But of course she had no reason to hide her suspicions from God. He already knew her mind.

She answered herself. *And what about you, Helen? He is a saint compared to what you once were.*

Helen turned her thoughts back to prayer. *But why have you drawn me into this? What could you possibly want from my silly walking? Not to complain, but really it is rather incredible.* She smiled. *Ingenious, really. But still, you could certainly do as well without this exercise, couldn't you?*

Again he didn't answer. She had once read C. S. Lewis's explanation for why God insists on having us do things like pray when he already knows the outcome. It is for the experience of the thing. The interaction. His whole endeavor to create man centers around desire for interaction. Love. It is an end in itself.

Her walking was like that. It was like walking with God on Earth. The very foolishness of it made it somehow significant. God seemed to enjoy foolish conventions. Like mud on the eyes, like walking around Jericho, like a virgin birth.

She mumbled her prayer now. "Okay, so he is worthy of your love. Go ahead, dump some of the stuff over him. Let's have this over with. Lay him out. Drop him. You could do that. Why don't you do that?"

He still wasn't answering.

She closed her eyes momentarily. *Father, you are holy. Jesus, you are worthy.*

Worthy to receive honor and glory and power forever. Your ways are beyond finding out. A tingle ran through her bones. This was actually happening, wasn't it? She was walking around physically empowered by some unseen hand. At times it seemed unbelievable. Like . . . like walking on water.

You are God. You are the Creator. You have the power to speak worlds into existence, and I love you with all of my heart. I love you. I really do. She opened her eyes. *I'm just confused at times about the man who lives in that house,* she thought.

That's your house, Helen.

The inner voice spoke rather clearly that time, and she stopped. The house loomed ahead, three doors down, like an abandoned mortuary, haunted with death. And it was not her house. She did not even want the house.

That's your house, Helen.

This time Helen could not mistake the voice. It was not her own mind speaking. It was God, and God was telling her that Kent's house was actually hers. Or was meant to be.

She walked forward, rather tentative now. High above, the sun shone bright. A slight breeze pressed her dress against her knees. Not a soul was in sight. The neighborhood looked deserted. But Kent was in his house, behind those pulled blinds. The silver car parked in the driveway said so.

"Is that my Lexus too?" The corner of her mouth twitched at her own humor. Of course, she did not want the Lexus, either.

This time God answered. *That's your house, Helen.*

And then she suddenly knew what he meant. She stopped two doors down, suddenly terrified. Goodness, no! I could never do that! The walking is one thing, but *that?*

Helen turned on her heels and walked away from the house. Her purpose here was over. At least for the day. An unsteadiness accompanied her strides now. *That's your house; that's your house.* That could mean anything.

But it didn't mean anything. It meant only one thing, and she had the misfortune of understanding exactly the message.

Helen walked for an hour, mumbling and begging and praying. Nothing changed. God had said his piece. Now she was saying hers, but he was not speaking anymore.

She was on her way back home, less than an hour from her house—her *real* house—before she found some peace over the matter. But even then it was only a thimbleful. She began to pray for Kent again, but it was not as easy as it had been on the first part of the trip.

Things were about to get interesting. Maybe crazy.

⌘

The second real bump in Kent's road came two days later, on Wednesday morning, on the heels of the cop-in-the-bookstore bump.

The day started out well enough. Kent had risen early and shaved clean to the bone. He smiled and nodded a greeting to several tellers on his way through the lobby. He even made eye contact with Sidney Beech on his way in, and she smiled. A sexy smile. Things were most definitely returning to normal. Kent whistled down the hall and entered the Information Systems suite.

Betty sat in typical form, tweezers in hand. "Morning, Betty." Kent forced a smile.

"Morning, Kent," she returned, beaming. If he wasn't mistaken there was some interest in her eyes. He swallowed and stepped past.

"Oh, Kent. They're meeting in the conference room down the hall. They're waiting for you."

He spun around. "There's a meeting this morning? Since when?"

"Since Markus got back from San Jose yesterday with new marching orders, he says. I don't know. Something about taking more responsibility."

Kent retraced his steps and entered the hall, trying to calm himself. This was out of the ordinary, and anything out of the ordinary was bad. His plan would work under existing circumstances, not necessarily under ones altered to meet some new marching orders.

Settle down, Buckwheat. It's just a meeting. No need to go in there and sweat all over the table. Kent took a breath and walked into the conference room as casually as possible.

The others rocked their chairs around the long table, wasting time, in good spirits. Borst had taken the head of the table and leaned back. His navy vest strained against its buttons. If one of those popped it might just poke Mary in the eye. She sat adjacent to Borst, leaning admiringly toward him. You'd think the two were best friends by their body language.

Todd sat opposite Mary, his head thrown back midhowl at some brilliant comment Borst had evidently graced them with. It was Todd's hoot that covered the sound of the door opening and closing, Kent guessed. Cliff sat two chairs down from Mary, facing Borst, grinning his usual pineapple-eater smile.

"Kent! It's about time," Borst boomed. The others thought that funny and lengthened their laugh. He had to admit, the jovial atmosphere was almost contagious. Kent smiled and pulled out a seat opposite Cliff.

"Sorry. I didn't know we were meeting," he said.

They gathered themselves and dug in. Borst started by fishing for a few compliments, which the others readily served up. Kent even tossed him one. Some ridiculous comment about how perceptive the supervisor had been to bring in Cliff.

Mostly the discussion centered on preserving control of AFPS. Evidently the main Information Systems division at the administration branch in California was talking about flexing its muscles. Or, as Borst put it, *going for a power grab.*

"That's all it is, and we know it," he said. "They have a dozen greedy engineers up there who feel left out, so now they want the whole thing. And I have no intention of giving her up."

Kent had no doubt that the words were not original with Borst. They were Bentley's. He pictured Porky and Porkier yapping up a frenzy on the flight home.

"Which means we have to run a tight ship; that's all there is to it. They're looking for weaknesses in our operation as we speak. In fact, three of them are flying down next Friday to survey the territory, so to speak."

"That's crazy!" Todd blurted out. "They can't just waltz in here and take over."

"Oh, yes they can, Todd. That's a fact. But we're not going to let them."

"How?" Mary asked, wide eyed.

"Exactly. How? That's what we're going to figure out."

"Security," Cliff said.

It was only then that the meaning of this little discussion came home to Kent. Like a flash grenade tossed into his skull. Whether the delay had been caused by tequila residue or his fascination at watching Borst's fat lips move was a tossup. But when understanding did come, Kent twitched in his chair.

"You have something to say about that, Kent?" Borst asked, and Kent knew they had all seen his little blunder. To exasperate the matter, he asked the one question only a complete fool would ask in the situation.

"What?"

Borst glanced at Cliff. "Cliff said security, and you looked like you wanted to add to that."

Security? Good grief! Kent scrambled for recovery. "Actually, I don't think they stand a chance, sir."

That got a smile from them. *That's our boy, Kent.* All of them except Cliff. Cliff scrunched his eyebrows. "How's that?" he asked.

"How's what?"

"How is it that the guys from California don't have a snowball's chance in hell of taking control of AFPS?"

Kent leaned back. "How are they going to maintain a system they know nothing about?" Of course the whole notion was ridiculous. Any good department could work its way through the program. In fact, Cliff was well on his way to doing just that. He said so.

"Really? I've been here three weeks, and I've found my way around the program well enough. The code's not even under active security measures."

The room fell to dead silence. This was not going well. Tightened security could very well bring his entire plan to its knees. Kent felt a trickle of sweat break from his hairline and snake past his temple. He casually reached up and scratched the area as if a tickle annoyed him there.

"I thought you were going to take care of restricted security," Borst said, staring directly at Kent.

"We have restricted codes at every branch. No one can enter the system without a password," he returned. "What else do you want?"

"That covers financial security, but what about security from hackers or other programmers?" Cliff asked evenly. The newcomer was becoming a real problem here.

All eyes were on Kent. They were asking about ROOSTER without knowing it, and his heart was starting to overreact. He had programmed ROOSTER precisely for this purpose.

Then Cliff threw even the *not knowing* part into question. "Actually it looks like someone started to put a system into place but never finished. I don't know; I'm still looking into it."

The kid was on to ROOSTER! He'd found something that led to the link. It was all Kent could do to stay seated. This was it, then. If he didn't stop them now, it was over!

"Yes, we did start a few things awhile back. But if I recall correctly, we discarded the code long ago. It was barely a framework."

Cliff held Kent in a steady gaze. "I'm not so sure it's gone, Kent. I may have found it."

Kent's heart felt like it might explode. He forced a nonchalant look. "Either way, it was far too clumsy to accomplish anything under the current structure." Kent shifted his gaze to Borst. "Frankly, I think you're approaching this all wrong, Markus. Sure, we can look at tightening security, but that's not going to stop a power grab, as you put it. What you need is some political clout."

Borst lifted his eyebrow, and his forehead rode up under his toupee a fraction. "Yes? And?"

"Well, you have some power now. Probably more than you know. You insist on maintaining control under the fairness doctrine. You were responsible for the program's creation as a dedicated employee. It's simply unfair for the big giant to come sweeping in and take your baby away, thereby minimizing any additional advances you might have realized had it remained under your control. I think you could get a lot of ordinary employees to back you on a position like that, don't you?"

The smile came slowly, but when Borst got it, his mouth spread from ear to ear. "My, you are not so dumb, are you, Kent?" He glanced at the others. "By golly, that's brilliant! I think you are absolutely right. The little man against the big corporation and all that."

Kent nodded. He spoke again, wanting to nail this door shut while the hammer was in his hand. "If the boys in California want AFPS, no security is going to slow them down. They'll just take the whole thing and stomp the living daylights out of anyone who stands in their way. You have to put a political obstacle in their way, Markus. It's the only way." Cliff had lost his plastic grin, and Kent wondered about that. What difference did it make to the newcomer how this went down? Unless he knew more than he was letting on.

"I'm surprised Bentley didn't think of that," Borst wondered aloud. He blinked and addressed the group. "Anyway, I think I should take this to him immediately." He was already on his feet. Like the young eager student off to find his professor. Cliff held Kent's gaze for a moment without smiling. He turned to Borst.

"May I suggest we at least handle the security issue since it has been raised?" Cliff asked.

"Yes, of course. Why don't you take the lead on that, Cliff?" he said. But his mind was already in Bentley's office. "I've got to go."

Borst left, wearing a smirk.

Cliff had found his grin again.

Kent blinked. That last exchange had effectively dropped a bucket of heat on his head. It was still leaking down his spine when the others stood and wordlessly followed Borst's lead, exiting the room.

That was it. Cliff knew something. Kent lowered his head and began to rub his temples. It was unraveling. It was coming apart. In the space of ten minutes his link to sanity had been casually snipped free by some snowboarder from Dallas who knew more than he had any business knowing.

Think! Think, think, think, boy!

Okay, this is not the end. This is just another little bump. A challenge. Nobody is better at challenges than you, boy.

Kent suddenly wanted out of the building. The thought of going back to his office and having Cliff walk in with his grin scared him silly. He wanted to see Lacy.

He wanted a drink.

22

Kent spent most of the afternoon walking through the office trying to hide the pallor of death he knew grayed his face.

He took a late lunch by himself and was about to enter Antonio's when he saw Cliff. At least he thought it looked like Cliff. The junior programmer walked toward the corner across the street, and Kent's heart began to palpitate madly. It was not the sight of the snowboarder that had him suddenly fixed to the concrete; it was the sight of the pinhead walking beside Cliff, yapping with the traitor as if they were old buddies. The cop! It was the pinhead cop with slicked-back hair and wire-frame glasses!

Or was it? And then they were gone.

Kent ordered a salad for lunch and left after eating only the two black olives that came perched on top. Imagine the cop showing up here, of all places. And talking to Cliff! Unless that hadn't been the cop *or* Cliff up there. It was for this conclusion that Kent finally angled, and he angled for it hard. He was seeing things in his anxiety. Boulders were beginning to fall from the sky; only they weren't boulders at all. They were sparrows, and they weren't falling from the sky. They were flying happily about.

Get a grip, Kent.

When he got home that night he made straight for the cabinet and pulled out a bottle of tequila. Three shots and a shower later, he still had not managed to shake the sickness in his chest. His head hurt from the day's brain twisting. Thing of it was, this particular challenge was not his challenge at all. It was Cliff's challenge. If Cliff found ROOSTER, the game was over. And there was nothing Kent could do to change that. Nothing at all.

He had just poured his fourth shot when the doorbell rang for the first time in a week. Kent jerked. The shot splashed over his hand, and he cursed. Fortunately he was near the kitchen sink, and a quick run of water washed the liquor down the drain. Who could possibly be ringing his doorbell at eight in the evening?

The answer should not have surprised him. He swung the door open to a frowning Helen. A large travel bag hung from her shoulder.

"Helen! Come in," he said. *Helen, take a hike,* he thought.

She came in without answering and set her bag on the floor. Kent looked at the black duffel bag, thinking at first that she had lost her interest in running after all and was returning the shoes. But he could see already that there was more than footwear in that bag.

"Kent," Helen said, and she smiled. He thought the smile might have been forced.

"What can I do for you?" he asked.

"Kent," She took a deep breath, and suddenly Kent knew this was not just a courtesy visit. "I need to ask you a favor, Kent."

He nodded.

"If I needed you for something—really needed—would you help me?"

"Sure, Helen. Depending on what it was you needed me for, of course. I mean, I'm not exactly the wealthiest man on the earth." He chuckled, all the while scrambling to guess her next move. She was setting him up; that much was clear. She was going to ask him to help clear out her garage or some other horrendous task he could do without.

"No, it won't cost you a penny. In fact, I don't mind paying rent. And I'll buy half the groceries. That should save you some money."

He smiled wide, wondering where this could possibly be leading. Surely she didn't expect to move in with him. She hated his guts. In a mother-in-law sort of way. No, she was angling for something else, but his mind was drawing a blank.

"What's the matter, Kent? Cat got your tongue? Oh, come on now." She walked past him into the living room, and he followed her. "It wouldn't be so bad. You and me living together."

Kent pulled up, flabbergasted. "What!"

She turned to him and looked him square in the eye. "I'm asking you if I can move in, young man. I have just lost a grandson and a daughter, and I've decided that I simply cannot live on my own in that great big house." She shifted her stare. "I need company," she said.

"You need company?" Heat washed down Kent's back. "I don't mean to be rude or anything, but I'm not exactly good company these days. I'm the devil, remember?"

"Yes. I do remember. Nonetheless, I would be so grateful if you would let me use one of your spare bedrooms downstairs here. The sewing room across from Spencer's room, perhaps."

"Helen, you can't be serious!" Kent rounded the couch and walked away from her. This was absurd! What could she possibly be thinking? She would ruin everything! An image of him sneaking to the kitchen for a drink winked through his mind. She would give him hell. "There's no way it would work."

"I'm asking you, Kent. You're not going to turn out family, are you?"

Kent turned back. "Come on. Stop this, Helen. This is crazy. Just plain stupid! You'd hate it here! We have nothing in common. I'm a *sinner*, for God's sake!"

She didn't seem to hear him. "I can do the dishes too. Goodness, just look at that kitchen. Have you even touched it since I was here last?" She waddled off toward the breakfast bar.

"Helen! No. The answer is no. You have your own home. It's yours for a reason. This is my home. It is *mine* for a reason. You can't stay here. I need my privacy."

"I'm walking every day now, Kent. Did I tell you that? So I'll be gone early in the morning for my walk. You'll be gone by the time I get back, but maybe we can have dinner together every evening. What do you think?"

Kent stared at her, at a loss for words at her insane behavior. "I don't think you're listening. I said no! N-O! No, you can't stay here."

"I know the sewing room is full of stuff right now, but I will move it myself. I don't want to put you out." She walked around the bar and turned the faucet on. "Now, you know I can't stand television. It's the box from hell, you know. But I thought you could watch the one upstairs in your sitting room." She twisted the sink tap and ran water over her wrist, testing its temperature. "And I'm not crazy about drinking, either. If you want to drink any alcohol I'd prefer you did that upstairs as well. But I like music, you know. Heavy music, light music, any music as long as the words—"

"Helen! You're not listening!"

"And you're not listening!" she said. Her eyes seemed to reach out with knives and hold him at the neck. His breathing shut down.

"I said I need a place to stay, dear son-in-law! Now, I gave you my daughter for a dozen years; she warmed your bed and ironed your shirts. The least you can do is give me a room for a few nights. Is it really too much to ask?"

Kent nearly buckled under the words. It occurred to him that his mouth was open, and he closed it quickly. The tequila was starting to speak, moaning lazily through his mind. He thought that maybe he should just pull the plug now. Go out and use that nine-millimeter on his own head. End the day with a bang. At the very least he should be screaming at this old wench who had played mother-in-law in his old life.

But he could not scream because she was holding him in some kind of spell. And it was working. It was actually making him think that she was right.

"I . . . I don't think—"

"No, stop thinking, Kent." She lowered her voice. "Start *feeling* a little. Show some kindness. Let me take a room." Then she smiled. "I won't bite. I promise."

He could think of nothing to say. Except okay. It just came out. "Okay."

"Good. I will bring the rest of my belongings in from the car tomorrow after I've had a chance to clean out the sewing room. Do you like eggs, Kent?"

The woman was incredible. "Yes," he said, but he hardly heard himself say it.

"Oh, but that's right. I will have to leave before you get up. I walk at sunrise. Well, maybe we can have an egg dish one evening."

For a minute they faced each other in silence. Then Helen spoke, her voice soft now, almost apologetic. "It'll be okay, Kent. Really. In the end you will see. It will be okay. I guess you've already learned that we can't control everything in life. Sometimes things happen that we just didn't plan on. You can only hope that in the end it will all make sense. And it will. Believe me. It will."

Kent nodded. "Maybe," he said. "You know your way around. Make yourself at home."

Then he retreated to the master bedroom upstairs, grateful that he had stashed a bottle in the sitting room. It was early; maybe he should call Lacy. Or maybe drive up to see her. The idea touched off a spark of hope. Which was good, because hope had been all but dashed today.

༺ঞ্চৡ༻

Lacy cleaned madly, fighting butterflies all the while and chastising herself for feeling any anxiety at all. So she was about to see Kent again. So he was coming to her condo this time. So he had brought that heat wave with him on Monday night. Her rekindled relationship with him was simply platonic, and she would keep it that way. Absolutely.

"Lacy, I need to talk," he'd said, and by the sound of his strained voice, he did need something. *Lacy, I need.* She liked the sound of that. And it was okay to like the sound of someone's platonic voice over the phone.

Indirect lighting cast a soft hue over the leather sofa angled under a vaulted ceiling. The fireplace sat black and spotless. An eight-by-ten picture of her late husband, John, stood at the hearth's center, and she considered removing it but quickly discarded the notion as absurd. Possibly even profane.

She donned jeans and a canary blouse, retouched her makeup carefully, opting for ruby lipstick and a light teal eye shadow, then made coffee. Her hand spooned the grounds with a slight quiver, and she mumbled to herself. "Lighten up, Lacy."

The doorbell chimed just as the coffee maker quit sputtering. Lacy took a deep breath and opened the door. Kent wore jeans and a white T-shirt that looked as if it might have been left in the dryer overnight. He grinned nervously and stepped in. His eyes were a little red, she thought. Maybe he was tired.

"Come in, Kent."

"Thanks."

He scanned the room, and she watched his eyes in the light. A small cut on his cheek betrayed a recent shave. They sat at the dinette and launched into small talk. How was your day? Good, and yours? Good. Good. But Kent was not looking so good. He was forcing his words, and his eyes jerked too often. He was having a bad day; that much he was not hiding. Better or worse than Monday, she did not know yet, but he was obviously still fighting his demons.

Lacy poured two cups of coffee, and they sipped through the small talk. Ten minutes passed before Kent shifted in his seat, and Lacy thought he was about to tell her why he wanted to see her again so soon. Other than maybe just wanting to see her. Unless her antenna had totally short-circuited over the last decade of marriage, there was some of that. At least some, regardless of all this platonic talk.

He stared at his black coffee, frowning. Her heart tightened. Goodness, he looked as though he might start crying. This was not just a bad-day thing. Something big had happened.

Lacy leaned forward, thinking she should reach out and take his hand or something. But he might misread her intentions. Or *she* might misread her intentions. She swallowed. "What's wrong, Kent?"

He shook his head and lowered it. "I don't know, Lacy. It's just . . ." He slid his elbow on the table and rested his forehead in his palm, looking now as if the blood had been siphoned from his face.

Now Lacy was worried. "Kent. What's going on?"

"Nothing. It's just hard, that's all. I feel like my life is unraveling."

"Your life *has* unraveled, Kent. You just lost your family, for heaven's sake. You're supposed to feel unraveled."

He nodded unconvincingly. "Yeah."

"What? You don't buy that? You think you're the man of steel who can just let these little details run off your big strong shoulders?" *Whoa, a bit strong there, Lacy. He* is *a wounded man. No need to kill him off with good intentions.*

Kent looked up slowly. There was a look in those eyes that brought a strange thought to Lacy's mind. The thought that Kent might actually be drinking. And maybe not just a little. "It isn't that. I know I'm supposed to be grieving. But I don't *want* to grieve," he growled through clenched teeth. "I want to make a new life for myself. And it's my new life that's driving me nuts. It hasn't even started, and it's already falling apart."

"Nothing's falling apart, Kent. Everything will work out; you'll see. I promise."

He paused and closed his eyes. Then, as if a spark had ignited behind his blue eyes, he suddenly leaned forward and grabbed her hand. A bolt of fire ripped through her heart. "Imagine having all this behind you, Lacy. Imagine having all the money you could dream of—starting over anywhere in the world. Don't you ever wonder what that would be like?"

He glanced at his hand around hers, and he pulled back self-consciously.

"Honestly? No," she answered.

"Well, I do. And I could do it." He gripped his right hand into a fist. "If it wasn't for all these fools who keep sticking their noses in my business . . ." Now it was more rage than anger lacing his voice, and he shook slightly.

Lacy blinked and tilted her head. He was making no sense. "Excuse me. What are we talking about here? *Who* are we talking about? You still work at the bank, right?"

"The cop at the bookstore for one thing. I can't shake him."

"You can't shake him? You've seen him again?"

"No, well yes—or maybe. I don't know if I really saw him again, but he's right there, you know. Riding along in my mind."

"Come on, Kent. You're overreacting now. For all you know, he was some kook pretending to be a cop. You don't know anything about this investigation of theirs."

He snapped his eyes to hers. "Pretending?"

"No, I don't know. I'm just saying *you* don't know. I'm not actually saying he was a kook, but there's no reason to walk around in this fear of yours when you hardly know a thing about the man. You have nothing to hide."

He blinked a few times quickly and bobbed his head. "Yeah. Hmm. Never thought of that." His glassy eyes stared at her cup now. Poor guy was upside down.

"Cliff's driving me nuts. I could kill the guy."

"Cliff, the new programmer? I thought you liked him. Now you're talking about killing the kid?" Lacy stood and walked to the coffee machine. "You're sounding scary, Kent."

"Yeah, never mind. You're right. I'm okay. I'm just . . ."

But he wasn't okay. He was sitting with his back to her, rubbing his temples now. He was coming unglued. And by the sounds of it, not from his wife's death, but from matters that followed no rhyme or reason. She should walk over there and knock some sense into his head. Or maybe go over there and hold him.

Her stomach hollowed at the thought. *A woman does not hold a man in a platonic relationship, Lacy. Shake his hand, maybe. But not hold him, as in, Let me put my hands on your face and stroke your cheek and run my fingers through your hair and tell you that everything—*

Something hot burned her thumb.

"Ouch!" Lacy snatched her hand to her mouth and sucked on the thumb. She had overfilled the cup.

Kent turned to her. "You okay?"

"Yes." She smiled. "Coffee burn." She returned to her seat.

"Helen moved in with me," he said.

Lacy sat back down. "Your mother-in-law? You're kidding! I thought you two were at each other's throats."

"We were. We are. I'm not even sure how it happened—it just did. She's staying in the sewing room."

"For how long?"

"I don't know." He was shaking his head again, and this time a tear had managed to slip from his right eye. "I don't know anything anymore, Lacy." Kent suddenly dropped his head onto folded arms and started to sob quietly. The man was stretched beyond his capacities.

Lacy felt her heart contract beyond her control. If she wasn't careful the tears would be coming from her eyes as well. And then one did, and she knew she could not just watch him without offering some comfort.

She waited as long as her resolve would allow. Then she stood unsteadily from her chair and stepped to his side. She stood over him for a brief moment, her hand lifted motionlessly above his head. His wavy blond hair rested against his head just as it had years ago, halfway down a strong neck.

Lacy had one last round with the inner voice that insisted she keep this relationship purely platonic. She told the voice to stretch its definition of *platonic*.

And then she lowered her hand to his head and touched him.

She could feel the electrical impulse run through his body at her touch. Or was it running through *her* body? She knelt and put her arm around his shoulder. His sobs shook him gently.

"Shhhh." Her cheek was now wet with tears. "It will be okay," she whispered.

Kent turned into her then, and they held each other.

That's all they did. Hold each other. But they held each other for a long time, and when Kent finally left an hour later, Lacy had all but decided that *platonic* was a word best left in the textbooks. Or maybe just erased altogether. It was a silly word.

23

Kent dragged himself to work Thursday morning, swallowing continually against the dread that churned in his gut. It reminded him of the time he'd been audited by the IRS three years earlier. He'd felt like a stranded Jew interrogated by the Gestapo. Only this time things were clearly worse. Then, he'd had nothing to hide beyond the moving deduction he'd possibly inflated. Now he had his whole life to hide.

His eyes had taken to leaking again—as they had those first few weeks after Gloria's death. The tears came without warning, blurring traffic signals and dissolving his dashboard to a sea of strange symbols. A dull ache droned through his head—a reminder of the "nightcaps" he'd indulged himself in after returning from Boulder. If it wasn't for the single thread of hope that strung through his mind, he might have stayed home. Downed some more nightcaps. Of course, he would have to tread lightly now that Helen had managed to work her way into his life. Things seemed to be coming apart at the seams again, and he had hardly begun this mad plan of his.

As it was, those words Lacy had spoken the previous evening triggered a new thought. A most desperate plan, really, but one to which he could cling for the moment. "For all you know he was some kook pretending to be a cop," Lacy had said. It was true that the cop had not shown his badge, and everyone knew that a business card could be had in half an hour at Kinko's. Still, he had known too much to be pretending. That was not it. But the comment had spawned another thought that centered around the word *kook*. And it had to do with Cliff, not the cop.

From all indications, it seemed that Cliff was on to him. Somehow that little snoop had gotten a hair up his nose and decided something needed exposing. So then why not undermine the kid? Showing him to be a kook might be a tad difficult; after all, the guy had already demonstrated his competence as a programmer. But that didn't mean he was squeaky clean. For starters, he was a snowboarder, and snowboarders were not textbook examples of conformists. There had to be some dirt out there on Cliff. Just enough to spin some doubts. Even a rumor with no basis at all. *Did you know that Cliff is the ringleader for the Satanist priesthood that murdered that guy in Naperville?* Didn't matter if there was such a priesthood or a murder or even a Naperville. Well, maybe it mattered a little.

By the time Kent got to work he knew precisely how he would spend his morning. He would spend it dragging Cliff into the dirt. And if need be, he would create the dirt himself with a few clicks of his mouse. Yes indeed, twenty years of hard study and work were gonna pay off this morning.

His ritual *Good mornings* came hard, like trying to speak with a mouthful of bile. But he managed them and rushed into his office, locking the door behind him. He made it halfway to his chair when the knock came. Kent grimaced and considered ignoring the fool—whichever fool it was. It didn't matter; they were all fools. It was probably Cliff the hound out there, sniffing at his door.

Kent opened the door. Sure enough, Cliff stood proud, wearing his ear-to-ear pineapple-eating grin.

"Hey, Kent. What are you doing this morning?"

"Work, Cliff." He could not hide his distaste. The realization that he was sneering at the man flew through his mind, but he was powerless to adjust his facial muscles.

Cliff seemed undeterred. "Mind if I come in, Kent? I've got some things you might want to look at. It's amazing what you can find if you dig deep enough." Cheese.

Kent's right hand nearly flew out and slapped that smiling face on impulse. But he held it to a tremble by his side. Things had evidently just escalated. It could very possibly all come down to this moment, couldn't it? This snowboard sniffer here may very well have the goods on him. Then a thought dropped into his mind.

"How about one o'clock? Can you hold off until then?"

Cliff hesitated and lost the grin. "I would prefer to meet now, actually."

"I'm sure you would, but I have some urgent business to attend to right now, Cliff. How about one o'clock?"

"And what kind of urgent business is that, Kent?"

They stared at each other without speaking for a full ten seconds.

"One o'clock, Cliff. I'll be right here at one."

The programmer nodded slowly and stepped back without answering. Kent closed the door, immediately breathing heavily. He scrambled for the desk, frantic, his knees weak. It was the end. If he had any sense at all he would leave now. Just walk out and leave Niponbank to its own problems. He had not broken any laws yet; his coworkers could do little but gossip. He would become "that poor man who lost his wife and son and then his mind." Too bad, too, because he showed so much promise. Borst's right-hand man. The thought made him nauseous.

This whole notion of stealing twenty million dollars had been foolishness from the beginning. Insane! You just don't think up things like that and expect to pull them off. He grabbed a tissue from a box on his desk and wiped at the sweat wetting his collar.

On the other hand, if he did leave he might very well kill himself. Drink himself to death.

Kent wiped his palms on his slacks and stabbed at the keyboard. A moment later he was into the human resources secure-data files. If anyone caught him in the files without authorization, he would be fired on the spot. He ran a query on Cliff Monroe. A small hourglass blinked lazily on his screen. This exercise now seemed like a stupid idea too. What did he expect to do? Run out into the hall, ranting and raving about the programmer who was really a werewolf? Maybe the bimbos in the lobby would believe him. *Honest, guls! He's a werewolf! Spread the word —quick, before my one o'clock meeting with him.*

A record popped on the screen, showing a home address on Platte Street in Dallas, a social security number, and some other basics. According to the record, Cliff had been employed exactly one week before his transfer to Denver in response to a request placed by Markus Borst. The reason was listed as "Replacement." So Borst had not expected to see him back. *Surprise, Baldy! Here I am!*

The rest of Cliff's record noted a basic education with high scores, and a list of previous employers. The kid had worked with the best, according to his short history. *Well, not for long, fella.*

Kent glanced back at the door quickly. *Here goes nothing.* He deleted the employment history from Cliff's record with a single keystroke. Then he quickly changed the file number so that no corresponding paper file would match this record, and he saved the modifications. In the space of ten seconds he had erased Cliff's history and lost the hard copy file. At least for a while.

He leaned back. Simple enough, if you knew what you were doing. Although the crashing of his heart belied that fact. Now the real test.

Kent picked up the phone and dialed Dallas. He was patched through to a Mary in human resources.

"Good morning, Mary. Kent Anthony here from IS in Denver. I'm checking on the qualifications of an employee. A Cliff Monroe, file number 3678B. Can you pull that up for me?"

He stared at the modified file on his screen.

"Yes, what can I help you with?"

"I'm trying to determine his employment history. Can you tell me where he worked before taking a job with us?"

"Just a second . . ." Kent heard the faint sound of keys clicking. "Hmm. Actually, it looks like he has no history. This must be his first job."

"You're kidding! Isn't that a bit odd for a high-level programmer? Can you tell me who hired him?"

Mary clicked for a minute and then flipped through some papers before answering. "Looks like Bob Malcom hired him."

"Bob? Maybe I should talk to Bob. He works there?"

"Sure. Talk to Bob. Does seem a bit odd, doesn't it?"

"Can you transfer me?"

"Sure, hold on."

It took a full five minutes of refusing to leave a message and holding to finally get the man on the phone.

"Bob Malcom."

"Bob, this is Kent Anthony from Denver. I'm looking into the employment history of a Cliff Monroe . . ." He went through the spiel again and let Bob look around a bit. But in the end it was the same.

"Hmm. You're right. It does say that I hired him, but, you know, I don't remember . . . Hold on. Let me look at my log."

Kent leaned back. He bit at his index fingernail and stared at the screen.

Bob's voice crackled again. "Yep, we hired him. So it says. How long did you say he's been working there?"

Kent scooted to the edge of his seat. "Six weeks."

"On what kind of project?"

"AFPS."

"The new processing system? And you have management control over him?" Suddenly Bob's voice rang with a note of concern.

"No, I'm not his direct supervisor; I'm just running a query to understand his qualifications for a project he's working on for me. And yes, it *is* the new processing system. Is there a problem with that?"

"Not necessarily. But you can never be too careful." He paused as if thinking things through.

It sounded too good to be true. Kent was trembling again, but now with waves of relief at this sudden turn of fortunes. "What do you mean?"

"I'm just saying you can never be too careful. It's odd we sent someone without an employment history to such a sensitive assignment. You never know. Look, I'm not ready to say that Mr. Monroe is anything but what he appears to be; I'm just saying until we know for sure, we should be careful. Corporate espionage is big business these days, and with the implementation of that system of yours up there—who knows? I'll tell you what. Why don't you have Mr. Monroe give me a call?"

No, that wouldn't do. "Actually, Bob, if there's any possibility that what you're saying proves to have merit, I'm not sure we want to tip Mr. Monroe off."

"Hmm. Yes, of course. You're right. We should begin a quiet investigation right away."

"And we may want him recalled in the meantime. I'll check with the department supervisor, but seeing as he's on temporary-replacement assignment anyway, I don't see any sense in keeping him in a sensitive position. AFPS is too valuable to risk, at any level."

"Reassign him?"

"Reassign him immediately," Kent insisted. "Today. As soon as I've talked to Borst, of course."

"Yes. Makes sense. Call me then."

"Good. In fact, maybe you could send him on an errand. Run to the bookstore or something—get him out of here while we sort this out."

"I'll call him as soon as we hang up."

"Thank you, Bob. You're a good man."

Kent hung up feeling as though the world had just been handed to him on a platter. He stood and pumped his fist. "Yesss!" He walked around his office, thinking through his next play. He would tell Borst about the possibility that they had a spy working under their noses. It was perfect! Cliff the kook, a spy.

Twenty-five minutes later it was all over. Kent talked to Borst, who nearly lost his toupee bolting from his seat. Of course, he had to call Bob himself— make sure this removing of Cliff happened immediately, barking orders like he owned the bank or something. Kent watched, biting his cheeks to keep the grin from splitting his face.

The plan proceeded flawlessly. Cliff left on some errand for Bob at eleven, after popping his head into Kent's office to remind him of the one o'clock, clueless as to his impending demise. It was the last they would see of him for at least a few days while Human Resources checked out this whole business. They would discover that Cliff's file had mistakenly been wiped out, possibly, but by then, it would not matter.

Borst changed the access codes to AFPS within the hour. Cliff Monroe was history. Just like that. Which meant that for now, all was back to a semblance of order. As long as ROOSTER had not yet been discovered, there was no reason not to continue.

Actually, there was plenty of reason not to continue. In fact, every reasonable bone in his body screamed foul at the very thought of continuing.

It was noon before Kent found the solitude he needed to check on ROOSTER's status. He virtually dove at the keyboard, punching through menus as if they did not exist. If Cliff had discovered the link, he would have left tracks.

Kent held his breath and scrolled down to the MISC folder containing ROOSTER. Then he exhaled long and slow and leaned back in his chair. The file had been opened one week earlier at 11:45 P.M. And that was good, because that had been him, last Wednesday evening.

A small ball of hope rolled up his chest, ballooning quickly. He closed his eyes and let the euphoria run through his bones. Yes, this was good. This was all he had. This was everything.

The pinhead cop's face suddenly flashed before him, and he blinked it away. The authorities had not made further contact, and he had decided that Lacy was correct about one thing—they were just doing their job. At least that's what he insisted on believing. They simply could not know about ROOS-TER. And without ROOSTER, they had nothing. Nada. This bit about Spencer was absolute nonsense. Why Pinhead had even gone on about everything one day being found out, Kent had no clue. Certainly the man was not a psychic. But no other explanation fit. And psychics were nothing more than con men. Which meant that nothing fit. Pinhead simply did not fit into any reasonable picture.

Once he executed the plan, the point would be moot anyway. Cops would be crawling all over the bank.

He had to do this now, before some other menace cropped up. Before some other propeller-head walked into his life, flashing a pineapple-eating grin. And *now* meant within a week. Or next weekend. Which meant beginning now.

∽≈∾

"You what?"

"I moved in with him."

"You moved in with Kent?" She did not answer. "Why?"

"I had no choice in the matter. Actually, I did have a choice. I could have ignored him."

"Kent asked you to move in?"

"No. I meant I could have ignored God. He told me to move in. And don't think I wanted to, either. Believe me, I fought this one."

Bill Madison shook his head slowly. Helen had been walking for over two weeks now. Eight hours, twenty miles a day, without any signs of weakness. It was Jericho all over again, and Bill was not sleeping so much these days. His wife had accused him of being distracted on several occasions, and he had not bothered to deny it. Neither had he bothered to tell her about Helen's little daily ventures out into the concrete jungle. It seemed somehow profane to talk idly about the matter. And he would be less than honest to deny that a small part of him wondered whether she had somehow conjured up the whole thing. A senile intercessor suffering from delusions of walking in God's power. It was not unthinkable. Actually more plausible than believing her.

But that was the problem—he did believe her. In fact he had *seen* her.

"So how did you talk him into that?"

"It wasn't pleasant."

"I'm sure it wasn't." He paused, choosing his questions carefully. They spoke every other day, give or take, and Bill found himself begging time to skip forward to their conversations. Once on the phone, he fought for every minute. Invariably it was she who ended the discussion.

"I'm surprised he didn't flatly refuse."

"He did."

"I see. And still you're there. How is he?"

"He's no nearer the truth than he was a decade ago," she returned flatly. "If I were walking in circles and he was the wall of Jericho, I might feel like we had come to the end of the first day."

"You think it's that far off?"

"No. I'm not *thinking*. It is how I *feel*."

He smiled. "Surely there must be a crack in that armor of his. You've been breathing down his neck as you say, for weeks. You are specifically called to intercede for the man; surely that means God will hear you. *Is* hearing you."

"You would think so, wouldn't you? On the other hand, you are specifically called to pray for *your* loved ones, Pastor. Does God hear my prayers any more than he hears your prayers?"

"I don't know. I would have said *no* a month ago, but I would also have thought you crazy a month ago."

"You still do at times, don't you, Bill?" He couldn't answer. "It's okay. So do I. But you are right; God is hearing me. We are both deriving a lot of pleasure from this little episode now that I've settled into an acceptance of the matter."

"You've always interceded for others, Helen. In many ways this is not so different."

"Yes, in many ways. You are right. But in one way it's very different. I am now walking in faith, you see. Quite literally. I am living intercession, not simply praying. The difference is like the difference between splashing through the surf and diving into the ocean."

"Hmmm. Good analogy. That's good."

"He's drinking, Bill. And he's slipping. Like a slug headed for the dark creases."

"I'm sorry, Helen. I'm sure it must be hard."

"Oh, it's not so hard anymore, Pastor. Actually the walking helps. It's . . . well, it's like a bit of heaven on Earth, maybe. It's the stretching of the mind that wears one thin. Have you been feeling thin lately, Bill?"

"Yes. Yes, I have. My wife thinks I need a break."

"Good. We have too many of the thick headed among our ranks. Maybe one of these days you'll be thin enough to hear."

"Hmm."

"Good-bye, Bill. I have to fix him dinner. I promised I would. We're having egg foo yung."

24

Kent saw Helen at each evening meal, but otherwise only the spotless kitchen remained as a clue that another person shared the house. By the time he dragged himself from bed each morning, she was gone. Walking, she said, although he couldn't imagine why a woman Helen's age chose 5 A.M. for her daily walk. By the time he wandered home about six, the evening meal was either on the table or simmering on the stove.

He'd peeked into the sewing room once, just to see what she had done with it. The bed had been neatly made with a comforter he'd never seen before; a small pile of laundry rested at the foot, waiting to be put away. Otherwise there was hardly a sign that Helen occupied the spotless room. Only the nightstand beside the bed betrayed her residence there. There, her Bible lay open, slightly yellowed under the lamp. A white porcelain teacup sat nearby, emptied of its contents. But it was the crystal bottle that made him blink. She had brought this one knick-knack from that hutch in her house and set it here beside her bed. Her most prized possession, Gloria had once told him. A simple bottle filled with only God knew what. Kent had closed the door without entering.

He had come home Tuesday evening to the sound of what he would have sworn was Gloria singing. He'd called her name and run to the kitchen only to find Helen bent over the sink, humming. If she'd heard him, she did not show it. He had retreated to the bedroom for a quick snip at the bottle without her knowing.

The meals themselves were a time of clinking and smacking and polite talk, but not once did Helen engage him in any of her religious dogma. She'd made a conscious decision not to, he thought. In fact, by the way she carried herself, on several occasions he found himself wondering if she had succumbed to some new drug that kept her in the clouds. Her eyes seemed to shine with confidence, and she smiled a lot. Possibly she was misreading one of her prescriptions and overdosing.

If so, she had lost neither her wit nor her analytical skills. He had engaged her about her knee-high socks once and found that out immediately.

"Those socks look silly with a dress. You *do* know that, don't you?"

"Yes, I had noticed that. But they keep my legs warm."

"And so would pants."

"No, Kent. You wear the pants in this family. I wear the dress. If you think these socks look silly, think of how a dress would look hanging off your hips."

"But it doesn't *have* to be that way," he said with a chuckle.

"You're right. But to be perfectly honest with you, it's the only way I can get men to look at my legs these days."

He drove up to the house on Thursday, eager to discover what Helen had prepared for dinner. The sentiment caused him to stop with the car door half open. The fact was, he looked forward to walking into the house, didn't he? It was the only thing he really looked forward to now besides the plan. There was always the plan, of course.

And there was Lacy.

They had steak that night.

Kent forged ahead, tiptoeing through the hours, refining his plan, calling Lacy, drinking. Quite a lot of drinking, always late at night, either in his upstairs sitting room or at the office, maintaining his pattern of late nights at work.

They all took Cliff's departure in stride, talking ad infinitum about how the competition had tried to steal AFPS and almost got away with it. The speculation only fueled their perceptions of self-importance. That anyone would go to such lengths to infiltrate their ranks came off as yet one more feather in Borst's cap. The distraction proved a perfect cover for Kent's last days among them.

Step by step, the perfect crime began to materialize with stunning clarity. And that was no illusion. He had breezed through graduate school, testing with one of the sharpest analytical minds this side of Tokyo. Not that he dwelled on the fact; he just knew it. And his mind told him a few things about his plan. It told him that what he was planning was most definitely a crime, punishable by severe penalties. If he did fail, it would be the end of him. He might as well take a cyanide capsule with him in the event things went wrong.

His mind also told him that the plan, however criminal, however heinous, was absolutely brilliant. Crime-of-the-century stuff. Enough to bring a smile to any cop's mouth; enough to boil any breathing man's blood.

And his mind told him that when it was over, if he succeeded, he would be one rich fool, living in a new skin, free to suck up whatever pleasures the world had to offer. His heart pounded at the thought.

There was simply nothing he had overlooked.

Except Lacy. He had overlooked Lacy. Well, not Lacy herself—she was becoming hard to overlook. In fact, it was the difficulty of overlooking her that he had overlooked.

They talked every evening, and he had become increasingly aware of the way his gut knotted each time he thought about picking up the phone to call her. It had been the way she touched him on his last visit, holding his head as though it might break, feeling her breath in his ear. Long-lost memories had flooded his mind.

The following evening's phone call had driven the stake further into his heart.

"You okay, Kent?"

"Yes. I'm better. I don't know how to thank you, Lacy. I just . . ." And then he had started to blubber, of all things. Cried right then on the phone, and he hardly knew why.

"Oh, Kent! It will okay. Shhh, shhh. It will be okay. I promise."

He should have dropped the phone in its cradle then and walked away from her. But he could not. The calls this whole week had been no better. No more tears. But the gentle words, though not overtly affectionate, could hardly hide the chemistry brewing between them.

And now Friday had arrived. Which was a problem, because Lacy didn't exactly fit into his plan, and his plan started tomorrow.

Helen asked him if anything was wrong during the evening meal, and he shook his head. "No, why?"

"No reason, really. You just look troubled."

It was the last she said of the matter, but her words rang annoyingly through his mind. He had expected to be ecstatic on the eve of the big weekend. Not troubled. And yet he *was* ecstatic in some ways. It was the Lacy thing that tore at his heart.

Kent retired to his room and downed three shots before working up the courage to call her.

"Kent! I'm so glad you called! You would not believe what happened to me at work today." Her voice might just as well have been a vise clamped around his heart, squeezing.

"Oh? What happened?"

"They asked me to enter management school. They want to groom me for management."

"Good. That's good, Lacy." He swallowed. It could have been him six years ago, starting his climb up the ladder. And he'd climbed right to the top . . . before they decided to push him over.

"Good? It's *great!*" She paused. "What's wrong, Kent?"

"Nothing. Really, that's great."

"You sound like you just swallowed a pickle. What's wrong?"

"I need to see you, Lacy."

Her voice softened. "Okay. When?"

"Tonight."

"Right now?"

"Yes."

"Is there a problem?"

"No." Kent was having difficulty keeping his voice steady. "Can I drive up?"

She hesitated, and for some reason that worsened the ache in his chest.

"Sure," she said. "Give me an hour."

"I'll see you in an hour, then."

Kent hung up feeling as though he had just thrown a switch to an electric chair. His own electric chair. But by the time he pulled up to her condo, he had resolved the issue. He would do what needed to be done, and he would do it the *way* it needed to be done. He took a slug of tequila from the bottle in the passenger seat and pushed his door open.

God, help me, he thought. It was a prayer.

∽∼∾

They sat at her dinette table again, opposite each other, as they had done nearly two weeks earlier. Lacy wore jeans and a white shirt advertising Cabo San Lucas in splashy red letters. Kent had come wearing faded denims and loafers. His blue eyes had not lost their red sheen. The faint, sweet smell of alcohol drifted around him. He had grinned shyly and avoided contact with her upon entering. Not that she had expected a hug or anything. But that said something, she thought. *What it said*, she had no clue.

For ten minutes they made small talk that would have carried more grace on the phone. Then Kent settled into his chair, and she knew he wanted to tell her something.

"Do you ever feel guilty about wanting to move on?" Kent asked, staring at his coffee.

Lacy felt her heart strengthen its pulse. *Move on?* she thought. *You want to move on? I'm not sure I'm ready to move on yet. At least not in a relationship with another man.* "What do you mean?" she asked and lifted her cup to her lips.

"Move on. Get past . . . John." He nodded to the mantel. "Forget about your past and begin over. You ever feel like that?"

"In some ways, yes. I'm not sure I've ever wanted to *forget* John, though. But we do have to get on with life." She looked at those baby blues, and suddenly she wanted him to just come out and tell her that he did want to move on—and move on with her. She would hold him back, of course. But she wanted to be wanted by him.

He was nodding. "Yes. Only . . . maybe even wanting to put the past totally aside. Because as long as you have those memories you can never really be new. You ever feel like that? Even a tiny bit?"

"Probably. I just never thought about it in those terms."

"Well, now that you are, does it make you feel bad? You know, for not wanting to remember the past."

Lacy thought about the question, thinking it a tad strange. "I'm not sure. Why?"

"Because I'm thinking about starting over," he said.

"Oh? And how would you do that?"

The corners of his mouth lifted barely. His eyes brightened. "If I told you, would you swear to secrecy?"

She did not respond.

"I mean, absolute secrecy. Tell no man, ever—or woman, for that matter. Just you and I. Could you swear to that on John's grave?"

Lacy recoiled at the question. John's grave? Kent was still grinning mischievously, and Lacy sat straighter. "Why? I mean, I think so. It depends."

"No, I need a definite yes. No matter what I tell you, I want you to swear to guard it. I need that confidence in you. Can you do that?"

In any other circumstance Lacy would be telling him she couldn't put herself in that situation without knowing more. But that's not what came out of her mouth.

"Yes," she said. And she knew it was the truth. No matter what he said, she would guard it as her own.

Kent watched her carefully for a few seconds. "I believe you," he said. "And if you ever break this promise, you will be putting me in the grave, right beside my wife. I want you to understand that. Acknowledge that."

She nodded, thoroughly confused as to his direction.

"Good." He took a long drink of coffee and set the cup down carefully, dead serious. "I'm going to start over, Lacy. Completely." He waited, as if he'd just revealed a sinister secret and expected her to drop her jaw to the table.

"That's good, Kent."

Kent lowered his head and looked at her, past her arching eyebrows. His lips curled in a wicked grin. "I'm going be rich, Lacy."

She thought he might burst with this thing. And so far, it was nothing worthy of his behavior. Unless it really was about her and he was showing attraction in some strange, deluded manor. *I'm going to get rich, Honey, so you and I can live a new life together.*

"I'm going to steal twenty million dollars."

"Come on, Kent. Be serious."

"I'm as serious as a heart attack, Honey."

She heard his words the way one might see a bomb's distant mushroom cloud, but it took a second for the impact to reach in and shake her bones. Her first thought was denial. But it fled before his glare, and she knew he was just that: as serious as a heart attack.

"You're going to *steal?*"

He nodded, grinning.

"You're going to steal twenty *million?*"

He nodded, still wearing that thin grin. "That's a lot of money, isn't it? It's the amount that I stood to earn from my bonus if Borst and Bentley hadn't pilfered it." He said the names through a sudden snarl. And then, more matter-of-factly, he added, "I'm going to take it."

Lacy was flabbergasted. "But how? From them? You can't just steal twenty million dollars and not expect to get caught!"

"No? I'm not touching Borst and Bentley, at least not at first. Even if they had that kind of money, you're right—it would be suicide to take such a sum from anyone."

He lifted the cup again, slowly, staring into it, and he spoke just before the rim touched his lips. "Which is why I will take it from no one." He drank, and she watched him, caught up in his drama.

She thought he had flipped his lid—all theatrical and making no sense at all. He lowered the cup to the table, landing it without a sound. "I will take it from one hundred million accounts. Next month, one hundred million interbank ATM service fees will be slightly inflated on selected customers' statements. Not a soul will even suspect a theft has occurred."

She blinked at him several times, trying to understand. And then she did. "They will see it!"

"Service fees are not reconciled, Lacy. When was the last time you even checked on the accuracy of those little charges?" He raised an eyebrow. "Hmm?"

She shook her head. "You're crazy. Someone will notice. It's too much!"

"The banks will not know except through the odd customer who complains. When someone complains, what do they do? They run a query. A query that I will be able to detect. Any account queried, regardless of the nature of that query, will receive a correction. In the world of computing, anomalies do occur, Lacy. In this case, the anomaly will be corrected on all accounts in which it is detected. Either way, the transactions will be nontraceable."

"But that's impossible. Every transaction is traceable."

"Oh?" He let it stand at that and just stared at her, his head still angled in a rather sinister manor, she thought.

Lacy stared at Kent and began to believe him. He was, after all, no idiot. She didn't know the inner workings of a bank's finances, but she knew that Kent did. If anybody could do what he suggested, he could. Goodness! Was he actually planning on stealing twenty million dollars? It was insane! Twenty *million* dollars! Her heart thumped in her chest.

She swallowed. "Even if you could pull it off, it's . . . it's wrong. And you know how it feels to be wronged."

"Don't even begin to compare this with my loss," he shot back. "And who is being wronged here? You think losing a few cents will make anyone feel *wronged*? Like, *Oh, my stars, Gertrude! I've been robbed blind!* Besides, you have to know something in order to feel anything about it. And they will not know."

"It's the principle of it, Kent. You're stealing twenty million dollars, for heaven's sake! That's wrong."

His eyes flashed. "Wrong? Says who? What's happened to me—now, *that's* wrong. The way I'm looking at it, I'm just getting centered again."

"That doesn't make it right." So this was what he'd come to tell her. That he was about to become a world-class criminal. Mafia type. And she'd bared her soul to the man.

She frowned. "Even if you pull it off, you'll spend the rest of your life running. How are you going to explain all that money? It'll catch up to you one day."

"No. You see, actually that's what I came to tell you. Nothing will ever catch up to me, because I don't plan on being around to be caught up to. I'm leaving. Forever."

"Come on, Kent. With international laws and extradition treaties, they can track you down anywhere. What are you going to do, hide out in some tropical jungle?"

His blue eyes twinkled. She furrowed her brows.

He just smiled and crossed his legs. "We'll see, Lacy, but I wanted you to know that. Because tonight may be the last time you see me."

Then she understood why Kent had come. He had not come to ask her to share his life; he can come to say good-bye. He was tossing her out of his life as he had done once before. He had bound her to this secret of his—this crime—and now he intended to heave her overboard.

The realization spread over her like a flow of red-hot lava, searing right through to her bones. Her heart seized for a few moments. She knew it! She knew it, she knew it, she knew it! She'd been a fool to let him anywhere *near* her heart.

Kent's face suddenly fell, and she thought he had sensed her emotions. The instinct proved wrong.

"There will be a death involved, Lacy, but don't believe what you read in the papers. Things will not be what they seem. I can promise you that."

She recoiled at his admission, now stunned by the incongruity facing her. *You promise me, do you, Kent? Oh, well, that fills the cockles of my heart with delight, my strapping young monster! My blue-eyed psycho . . .*

"Lacy." Kent's voice jarred her back to the table. "You okay?"

She drew a breath and settled in the chair. It occurred to her that the time she had spent hurriedly doing her face and cleaning the condo had been wasted. Entirely. "I don't know, Kent. Am I supposed to be okay?" She eyed him pointedly, thinking to thrust a dagger there.

He sat up, aware for the first time, perhaps, that she was not taking all of this with a warm, cuddly heart. "I'm sharing something with you here, Lacy. I'm *exposing* myself. I don't just walk around flashing for the public, you know. Lighten up."

"Lighten up? You waltz into my place, swear me to secrecy, and then dump all over me! How dare you? And you just want me to lighten up?" She knew that nasty little quiver had taken to her lips, but she was powerless to stop it. "And don't assume everyone you flash will like what they see!"

Lacy felt a sudden furious urge to reach out and slap him. *Don't be an imbecile, Kent! You can't just run off and steal twenty million dollars! And you can't just run off, period! Not this time!*

And then she did. In a blinding fit of anger she just reached out and slapped him across the cheek! Hard. *Smack!* The sound echoed in the room as if someone had detonated a small firecracker. Kent reeled back, grabbing at the table for support and gasping in shock.

"Whaa—"

"Don't you *what* me, Kent Anthony!" Heat washed down Lacy's neck. Her hand was stinging. Maybe she had swung a bit hard. Goodness, she had *never* slapped a man! "You're killing me here!"

His eyes flashed with anger, and he scowled. "Look. *I'm* the one who's going out on the line here. I'm risking my neck, for Pete's sake. I'm sorry I've burdened you with my life, but at least you don't have to live it. I've lost everything!" His face throbbed red. "Everything, you hear me? It's either this or suicide, and if you don't believe me, you just watch, Honey!" He jerked away from her, and she saw that his eyes had blurred with tears.

Lacy gripped her fingers into a fist and closed her eyes. *Okay, slow down, Lacy. Relax. He's just hurt.* You're *hurt.* She put her palms flat on the table, took several long pulls of air, and finally looked up at him.

He was staring at her again with those blue eyes, searching her. For what? Maybe she had mistaken his signals all along. Maybe those baby blues were looking at her as a link to reality, a partner in crime, a simple companion. God knew he was living in a void these days. And now she knew why—he was stepping off a cliff. He was playing with death. It was why the meeting with the cop had him wringing his hands.

She should be angry with herself more than with him, she thought. He had not misled her; she had simply been on the wrong track. Thinking foolish thoughts of falling in love with Kent again, while he had his eyes on this—this crime of new beginnings. And a death. Good heavens! He was planning on killing somebody!

"I *will* have to live with it, Kent," she said gently. "Whatever happens to you, happens to me now. You see that, don't you? You've climbed back into my heart." She shrugged. "And now you've just made me an accomplice, sworn to secrecy. You can understand how that might upset me a little, can't you?"

He blinked and leaned back. She could see that the thought was running through his mind for the first time. *Goodness. Men could be such apes.*

She rescued him. "But you're right. You're going to live the brunt of it all. So I may not see you again? Ever?"

He swallowed. "Maybe not. I'm sorry, Lacy. I must sound like a fool coming here and telling you all of this. I've been insensitive."

She held up a hand. "No, it's okay. It's not something I asked for, but now that it's done, I'm sure I can handle it." She looked at him and decided not to press the issue. Enough was enough. "And I shouldn't have slapped you."

"No, I guess I had that coming."

She hesitated. "Yes, I guess you did."

He gave off a nervous *humph*, off balance now.

"So, you really think striped pajamas and a buzz cut will disguise you, Kent? Maybe a ball and chain to boot? It'll be a new life, all right. Don't worry. I'll visit you often." She allowed a small grin.

He chuckled, and the tension fell like loosened shackles. "No way, Honey. If you think I'm going to prison, you obviously don't know me like you think you do."

But that was the problem. She did know him. And she knew that one way or another, his life was about to change forever. And with it, possibly hers.

"You're right. Well, I would wish you luck, but somehow it doesn't quite feel right, if you know what I mean. And I can't very well wish you failure, because I don't really go for watching people jerk and foam in electric chairs. So, I'll just hope that you change your mind. In the meantime, my lips are sealed. Fair enough?"

He nodded and grinned.

They drank coffee and talked for another hour before Kent left. He pecked her on the cheek at the door. She did not return the kiss.

Lacy cried a lot that night.

25

Saturday.

Stealing twenty million dollars, no matter how well planned, engenders undeniable risks. Big, monstrous risks. Although Kent had rehearsed each phase of the two-day operation a thousand times in his mind, the actual execution would involve dozens of unforeseen possibilities. The least of these was probably the likelihood of a Volkswagen-sized asteroid striking downtown Denver and ending his day along with a few million others'—not much he could do about that. But somewhere between *Armageddon Two* and the real world lay the lurking monsters that seemed to ruin every crook's good intentions.

Kent let the booze knock him out late Friday night. After his little confessional with Lacy he deserved a good, long drink. Besides, with nerves strung like piano wires, he doubted sleep would come any other way. There would be no drinking for the robbery's duration, which meant he would have to lay off for a few days. Or maybe forever. The nasty stuff was beginning to show.

When consciousness returned at six o'clock Saturday morning, it came like an electric shock, and he bolted from bed.

It was Saturday! *The* Saturday. Six o'clock? He was already late! He stared around his bedroom, straining his eyes against a throbbing headache. His sheets lay in a wrinkled mess, wet from sweat.

A chill flashed down his spine. Who did he think he was, off to steal twenty million dollars? *Hello there, my name is Kent. I am a criminal. Wanted by the FBI.* The whole notion suddenly struck him as nonsense! He decided then, sitting in his bed, wet with cooling sweat at a hair past six Saturday morning, to discard the whole plan.

Seven deliberate seconds passed before he rescinded the decision and threw his sheets from his legs. Twenty million good old American greenbacks had his name on them, and he wasn't about to let them go to Borst and Tomato-Head.

The trip to Salt Lake City would take nine hours, which left him two hours to dress, confirm the order for the *fish,* and retrieve the truck.

Kent ran into the bathroom, cursing himself for the alcohol. He dipped his head under the tap, ignoring the pooling water at his beltline. No time for a shower. He wasn't planning on running into anyone who would mind anyway.

He dressed on the fly, pulling on a baggy shirt and khaki slacks. Within ten minutes of his first jolt in bed, Kent was ready to leave. For good. The thought stopped him at his bedroom door. Yes, for good. He had no plans of returning to the house again—a prospect he'd thought might bring on some nostalgia. But scanning the room now, he felt only anxious to leave.

It had to look as if he'd left with the full intention of returning, which was why he took nothing. Absolutely nothing. Not a tube of toothpaste, not an extra pair of socks, not even a comb. It was always something simple that tipped off the investigators. Truly brain-dead criminals like those from Stupid Street might empty their bank accounts the day before planning a getaway. Those with no mind at all might even run around town kissing loved ones good-bye and grinning ear to ear about some secret. *Gosh, I'm sorry, Mildred. I just can't tell you. But believe me, I'm gonna be soakin' up the sun in Hawaii while you're here workin' like an idiot for the rest of your miserable life!*

That pretty much summed up his little confessional with Lacy. Goodness! Kent shivered at the thought, wondering if his little trip to Boulder might be his undoing. If the visit had been a mistake, it would be his last. He swore it then, surveying his room for the last time.

He ran into the sitting room and turned on the television. He left his bed unmade; the toothpaste lay on the vanity, capless and dribbling. A John Grisham novel rested, dog-eared, on the nightstand, bookmarked at the ninth chapter. He ran down to the kitchen and scribbled a note to Helen.

Helen,

I'm headed for the mountains to fish—clear my head. Won't be back 'til late. Sorry about dinner. If I catch anything, we can fry it up tomorrow.

Kent

He reread the note. Good enough.

Kent left through the front door, casually opened the garage and pulled out his fishing tackle. Bart someone-or-other—Mathews, he thought, Bart Mathews—waved from his riding mower three lawns up. Kent waved back, thinking that the gods were now smiling on him. Yes, indeed, Kent Anthony left his house on Saturday with one thing on his mind. Fishing. He went fishing. Kent lifted his rod in a motion that said, *Yes sir, Bart—I'm going fishing, see? Remember that.* He smiled, but his hands were trembling. He tossed the pole in the backseat, on top of a closed box he'd loaded in the wee hours last night.

Kent backed the silver Lexus into Kiowa Street for the last time and sped from suburban Littleton, blinking his eyes against nagging whispers telling him that he was nuts. *Nuts, nuts, nuts.* Maybe he should *un*-rescind the decision to rescind the decision to abort. Now, there was some clear thinking.

On the other hand, how many would-be criminals had found themselves in precisely this situation—on some precipice overlooking the actual drop and thinking the cliff suddenly looked awfully high? And there was no bungee cord to yank him back if he went into freefall, no rip cord to pull in case he decided to bail out. It was straight down to see if you could land just right and roll out of it. The facts said that 99 percent ended up splattered on the rocks below, bird meat. The facts, the facts. The facts also said that every single one of those greenbacks was waiting to go home to Papa. And in this case, he was Papa.

Besides, at some point you suddenly realized you were already there, over the cliff, falling free, and Kent decided he'd now reached that point. He'd reached it two months earlier when all hell first broke loose.

It took him forty-five minutes to reach Front Range Meat Packers. He had selected the company ten days earlier for several reasons. At least that was the story he was telling himself these days. It might be more accurate to say that he had *chanced* upon the company, and then only because of the dreams.

The dreams. Ah, yes, the dreams. Although he could hardly remember the details of the dreams when he awoke, their general impressions lingered through the day. Brilliant general impressions, like the one that suggested he find his truck on the outskirts of town, near the Coors beer-processing plant. It was as if the alcohol delivered him to a deep sleep where things became clear and memories were bright once again. He'd awakened in the middle of a dream once and found himself shaking and sweating because it really felt like someone was in the dream with him, giving him a tour.

The dreams had played on his mind like fingers across a keyboard, stretching out tunes that resonated with his own brilliance. In fact, he'd finally concluded that they were just that: his own brilliance, shocked into high gear by the events that had pushed him. Pure logic found in the quiet of sleep.

And there were several very logical reasons why the Front Range Meat Packers plant met his needs. First, and possibly most important, it was located far off the beaten track in a large warehouse district south of 470. The metal structure evoked images of the Mafia cover operations he'd seen in a dozen movies. It was also closed on the weekends, leaving a hundred short-box refrigerated trucks parked in the sprawling lot, soaking up the sun's rays until Monday. He'd walked through the lot on Tuesday, wearing glasses and sporting a slicked-back hairdo that did a good enough job of changing his appearance, he thought. He had played a meat buyer from startup Michael's Butcher Shop in East Denver, and he'd played the part well. He'd also been given a lesson on exactly why Iveco refrigerated trucks were still the best units on the road. "No chance of the meat spoiling in here. No way," meatpacker Bob "the Cruiser" Waldorf had insisted, stroking a three-inch goatee.

Which was why he needed a truck in the first place. To keep the meat—the *fish*—from spoiling.

Kent now drove up to the warehouse complex and scanned it nervously. The grounds lay deserted. He snaked the Lexus into an alley and rolled toward the adjacent complex. Gravel crunched under tires; sweat leaked down his neck. It occurred to him that the unexpected presence of a single fool here could close down the operation. There could be no witness to his visit.

The adjacent lot housed a hundred ten-by-thirty storage cubicles, half of which were empty, their white-flecked doors rusted, dented, and tilting. It was a wonder the business found willing renters for the other half of the cubicles. That was another reason he had chosen this particular location: It offered a hiding place for the Lexus.

Kent nosed the car up to space 89 and turned the motor off. Silence rang in his ears.

This was it. Technically speaking, up until now he had not actually committed any crime. Now he was about to break into a storage bin and hide his car. Not necessarily something they would fry him for, but a crime nonetheless. His heart pounded steadily. The alley on either side lay clear.

Okay. Do this, Kent. Let's do it.

Kent pulled on leather gloves and stepped from the car. He pried the roll door up with considerable effort. Its wrenching squeal echoed through the concrete cubical, and he winced. Goodness, he could have just as easily put a flashing red light atop the thing. Kmart special. One crime being committed here! Come one, come all.

But no one came. Kent hopped back into the Lexus and pulled it into the space. He grabbed his briefcase and pulled the door closed, wincing again at its screech. Still the alley remained empty. He knelt quickly, withdrew a small rivet gun from his briefcase, popped a rivet on either side of the tin door, and replaced the gun.

He left space 89 and walked briskly for Front Range Meat Packers, scouring the compound in every direction for the one fool who would ruin everything. But the compound sat still and empty in the morning light.

Kent had run through a thousand methods for stealing a vehicle—crime number two in this long string of crimes he was about to commit. It wasn't until Cruiser had offered his explanation for the five trucks outside the main compound's security fence that Kent had landed on the current plan. "See, out of a fleet of 120, those are the only 5 that are inoperable right now."

"What? Breakdowns?" Kent had said, half kidding.

"Actually, truck 24, the one on the end, is in for a routine tune-up. We take good care of our trucks. Always have, always will."

It had been a gift. Kent stood by Cruiser, frozen for a moment, sure that he'd been here before—standing next to Cruiser while the keys to the kingdom were handed over. A déjà vu from one of those dreams, perhaps. There were other ways, of course. But in an operation strewn with complications, he had no intention of turning down the offering. He'd returned Thursday night and broken into the truck with a coat hanger. If they discovered Friday that truck 24 had been left open, they would probably move it. But it was a risk he had taken gladly. The process of breaking into the truck had taken him two full hours. He couldn't very well take two hours in broad daylight struggling on the hood with a coat hanger.

Truck 24 sat, unmoved, and Kent covered the last thirty yards over the graveled lot in a run. He grabbed the truck's door handle, held his breath, and pressed the latch. The door opened. He sighed with relief, tossed his briefcase on the bench seat, and climbed up, shaking like a leaf. A small ball of victory swelled in his chest. So far, so good. Like taking candy from a baby. He was in the cab, and the coast was clear!

One of the primary benefits of spending six years in higher learning institutions was learning how to learn. It was a skill that Kent had perfected. And one of the things he'd learned as of late was how to hot-wire a truck. Specifically an Iveco 2400 refrigerated truck. Not from a book entitled *How to Hot-Wire Your Favorite Truck*, no. But from a book on safeguarding your property, along with an engineering manual, an auto mechanic's electrical guide, and, of course, an Iveco 2400 repair manual—each source lending a few details to his collective learning experience. In the end, he knew precisely how to hot-wire an Iveco 2400. The procedure was supposed to be a thirty-second affair.

It took Kent ten minutes. The Phillips head he'd brought was a tad small and wanted to slip with every rotation. When he finally freed the panel under the dash, the wires were so far behind the steering column that he nearly ripped the skin from his fingers prying them out. But in the end his learning experience proved valid. When he touched the red wire to the white wire, the truck rumbled to life.

The sudden sound startled Kent, and he jerked up, promptly dropping the wires and hitting his head on the steering wheel in one smooth motion. The motor died.

Kent cursed and righted himself on the seat. He gazed about the compound, breathing heavily. The coast was still clear. He bent over and restarted the truck. His hands were sweating in the leather gloves, and he briefly considered pulling them free. But a dozen episodes of *Forensics* crashed into his mind at once, and he rejected the notion.

He shoved the truck into reverse, backed it into the lane, and nosed it toward the complex's exit a hundred yards off. One look and any reasonable person would have known that the driver perched behind the wheel in truck 24, sneaking toward the exit gate, was not your typical driver headed out for deliveries. For one thing, typical drivers don't sit like ice sculptures on the front edge of the seat, gripping the wheel as if it were the safety rail on a roller-coaster ride. For another, they don't jerk their heads back and forth like some windup doll gone berserk. But then, none of that mattered, because there were no reasonable people—or for that matter, *any* people—to see Kent creep from the lot in truck 24.

Within three minutes he was back on the thoroughfare, headed west, anxious and sweaty and checking the mirrors every five seconds, but undiscovered. He studied the gauges carefully. The company had seen fit to leave truck 24 full of fuel. *Way to go, Cruiser.* Kent flipped on the cooling unit and rechecked the gauges. In fact, he rechecked the gauges fifteen times in those first ten minutes, before finally settling down for the seven-hour drive to Salt Lake City.

Only he didn't really settle down. He bit his nails and walked through every detail of his plan for the thousandth time. Now that he'd actually jumped over this cliff, the ground below was looking a little more rugged than before. In fact, having executed a brilliant plan that left absolutely nothing to chance, it occurred to him that he had virtually *depended* on chance up to this point. The chance that his alarm clock would actually work that morning. The chance that no one would be at Front Range Meat Packers on a Saturday morning, regardless of the fact that they were closed. The chance that the Iveco had not been moved into the secure compound. The chance that he could actually get the Iveco started.

And now Kent began to imagine the road ahead strewn with chances . . . with flat tires and traffic delays and power outages and routine pullovers. With boulders falling from the nearby cliffs and closing the road. Or worse, squashing his truck like a roach. That one would be God's doing—if indeed Gloria had been right and there was a God. Unless it was an earthquake's doing, in which case it would be Mother Nature reaching out to express her opinion of the matter.

Don't, son. Don't do this.

He glanced at the speedometer, saw that he exceeded the posted sixty miles-per-hour speed limit, and eased his foot from the accelerator. Getting pulled over for a speeding ticket, now, that would be a story for Stupid Street.

Kent reached the preselected dirt turnoff thirty minutes later and pulled into a grove of trees blocking the view to the interstate. It took him no more than five minutes to pull out the large magnetic signs he'd hidden in the tall grass midweek and slap them into place along each side of the truck. He studied his handiwork. For the next twenty-four hours, Front Range Meat Packers truck 24 would be known as McDaniel's Mortuary's truck 1. The signs along each side said so. In black lettering that was quaint and unobtrusive but clear and definite, so there would be no doubt.

Kent pulled back onto the highway and brought the truck up to full speed. Yes, he was most definitely over the cliff now. Falling like a stone.

26

Finding the right body, the "fish," and arranging for the pickup had taken Kent the better part of a week. He'd approached the challenge in two parts. First, setting up a plausible body pickup and second, actually finding the body itself.

Although he'd established McDaniel's Mortuary as a legitimate business only two weeks earlier, to look at the ghost company's Web site you would think it was one of the older houses in the West. Of course, local mortuaries would be the first to identify a new player that suddenly appeared in their territories, so he'd been forced to use distance as a buffer against recognition. It wasn't likely that independently owned mortuaries in Los Angeles, for example, would be familiar with funeral homes in Denver.

The company of choice also needed to be large enough to handle transfers to and from other cities on a regular basis. The request for a particular body on ice could not be an unusual occurrence. In addition, the mortuary had to be computerized, allowing Kent some kind of access to its data files.

These first three restrictions narrowed the field of eligible mortuaries from 9,873 nationally to 1,380. But it was the fourth requirement that put the breaks on eligibility for all but three unwitting participants. The mortuary had to be in possession of the right body.

The right body. A body that was six-feet-one-inch tall, male, Caucasian, with a body weight of between 170 and 200 pounds. A body that had no known surviving relatives. And a body that had no identifiable dental records outside of the FBI's main identification files.

In most cases mortuaries hold cadavers no longer than two or three days, a fact that limited the number of available bodies. For a week, Kent ran dry runs, breaking into the networks using the Web, identifying bodies that fit his requirements.

The process was one of downloading lists and cross-referencing them with the FBI's central data bank—a relatively simple process for someone in Kent's shoes. But it was arduous and sweaty and nerve-racking nonetheless. He ran the searches from his system at home, sipping at the tall bottle next to his monitor while he waited for the files to download.

On Tuesday, he'd found only one body, and it was in Michigan. That had put the jitters right though him, and it had taken nearly a full bottle of the hard drink to bring them under control.

On Wednesday, he'd found three bodies, one of which was actually in Denver. Too close to home. The other two were in California—too far. But at least there were three of them.

On Thursday, he'd found no bodies, and he had shattered his keyboard with a fist, a fit he immediately regretted. It ruined both his right pinkie—which had taken the brunt of the contact, somewhere between the letters J and U by the scattered keys—and his night. There were no twenty-four-hour keyboard stores that he was aware of.

Friday he'd found three bodies, to shuddering sighs of relief. Two on the East Coast and one in Salt Lake City. He downed two long slugs of liquor at the find. Tom Brinkley. *Thank you, Tom Brinkley. I love you, Tom Brinkley!*

Tom Brinkley had died of a gunshot wound to the stomach, and according to the records, no one seemed to have a clue about him beyond that. From all indications the man had shot himself, which also indicated to Kent that there *was* at least one other thing known about the man. He was an idiot. Only an idiot would attempt suicide with a bullet through the gut. Nevertheless, that is precisely what the authorities had concluded. Go figure.

Now poor Tom's body sat awaiting cremation in Salt Lake's largest mortuary, Peace Valley Funeral Home. Kent had tagged his "fish" then—processed an order for a transfer of the catch to McDaniel's Mortuary in Las Vegas, Nevada. Reason? Relatives had been located and wished a local burial. *Now I lay my fish to sleep.* The funeral home had informed him by e-mail that the body had already been stripped and prepared for cremation. *Not a problem. Will pick up as is.* It was in a sealed box. Did he want it in a body bag? A body bag was customary. *Not a problem. Will pick up as is.*

He scheduled a "will call" Saturday between 3 and 5 P.M. He would pick up the fish then. Only he knew it was not a fish, of course. It was just one of those interesting quirks that a mind gone over the edge tends to make. It was a dead body, as cold as a fish and possibly gray like a fish, but certainly not a fish. And hopefully not slimy like a fish.

He confirmed the order an hour later from a pay phone. The girl who answered his questions had a bad habit of snapping chewing gum while listening, but otherwise she seemed cooperative enough.

"But we close at five. You get here a minute past, and you won't find a soul around," she warned.

It had taken a mere forty-five minutes with his fingers flying nervously over the keyboard to make the changes to Tom Brinkley's FBI file. The tingles of excitement had shortened his breath for an hour following. Actually *that* had been the first crime. He'd forgotten. Breaking into the FBI files was not a laughable prank. It had not seemed so criminal, though.

Kent let the memories run through his mind and kept his eyes peeled as he negotiated I-70 west. The trip over the mountains was uneventful, unless you considered it eventful to bite your nails clean off every time a patrol car popped up in your rearview mirror. By the time Kent reached the outskirts of Salt Lake, his nerves had frayed, leaving him feeling as though he'd downed a dozen No-Doze tablets in a single sitting. He pulled in to a deserted rest stop, hurried to the back of the truck, and popped the refrigerated box open for the first time.

A cloud of trapped vapor billowed out, cold and white. The cooler worked well enough. Kent pulled himself up to the back bumper and then into the unit and waved his hand against the billows of vapor. The interior drifted into view about him. Metal shelves arose on the right. A long row of hooks hung from the ceiling on the left like claws begging for their slabs of meat. *For their fish.*

Kent shivered. It was cold. He imagined the gum-snapping gal at Peace Valley Funeral Home, clipboard in hand, staring up at those hooks.

"What are those for?"

"Those? Oh, we find that bodies are much easier to carry if you take them from their caskets and hook them up. You guys don't do that?"

No, the hooks would not do. But then, he was not some white-trash bozo from Stupid Street, was he? No sir. He had already planned for this eventuality. Cruiser had told him that all trucks carried thermal blankets to cover the meat in case of emergency. Truck 24's blankets lay in a neat stack to Kent's right. He pulled them off the shelf and strung two along the hooks like a shower curtain. A divider.

"What are those for?"

"Those? Oh, that's where we hide the really ugly ones so people don't throw up. You guys don't do that?"

Kent swallowed and climbed out of the cooler box. He left the rest stop and slowly made his way to the mark on his map that approximated the funeral home's location. To any other vehicle parked beside him at a light, he resembled a mortuary truck on a Saturday run. Right? The magnetic signs were dragging on the street, exposing the meat packer's logo, right? Because that would look obscene. So then why did he have such a hard time looking anywhere but straight ahead at stoplights?

Liberty Valley's wrought-iron gates loomed suddenly on Kent's left, bordered by long rows of pines. He caught a glimpse of the white building set back from the street, and his heart lodged firmly in his throat. He rounded the block and approached the main gate again, fighting the gut-wrenching impulse to drive on. Just keep on driving, right back to Denver. There was madness in this plan. Stealing a body. *Brilliant software engineer loses sanity and steals a body from funeral home. Why? It is yet unknown, but some have speculated that there may be other bodies, carved up, hidden.*

Then the gate was there in front of him, and Kent pulled in, clearing his throat of the knot that had been steadily growing since entering this cursed city.

The long, paved driveway rolled under him like a black snake. He followed a sign that led him to the rear, where a loading bay sat empty. A buzz droned in his head—the sound of the truck's wheels on the pavement. The steady moan of madness. He backed up to the door, pulled the parking brake, and left the engine running. He couldn't very well be seen fiddling with wires to restart it.

He set himself on autopilot now, executing the well-rehearsed plan. From his briefcase he withdrew glasses and a mustache. He fixed them quickly to his face, checked his image in the rearview mirror, and pulled out his clipboard.

A blonde-headed girl with a pug nose pushed open the rear door of the funeral home on his second ring. She was smacking gum.

"You from McDaniel's?"

He could feel the sweat breaking from his brow. He pushed his glasses back up his nose. "Yes."

She turned and headed into the dim storage area. "Good. You almost didn't make it. We close in fifteen minutes, you know."

"Yeah."

"So, you from Las Vegas?"

"Yeah."

"Never heard of McDaniel's. You ever win big money?"

Big money? His heart skipped a beat. What could she know of big money?

She sensed his hesitation and glanced over at him, smiling. "You know. Las Vegas. Gambling. Did you ever win big?"

"Uh . . . No. I don't gamble, really."

Coffins rose to the ceiling on all sides. Empty, no doubt. Hopefully. She led him to a huge side door made of steel. A cooler door.

"I don't blame you. Gambling's a sin." She popped the door open and stepped through. A dozen coffins, some shiny and elaborate, some no more than plywood boxes, rested on large shelves in the cooler. The girl walked over to one of the plain boxes, checked the tag, then slapped it.

"This is it. Grab that gurney there, and it's all yours."

Kent hesitated. The gurney, of course. He grabbed the wheeled table and pushed it parallel to the casket. Together they pulled the plywood box onto the gurney, a task made surprisingly easy by rollers on the shelf.

The girl slapped the box again. Seemed to like doing that. "There you go. Sign this, and you're all set."

Kent signed her release and offered a smile. "Thanks."

She returned the smile and opened the door for him.

Halfway back to the outer door he decided it might be best if she did not watch him load the body. "What should I do with the gurney when I'm done?" he asked.

"Oh, I'll help you."

"No. No problem, I can handle it. I should be able to—I've done this enough. I'll just shove it back through the door when I'm done."

She smiled. "It's okay. I don't mind. I need to close down anyway."

Kent thought about objecting again but decided it would only raise her curiosity. She held the door again, and he rolled the brown box into the sun. From this angle, with the truck parked below in the loading dock, he caught sight of the Iveco's roof. And it wasn't a pretty sight.

He jerked in shock and immediately covered by coughing hard. But his breathing was suddenly ragged and obvious. Large red words splashed across the roof of the Iveco's box: Front Range Meat Packers.

He flung a hand toward the bottom of the truck's roll door, hoping to draw her attention there. "Can you get the door?" If she saw the sign he might need to improvise. And he had no clue how to do that. Stealing bodies was not something he had perfected yet.

But Miss Gum-Smacker jumped to his suggestion and yanked the door up like a world-class chain-saw starter. She'd obviously done that a few times. Kent rolled the gurney down the short ramp and into the truck, gripping the ramp's aluminum railing to steady his jitters. As long as they remained down here, she would not have a chance to see the sign. Now, when he drove off . . . that would be a different story.

It occurred to him then that the casket would not fit on the shelves designed for meat. It would have to go on the floor.

"How do you lower this?" he asked.

She stepped in and looked at him with a raised brow. "You're asking me how to lower a gurney?"

"I usually carry ours—battery powered. All you do is push a button. But this is a new rig. It's not outfitted properly yet." Now, *there* was some quick thinking. Powered gurneys? There must be such a thing these days. She nodded, apparently satisfied, and lowered the contraption. Together they slid the coffin off and let it rest on the floor. Now to get her back into the warehouse without looking back.

"Here, let me help you," he said and walked right past her to the warehouse door, which he yanked open.

She wheeled the gurney up after him and pushed it through the door. "Thanks," she said and walked into the dim light.

"Thank you. Have a great weekend."

"Sure. Same to you."

Kent released the door and heard its lock engage. He glanced around and ran for the cab, trembling. What if she were to come back out? *Hey, you forgot your clipboard.* Only he hadn't forgotten it. It was in his right hand, and he tossed it onto the bench seat. With a final glance back, he sprang into the truck, released the brake, and pulled out of the loading dock, his heart slamming in his chest.

He'd crossed the parking area and was pulling onto the long, snakelike drive before remembering the rear door. It was still open!

Kent screeched to a halt and ran to the back, beating back images of a shattered box strewn behind the truck. But not this day; this day the gods were smiling on him. The box remained where he'd left it, unmoved. He pulled the door closed, flooded with relief at small favors.

He pulled out of Liberty Valley's gates, shaking like a leaf. A full city block flew by before he realized that the jerking motion under him resulted from a fully engaged parking brake. He released it and felt the truck surge forward. Now, that was a Stupid Street trick if there ever was one. He had to get control of himself here!

Two blocks later the chills of victory began their run up and down his spine. Then Kent threw back his head and yelled out loud in the musty cabin. "Yes!"

The driver in the Cadillac beside him glanced his way. He didn't care. "Yes, yes, yes!"

He had himself a body. A fish.

27

Helen scanned the note again and knew it said more than it read. This fishing business was hogwash, because it didn't bring a smile to her face as in, *Oh, good. He's gone to catch us some trout. I love trout.* Instead, it brought a knot to her gut, as in, *Oh, my God! What's he gone and done?*

She had felt the separation all day, walking the streets of Littleton. It was a quiet day in the heavens. A sad day. The angels were mourning. She still had energy to burn, but her heart was not so light, and she found praying difficult. God seemed distracted. Or maybe *she* was distracted.

Helen had walked the same twenty-mile route five days now, stopping briefly at the hot-dog stand at Fifth and Grand each day for a drink and a quick exchange with its proprietor, Chuck. She'd suspected from the first words out of Chuck's mouth that he was a man holed up in his religion.

Today she had helped him out of his shell.

"You walk every day, Helen?"

She'd nodded.

"How far?"

"A long way. Longer than I can count."

"More than a mile?"

"I can count a mile, young man."

"Longer?"

"Longer than I can count."

He'd chuckled nervously. "Ten miles?"

She sipped at the lemonade he'd served her. "Longer."

"Twenty?" he asked incredulous.

She shrugged. "I don't know for sure."

"But that's impossible! You walk twenty miles *every* day?"

She looked right into his eyes then. "Yes, I'm an intercessor, Chuck. You know what that is, don't you? I will walk as long as he requires me to."

He glanced around quickly. "You mean you pray?"

"I pray, and I walk. And as long as I'm walking and praying I don't feel strain on my legs at all." She eyed him steadily. "How does that sound, Chuck?"

He stood there with his mouth open, possibly thinking that this kind woman he'd served over the last five days was stark-raving mad. "Sound strange? Well, there's more, Chuck. I see things too. I walk on legs that have no business walking, and I see things." It was the first time she had been so vocal about this business to a stranger, but she could hardly resist.

She pointed to the overcast sky and gave it a faraway look. "You see those clouds there? Or this air?" She swept her hand through the air. "Suppose you could tear away this air and expose what lay behind. What do you think you would find?"

Chuck the hot-dog man was stuck in the open-mouth, wide-eyes look. He did not answer.

"I'll tell you what you would find. A million beings peering over the railing at the choices of one man. You would find the real game. Because it's all about what happens on the other side, Chuck. And if you could tear the heavens apart, you would see that. All this other stuff you see with those marbles in your head are props for the real game." She flashed him a grin and let that sink in. "At least, that's one way of looking at it all. And I think there is a game over your soul as well, young man."

She had left him like that, holding a hot dog in one hand with his mouth gaping as if he were ready to shove it in.

It had been the high point of the day, actually, because she knew Chuck's life would change now. But the balance of her walk had been a somber one.

Back at home, Helen picked up the phone and called Pastor Bill at home.

"Bill Madison here."

"He's gone off the deep end, Bill."

"Helen?"

"Yes."

"What do you mean?"

"Kent's gone off the deep end, and I smell death in the air. I think he may be in trouble."

"Whoa. You think he may *die?* I didn't think he *could* die in this thing."

"I didn't either. But there's death in the air. And I think it's his death, although I don't know that. There was a lot of silence in the heavens today."

"Then maybe you should warn him. Tell him about this. You haven't been . . . you know . . . told not to, have you?"

"No. Not specifically. I've had no desire to tell him, which usually means that I shouldn't. But I think you may be right. I think I will tell him the next time I see him."

They let the phones rest silent for a moment.

"Helen, are you walking tomorrow?"

"Did you awake this morning, Bill?"

"What? Of course I did."

"The answer to your question should be as obvious, don't you think? I walk every day."

He continued after regrouping himself. "Would you mind if I walked with you for a spell tomorrow? Before church?"

"I would like that, Pastor."

"Good. Five o'clock?"

"Five-thirty. I sleep in on Sundays."

༜

If Kent thought he could have managed it, he would have driven straight back to Denver. But his body was in no condition to pull a twenty-four-hour shift without sleeping. He had to rest somewhere. At least, that was the way he'd planned it on paper.

He pulled into Grady's Truck Stop two hours outside of Denver, near midnight. A hundred sleeping rigs lined the graveled lot to the west of the all-night diner, and he pulled the little Iveco between two large, purring diesels. So far, so good. No flat tires, no routine pullovers, no breakdowns, no boulders from the sky. He could easily be a real driver for a mortuary, handling just one more body in a series of a hundred.

Kent locked the truck up and walked briskly toward the café. The cool night air rushed softly under the power of the towering trucks on all sides. What were the odds of being recognized in such a remote spot? He paused by the front wheel of a black International tractor-trailer and studied the diner thirty yards away. It stood there all decked out in neon like a Christmas tree. Two thoughts crossed his mind simultaneously, and they brought his pulse up to a steady thump.

The first was that the Iveco back there did not have a lock on the rear door. That had been an oversight on his part. He should have bought a padlock. A grisly wino on the prowl would find his little Iveco easy pickings. Only when the vagrant got back to his lair would he and his cohorts discover that the brown box did not contain rifles or beef or a priceless statue or any such treasure, but a cadaver. A smelly old fish. A dead body—not fit for the eating unless you were on an airplane that went down in the Andes and it was either you or the bodies.

The second thought was that entering Grady's diner, all lit up like a Christmas tree, was starting to seem like one of those stupid mistakes a criminal from Stupid Street might make. *"Yes sir, everything was going perfect until I ran into Bill at Grady's Diner, and he asked me what I was doing at one in the morning toting a cadaver around in a meat truck. Imagine, Bill at Grady's Diner! Who would have possibly thought?"*

Anybody with half a brain would have thought, that's who would have thought! He should have brought his own food. Although he *was* two hours out of Denver. Who that he knew could possibly be here at midnight? But that was just the point, wasn't it? What would *he* be doing here at midnight?

Kent slunk back into the shadows and climbed into the cab he'd made home for the last sixteen hours. He lifted a 7-Up can he'd purchased four hours earlier at the Utah border and swallowed the flat dregs in one gulp. There would be plenty of time for food and drink later. Now he needed sleep.

But sleep did not come easily. For one thing, he found himself craving a real drink. Just one quick nip to settle the nerves. Grady's could probably oblige him with at least a six-pack of beer.

"Don't be a fool," he muttered and lay down on the bench seat.

It was then, parked outside of Grady's, two hours from Denver, that the first major flaw in his plan presented itself to him like a siren in the night. He jerked upright and stared, wide eyed, out the windshield.

Helen! Helen had moved in *after* he'd laid out the timetable. When the rest of his plan was put into play, they would question her, and that questioning rang through his head now, clear and concise—and as condemning as a judge's gavel.

"You're saying he left you a note stating he's going fishing on Saturday but he never comes back? Not even on Sunday?"

"Yes, officer. As far as I can tell."

"So he goes fishing—we know that from the neighbor who saw him—and goes straight to the office in his fishing gear thirty-six hours later, without bothering to come home. No pun intended here, but doesn't that smell a little fishy?"

He had decided not to return for the simple reason that he had the body to contend with. He couldn't very well drive up to his house in the meat truck. Neither could he drive around town with a body in the trunk of the Lexus for a whole day. At some point things would be smelling more than just fishy.

But that was before Helen.

An alarm went off in his head. *Stupid, stupid, stupid!* He had to get to Denver. Get home somehow.

Kent brought the truck to life and roared back to the freeway, once again bouncing on the edge of the seat like some kind of idiot.

An hour later, rumbling into the outskirts of suburban Denver, he conceded to the only plan that made sense in the morning's wee hours. A new element of risk threatened now, but nobody ever said stealing twenty million would be light on the risk factor.

Kent slowly wound his way back to the Front Range Meat Packers compound south of 470 and entered the industrial maze of metal buildings. He killed the lights and crept forward, his eyes peeled for motion, his muscles rigid, his fingers wrapped white on the wheel.

Two minutes later, Kent eased the Iveco into its original space and pulled the ignition wires free. The engine sputtered to silence. By the watch on his right wrist, it was two o'clock in the morning.

For five minutes he sat in the silence, allowing the distant highway drone to settle his nerves. He finally climbed from the truck and walked behind. The roll door remained latched. He eased the lever up and pulled the door up. The box lay on the floor, swirling in a cold mist. He closed the door.

It took him another fifteen minutes to repair the cut wire in the steering column and return the cab to its original condition. Satisfying himself that he no longer needed access to the cab, he locked the doors and shut them quietly. Come Monday morning, if Cruiser had an inkling to pull truck 24 in for service, he would hopefully find her just as he'd left her. Now, if the truck would be kind enough to keep his body hidden and free from rot for another twelve hours without its cooling unit in operation, all would be well.

Kent had made it halfway back to the storage unit housing the Lexus before realizing he'd left the McDaniel's Mortuary signs on the truck. He hastily retreated and tore them free, cursing himself for the oversight. If he could have stopped somewhere and flogged the stupidity from his mind he would have done it without consideration. Evidently he was discovering what most criminals discover midcrime: Stupidity is something that comes upon you *during* the crime, not before. Like the rising sun, you cannot escape it. You can only hope to do your dirty deed before it fries you.

Kent headed back to the storage units, hauling his briefcase in one hand and the rolled-up signs in the other. Sweat soaked his shirt, and he let stealth slip a little. You can't very well pretend to be invisible lugging ten-foot rolls of vinyl under your arm. He plopped the load on the asphalt before the storage door, retrieved the rivet poppers from his briefcase, and made quick work of the fasteners he'd installed earlier.

The Lexus gleamed silver in the moonlight, undisturbed. Kent stuffed the signs in the trunk, tossed the briefcase into the passenger seat, and climbed into the familiar cockpit. He made it all the way to the industrial park's entrance before flipping on his lights. It was 2:38 Sunday morning when he finally entered highway 470 and headed for home, wondering what other small mistake he had made back there.

Yet he had made it, hadn't he? No, not really—not at all. Really he had not even started.

Kent left his Lexus on the street where it would be seen—right in front of the red *No Street Parking* sign by his house. The small black letters below promised that violators would be towed, but they'd never actually hauled any car off that he knew of, and he doubted they would begin on a Sunday.

He entered the house, flipped his shoes off at the front door, made a little noise in the kitchen, moved a few items around, and headed for his bedroom. The trick was to clearly show his presence without actually engaging Helen. He did not want to engage Helen. Not at all.

And, considering the old lady's walking obsession, which he assumed was an everyday affair, missing her might not be so difficult. On the other hand, today was Sunday. She might not walk on Sundays. If she did not, she would at least leave for church. He would have to be gone by noon.

Kent locked the door to the master suite, peeled off his clothes, and fell into bed. He slowly drifted into a fitful sleep.

28

Helen slipped out onto the porch after the doorbell's first ring.

"He's here, Bill."

The pastor did not respond immediately.

"Let's walk." She stepped past him and strolled to the street. The silver Lexus sat along the street beside the driveway. She turned left at the sidewalk and walked briskly past it.

"He came home last night."

"He catch any fish?" Bill asked, beside her now.

"Don't know. He's hiding something."

"Hiding what? How do you know?"

"I don't know what he's hiding, but I'm going to find out the minute I get home. They're on pins and needles up there; that's how I know. Death is in the air. I can feel it."

"You mind if we slow down a little, Helen? You're walking pretty fast here."

"We have to walk fast. I'm cutting it short today. Real short. I've got to get back there." She glanced down at her Reeboks and noted they were wearing thin in the toes.

"You want to pray, Bill?"

"Sure."

"Pray, then. Pray out loud."

⁓⁓⁓

Kent awoke with a start. Something was wrong. His chest felt as though a jackrabbit had taken up residence there and was testing its thumpers. Only this was his heart—not some bunny. Which meant he'd had another dream. He could remember nothing—not even why he was in his own bed. Then he remembered everything, and he leapt from the bed.

Yesterday he had stolen a truck, driven to Utah, stolen a dead body, and returned to Front Range Meat Packers, where the body now lay dead; slowly warming in the back of truck 24. He'd come back to the house because of Helen. Dear Mother-in-law Helen.

It was this last tidbit that had awakened him to the drumming of Thumper's feet—this bit about Helen. He could not allow Helen to see him. And that was a problem because Helen was close. Imminent. Maybe at the bedroom door right now, waiting for the sound of his stirring.

He grabbed the khaki slacks and shirt he'd thrown off last night and pulled them on. For the second morning in a row he faced the task of leaving the room as though he fully intended to return. He made a quick circuit, rubbing some toothpaste on his teeth with his forefinger and tossing the tube in the drawer; throwing the covers loosely over the bed, half made; moving the Grisham novel forward a few pages. And he did all of it without knowing precisely what he was doing.

No matter—Helen was coming.

Kent cracked the door and listened for the sound of movement downstairs with stilled breath. Nothing. Thank God. He slipped into the hall and flew down the steps two at a time. In a matter of sixty seconds flat he managed to pull out the orange juice, slop some peanut butter on a bagel, down half of both, and hopefully leave the general impression that he had enjoyed a leisurely breakfast on a Sunday morning. He snatched up a pen and, taking a deep breath to still his quivering hand, wrote over the note he'd left yesterday.

Hi, Helen.
  Sorry I missed you. Had a great day fishing. All too small to keep. If not home by six, don't wait.

                    Kent

Kent laid the note on the counter and ran for the entrance. The microwave clock read 9:30. He opened the front door carefully, begging not to see Helen's smiling mug. Sunlight stung his eyes, and he squinted. His Lexus sat idle on the street. Helen's yellow Pinto was parked in the garage and a third car, a green Accord, sat in the driveway behind the Pinto.

A friend's car. In the house? No, he had not heard a sound. Helen was out walking with a friend who owned a green Accord. Which meant Helen would be walking down the street with said friend, ready to run off to church. And church started at ten, didn't it?

Kent pulled the door shut and walked for his Lexus, head down, as nonchalantly as possible. If they were down the street, he would ignore them. Had to. Why? Because he just had to. He'd awakened with that realization buzzing through his skull, and it hadn't quieted just yet.

He brought the Lexus to life without looking up. It was when he started the U-turn that he saw them—like two figures on the home stretch of the Boston Marathon, arms pumping. He knew then what it felt like to jump out of your skin, because he almost did. Right there in the tan leather seats of the Lexus. Only his frozen grip on the steering wheel kept him from hitting his head on the ceiling, which was good because they might have seen the movement. You can't just throw your arms up in surprise and then pretend not to see someone—it just doesn't come off as genuine. Kent's foot jerked a little on the accelerator, causing the car to lurch a tad, but otherwise he managed to keep the turn tight and smooth.

He had a hard time removing his eyes from Helen. She and the man were about a block off, leaning into their walk, waving at him now. She wore a yellow dress that fluttered in the breeze, clearly exposing those ridiculous knee-socks pulled up high.

Should he wave back? It was obviously a *Stop-the-car* wave by its intensity, but he could pretend he'd mistaken it for a *Have-a-good-day* wave and return it before roaring off into the sunset. No, better to pretend not to have seen at all.

Kent's foot pressed firmly on the gas pedal, and he left them just breaking into a run. His neck remained rigid. Goodness, what did they know? They pulled up and dropped their arms. *"Sorry, guys, I just didn't see you. I swear I didn't see a thing. You sure it was me?"*

But he wouldn't be asking that question anytime soon, would he? Never. He glanced at the dash clock: 9:35. He had ten hours to burn.

It took Kent a good ten minutes to calm down, nibbling on blunted fingernails, thinking. Thinking, thinking, thinking. In the mirror his face stared back unshaven and wet. He should have cleaned up a little—at least thrown on some deodorant. Only a slob or a man in a great hurry would neglect basic body care. And he was beginning to smell. Kent sniffed at his armpit. No, beginning was far too kind. He reeked. Which would not present a significant problem unless he ran into someone who took note. And even then what could they do? Call the local police and report the reeking swamp thing tooling about town in the silver Lexus? Not likely. Still, it might leave an impression in some clerk's head.

"Did he appear normal to you?"

"No sir, officer, I daresay not. Not unless you consider walking around with radishes for eyes and smelling of rotted flesh at thirty feet normal."

"That bad, huh?"

"That bad."

Kent decided he would drive to Boulder for a burger. He had the time to burn, and on further thought, he needed the miles on his car. It had just gone on a fishing trip.

Two hours later he pulled into a truck stop ten miles south of Boulder, where he managed to splash some water under his pits and purchase a dry sandwich without incident. He spent three hours on the back lot mulling over matters of life and death before pulling out and cruising back toward Denver the long way. And did he use his credit card? No, of course he didn't use his credit card. That would be brain dead. Stupid, stupid. And he was done being stupid.

Darkness had enveloped Denver by the time Kent nosed the Lexus back into the industrial park holding Tom Brinkley's dead body.

Matters were considerably simpler this time around. He shut off his lights, thankful for a three-quarter moon, and idled through the alleys to the back fence. Truck 24 sat faithfully next to its two cousins, and Kent squeezed his fist in satisfaction. "You'd better be there, baby," he whispered, staring at the truck's roll door. "You'd better be right where I left you." This, of course, was spoken to the dead body, hopefully still lying in the plywood box. And hopefully not yet rotting. Things were smelling bad enough already.

Kent backed the Lexus to within two feet of the truck, hopped out, and popped the trunk. He pulled on a pair of surgical gloves, unlatched the Iveco's door, and yanked up. A heavy musty smell filled his nostrils—musty more like wet socks than musty like a dead body, he thought, although he'd never smelled musty like a dead body before. Still, it was not the smell he'd read about.

The back of the truck opened like a yawning jaw, dark to the throat, with a tongue resting still and brown in the middle. Only the tongue was the box. Kent exhaled in relief.

He pulled a crowbar from his trunk and jumped into the truck. The coffin had been screwed shut, making the prying-open part of the plan a little noisy, but within three minutes the lid lay at an angle, daring him to topple it off.

The sensations that struck next had not been well rehearsed. In fact, not planned at all. Kent had his hand under the lid, ready to flip it casually off, when it occurred to him that he was about to stare into the face of the fish. But it wasn't a fish at all. It was a dead body. He froze. And he wasn't going to just *stare,* but he was going to touch and lift and hoist that cold, gray flesh around. A chill cooled his neck.

A few seconds tripped by in silence. He should get the plastic first.

Kent jumped from the truck and grabbed a roll of black plastic from the car's trunk. He climbed back into the truck and stood over the coffin. *Now or never, buddy. Just do it.*

He did it. He kicked the lid off and stared into the coffin.

Tom Brinkley lay gray and slightly swollen with a hole the size of a fist in his gut. His hair was blond, and his eyes were open. For a full five seconds Kent could not move. It was those two eyes staring at him like marbles—glinting with life in the moonlight, but dead. Then the scent wafted past his nostrils. Faint, oh, so very faint but reaching right through to his bones, and his stomach was not responding so happily.

By the looks of it, Tom Brinkley's stomach had not responded so happily, either. It appeared as though he'd used a bazooka to end his life, judging by the size of that hole. His message to the funeral home flashed through his mind. *Not a problem. Will pick up as is.* Now he was staring at *"as is,"* and it *was* a problem.

Kent spun away and grabbed the metal shelving. Goodness, this was not in the plan. *It's just a body, for heaven's sake! A dead thing, like a fish, with a big hole in its stomach. Get on with it!*

And what if he couldn't get on with it? What if he simply did not have the stomach to slump this body around? He stared at the gloves on his hands; they would shield him from any lingering disease. Any danger he imagined was only in his mind. Right?

The thought forced Kent into a state of bumbling overdrive. He grabbed a lungful of air, whirled back to the body, reached into the coffin, and yanked Mr. Brinkley clean out in one smooth motion.

Or so he'd intended.

Problem was, this cadaver had lain dormant for a good forty-eight hours and was not so eager to change its position. They call it rigor-mortis, and the dead man had found it already.

Kent had not aimed his hands as he dived into the casket; he'd just grabbed, and his fingers had closed around a shoulder and a side of ribs, both cold and moist. The body came halfway vertical before slipping from Kent's grip. Mr. Brinkley turned lazily and landed on the edge of the coffin. His stiff upper torso slipped clean out and landed on the truck's floor boards with a loud, skull-crushing thud. Now the body slumped over the casket, belly down and butt up in the moonlight with its hands hanging out of the rear as though paying homage to the moon.

Kent swallowed the bile creeping up his throat and leapt from the truck, grunting in near panic. If there really was a God, he was making this awfully difficult. None of the books had made mention of the clammy, slippery skin. Had he known, he would have brought towels or something. Of course the books had not featured chapters on the preferred methods of lugging around dead bodies. Usually these things stayed peacefully on their tables or in their caskets.

Standing on the ground, he glanced up at the body in the back of the truck. It was gray in the dim light, like some kind of stone statue memorializing butts. Well, if he didn't get that butt into the trunk soon, there'd be a dozen cops shining their flashlights on that monument, asking silly questions. Questions like, *"What are you doing with Mr. Brinkley, Kent?"*

He turned gruffly to the job at hand, clamped his hands around each wrist, and pulled hard. The cadaver flopped out of the box and slid easily enough, like a stiff fish being dragged along the dock. He pulled it halfway out before bending under its midsection. The thought of that hole in Mr. Brinkley's stomach made him hesitate. He should have rolled the old guy in plastic.

The plastic! He'd left it by the coffin. Dumping the body into the Lexus without covering it would most definitely be one of those idiotic things Stupid Street criminals did. If they ever had an inkling to look, forensics experts would have a field day in there. Kent shoved the body back into the truck, snatched the plastic, and spread it quickly along the trunk floor, draping it over the edges. He bent back into the truck again for the wrists and yanked Mr. Brinkley's naked body out again.

In a single motion, refusing to consider what that hole might be doing to his shirt, Kent hoisted the cadaver onto his shoulder, turned sideways, and let Mr. Brinkley drop into the trunk. The body flipped on descent and landed with a loud thump, butt down. The head might have put a dent in the metal by that sound. But it was covered with plastic, so no blood would smear on the car itself. Besides, dead bodies don't bleed.

Sweat dripped from Kent's forehead and splattered onto the plastic. He glanced around, panting as much from disgust as from exertion. The night remained cool and still; the moaning of the distant highway filtered through his throbbing ears. But there were no sirens or helicopters or cop cars with floodlights or anything at all that looked threatening. Except that body lying exposed beside him, of course.

He quickly forced the head and feet into the trunk, careful not to allow contact with the exposed car. The legs squeaked and then popped on entry, and he wondered if that was joints or solid bones. Had to be joints—bones would never break so easily.

The eyes still stared out of Tom Brinkley's skull like two gray marbles. By the looks of it, his nose might have taken the brunt of that face plant in the truck. Kent yanked the black plastic over the body and shut the trunk.

Then there was the matter of the casket. Yes indeed, and he was prepared for that little problem. He pulled a blanket from the backseat, threw it over the car, retrieved the plywood coffin from the Iveco, and strapped it onto the top of his car with a single tie-down. Not to worry—it was not going far.

He quickly tidied the truck, closed the rear door one last time, and drove off, still guided by moonlight alone. He unloaded the casket into an abandoned storage bin, two down from where he'd parked the Lexus earlier. Whoever next braved the cubicle would find nothing more than a cheap plywood casket ditched by some vagrant long ago.

By the time Kent hit the freeway, it was almost 9 P.M.

By the time he made his first pass of the bank it was closer to ten.

He told himself he made the pass to make sure the lot lay vacant. But seeing the bank looming ahead as he made his way down the street, he began reconsidering the entire business, and by the time he reached the parking lot, his arms were experiencing some rigor mortis of their own. He simply could not turn the wheel.

The white moon bore down like a spotlight in the sky, peering steadily between passing black clouds. The bank towered dark against the sky. The streets were nearly vacant, but each car that did drive by seemed somehow intent on the Lexus. Kent imagined that it was because the car's tailpipe was dragging with Mr. Brinkley hiding like a lead weight back there. Or maybe he'd left a finger poking out of the trunk. He took a deep breath to calm himself. No, the tailpipe wasn't dragging or even sagging. And the finger-in-the-trunk thing was ridiculous. The lid would not have closed with anything so thick as a finger sticking out. Hair perhaps? Kent glanced in the side mirrors but saw no hair flapping in the wind.

"Get a grip, man!" he growled. "You're acting stupid!"

Kent drove three blocks past the bank before turning onto a side street to circle around. The objections were screaming now. Taking the truck—that had been nothing. Stealing the body—child's play. This, now *this* was where it all hit the fan. Only a complete imbecile would actually attempt this. Or someone who had nothing to live for anyway. Because attempting this might very well end in death. *You know that, Kent, don't you? You might die tonight. Like Spencer.*

His palms were slippery on the leather steering wheel, and he wondered if forensics could pick that up. He would have to wipe the sweat off the seat as well. He didn't want some ambitious rookie investigator concluding he'd arrived in a state of distress, leaking buckets of sweat all over the seats. Then again, he had lost his wife and child; he had reason to be distressed.

Kent approached the bank from the rear and rolled into his parking spot at the back corner by the alley. *Okay, boy. Just chill. We're just going to walk in there and take a quick look. You come here all the time at night. Nothing unusual yet. You haven't done anything wrong yet. Not much anyway.*

Kent took a deep breath, stepped from the car, briefcase in hand, and walked for the back entrance. His hand shook badly inserting the key. What if they had changed the lock? But they hadn't. It swung open easily to the sound of a quiet chirping. The alarm.

He stepped in and punched in the deactivation code. Now the alarm company knew that Kent Anthony had entered the building through the rear door at 10:05 P.M. Sunday night. No problem—that was part of this little charade. The rear offices were not monitored by video equipment like the rest of the bank; he was a free bird back here.

Kent walked through dark halls, stepping quickly by the light of glowing exit signs. He found his office exactly as he had left it, untouched and silent except for the *whir* of his computer. The exotic fish swam lazily; red power lights winked in the darkness; his high-back leather chair sat like a black shadow before the monitors. Kent's hands trembled at his sides.

Kent flipped the light on and squinted at the brightness. He set his briefcase on the desk and cracked his knuckles absently. By his estimation, he would need five hours in the building to pull this off. The first four hours would be relatively simple. Just walk into the advanced processing system using ROOSTER, execute the little BANDIT program he'd been fine-tuning for the last three weeks, and walk away. But it was the walking away part that had his bones vibrating.

Kent made one last pass through the halls, satisfying himself as to their vacancy. And then it was suddenly now-or-never time, and he walked briskly back toward his office, knowing it had to be now.

It's okay, boy. You haven't done nothin' yet. Not yet.

He withdrew a disk from his briefcase, inserted it into the floppy drive, took one last long pull of air, and began punching at the keyboard. Menus sprang to life and then disappeared, one after the other, a slide show of reds and blues and yellows. He located ROOSTER and executed it without pausing. Then he was into AFPS, through ROOSTER's hidden link, like a ghost able to do anything at will without the mortals knowing.

He'd already determined his will. His will was to confiscate twenty million dollars. And stealing twenty million dollars all came down to a few keystrokes now.

He stared at the familiar screen of programming code for a long minute, his quivering fingertips brushing lightly on the keys, his heart pounding in his ears.

It's okay, boy. You haven't done . . .

Yeah, well, I'm about to.

He entered the command line: RUN a:\BANDIT.

Then do it. Just do it.

He swallowed and depressed the ENTER key. The floppy drive engaged, the hard drive spun up, the screen went blank for a few seconds, and Kent held his breath.

A string of numbers popped up, center screen, and began spinning by like a gas pump meter gone berserk. The search was on. Kent leaned back and folded his hands, his eyes lost to the blur of numbers.

The program's execution was simple, really. It would systematically scan the massive electronic web of banking and identify accounts in which charges had been levied for interbank ATM use. Example: Sally, a Norwest bank customer, uses her cash card at a Wells Fargo cash machine and is charged $1.20 for the use of Wells Fargo's ATM. The fee is automatically taken from her account. Sally gets her statement, sees the charge, and adds it to the line that reads "Service Charges" on her reconciliation form. Case closed. Does Sally question the charge? Not unless Sally is a kook. BANDIT would search for one hundred million such transactions, add twenty cents to the fee charged by the host bank, and then neatly skim that twenty cents off for deposit into a labyrinth of accounts Kent had already established. In Sally's case, neither Norwest nor Wells Fargo would be short in their own reconciliation. They would receive and be charged precisely what they expected: $1.20. It would be Sally who was out twenty cents, because her statement would show a service charge not of $1.20 but of $1.40. The additional twenty cents she paid would be unwittingly donated to Kent's accounts while the balance of $1.20 happily made its way to Wells Fargo. No one would be the wiser.

But say Sally *is* a kook. Say she calls the bank and reports the mistake: a $1.40 charge instead of the customary $1.20 rate advertised in the bank's brochures. The bank runs a query. BANDIT immediately identifies the query, dispatches a gunman to Sally's house, and puts a slug in her head.

Kent blinked. The numbers on the screen continued to spin in a blur.

Okay, not quite. BANDIT would just return Sally her precious hard-earned twenty cents. But it was here, in the method Kent had devised to return Sally her money, that his real brilliance shone. You see, BANDIT would not just return the money lackadaisically and apologize for the blunder. Too many blunders would raise brows, and Kent wanted to keep those eyebrows down. Instead, BANDIT acted like a self-erasing virus, one that detected the query into Sally's account, and did its dirty deed of returning the twenty cents immediately, before the query returned the details of Sally's account to the operator's screen. By the time the banker had Sally's latest bank statement on the screen, it would show that the customary bank charges of $1.20 had been levied. The computer would then spit out a comment about an internal self-correcting error, and that would be that. In reality, there would undoubtedly be some deeper probes, but they would find nothing. The transactions would be executed through the back door and their trails neatly erased, thanks to AFPS. Of course, the safeguard was AFPS itself—those who entered AFPS normally left their prints at every keystroke.

Normally. But not with ROOSTER.

Either way, it really did not matter. The last hour of this operation would neutralize everything. Meanwhile, he had a body rotting in his trunk. Kent let the computer spin while he chewed his fingernails and paced the carpet. He might have shed a full gallon of sweat in those first three hours, he did not know—he hadn't brought a milk jug along to catch it all. But it did a fine job of soaking his shirt clean through.

It took three hours and forty-three minutes for the program to find its intended victims. The clock on Kent's office wall read 1:48 when the program finally asked him if he wished to get it on—transfer this insanely huge amount of money into his accounts and enter a life on the run from the long arms of the United States justice system. Well, not in so many words. There was actually only one word on the screen: TRANSFER? Y/N. But he knew what the program was really asking by that simple word, because he had written that word.

His hand hovered over the Y that would actually alter the accounts and transfer the money into his own—a process he'd calculated to take roughly thirty minutes. He pressed it, conscious of the small click in the key. The words vanished to black, replaced by a single word blinking on and off: PROCESSING.

Kent backed from the desk and let the computer do its deed. *Yes indeed, BANDIT, rob them blind.* His heart beat at twice its customary pace, refusing to calm. And he still had that clammy body to deal with.

Kent crept out to the Lexus, glancing around nervously for the slightest sign of an intruder. Which struck him as ironic because *he* was the intruder here. He popped the trunk and quickly peeled the plastic away from Mr. Brinkley's body. He had to be quick now. It wouldn't do to have a passerby seeing him hauling a flopping body from the trunk. Backing the car into the alley would have been easier, but it also would have left tire tracks that didn't belong. One of those Stupid Street moves.

The cadaver stared up at the moon with its wide, gray eyes, and Kent shuddered. He reached in, swallowing hard, wrapped both arms around the cold torso, and yanked. The body came out like a bloated sack of grain, and Kent staggered under its weight. The head bounced off the rear bumper and came within an inch of leaving a slab of skin on the asphalt, which would have been a problem.

Move it, man! Move it!

Kent hoisted the body and flipped it into the crooks of his arms as he turned. The trunk would have to remain open for the moment. He staggered down the alley, wheezing like ancient bellows now, fighting to keep the contents of his stomach where they belonged. If he'd eaten more over the last day, it might have come up then while he staggered down the alley, eyes half closed to avoid seeing what lay across his arms. Mr. Brinkley bounced naked and gray. Butt up.

The cadaver nearly fell from his grasp once, but he recovered with a lifted knee. He lost his firm grip on the body, however, and had to run the last few yards before the fish slipped all the way out of his arms.

The rear door proved another challenge altogether. Kent stood there, bent over, straining against the dead weight, knowing that if this thing fell it would leave evidence. Dead body evidence.

Problem was, his hands were trembling in their task of keeping Mr. Brinkley from landing on his toes, and the door was closed. He would have to get the body onto his shoulder—free up a hand.

"Oh, man!" He was whispering audibly now. "Oh man, oh man!" The words echoed ghostly down the alley.

It took him three panicked attempts to heave the naked body up by his head, and by the time he finally managed to snake a shoulder under it, his breathing was chasing those words. The body's flesh felt soft on his shoulder, and visions of that hole in the cadaver's gut filled his mind. But Mr. Brinkley's spare tire was sucking up to his right ear, and the realization put him into gear.

Kent opened the door and staggered through, fighting chills of horror. The thought that he'd have to wipe that door handle managed to plant itself firmly in his mind. He had dead flesh on his hands.

He ran for his office with the body bouncing on his shoulder. Groans accompanied each breath now, but then who was listening?

He heaved the body from its precarious perch the second he lurched through his office door. It fell to the gray carpet with a sickening dead-body thump. Kent winced and pushed the door shut. His face still twisted with disgust, he paced back and forth in front of the body, trying to gather himself.

To his right, the computer screen still winked through its dirty deed.

PROCESSING, PROCESSING, PROCESSING . . .

He needed fresh air. Kent ran from the bank and walked back to the car, thankful for the cool air against his drenched shirt.

He removed a green-and-red cardboard box, which had only two weeks ear-lier held twelve bottles of tequila, from his rear seat and carefully cleaned out the trunk. Satisfied that the Lexus carried no physical evidence of the body, he stuffed the plastic into the box and walked to a tangle of pipes and knobs poking from the concrete halfway down the alley. The smallest of these controlled the bank's sprinkler system. He twisted a valve and shut it down.

From the tequila box Kent removed a pair of running shoes and replaced his own loafers with them. A few stomps down the alley insured they would leave a print. Evidence. He wiped the rear door handle carefully and reentered the bank.

The body lay face up, naked and pasty when he stepped into his office. He shivered. The computer screen still flashed its word: PROCESSING, PROCESSING . . .

Kent stripped off his clothes, until he stood naked except the running shoes. He started to dress Mr. Brinkley but quickly decided that he could not tolerate being naked in the same room with a naked dead man. Granted, he would put up with whatever it took to do this deed, but bending naked over a dead naked body was not in the plan. He would dress first. He snatched a pair of loose jeans and a white T-shirt from the green-and-red box and pulled them on. Then he turned back to the body.

Dressing a dead body proved to be a task best done with a vengeance—any-thing less had him cursing. The body's stiffness helped, but the dead weight did not. He forced his white boxers over Mr. Brinkley's midsection first, holding his breath for most of the operation. Relieved, he struggled with the slacks, rolling the body around, and tugging as best he could. He had the shirt nearly over the cadaver's chest when a blip sounded at the computer.

Kent snapped his head up. TASK COMPLETE, the screen read. $20,000,000.00 TRANSFERRED.

A tremble seized his bones. He returned to the body, tearing about it now. His watch went on the wrist, his socks and shoes on the feet.

Satisfied, he withdrew his floppy disk from the drive and exited the program. A fleeting thought skipped through his head. The thought that he had just trans-ferred twenty million dollars into his personal accounts successfully. The thought that he was a very rich man. Goodness!

But the overpowering need to flee undetected shoved the thought from his mind. He emptied half the contents from his briefcase into the tequila box. The incriminating half. What remained in the briefcase represented the work of a dedicated programmer including a personal reminder to speak to Borst Monday morning about efficiency issues. Yes sir, show them he fully expected to return to work on Monday, the morning after a casual fishing trip and a late night at the office.

Kent yanked the cadaver, now fully dressed in his clothes, to a standing position so that it leaned against his chair like some kind of wax museum piece. Here rigor mortis was his friend. He had buttoned the shirt wrong, he saw, and the slacks were hitched up high on one side. Mr. Brinkley looked like some kind of computer nerd short the pocket protector. But none of this mattered.

The corpse stared wide eyed at the poster of the white yacht. Now that Kent thought about it, he should have closed those bug eyes like they did when someone died on television.

He backed to the door, surveyed his work, and pulled the nine-millimeter semiautomatic Uncle Jerry had given him from the box. *Okay boy, now you're gonna do this.* He lifted the pistol. Once he pulled the trigger, he would have to fly. No telling how far the report might travel.

But Mr. Brinkley was having none of it. At least not yet. He suddenly slipped to the side and toppled to the floor, stiff as a board.

Kent cursed and bounded over to the body. He jerked Mr. Brinkley upright and planted him in place. "Stay put, you old fish," he mumbled through gritted teeth. "You're dying standing up, whether you like it or not."

He crouched and squinted. The gun suddenly bucked in his hand. *Bang!* The report almost knocked him from his feet. Panicked, he fired twice more, quickly, into the body—*Bang! Bang!* The body stood tall, still staring dumbly forward, oblivious to the bullets that had just torn through its flesh.

Kent swallowed and tossed the weapon back into the box. Shaking badly now, he staggered forward and yanked a two-gallon can from the box. He gave Mr. Brinkley a nudge and let him topple to the floor. He emptied the flammable mixture onto the body and then doused the surrounding carpet. He scanned the office, picked up the box, and backed to the door.

It occurred to Kent, just before he tossed the match, that he was about to go off the deep end here. Right off into some abyss, spread-eagle. He struck the match and let it flare. What on Earth was he about to do? He was about to put the finishing touches on the perfect crime, that's what he was about to do. He was about to kill Kent Anthony. He was about to join Gloria and Spencer in the ground, six feet under. At least that was the plan, and it was a brilliant plan.

Kent backed into the hall and tossed the match.

Whoomp!

The initial ignition knocked him clear across the hall and onto his seat. He scrambled to his feet and stared, unbelieving, at the blaze. A wall of orange flames reached for the ceiling, crackling and spewing black smoke. Fire engulfed the entire office. Mr. Brinkley's body lay like a log, flaming with the rest, like Shadrach or Meshack in the fiery furnace. The accelerant mixture worked as advertised. This cadaver was going to burn. Burn, baby, burn.

Then Kent fled the bank. He burst through the back door, tequila box in hand, heart slamming. His Lexus sat parked around the corner to his left. He ran to his right. He would not need the car again. Ever.

He'd run three blocks straight down the back alleys before he heard the first siren. He slowed by a trash bin, palmed the gun, and ditched the box. Behind him a cloud of smoke billowed into the night sky. He had known the old wood-frame building would go up, but he had not expected the fire to grow so quickly.

Kent looked back four blocks later, eyes peeled and unblinking. This time an orange glow lit the sky. A small smile of wonder crossed his face. Sirens wailed on the night air.

Five minutes later he entered the bus depot on Harmon and Wilson, produced a key to locker 234, and withdrew an old, brown briefcase. The case held eleven thousand dollars in twenty-dollar bills—traveling expenses—a bus ticket, a stick of deodorant, a toothbrush with some toothpaste, and a passport under his new name. It was all he owned now.

This and a few dozen accounts holding twenty million dollars.

Then Kent walked out into the street and disappeared into the night.

29

Helen brought two glasses of ice tea into her living room and handed one to Pastor Madison. Returning to her own home was the one small blessing in this latest turn in events. No need to stay at Kent's if he was gone.

"Thank you, Helen. So . . ."

"So," she repeated.

"So they've concluded the fire resulted from a freak robbery attempt. You read this story?" he asked, lifting the *Denver Post* in one hand.

"Yes, I saw that."

The pastor continued anyway. "They say evidence from the scene clearly shows a second party—presumably a robber. Evidently this guy found the rear door open and entered the bank, hoping for some easy cash. Unfortunately, Kent was there, 'working late on a Sunday night, not unusual for Kent Anthony. The thirty-six-year-old programmer was well known for working odd hours, often into the early hours of the morning.'"

"Hmmm," Helen offered.

"It says that the investigators speculate that the robber stumbled into Kent, panicked, and shot him dead. He then returned and torched the place—probably in an effort to erase evidence of his presence. He's still at large, and the search continues. The FBI has no current suspects. No actual robbery was committed . . . They estimate the fire damage to reach three million dollars, a fraction of what it could have been, thanks to the rapid response of the fire department." He lowered the paper and sipped at his tea.

"And of course, we know the rest, because it's just about the funeral."

Helen did not respond. There was not much to say anymore. Things had dropped off her plateau of understanding. She was guided by the unknown now. By the kind of faith she had never dreamed possible.

"What's happening to his belongings?" Bill asked.

"His will leaves it all to Gloria and Spencer. I suppose the state will get it now—I don't know and quite frankly, I don't care. From what I've seen, there's no use for this stuff in the next life anyway."

He nodded and sipped again. For a while they sat in silence.

"I have to tell you, Helen. This is almost too much for me."

"I know. It seems difficult, doesn't it?"

Bill cocked his head, and she knew he was letting his frustration get the better of him. "No, Helen. This does not *seem* difficult. Not everything is about *seeming* this way or that way. This *is* difficult, okay?" He shifted uncomfortably. "I mean, first Kent's wife dies of a freak disease, and that was unfortunate. I understand these things happen. But then his son is killed in a freak accident. And now we've hardly put away the funeral garb, and *he's* murdered in some freak robbery attempt. Strange enough? No, not quite. Meanwhile you, the mother, the grandmother, the mother-in-law, are walking around—quite literally—talking about some game in heaven. Some master plan beyond normal human comprehension. To what end? They're all dead! Your family is all dead, Helen!"

"Things are not always what . . ."

". . . what they seem," Bill finished. "I know. You've told me that a hundred times. But some things *are* what they seem! Gloria *seems* quite dead, and guess what? She *is* dead!"

"No need to patronize me, young man." Helen smiled gently. "And in reality, she's more alive now than dead, so even there you are less right than wrong. In practical terms, you might be right, but the kingdom of heaven is not what most humans would call practical. Quite the opposite. You ever read the teachings of Christ? 'If a man asks for your tunic, give him your cloak as well.' You ever do that, Bill? 'If your eye causes you to sin, pluck it out.' You see anybody smash their television lately, Bill? 'Anyone who does not take up his cross'—that's death, Bill—'and follow me is not worthy of me . . . Let the dead bury the dead.' And it was God speaking those words, as a guideline by which to live life."

"Well, I'm not talking about the teachings of Christ here. I'm talking about people dying without apparent reason."

Helen searched him deep with her eyes, feeling empathy and not knowing really why. He was a good man. He simply had not yet seen what was to be seen. "Well, I *am* talking about the teachings of Christ, Bill, which, whether you like it or not, include death. His own death. The death of the martyrs. The death of those on whose blood the church is built."

She looked away, and suddenly a hundred images from her own past crashed through her mind. She swallowed. "The reason you look for is here, Pastor." She waved her hand slowly through the air. "All around us. We just don't often see it clearly, and when we do, it is not often as we think it should appear. We're so bent on stuffing ourselves full of life—full of *happiness*—that we lose sight of God. Make up our own."

"God is a God of joy and peace and happiness," he offered.

"Yes. But the Teacher did not have in mind sitcoms that make you laugh or happy sermons about what a breeze the narrow road really is. Heavens, no. What is pure, Bill? Or excellent or admirable? The death of a million people in the Flood? God evidently thought so. He is incapable of acts that are not admirable, and it was he who brought about the Flood. How about the slaying of children in Jericho? There are few Bible stories that are not as terrible as they are happy. We just prefer to leave out the terrible part, but that only makes the good anemic." She turned from him and gazed at the picture of Christ in crucifixion.

"We are encouraged to *participate* in the sufferings of Christ, not to pretend they were feel-happy times. 'Take this in remembrance of me; this is my blood, this is my body,' he said. Not, find yourselves an Easter bunny and hunt for chocolate eggs in remembrance of me. We are told to *meditate* on Scripture, even the half that details the consequence of evil, the conquest of Jericho and all. Not to pretend our God has somehow changed since the time of Christ. Obviously, Paul's idea of admirable and noble is quite different from ours. God forgive us, Bill. We have mocked his victory by whitewashing the enemy for the sake of our neighbor's approval."

He blinked and drew a deep breath. "Imagine me talking like that from the pulpit. It would scare the breath out of most of them." He lowered his head, but his jaw was clenched, she saw. Suddenly those images from her past were crashing through her mind again, and she closed her eyes briefly. She should tell him, she thought.

"Let me tell you a story, Bill. A story about a man of God unlike any I have known. A soldier. He was my soldier." Now the emotions flooded her with a vengeance, and she noted her hands were trembling. "He was from Serbia, you know, before he came to the States. Fought in the war there with a small team of special forces. He served under a lieutenant, a *horrible* man." She shuddered as she said it. "A God hater who slept with the devil."

She had to stop for a few moments. The memories came too fast, with too much intensity, and she breathed a prayer. *Father, forgive me.* She glanced up at the red bottle in her hutch, sitting, calling from the past. From the corner of her eye she saw that Bill was staring at her.

"Anyway, they walked into a small town one day. The commander led them straight to the church at the center. The soldier said that he knew with one look into the lieutenant's eyes that he had come with cruel intentions. It was a gross understatement."

She swallowed and plowed on before this thing got the best of her. "The commander had them gather the townspeople, about a hundred of them, I think, and then he began his games." Helen looked up at the cross again. "The priest was a God-fearing man. For hours the commander played his game—bent upon forcing the priest to renounce Christ before the townsfolk. The horror of those hours was so reprehensible that I can hardly speak of them, Bill. To hear of them I would weep for hours."

Tears slipped from Helen's eyes and fell to her lap.

"The soldier was appalled by what he saw. He tried in vain to stop the lieutenant—almost lost his own life. But in the end the priest died. He died a martyr for the love of Christ. There is a monument to him in the town now. It is a cross rising from a green lawn bearing the inscription, 'No Greater Love Has Any Man.' The day after the priest's death, they collected some of his blood and sealed it into several small crystal bottles, so they would not forget."

She stood and walked to the hutch. She'd told no one other than her daughter of this, but it was time, wasn't it? Yes, it was time she spread this seed. Her breathing was coming thick as she pulled open the glass doors. She placed her fingers around the small bottle and pulled it out. The container was only slightly larger than her hand.

Helen returned to her seat and sat slowly, her mind swirling with the images. "The soldier went back to the village the next day to beg for their forgiveness. They gave him one of the bottles filled with the martyr's blood." Helen held the bottle out on her palm. "Never to worship or to idolize, they told him. But to remind him of the price paid for his soul."

It was not the whole story, of course. If the pastor knew the whole story he would be slobbering on the floor in a pool of his own tears, she thought. Because the whole story was as much her story as the soldier's, and it stretched the very limits of love. Perhaps one day she would tell him.

"The experience profoundly changed his life," she said, looking at Bill. His eyes were misty, staring at the floor. "And ultimately it changed my life, and Gloria's and Spencer's and even yours and countless others. And now Kent's, possibly. But you see, it all began with death. The death of Christ, the death of the priest. Without these I would not be here today. Nor would you, Pastor. It is how I see the world now."

"Yes." He nodded, gathering himself. "You do see more than most of us."

"I see only a little more than you, and most of that by faith. You think I wear the face of God?"

He blinked, obviously unsure if he was meant to answer.

"You see me walking around, disturbed, worried, with a furrowed brow. You think it's the face of God? Of course not! He is furious at sin, no doubt. And his heart aches over the rejection of his love. But above it all he rolls with laughter, beside himself with joy. I see only the hem of his garment and then only at times. The rest comes by faith. We may have different giftings, but we all have the same faith. Give or take. We are not so different, Pastor."

He stared at her. "I've never heard you say those things."

"Then maybe I should have spoken sooner. Forgive me. I can be a bit mule-headed, you know."

He smiled at her. "Don't worry, Helen. If you're a mule, may God smite our church with a thousand mules." They chuckled.

For several minutes they just sat there and thought in silence. Their glasses clinked with ice now and then, but the gravity of the moment seemed to want its own space, so they let it be. Helen hummed a few bars of "Jesus, Lover of My Soul" and stared out to the field beyond her house. Autumn would come someday. What would walking be like then?

"Are you still walking?" Bill asked the question as if it had been the real reason for his visit and he was just now getting around to it.

"Yes. Yes I am."

"The full distance?"

"Yes."

"But how? I thought you were walking and praying for Kent's soul?"

"Well, that's the problem. That's where things don't seem to be what they seem. I'm still walking because I've felt no urge not to walk and because my legs still walk without tiring and because I still want to pray for Kent."

"Kent is dead, Helen."

"Yes. So it seems. But the heavens are not playing along. I walked that first day after the fire, seeking release. It was to be expected, I thought. But I found no release."

She glanced at him and saw that he'd tilted his head, unbelieving.

"And then there's the dream. Someone's still running through my head at night. I still hear his breathing, the soft pounding of feet through the tunnel. The drama is still unfolding, Pastor."

Bill gave her a small, sympathetic smile. "Come on, Helen. I talked to the lead investigator myself two days ago. He told me very specifically that the coroner clearly identified the body as belonging to Kent Anthony. Same height, same weight, same teeth, same everything. FBI's records confirmed it. That body we buried three days ago belonged to Kent. Maybe he needs help in some afterlife, but he is no longer of this earth."

"They did an autopsy, then?"

"An autopsy of what? Of charred bones?"

"DNA?"

"Come on, Helen. You can't actually believe . . . Look, I know this is hard on you. It's been a terrible tragedy. But don't you think this is going a little too far?"

Her eyes bore into his with an unmoving stare. "This has nothing to do with tragedy, young man. Am I or am I not walking eight hours a day without tiring?"

He didn't answer.

"Is it some illusion, this walking of mine? Tell me."

"Of course it's no illusion. But—"

"Of course? You sound pretty sure about that. Why is God making my legs move like this, Pastor? Is it that he has discovered a new way to make the tiny humans below move? 'Hey look, Gabriel, we can just wind them up and make them walk around forever.' No? Then why?"

"Helen . . ."

"I'm telling you, Pastor, this is not over. And I mean, not just in the heavens, but on Earth it's not over. And since Kent was the main object of this whole thing, no, I don't think he is necessarily dead."

She turned away from him. Goodness, listen to her. It was sounding absurd. She had peeked in the coffin herself and seen the blackened bones. "And if you think it makes sense to me, you are wrong. I'm not even saying he *is* necessarily alive. It is just easier to believe he's alive, given the fact that I'm still praying long days for him." She turned back to him. "Does that make sense?"

Bill Madison took a deep breath and leaned back in his chair. "Well, Helen." He shook his head. "I guess so."

They sat in silence for a few minutes, staring off in different directions, lost in thought. His voice broke the stillness.

"It's very strange, Helen. It's otherworldly. Your faith is unnerving. You're giving your life to impossibilities."

She looked up and saw that his eyes were closed. A lump rose in her throat. "It's all I have, Bill. It's all anybody really has. It's all Noah had, building his impossible little boat while they mocked him. It's all Moses had, holding his rod over the Red Sea. It's all Hosea had and Samson and Paul and Stephen and every other character of every other Bible story. Why should it be so different for us today?"

She saw his Adam's apple bob. He nodded. "Yes, I think you're right. And I fear my faith is not so strong."

He was beginning to see, she thought. Which meant his faith was stronger than he realized. It could use a nudge. She'd read somewhere that eagles would never fly if their mothers did not push them from their nests when they were ready. Even then they would free-fall in a panic before spreading their wings and finding flight.

Yes, maybe it was time the pastor got a little shove.

"Would you like to see more than you've seen, Bill?"

"See what?"

"See the other side. See what lies behind what you see now."

He stiffened a little. "What do you mean, *see?* It's not like I can just flip on a light and see—"

"It is a simple question, Bill, really. Do you want to see?"

"Yes."

"And you would be willing to let go a little?"

"I think so. Although I'm not sure how you let go of something you can't see."

"You forget about how important you are, put aside your narrow field of vision; you open your heart to one thing only. To God, in whichever way he chooses to reveal himself, regardless of how it might seem to you. You let go."

He smiled nervously. "Sounds a bit risky, actually. You can't just throw out all doctrine for some experience."

"And what if that experience is God, the creator? What is more important to you, an encounter with God or your doctrine?"

"Well, if you put it that way—"

"As opposed to which way?"

"You've made your point. And yes, I think I could let go a little."

She smiled slowly. "Then let's pray."

Helen watched him close his eyes and bow his head. She wondered how long the posture would hold. "Father in heaven," she prayed aloud and closed her own eyes, "if it would please you, open this child's eyes to see what you have called him to. May he have the power to see how wide and how deep and how high your love is for him."

She fell silent and closed her eyes to darkness. *Please Father, let him feel your presence. At least that, just a taste of you, God in heaven.*

An image of Kent filled her mind. He walked down a long, deserted street, aimless and lost. His hair was disheveled, and his eyes peered blue above dark circles. For a moment she thought it might be his spirit, like some kind of ghost wandering the streets of her mind. But then she saw that it was him, really him, bewildered by the vacancy of the street on which he walked. And he was lonely.

She forgot about the pastor for the moment. Maybe she should walk. Maybe she should just leave Bill and go for another walk—pray for Kent. Yes, at least that. Her heart swelled in her chest. *Oh God, save Kent's soul! Do not hide your face from this man you made. Open his heart to your spirit. Speak words of love to his ears, drop your fragrance in his mind, dance before his eyes, show him your splendor, wrap your arms around him, touch his cold skin with a warm touch, breathe life into his nostrils. You fashioned him, did you not? So now love him.*

But I have.

Helen dropped her head at the words and began to weep. *Oh God, I'm sorry. You have! You have loved him so much. Forgive me!*

She sat bunched in her chair for several long minutes, feeling waves of fire wash through her chest. It was a mixture of agony and desire—a common sentiment these days. The heart of God for Kent. Or at least a small piece of it. The piece he chose to reveal to her.

She suddenly remembered Bill and snapped her head up.

He sat on the green chair, head bent back like a duckling begging food. His Adam's apple stuck out prominently on his neck, his jaw lay open, his mouth gaped wide, his nostrils flared. And his body shook like a ragged old cloth doll. Something somewhere had been opened. His eyes, maybe.

Helen relaxed and leaned back into her cushions. A smile split her face wide. Now he would understand. Maybe not any details of Kent's plight, but the rest would come easier now. Faith would come easier.

Tears fell in streams down the pastor's cheeks, and she saw that his shirt was already wet. Looking at the grown man reduced to a heap of emotions made her want to scream full throated. It was that kind of joy. She wondered how it was that she had never had a heart attack. How could a mortal, like Bill there, all inside out, endure such ravaging emotion, busting up the heart, and not risk a coronary? She smiled at the thought.

On the contrary, his heart might very well be finding some youth. Her legs had, after all.

Helen began to rock gently. "Do you want to see, Bill?" she whispered.

30

Lacy Cartwright nibbled at her fingernail, knowing it was an unseemly habit and not caring. The truth be known, she had not cared for much during the last week. She glanced at the clock: 8:48. In twelve minutes the doors of Rocky Mountain Bank and Trust would open for customers.

Jeff Duncan caught her eye from across the lobby, and she smiled politely. Now, there was a man who was maybe more her type after all. Not so impulsive as Kent, but alive and well and here. Always here, not running in and out of her life every twelve years. Not pulling some impossible disappearing trick and expecting her to just get on with life. But that was just the problem—Lacy honestly didn't know if Kent had really disappeared or not. And what she did know was giving her waking fits.

Kent had come to her two nights before the big fire in Denver; that much she had not imagined. He had sat across from her and told her that he was going to do pretty much what happened. Or at least what *could* have happened. But reading the papers, what happened was not what *could* have happened at all. In fact, what happened, according to the papers, was precisely what Kent had said would happen. A robbery attempt, a death, and most important, his disappearance. He had neglected to mention that it would be *his* death, of course, but then she doubted he'd planned that much.

Then again, what actually happened was anybody's guess, and she found herself guessing that something else entirely had happened. Maybe Kent had not been surprised by some wandering robber that night, because maybe Kent himself *was* the robber; he'd suggested as much himself. So then what seemed to have happened must not have happened at all. Which was downright confusing when she thought too much about the matter.

Either way, he had left her again. Maybe this time for good. Well, good riddance.

There was one way to determine if that charred body in the Denver bank fire belonged to Kent Anthony or to some other poor soul everyone *thought* was Kent Anthony. If Kent had actually pulled off this incredible theft of which he'd spoken, he had done it brilliantly, because as of yet, no one even suspected there *had* been a theft. On the other hand, no one knew to look, much less *where* to look. All eyes were on the fire damage and the search for a loose murderer, but no one had mentioned the possibility that a robbery *had* actually occurred. And no wonder—nothing had been taken. At least not that they knew.

But she, Lacy Cartwright, might know differently. And if she did discover that Kent was alive and well and extremely wealthy—would she be compelled to tell the authorities? It was the question that had kept her tossing at night. Yes, she thought so. She would have to turn him in.

If he was indeed alive and if he had left even the slightest of trails, she would find it on the computer screen before her, in some log of ATM transaction fees. Fortunately or unfortunately, depending on the hour, eight days of looking had shown her nothing. And slowly, her anger at him rose to a boil.

"Morning, Lacy."

Lacy started and jerked her head up. Jeff smiled broadly at her reaction. "Strung a bit tight this morning, are we?"

She ignored him.

He chuckled. "I guess. Well, welcome back to the land of the living."

The comment momentarily thrust Lacy back into the land of the dead. "Yeah," she responded politely, shifting her eyes from him. Maybe that was the problem here, she thought. Maybe this land of the living here in the bank with all the customers and meaningless talk and overstuffed maroon sitting chairs was more like death, and the land that Kent had trotted off to was more like life. In a way she was a bit jealous, if indeed he was not actually in hell but roaming the earth somewhere.

Jeff leaned on the counter. "You coming to Martha's party this weekend? It might be a good thing, considering the fact that all the top brass will be in attendance."

She pulled herself back to this reality. "And this should bring me to my knees? When is it?" Actually she had no plans to attend the affair and knew precisely when it was, but Jeff was the kind of guy who liked giving out information. It made him feel important, she guessed.

"Friday at seven. And yes, you might consider paying a little homage."

"To them or to you?"

He smiled coyly. "But of course, I'll be there as well. And I'd be disappointed if you were not."

She smiled kindly. "Well, we'll see." Maybe it would be a good idea, after all. Get her mind off this Kent madness. "I'm not crazy about parties doused in alcohol." She studied his face for reaction.

"And neither am I," he said without missing a beat. "But, like I said, the brass will be there. Think of it as a career move. Reaching out to those who determine your future. Something like that. And of course, an opportunity to see me." He winked.

Lacy stared at him, surprised by his boldness.

Jeff shifted awkwardly. "I'm sorry, I didn't mean to be so—"

"No. It's okay. I'm flattered." She recovered quickly and smiled.

"You sure?"

"Yes, I'm sure."

"Well, I'll take that as a sign of promise."

She nodded, unable to answer for the moment.

Evidently satisfied that he'd accomplished his intentions in the little exchange, Jeff stepped back. "I have to get back to work. Mary Blackley is waiting anxiously for my call, and you know Mary. If it's one penny off, she's ready to declare war." He chuckled. "I swear, the old lady does nothing but wait by her mailbox for her statement. I can't remember a month when she hasn't called, and I can't remember a single complaint that has borne true."

Lacy pictured the elderly, hook-nosed lady wobbling through the doors, leaning on her cane. She smiled. "Yeah, I know what you mean. What is it this time? A missing comma?"

"Some ATM fee. Evidently, we're robbing her blind." Jeff laughed and retreated across the floor.

The heat started at the base of Lacy's spine and flashed up through her skull as if she'd inadvertently hit a nerve. *Some ATM fee?* She watched Jeff clack along the lobby floor. The clock above his head on the far wall read 8:58. Two minutes.

Lacy dived for her keyboard, hoping absently that no one noticed her eagerness. She ran a quick search for Mary Blackley's account number, found it, and keyed it in. She ran a query on all service charges. The screen blinked to black, seemed to hesitate, and then popped up with a string of numbers. Mary Blackley's account. She scrolled quickly down to the service charges levied. She lifted a trembling finger to the screen and followed the charges . . . six ATM transactions . . . each one with a fee of $1.20. A dollar-twenty. As it should be. Mary Blackley was chasing ghosts again. Unless . . .

She straightened and ran a search on the first transaction fee. According to the record that popped up, Mary had used her card at a Diamond Shamrock convenience store and withdrawn forty dollars on August 21, 1999, at 8:04 P.M. The servicing bank, Connecticut Mutual, had charged her $1.20 for the privilege of using its system.

So then, what could have prompted Mary to call?

Lacy backed out of the account quickly and walked across the lobby to Jeff's cubicle. He was bent over the keyboard when she stuck her head in and smiled.

"Lacy!" He made no attempt to hide his pleasure at seeing her materialize in his doorway.

"Hi, Jeff. Just walking by. So, you straighten Mary out?"

"Nothing to straighten out, actually. She was not overcharged at all."

"What was her problem?"

"Don't know. Printing mistake or something. She was actually right this time. Her statement did have the wrong fee on it—$1.40 instead of $1.20." He lifted a fax from his desk. "But the statement in the computer shows the correct fee, so whatever happened didn't really happen at all. Like I said, a printer problem, maybe."

Lacy nodded, smiling, and turned away before he could see the blood drain from her face. A customer stepped through the doors, and she made her way back to the tellers' windows, stunned and lost and breathing too hard.

She knew what had happened then with a dreadful certainty. Kent had done that! The little weasel had found a way to take Mary's twenty cents and then put it back as he had said he would. And he had done it without tipping his hand.

But that was impossible—so maybe that was not what had happened at all.

Lacy returned to her station and lifted the closed sign from her window. The first customer had to address her twice before she acknowledged.

"Oh, I'm sorry. What can I do for you today?"

The older woman smiled. "No problem. I know the feeling. I would like to cash this check." She slid a check for $6.48 made out to Francine Bowls across the counter. Lacy punched it in on autopilot.

"God, help me," she muttered aloud. She glanced at Mrs. Bowls and saw her raised eyebrow.

"Sorry," she said.

Mrs. Bowls smiled.

Lacy did not.

31

One Month Later
Wednesday

Kent sat on the edge of the lounge chair, staring at the Caribbean sunrise, his stomach in knots over what he was about to do.

He rested his hands on the keyboard and lifted his chin to the early morning breeze. The sweet smell of salt swept past his nostrils; a tall tumbler filled with clear liquor sparkled atop a silver platter beside the laptop. The world was his. Or at the very least this small corner of the world was.

From his perch on the villa's deck, Kent could see half of the island. Luxurious villas graced the hills on either side like white play blocks shoved into the rock. Far below, sun-bleached sand sloped into emerald seas that slapped gently at low tide. The ocean extended to a cloudless, deep-blue horizon, crystal clear in the rising sun. The Turks and Caicos Islands rose from the Caribbean Sea like brown rabbits on the blue ocean, a fitting likeness, considering the number of inhabitants there who were on the run. Whether fleeing taxes or the authorities or just plain life, there were few destinations better suited to a man on the lam.

But none of this mattered at the moment. All that mattered now was that some satellites had graced him with a clear connection. After all these weeks of lying low, he was rising from the dead to wreak just a little havoc in the lives of those two fools who'd taken him for a sucker not so long ago. Yes indeed. This was all that mattered for the moment.

Kent lowered his eyes to the laptop's screen and ran his fingers over the keys, taking the time to consider. It was a commodity he had plenty of these days. Time.

He'd paid $1.2 million cash for the villa four days earlier. How the builders had managed to erect the house in the first place remained a mystery, but nothing short of a monster sledge hammer swung from heaven would knock this small fortress from its moorings. On either side, tall palms bustled with a dozen chirping birds. He turned back to the living area. Large flagstones led to an indoor dipping pool beside the dining area. With the flip of a single switch the entire front wall could be lowered or raised, offering either privacy or exposure to the stunning scenery below. The previous owners had constructed a dozen such villas, each extravagant in its own way. He'd never met them, of course, but the broker had assured Kent that they were of the highest caliber. Arabs with oil money. They had moved on to bigger and better toys.

Which was fine by him—the villa offered more amenities than he imagined possible in a four-thousand-square-foot package. And it now belonged to him. Every stick of wood. Every brick. Every last thread of carpet. Under a different name, of course.

Kent took a deep breath. "Okay, baby. Let's see what our two porky friends are doing." He began what he called phase two of the plan, executing a series of commands that took him first into a secure site and then to Niponbank's handle. He then entered a request that took him directly into a single computer sitting idle, asleep in the dark corner of its home, as well it should be at 4 A.M. mountain time. Borst and company had moved to a different wing of the bank following the fire, but Kent had found him easily enough. Beginning within the week of the theft, he had made breaking in to both Borst's and big-boss Bentley's computers a regular routine.

There was always the off chance that someone intelligent was at one of the two computers at 4 A.M.—someone with the capability to detect the break-in in real time—but Kent lost no sleep over the possibility. For starters, he'd never known Borst to work past 6 P.M., much less in the wee morning hours. And if he would be in there, poking around his computer at four in the morning, Porky was not so stuffed with intelligence as he was with other things. Such as pure, unadulterated drivel.

Kent entered Borst's computer through a backdoor and pulled the manager's hard drive up on his screen. The directory filled his screen in vivid color. Kent chuckled and sat back, enjoying the moment. He was literally inside the man's office without the other having a clue, and he rather liked the view.

He lifted a crystal glass from the table and sipped at the tequila sunrise he'd mixed himself. A small shudder ran through his bones. A full thirty days had passed since his night of terror in the bank, lugging that ridiculous body around.

And so far every detail of his plan had fallen into place as planned. The realization still made regular passes through his mind with stunning incredulity. To say that he had pulled it off would be a rather ridiculous understatement.

Kent removed his eyes from Borst's directory and looked out at the emerald seas far below. So far he was batting a thousand, but the minute he touched these keys a whole new set of risks would raise their ugly little heads. It was why his gut still coiled in knots while he presented himself to the seascape as a man in utter tranquillity. An odd mixture of emotions to be sure. Fully pleased at himself and thoroughly anxious at once.

The events of the days leading up to this one slipped through his mind. No need to be overzealous here—he still had time to abort phase two.

He'd escaped Denver easily enough, and the bus trip to Mexico City had flown by like a surrealistic scene on the silver screen. Yet once in the massive city, a certain deadening euphoria had taken to his nerves. He'd rented a room in an obscure dump some enterprising soul had the stomach to call a hotel and immediately set about finding the plastic surgeon he'd made contact with a month earlier. Dr. Emilio Vasquez.

The surgeon readily took a thick wad of money and set about giving Kent a new look. The fact that Kent's "new look" should have required four operations instead of the one did not deter Vasquez in the least. It was, after all, his trademark—doing to a man's face in one operation what took most plastic surgeons three months. It was also why Kent had chosen the man. He simply did not have three months. The rest of his plan was begging for its execution.

Four days after the big fire Kent had his new look, hidden under a heavy mask of white gauze, but there, Dr. Vasquez promised him. Definitely there. The twinkle in the surgeon's eyes had worried him. It was the first time he'd considered the possibility that he might spend the rest of his life looking like something out of a horror comic. But done was done. He'd sequestered himself in the hotel room, willing the cuts beneath the facial bandages to heal. It was a time that both stretched his patience and settled his nerves at once.

Kent lifted the chrome platter from the table and stared at his reflection. His tanned face looked like a Kevin, he thought. Kevin Stillman, his new assumed name. The nose was fuller, but it was the jaw line and brow work that changed his face so that he hardly recognized his own reflection. The plastic surgeon had done an exceptional job—although the first time Dr. Vasquez had removed the bandages and proudly shoved a mirror to his face he'd nearly panicked. Then, the red lines around his nose and cheekbones brought to mind frightening images of Frankenstein. Oh, he looked different, all right. But then, so did a skinned plum. He started to drink heavily that night. Tequila, of course, lots of it, but never enough to knock him silly. That would be stupid, and he was over being stupid.

Besides, too much liquor made the computer screen swim before his eyes, and he'd spent a lot of time staring at the laptop those first two weeks. Whereas ROOSTER allowed him undetected access into the banking system, it was that second program, the one called BANDIT, that had actually done the deed. When he had inserted his little disk into the drive that night at the bank and executed his theft, he'd left a little gift in each target account from which he'd taken twenty cents. And by all accounts the program had executed itself flawlessly. Indeed, BANDIT worked on the same principles as a stealth virus, executing commands to hide itself at the first sign of penetration. But that was not all it did. In the event the account was even so much as queried, it would first transfer twenty cents from one of Kent's holding accounts back into the target account, and then it would immediately remove itself permanently. The entire operation took exactly one and a half seconds and was over by the time the account-information screen popped to life on the operator's monitor. In the end it meant that any queried account would show erroneous charges on printed statements but not in the accounts themselves.

Kent's little virus executed itself on 220,345 accounts in the first two weeks, refunding a total of $44,069 dollars during that time. The virus would lay dormant in the rest of the accounts, waiting until September 2000 to be opened. They would obediently delete themselves if not activated within fourteen months.

It took two full weeks before he felt comfortable enough to make his first trip to the bank in Mexico City. The lines on his face were still visible, but after applying a pound of makeup he succeeded in convincing himself that they were virtually undetectable. And he was at the point of driving himself crazy in the hotel room. It was either risk a few raised brows in the bank or hang himself with the bedsheets.

The banking official at Banco de Mexico had indeed raised his brow when Kent visited under the name Matthew Brown. It was not the way Mr. Brown looked that had him jumping, it was the five-hundred-thousand-dollar cash withdrawal he'd executed. Of course the official had almost certainly reported the unusual amount—even banks that promise discretion keep a log of such transfers.

But Kent hardly cared. The maze of accounts through which the money had traveled over the last two weeks would require pure fortune to unravel. If any man were able to track the funds back to either Kent Anthony or the fire in Denver, they deserved to see him fry.

But that just wasn't going to happen.

That first five hundred thousand dollars brought a thrill to Kent's bones that he had not felt for months. He'd popped the latches of the black case he'd purchased for just this occasion and dumped the cash onto the moth-eaten bedspread in the hotel room. Then he'd stripped the piles of their rubber bands and physically rolled through them, tossing the bills into the air and letting them float lazily to the floor while pumping his fists and hooting in victory. It was a wonder the neighbors did not come pounding on his door. Possibly because there were no neighbors foolish enough to pay five hundred pesos a night to sleep in the miserable dump. He touched every bill, he thought, counting and recounting them all in a hundred different configurations. Of course he'd had little else to do then besides monitor the computer—that was his reasoning. Then he'd discarded his reasoning and celebrated by drinking himself into a two-day stupor.

It was his first alcoholic binge.

He started his well-rehearsed withdrawal plan then, flying first to Jakarta, then to Cairo, then to Geneva, then to Hong Kong, and finally here, to the Turks and Caicos Islands. At each stop he'd traveled under false identification papers, withdrawn large sums of money, and departed quickly. After each visit to a bank he'd taken the liberty of waltzing into its system using ROOSTER and isolating the links to the closed account. Bottom line, even if the local banking officials wanted to know more about the strange man who'd emptied their daily cash reserves with his massive withdrawal, they would find nothing.

He'd arrived a week ago in the islands packing just over six million dollars. All of it in cash, every last dollar untraceable. He'd become Kevin Stillman then and bought the villa. Fourteen million dollars, give or take, still waited around the world, gathering interest.

Yes indeed, to say that he'd pulled it off might very well be the century's greatest understatement. He had *rocked!* A dead man had ripped off twenty million bucks right under the nose of the almighty United States banking system, and not a soul suspected it was even gone!

That had been phase one.

Phase two had started one week after the fire, two days after Kent had received his new face. And it was phase two that was responsible for these raging emotions of insecurity now charging in to disturb the peace.

Maybe he should have been satisfied to take the $20 million minus the $44,069 and call it even. But in reality the thought hardly even occurred to him. This was not simply a matter of his getting what was coming to him; it was also a matter of Borst and Bentley getting what was coming to *them*. Some would call it revenge. Kent thought of it as justice. Putting things back the way they were meant to be. Or at least one version of how they were meant to be.

It was why he had planted a copy of ROOSTER on both Borst's and Bentley's hard drives several nights before executing the theft. And it was why he had made that first visit to their computers one week after the fire.

They already had routine access to AFPS, of course, and now they had untraceable access as well without knowing it. Only it was Kent in there doing the accessing, using their computers from remote stations. And the stuff he was accessing was not the stuff he was supposed to be accessing. Or rather it was not the kind of stuff *they* should be accessing. Naughty, naughty.

Over the course of three weeks, Kent had helped them steal money on seven different occasions. Small amounts of money—between three and five hundred dollars per whack—just enough to establish a trail. That was his little contribution to their burgeoning wallets, although to look at their private balances they certainly needed no help from him. Their contributions had been to keep the money. So far anyway. Whether because they were exceedingly greedy or because they simply did not know, Kent neither knew nor cared.

He considered all of this, set his drink back on the silver tray, and pressed his fingers together contemplatively. It had gone so smoothly that it would slip through the most sensitive digestive system unnoticed.

So then why the jitters?

Because everything up to this point had been a warmup of sorts. And now the computer sat on his table, wanting him to push the final buttons.

Kent grunted and wiped the sweat from his palms. "Well, we didn't come all this way to weasel out in the end, did we?" Of course not. Although it would certainly not hurt. And it would certainly be the wisest course, all things considered. It would . . .

"Shut up!" he snarled at himself.

Kent leaned forward and worked quickly now. He brought up ROOSTER from Borst's hard drive and then entered AFPS. He was into the bank's records.

Now the excitement of the moment brought a quiver to his bones. He brought up Borst's personal account and scanned the dozens of transactions recorded over the last few weeks. All seven deposits accommodated by him were still present. Thank heaven for small favors! He grinned and scanned down.

There were a few other deposits there as well. Large deposits. Deposits that made Kent squint. The bank was obviously paying him for AFPS. Nothing else could possibly account for a two-hundred-thousand-dollar balance.

"Not so fast, Fat-Boy," Kent muttered.

He selected *all* of the deposits with a single click of the mouse, ten in all including his own, and removed them from Borst's account to a holding account he'd built into ROOSTER. The account balance immediately dropped to an overdrawn status. Overdrawn by the $31,223 in checks Borst had written this month. He was spending his hard-earned money quickly. Well, this would give him pause.

And *this . . . will give you a hernia!*

Kent broke into the bank's primary accounting system, selected the primary bank reserves, and transferred five hundred thousand dollars to Borst's account. Using ROOSTER of course. He didn't want the authorities to know what had happened to the money. Not yet.

He posted a flag on the federal account and retreated to Borst's account. In the morning some lucky operator at Niponbank's headquarters in Japan would bring his computer up to find a nasty flag announcing the overnight disappearance of a half-million dollars from the bank's main account. Bells would clang, horns would blow, nostrils would flare. But nobody would discover the fate of the money, because it was as of yet unfindable. That was the beauty of ROOSTER.

Kent squirmed in his chair. Borst's account now showed a very healthy balance of over four hundred thousand dollars. He stared at the figure and considered leaving it. The ultimate carrot for Mr. Borst. Go ahead. Spend it, baby.

He discarded the notion. A plan was a plan. Instead he transferred the money to the same hidden account he'd set up for the other deposits, returning Borst's account to an overdrawn status. The man was going to wake up to the shock of his life.

Kent smirked, exceedingly happy for the moment.

He retreated from Borst's account and ventured into Bentley's. There he repeated the same steps, placing all of the bank president's money into another hidden account prepared for the occasion.

The porky twins were now very, very broke.

It was time to get out. Kent pulled out of the system, broke his connection, and sat back in the lounger. Sweat ran down his chest in small rivulets, and his hands were shaking.

"See how it feels, you greedy pigs," he sneered. And then he lifted his glass and threw back the remaining liquor.

Yes indeed. It was all going exactly as planned. And to this point, not a soul knew a thing.

Except Lacy, possibly. He'd said a bit much to her that night.

Or possibly that pinhead cop.

The emotion hit him then, full force, as if a lead weight had been neatly aimed from heaven and dropped on the half-naked man lounging on the deck so smugly down there. It felt as though a hole had been punched through his chest. A vacancy. The gnawing fear that it had all gone too smoothly. That in the end this dream facing him in the eyes would not be a dream at all but some kind of nightmare dressed up in sheep's clothing. That trying to live now, surrounded by his millions but without Gloria or Spencer . . . or Lacy . . .

He shook his head to clear the thought. On the other hand, there was no evidence at all that Lacy or the cop knew anything. And someday soon, perhaps, there would be another Gloria or another Lacy. Maybe. And another Spencer.

No, never another Spencer.

Kent rose, snatched the glass, and strode for the kitchen. It was time for another drink.

32

Two thousand miles northwest that same evening Lacy Cartwright stood over her stove struggling to flip the massive omelet she'd concocted in the shallow frying pan. She had no idea how she was going to eat the beast, but its aroma was staging a full assault on her senses, and she swallowed her saliva.

Her mind drifted back to the party Jeff Duncan had insisted she attend. The affair had been far too telling. She'd left after an hour of the foolishness and had to fend off a dozen questions the next workday. In the end she had succumbed to a little white lie. She had gotten sick. Which was, after all, true in heart-matters. Because she was still sick over this whole robbery issue. She knew he had done it—knew it like she knew the weasel was sitting on some beach somewhere, soaking up the rays.

She ground her teeth, turned off the stove, and flopped the eight-inch egg patty on a plate. If the idiot was still alive, off living with his millions, she hated him for it. If he was dead, having attempted such a fool thing, she hated him even more. How could anybody be so insensitive?

Lacy sat at the dinette and forked her omelet. She had decided a week ago that she should go to the authorities, even though she had promised not to tell. Give the little information that she had to the lead investigator. *"Hey, FBI man, you ever consider that maybe it was Kent Anthony who was the real robber?"* That would set them on a new track. Problem was, she could not be absolutely certain, which relieved her of any obligation, she thought. So she might very well tell them, but if she did, she would take her time.

Meanwhile, she had to get back to a normal life. The last time she remembered feeling in any way similar to this was after Kent had severed their relationship the first time. For a week she had walked around with a hollow gut, trying to ignore the lump in her throat and furious all at once. This time it was going on three weeks, and that lump kept wanting to lodge itself in her windpipe.

She had loved him, Lacy thought, and lowered her lifted fork. She had actually fallen in love with the man. In fact, to get right down and honest about the matter, she had been crazy about him. Which was impossible because she really hated him.

"Oh, God, help me," she muttered, rising and crossing to the ice box. "I'm losing my mind."

She returned to her seat with a quart of milk and drank straight from the carton. Impossible habit, but seeing as there was no one to offend at the moment, she carried on anyway. Now if Kent were here—

Lacy slammed the carton on the table in a sudden fit of frustration. Milk cleared the spout a full six inches before splashing to the table. Good grief! Enough with this Kent foolishness!

She jabbed at the omelet and stuffed a piece in her mouth, chewing deliberately. For that matter, enough with men, period. Lock 'em all in a bank somewhere and burn the whole thing to the ground. Now, that might be a bit harsh really, but then maybe not.

What in the world would Kent do with twenty million dollars? The sudden chirp of the doorbell startled her. Who could be visiting her tonight? Not so long ago it might have been Kent. Heavens.

Stop it, Lacy. Just stop it!

She walked for the door and pulled it open. A dark-haired man with slicked-back hair and wire-framed spectacles stood there, grinning widely. His eyes were very green.

"May I help you?"

He flipped a card out of his breast pocket. "Jeremy Lawson, seventh precinct," he said. "Do you mind if I ask you a few questions?"

A cop? "Sure," she muttered, and stepped aside.

The middle-aged man walked in and looked around the apartment, offering no reason for his being there.

Lacy shut the door. Something about the cop's appearance suggested familiarity, but she could not place him. "How can I help you?"

"Lacy, right? Lacy Cartwright?"

"Yes. Why?"

"I just want to make sure that I have the right person before I fire away, you know." He was sill wearing the wide grin.

"Sure. Is there a problem?"

"Oh, I don't know really. I'm doing a little looking into a fire down in Denver. You hear about that blaze that burned down a bank about a month ago?"

Whether or not it showed Lacy did not know, but she felt as though her head swelled red at the question. "Yes. Yes, I did read about that. And what does it have to do with me?"

"Nothing, maybe. We're just talking to people who might have known the gentleman who was killed in the fire. Do you mind if we sit, Miss Cartwright?"

Kent! He was investigating Kent's death! "Sure." She motioned to the sofa and took a seat in the armchair opposite. What was she to say?

Now that she looked at him carefully she saw why Kent had referred to him as a pinhead. His head seemed to slope to a point covered neatly in black shiny hair.

"Just a few questions, and I'll be out of your hair," the cop said, that smile stubbornly stuck on his face. He pulled out a small notebook and flipped it open. "I understand that you knew Kent Anthony. You spent some time with him in his last few weeks. Is that right?"

"And how did you discover this?"

"Well, I can't very well spill my trade secrets, now, can I?"

Lacy settled in her chair, wondering desperately what he knew. "Yes, I saw him a few times."

"Did his death surprise you?"

She scrunched her eyebrows, "No, I was expecting it. Of course it surprised me! Am I a suspect in the case?"

"No. No, you're not."

"So what kind of question is that? How could I not be surprised by his death unless I somehow knew about it in advance?"

"You may have expected it, Lacy. Can I call you Lacy? He was depressed, right? He'd lost his wife and his son in the months preceding the fire. I'm just asking you if he seemed suicidal. Is that so offensive?"

She breathed deeply. *Calm down, Lacy. Just calm down.* "At times, yes, he was upset. As would be anyone who'd suffered as much as he had. Have you ever lost a wife or a son, detective . . ." She glanced at his card again. "Lawson?"

"I can't say that I have. So you think he was capable of suicide, then? Is that your position?"

"Did I say that? I don't remember saying that. I said that at times he was upset. Please don't turn my words around."

The cop seemed thoroughly undeterred. "Upset enough to commit suicide?"

"No, I wouldn't say that. Not the last time I saw him."

He lowered his voice a notch. "Hmmm. And did you know about his little difficulties at work?"

"What difficulties?"

"Well, if you knew, you would know what difficulties, now, wouldn't you?"

"Oh, you mean the bit about his boss betraying him while he was mourning the death of his wife? You mean that tiny speck of trouble?"

The cop studied her eyes for a moment. "So you did know."

She was matching him tit for tat without really knowing why. She had no reason to defend Kent. He'd dumped her, after all. Now, if Lawson came right out and asked certain questions, she didn't know what she would say. She couldn't very well lie. On the other hand, she had promised Kent her silence.

"You knew him well, Lacy. In your opinion—and I'm just asking your opinion here, so there's no need to jump up and down—do you think he was capable of suicide?"

"Do you suspect he committed suicide? I thought they concluded that a robber had murdered him."

"Yes. That's the official line. And I'm not saying it's wrong. I'm just doing my best to make sure everything fits. You know what I mean?"

"Sure."

"So then, yes or no?"

"Suicide?"

He nodded.

"Capable, yes. Did he commit suicide? No."

The cop lifted an eyebrow. "No?"

"He was a proud man, Detective Lawson. I think it would take the hand of God to bring him to his knees. Short of that, I don't think he was capable of giving up on anything, much less his life."

"I see. And from what I've heard, I would have to agree with you. Which is why I'm still on the case, see?" He stopped as if that should make everything crystal clear.

"No, actually I don't see. Not in the least."

"Well, if it were a suicide there would be no need for further investigation. Suicide might be an ugly thing, but it's usually an open-and-shut case."

She smiled despite herself. "Of course. And being murdered causes guys like you a lot more work."

He smiled. "If he was murdered there would be no need to investigate *him*. We'd be looking for the murderer, wouldn't we?"

"Then it seems to me that you're barking up the wrong tree, Detective Lawson."

"Unless, of course, your friend Kent was not murdered. Now, if he did not commit suicide and he was not murdered, then what are we left with?"

"A dead body?" Mercy, where was he headed?

Lawson shoved his little notebook back into his pocket, having written maybe two letters on the open page. "A dead body! Very good. We'll make a detective out of you yet." He stood abruptly and headed for the door. "Well, I thank you for your time, Miss Cartwright. You've answered my questions most graciously."

He was hardly making sense now, she thought. She stood with him and followed him to the door. "Sure," she muttered. What did he know? Every bone in her body screamed to ask the question. *Did you know we were in love, Officer? Did you know that?* No, not that!

He had his hand on the door before she spoke, unable to restrain herself.

"Do *you* think he's dead, Detective?"

He turned and looked her in the eyes. For a long moment they held eye contact. "We have a body, Miss Cartwright. It is burned beyond recognition, but the records show that what is left belongs to Mr. Kent Anthony. Does that sound dead to you? Seems clear enough." He flashed a grin. "On the other hand, not everything is what it seems."

"So why all the questions?"

"Never mind the questions, child. We detective types practice long and hard at asking confusing questions. It throws people off." He smiled warmly, and she thought he was sincere. She returned the smile.

He dipped his head. "Good evening, Mrs. Cartwright."

"Good night," she returned.

He turned to leave and then hesitated, turning back. "Oh, one last question,

Lacy. Kent never mentioned any plans he had, did he? Say some elaborate plan to fake his death or any such thing?"

She nearly fell over at the question. This time she knew he saw her turning red under the gills. He could hardly miss it.

And then he simply flipped a hand to the air. "Never mind. Silly question. I've bothered you enough tonight. Well, thank you for your hospitality. Coffee might have been nice—we detectives always like coffee—but otherwise you did just fine. Good night."

With that he turned and pulled the door closed behind him.

Lacy sidestepped to the chair and sat hard, heat sweeping over her. Lawson was on to him! The detective was on to Kent! He had to be! Which meant that Kent was alive!

Maybe.

༄

Kent drove his new black Jeep down the hill to the town at seven, just as the orange sun sank behind the waves. The sound of calypso drums and laughter carried on the warm breeze. Brent the real-estate broker had recommended the Sea Breeze. "The finest dining south of Miami," he'd said with a twinkle in his eye. "A bit draining on the wallet but well worth it." Kent could use a little draining on his wallet. It was feeling a tad heavy.

He mounted the wooden steps and bounded up the flight. A fountain gurgled red water from a mermaid's lips just inside the door. Like some goddess drunk on the blood of sailors. He turned to the dim interior. Through a causeway a fully stocked bar already served a dozen patrons perched on tall stools. Mahogany stairs wound to the upper level to his right.

"Welcome to the Sea Breeze, sir. Do you have reservations?"

Kent faced the hostess. Her black hair lay long on bare shoulders. She smiled carefully below dark eyes, and an obscure image of red water spewing from *those* round lips slinked though his mind. Miss Mermaid in the flesh. Her nametag read "Marie."

"No. I'm sorry, I didn't realize that I needed reservations."

"Yes. Maybe you could return tomorrow night."

Tomorrow? Negative, Black Eyes. "I'd rather eat tonight, if you wouldn't mind," Kent returned.

Marie blinked at that. "I'm sorry, maybe you didn't understand. You need a reservation. We are full tonight."

"Yes, evidently. How much will a table cost me?"

"Like I said, sir, we don't—"

"A thousand?" Kent lifted his eyebrow and pulled out his wallet. "I'm sure that for a thousand dollars you could find me a table, Marie. In fact for a thousand dollars you could possibly find me the best table in the house. Am I right? It would be our secret." He smiled and watched her black eyes widen. He felt the subtle power of wealth run through his veins. In that moment he knew that for the right price, Miss Mermaid Marie here would lick the soles of his sandals.

She glanced around and smiled. Her breathing had quickened by the rise and fall of her chest. "Yes. Actually we might have an opening. I apologize, I had no idea. This way."

Marie led him up two flights of stairs to a glass-enclosed porch atop the restaurant. Three tables rounded out the room, each delicately laid with candles and flowers and crystal and silver. The musty scent of potpourri hung in the air. A party of well-groomed patrons sat around one of the tables, drinking wine and nibbling at what looked to be some sea creature's tentacles. They looked at him with interest as Marie sat him across the circular room.

"Thank you," Kent said, smiling. "I'll add it to your tip."

She winked. "You are kind, Mr. . . . ."

"Kevin."

"Thank you, Kevin. Is there anything else I can do for you at this time?"

"Not at the moment, Marie, no. Thank you."

She turned with a twinkle in her eyes and left the room.

The two waitresses who served him had obviously been told of his generosity and were unabashed in their attempts to please. He ordered lobster and steak and wine, and they were delicious. As delicious as they had been three months earlier when he had ordered the same in celebration with Gloria at the completion of AFPS. He lifted his glass of wine and stared out at the dark seas, crested with moonlit waves. *Well, I did it, Honey. Every bit and more, and I wish you were here to enjoy it with me.*

It settled on him as he ate that the food, though quite good, did not taste any different than it had when he'd paid twelve dollars for it back at Red Lobster in Littleton. The Heinz 57 sauce certainly came from the same vat. In fact the wine probably came from the same winery. Like different gasoline stations selling branded gas that anyone with half a brain knew came from the same refinery.

Kent finished the meal slowly, intent on relishing each bite, and uncomfortably aware that each bite tasted just as it should. Like lobster and steak should. The wine went down warm and comforting. But when he was done he did not feel as though he'd just eaten a thousand dollars' worth of pleasure. No, he'd just filled up his tank.

In the end he tipped heavily, slipped Marie her thousand dollars, and retired to the bar, where tequila was more in order. Steve, the bartender, must have heard of his tipping, because he eased right on over and set up a glass.

"What'll it be, sir?"

"Cuervo Gold. Straight up."

Steve poured the liquor into the glass and started polishing another. "You passing through?"

"You could say that. I own a place up the hill, but yes, I'll be in and out."

The man stuck out his hand. "Name's Steve Barnes. It's good to have you on the island."

"Thanks. Kevin Stillman."

The man hung around and asked a few more questions to which Kent gave short, pert answers. Eventually Steve wandered off to the other customers, who were talking about how some tourist had fallen off a fishing boat and gotten entangled in a net. Kent smiled once, but beyond the hint of humor, he found himself odd man out, and the hole in his chest seemed to widen. Maybe if he pulled out a few hundred and waved it around them. *"Hey guys, I'm rich. Stinking rich. Yes indeed, you may come over and lick my toes if you wish. One at a time, please."*

By the time Kent pulled into his circle drive back at the villa, his mind was numbed by the alcohol. Which was a good thing, he thought. Because something inside his mind had started to hurt, watching those fools carry on down at the pub.

But there was tomorrow, and tomorrow would be a day of reckoning. Yes indeed. Never mind the fifteen hundred bucks he'd just tossed down for dinner. Never mind the foolishness of those still surrounding the bar, gabbing with Steve the bartender.

Kent fell onto the covers. Tomorrow night he would turn the screws.

Sleep came within the minute.

33

Thursday

Markus Borst ran through the bank, huffing and puffing and not caring who saw him in the state of terror that obviously shone from his face like some kind of shiny red Christmas bulb.

He was not accustomed to running, and it occurred to him halfway through the lobby that he must look like a choo-choo train with his short legs pumping from the hips and his arms churning in small circular motions. But the gravity of the situation shoved the thought from his mind before it had time to set up. A dozen eyes glared his way, and he ignored them. What if Price was not in his office? Heaven help him! Heaven *help* him!

He met Mary as he was charging around the corner leading to Price Bentley's office, and she jumped with a cry. "Oh!" A sheet of paper fluttered from her grasp, and she bolted back. "Mr. Borst!"

"Not now!" he said. He rushed past her and slammed through the bank-branch president's door without bothering to knock. There was a time to knock and there was a time not to knock, and this was the latter if there ever was a time for the latter.

Price Bentley sat behind his big cherrywood desk, his bald head shining red under the bright fluorescent tubes above. His eyes widened in shock, and he came halfway out of his seat before his thighs intersected the bottom edge of his desk, propelling him back into his black leather chair. He immediately grabbed his legs and winced.

Bentley cursed. "What in the blazes are you doing, Borst! *Man* that hurt!" He opened his eyes and blinked rapidly at Borst. "Close the door, you fool. And straighten out that thing on your head! You look ridiculous!"

Borst hardly heard him. He slammed the door shut instinctively. "The money's gone!"

"What? Lower your voice and sit down, Borst. Your wig is slipping, man. Fix it."

Borst jerked his hand up to his head and felt the toupee. It had fallen halfway down his right ear. An image of that choo-choo train pumping through the lobby with a hairpiece slipping down one cheek flashed through his mind. Perhaps he'd frightened Mary with it. A flush of embarrassment reddened his face. He yanked the thing off and stuffed it in his breast pocket.

"We have a problem," he said, still breathing hard.

"Fine. Why don't you run through the lobby tooting a horn while you're at it. Sit down and get ahold of yourself."

Borst sat on the edge of the overstuffed chair, facing Bentley.

"Now, start from the beginning."

The branch president was coming across as condescending, and Borst hated the tone. It was *he*, after all, who had brought this whole idea to Bentley in the first place. He'd never had the guts to shove some of the man's medicine back into his face, but sometimes he sure had the inkling.

"The money's gone." His voice trembled as he said it. "I went into my personal account a few minutes ago, and someone's wiped out all the deposits. I'm overdrawn thirty thousand dollars!"

"So there's been a mistake. No need to come apart at the seams over an accounting snafu."

"No, Price. I don't think you understand. This is not some simple—"

"Look, you fool. Mistakes happen all the time. I can't believe you come storming in here announcing your stupidity to the whole world just because someone put a decimal in the wrong place."

"I'm telling you, Price. This is not—"

"Don't tell me what it is!" Bentley stormed. "This is *my* bank, isn't it? Well, when it's your bank you can tell me what it is. And stop calling me Price. Show some respect, for Pete's sake!"

Borst felt the words slapping at his ears as if they had been launched from a blast furnace. Deep in his mind, where the man in him cowered, a switch was thrown, and he felt hot blood rush to his face.

"Shut up, Price! Just shut up and listen. You're an insolent, bean-brained hot-head, and you're not listening. So just shut up and listen!"

The president sat back, his eyes bulging like beetles. But he did not speak, possibly from shock at Borst's accusations.

"Now, whether you like it or not, regardless of whose bank this is or is not, we have a problem." Borst swallowed. Maybe he had gone too far with that attack. He shrank back a tad and continued.

"There is no *simple* accounting mistake. I've already run the queries. The money is not misplaced. It's gone. All of it. Including the small deposits. The ones—"

"I know which ones. And you ever talk to me like that again, and we're finished." The president stared at him unblinking. "I can do to you what we did to Anthony with a few phone calls. You'd best remember that."

Borst's ears burned at the insinuation, but the man was right. And there was nothing he could do about it. "I apologize. I was out of line."

Evidently satisfied that Borst was properly chastised, Bentley turned to his terminal and punched a few keys. He squinted at the screen for a moment and then went very still. A line of sweat broke from his brow, and his breathing seemed to thicken.

"You see," Borst said, "it's just gone."

The president swallowed deliberately. "This is not your account, you fool. It's mine. And it's overdrawn too."

"See!" Borst slid to the front of his chair. "Now, what's the chance of that? Both of our accounts wiped out! Someone found the deposits and is setting us up!"

"Nonsense!" Bentley swiveled back to Borst, dropped his head, and gripped his temples. He stood and paced to the window, rubbing his jaw.

"What do you think?"

"Shut up. Let me think. I told you that keeping those small deposits was a bad idea."

"And who says we've kept them? It's been less than a month. They were put there without our knowing; we were going to report them, right? That wouldn't warrant *this*," Borst said.

"You're right. And you ran a full query, right? There's no trace of where it went?"

"None. I'm telling you, someone took it!"

Bentley sat down, hard. His fingers flew across the keyboard. Menus popped to life and disappeared, replaced by others.

"You won't find anything. I've already looked," Borst said.

"Yeah, well now *I'm* looking," Bentley snapped back, undeterred.

"Sure. But I'm telling you, there's something wrong here. And you know we can't just report it. If there's an investigation, they'll find the other money. It won't look right, Price."

"I told you not to call me Price."

"Come on! We're each a few hundred thousand dollars upside down here, and you're bickering over what I call you?"

Bentley had finished his queries. "You're right. It's gone." He slammed his big fist on the desk. "That's impossible! How's that possible, huh? You tell me, Mr. Computer Wizard. How does someone just walk into an account and wipe it out?"

A buzz erupted at the base of Borst's skull. "You would need a pretty powerful program." He stiffened in his chair. "AFPS could do it, maybe."

"AFPS? AFPS would leave a trail as wide as I-70."

"Not necessarily. Not if you know the raw code."

"What are you saying?"

"I'm not sure. I'm not even sure how it could be done. But if there were a way, it would be through the alteration of the code itself."

"Yeah, well that's not good news, Borst. And do you know why that's not good news? I'll tell you why. Because you, my dear friend, are in charge of that code! You're the brilliant one who pieced this thing together, right? Now either you stole from yourself, and from me, or someone else is using your program to rob you blind."

"Don't be ridiculous! Those monkeys in there wouldn't have the stomach much less the experience to do anything like this. And I certainly did not mess with my own account."

"Well, somebody did. And you'd better find that somebody, or it won't go nicely for you. Do you understand me?"

Borst looked up at the president, stunned by the suggestion. "Well, if it doesn't go nicely for me, you can bet it won't go nicely for you."

"And *that,* my dear, fine-feathered friend, is where you are wrong." Bentley jabbed his desk with his finger, making a small thumping sound each time it landed. "If this goes down, you'll take the fall, the whole fall, and nothing but the fall. And don't think for a minute I can't do it."

"We will deny it," Borst said, dismissing Bentley's threats.

"Deny what?"

"We deny that we know anything about our accounts at all. We ignore all of this and come unglued when the first sign of trouble crops up."

"And like you said, if they run an investigation we could have a hard time answering their questions."

"Yes, but at least it's only an *if.* You have a better suggestion?"

"Yes. I suggest you find this imbecile and put a bullet in his brain."

They stared at each other for a full thirty seconds, and slowly, very slowly, the magnitude of what they might be facing settled on both of them. The macho stuff vacated their minds, replaced by a dawning desperation. This was not a problem that would necessarily go away at the push of a button.

When Borst emerged from the room thirty minutes later, his head was bald and his face was white. But these issues were of little concern to him now. It was the pressure on his brain that had him swallowing repeatedly as he walked back to his office. And nothing, absolutely nothing, he could think of seemed to loosen the vise that now held his mind in its grip.

∽∾∾

Kent awoke midmorning and slogged out to the deck, nursing a bit of a headache. He squinted against the bright blue sky and rubbed his temples. The ocean's distant crashing carried on the wind, but otherwise silence hung heavily in the air. Not a voice, not a bird, not a motor, not a single sound of life. Then he heard the muted thud of a hammer landing on some new home's wood frame down the way. And with that thud the hole in Kent's chest opened once again. A sobering reminder that he was alone in the world.

He glanced at his watch, suddenly alert. Ten o'clock Friday morning. His lips twitched to a faint grin. By now Borst and Bentley would have discovered the little disappearing trick. Now you see it; now you don't. He imagined they'd be sweating all over their desks about now. What they didn't know was that the trick was just beginning. Act one. Strap yourselves in, ladies and gentlemen. This one will rock your socks. Or perhaps steal them right off your feet without your knowing the better.

He swallowed and thought about mixing himself a drink. Meanwhile, he was wealthy, of course. Must not forget that. How many people would give their children to have what he now had? An image of Spencer, riding his red skateboard, popped into his mind. Yes, a drink would be good.

Kent mixed himself a drink and meandered out to the deck. The soft sound of waves rushing the shore carried on the breeze. He had ten hours to burn before placing the phone call. He couldn't sit around drinking himself into a stupor this time. Not with that conversation coming on tonight. He would have to stay clear headed. Then perhaps he should clear his head out there on the waves.

An hour later Kent stood by the pier, gazing down the long row of boats, wondering how much they would bring. A small chill of excitement rippled through his gut.

"Whoa there, mate!" The voice spoke with an Australian accent.

Kent whirled to face an older seaman pushing a dolly stacked with provisions down the plank. "If you'll step aside, son, I'll be by quicker than a swordfish on a line." He grinned, splitting the bristly white hair that masked his face. Years of sun had turned the man's skin to leather, but if the shorts and tank top were any indicator, he wasn't too concerned.

"Sorry." Kent stepped aside to let the man pass and then followed him up the pier. "Excuse me."

"Hold your head, son," the man croaked without looking back. "I've got a bit of a load, as you can see. I'll be with you in a jiffy. Have yourself a beer."

Kent smiled and trailed the man to a large white boat near the end of the pier. *Marlin Mate.* She was a Roughwater, the little silver plaque on her bow said. Maybe fifty feet in length.

"This your boat?" Kent asked.

"You don't hear too well, do you? Hold your head, mate." The seaman hauled the dolly over the gangplank and into the cabin, grumbling under his breath. This time Kent lost his grin and wondered if the old man's head was out to sea. He could certainly use a little fine-tuning in the social-graces department.

"Now there," the man said, coming from the cabin. "That wasn't such a long wait, was it? Yes, this is my boat. What can I do for you?" The sailor's blue eyes sparkled with the sea.

"What does something like this go for?" Kent asked, looking her up and down.

"Much more than you would think. And I don't rent her out. If you want a day trip, Paulie has—"

"I'm not sure you're answering my question. It was quite simple, really. How much would a boat like this one cost me?"

The man hesitated, obviously distracted by the strong comeback. "What's it to you? You plan on buying her? Even if you could afford her, she's not for sale."

"And what makes you think I can't afford her?"

"She's pricey, mate. I've worked her for half my life, and I still hold a decent note on her." Leather Face smiled. He'd misplaced two of his front teeth. "You got five hundred thousand dollars hanging loose in your pocket there?"

"Five hundred, huh?" Kent studied the boat again. It looked almost new to him—if the Australian had owned it for as long as he let on, he'd cared for her well.

"She's not for sale."

Kent looked back to the old man, who had flattened his lips. "How much do you want for her? I pay cash."

The man looked at him steadily for a moment without answering, probably running through those little note balances in his mind.

"Five-fifty, then?" Kent pushed.

Leather Face's baby blues widened. For a long minute he did not speak. Then a smile spread his cracked face. "Seven hundred thousand U.S. dollars, and she's all yours, mate. If you're crazy enough to pay that kind of dough in cash, well, I guess I'll have to be crazy enough to sell her."

"I'll pay you seven hundred on one condition," Kent returned. "You agree to keep her for a year. Teach me the ropes and take care of her when I'm not around."

"I'm no steward, mate."

"And I'm not looking for a steward. You just let me tag along, learn a few things, and when I'm gone you run her all you like."

The old man studied him with piercing eyes now, judging the plausibility of the offer, Kent guessed. "You show me the cash, I'll show you the boat. If I like what I see and you like what you see, we got us a deal."

Kent was back an hour later, briefcase in hand. Leather Face—or Doug Oatridge as he called himself—liked what he saw. Kent just wanted to get out to sea, feel the breeze through his hair, drink a few beers, distract himself for a few hours. Kick back on the deck of his yacht while Borst and Bentley chewed their fingernails to the knuckles.

By midday they were trolling at twenty knots, precisely. A permanent smile had fixed itself on Doug's face as he feathered the murmuring engine through the sea-water. Thinking about the cash, no doubt. They sat on cushioned chairs, eating sandwiches and drinking ice-cold beer. The sun had dipped halfway when the first fish hit. Ten minutes later they hauled a four-foot tuna over the side and shoved it into the holding tank. What they would do with such a creature, Kent had no clue—maybe carve it up and fry it on the grill, although he'd never liked tuna. Give him swordfish or salmon, disguised with chicken broth, but keep the smelly stuff. Three more of the fish's cousins joined him in the tank over the next half-hour, then they stopped taking the bait. Doug was talking about how tuna ran in schools, but Kent was thinking the fish had just grown tired of the senseless self-sacrifice.

The perfect day's only damper came on the trip home, when Kent made the mistake of asking Doug how he'd come to own the boat in the first place. The old man had evidently both grown accustomed to Kent and loosened under the influence of a six-pack, and his story ran long. He'd been married twice, he said, first to Martha, who had left him for some basketball player on a beach court in Sidney. Then to Sally, who had borne them three sons and tired of them all after ten years. It was an inheritance of a hundred thousand dollars that had brought Doug to the islands with his sons, in search of a boat with which to begin life anew. He'd purchased *Marlin Mate* then. Two of his sons had left the island within the first year—off to America to find their own lives. The youngest, his little Bobby, had been swept overboard in a storm one year later.

The old man turned away and stared misty eyed to the sea, having dropped his tale like a lead weight into Kent's mind. The beer in Kent's hand suddenly felt heavy. The afternoon grew quiet beyond the splashing wake. Kent imagined a small boy cartwheeling off the deck, screaming for Daddy. A knot rose into his throat.

They docked the boat an hour later, and Kent showed as much interest as he could muster in the procedure. He shook the old man's hand. Did he want to go out tomorrow? No, not tomorrow. Could he take the boat out tomorrow then? Yes, of course. Do what you like, Doug. He thumped the man on the back and smiled. In fact, keep the stupid boat, he thought, but immediately reined in the absurd notion.

"Hey, me and the mates are going to do some drinking tonight. You want to come? There'll be dames."

"Dames?"

Doug flashed a toothless smile. "Girls, mate. Beach bunnies in their bikinis."

"Oh yes, of course. Dames. And where are we having this party?"

"Here on the boat. But not to worry, mate. The first man to puke gets thrown overboard."

Kent smiled. "Well, that's comforting. Maybe. We'll see."

34

Despite his need for a clear mind, Kent downed two stiff drinks before his eight o'clock phone call. It wouldn't do to have his teeth clattering against the receiver, either, and his nerves had tightened as the hour approached.

Darkness had settled over the island. From the villa's deck the sea looked black below, split by a long shaft of white cast by the bright moon. A spattering of lights twinkled along the hillside on either side. It was hard to imagine that across that sea the sun had already risen over a bustling city called Tokyo. He'd seen pictures of the tall, chrome building that housed Niponbank's headquarters, smack-dab in the middle of the busiest part of town, but he could hardly picture the crowded scene now. The serene one before him had lulled him into a foggy state. Or perhaps the drinks had done that.

A small bell chimed behind him, and Kent started. It was time.

He grabbed the cordless phone from the table and stared at its buttons. His heart pounded like a tom-tom in his ears. For the first time in over a month he was about to expose himself. And for what?

Kent cleared his throat and spoke with a gruff voice, the voice he had decided would be his to complete his disguise. "Hello, this is Bob." Too high. He'd done this a thousand times. "Hello, this is Bob."

Get on with it, man.

He punched the numbers in quickly.

An electronic voice answered his call. "Thank you for calling Niponbank. Please press one if you wish to be served in Japanese. Please press two if you wish to be served in English." *Please press three if you are calling to turn yourself in for grand larceny.*

Kent swallowed and pressed two.

It took all of ten minutes to find the right individual. A Mr. Hiroshito—the one banking executive Kent knew who could quickly get him to the real power mongers at the top. He knew Hiroshito because the high-level man had visited Denver once, and the bank had spent a day dancing around him like crows around fresh road kill.

"Hiroshito." The man said his name like it was an order to attack.

Chill, my friend. "Mr. Hiroshito, you don't know me, but you should. I'm—"

"I am sorry. You must have the wrong connection. I will put you through to the operator."

Kent spoke quickly before the man could pass him off. "Your bank is missing one million dollars, is it not?"

The phone filled with the soft hiss of distant static. Kent was not sure if the man had transferred him. "Hello."

"Who is this?"

"I am the person who can help you recover the million dollars that was missing from your ledgers yesterday. And please don't bother trying to trace this phone call—you will find it impossible. Do I have your attention?"

Hiroshito was whispering orders in Japanese behind a muted receiver. "Yes," he said. "Who is this? How do you know of this matter?"

"It is my business to know of such matters, sir. Now, I will lay this out for you as quickly and as plainly as possible. It would be best if you could record what I say. Do you have a recorder?"

"Yes. But I must know who you are. Surely you cannot expect—"

"If you choose to accept my terms, you will know me soon enough, Mr. Hiroshito. That I can promise you. Are you recording?"

A pause. "Yes."

Here goes nothing. Kent took a deep breath.

"Yesterday a million dollars was stolen from Niponbank's main ledger, but then, you know this already. What you don't know is how I know this. I know this because a certain party within your own bank, who shall remain nameless, tipped me off. This is relatively unimportant. What *is* important, however, is the fact that I managed to break into your system and verify the missing balance. I was also able to track the first leg of the outbound transaction. And I believe I will be able to uncover the theft in its entirety.

"Now, before you ask, let me tell you what you are going to ask. Who in the world am I to think I can track what the engineers in your own bank cannot track? I am a number: 24356758. Please write it down. It is where you will wire my fee if I successfully expose the thief and return your money. As I'm sure you can appreciate, I must protect my actual identity, but for the sake of convenience you may use a fictitious name. Say, Bob. You may call me Bob. From now on, I am Bob. I can assure you that Bob is quite proficient at electronic data manipulation. Without question one of the world's finest. You have not heard of him only because he has always insisted on working in complete anonymity. In fact, as you will see, he depends on it. But there is no man better suited to track down your money; that much I can assure you with absolute confidence. Do you understand thus far?"

Hiroshito did not expect the sudden question. "Y . . . yes."

"Good. Then here are Bob's terms. You will grant him unlimited access to any bank he deems necessary for his investigation. He will both return your money and uncover the means with which the perpetrator took your money. You obviously have a hole in your system, my fine friends. He will not only return your money; he will close that hole. If and only if he is successful, you will transfer a 25 percent recovery fee into the Cayman account I recited earlier: 24356758. You will wire the money within one hour of your own recovery. In addition, if he is successful, you will grant him immunity in connection with any charge related to this case. These are his terms. If you accept them, I can assure you he will recover your money. You have exactly twelve hours to make your decision. I will call you then for your decision. Do you understand?"

"Yes. And how is this possible? How can we be sure you are sincere, Mr. . . . uh . . . Bob?"

"You can't. And once you've had time to think about it, you'll see that it does not matter. If I am unsuccessful, you pay nothing. But you must ask yourself how I know what I know. No one knows the workings of electronic high finance like I do, Mr. Hiroshito. I am simply the best. Please take this message to your superiors immediately."

"And how do I know—?"

"You know enough already," Kent interrupted. "Play the tape for the main man. He'll agree to my terms. Good day."

Kent hung up to a stammering Hiroshito and exhaled slowly. His hands were trembling, and he pulled them into fists. Man, that had felt good! He took a long drink from his glass, slammed the tumbler onto the table, and pumped a fist in victory. "Yes!"

Of course it was not victory. Not yet. But it was the deed. It was the plan. The thrill of the hunt, as they say. Within the hour the whole snobby bunch of them would at least suspect that there existed a man who possessed the electronic wizardry to waltz into their systems and do what he willed. A lunatic who called himself Bob. Now *there* was power! Not just being able to *do* it, but being settled in the knowledge that others *believed* he could do it.

Kent made his way to the bathroom on shaky legs. In twelve hours he would have his answer. And if they said no? If they said no, he might very well go in there and take another million. Then call them back and ask them if they might reconsider. *Ha!*

Yes indeed. Now *there* was power!

∽⌒∽

Kent attended Doug's party on the *Marlin Mate* later that night for lack of appealing alternatives. Actually, the thought of standing on a swaying boat with twenty people held little appeal itself. Never mind that there would be "dames." Half-naked dames at that. Never mind that there would be booze. It was all sounding rather bleak now. But staying home alone drumming his fingers on the table held even less appeal, so he took the Jeep to the pier and boarded the swaying boat.

The Aussie knew how to party. It was perhaps the only skill he'd mastered aside from skippering. As promised, a dozen girls smelling of coconut oil slithered about the twin decks. At some point, Doug must have dropped the nugget that the blond-haired man sitting quietly on the upper deck was flush with cash, because the women began to mill about Kent with batting eyes and pouting lips.

For the first hour, Kent quite enjoyed the attention. It was sometime near midnight, however, that a thought dawned on him. He was not attracted to these bathing beauties. Maybe the booze had messed with his libido. Maybe the memory of Gloria was simply too fresh. Maybe the hole in his chest had sucked the life right out of him—neutered him. The realization fell over him like a wet blanket.

By the time he dragged himself back up the hill at two in the morning, the booze had robbed his ability to consider the matter any further. It was the last time he would party with Doug and his dames.

When Kent rejoined the land of the conscious it was to a relentless chirp sounding in his ear. A whistle blowing down the alley. He spun around, except that he couldn't spin at all because Mr. Brinkley's dead body was hanging off his shoulders, butt up, gray in the moonlight. He nearly capsized in his lumbering turn.

Tweep, tweep, tweep!

His heart pounded like a drum to that piercing alarm. They had found him! A figure ran through the shadows toward him, his hand extended accusingly, blowing his whistle.

Tweep, tweep, tweep!

He and Mr. Brinkley had been caught with their pants down behind the bank! At least Mr. Brinkley had. The rest of this nonsense about buying a villa and sailing on his yacht had been a dream. He was still back at the bank!

And then the whistle-blower's face emerged from the shadows, and Kent's heart slammed into his throat. It was the vagrant! And it wasn't with a two-dollar tin whistle that he was sounding the alarm; it was with that long tongue of his, sticking out and curled like a bamboo reed.

Kent bolted up, sticky with sweat, breathing hard.

Tweep, tweep, tweep.

He reached over and smacked the alarm beside his bed.

Eight o'clock! He sprang from the bed and splashed cool water over his face. Hiroshito and company were waiting by the phone—at least he hoped they were. Ready to deal. And if not he would go ahead and rock their world a little. Sound his own wake-up call. *Tweep, tweep!* Maybe he'd take five million next time! That would put them on their seats. Of course he'd have to give it all back—this was not like taking twenty untraceable cents from millions of unsuspecting donors; this was plain old larceny. They'd be crawling over this like ants on honey. And they'd eventually find the link. Which was why he had to get on the phone and strike a deal to find their money *his* way before they found it *their* way. Kent to the rescue.

He snatched up the phone and dialed the number. This time it took less than sixty seconds before Mr. Hiroshito's sharp voice crackled in his ear.

"Hello."

"Mr. Hiroshito. It is Bob. You remember me?"

"Yes. I have someone here who would like to speak to you."

Kent sat on the deck chair facing the blue-green sea. "Sure."

Another voice spoke into the phone, this one sly like a loan shark and defi-nitely Caucasian. "Bob? Are you there, Bob?"

"Yes." The man's tone reminded Kent of a bossman smirking on some gang-ster movie.

"Okay, Bob. I don't know who you are, and frankly, I don't care. But *you* know who we are, and you should know that we don't deal with extortionists and blackmailers. So why don't you just cut the charades and talk to us straight instead of playing peekaboo, okay, pal?"

Kent ground his teeth, flooded with the sudden urge to hurl the phone over the railing. Maybe fly over to Tokyo and smack some sense into Mr. Cheese Whiz. He crossed his legs and breathed deliberately.

"I'm sorry, Mr. . . ."

A pause. "Call me Frank."

"I'm sorry, Frank, but you have this all wrong. I apologize for the mix-up. You must have been out of the room when they played the tape. Nobody as bright as you sound would have the stomach to threaten a man in my position. Listen to the tape, Frankie. I'll call back in ten minutes." Kent hung up.

His chest was thumping. What was he doing? Frank had obviously listened to the tape already—it was why he had used the term *extortion*. Because frankly, when you got right down to it, this was as close to extortion as kidnapping. He had kidnapped their system, and they knew it. And what he was really proposing was that he would turn over the key to their system (that would be ROOSTER) in exchange for immunity. That and $250,000.

Kent retreated to the kitchen and poured a drink, a tequila sunrise minus the citrus and the ice. Cuervo Gold straight up. If ever there was a time he needed a drink, it was now.

When he called ten minutes later, they put him directly through.

"Bob?" It was Frank, and he was not sounding so slick.

"Did you listen to the tape, Frank?"

"Of course I listened to the tape!" the other man yelled. "Now, you listen to me . . ."

"No, you listen to me, Buckwheat! If you think for a minute that I cannot do what I claim I can do, then simply reject my terms. Don't come at me with all this strong-arm baloney. Either you hire me for a 25 percent recovery fee and immunity, or you don't. Is this too difficult to understand?"

"And how do we know that it wasn't *you* who stole the money in the first place?"

"Not a bad idea, Frankie. Except this is no ransom. Or maybe you didn't listen to the whole tape. I've agreed to turn the perpetrators over to you, and that wouldn't be me. More important, your payment of this recovery fee is contingent upon my closing the security breach through which they were able to gain access to your million dollars. You obviously have a gaping hole somewhere in your system. It was one million this time. Who's to say that it won't be ten million the next?"

"I'm not sure whether to take that as a threat or a warning, Bob."

"Take it as a warning. Don't be a fool, Frankie. I'm not your thief. Think of me as your cybercop. I don't come cheap, granted, but then, I only charge if I deliver. Do we have a deal, or don't we? I have other clients waiting."

The phone hissed for a few long seconds. They were talking, and Kent let them talk.

When a voice spoke again, it was Hiroshito's. "We will accept your terms, Mr. . . . Bob. You have two weeks to find the security breach and recover our money. Is there anything that you require of us at this time?"

"No. I will contact you Monday morning with a list of banks to which I need free access. Until then, rest well, my friends, You have chosen wisely."

"I hope so, Bob. This is most unusual."

"We no longer live in a world of stagecoach robbers slinging Winchesters, Mr. Hiroshito. Now it's the keyboard we have to worry about." The phone sat silently in his hand, and he wondered if the Japanese banking executive made any sense of the comparison.

"Good-bye."

"Good-bye."

Kent dropped the phone on the table and breathed deep. He had done it! Hey, a life of crime might not be such a bad thing. *Stick 'em up, baby!*

Of course he would not give Mr. Hiroshito a list of banks to which he needed access, because he had no intention of visiting a list of banks. He would make one stop, and one stop only. And that bank was located in Denver, Colorado.

On Monday he would step back into his old stomping grounds. Back to Stupid Street. The audacity of the plan struck Kent then as he gazed out to the lapping waves far below. It was lunacy! Terrifying, really. Like a killer returning to the scene of the crime just to see if the cops had found anything. *"Hey guys! It's me! So what do you think? Pretty clever, huh?"*

Kent rose unsteadily and made for the bottle on the kitchen counter. This called for another drink. There was no way he was going to return to Stupid Street completely sober.

35

Helen walked with Bill Madison under the swaying oaks, five miles from home and going strong. The park rustled with windblown leaves, yellowed in midfall. An overcast sky grayed the early afternoon, but the light was burning bright in her heart, she thought. Brighter by the day. Which meant that something was up.

"I really need to buy some new walking shoes," she said.

Bill strutted by her side, dressed in green sweats and a pair of running shoes he'd purchased for his afternoon walks with her. That day in her living room had changed the pastor's life. The heavens had torn open for him, and he'd become a new man. He'd announced the next morning that he would like to join her in the afternoons when his schedule permitted. In fact, he'd make sure his schedule did permit. The way he told it, if he joined her on the last leg of her journey, he'd be able to keep up just fine. And keep up he had, brimming with an enthusiasm that in fact spilled over to her.

"How many pair have you been through? How long have you been walking now, anyway? Two—three months?"

"Three. I've been walking three months, give or take. And I guess I've gone through about ten pairs of shoes. Same legs though. I haven't traded those in yet."

He chuckled. "No, I guess you haven't."

They walked on for a hundred feet before Helen told him what had been on her mind for the past few miles. "We are nearing the end, I think."

He turned, surprised. "The end? As in the end of the walking?"

"Yes." She smiled. "It's quite something, you know—having the Spirit of God filling your bones like a miracle drug. It gives the notion of walking in the Spirit new meaning."

"Yes, I can see that. You know, when I first saw that vision in your living room, I couldn't get over how clear everything was. All the questions just evaporated. *Poof,* they were gone. God is obviously God, and heaven obviously exists, and every word spoken here on Earth turns a head up there. But I have to tell you, things are not always so clear down here, even after that kind of encounter. Time dims the memory, and what was so bright only a couple of weeks ago starts to cloud a little. That make sense?"

Helen nodded. "Crystal clear."

"Well, if it wasn't for your walking—this incredible thing God has done to your legs—I might honestly think you had lost your mind, praying every day for a dead man."

"We've been over this, haven't we?"

"Yes. But not lately. You still think he's alive?"

"I'm past thinking too clearly, Pastor. There's a word from God—'Lean not on your own understanding, but trust in God'—you know it?"

"Sure."

"I've learned what that means. My own mind tells me all kinds of things that would make a grown man want to climb into a hole. You think the idea of a sixty-four-year-old lady walking in tube socks and a dress, twenty miles a day, praying for a dead man, is not strange? It is quite absurd. So absurd that whole theologies have been constructed to push such events into a different time zone. As if God woke up one day and suddenly realized that the way he'd been doing things all along, with falling walls and talking donkeys and burning bushes, was really quite childish. Men have grown too smart for that, yes?" She chuckled. "So when I get to the end of my walk each day, I still have to pinch myself. Make sure it's all real. Because my mind is not so different from yours, Bill. It wants to reject some things."

"It's good to know that you're as human as I am. Maybe that's one reason God has given you this physical sign. Helps you keep the faith."

"I'm sure it is."

"So you think Kent is still alive, then?"

"We've come back to that question, have we? Let's put it this way, Pastor. Wherever Kent is, he needs my prayers. The impulse to pray has not dimmed."

"Which basically means he must be alive."

"So it seems."

"But it's all coming to an end, you say."

She closed her eyes for a moment and considered the lightness of her spirit. Although she had not had any visions for over a week now, there was an expectancy riding in the air. A lightness. A brightness, hovering just beyond the clouds. How she knew it was all going somewhere rather quickly remained a small mystery. But she did.

"I think so, yes. How it will end, I have no clue. My spirit is light, but that may be for my sake rather than his. I just don't know. One thing I do know, however. When these legs begin to wobble with fatigue, it is the end."

The pastor did what he had often taken to doing these days. He broke into a prayer. "Jesus, we love you. Father, you are sovereign, your ways beyond finding out. Thank you for choosing to dwell in us. You are mighty, you are holy, you are awesome in your power."

No matter how this ended, Helen thought, the little Community Church on the corner of Main and Hornberry was in for a little jolt. Which was not so bad. Not so bad at all.

<hr>

Kent peered through the oval window to the darkness. A strobe on the airliner's wingtip lit the fuselage every three seconds, and he half expected to see the vagrant clinging to the silver wing on one of those flashes. Welcome to the Twilight Zone. The engine's steady drone dropped in pitch as the lumbering jet descended through the black skies. A sea of pinpricks sparkled ten thousand feet below them. Denver was lit up like a Christmas tree in October.

Kent rattled the ice in his glass and sipped at the tequila. He'd lost count of the little bottles Sally, the first-class bombshell stewardess, had brought him over the last few hours—enough to ease the sense of dread that had lodged itself in his chest somewhere over the Atlantic. It had felt akin to being trapped between a brood of vipers and a cliff overlooking a black void. Denver would be the coiling snakes, of course. They would be hissing and snapping at his heels if he was not careful.

But it was the cliff at his back that had him calling for the small liquor bottles. The dread he'd wrestled with back there on the island, staring at the blue seas those last two days while awaiting his flight stateside. The truth be told, he was growing tired of paradise on the hill before he'd really had a chance to live the good life. A gloom had settled over the villa by midday Friday, and it had refused to budge.

The problem was quite simple, actually: Kent could find nothing that captured his fancy, sitting high on the hill, nestled in his own private Shangri-la. It was all feeling like day-old soda. No matter how often he told himself that he ought to be thrilled with the new yacht—it was a lifelong dream, for heaven's sake—he could not bring himself to crawl down the hill to take her out again. The realization prompted a slowly moving panic that had gnawed at him with building persistence. The kind of panic you might expect after reaching a coveted destination for which you had sold your firstborn only to discover that the condo on the beach was really a roach-infested shack on a muddy river.

By Saturday the villa felt more like a prison than a resort. The tropical sun seemed like a relentless blast furnace, the quiet like a desperate solitude. And all the while he could not find release, a situation that only served to fuel the growing panic. Madness. Madness in paradise: human nature's grand joke. *When you finally arrive, my friends, you will find the Joker, wearing a frown.*

In the end he'd washed it away with tequila. Lots of tequila.

Sunday came slowly, but it came. Kent packed a million dollars in cash about his body and luggage and boarded his flight, indirectly bound for Denver.

The airliner settled onto the asphalt with a squeal of rubber, and Kent closed his eyes. He was Kevin, now. Kevin Stillman. *Remember that, Buckwheat. Kevin, Kevin, Kevin.* His passport said he was Kevin, his business card said he was Kevin, and a dozen accounts scattered to the four corners, each stuffed with cash, all said he was Kevin. Except at the bank—there he would be Bob.

The huge tower clock in Denver International Airport said it was ten o'clock by the time Kent left the rental desk to collect his Lincoln Towncar. It was black, fittingly. An hour later he took a room in the downtown Hyatt Regency ten blocks from the bank, walking through the lobby on pins and needles, fighting off the fear that someone might recognize him. The sentiment was thoroughly unfounded, of course. He looked nothing like the Kent of old. In fact he was *not* the Kent of old. He was Kevin Stillman, and Kevin Stillman had a new face— broader and well tanned, topped with brown hair. He was not the lanky blond some had once known as Kent Anthony. Goodness, if the prospect of being caught in this remote hotel lobby brought sweat to his forehead, what would a walk through the bank do?

TED DEKKER

He made the call to Japan at eleven that night. Hiroshito was where all hard-working banking executives were expected to be first thing Monday morning Japan time—in his office.

"Mr. Hiroshito?"

"Yes."

"It's Bob. You do remember me?"

"Yes."

"Good, I will need access to the bank president at your main Denver branch at 9 A.M. mountain time. His name is Bentley. Mr. Price Bentley. Will there be a problem with this request?"

Hiroshito hesitated. "Nine? The bank opens at eight. It is short notice."

"Not too short, I am sure. You have the capability of transferring a million dollars in much less time. Surely you have the capability of making a phone call."

"Of course. He will be ready."

"Thank you, sir. You are very helpful." Kent hung up and made for the liquor cabinet. He managed to drift off near midnight, pretty much inebriated.

⌘

The sounds of rush hour filtered through the room's window when he awoke at seven. He was in Denver! Monday morning!

Kent bounded from the bed and showered, his spine tingling with anticipation. He donned a black double-breasted suit, the first he'd worn in six weeks, by his accounting. He'd chosen a white shirt accented by a teal tie—strictly business. Bob was about to do some business.

By the time he reached the towering bank he was sweating profusely. He pulled the Towncar into a space three down from his old parking spot and turned off the ignition. Silence engulfed the cab. To his right the alley gaped with a red brick mouth, blackened slightly. That would be his handiwork. The memories strung through his mind like Polaroids on a string. He dabbed his forehead and wiped at his neck with a napkin he'd taken from the hotel lounge. Couldn't very well go in there looking as though he'd just come from the sauna.

What if, by some strange force at work in their memories, they *did* recognize him? Something about his hairline or his vocabulary or the sound of his voice. What if it struck a bell in their empty noggins, and they actually identified him?

299

He cleared his throat and tried the voice. "Hello." It came out squeaky, and he tried again, intentionally lowering it. "Hello, there. I'm Bob."

Kent bit his lip, slipped on black glasses, and stepped from the car, closing his hands against a tremble that had taken over his fingers. He straightened his suit and looked up at the rising steps. Customers already streamed in and out of the revolving doors. He took three long, deep breaths and strode forward. *It's now or never, Buckwheat. Buckwheat Bob. Suck it up. Think of what they did to you.*

Kent did that. He clenched his jaw and bounded up the steps, grasping madly at the sudden surge of confidence. He stepped through the revolving doors like a rooster on the hunt and stopped dead in his tracks.

It all crashed down on him with a vengeance: Zak the security guard, pacing with sagging eyes; the long row of tellers, mechanically pushing and pulling slips of paper across the green counter; the tall sailboat suspended in the middle of the lobby; a sea of muted voices murmuring on about dollars and cents; the smell of a dozen perfumes, all mixed into a potpourri of scents.

If Kent's skin had been invisible they would have all seen his heart bounce up into his throat and stick there, a ball of quivering flesh. He suddenly knew with absolute certainty that this was all a mistake. A huge monstrous mistake. He very nearly spun on his heels for a hasty getaway then. But his muscles were not responding so quickly, and he hesitated. And by then it was too late. Because by then Sidney Beech was walking directly for him, smiling as if to welcome him back into the fold.

"May I help you?" she asked, which was not what Sidney Beech normally did with just any yahoo who wandered into the bank. It was his Blues Brothers look, he quickly decided. He still had the shades on, a good thing—if she could have seen his bulging eyes she might have called security instead of wandering over with that grin on her face.

"Excuse me, can I help you with something?"

Kent cleared his throat. *Strictly business, Bob. Don't be a wuss.*

"Yes. I'm here to see a Mr. Bentley. Price Bentley."

She cocked her head, in a polite way of course. "And you are?"

"Bob."

She waited for more.

"He's expecting me," Kent said.

"Bob?"

"Bob."

"I'll let him know you are waiting, Bob. If you'd like to have a seat in our lounge . . ."

"You may tell him that I'm on a tight schedule. I don't intend on lounging around waiting for him."

She lifted an eyebrow, unable to hide a slight grin. "Of course." Sidney motioned for the overstuffed chairs and strutted off toward Bentley's office, to tell him of the kook that had just walked in, no doubt.

Kent meandered over to the ship and studied the structure, feigning interest. Several tellers watched him curiously. Perhaps he should remove the black glasses. And maybe he should have purchased some of those colored contact lenses—his blues eyes might bare his soul.

Sidney was clacking up behind him. This was it then. He let her come.

"Bob?"

He turned and ground his teeth. *Strictly business, Bob.*

"He will see you now." She had lost the grin.

Kent strode for the office without waiting for her to show the way then realized it would be a mistake. How would he know? He turned to her. "This way?"

"Around the corner," she said.

Better. He walked for the office, tall and mean, looking like a cybercop ought to look, gaining confidence with each step.

Kent put his hand on the brass knob, took a single deep breath, pushed the door open without knocking, and stepped in. The oversized branch president sat behind his desk like a bowl of firm jelly. His oblong face had swelled, Kent thought. The man was eating well on his newfound wealth. Bentley's suit buttons still stretched as he sat. He still wore his collar tight so that it pinched off his head to resemble a tomato. His big cherrywood desk still sat neat and stately. The air still smelled of cigar smoke. Only the look in Bentley's eyes had changed from Kent's last visit. And he wasn't sure if the man's eyes bulged from fear or from offense.

"Price Bentley?"

"Yes." The man extended a hand over the desk. His face split with a manufactured grin. "And you must be Bob. I was told you would be visiting us."

"You were, were you?" Kent shut the door behind him. He removed his sunglasses with a casual flip and ignored Bentley's extended hand. "Get on the horn and call Borst," he said. "I need him here too."

That controlled grin flattened to concern. "Borst? What does he have to do with this?"

"What does he have to do with *what*, Bentley?" Kent stared into the man's eyes, and a small tremor of revulsion swept through his bones. "You don't even know why I'm here, correct? Or am I wrong?"

He did not respond.

"Pick your jaw off the table and call him," Kent said. "And tell him to hustle. I don't have all day."

Bentley called Borst and set the phone down. It missed its cradle and clattered to the president's lap. He snatched it up and clanked it in its proper place. "He's on his way."

Kent watched the pathetic man, expressionless.

"Is there anything I can get for you?"

"Do I look like I need something?" Kent placed his hands behind his back and walked past Bentley toward the far window. "What did they tell you?"

The president cleared his throat. "They said you were investigating something for them."

"Investigating, huh? And did they tell you *what* I was investigating?"

The door burst open, and Borst barged in, his face flushed. "Oh. Excuse me. I got here as soon as I could."

"Sit down, Markus." Bentley said, rising. "This is Bob . . . Bob . . . uh . . . I'm sorry, I don't know your last name."

Kent faced them. "Just Bob to you. Morning, Mr. Borst. Good of you to join us." He looked at Bentley and nodded toward the guest chair beside Borst. "You might as well have a seat over by Borst, if you don't mind."

The president lifted an eyebrow. "In the guest chair? Why?"

"Because I told you to sit there. I want you to sit down beside Borst. Is that so difficult to understand?"

Borst turned white. Bentley's face flashed red. "Look, I think you—"

"Frankly I'm not really interested in what you think. I have no intention of standing here in some jaw-flapping contest with you. Now, when I say sit, you will sit. And if I tell you to open up your shirt and expose your hairy belly, you will do just that. Is this a problem? If so, you say so now, and I'll pick up that phone. But if you're interested in keeping the grossly inflated salary you've somehow managed to wrestle out of our Japanese friends, you should do precisely what I say. Are we clear?"

Bentley's tomato head seemed to swell. Kent looked at Borst and winked. "Right, Borst?"

His old boss did not respond. He might have swallowed his tongue, Kent thought.

"Now, if you don't mind, please sit over by your partner in crime there."

Bentley hesitated a moment and then stormed around the desk to sit heavily beside Borst. The large man's expression teetered between rage and fear.

Kent continued. "Now, before I go any further I want both of you to understand a few things. First, I want you to understand that I'm just doing a job here. You two could be the king and his court jester, for all I care. It makes little difference. My job is to uncover the truth. That's it."

Kent paced across the room, keeping them in his sight as he turned.

"Second, you may not approve of my approach, but obviously the people who hired your miserable necks do, or I wouldn't be here. So keep your lips closed unless I ask you to open them. *Capisce?*"

They stared at him, obviously steaming at his audacity. "You see, now, that was a question. It is appropriate to open your lips in a response when I ask a question. Let's try it again, shall we? I say *Capisce,* which is Italian for *understand,* and you say . . ."

The fear had left Bentley's eyes, for the most part. Now it was just a snarl twisting those fat lips. Borst responded first. "Yes."

Bentley dipped his head but did not speak. It would have to do for the moment.

"Good. Now, I know that you're both big shots in this bank. You're used to having a dozen or so employees follow you around eager to shine your shoes if you are so inclined. Am I right? You don't have to answer that one. Either way, I am not one of those people. Do we have this straight, or should I start over?"

Borst nodded. Bentley's lips twitched.

"Good enough. I'm here because someone obviously suspects that you two have been involved in some hanky-panky. Have you?"

The sudden question caught them off guard. Again Borst answered first. "No! Of course not."

"Shut up, Borst!" Bentley had caught his breath. "I don't think we have to answer your questions without our attorneys present, Mister."

"Is that so?" Kent arched an eyebrow. "Has anyone ever told you that your head is rather large, Bentley? Hmm? I mean, not just figuratively, but physically. I look at you, and I think . . ." He lifted a finger to his chin and looked off to the ceiling. ". . . tomato. Yes, tomato. That's what I've been standing here thinking. My, this fellow has a head that really, really looks like a tomato. Well, you listen up, Tomato-Head. There's a little document that you signed when you agreed to your bloated salary. It's called an employment agreement. I think you will find a clause in your agreement that pretty much gives me, the bank that is, full rights to investigate any matter suspect of hanky-panky. I think the word in the agreement is actually *fraud*. Same difference. Now, if you feel at a later date that we have treated you unfairly, you are free to sue to your heart's content. But until then let's keep things in perspective, shall we? Now, please answer my question. Have or have you not, Mr. Price Bentley, been involved in hanky-panky here at the bank?"

"No." He had collected himself during that long diatribe, which was fine by Kent. A bit of a fight would not be so bad.

"No. Very good. Then I'm sure you have some exceptional explanations for my concerns. Let's start with you, Borst. By the way, please remove your toupee. I find it rather distracting."

Borst's face flushed pink, and he looked up with a sheepish smile.

Kent nodded and waved a hand toward the black toupee. "Go ahead. Rip it off, my friend."

His old boss realized then that he was serious, and his jaw fell open. "You . . . you . . . that's absurd!" he sputtered.

"Either way, please remove it. It's keeping me from concentrating on my job here."

Borst spun toward Bentley, who ignored him.

Kent pushed the point. "Hurry, man. We don't have all day. Just pull it off."

Borst reached up and pulled the hairpiece from his bald head. His face now beamed the shade of red found in a grocer's meat department.

"Good. So then, my friend, were you aware that some money is missing from the bank? Stolen electronically?"

Borst's breathing came raggedly now. "No."

"No? That's funny, because it did indeed find its way into your personal account. Odd. And you, of all people, should know that money does not just float around the system of its own accord. In fact, isn't it your job to see that it does not?"

The man did not respond.

"Now would be a good time to move your lips, Borst."

"No. I mean, yes. Sort of . . ."

"Well, which is it? Aren't you in charge of this new funds processing system everyone is raving about? AFPS?"

"Yes."

"And you designed it, did you not?"

"No. No, *that* is not true!"

Bentley spoke again, furious now. "Will you keep your trap shut, Borst!"

Kent smiled. "Fighting among friends. How tragic. Which is it, Bentley? Yes, he did design AFPS, or no, he did not?"

"I barely even knew the program!" Borst blurted. "I oversee programmers, see, so I might not be as proficient about moving money around as you think. I swear I had no idea how that money got into our accounts!"

"Shut up, Borst!" Spittle flew from Bentley's lips as he spoke. "Listen to what you're saying, Meathead!"

Kent ignored the president. "But you *did* know about the money. And you knew about the money in Tomato-Head's account as well, which means he also knew about it. But we'll come back to that. I want to pursue this line of crock you're feeding me on AFPS." He wagged a finger at them. "Didn't you two take credit for its development? Didn't you sign an affidavit claiming primary responsibility for the conception and implementation of the system? I mean, the last I checked, a lot of money was headed your way as a result of the bank's bonus program. Are you telling me there was some hanky-panky in that as well? Why don't you answer that, Bentley?"

The president looked as though he had indeed tied a noose about his neck and cinched it tight. "Of course I signed an affidavit stating I was primarily responsible for the system's development. And I was. Borst was as well. You just have him tied in knots with this dog and pony show of yours. So what do you say we get down to your real concerns, Bob? What exactly are you suggesting we did or did not do?"

"Oh, my goodness. He shows some intelligence at last. Did you hear him, Borst? Didn't that come off quite nicely? I'll tell you what I'm suggesting. I'm suggesting that you and Borst here are hiding some things. For starters, money transfers were illegally issued, neatly depositing several thousand dollars in each of your accounts, and I don't buy Borst's assertion that he had no idea where that money came from. Nobody could be such an idiot. So I guess I'm suggesting, Mr. Price Bentley, that you just got caught with your hand in the cookie jar. For starters, that is."

"And I'll tell *you* that that is the most ridiculous suggestion I've ever heard. You come walking in here, spouting these absurd accusations of fraud. How dare you!"

Kent stared Bentley down for a full ten seconds. He turned to his old boss. "Borst, will you please tell Mr. Bentley here that he's starting to get under my skin. Will you tell him that I already have enough hard evidence to have him put in the slammer for a few years, and if he doesn't back off, I might do just that. And tell him to cool down. He really is looking more and more like a tomato, and I'm afraid I might just walk over there and bite into him by mistake. Go on, tell him."

Borst blinked. He was obviously completely out of his league here. "Come on, Price. Settle down, man."

Bentley snorted, but he did not attack.

"Good." Kent turned back to the president. "Now, I'll tell you what, Bentley. I really did not come all the way from the Far East to slap your wrists over a couple thousand dollars. If that were the case it would be local security in here, not me. No sir. I'm after much bigger fish. But now you've hurt my feelings with this big talk of yours, and I'm not sure I want to bring you in on my little secret anymore. I'm tempted to just walk out of here and file a report that will nail your hide to the wall. And I could do it too."

He drilled Borst with a stare and returned to Bentley. "But I'll tell you what I'm willing to do. I'm willing to let the small deposits slip and tell you what I really need from you if you'll just apologize for your nasty attitude. How's that? You put your hands together as if you're praying and tell me you're sorry, and I'll forgive this whole mess. Both of you."

They looked at him with wide eyes and gaping mouths. Borst put his hands together and looked at Bentley. The president appeared to have frozen solid.

"Come on, Price," Borst whispered.

The humiliation of the moment was really too much for Kent himself. Two grown men, begging apologies without just cause. At least none they knew of. They had nothing to do with those small deposits, and all three of the men in the room knew that. Still, Bentley was no idiot. He could not know *what* "Bob" knew.

It took a good thirty seconds of silence before Bentley slowly clasped his hands as if in prayer and dipped his head. "I'm sorry. I spoke in haste."

"Yes. I'm sorry too," Borst echoed.

Kent smiled. "Well, that's much better. I feel so much better. Don't you?" They were undoubtedly too stuffed with humiliation to respond.

"Good, then. And please keep this attitude of contrition about you as long as I am present. Now, let me tell you why I'm really here. Last week, someone stole one million dollars from the bank through a series of ghost transactions. Transactions similar in nature to the deposits made to your accounts. And quite frankly, I'm really quite convinced that you two did it. I think you two have a bunch of money stashed somewhere and that you've used some variation of AFPS to do it."

Their faces went white together, slowly, as the blood slowly vacated. Their mouths gaped.

Kent spoke before they could. "Now, I know what you're thinking. You're thinking that I just told you differently not two minutes ago. You're thinking that I just promised to let things slide if you made that silly apology. And you're absolutely right. But I was lying. You two are quite the liars yourselves, aren't you? You really should have seen it coming."

They sat woodenly, thoroughly seized by shock. Kent firmed his jaw and glared at them. "Somewhere in the deepest folds of cyberspace there's a lot of money hiding, and I guarantee it; I'm gonna find that money. And when I do, I'm going to find your grimy fingerprints all over it. You can bet your next twenty years on that. I figure it'll take me about two weeks. In the meantime, I'll get you a number in case your memory improves and you suddenly want to talk sense."

He walked past them to the door and turned back. Borst was moving his lips in horrified silent protest. Bentley's head had swelled like a tomato again.

Kent dipped his head. "Until then, my fat friends. And I don't mind telling you, that apology really was a special moment for me. I will remember it always."

With that Kent shut the door behind him and left, hardly able to contain himself. He slipped on the dark glasses while still in the lobby, nodding to Sidney Beech as he passed. Then he was through the revolving glass doors and facing Broadway.

Man, that had felt good. Time for a drink.

36

The hole in Kent's chest had returned shortly after noon on Monday, just three hours after his little victory over the porky twins. He was not done with them, of course, but it would be two weeks before he walked back into their lives. Two weeks with nothing to do but wait. Two weeks of empty space.

He could return to the island and live it up with Doug and friends. But the idea felt like death warmed over. Why retreat to solitude? Why not try to shake this emptiness by filling his life with a few things here? Maybe he ought to take a drive up to Boulder.

What was he thinking?

Kent decided to catch a flight to New York. He made the decision impulsively, with a slug of tequila burning his throat. Why not? Money was no object. He could hop the *Concorde* to London if he so desired. And sitting around Denver beating back memories of his past would drive him to the grave.

He checked out of the Hyatt, paid cash for a thousand-dollar ticket to New York, and was airborne by four that afternoon.

The Big Apple was just another clogged city, but it did offer its advantages. Bars, for instance. There were pubs and lounges on virtually every corner around Kent's Manhattan hotel. Kent settled for the one in the hotel— O'Malley's Pub—and retired in a daze at 1 A.M. Tuesday morning.

He woke just before noon, lost in a dark room, wondering where he was. New York. He had flown to New York. Only God knew why. To escape Denver or some such nonsense. He rolled over and shut his eyes. He imagined there would be a dozen messages on the phone number he'd called over to Bentley's assistant before leaving Denver. The president and his cohort were probably coming apart at the seams trying to get hold of him. Yes, well he would let them sweat. Let them die a few deaths, see how it felt.

Kent forced himself out of bed at one, determined to find a distraction beyond the bottle. Goodness, he was chugging alcohol as if it were a runner's water. He had to get hold of himself here.

The bellboy told him that the opera was always a stretching experience.

He attended the opera that night. The sound of the lead vocalist's crooning nearly had him in tears. For some ungodly reason the woman became Lacy in his mind's eye, mourning the loss of her lover. That would be him. He could not follow the plot, but that the play was a story of death and sorrow could hardly be missed.

Kent woke Wednesday to a refreshing thought. Refreshing, not in the sense that he particularly enjoyed it, but refreshing in that it pulled him out of the doldrums—like a bucket of ice water tossed into a hot shower. It was a simple thought.

What if they're on to you, my friend?

He bolted up in bed and grabbed the bedspread. What if, back there in Denver, someone had put a few things together? Like that cop who'd interrupted his reading time at the bookstore. What had become of him? Or Bentley himself, sitting there wheezing like a camel, what if he'd seen something in his eyes? Even Borst, for that matter. No, not Borst. The man was too stupid.

He rolled out of bed, his stomach churning. Or what of Lacy? He had actually told her, for heaven's sake! Most of it anyway. Coming here to the United States had been idiotic. And going back to the bank, now, there was a move straight off of Stupid Street. What had he been thinking! Had to get the nasty boys, yes sir. Extract a slice of revenge.

Kent dressed with a tremor in his bones and headed for the bar. Problem was, the bar hadn't opened yet. It was only 9 A.M. Back to the hotel room to down a few of those small bottles in the cabinet. He spent the day watching golf in his hotel room, sick with anxiety and bored to death for the duration.

He managed to slap some sense into himself the next day by reviewing each and every step of his plan. The simple fact of the matter was that it had been rather brilliant. They had buried Mr. Brinkley's charred body, convinced it belonged to Kent Anthony. Unless they exhumed that body, Kent was a dead man. Dead men do not commit crimes. More important, there had been no crime. Ha! He had to remember that. No theft and no thief. No case. And he was the rich fool who had masterminded it all. A very wealthy man, dripping in the stuff.

It was that day, Thursday, in the bustling city of New York, that Kent began to understand the simple facts of a wealthy life. It all started after a two-hundred-dollar lunch down the street from the hotel, at Bon Appétit French Cuisine. The food was good; he could hardly deny that. For the price, it had better be good. But it occurred to him while stuffing some cupcake-looking pastry into his mouth, with his stomach already stretched far beyond its natural limits, that these French morsels, like most morsels, would come out in much worse shape than they went in. And in all honesty, they did not bring him much more pleasure than, say, a Twinkie at twenty cents a pop. It was a little fact, but it left the restaurant with Kent.

Another little fact: No matter how much money he carried in his wallet, individual moments did not change. Hopes and dreams might, but the string of moments that made up life did not. If he was walking down the hall, placing one foot in front of the other, he was doing just that, regardless of what his wallet packed. If he was pushing the call button for the elevator, it was just that, no more and no less, regardless of the number of bills in his back pocket.

But it was that night, approaching the midnight hour while drinking in O'Malley's Pub, that the full weight of the matter presented itself to him in one lump sum. It was as though the heavens opened and dropped this nugget on him like an ingot of lead. Only it didn't come from the skies. It came from the mouth of a fellow drinker, ready to impart his wisdom.

Kent sat next to the man who called himself Bono—after the U2 singer, he said—an ex-Orthodox priest, of all things. Said he left the Greek church because it left him dry. The man looked to be in his forties, with thick eyebrows and graying hair, but it was his bright green eyes that had Kent wondering. Since when did Greeks have green eyes? Together they knocked back the shotglasses. Actually, Kent was putting them away. Bono contented himself with sipping at a glass of wine.

"You know, the problem with those Wall Street yuppies," Bono offered after a half-dozen shots, "is that they all think there's more to life than what the average man has."

"And they'd be right," Kent returned after a pause. "Average is lazy, and lazy is not much."

"Whoa, so you are a philosopher, are you? Well, let me ask you something, Mr. Philosopher. What's better about busy than lazy?"

It was a simple question. Even awkwardly simple, because everyone knew that busy was better than lazy. But at the moment, Kent was having difficulty remembering why. It was possibly the booze, but it was just as possibly that he had never really known why busy was better than lazy.

He did what all good fools do when presented with a question they cannot answer directly. He raised his voice a tad and threw the question back. "Come on! Everybody knows that being lazy is stupid."

"That's what you said. And I asked you, why?"

Bono was no fool. He'd been here before. "Why? Because you cannot excel if you're lazy. You will go nowhere."

"Excel at what? Go where?"

"Well, now. How about life? Let's start with that. I know it's not much, but let's start with excelling at that little event."

"And tell me what that feels like. What does *excelling at life* feel like?"

"Happiness." Kent raised his shotglass and threw it back. "Pleasure. Peace. All that."

"Ahh. Yes, of course. I had forgotten about happiness, pleasure, and peace and all that. But you see, the average man has as much as the Wall Street yuppie. And in the end, they both go into the same grave. That *is* where they go, isn't it?" The man chuckled.

It was then, at the word *grave,* that the buzzing had first started again in Kent's skull. "Well, most have a good eighty years before the grave," he said quietly. "You only live once; you might as well have the best while you do it."

"But you see, that's where you and the yuppies on Wall Street are mistaken," Bono insisted. "It makes a fine fantasy, no argument there. But when you've had it all—and believe me, I have—wine still tastes like wine. You might drink it out of a gold chalice, but even then you realize one day that you could close your eyes and honestly not know whether the cold metallic object in your hand is made from gold or tin. And who decided that gold is better than tin anyway? In the end we all go to the grave. Perhaps it is beyond the grave where life begins. You know anyone who's gone to the grave lately?"

Kent swallowed and flung back another shot. Lately? His vision doubled momentarily. He leveled a rather weak objection. "You're too pessimistic. People are full of life. Like that man laughing over there." He motioned to a man in a far booth, roaring with his head tilted back. "You think he's not happy?" Kent smiled, thankful for the reprieve.

Bono gazed at the man and grinned. "Yes. Today Clark looks quite happy, doesn't he?" He turned back to Kent. "But I know Mr. Clark. He's a pig-head. Recently divorced and rather smug with the notion because he no longer has to deal with his brats. He's got three of them—six, ten, and twelve—and he can hardly stand them. Problem is, he spends most of his waking hours feeling guilty for his remarkably selfish disposition. He's been trying to wash it all away with the bottle for a year now. Trust me. He will leave this place tonight and retreat to a wet pillow, soaked in tears." Bono took a sip from his glass, evidently satisfied for having made his point. "Look under any man's sheets, and you'll find a similar story. I guarantee it, certifiable."

Kent had lost his interest in arguing the point. He was too busy trying to shake loose the fingers of heat climbing into his brain. The man had hit a nerve. Clark there could easily be him, drowning his failure in the bottle, bent upon pleasure and finding none. Except that he did not hate his son, like Pig-Head did. In fact he would have killed for his son—would've gladly given up every red cent for Spencer's life. The thought brought a sliver of light to Kent's mind.

Bono stood. He slid his glass across the counter and exhaled with satisfaction. "Yessiree. I'm telling you, this life is quite pitiful. No man can escape it." He tilted his head and lifted his brows so that his green eyes bulged down at Kent. "Unless, of course, you understand what lies beyond the grave." He smiled wide and slapped Kent on the back. "But then, I'm sure you know all about that, don't you, Kent?" He sauntered from the pub without looking back.

The words echoed in Kent's for an hour, and no amount of tequila quieted them. Kent drank for another hour by himself before wandering back to his hotel suite. Somewhere in that hour he began to miss Gloria. Not just *wish-she-were-sitting-with-me* missing, but *blurry-eyed-I'm-lost-without-her* missing. It was all these thoughts about the grave that the green-eyed Bono had deposited on him; they brought pictures of Gloria calling to him from some great unseen horizon. And what if there was some truth to all her babble of God? That thought shoved a fist-sized lump into his throat.

Well, Gloria was dead. Dead, buried, and beyond the grave, wherever that was. But there was Lacy—she too knew of the grave. And she knew of God. Still, Lacy could never be Gloria. Kent finally drifted off to sleep, his mind all mixed up with pictures of Gloria and Lacy.

37

Rather than take a room in another hotel, Kent found a furnished executive suite upon his return to Denver Friday afternoon. The agent had hesitated when Kent forked over the ten thousand security deposit in cash, but he had taken it, and Kent had moved in, an event that consisted of nothing more than stepping through the door with the keys in one hand and a single garment bag hanging from his shoulder.

The suite reminded him of the kind you see on futuristic shows, stark and shiny, decorated in black and white. The furniture was all metal, glass, or leather—rather cold for his tastes. But at least it was clean. More important, it was fully stocked, from a flat-screen entertainment center to place settings for eight.

Kent mixed himself a stiff drink, pulled an ugly-looking, black, wrought-iron chair out from under the glass table, and flipped open his laptop. The Toshiba had seen its share of activity over the last six weeks. He powered it up and logged on. Communication on the laptop was through a satellite connection—never a land line. He may have executed a few dumb moves here and there, but not when it came to computing. Here, at least, in his thieving and hiding, he had covered his tracks impeccably, thanks in large part to this baby.

The message box he'd left Bentley was indeed overflowing with messages. There were a dozen or so from Bentley, ranging from the earliest nearly a week old, insisting that he meet with them again, to the latest, left on Friday, screaming about lawsuits and counter lawsuits and what else Kent did not know because he spun quickly through the rest of the voice mail. Phase two was unfolding as planned. Let them sweat.

The last message was from an unidentified number, and Kent sat up when the voice spoke low over his speakers. A chill flashed down his spine. He knew the voice!

"Hello, Bob. You don't know me . . ." *Oh yes I do! Yes, I do.* ". . . but I would very much appreciate bending your ear for a few minutes on this case at the bank. Price Bentley told me I could reach you here. I'm a law enforcement officer working a few angles on a related matter. Please call me as soon as possible to set up a meeting. 565-8970. Thanks, pal. Oh, ask for Germy."

A cop! Pinhead? Impossible! Germy? What kind of name was *Germy?* But he could swear he'd heard that voice before. And it was a cop.

Kent placed his hands over his face and tried to think. What if the cop was indeed on to him? But he'd already decided that was impossible. No theft, no thief, no crime, no problem. Only this *was* a problem, because he was sitting alone in his new apartment, sweating like boxer.

He should pretend the message had never come through. And risk raising the cop's curiosity? No. He should call the man and weasel his way out of an appointment.

Kent snatched up the phone and dialed the number. A lady answered. "Seventh precinct, may I help you?"

Seventh precinct! "Yes . . ." His heart was thumping in his ear. "I was told to call a cop at this number. A Germy?"

"Oh, you must mean the new guy: Jeremy. Hold please."

Pinhead!

The receiver barked before Kent could do anything like slam the phone down. "Jeremy here. What can I do for you?"

"Ah . . . Yes. This is . . . Bob. You left a message for me."

"Bob! Yes, of course. Thank you for calling back so quickly. Listen, I just have a few questions about this business at the bank. Do you have any time to grab a cup of coffee? Say tomorrow morning? Ten-ish?"

What could he say? *No, not ten-ish. Ten-ish is when I start on the bottle, see? How about never-ish?*

"Sure," he said.

"Great! It won't take but a few minutes. How about at the Denny's at Broadway and Fifth? You know where that is?"

"Sure."

"Good. I'll see you at ten tomorrow morning."

314

"Sure."

The phone went dead. Sure? Gulp.

Kent did not sleep well Friday night.

❧

How the time managed to crawl by, Kent did not know, but it did, like a snail inching its way across a nine-foot razor blade. He awoke at five Saturday morning, although opened his eyes might be a better way to characterize the event, because he'd never really fallen asleep. A shower, a cup of coffee, a few shots of tequila for the nerves, and two miles of pacing across the black-and-white-checkered linoleum delivered him reluctantly to the appointed hour. He found himself parked outside of Denny's at ten o'clock without knowing precisely how he'd gotten there.

Kent slipped on his black shades and walked in. It might look ridiculous for a grown man to wear sunglasses indoors, but he'd decided sometime past midnight that ridiculous was better than incarcerated.

Detective Jeremy sat in a nonsmoking booth, staring at Kent as he entered. And it was indeed Pinhead. Complete with slicked black hair and wire-frame glasses. He was grinning wide. *"Hello, Kent. You are Kent, aren't you?"*

Kent swallowed and crossed to the booth, mustering every ounce of nonchalance remaining in his quivering bones.

"Bob?" The detective half rose and extended a hand. "Good of you to come."

Kent wiped his palm and took the hand. "Sure." He sat. Pinhead smiled at him without speaking, and Kent just sat, determined to act normal but knowing he was failing miserably. The cop's eyes were as green as he remembered them.

"So, I guess you're wondering why I've asked you to meet me?"

Kent shrugged. "Sure." He needed another word badly.

"Price Bentley tells me that you're investigating a robbery at the bank. You're a private investigator?"

"I suppose you could call me that." *Cybercop,* he almost said, but decided it would sound stupid. "At this point it's strictly an internal matter."

"Well, now, that depends, Bob. Depends on whether it's connected."

"Connected to what?"

"To my investigation."

"And what might that be, Jeremy?" That was better. Two could be condescending.

"That would be the bank fire a month or so ago."

Every muscle in Kent's body went rigid. He immediately coughed to cover. "The bank fire. Yes, I heard about that. To be honest, arson was never my thing."

"Mine neither. Actually I'm following up the murder. Do you always wear sunglasses indoors, Bob?"

Kent hesitated. "I have a light sensitivity in my left eye. It acts up on occasion."

Jeremy nodded, still grinning like a chimpanzee. "Of course. Did you know the victim?"

"What victim?" *That's it—remain cool, Buckwheat. Just play it cool.*

"The gentleman murdered in the bank robbery? You know, the fire."

"Bank robbery? I didn't know there was a robbery."

"So they say. *Attempted* robbery, then. Did you know him?"

"Should I have?"

"Just curious, Bob. No need to be defensive here. It was a simple-enough question, don't you think?"

"What exactly do you need from me, Jeremy? I agreed to meet with you because you seemed rather eager to do so. But I really don't have all morning to discuss your case with you. I have my own."

"Relax, Bob. Would you like some coffee?"

"I don't drink coffee."

"Shame. I love coffee in the morning." He poured himself a steaming cup. "For some it's the bottle; for me it's coffee." He sipped the hot, black liquid. "Ahh. Perfect."

"That's wonderful. My heart is glad for you, Jeremy. But you're starting to annoy me just a tad here. Can we get on with it?"

The detective just smiled, hardly missing a beat. "It's the possible connection that has me worried. You see, whenever you have two robberies or *attempted* robberies in one bank during the span of six weeks, you have to ask yourself about the connections."

"I hardly see the similarity between a common thief who happened upon an open door and the high-tech theft I'm investigating."

"No. It does seem rather unlikely. But I always turn over every stone. Think of yourself as one of those stones. You're just being turned over."

"Well, thank you, Jeremy. It's good to know that you're doing your job with such diligence."

The detective held up his cup as if to toast the notion. "My pleasure. So, did you know him?"

"Know him?"

"The victim, Bob. The programmer who was killed by the common thief."

"Should I have?"

"You already asked that. Yes or no would be fine."

"No, of course not. Why should I know a programmer who works in the Denver branch of Niponbank?"

"He was responsible for AFPS. Were you aware of that?"

Kent blinked behind the shades. *Watch it, Buckwheat. Tread easy.* "It was him, huh? I figured it couldn't have been Bentley or Borst. So they cheated someone for that bonus after all."

"All I know is that it was Kent Anthony who developed the system, pretty much from the ground up. And then he turns up dead. Meanwhile Bentley and company end up pulling down some pretty healthy change. Seems odd."

"You're suggesting Bentley might have had a finger in the programmer's death?" Kent asked.

"No. Not necessarily. He had nothing to gain by killing Kent. I just throw it out there 'cause it's another stone that needs turning."

"Well, I'll be sure to turn over my findings if they seem to shed any light on the fire. But unless Bentley and company are somehow implicated in the fire, I don't see how the two cases tie in."

"Yes, you're probably right." The detective downed his coffee dregs and looked out the window. "Which leaves us pretty much where we started."

Kent watched him for a moment. By the sounds of it, Pinhead was not turning out to be such a threat after all. Which made sense when you thought about it. The theft had been perfectly planned. There was no way that anyone, including Detective Pinhead here, could even suspect the truth of the matter. A small chill of victory ran up Kent's spine.

He smiled for the first time, confident now. "And where would that be? Tell me, where did we start? I'm a bit lost."

"With a crime that simply does not fit the players involved. If Bentley and Borst don't fit, then nothing fits. Because, you see, if you knew the man, you would know that Kent Anthony was not the kind of man who would leave a door unlocked for a pistol-toting thief. He was not nearly so stupid. At least not according to his friends."

"Friends?" The question slipped out before Kent could hold it back.

"Friends. I talked to his girlfriend up in Boulder. She had some interesting things to say about the man."

The heat was suddenly flashing though Kent's skull. "Anybody can make a simple mistake," he said, knowing it sounded weak. He certainly could not defend a man he supposedly did not know. "In my experience the simplest explanation is usually the correct one. You have a body; you have slugs. He may have been an Einstein, but he's still dead."

Pinhead chuckled. "You're right. Dead is dead." He mulled that over. "Unless Kent is not dead. Now, maybe that would make more sense." The man drilled Kent with those green eyes. "You know, not everything is what it seems, Bob. In fact I am not what I seem. I'm not just some dumb, lucky cop."

Kent's face flushed red; he felt panic-stricken. His chest seemed to clog. And all the while Pinhead was looking directly at him. He was suddenly having a hard time forming thoughts, much less piecing together a response. The cop removed his gaze.

"My case and your case could be connected, Bob. Maybe we're looking for the wrong guy. Maybe your high-tech phantom and my dead guy are really the same person! A bit far-fetched but possible, don't you think?"

"No. That's not possible!"

"No? And why is that not possible?"

"Because I already know who did it!"

The cop arched a brow. "Who?"

"Bentley and Borst. I'm putting the finishing touches on the evidence, but within a week I can assure you, fraud charges will be filed."

"So quickly? Excellent work, Bob! But I really think you ought to rethink the matter. With my theory in mind, of course. It would be something, wouldn't it? Kent alive and kicking with a dead man in his grave?" He dismissed the theory with his hand. "Ah, but you're probably right. The two cases are probably not connected. Just turning over every stone, you know."

At the moment Kent felt like taking one of Jeremy's stones and shoving it down the detective's throat. *Try that for a theory, Pinhead!* But he could hardly breathe, much less reach over there and wrestle the man's mouth open.

"Well, I surely do appreciate your time, Bob. Maybe we will meet again. Soon." The detective smiled.

With that he stood and left, leaving Kent soaking under the arms and frozen to his seat.

This was a problem. Not just a little challenge or a bump in the road, but the-end-of-the-world-as-we-know-it kind of problem. Coming here had been a mistake. Coming back to this *country* had been a mistake. Going to the bank—that had been idiotic!

Still, there was no evidence, was there? No, no evidence. It was Pinhead's theory. A stupid theory at that.

Then a simple little picture popped into his mind and crushed what little hope he had left. It was a picture of Lacy, sitting on her couch, hands folded, knees together, facing Pinhead. She was talking. She was telling her little secret.

Kent dropped his head into his hands and tried to still his breathing.

38

Kent stood by the pillar just outside Macy's in a Boulder mall on Monday evening and stared at the woman, his heart beating like a kettle drum, his palms wet with balls of sweat.

Sometime on Saturday, he'd come to a new realization about life. It was a notion so profound that most people never understood it properly. It was the kind of truth one encounters only in moments when he is stretched beyond all limits, as Kent had been after that little encounter with Pinhead. And it was simply this: When you really got right down to it, life sucked.

The problem with most people was that they never really got right down to it. They lived their lives *thinking* of getting right down to it, but did they ever actually get right down to it? No. *"Next year, Martha, I promise, next year we're gonna sell this rattrap, buy that yacht, and sail around the world. Yes sir."* People's dreams acted as a sort of barrier between life and death. Take them away—let people actually live those dreams—and you would be mopping up the suicides by the dumpster full. Just look at those few who did live their dreams, like movie stars or rock stars—the ones who really have the money to get right down to it—and you'll find a trail of brokenhearted people. Brokenhearted because they'd discovered what Kent was discovering: When you really got right down to it, life sucked.

That fact had delivered Kent to this impossible place, standing by the pillar just outside Macy's Monday evening and staring at a woman, his heart beating like a kettle drum, his palms wet with balls of sweat.

Lacy sighed, obviously unsatisfied with the discount rack's selection. She walked toward him. Kent caught his breath and turned slowly away, straining for nonchalance. In the hour that he had been tailing her, she had not recognized him, but then she had not studied him either. Twice she'd caught his eye and twice he had brushed on as though uncaring. But each time his heart had bolted to his throat, and now it was doing the same.

He bent for a *Shopper's Guide* on a bench and feigned interest in its cover. She walked by him, not three feet away. The sweet scent of lilac drifted by his nostrils, and he closed his eyes. It was all insanity, of course, this stalking. Not just because someone might notice the sweating man staring at the beautiful single woman and call security, but because he was indeed *stalking*. Like some kind of crazed loony, breathing heavily over a woman's shoulder, waiting for his chance.

He had driven to Boulder that afternoon, parked his car a hundred yards from Lacy's apartment, and waited. She had returned from work at six, and he had spent a good hour chewing at his nails, contemplating walking up to her door. Thing of it was, Gloria kept traipsing through his mind. For some reason not quite clear to him, he was feeling a strange guilt about Gloria. More so now, it seemed, than when he had spent time with Lacy before the robbery. Perhaps because then he had had no real intentions of pursuing Lacy. Now, though, faced with this crazy loneliness, he was not so sure.

She'd left the condo and driven here. His greatest regret in stalking her was the decision to leave the bottle of tequila in the car. He could have excused himself to the bathroom a dozen times for nips. But returning to retrieve the bottle from the car would take far too long; she might disappear on him, a thought suddenly more unnerving than staying dry for a few hours.

He twisted his head and watched her from the corner of his eye. Lacy wore blue jeans. She seemed to float along the shiny marble floor, her white running shoes gliding along the surface, her thighs firm beside her swinging brown purse. The lime-green sweater was perhaps a cardigan, resting loosely over her shoulders, its collar obscured by her blonde hair. Her lips seemed to pout, smiling on occasion; her hazel eyes darted over the selections; her fingers walked through the clothing carefully.

Kent watched her walk toward the food court. He wiped his forehead with the back of his hand and stepped cautiously after her. She wandered past shiny windows, casually glancing at their displays without bothering to enter. Kent stepped into a sports store, grabbed a beige flannel shirt from the sale rack, and hurriedly purchased it. He went straight to the shop's dressing room and changed into the new shirt before hurrying past a confused salesclerk to catch Lacy. The red shirt he'd worn went in the nearest trash bin. *You see, Lacy, I've learned a few tricks. Yes, sir, I'm a regular sneaky guy. You gotta be sneaky to steal twenty million, you know.*

He found her in the food court. She sat cross-legged, slowly eating an ice cream cone. He watched it all while peeking around a mannequin in Gart Brothers Sporting Goods across the lobby. There was nothing sexual in his desire—nothing perverse or strange or obsessive. Maybe obsessive. Yes, actually it was obsessive, wasn't it? He blinked at the thought and removed his eyes from her. How else could you characterize stalking a woman? This was no date. *Goodness, you're losing it, Kent.*

A wave of heat washed down Kent's back, and he left the mall then, feeling small and puny and dirty for having driven there. For having peeked at her from the shadows. What was he thinking? He could never tell her the truth, could he? She would be compelled to turn him in. It would be over—all of it.

And Gloria! What would Gloria say to this?

She's dead, *bozo!*

He drove back to Denver, wondering why he should not take his own life. Twice he crossed overpasses wondering what a plunge through the rail might feel like. Like an amusement ride, falling weightlessly for a moment, and then a wrenching crash. The grave. The end. Like Bono had said, in the end it's all for the grave anyway.

Kent shook his head and squeezed his eyes against the mist blurring his vision. He grunted to clear his throat of its knot. On the other hand, he wasn't in the grave yet. He had money, more than he could possibly spend; he had freedom from any encumbrances whatsoever. No wife, no children, no debt, no nothing. That was worth a smile at least, wasn't it? Kent smiled, but the image staring back at him from the rearview mirror looked more like a jack-o'-lantern than the face of a contented man. He lost the charade and slouched in his seat.

The evening took a turn for the better near midnight, two pints of tequila later. He lounged with glass in hand on the black-leather recliner facing a black television screen in the sleek apartment. The memory of his little stalking trip to Boulder sat like an absurd little joke on his brain.

Because of some obsession. Some pearls of wisdom from a Greek named Bono. Yes indeed, life sucked.

Well, it would be the last time he stalked anyone, he thought wryly. He would drive off one of those overpasses at a hundred miles per hour in the Lincoln before doing anything so foolish again. He had the world at his fingertips, for Pete's sake! Only an absolute loser would slink back for another peek. *"Peekaboo, I see you. My name's Kent, and I'm filthy rich. Would you like to share my life? Oh, yes, one small nugget for the hopper—my life really sucks, but not to worry, we will soon be in the grave anyway."*

Kent passed out on the leather recliner sometime before the sun rose.

39

Lacy sat alone in Wong Foo's Chinese Cuisine Thursday evening, nibbling at the noodles on her plate. Indirect lighting cast a dim orange glow across her table. A dozen heavy wooden carvings of dragons stared down from the low-hung ceilings. Cellulose walls lent an aura of privacy to the room. Glasses clinked with iced drinks, and voices murmured softly all about her, behind those paper partitions; somewhere a man spoke rapidly in Chinese. The smell of oriental spices circulated slowly.

A man sat alone in a booth ten meters to her right, reading the paper and sipping at noodle soup. They had noticed each other shortly after he had been seated not ten minutes earlier, and his bright blue eyes reminded her of Kent at first sight. He'd smiled politely, and she'd diverted her gaze. Freaks were everywhere these days. *You don't know that, Lacy. He may be a regular Clark Kent.* Actually, all men were pretty much looking like freaks these days.

Lacy dipped her spoon into the hot-and-sour soup and sipped at the liquid. She was having some difficulty shaking Kent's image. *Why* she could not shake his image, she could not fully understand. The first week was understandable, of course. The second, maybe even the third as well. But he had been gone for over a month now, for heaven's sake. And still he left tracks all through her thoughts every day. It was nonsense. Perhaps it was the thought of him living like a king after having the audacity to rub his plans in her face.

She peered at the man reading the newspaper and found him looking at her again. Goodness. She shot him a contemptuous grin this time. *Not too bold there, Lacy. He might get the wrong idea.* Looked like a decent-enough fellow. Blue eyes like Kent's—*See, now, there I go again*—and a face that reminded her of Kevin Costner. Not bad looking actually.

He had his head buried in that paper again, and Lacy steered her mind back to the plate in front of her. She had not heard from the detective again, and neither had she made any attempt to call him, because as the days passed, the notion began to sound somewhat misguided. She certainly had found no absolute collaborating evidence suggesting Kent's theft. And even if she had, she'd made a promise to him. Not that she *should* be bound by any promise after what he had done. There had been four incidents of mismatched bank statements, but no one seemed to give them any mind. Printer error or something. Whatever it was, it had corrected itself.

Yes indeed. The only thing that had not self-corrected was her mind. And she was beginning to think it might need some professional examination. Lacy lifted her fork and savored a bite of gingered chicken. The dragons glared down at her with glassy yellow eyes, as if they knew something she did not.

They were not the only things staring at her, she thought. The pervert was staring at her again. From the corner of her eyes she could see his face turned her way. Her pulsed spiked. Unless he wasn't really staring at her at all and it was just her imagination.

She turned slowly to him. No, it was not her imagination. He yanked his eyes away as her own zeroed in on him. What kind of guy was this? She should possibly leave before he began wagging his tongue at her.

Then his blue eyes rose to meets hers again, and they held for a long second. Lacy's heart paused for that second. And before it restarted, the man rose from his seat and walked toward her.

He's leaving, she thought. *Please tell me he's leaving!*

But he didn't leave. He walked right up to her table and placed a hand on the back of the chair opposite hers.

"I'm sorry, ma'am. I couldn't help but notice you sitting all alone." He smiled kindly, quite handsomely actually. But then Ted Bundy had been quite handsome. His voice came like honey to her mind, which surprised her. A thin sheen of sweat beaded his forehead. She imagined him breathing heavily in the corner. Lacy stared at the stranger without speaking, *unable* to speak really, considering the contradictions this man represented.

He attempted a smile, which awkwardly lifted one side of his face. "I know this may sound unusual, but do you mind if I have a seat?" he asked.

A hundred voices screamed in unison in her head: *Don't be a fool! Go wag your tongue at some streetgirl! Beat it!*

The stranger did not give her a chance to speak her thoughts. He sat quickly and folded trembling hands. She instinctively pulled back, stunned by his boldness. The man did not speak. He breathed deliberately, watching her in awe, with a slight smile curving his lips.

Goodness! What was she thinking, allowing this man to sit here? His eyes were striking enough, like blue sapphires, wide and adoring. *God, help me!*

"Can I help you?" she asked.

He blinked and sat a little straighter. "I'm sorry. This must seem awfully strange to you. But . . . does anything . . ." He fidgeted uncomfortably. "I don't know . . . strike you as odd?"

Lacy was finding her senses, and her senses were telling her that this man rang bells that echoed right through her skull, as if it were churchtime at the cathedral. They were also telling her that this man had a few loose bells himself.

"Actually, *you* strike me as odd. Maybe you should leave?"

That took the curl out of his gimpish smile. "Yeah? Well, maybe I'm not as odd as you think. Maybe I'm just trying to be friendly, and you're calling me odd. Is that what you think of friendly people? That they're odd?"

Tit for tat. He didn't seem so harmful. "People don't normally wander around Chinese restaurants looking for friendly conversation. Forgive me if I sound a bit concerned."

"People aren't usually friendly, is what you're saying. Well, maybe I'm just trying to be friendly. You consider that?"

"And maybe I don't need any new friends."

He swallowed and studied her for a moment. "And maybe you should think twice before rejecting a friendly neighbor."

"So now you're my neighbor? Look, I'm sure you're a wonderful man . . ."

"I'm just trying to be friendly, ma'am. You should never bite the hand that feeds you."

"I wasn't aware that you had fed me."

He reached over, picked up her bill, and slid it into his pocket. "You are aware now."

Lacy leaned back, struck by the absurdity of the exchange. "I don't even know you! I don't even know your *name*."

"Call me . . . Kevin." The stranger smiled. "And honest, I'm just an ordinary guy who looked across the room and saw a woman who looked like she could use some friendship. What's your name?"

She eyed him carefully. "Lacy." The bells were still gonging in her mind, but she could not place their significance. "And you can't tell me that walking up to a woman in a Chinese restaurant and asking to sit isn't rather strange."

"Maybe. But then, they say all is fair in love and war."

"So then that makes this a war? I'm not looking for a fight, really. I've had my share," she said.

"You have? Not with men, I hope."

"You're right. Men don't fight; they just leave." The crazy discourse was suddenly feeling a bit therapeutic. "You the love-'em-and-leave-'em type, Kevin?"

The man swallowed and grew very still. A pause seemed to settle over the restaurant. "No, of course not."

"Good, Kevin. Because if you were the love-'em-and-leave-'em type, I would throw you out the door myself."

"Yes, I'll bet you would." He shifted in his seat. "So we're sworn off men, then, are we?"

"Pretty close."

He eyed her carefully. "So . . . what happened?"

She did not respond.

∽◦∾

Of course Kent knew precisely what had happened. She was speaking about him. He had courted her, earned her trust, and then dropped her on her seat. And now this.

On Monday he had sworn to kill himself rather than stalk her again. On Wednesday he had broken that promise. He had allowed himself to live despite slinking back to Boulder to sneak a peek. She had gone grocery shopping that night, and he had slipped between the aisles on the edge of panic for the duration.

But this . . . He would pay for this madness. But it no longer mattered. He no longer cared. Life had somehow lost its meaning. He had followed her to the restaurant; taken a seat in plain view, and then approached her table. It had felt like stepping out on a tightrope without a net.

And now he'd had the audacity to ask her what happened. His palms were sweating, and he wiped them on his knees. The electricity between them had his heart skipping beats.

She was not responding, and he repeated the question. "So what happened?"

"No offense, *Kevin,* but if you want to befriend a lady at a restaurant, it's not necessarily advisable to strut up and drop the old *So-what's-happened-in-your-love-life-lately?* line. Comes across like something a pervert might say."

That stung, and he flinched visibly. *Whoa boy, don't expose yourself so easily.*

"You look surprised," Lacy said with a tilt of her head. "What did you expect? That I would lie down on a couch and tell you my life history?"

"No. But you don't have to bite my head off. I just asked a simple question."

"And I just more or less told you to mind your own business."

So, she was bitter and letting it ooze from her seams. She was right; he should have expected nothing less. "Okay look, I'm sorry if my introducing myself caused such offense, but maybe—just maybe—not everyone in the world is as cynical as you think. Maybe there are a few decent people around," Kent said, building his volume. Of course the whole thing was a crock, and he knew it as he spoke. He was about as decent as a rat.

She looked at him for a moment and then nodded slowly. "You're right. I'm sorry. It's just not every day that a man walks up to me and plops down like this."

"And I'm sorry. It was probably a dumb thing to do. I just couldn't help noticing you." She was softening. That was good. "It's not every day you come across a beautiful woman sitting alone looking so lost."

Lacy looked to the side, suddenly awash with emotion. He watched it descend on her like a mist. Watched her swallow. His own vision blurred. *Lacy, Oh, Lacy! It's me! It's Kent, and I love you. I really do!* His throat burned with the thought. But he could never go so far. Never!

"I'm so sorry," he said.

She sniffed and wiped her eyes quickly. "No. Don't be sorry. Actually, I think I'm in love with another man, Kevin."

Heat flashed over Kent's skull. Another man?

"I'm not even sure I could befriend you. In fact, I'm crazy about him"

Goodness, this was impossible! "Yes," he said. But he felt like saying no. Screaming, *No, Lacy! You can't love another man! I'm right here, for Pete's sake!*

"I think you should leave now," she said. "I appreciate your concern, but I'm really not looking for a relationship. You should go."

Kent froze. He knew she was right; he should leave. But his muscles had locked up. "Who?" he asked.

She looked at him, startled. "Who?" Her eyes bore into him and for a moment he thought she might lash out at him. "A dead man, that's who. Please go," she said. "Please go now," she insisted.

"A dead man?" his voice rasped.

"Go now!" she said, leaving no doubt as to her intentions.

"But . . ."

"No! Just go!"

Kent stood shakily to his feet, his world gray and fuzzy. He walked past her toward the door, right past the cashier without thinking to pay for their meals, right out into the street, hardly knowing he'd exited the restaurant.

Lacy was still in love with him. With Kent!

And this was good? No, this was bad. Because he was indeed dead. Kent was dead. And Lacy had not shown the least morsel of interest in Kevin, with his surgically altered cheeks and larger nose and sharper chin.

The realization fell on him like a boulder rolled from a cliff. He had truly died that night at the bank! Kent was truly dead. And Lacy was on the verge of death— at least her heart was. Any lingering hopes for love between them were now lost to the grave. End of story.

Kevin would have to find his own way. But Kevin didn't want to find his own way. Kevin wanted to die. Kevin didn't even exist.

He was *Kent! Kent, Kent, Kent!*

But Kent was dead.

It was the low point of his day. It was the low point of his month. It might very well be the low point of his life—although that day Gloria had died and that day Spencer had died, those had been low as well. Which was a problem because before coming here tonight, he had already been sliding along the bottom. Now the bottom was looking like the sky, and this tunnel he was in was feeling like the grave.

Kent's mind drifted to Spencer and Gloria, rotting six foot under. He might have to join them soon, he thought. Life up here above the grass was becoming quite difficult to manage. He trudged down the street thinking of options. But the only two he could wrap his mind around were trudging and dying. For the moment he would trudge, but maybe soon he would die. Either way, that woman back there was dead.

He knew that because he had killed her. Or he might as well have.

40

Kent stormed up Niponbank's sweeping steps Friday morning at ten, grinding his teeth and muttering under his breath. A fury had descended upon him in the wee hours of the morning. The kind that results from stacking up circumstances on the grand scale of life and then stepping back for a bird's-eye view only to see one end of the brass contraption dragging on the concrete and the other end swinging high in the sky. How much could a man take? Sure, on the one hand there was the brilliant million-dollar larceny bit, teetering up there on one side of the scale. But it was alone, hanging cold in the wind, forced into the loft by a dozen inequities piled high on the other side.

Lacy, for example. Or, as Kent saw the image, Lacy's firm jaw, snapping at him, barking for him to go. *"Just go! Now!"* Then there was the cop, an ear-to-ear grin plastered on that pointy head. Pinhead. *"You wanna know what I think, Bob? Or is it Kent?"* And there was Bono, spouting his wisdom of the grave, and Doug the Aussie, smiling toothlessly on the yacht that had killed his last son, and Steve the bartender hovering like a vulture. The images whispered through his mind, weighing the scales heavily, slowly pushing his blood pressure to a peak.

But it was the final few tidbits that had awakened him an hour earlier, panting and sweating on the covers. The ones he'd somehow managed to bury already. Gloria, swollen and purple and dead on the hospital bed; Spencer bent like a pretzel, cold as stone. Borst and Bentley, sitting behind their desks, smiling. *Welcome back, Kent.*

Somehow, all the images distilled down to the one of the porky twins sitting there, wringing their hands in the pleasure of their *deed.*

Which was why he found himself storming up Niponbank's sweeping steps Friday morning at ten, grinding his teeth and muttering under his breath.

He pushed through the revolving door and veered immediately right, toward the management offices. No nostalgia greeted him this time, only an irrational rage pounding through his veins. Sidney was there somewhere, clacking on the marble floor. But he barely registered the sound.

Bentley's door was closed. Not for long. Kent turned the knob and shoved it open, breathing as hard now from his climb up the steps as from his anger. A dark-haired woman sat cross-legged in a guest chair, prim and proper and dressed in a bright blue suit. Both snapped their heads up at his sudden entry.

Kent glared at the woman, stepped to the side, and flung a hand toward the door. "Out! Get out!"

Her jaw fell open and she appealed to Bentley with round eyes.

Bentley shoved his seat back and clutched the edge of his desk, as though poised to leap. His face had drained of color. He moved his lips to form words, but only a rasp sounded.

The woman seemed to understand. She could not possibly know what was happening here, but she wanted no part of it. She stood and hurried from the room.

"Get Borst in here," Kent said.

"He . . . he was already coming. For a meeting." The boy in Bentley was showing, like a man caught with his pants down. But if Kent's previous encounters with him were any indication, the man would gather himself quickly.

Borst walked into the room then, unsuspecting. He saw Kent and gasped.

"Good of you to join us, Borst. Shut the door." Kent closed his eyes and settled his nerves.

His former boss shut the door quickly.

"Why didn't you return my calls?" Bentley demanded. He was finding himself.

"Shut up, Bentley. I really have no desire to subject myself to more of your nonsense. I can take my share of punishment, but I'm no sadomasochist."

"And what if I had information critical to your investigation? You can't expect to walk out of here hurling your accusations and then just leave us hanging dry!"

"I did, didn't I? And short of a signed confession, nothing you could possibly tell me would prove critical to my investigation. Take my word for it. But I'll tell you what. I'll give you a chance now, how's that?"

Bentley stared at him, flabbergasted.

"Come on, out with it, man. What was so important?"

Still nothing. He had the man off center. No sense stalling.

"I didn't think so. Now, go over there and sit next to Borst."

"I—"

"Sit!"

The man jerked from his seat and shuffled over to where Borst sat, still white as a marshmallow on a stick.

"Now, for your sakes I'm going to keep this short. And I don't want to see you two slobbering all over the chairs, so save your comments for the authorities. Fair enough?"

They sat woodenly, unbelieving.

"Let me start at the beginning. I've put my findings in writing to the men who sign your checks, but I figure we have about ten minutes to chat about it before the Japanese come screaming across that phone. You ever hear cursing in Japanese, Borst? It isn't soothing stuff."

Kent took a breath and continued quickly. "For starters, you two had very little to do with AFPS. Its actual development that is. You evidently learned how to use it well enough. But in reality you did not deserve credit for its implementation, now did you? Don't bother answering. You did not. Which is a problem because, in claiming credit for another man's work you violated your employment agreements. Not only ground for immediate dismissal, but also requiring repayment in full of any monetary gain from the misrepresentation."

"That's not true!" Bentley said.

"Shut up, Bentley. Kent Anthony was solely responsible for AFPS, and you two know it as well as you know you're in this, neck deep." He drilled them with his eyes and let the statement settle in the room. "Lucky for you Kent seemed to meet an untimely demise a month after your little trick."

"That's not true! We had nothing to do with Kent's death!" Borst protested. "Taking a little credit is one thing, but we had nothing to do with his death!"

"You take a man's livelihood, you take his pride. Might as well be dead."

"You can't make any of this stick, and you know it!" Bentley said.

"We'll let the Japanese decide what sticks and what doesn't. But I'd spend just a little more time thinking about the million-dollar problem than about the Kent Anthony problem. Pretty clever, really. It took me the better part of a week to crack your little scheme."

A quiver had taken to Bentley's face, now red like a tomato again. "What are you talking about?"

"You *know* what I'm talking about, of course. But I'll tell you anyway. The way I figure it, Borst here developed this little program called ROOSTER. It looks like a security program for AFPS. Problem is, it was never released with the rest of the code. In fact it resides on only two computers throughout the entire system. That's right, the computer on Markus Borst's desk and the one on Price Bentley's desk. Interesting, given the fact that these two yahoos are the ones who ripped off Mr. Kent Anthony of his just reward. But even more interesting when you discover what the program is capable of. It is a ghost link to AFPS. A way into the system that's virtually undetectable. But I found it. Imagine that."

"But . . . But. . . ." Borst was sputtering.

"Shut up, Borst! That ain't the half of it." Kent delivered his indictment in long staccato bursts now. "It's how the program was used that tops the cake. Actually very clever, that one. A run of small, untraceable transfers to see if anyone notices and then hit them with the big one. *Bam!*" Kent smacked his palm with a fist, and they both jumped.

"One million dollars in a single shot, and no one knows where it's gone to. Unless you peek inside the accounts hidden conveniently on Borst's and Bentley's computers! Why lookie here! A million dollars all neatly tucked away for a rainy day. Not a bad plan."

"That's impossible!" Bentley was steaming red and dripping wet. "We did none of that! You can't be serious!"

"No?" The rage Kent had felt first while stomping up the bank's steps roared to the surface. He was suddenly yelling and jabbing his finger at them, and he knew that he had no reason to yell. They were both sitting five feet from him. "No? Well you're wrong, Porky! Nothing, and I mean *nothing,* is impossible for greedy slobs like you! You confiscate another man's fortune and guess what— someday you can expect yours to be confiscated as well!" He breathed hard. *Easy, boy.*

"It's all there, you idiot." He pointed at Bentley's computer. "Every last detail. You can read it like a mystery novel. Say what you want, but the data does not lie, and they already have the data. You two are going down!"

They gawked at him, thoroughly stunned.

"Do you understand this?" Kent asked, stabbing his forehead. "Is this information sinking in, or are you madly trying to think of ways to save your miserable necks?"

They couldn't respond, by the looks of it. Borst's eyes were red and misty. He was badly unraveled. Bentley was leaking smoke out of his ears—invisible, of course, but just as apparent.

Kent lowered his voice. "And let me tell you something else. The evidence is incontrovertible. Trust me; I put it together. If you want to get out of this you're gonna have to convince the jury that some ghost from the past did it all in your place. Perhaps you could blame it on that programmer you screwed. Maybe Kent Anthony's ghost has come back to haunt you. But short of an insanity plea along those lines, you're toast."

They still were not talking. Kent felt like saying more, like slapping them both back to life. But he had said what he'd come to say. It was the card he'd dreamed of playing for many long nights, and now he'd played it.

Kent strode for the door, past Bentley and Borst who sat unmoving. He hesitated at the door, thinking to put an exclamation mark on the statement. Maybe knock their heads together. *Thump! And don't forget it either!*

He resisted the impulse and walked from the bank. It was the last time he would see them. What happened to them now would be up to someone else, but in any scenario, things would not go easy for the porky twins. Not at all.

41

Helen walked alone on Monday, beside herself with contentment, unable to settle the grin bunching her cheeks. Light was crackling around the seams of heaven. She knew that because she closed her eyes and saw it almost without ceasing now. Yesterday, even Bill had seen the phenomenon. Or felt it, really, because it wasn't about physically seeing. It was more like *knowing* God's love, which in itself took a supernatural power. She mulled over one of the apostle Paul's prayers: "And I pray that you may have the power to grasp how wide and long and high and deep is the love of Christ . . ." It was something not easily grasped, that love. Something imagined with a certain degree of confidence, really. Certainly not heard or touched or seen or tasted or smelled. Not usually, anyway.

The light was like that, not easily grasped. But Pastor Bill was getting a grip on things these days. He was getting better at imagining the world beyond what most see and touch and taste. And he was imagining with belief. Faith. Believing having not seen, as the apostle put it.

Helen hummed the hymn "Jesus, Lover of My Soul." It was the martyrs' song, she thought. Everyone she knew who had carried that song had died for God. *Let me to Thy bosom fly . . .*

In all honesty she was not certain why the light was shining so brightly beyond the sky, but she had an idea. Things were not what they seemed. The death of her daughter, Gloria—such a devastating experience initially—was not such a bad thing at all. Neither was the death of Spencer such a bad thing. She had said so to Bill a dozen times, but now Helen was feeling the truth. Their lives were like seeds, which, having died in the ground, were now bearing a splendor unimaginable in their former puny vessels. Like the martyr who had been slain in Serbia. Somehow the seed was bearing fruit decades later in lives not yet born when that priest gave his life. How that fruit actually looked she did not know yet. She could not see as much. But the light spilling out of heaven was being pushed by peals of laughter.

"Good God, take me!" she mumbled and skipped a step. Her heart pounded with excitement. "Take me quickly. Let me join them, Father."

She had heard many times of how the martyrs walked willingly to their deaths, overjoyed and eager to find the life beyond. She herself felt the same way for the first time in her life, she thought. It was that kind of joy. A complete understanding of this life stacked up against the next life. And she would gladly jump into the next if given the opportunity.

Now this death of Kent, it was not quite so clear. He had died; he had not died. He would die; he would live; he would love; he would rot in hell. In the end she might never even know. In the end it was between Kent and God.

In the end Kent was every man. In the end the pounding feet in her dreams were the feet of every man, running from God.

She knew that now. Yes, there was this grand commotion over Kent in the heavens because of the challenge cast. Yes, a million angels and as many demons lined the sky, peering on his every move. But it was the same for every man. And it was not a game, as she had once suggested to the pastor. It was life.

"Glory!" she yelled, and immediately spun around to see if anybody had been surprised by that. She could see no one. Too bad—would've been nice to treat another human to a slice of reality. She chuckled.

Yes indeed. What was happening here in this isolated petri dish of her experience was no different from what happened in one form or another to every last human being who lived on God's green Earth. Different in the fact that she had been enabled to participate with her walkathon intercession, perhaps. Different because she saw more of the drama than most. But no different up there where it counted.

The truth of it all had descended upon her two days earlier, and now she wanted one thing like she had never wanted anything in the sixty-four years her little heart had managed to beat. She wanted to cross that finish line. She wanted to step into the winner's circle. She wanted to walk into glory. If given the choice to live and walk or to die and kneel before the throne, she would scream her answer: "the throne, the throne, the throne!" Jumping like a pogo stick. She would do it in her running shoes and tall white socks, not caring if a park full of baseball players saw her do it.

She wanted it all because now she knew without the slightest sliver of doubt that it was all about God's love—so desperate and consuming for every man. And she also knew that Gloria and Spencer were swimming in God's love and screaming with pleasure for it.

"God, take me home," she breathed. "Take me quickly."

Frankly, she didn't know how Kent could resist it all.

Maybe he wouldn't. Maybe he had.

Either way, the light was bright and crackling around the seams.

"Glory!" she chirped and skipped again.

<hr/>

It struck Kent that Sunday, two days after Lacy had spit him out like raw quinine, that it had been almost two months since he'd become a millionaire. Actually it didn't *strike* him at all, because the thought barely crept through his mind, like a lethargic slug hoping for safe passage. He rolled over and noted that he'd slept on top of the covers again. A dim light glowed around the room's brown drapes, and by the sounds of traffic he knew it was well past morning. Not that it mattered—day and night had lost their significance to him now.

It is said that money cannot buy happiness. It is one of those axioms often spoken but rarely believed for the simple reason that money does indeed seem to bring with it a measure of happiness. At least for a while. Bono's assertion that all paths end in the grave might be true, but in the meantime, surely money might ease the journey. It was the *meantime* part that Kent was having difficulty with. Because for Kent, the conclusion of the matter—the bit about the grave—took up early residence inside him. Like a hole in his chest.

It was all a bit unusual, possibly. Not in the least fair, it seemed. But hollow and black and sickening just the same. And this all without Pinhead the cop entering the picture. Throw his mug into the mix, and it was flogging desperation.

Kent had walked long and slow that Thursday night, away from Lacy. A limousine stuffed with squealing teenagers had nearly run him over at one point. The near-miss had nearly scared him out of his skin. He had hailed a taxi then and returned to the dungeon in Denver. The sun was already graying the eastern sky when he paid the driver.

Friday. Friday had been the big day of living dangerously, taking out his last few breaths of fury on the porky twins and then submitting his findings to the bank. They had delivered his fee as agreed. Bentley and Borst would undoubtedly find their just reward. Revenge is sweet, so they say. Kent didn't know who *they* were, but he knew now that they knew nothing. His victory was hardly more than a distant memory by two o'clock that afternoon.

He spent a good portion of the next two days—or nights, really, because he didn't roll out of bed until 5 P.M.—trying to plot a comeback. Not a comeback to Lacy; she was dead to him. But a comeback to life. He had eighteen million dollars stashed, for heaven's sake. Anybody who had eighteen million dollars stashed without knowing how to spend it was the better part of a moron. The things one could do with such wealth. Granted, Bill Gates might consider the cash chicken feed, but then Mr. Bill was in a different reality altogether. Most normal human beings would have trouble finding ways to spend even one million dollars, short of purchasing some jet or yacht or some other toy that cost the world.

Kent had considered doing just that. Buying another bigger, fancier yacht, for example, and sailing it to a deserted tropical cove. The idea actually retained some luster for the better part of a beer before he discarded it. He had already purchased one yacht, and he had left it behind. Maybe he'd buy a small jet. Fly around the world. Of course he would be landing and partying at all stops, discovering the local flavors and laughing with the natives. On the other hand, most local flavors were available at specialty restaurants around town—no need to traipse around the world. And laughter was not coming so easily these days.

Perhaps he could visit a few great sporting events. Sit in the stadium with the other rich folk who could afford to drop a few C notes for the pleasure of watching men bat, or throw, or bounce a ball around. Yes, and maybe he could take his own ball and play catch with a few celebrities. *Gag.* Thing of it was, three months ago the idea would have thrilled him. Now that he had the money, he could not remember why.

On Monday another emotion found its way into Kent's mind. Panic. An unearthly desperation at the prospect of finding no solution to this dilemma. A day later the panic settled into a dull hopelessness. He stopped feeling then and just continued his trudging through what he now saw clearly as the wastelands of life. Life without Gloria and Spencer. Life without Lacy. Life without Kent. Life without any meaning at all.

Kent climbed from bed on Wednesday and pulled the drapes aside. A light drizzle fell from a dark, gray sky. Could be morning, could be afternoon, could be evening. Looked nasty whatever time it was. He dropped the heavy curtain and trudged to the bathroom, shoulders drooping. The fluorescent bulb blinked brightly, and he squinted. Toothpaste stains ringed the sink, and he thought it might be good to clean the bathroom. He'd slept in the apartment for almost two weeks now without cleaning the kitchen or the bathroom. What would Helen say to that?

Helen, dear old Helen. A lump rose to his throat at the thought of the woman. So sincere, so steady, so sweet, so gentle. Well, not always so sweet or gentle, but sincere and truthful. She'd likely walk in here and land a loud slap on his cheek.

A tear sprang to Kent's eye. What was this? He was actually missing the old wench? Maybe, maybe not, but either way the tear felt good, because it was his first tear in five days. Which meant that his heart was still alive in its prison of bones.

But the sink and the kitchen and the rest of it could wait. Helen was not here. In fact, no one was here. Nor would anyone be here soon. He could buy the place and burn it to the ground. That would clean it up good. Yes, maybe he'd do that when this was over.

When what is over, Kent?

He looked up at the mirror and stared at his disheveled reflection. The face Lacy had rejected. Three days' stubble. Maybe four days'. The face of Kevin Stillman, still bearing scars from the surgery, if you knew where to look.

When what is over, Kent?

The lump swelled in his throat, like a balloon. Another tear slipped from his right eye. *I'm sorry, Gloria. God, I'm sorry.* His chest was aching. *I'm sorry, Spencer.*

Yes, and what would Spencer think of you now?

His shoulders shook, and the mirror dissolved in a single sob. *I'm so sorry.*

It's over, Kent.

He sucked at the air and caught his breath. The notion popped in his mind with sudden clarity. Yes, it was over, wasn't it? There was nothing left to do anymore. He had spent his life. He had drained it of meaning. Now it was time to step aside and let the others have a try.

It was time to stop trudging. It was time to die.

Yes, it's time to die, Kent.

Yes, let the other fools bloody their fingers climbing up life's cliff. Let them claw over the edge to find the wastelands stretching like a dusty graveyard. In the end it was all the same. In the end it was the grave.

Yes. You've come home, Kent. Welcome home, Kent.

It was the first touch of peace Kent had felt in weeks, and it tingled down his spine. *Now I lay me down to sleep . . .* Right beside the others who wasted their lives climbing this cliff called life and then lay down to die on barren wastelands. Salmon fighting their way up the river. Lemmings rushing to the cliff. Humans dying in the wastelands. It all made sense now.

Kent brushed his teeth. No sense dying with dirty teeth. He dropped the toothbrush half finished and spat the foam from his mouth. He didn't bother running any water to clean the mess.

The easiest way to slip into the grave would be through some sort of overdose; he'd thought so a hundred times. But thinking of it now, it seemed there ought to be more to the matter. It could be a month before they found his rotting body, maybe longer. Maybe he'd do the deed in a place that made a statement. The bank, for instance. Or in the steeple of a church. On the other hand, did he care? No, he did not care at all. He simply wanted out. Done. Over. He wanted to end. Find Bono's graveyard. Find a priest . . .

Confess.

Kent was halfway across the room, headed nowhere, when the thought dropped into his head. He pictured Bono telling him that. *"Confess, my son."* The word hollowed his chest. It seemed to carry a sense of purpose. And a suicide with purpose felt better than a senseless one. It would be something like leaning over that cliff and calling down to the million fools struggling up the stone face. *"Hey, fellas, there ain't nothin' up here but ashes and tombstones. Save yourselves the energy."*

Confess to a priest. Find a church, find a man of the collar, confess the crime, then drift off to the wasteland. Maybe meet Helen's God. The thought brought a tightness to his chest again. *I'm sorry, Helen.* Dear old Helen.

Kent sat on the bed and rested his forehead on his hands. An image of Helen filled his mind, and he swallowed against the knot in his throat. She was pointing to the bare spot above his fireplace—the spot that had once graced a painting of Christ. *"You crucified him, Kent,"* Helen was saying. Only she wasn't yelling it or stuffing it down his throat. She was crying and smiling.

"Yes," he muttered beneath his breath. A tear slipped down his cheek. "And now I'm going to crucify myself, Helen."

42

Helen called Bill at six that morning, pacing in small circles while she waited for him to answer. "Come on, Bill."

The dream had changed last night. The sound of running had quickened; the breathing had come in gasps. She had awakened wet with sweat and rolled from bed, the fingers of panic playing on her spine.

"Get up, Bill. Pick up the phone!"

A groggy voice spoke through the receiver. "Hello."

"Something's up, Bill."

"Helen? What time is it?"

"It's already six, and I should've been walking half an hour ago, but I started praying in my kitchen and I'm telling you, I could hardly stand it."

"Whoa, slow down, Helen. Sorry, I had a late appointment last night."

She stopped her pacing and peered out the window. A fine drizzle fell from a dark gray sky. "I don't know. But it's never been like this before."

"Like what, Helen. What are you talking about?"

"There's electricity in the air. Can't you feel it?" Helen moved her arm through the air and felt her hair stand on end. "Heavens, Bill, it's everywhere. Close your eyes and calm yourself. Tell me if you feel anything."

"I'm not the one who needs calming—"

"Just do it, Pastor."

The phone went dead for a moment before he came back on. "No. I'm sorry. I see only the backs of my eyelids over here. It's raining outside."

"It feels like heaven is about to tear loose, Bill. Like it's a bag of white-hot light, bursting at the seams over here."

He didn't answer right away, and she was suddenly impatient. She should be out walking and praying. The thought brought another shiver to her bones. "Glory," she whispered. Bill's breathing suddenly went ragged in the receiver.

"Helen . . . ?" his voice warbled.

Her pulse quickened. She spun from the window. "Yes? You see something?"

"Helen, I think something is going to happen . . . Oh, my God! Oh, my God!"

"Bill!" She knew it! He was seeing something right now. Had to be! "Bill, what is it? Tell me!"

But he just mumbled on. "Oh, my God. Oh, my God." His voice wavered over the phone, and Helen fought a sudden urge to drop the receiver and rush to his house. He was over there seeing into the other side, and she was standing here on this side, holding this ridiculous phone and wanting to be *over there*.

"Come on, Bill," she suddenly blurted. "Stop mumbling and tell me something!"

That put the pause in him. But only for a moment. Then he started again. "Oh, my God! Oh, my God!" It was not anything akin to swearing. Quite the opposite. This much Helen knew with certainty: Pastor Bill Madison was peeking into the heavens this very minute. And he was desperately yearning for what he was seeing, yes sir. The truth of it oozed from his shuddering voice as he cried to his God. "Oh, my God! Oh, my God!"

He fell silent suddenly.

Helen took a deep breath and waited a few seconds before pressing again. "What was it, Pastor? What did you see?"

He was not talking. Perhaps not listening, either.

"Bill . . ."

"I . . . I don't really know," came the weak reply. "It just came like a blanket of light . . . like last time, only this time I heard laughter. Lots of laughter."

"Ha! You heard it, did you? Well, what did I tell you? You see? Have you ever in your life heard such laughter?"

He laughed a crazy little chuckle. "No. But who is it? Who's laughing? . . . Do you think it's *God?*"

Helen lifted her arm and saw that the hair stood on end. She should walk. She needed to walk *now!* "The laughter is from humans, I think. The saints. And maybe from angels as well."

"The saints are laughing? *Laughing,* huh? And what about God? Did I see him in there?"

"I don't know what you saw, Bill. I wasn't there. But God is responsible for the light, and you saw the light, right? I think he is mostly loving and being loved and laughing—yes, laughing too—and weeping."

"And why, Helen? Why are we seeing these things? It's not common."

"No, it's not common. But it's real enough. Just like in biblical times, Bill. He's nudging our stubborn minds. Like my walking—impossible yet true. Like Jericho. Like two-thirds of the Scriptures, impossible yet true and here today. He has not changed, Bill." She gazed back out the window. "He has not changed."

"Yes. You are right. He has not changed."

"I have to go, Pastor. I want to walk."

"Yes, you should walk. It's supposed to snow today, they say. First snow of the season. You dress warm, okay?"

Snow? Goodness, that would be something, walking in the snow. "I'll be fine. My legs are not so concerned with the elements these days."

"Go with God, Helen."

"I will. Thank you, Bill."

Helen grabbed a light jacket on the way out and entered the gray morning air. Streetlights glowed like halos in a long string down the glistening pavement. One of those Volkswagen bugs drove by, its lights peering through the mist. The sound of its wheels running over the pavement sounded like tearing paper. She pulled on the jacket and walked into the drizzle, mumbling, hardly aware of the wet.

Father, thank you, thank you, thank you. Her body shivered once, as a chill swept through her bones. But it was not the cold; it was that light, crackling just behind the black clouds, that set off the tremor. True enough, she could not actually see it, but it fizzled and snapped and dazzled there, just the same. Her heart ran at twice its customary clip, as if it too knew that a rare power streamed through the air, unseen but fully charged.

Perhaps the prince of this earth wanted to put a damper on things. Soak his domain with a cold, wet blanket in an attempt to mask the light behind it all. But she was not seeing the blanket at all. She was seeing that light, and it felt warm and dry and bright. *Glory.*

Helen glanced at her white running shoes, stabbing forward with each stride. They flung droplets out ahead of her, christening the sidewalk like a priest flinging water on a baby's head. *Blessed be these feet, walking by the power of God.* It might have been a good idea to pull on long pants and a sweater, but she was not following good ideas these days.

She had run out of words in this prayer-walking weeks ago. She might have prayed through the entire Bible—she didn't know. But now it was just her heart yearning and her mouth mumbling. *You made this earth, Father. It's yours. There's no way a few drops will stand in your way! Goodness, you parted a whole sea for the Israelites—surely this here is nothing. In fact, maybe it's your rain. How about that?*

Helen lifted her hands and grasped at the drops, smiling wide. For a brief moment her chest felt as though it might explode, and she skipped for a few steps. Another car with lights glaring whisked by, its tires hissing on the wet street. It honked once and sped on. And no wonder; she surely looked like a drowned rat with her matted hair and drooping wet dress. *Crazy old woman, walking in this stuff. She'll catch her death!*

Now *there* was a thought. *Take me, Father. I'll gladly come. You know that, don't you? Don't get me wrong here. I'll do whatever you wish of me. But you know I'd die to be with you. To be rid of this flesh and this old wrinkled face and this hair that keeps falling out. Not that it's so bad, really. I thank you for it; really I do. And if you'd want me to, I'd bring it with me. But I'll tell you this, my God: I would give anything to be there with you. Take me any way you choose. Strike me dead with a bolt of lightning, roll me over with a monster truck, send a disease to eat away my bones—any way, just bring me home. Like those before me.*

She jumped once and swung her arm—a grandma-style victory whoop. "Glory!" This was how the martyrs had felt, she thought. Marching to Zion!

The sky slowly but barely brightened as the hours faded. Helen walked, scarcely conscious of her route. The path took her due west along side streets. She'd been here before, numerous times, and she knew the four-hour turnaround point well. If she took a loop around the fountain at 132nd and Sixth, she would end up back at home eight hours after her morning departure. The fat Buddha-looking statue at the fountain's center would be wet today, the goldfish swimming at its feet doubly doused.

Helen groaned at the thought of rounding the fountain and heading home. It should have come as a comfort with all the rain drenching her to the bone and the dark sky foreboding a storm, but it didn't. Not today. Today the thought of heading home made her heart sink. She wanted to hike right over the distant, crackling horizon like Enoch and climb under the black clouds. She wanted to find the light and join in the laughter. *Glory!*

The traffic was light, the normal straggle of pedestrians absent, the shops eerily vacant. Helen approached Homer's Flower Shop on the corner of 120th and Sixth. The old man stood under his eaves with folded arms and raised brows as she came near.

"They say snow's coming, you know. You shouldn't be out here."

"I'm fine, old man. This is no time to stop. I'm near the end now." He squinted at the comment. Of course, he could have no idea what she referred to, but then, a little mystery now and then never hurt anybody.

"Don't say I didn't warn you, old lady," he said.

She was even with him now and kept her head turned to meet his stare. "Yes, indeed. You have warned me. Now hear the warning of God, old man. Love him always. With every last breath, love him madly."

He blinked and took a step back. She smiled and walked on past. Let him think that one through. *Love God madly. Glory!*

She'd come to a string of street merchants who'd packed it in for the day, all except for Sammy the cap man who, truth be said, was more a homeless freeloader than an actual merchant, but nobody was saying so. Those who knew him also knew that he had sincerely if unsuccessfully tried at this life's game. Sometimes the ball rolls that way. He'd left a dead wife and a bankrupt estate in his wake. No one seemed to mind forking over a ten-dollar bill for a cheap, two-dollar cap— not when it was Sammy collecting the money. He stood under the eaves beside two large crates filled with his hats.

"What on Earth are you doing out here in the rain, Helen?"

She veered under the overhang. "Morning, Sammy. I'm walking. You have a cap for me today?"

He tilted his head. "A hat. You're soaked to the skin already. You think a cap will help now? Snow's coming, you know."

"Exactly. Give me one of those green ones you had out the other day."

He eyed her carefully, trying to decide if this bit of business was meant in sincerity. "You got a ten on you?"

"No, but I'll have it tomorrow."

Sammy shrugged and dug out a green hat sporting a red-and-yellow parrot on its bill. He handed it over with a smile, playing the salesman's role now. "It'll look great with that yellow dress. Nothing quite so appealing as a woman wearing a hat—dress or pants, rain or shine, it don't matter. It's the hat that counts."

She pulled it on. "Thanks, Sammy," she said and turned up the sidewalk.

Truth be told, she did it for him. What good would a hat do her? Although now that she had stretched it over her head, the bill did keep the drizzle from her eyes. "Glory!"

The horizon fizzled and crackled with light—she could feel it more than see it with her eyes, but it was real just the same. And she knew that if she could reach up there and pull those clouds aside she'd find one giant electrical storm flooded with laughter.

Helen walked on toward the turnaround point, toward the horizon, toward that sputtering light beyond what Homer or Sammy saw. If anybody was watching her on a regular basis they would notice that today her pace was brisker than usual. Her arms swung more determinedly. On any other day she might look like a crazy old woman with outdated fashion sensibilities, out for a walk. Today she looked like an ancient bag lady who'd clearly lost her mind—maybe with a death wish, soaked to the bone, marching nowhere.

Helen walked on, humming now. She stabbed the air with her white Reeboks, stopping on occasion to pump her fist and blurt out a word.

"Glory."

43

Kent drove to the liquor store at three in the afternoon, two hours after he had awakened and discovered he had only half a bottle of tequila left. He had decided it would be with booze and a bullet that his world would end, and half a bottle was not enough. He would drink himself into a state just this side of comatose, place the barrel of the nine-millimeter to his temple, and pull the trigger. It would be like pulling an aching tooth from society's jaws. Just enough anesthetic to numb the nerve endings and then rip the rotting thing out. Except it was his life decaying, not just some bony incisor.

He navigated the streets in a daze, peering lethargically past the drizzle. Sleet and the occasional snowflake mixed with the rain. The sky loomed dark and ominous. Decay was in the air.

He bought three bottles of the best tequila Tom's Liquor sold and tipped Tommy three hundred dollars.

"You sure? Three hundred dollars?" The man stood there with the bills fanned out, offering them back as if he thought they might be contagious.

"Keep it," Kent said and walked out of the store. He should have brought a couple hundred *thousand* from his mattress stash for the tip. See what Tommy would say to that. Or maybe he'd give the rest of the money to the priest. If he could *find* a priest to hear him. One final act of reconciliation for Gloria's sake. For Helen's sake.

He drove back to the apartment and pulled out the pistol. He'd shot it into the dead body at the bank a few times—three times actually, *blam, blam, blam* — so he wasn't terribly surprised to find six bullets in the nine-round clip. But it would only be one *blam* this time. He felt the cold steel and played with the safety a few times, checking the action, thinking small thoughts like, *I wonder if the guy who invented safeties is dead. Yes, he's dead and his whole family is dead. And now he's going to kill me. Sort of.*

Kent turned off all the lights and opened the drapes. The red numbers on the clock radio read 4:29. Snow now drifted silently past his window. The earth was dying slowly, begging him to join her.

It's time to lie down, Kent.

Yes, I will. As soon as I confess.

But why confess?

Because it seems decent.

You're going to blow your brains against the wall by the bed over there! What does decent have to do with that?

I want to. I want to tell a priest that I stole twenty million dollars. I want to tell him where to find it. Maybe he can use it.

You're a fool, Kent!

Yes, I know. I'm sick, I think.

You are human waste.

Yes, that's what I am. I'm human waste.

He backed to the bed and opened a bottle. The fiery liquid ran down his throat like fire, and he took a small measure of comfort in the knowledge that he was going to stop feeling soon.

He sat on the bed for an hour, trying to consider things, but the considering part of him had already gone numb. His eyes had dried of their earlier tears, like ancient abandoned wells. He was beginning to wonder if that voice that had called him human waste was right about blowing off the confession. Maybe he should stick to blowing off his head. Or maybe he should find a church—see if they even heard confessions of a dying man on dark wintry afternoons.

He dragged out the phone book and managed to find a listing of Catholic churches. Saint Peter's Cathedral. Ten blocks down Third Street.

Kent found himself on the road driving past the darkened cathedral thirty minutes later. The sign out front stated that confessions were heard until 7 P.M. each night, excluding Saturdays, but the dark stained-glass windows suggested the men of God had made an early retreat. Kent thought perhaps the sign should read, *"Confessions heard daily from 12:00 to 7:00 except on dark wintry days that depress everyone including priests who are really only men dressed in long black robes to earn their living. So give us all a break and go home, especially if you are suicidal.*

Don't bother us with your dying. Dying people are really just human waste. Priests are just ordinary people, and dying people are human waste." But that would hardly fit on the placard.

The thought drifted through his mind like wisps of fog, and it was gone almost before he realized he'd thought it. He decided he might come back later to see if the lights had been turned on.

Kent went back to his dark apartment and sat on the edge of his bed. The tequila went down smoothly now, not burning so much. It was five o'clock.

44

The Buddha-belly fountain came and went, and Helen did not stop.

It was as simple as that. She had passed the fountain at 11 A.M., and every other day she had turned around at the four-hour mark, but today she didn't want to turn around. She wanted to keep walking.

She could hear the water gurgling a full block before coming up on Mr. Buddha, and the impulse struck her then.

Keep walking, Helen.

I'm four hours from home if I turn now. I should keep walking?

Just keep right on walking.

Past the fountain? To where?

Past the fountain. Straight ahead.

Until when?

Until it's time to stop.

And how will I know that?

You will know. Just walk.

So she had.

That first step beyond her regular turning point felt like a step into the deep blue. Her heart raced, and her breathing thickened, but now it was not due to light spilling from the seams. This time it was from fear. Just plain, old-fashioned fear.

Certain facts presented themselves to her with convincing authority. Like the fact that every step she took west was one more step she would have to repeat later, headed east. Like the fact that it was now starting to snow, just like the weatherman had forecasted, and she wore only a thin jacket that had been soaked before the rain turned to snow. Like the fact that she was a lady in her sixties, marching off in a storm toward a black horizon. Like the fact that she did indeed look ridiculous in these tall, red-striped socks and wet, dirtied running shoes. In general, like the simple fact that she had clearly graduated from the ridiculous to the absurd.

Still she walked on, fighting the thoughts. Her legs did not seem to mind, and that was a good thing. Although they could hardly know that she was taking them farther from their home instead of closer. The first hour of walking into the cold, wind-blown snow had been perhaps the hardest hour Helen had lived in her sixty-plus years. Actually, there was no *perhaps* about it; nothing had been so difficult. She found herself sweating despite the cold. The incredible joy she'd felt when first walking a few hours earlier had faded into the gray skies above.

Still, she had placed one foot in front of the other and plodded on.

The light returned at three. Helen was in midstride when her world turned. When her eyes snapped open and she saw clearly again. That was exactly what happened. Heaven did not open up to her—*she* opened up to heaven. Perhaps it had taken these last four hours of walking blindly without the carrots of heaven dangling out in front to set her mind straight.

Either way, her world turned, midstride, and she landed her foot and froze. A crackle of light stuttered behind the walls of gray in her mind. Tears sprang to her eyes like a swelling tide. She remained still, her legs scissored on the sidewalk like a girl playing hopscotch. Her shoulders shook with sobs.

"Oh thank you, Father! Thank you!" She moaned aloud, overcome by the relief of the moment. "I knew you were there. I knew it!" Then the joy came, like a tidal wave right up through her chest, and she squeezed her hands into fists.

Just walk, Helen. Walk on.

It's been more than eight hours. It's getting dark.

Walk.

She needed no further urging.

I will walk.

She broke into a long stride. *One, two. One, two.* For a moment she thought her heart might burst with the exhilaration that now throbbed through her chest. *One, two. One, two. I will walk on. I will walk on.*

Helen strode down the sidewalk, through the strange neighborhood, toward the ominous horizon, swinging her arms like some marching soldier on parade. Snowflakes lay like cotton on her green hat and clung in lumps to her hair. She left footprints in the light snow covering the sidewalk. *Goodness, just wait until I tell Bill about this, she thought.* "I just kept going, Bill, because I knew it was what he wanted. Did I consider the possibility that I had lost my mind? Sure I did. But still I knew, and he showed me just enough to keep me knowing. I just walked."

Helen had walked another five blocks when the first pain shot up her right thigh.

She had not felt pain during weeks of walking. Now she felt the distinct sensation of pain, sharp and fleeting but unmistakable. Like a fire streaking through the femur toward her hip and then gone.

She gasped and pulled up, clutching her thigh, terrified. "Oh, God!" It was all she could say for a moment.

Walk.

Walk? Her jaw still gaped wide in shock. She rocked back on her good leg. I just had a leg cramp. I had pain! I'm twenty miles from home, and it's ending. It's over!

Walk. The impulse came strong.

Helen closed her mouth slowly and swallowed. She gazed about, saw that the street was clear of gawkers, and gingerly placed weight back on her right leg. The pain had gone.

Helen walked again, tentatively at first but then with gaining confidence. For another five blocks she walked. And then the pain flared through her femur again, sharper this time.

She gasped aloud and pulled up. "Oh, God!" Her knee quivered with the trauma.

Walk. Just keep walking.

"This is pain I'm feeling down here!" she growled angrily. "You are pulling your hand away from me! Oh God, what's happening?"

Walk, child. Just walk. You will see.

She walked. Halting at first until she realized the pain had left, as before.

It roared back with a vengeance six blocks later. This time Helen hardly stopped. She limped for ten yards, mumbling prayers through gritted teeth, before finding sudden relief.

The pain came every five blocks or so, first in her right leg and then in her left leg, and after an hour, in both legs simultaneously. A sharp, shooting pain right up each bone for half a dozen steps and then gone for a few blocks only to return like clockwork. It was as if her legs were thawing after months in the deep freeze and a thousand miles of pain was slowly coming due. Each time she cried out to God, her face twisted in pain. Each time he spoke to her quietly. *Walk. Walk, child.* Each time she put her foot forward and walked on into the falling darkness.

Three things contributed to her relentless journey despite its apparent madness. First was that quiet voice whispering through her skull. *Walk, child.* Second was the light—it had not fled. The blackening skies crackled with light in her mind, and she could not ignore that.

The third thought that propelled her forward was the simple notion that this might very well be the end. *The* end. Maybe she *was* meant to walk right up to the horizon of heaven and enter glory. Like Enoch. There might not be a flaming chariot to whisk her away. That had been Elijah's treat. No, with Helen it would be the long walk home. And that was fine by her. *Glory!*

The sun left the city dark by five-thirty. An occasional car hissed by, but the early storm had left the streets quiet. Helen limped on into the black night, biting her lower lip, mumbling against the voices that mocked her.

Walk, child. Walk on.

And she did walk on. By six o'clock both legs were hurting without relief. The soles of her feet felt as though they might have caught fire. She could distinctly imagine, if not actually hear, the bones in her knees grinding with each step. Her hips joined in the protest soon after. What began as a dull ache around her upper thighs quickly mushroomed to sharp pangs of searing pain throughout her legs.

Walk, child. Walk on.

Still she walked. The snow fell in earnest now, like ashes from a burnt sky. Helen kept her eyes on the ground just in front of her feet mostly, concentrating on each footfall as her destination—one . . . two, one . . . two. When she did look up she saw a dizzying sea of flakes swirling around the streetlights. The night settled quietly. Biting cold now numbed her exposed knees, and she began to shiver. She tucked her hands under her arms in an attempt to keep them warm, but the new posture threw her balance off, nearly sending her to the ground, and she immediately withdrew them. Oh, God! Please, Father. I have lost my mind here. This is . . . this is madness!

Walk, child. Walk on.

So she walked, but barely now, dragging one foot at a time, inching into the night. She lost all sense of direction, fighting through the landscape of her mind, aware of the pain ravaging her bones but no longer caring. At the eighth hour, back there, she had crossed the point of no return. She had stepped off the cliff and now fell helplessly onward, resigned to follow this still small voice or die trying. Either way the crackling light waited. And there would be laughter in the light. The notion brought a smile to her face, she thought, although she could not be sure because her face had gone numb.

The last fifty yards took twenty minutes—or an eternity, depending on who was counting. But she knew they were the last when her right foot landed on a cement rise of some kind and she could not pull herself up or over it. Helen fell to one knee, collapsed facedown, and rolled to her side.

If she'd been able to feel, she might have thought she had ground her legs to bloody stumps, judging by the pain she felt, but she could feel nothing at all. She was aware of snowflakes lighting on her cheek but no longer had the strength to turn away from them.

Then her world faded to black.

45

Desire for death is a unique sentiment, like a migraine sufferer's impulse to twist off his head in the hopes of banishing a throbbing headache. But Kent was still craving death—and increasingly so as the minutes ticked by in his dark apartment.

It might have been some deep-seated desire to delay his death that pushed him back to the church despite the falling snow. But if it was, it did not feel like any desire he'd ever felt. Nevertheless, he would do this one last deed. He would find his priest.

Snow rushed past his headlights, and it occurred to him that coming out for a priest on a night like this was nuts. But then, so was killing himself. He was a nutcase. The church's tall spiral reached into the night sky like a shadowed hand reaching for God. *Reach on, baby. Nothin' but black up there.*

He parked the car and stared at the dark cathedral. A monument to man's search for meaning, which was a joke because even the robed ones knew, way deep inside, that there was no real meaning. In the end it was just death. A dusty graveyard on the top of a cliff.

Get on with it, Kent.

Kent pushed the door open and slogged toward the wide steps.

The lump on the first step caught his attention immediately. A body lay curled like a fetus, covered with snow. Kent stopped on the sidewalk and studied the form. The priest had fallen down on the job—closed the temple up too early and now his God had dashed him on the steps. Or possibly a vagrant had come to find God and discovered a locked door instead. Either way the body did not move. It was the second dead body he'd seen recently. Maybe he should curl up and join this one.

Kent mounted the steps and climbed to the front door. It was locked. His mouth no longer had the will to swear or speak or even breathe, but his mind swore. He slogged down the steps, his mind still swearing long strings of words that no longer had meaning. He veered to the body and shoved it with his foot. *Death becomes me.* The snow fell from the vagrant's face. An old woman, smiling to beat all. A wide grin frozen on that pale face. She'd finally found her peace. And now he was on his way to find his own peace.

Kent turned from the body and walked for the car. An old memory crawled through his mind. It was dear old Helen, smiling with moist eyes in his living room. *You crucified him, Kent.*

Yes, dear Helen. But I will make amends soon enough. Like I told you, I'm going to kill my—

The next thought exploded in his mind mid-street, like a stun grenade. *That was Helen!*

His legs locked under him, stretched out for the next step.

Kent whirled back to the body. Ridiculous! That old woman lying over there was no more Helen than he was *God!* He turned back to his car.

If that wasn't Helen, then Helen has a twin.

He stopped and blinked. *Get a grip, Kent.*

And what if that is Helen by some freak accident, dead on the step?

Impossible! But suddenly the impulse to know trumped the rest of it.

Kent spun back toward the form and walked quickly. He bent and rolled the dead body to its back. Only it wasn't dead; he knew that immediately because its nostrils blew a few flakes from its upper lip in a long exhale. He jerked back, startled by the ghostly face smiling under a cap. His heart crashed against the walls of his chest. It *was* Helen!

It was not the grin or the face or even the hair. It was the yellow dress with small blue flowers, all but covered in snow, that made it so. The same yellow flowered dress she had worn to Gloria's funeral. The same yellow flowered dress she had worn to his door that first night moving in. That and the socks pulled to her knees.

He was staring at Helen, crumpled on the steps of this church, wearing running shoes clotted with frozen snow, smiling like she was in some kind of warm dream instead of freezing to death on this concrete slab.

Leave her.

I can't. She's alive.

Kent glanced around, saw that they were alone, and shoved his arms under Helen's limp body. He staggered to his feet with her dead weight hanging off each arm. The last time he'd done this, the body had been naked and gray and dead. He'd forgotten how heavy these things were. Well, the paramedics could deal with the crazy old fool as they saw fit.

Kent was halfway back to his car with Helen in his arms when that last thought crossed his mind. A swell of sorrow swept through his chest, and immediately he wanted to cry. For no reason that he could think of, really. Maybe because he had called her a crazy old fool and, really, she was no such thing. He looked down at the sagging body in his arms. No, this was no fool he carried. This was . . . this was precious. Helen, in all her eccentric craziness, somehow embodied a goodness. A tear came to his eyes, and he sniffed against it.

Get ahold of yourself, fool. And if she is goodness then what does that make you? Human waste.

Yes. Worse.

Yes, worse. Get rid of her.

Kent barely managed to open the passenger door without falling. He slid Helen onto the seat, slammed the door, and climbed in behind the wheel. She had fallen against the door, and her breathing came steadily now. A knot rose to his throat, and he shook his head. Thing of it was, she brought a strange sentiment out of him. One that had his windpipe aching. He missed her. That's what it was. He actually missed the old lady.

He started the Lincoln and pulled into the deserted street. The snow had eased to a powdery mist, visible only around a row of streetlights on the right. A white blanket lay undisturbed over parked cars and bushes and pavement alike. The sedan crept quietly over the snow, and Kent felt the fingers of death curl around his mind. It was death—death everywhere. A frozen graveyard. Kent swallowed hard. "God, let me die," he growled under his breath.

"Uhh . . ."

The groan from his right slammed into his consciousness like a bullet to the brain, and he reacted instinctively. He crammed his foot on the brake and pulled hard on the wheel. The Lincoln slid for the sidewalk, bumped into the curb, and stalled. Kent gripped the wheel with both hands and breathed heavy.

He whirled to the passenger's seat. Helen sat there, leaning against the passenger door with her head resting on her shoulder, cockeyed but wide eyed, and staring ahead past snow-encrusted brows. Kent's breath seemed to freeze in his throat. She was awake! Awake from the dead like a lost soul from the cast of a cheap horror movie.

Slowly she straightened her neck and lifted a hand to brush the snow from her face. Kent stared dumbly, thoroughly confused on how to feel. She blinked a few times in succession, climbing back into the land of the living, still staring out the windshield.

A small grunt came from Kent's throat, and it was this that clued her in to the fact that she was not alone. She turned to him slowly. Now her mouth was open as well. They locked like that for several long seconds, two lost souls gaping at each other in the front seat of a car, lost in a silent snowfall.

But Helen did not remain lost for long. No, not Helen.

She blinked again and swallowed. She breathed out deliberately, like the sigh of one disappointed. Perhaps she had not intended to wake up on the front seat of a car, staring at a stranger.

"Kent? You look different. Is that you?"

Well, then, perhaps not a stranger.

Kent more guffawed than answered. "Helen! What are you doing? You could have killed us!" It was an absurd statement considering his intentions, and having said it, he swallowed hard.

"You are Kent." She said it as a matter of simple fact. Like, "The sun has gone down."

"And how do you know I'm Kent?" He caught himself. "Even if I were?" But he'd already called her Helen, hadn't he? Good grief!

Either way, Helen was not listening. She was lost; he could see that in her eyes. She turned to the windshield without blinking. "Did you see it, Kent?"

He followed her eyes. The street still lay empty and white. Condensation was beginning to gather on the windshield from the hot breath. "See what?"

"See the light. Did you see the light? It was everywhere. It was heaven, I think." She spoke in awe.

The anger flared up his spine, but he bit his tongue and closed his eyes. "Helen . . . you were out cold and hallucinating. Wake up, you old religious coot. There's nothing but cold snow and death out there." Then he turned on her and let his anger swell past his clenched teeth. "I swear, I'm *sick* of all your crazy heaven and God talk!"

If he expected her to shrink, he should have known better. She turned to him with bright eyes. She did not look like an old woman who had just been dragged, half dead, from a snowstorm. "What if there *is* life out there, Kent?" Her lips flared red. "What if, behind this veil of flesh, there is a spiritual reality crackling with light? What if it was all created for a purpose? What if, behind it all, that Creator is craving relationship?" Tears sprang to her eyes.

"What if you were made to love him? What then, Kent?" Her eyes did not blink but turned to pools of tears. One of those pools broke, and a trail of tears ran down her right cheek.

Kent had his mouth opened to retort, to put her back in her place, before he realized he had nothing to say. Not to *this*. What she suggested could not be. He tried to imagine a God desperate for love, like some huge, smiling ball of light with outstretched arms. The image refused to hold shape. And if there was truth there in those words, if somehow there was a Creator who loved him so . . . he would kill himself anyway. He would slit his wrists in agony.

Kent turned from her and clenched his jaw.

"Kent." Her voice warbled soft to him.

Shut up, Helen! Just shut up! His mind screamed obscenities, locked in torment.

"Kent." She was begging. The small, stuffy cabin of the Lincoln seemed to throb with the beating of his heart. He wanted to reach over and slap her, but his hands had frozen on the wheel.

Kent cast her a sideways glance. Helen was trembling and weeping and melting on the seat before him. His heart screamed with pain. Her lips quivered with desire. A pleading smile.

She reached a shaking hand toward him. "Kent. Do you want to see?"

He could barely hear the words from her constricted throat. *"Kent, do you want to see?"*

No! No, no, no, I don't want to see! "Don't be a fool, Helen! You don't just turn on a light to see this God of yours!"

"No. But tonight is different. Do you want to see?"

No, no, no, you old hag! There is nothing to see! Tears blurred his vision.

What was happening to him? An ache tore at his heart, and he whimpered. Time seemed to cease then, in that moment of agony. *Oh, God! Oh, God! Do I want to see? Yes! Yes, I do want to see, don't I?* Kent slowly kneaded his skull with his fingers. He heard the word from his lips like a distant whisper. "Yes."

She touched his cheek.

A strobe exploded in Kent's skull. The horizon detonated with a blinding light, and he jerked upright. Everything stopped then. His heart seized in his chest; his blood froze in his veins; his breath stalled in his lungs. The world ended with one gasp.

And then it restarted with a blur of images that slammed him back in his seat and yanked his jaw open. Torrents of light cascaded into his mind and thundered down his spine. His body convulsed there on the leather Towncar seat as if seized by death throes.

But it was not death. It was life! It was the breath of God! He knew that the moment it touched him. Helen's creator was . . . was *whispering* to him. He knew that too. This raw emotion pounding through his body was just a whisper, and it said, *I love you, my beloved.*

"Oh, God! Oh, God, God!" He was screaming. Laughter drowned out his own cry—a pealing laughter that echoed across the sky. He knew that laughter! Voices from the past—a mother laughing in pleasure; a child giggling in long, high-pitched squeals of delight. It was Gloria and Spencer, there in the light, ecstatic. Kent heard their voices echo through his skull, and he threw his hand to his face and began to writhe in shame.

"Oh, God! Oh, God. I'm sorry!" It was true! The realization pummeled him like a battering ram to the chest. God! Helen's God. Gloria's God. Spencer's God. *The* God!

And he had said, *I love you, my beloved!*

The injustice of it all twisted Kent's mind, and he wormed in agony. The anguish of a mother having smothered her child. The desperation of a husband having tossed aside his bride for the whore. A wish for death.

A new surge of Helen's heaven crashed through Kent's bones, and he trembled under its power. *I love you, my beloved.*

Kent screamed. With every fiber still intact in his throat he screamed out for death, for forgiveness—but his vocal cords had seized with the rest now. They produced nothing more than a long, drawn-out groan. "Uuuuuuhhhhh . . ."

I have died already. I forgive you.

No, no, you don't understand! I am human waste. I do not know how to love. I am death!

You are my lover.

I am your hater! Kent's body buckled, and his forehead hit the steering wheel. Tears ran down his cheeks. The gross incongruity of these words swung like a steel wrecking ball against the sides of his skull.

You are my lover!

The notion that this being of white-hot love could want to love *him!* It could not be! He arched his neck and faced the Towncar's plush ceiling, his mouth stretched wide. It was then that he found his voice again. And he used it to roar, full throated. "Nooooooooo! I caaan't!"

Please love me. The whisper thundered through his body.

You were made to love him, a small voice said. Spencer's voice. Then it giggled.

Yes, Kent. Love him. That was Gloria.

Then Kent fell apart and heaved with sobs on the front seat beside Helen. In one twisted bundle of agony and ecstasy, of deep sorrow and bubbling joy, Kent loved God.

"Yes. Yes, yes, yes." He drank the forgiveness as if an overwhelming thirst had brought him to the edge of death. He gulped at the love like a fish desperate for oxygen. Except this was God filling him with breath, and it brought an unabashed quiver to each fiber of muscle still capable of movement. He reached out with every ounce of his being, every conscious thought, and he begged to be there with him.

For a few moments he *was* there with him. Or a part of God was down here in the Lincoln with him.

And then the light vanished, leaving Kent gasping for breath, draped over the steering wheel. He fell over Helen's lap and sobbed.

She stroked his head gently. Time lost its meaning for a while.

46

"So you saw him?"

Kent sat up, dazed. He looked at Helen and then back out the front windshield, misted now with condensation. "God!"

"Yes. Words just aren't adequate, are they?"

"So that was . . . God?" He knew it was. Without the slightest question.

"Yes."

Kent turned to her slowly. "Is it that way for everybody? How come I've never heard of this?"

"You've never heard about it because you've kept your ears closed. Is it that way for everybody? Yes and no."

He stared at her, wanting her to continue.

"No, not everyone will see what you have seen here tonight. At least not in the same way. But yes, in many ways, it is the same."

She turned to the windshield. "Let me tell you a story, Kent. You remember a story in the Bible about a man named Job?"

"I heard them, Helen. I heard Gloria and Spencer. They were laughing." A smile curved his mouth.

She smiled, bright eyed. "Yes, I know. You remember this man, Job? From the Bible?"

"They're in heaven, Helen," Kent returned, still distracted by the thought. "They're actually in heaven. With *him!*"

"Yes." She nodded. "Kent. I'm asking you a question here. Do you know of Job in the Bible?"

"The man who suffered?"

"Yes. Satan lost his challenge that he could make a righteous man curse God. You remember that?"

"Job remained faithful to God. And in the end he received twice the wealth. Something like that."

"It actually happened. He lost everything. His children, his wife, his wealth."

Kent turned to her, blinking.

She faced the dark sky. "Not so long ago, Satan cast another challenge before God. A challenge of reversals. This time he insisted that he could keep an unrighteous man from responding to God's love. *No matter how you draw him, no matter how you love him, no matter how you lure him,*" Satan said, *"I can keep this man from responding to your love."*

"You're saying this actually happened?"

"Yes." She looked at him and nodded, teary eyed now. "Yes. And God accepted the challenge. The heavens have been lined with a million creatures, intent on that man's every move for months. And today, God has won the challenge." Helen smiled.

"M . . . me?" Kent asked, stunned. *"I was this man?"*

"Yes."

The notion seemed absurd. "This was all engineered, then? How . . ."

"No, not engineered, Kent. You were drawn. In ways none of us may ever fully understand, you were drawn by the father. And you were pulled . . . in a thousand ways you were pulled by Satan. Away from God."

Kent's mind spun back over the last few months and saw a long string of events full of extremes. Death. But in death, laughter, because Gloria and Spencer were laughing up there. Wealth. But in wealth, death. Or very nearly death. A whole reality behind the stage of life.

"He must have switched strategies halfway through," Kent said absently.

"Satan?"

"Yes. Killing off my family didn't work, so he set out to make me rich."

She chuckled. "Yes, you're getting the picture."

He turned to her again. "But why me?"

She sighed and shook her head. A car drove by, its lights glaring like halos in the windshield. The dull thump of rock music for a moment and then silence once again.

"That's just it, Kent. Your case is unique because of what we were able to see. But otherwise it's not so different than the challenge made over the young man or woman behind the wheel of the car that just passed us."

"It's the same for everybody?"

"You think God loves any one man more than he loves another? Does he draw one more and another less? No. Over every man there is cast a challenge. It is as intense for every man. We just don't see it. If we could . . ." She shook her head. "My, my, my."

Kent's chest began to swell, and he thought he might be reduced to tears again. This changed everything. It seemed so obvious now. So right. The meaning of life all bundled up in a few statements and yet so few knew the truth.

"So then behind this . . . this flesh . . . this physical world, there is activity . . . enough activity to blow our minds." He shook his head, overwhelmed by the notion. "We see only the tip of it all. And then only if we open our eyes."

"We fight not against flesh and blood. And we fight a war that is fleeting. Believe me, this life will pass quickly enough, although sometimes not quickly enough, it seems. Then it will be forever. Somewhere."

"Why don't more people know this? Why has no one told me this?"

She turned to him. "You think Gloria never told you this? We prayed every Thursday morning for five years for this day. You were just too wrapped up in this world to notice."

"Yes, you are right. You are so right!"

"Today you start over, Kent."

Lacy!

He grabbed Helen's arm. "We have to get to Lacy!"

"Lacy?"

"Yes. She lives in Boulder." He started the car and pulled out into the street, sliding on the snow. "Do you mind? I need you there. She'll never believe me."

"Why not? It's a beautiful, snowy night for a drive. I was rather hoping for an entirely different destination, but I suppose Boulder will do for now."

47

Lacy answered the door dressed in a plaid flannel shirt that hung below her jeans. "May I help you?"

Kent stood behind Helen for the moment, his heart pounding like a locomotive in his chest. He saw Lacy's eyes shift to him, questioning at first, and then recognizing. "Hello, Lacy," Helen said. "May we come in?"

"You? Kevin, right? I met you in the restaurant. What do you want?"

Helen answered. "We are not who you might think. My name is Helen. Helen Crane. This is my son-in-law, Kent Anthony. I believe you know each other."

Lacy's eyes grew round.

Kent stepped around Helen, steadying a tremble that had parked itself in his bones since his eyes had been opened. "Hello, Lacy."

She stepped back. "That's . . . that's impossible! Kent's dead."

"Lacy. Listen to me. It's me. Listen to my voice." He swallowed. "I know I look a bit different; I've had a few changes made, but it's me."

Lacy took another step back, blinking.

"You hear me?" Kent pushed. "I told you the whole plan on a Friday night, sitting right there," he motioned to the dinette table, "drinking your coffee. Twenty million dollars, right? Using AFPS? You slapped me."

It was too much for her to reject, he knew. She stepped aside as though in a dream. Kent took it as a sign to enter and he did so cautiously. Helen followed and sat on the sofa. Lacy closed the door and stood facing him, unblinking.

The room stilled to silence. What could he possibly say? He grinned, feeling suddenly foolish and small for coming. "So, I don't know what to say."

She did not respond.

"Lacy. I'm . . . I'm so sorry." His vision swam in fresh tears. She was searching her memory banks, trying to make ends meet, reconciling conflicting emotions. But she was not speaking. He saw her swallow and suddenly it was too much for him. *He* had caused this. *He* might have changed, but the remnants of his life lay in ruins. Gutted shells, hollow lies, broken hearts. Like this heart here, beating but broken, possibly beyond mending.

Lacy's jaw clenched, and her eyes swam in pools of tears.

Kent closed his eyes and fought his own tears. Yes, indeed, she was not so happy; that much was obvious.

Her voice came barely above a whisper. "So. It *is* you. Do you know what you've done to me?"

He opened his eyes. She was still staring at him, still clenching her jaw. But some light had come to her eyes, he thought. "Yes, it is me. And yes, I've been a complete idiot. Please . . . please forgive me."

"And you came to me at the restaurant." Her jaw relaxed.

He nodded. "Yes. I'm sorry."

"Good. You should be. You should be terrified about now."

"Yes. And I am." She was going to reject him, Kent thought. She *should* reject him.

Lacy's eyes blazed. "And why did you come? Tell me why you came."

"Because . . ." It was hard, this dealing in love. First God and now her. He blinked. No, not hard at all. Not in his new skin. Hard in his old self, but in this new skin, love was the currency of life.

He said it easily then. "Because I love you, Lacy."

The words seemed to hit her with their own physical force. A tear broke from her eye. "You love me?"

Oh, what had he done to her? "Yes. Yes, I love you," Kent said. He walked right up to her and opened his arms, desperate for her love.

She closed her eyes and let him embrace her, hesitantly at first, and then she slid her arms around his waist and pulled herself into his chest, crying. For a long time they said nothing. They held each other tightly and let their embrace speak.

When Lacy finally spoke it was in a soft, resigned voice. "And I love you, Kent. I love you too."

48

Padre Cadione turned from the window, his face wet with tears at the tale his visitor had shared over the last two hours. They had shifted about the office, reposturing themselves as the story sped on, at times leaning against the wall, at times sitting behind the desk, but always intent. The confessor had told the story with exuberance, with many hand gestures, with tears, and often with a contagious grin splitting his face. And now the tale had ended, much to the father's dismay. But had it?

Beyond the window he could see the east guard tower, stoic against the blue sky. Cadione turned back to the man before him. His chest felt as though a vise had screwed down on his heart for the duration. The visitor sat cross-legged now, swinging one leg over the other, his hands folded on his lap.

"This is true? All of it?"

"Every word, Father."

The fan continued its swishing high above, drying the sweat gathered on Padre Cadione's neck. "You believe that God is capable of such a thing today, then?"

"I know it, Father!" The man stood to his feet and spread his hands wide. Cadione leaned back in his chair. "His love is greater than the greatest love man can imagine. The most extravagant expression of love is but a dim reflection of his own! We are made in his image, yes?"

"Yes." The padre could not help but smile with the man.

"You see, then! The greatest passion you are capable of only hints at his love."

"Yes." He nodded. "But how is it possible for a man to experience God in such a way? The experiences you speak of are . . . incredible!"

The visitor dropped his hands. "Yes, but they are real. I know."

"And how do you know?"

The light glinted off the visitor's eyes, and he smiled mischievously. "I know because I am he."

Padre Cadione did not respond immediately. He was who? The man in the story? But that was impossible! "You are *who?*"

"I am he. I am Kent Anthony."

The father's heart missed its rhythm. "Kent? Your file says your name is Kevin. Kevin Stillman."

"Yes, well, now you know the whole story, don't you? There are certain advantages to changing identities, my friend. It is the one thing they permitted me to keep when I confessed. A small consolation. And of course, I had to confess—you understand that, don't you? I *wanted* to confess. But there is no use living in the past. I am a new man. And I rather like the name."

The father's mind spun. "So then, you say that you personally glimpsed heaven? That this whole wager of Lucifer's was over your soul? You say heaven bent over backward to rescue your soul?"

"You think it is presumptuous?" the man said, smiling. "It is no less so than the challenge over your soul, Father. You just do not see it." He lifted a hand to make a point. "And I'll tell you something else. Everything is not what it seems. I knew early on that the vagrant in the alley was a man of dreams, but I did see him once, and I am not sure to this day whether he was real. But he was not an angel, I can assure you."

"You're saying he was sent from hell, then?"

"Can you think of a reason why not? Now, the others—I believe they were from heaven. I cannot be sure, of course. But the Scriptures do say that we entertain angels without knowing, do they not?"

"Others?"

"Cliff. I could find no record of him in the employment files when I looked for him at the end. And the detective. Detective Pinhead. There is no record of a Jeremy Lawson at the Seventh Precinct. I always suspected there was something with those two. Perhaps even Bono at the bar."

A knock rapped on the door.

"That seems . . ."

The man grinned wide. "Impossible? Not all things are what they seem, my friend."

"What happened to the money? To the bankers?"

"Borst and Bentley? Neither work for the bank now. I told the bank everything, of course. Last I heard they were wrapped up in court battles over the bonus money. They cannot win. And no bank will hire dishonest men. I pity them, really. As for the money, I liquidated everything and returned the money to each and every account from which it was taken, twenty cents at a time. Using ROOSTER, of course. Only the authorities and a few officials at the highest level even know what happened. The bank insisted I keep the $250,000 recovery fee. I tried to give it back, but they said I had earned it by exposing Borst and Bentley. And by developing AFPS, of course."

The rap sounded again. "Time's up, Chaplain."

"Come in," Cadione called, keeping his eyes on the man. The pieces to this puzzle locked in his mind, and he stood, frozen by them.

A uniformed guard walked through the door and stopped. "Come on. Let's go." The guard waved a night stick in Kent's direction. "Back to the cell."

The prisoner named Kevin, who was really Kent—Kent Anthony—turned to leave, still smiling at Padre Cadione.

"And what of Lacy?" Cadione asked, ignoring the guard.

Kent smiled. "I'll be up for parole in two years. If all goes well, we plan to be wed then. Maybe you could do the honors, Father."

He nodded. "Yes. And Helen?"

"Yes, Helen. You will have to meet Helen someday, Padre. She was not always the kind of woman she was in this story, you know. Her life story will make you weep. Perhaps someday when we have more time, I will tell you. It will make you see things differently. I promise."

"I would like that," the chaplain heard himself say. But his mind was spinning, and he was finding it difficult to concentrate.

The prisoner turned at the door and winked. "Remember, Father. It is true. Every last word is true. The same challenge has been cast over your soul. You should ponder that tonight before you sleep. We are all Jobs in one way or another."

They led him out, still smiling.

Padre Cadione staggered to his chair and sat hard. It had been a long time since he had prayed more than meaningless words. But that was about to change.

Everything was about to change.

OK, WE ADMIT IT.
There's truth in our fiction.

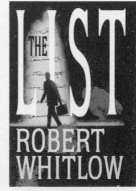

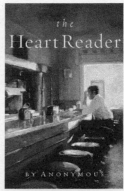

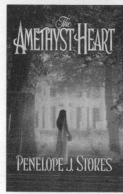

RATTENBURY

RATT

ENBURY

Terry Reksten

SONO NIS PRESS
VICTORIA, BRITISH COLUMBIA

1978

Copyright © 1978 by Terry Reksten

Canadian Cataloguing in Publication Data

Reksten, Terry, 1942-
    Rattenbury

        Includes index.
    ISBN 0-919462-58-8

        1. Rattenbury, Francis Mawson.
    2. Architects — Canada — Biography.
    NA749.R3R4   720'.92'4   C78-002169-X

Published by
SONO NIS PRESS
1745 Blanshard Street
Victoria, British Columbia

Designed and printed in Canada by
MORRISS PRINTING COMPANY LTD.
Victoria, British Columbia

To my mother

Acknowledgements

I am especially grateful to the staff of a number of museums, archives and libraries; the British Library; the Newspaper Library at Colindale; Oxfordshire County Council Library; the General Register Office, London; Bradford Metropolitan Library; Washington State Library; Saskatchewan Archives Board; Glenbow-Alberta Institute; Archives of the Canadian Rockies; Victoria Public Library; Oak Bay Municipality and the Provincial Archives of British Columbia. Without their interest and helpful suggestions the research for this book could not have been completed. And I am most grateful to the Canada Council for providing the grant without which much of the research would have been impossible.

Many individuals gave invaluable assistance in the preparation of this book. I owe a special debt of gratitude to Frank B. Rattenbury and Mrs. E. Burton (Mary Rattenbury) for providing me with a highly personal view of their father. And to Ainslie Helmcken and Miss C. Maclure and many other long-time Victoria residents who shared their reminiscences with me. Thanks are also due to Ian Whitely of the *Bournemouth Daily Echo* who helped me find Stoner, to Bert Parsons and Dixie Dean for their recollections of Alma, to Martin Segger, Al Kerr and Leonard McCann for sharing their information and their photographs with me, to Carolyn Smyly, Joan Wright and Brian Smith who helped in the beginning when it was so important, and to Eric Tomlinson for helping to tie up loose ends. And to Jim Munro who gave me encouragement when I needed it most.

Candy Wyatt deserves special thanks. A constant friend and long-suffering sounding board, she also suggested changes to and then typed the final manuscript. I appreciate her help so much that some-day I may find it in my heart to forgive her for the unbounded glee with which she pounced on yet another spelling mistake.

I hope Jane and Norah already know how much their patient acceptance of a slightly distracted mother has meant. And if my husband Don thinks for one moment that I could have completed this book without him, then he'd better think again.

Contents

Introduction

Five years ago when I first became interested in Francis Mawson Rattenbury I knew only that he was the architect of British Columbia's Parliament Buildings and Victoria's Empress Hotel and that he had been murdered in England. In the beginning I was only mildly curious. This man must have been one of the most respected and successful architects of his day. Why had he chosen to leave Victoria to live in anonymity in Bournemouth, an English seaside town that was in many ways similar to Victoria? And why had he been murdered?

The second question proved the easier one to answer. Rattenbury's murder had resulted in one of the most celebrated trials to be held in London's Old Bailey in the first half of the twentieth century. A transcript of the trial, edited by F. Tennyson Jesse, had been added to the "Notable British Trials" series in 1935. Rattenbury, it appeared, had become entangled in a strange and unlikely *ménage à trois* and the jealousies and passions of that relationship had led to his murder.

But again why had he left Victoria, the scene of his success, to settle in Bournemouth where he became known as just another retired colonial with a few interesting stories to tell? By the time I discovered the answer to that question, learning more about Rattenbury, his life and his career, had ceased to be a part-time diversion and become a full time preoccupation. For at least twenty years Rattenbury had been British Columbia's most prominent architect. Even a partial list of his buildings was impressive; office buildings for the Bank of Montreal in Victoria, Nelson and New Westminster; courthouses in Vancouver, Nelson, and Nanaimo; Victoria's Crystal Garden, the Calgary home of cattle baron Pat Burns; B.C.'s Government House. All landmark buildings and all designed by a man who never thought of himself solely as an architect. A man who dabbled successfully in politics and who proved himself to be a sensitive and visionary town planner. A man who crossed the Chilkoot in 1898 to promote his transportation company and a man who dreamt of being an empire builder and who risked a fortune in an attempt to make that dream a reality.

It seemed to me that Rattenbury was a fascinating character whose story deserved to be told, but researching this book presented certain difficulties.

The Five Sisters block in Victoria which housed Rattenbury's office burned to the ground in 1910 taking with it many of his plans and sketches, his business records and his correspondence. Without those records it is impossible to know the full extent of his architectural practice. But fortunately a number of his plans and rough sketches have managed to survive — some in the files of the Department of Public Works and others found hidden away in the attic of his home years after his death. And they were enough to clearly indicate the impatient genius of the man who drew them, a man who sketched monumental buildings with quick bold strokes and who became bored with the careful and clever detail work on which other architects based their reputations.

And fortunately too, Rattenbury held his own opinions in such high regard that he could see no reason for keeping them to himself. He often rambled on happily to reporters from the Victoria newspapers about his ideas on town planning or about the assured success of his latest business venture. He was particularly sensitive to criticism and more than one "Letters to the Editor" column was enlivened by his aggressive and uninhibited letters. In 1903 he wrote an open letter to Alderman Yates. Yates, a Victoria lawyer for whom Rattenbury had designed a small office block five years earlier, had had the temerity to suggest that Rattenbury seldom completed a building within the estimated cost. "You have no more right, Mr. Yates, to make such a sweeping assertion as reported, than I should have to say that you have muddled almost every case you have ever taken into court, although I may think so." That kind of outspokenness was typical of Rattenbury and although none of his personal correspondence has been found, his public letters are more revealing of his character than might ordinarily be expected.

Many long-time residents of Victoria remember Rattenbury but they are contemporaries of his children and being a generation removed they lack the insight that would have helped immeasurably in understanding and exploring his character. During the course of many interviews, a surprising and disappointing consistency emerged. Rattenbury was remembered as a man who doted on his children, particularly his daughter, but who felt a contemptuous dislike for his wife; a bad tempered man who became increasingly so as the years passed. Without exception the people I interviewed told me that their fathers had considered Rattenbury a genius but that they, as children, had found that he wasn't a very nice man to know. It was a distressingly one-dimensional picture. There is some evidence to suggest that in his younger days Rattenbury's fellows had found him rowdy good company and at least one man had benefited from his generosity but otherwise his character has received unanimously bad reviews.

And yet I can't help but admire him and feel some sympathy for him. If, as his competitors charged, his cunning rather than his talent accounted for much of his success then one must at least give him credit for having a finely calculating mind, for while his commission-winning tactics could be devious, there is no evidence to suggest that they were dishonest. His one true ambition was to be a man who counted. He wanted prominence, fame and wealth. He wanted to be someone who mattered and it made little difference to him whether he achieved his goal through architecture or by building a northern empire. To appreciate his passionate need to succeed is to begin to understand the narrow single-mindedness with which he pursued his goal.

I have avoided a detailed critical analysis of Rattenbury's buildings for two reasons. As someone with a general, rather than a specialized, interest I find the vocabulary of architectural criticism confounding and the subject both technical and complex. Even so, such an omission might be unforgivable were it not for the fact that Rattenbury simply wasn't a particularly original architect. He broke no new ground. He was never considered by himself or by others to be avant-garde or daringly creative. He succeeded by giving people what they wanted and despite changing tastes many of his buildings continue to be objects of public admiration. Rattenbury's skill lay not in attention to the finer details of design but in his ability to envision monumental buildings in spectacular settings, buildings which would have an immediate and unforgettable visual impact.

Rattenbury and Sam Maclure were Victoria's two most prominent architects. They worked out of adjacent offices in the Five Sisters block and they worked together on at least two projects; Cary Castle and Dr. Jones' home on Island Road in Oak Bay. But while Maclure's work has been the subject of books, photographic displays and numerous articles, Rattenbury's buildings have been virtually ignored by architects and art historians. The reason for this, according to Martin Segger, an acknowledged expert on Victoria's early architects, is that Rattenbury isn't particularly interesting from an architectural historian's point of view. What Rattenbury looked for was the opportunity to design huge, powerful buildings, impressive monuments which would dominate town and cityscapes. He worked at a time when the creation of a fine and impressive skyline was the mark of a good designer and many of his buildings could be considered good in that respect, says Segger. But in creating that impressive skyline he often produced buildings that lack dimension. Segger cites the Empress Hotel as an example of a building which appears like a cardboard cut-out against the sky. Rattenbury was a great dreamer and a monumental planner and while that might be great romantic stuff his buildings won't stand intensive scrutiny, whereas Maclure's can and do. The major difference between the two architects, according to Segger, is in their treatment of interior spaces and their attention to detail. Rattenbury's interiors tended to be confined and restricted not so much in terms of size but according to use. Maclure, by thinking in terms of volume rather than floor area, designed interiors which seemed much larger than they actually were, one room flowing into another creating a grand dramatic space in an otherwise modest house. Maclure was known to design every last moulding, developing a theme which would be carried throughout the house, while Rattenbury often left this kind of decision up to his contractor. Maclure visited his construction sites at least once a day, carefully checking all the work that had been done. His attention to detail was almost obsessive. Hatley Park, his largest commission, nearly drove Maclure berserk, says Segger. He couldn't leave well enough alone and Hatley Park was just too big.

Thinking big was Rattenbury's forte. He was not an architect who grew in ability, who gradually refined a style or a technique. His buildings were symbolic of his towering self confidence, products of a forceful personality rather than contemplative artistry. And so while his buildings might not bear close inspection, the man who designed them certainly does.

Part I

FRANCIS MAWSON RATTENBURY

1

Family Background and Training

Arrogant and boastful, driven by ambition, Francis Mawson Rattenbury was a talented architect who easily rose to the top of his profession. A visionary capitalist and skilled promoter, he pictured himself as an empire builder and if fate had not intervened he might
well have achieved his goal of becoming one of British Columbia's
richest and most powerful men. Residents of Victoria, B.C. who
remember him are quick to admit that he was a genius, but he
made few real friends, more than his share of enemies and those who
became close to him were left embittered by the experience. And
when he was murdered there were many who secretly felt that he
had got what he deserved.

Yet things might have turned out differently. His grandfather,
with whom Rattenbury shared many of the same talents and many
of the same faults, made a success of both his public and private life.
Both men were tall, blessed with a commanding physical presence
and almost hypnotic powers of persuasion. They brought to their
work the same single-minded enthusiasm and insatiable desire to
succeed, combined with a sometimes selfish disregard for the wel-
fare of their families. But his grandfather, John Rattenbury, died a
contented and revered man for he had devoted his life to God rather
than the pursuit of personal success and his excesses were praised as
evidence of exceptional religious ardour rather than condemned as
signs of ruthless personal ambition.

As a boy living in Manchester, John Rattenbury had fallen under
the spell of the local Methodist preacher. In 1825 when he was
nineteen and after the death of his unsympathetic father he had
thrown himself into preaching with an almost fanatical dedication.
As a brother minister recalled, "No minister ever felt the call to
preach more loudly than he . . ."[1]

And apparently few ministers had come so well equipped for their chosen vocation. "His physical advantages were great. Tall, with an abundance of flowing dark hair, he had a 'pulpit-presence' of the finest kind. His mobile features, his large, expressive, lustrous, yet dreamy eyes, quivering lips, and unspeakably tender, persuasive and pathetic utterance, were wonderfully in his favour."[2]

Reverend John Rattenbury knew instinctively how to manipulate his audience. He would begin quietly, seriously, earnestly "but soon kindled with his subject; and his hearers soon caught the contagion of his fervour, and broke out at first into low murmurs of delighted assent, which soon swelled into shouts of rapturous exclamations, so that the preacher's words were over and over again drowned by many-voiced bursts of Hallelujah! Glory! Praise the Lamb!"[3]

His religious ardour was not confined to the pulpit. Upon entering a drawing room and finding the inhabitants happily engaged in gossip or carefree repartee, he would determinedly steer the conversation to more sober topics and end by leading the chastened assembly in prayer. And when it came to Sabbath-breaking his outrage knew no bounds. Whether the guilty parties were hapless shopkeepers peddling their wares of a Sunday or drunkards turned out of a local gin-palace, he would accost them on the spot and gently but persistently lecture to them until their indignant oaths became cries for mercy.

His ministry was centred in the West Riding of Yorkshire, an area beset by social problems as the result of sudden change. For centuries the Riding had been the site of a flourishing cottage industry, wool being spun and woven into cloth by hand in scattered villages and lonely farmhouses. But now towns located in river-filled valleys near beds of waiting coal had become centres of the new industry created when steam power was adapted to the processing of wool. Farm workers, encouraged to leave the countryside by an agricultural depression, had flocked to these growing cities, spurred on by the promise of plentiful work. Almost overnight sleepy market villages became squalid cities, their skies leaden with the smoke from a growing forest of chimneys. Disease was rampant, the result of fouled streams, long hours of backbreaking labour in the mills and overcrowded, unsanitary living conditions. While many turned to drink to escape the grim realities of their existence, others found solace in religion. They filled the chapels on the Methodist circuit eager to hear the inspirational words of the travelling preachers.

A minister on the circuit was allowed to stay in any one place for no more than three years before being required to move on to the next town on the circuit and so Reverend Rattenbury's life became a succession of one grim industrial city after another. He was fortunate that when he married he chose a wife whose dedication to God's work matched his own.

During his stay in Sheffield from 1831-1833 he married Mary Owen, a pious and devout woman who had been attracted to the young preacher by his habitual godliness, his Christian simplicity and cheerfulness, and his natural and unpretentious courtesy — the same qualities that helped him rise from obscurity to his church's highest position, President of the Conference, some thirty years later. The daughter of Samuel Owen, a successful coal merchant and influential Methodist, Mary Owen accepted their transient life without complaint even though the family moved so often that no two of her children were born in the same place. Their first child, John Owen Rattenbury (Francis Rattenbury's father) was born in Macclesfield in 1836. Three years later Samuel was born in Leeds, followed by Sarah Anne in 1841 in York. Henry was born in Manchester in 1843 and Catherine in 1846 near Bradford.

In his home Reverend Rattenbury set an example of solemn prayerful piety. In his musical and powerful voice, with his pale handsome face lifted toward heaven, he prayed daily for each of his children in turn, listing their individual faults and needs and pleading with God to give them guidance. Although his easy understanding of their problems filled them with awe and at times covered them with embarrassment, his children, with one possible exception, adored him.

His third son, Henry, born with his feet firmly planted on the road to righteousness found his father's presence "pure sunshine in the house"[4] and never deviated from his life's ambition to follow his example. Becoming a minister at the age of twenty, Henry laboured on the Methodist circuit for forty years and while he could never match his father's dynamic appeal, he did become known as a conscientious pastor and just administrator.[5] Inspired by his example, two of his sons became Methodist ministers and his younger son, Harold Burgoyne Rattenbury, was elected to fill his grandfather's position as President of the Conference in 1949.

Henry may have found that his father's prayers at the family altar seemed to bring him "beneath the very wings of the holy and loving

God."[6] But for his older brother John, who all too often found himself the subject of those fervent prayers, they were an uncomfortable experience. John Owen Rattenbury seemed so out of place in that reverent family that his mother became more than a little concerned that he might follow in the footsteps of a quite different John Rattenbury — one to whom, she shuddered to think, her family might be related. In 1836 this John Rattenbury, a reluctantly reformed smuggler, had given up the sea and fondly recounted his boisterous career. He called his book *Memoirs of a Smuggler* and proudly reminded his readers that he had been known as the "Rob Roy of the West." So much did he enjoy smuggling that he had introduced his sons to the trade and proclaimed that while smuggling might be fraught with difficulties and danger it was a career "calculated to gratify a hardy and enterprising spirit, and to call forth the latent energies of the soul . . ."[7]

When Mary Owen Rattenbury read John's *Memoirs* she hurled the offensive book into the fire, for as well as sharing the same name, the portrait grinning merrily from the book's frontispiece showed that the "Rob Roy of the West" bore a distinct resemblance to her husband.[8] The fear that her oldest child might take after this roving pirate seemed to be confirmed when, at the first opportunity, John Owen Rattenbury cast himself loose from his family and sailed for New Zealand. But his restlessness was easily overcome and his desire for adventure easily met for in 1861 when he was twenty-five John Rattenbury returned to England and settled in Leeds where he met and courted Mary Anne Mawson.

The Mawsons, a large, solidly middle-class family, had made the most of Yorkshire's expanding economy. Mary Anne's father owned a prosperous printing business in Leeds and in the same city her uncles and cousins were engaged in the textile trade marketing the products of the busy woollen mills. In Bradford two of her brothers, William and Richard Mawson, were working with Henry Francis Lockwood in an architectural partnership which was proving to be outstandingly successful. It seemed likely that Mary Anne and her industrious family would have a steadying influence on John Owen Rattenbury.

On March 12, 1862 they were married in the Wesleyan Chapel in Leeds, John gaining both a devoted wife and a partnership in the firm of Mawson and Dewhirst, woollen merchants in the city. The couple settled down on Hyde Park Terrace in Headingley, a pleasant residential section of Leeds favoured by moderately successful business and professional men and for a time John Rattenbury tried to fit into the place that had been made for him in the world of commerce. When his first son, John, was born in 1864 he still listed his occupation as cloth merchant, but by the time his second son, Francis Mawson Rattenbury, was born on October 11, 1867 he had severed his connection with Rattenbury, Mawson and Dewhirst and become the local manager of the General Assurance Company. Ten years later, in a move that earned him the reputation of the family's black sheep, John Rattenbury gave up the role of a man of business and eased himself into the life of a self-styled artist and the family found it necessary to move down the street into a more modest, severely plain house. Francis Rattenbury's enrollment the following year in the Leeds Free Grammar School is a further hint that the family suffered financially from John's decision to devote himself to art. Affiliated with the Church of England, the school had been founded in the sixteenth century and under headmaster Reverend William Henderson it continued to perform its original function — providing, without fee, a classical education for those boys of the parish whose parents could not afford to pay for it.

Mary Anne may have been disappointed by her husband's apparent lack of ambition, but at least she still had the Mawsons on whom she could rely. It seems that they were prepared to offer Francis Rattenbury his father's former position with the firm of Mawson and Dewhirst for after completing the course of studies at the Leeds Free Grammar School, he was enrolled at Yorkshire College, a vocational school founded in the 1870's to channel students into the textile industry. But like his father, Francis Rattenbury found that learning the techniques of processing, dyeing and marketing wool held no appeal for him and he left the college without a diploma.

As well as an aversion to the textile trade, he had inherited from his father a facile ability to draw, to cover page after page with sure, accurate sketches. Hoping that he would learn to use this skill in a practical way, Mary Anne arranged for her bachelor brothers, William and Richard Mawson, to take him under their wing and in 1885, when he was eighteen, Francis Mawson Rattenbury left Leeds to become an articled student with the firm of Mawson and Mawson, architects in the city of Bradford.

7

It cannot have taken long for Rattenbury who was later to become an architect of imagination and vision, a dreamer of grand architectural dreams, to realize that the firm he had joined was now producing buildings of only mediocre quality. It had not always been so. In Bradford, Rattenbury was surrounded by the firm's past glories, the much admired public buildings designed by the Mawsons when they had been partnered with Henry Francis Lockwood. Later when he struck out on his own as an architect in Canada it was to these buildings designed long before he joined the firm that Rattenbury would point as evidence of the excellence of his training and of the wide range of his experience.

The association of Henry Lockwood and the Mawsons had begun in 1849 when William Mawson, who had just completed his articles in Leeds, and Lockwood, who had been practicing for some fifteen years in Hull, decided to form a partnership and move to Bradford where they felt the opportunities for enterprising architects were unsurpassed. While the booming textile industry had encouraged the growth of many towns, Bradford's growth had been explosive. In the fifty years since the turn of the century the town of 13,000 people had mushroomed into a city with a population of 103,000. In 1850 there were few large buildings in Bradford and Lockwood and Mawson knew they would have to be built soon.

They had completed work on their first Bradford commission, a workhouse for the Bradford Board of Guardians, and were preparing plans for the city's concert hall, when one winter afternoon in 1850 a certain Titus Salt called at their offices and told them of his plans to build a new mill at Shipley Glen some four miles from the centre of Bradford. Lockwood set to work on the preliminary sketches without suspecting that they would lead to the single most important commission the firm would ever be given.

The owner of several local textile mills, Salt was a capitalist with a conscience. During his term as mayor of Bradford in 1848 he had been confronted by the many social problems he, as an industrialist, had helped to create. Ignored by mill owners in their scramble for profits, the textile workers led squalid lives, blighted by disease, drunkenness, and deplorably inadequate housing. As mayor, Salt had found that there was little he could do to allay their suffering. Now he had decided to lead the way. He would build a model community, a showplace of enlightened capitalism on the banks of the Aire.

Calling at the architects' offices a few days later, Salt approved of the sketches and found his admiration increasing for Henry Lockwood, a cultured, quietly diligent man whose Liberal political views matched his own. The plan he gradually unfolded astounded the architects in its scope. As well as a factory equipped with all the modern inventions to combat the twin evils of air and water pollution, Salt proposed the building of an entire town complete with attractive homes for his workers and including many social amenities, such as schools, churches, a library, alms houses, a hospital and parks. It would not, however, boast any public houses or inns as Salt remained convinced that Demon Drink was at the bottom of all the ills of the nation. The community was to be planned down to the smallest detail, even to the prohibition of washing lines and hoardings. Nothing quite like it had ever been attempted before.[9]

The architects chose the same Italianate style for all the buildings, from the mill, its 250 foot chimney resembling an Italian bell tower, to the workers' houses with their gracefully arched windows and to further unify the design of the community they decided that all the buildings would be constructed of the same cream coloured brick and stone. Salt, proud of the new town, christened it Saltaire and both Lockwood and Mawson were honoured to have streets named after them.

As well as establishing their reputation, Saltaire would keep Lockwood and Mawson busy for the next twenty years. When William Mawson's younger brother, Richard, joined the firm in the mid-1850's he was a welcome addition to an extremely busy company. As well as their ongoing work on Saltaire, they were, with ecumenical enthusiasm, designing churches for the Congregationalists in Cleckheaton, the Methodists in Harrogate, and the Baptists in Scarborough.

Adding to the firm's prestige was the selection of Lockwood as one of the seven architects invited to compete for the design of the new Law Courts to be erected in London, placing him in the heady company of such well-known men as Barry, Scott, Waterhouse and Street, the top echelon of English architects of the time. The fact that he lost the contest to Street did little to diminish his reputation locally. The opinion voiced in Bradford was that Lockwood's design had shown "the greatest power, the greatest skill as an architect for arrangement, and the greatest idea of beauty as an artist."[10]

Lockwood and Mawson's guess that Bradford would engage in a madly energetic building boom proved correct. During the 1860's they won a wide variety of commissions ranging from the Victoria Hotel and the Kirkgate Market to the Wool Exchange, their success culminating when they were selected as architects for Bradford's Town Hall in 1870.

When the Town Hall was officially opened in 1873 all Bradford turned out to celebrate. An elaborate procession of eighteen bands and a great display of flags and standards, somewhat sodden by a heavy downpour, wound through the town. So important was the event in Bradford that the Prime Minister, Mr. Gladstone, had been invited to attend and, while he found better things to do, the guest list did include four members of parliament.

An impressive mixture of Franco-English and Italian Gothic styles, with statues of the thirty-five English monarchs from William the Conqueror to Queen Victoria peering down from niches in its second floor arcade, the Town Hall was the pinnacle of Lockwood and Mawson's career.

Their early success had been due to three factors: as Yorkshiremen they appealed to the regional loyalties of local concerns, they were on the spot when Bradford needed architects most, and they worked well together each providing necessary ingredients for a successful client-attracting formula. Lockwood was the most architecturally talented of the three and was recognized as the foundation of the firm's success.[11] William Mawson was an efficient business manager known for his practical ability.[12] Richard Mawson was a social asset, a well known sportsman[13] who made many important friends and connections through his many club memberships and who carefully eschewed political affiliations to counteract the effects of Lockwood's vocal Liberalism.

Encouraged by local success, they opened a branch office in London. And from 1871 when Henry Lockwood moved to the sunnier climes of Surrey, his health broken by the damp, dirty Bradford air, it was from this office at 10 Lincoln's Inn Fields that he practiced. With Lockwood's removal to London and all major buildings in Bradford completed, two necessary ingredients of the firm's success were gone. Business fell off as commissions they might have won in Leeds went to Cuthbert Broderick, an architect who had trained under Lockwood in Hull and whose Gothic designs had a wider appeal than did Lockwood and Mawson's Italianate.

When Henry Francis Lockwood died in 1878, he took with him the firm's creative spark. The two brothers formed a new partnership under the title Mawson and Mawson but in 1886, a year after Francis Rattenbury joined the firm as a student, William Mawson, his health failing, retired and Robert Hudson who had laboured anonymously with the Mawsons and Lockwood for 17 years was elevated to a full partnership.

During the six years Rattenbury spent with Mawson and Hudson the architects were engaged in projects of little impact or importance either locally or nationally. Later in an attempt to establish his credibility as an architect in Canada, Rattenbury could name with pride only two buildings on which he had worked and in both cases he found it necessary to exaggerate both his role in their design and the critical acceptance they had enjoyed.

One was the Town Hall of Cleckheaton, a mill town near Bradford. In 1887 after casting about for a fitting way to celebrate Queen Victoria's jubilee, the city fathers decided that the Queen would best be fêted by the erection of a new building to house municipal government. A competition was held to select the best design and Mawson and Hudson's entry entitled "Light and Air" was judged to be the most suitable. Rattenbury would later claim dual authorship of the design with his uncle, but he certainly received no credit for it at the time. And perhaps in later years he would just as soon not have been reminded of it, for Cleckheaton's Town Hall is an odd, strangely out-of-proportion building — not one of Mawson and Hudson's greater successes.

Contemporary opinion was not so harsh, but neither was it overly enthusiastic. When a professional journal, *The Architect*, noted that "The architects have sought to obtain picturesque grouping without excessive ornamentation, and the sketch plans show this desirable result has been achieved,"[14] Mawson and Hudson were so encouraged by this mildly favourable praise that they decided to submit their plans to the Royal Academy in 1891, hoping they would be selected for display at the Academy's annual exhibition of British architecture. Rattenbury would later boast about the Academy's ultimate selection of their design, but this honour wasn't necessarily all that it seemed. While other buildings brought effusive praise, little was said about their design. "The town-hall of Cleckheaton, by Messrs. Mawson and Hudson, is shown on too small a drawing. The architects have produced a very effective building without imposing a burthen on the inhabitants,"[15] *The Architect* damned with faint praise.

And the whole method of selection and the quality of the exhibits shown at the Academy was beginning to be questioned. The following year the display was roundly condemned by *The British Architect*. "The annual farce had once again been enacted. Some architects having again elected to send specimens of their work to Burlington House to uphold the credit of British Architecture, a certain number have been selected, and having been mixed up with studies of old works and drawings of stained glass, have produced a totally inadequate and misleading record of the quality of British Art in this department."[16]

Rattenbury also claimed to have made a substantial contribution to Mawson and Hudson's design for the municipal buildings to be erected at Oxford. The firm did not win the design competition, nor did it place among the five finalists, but Rattenbury, finding a way of turning a company failure into a personal success took comfort in the fact that their design had been highly recommended[17] by T. E. Collcutt, contest judge and architect of the buildings housing the Imperial Institute in London. Some would have found this cold comfort indeed for while Collcutt was a well-known architect, he was not universally admired. In commenting on his entries at the Royal Academy's exhibition of 1892, *The British Architect* was most uncharitable. "Mr. T. E. Collcutt gives a coloured view of the upper part of his Imperial Institute Tower, in which the want of force and substance is more apparent than ever." Another Collcutt design was found to be "an unpleasantly spotty ink view" and "one of those instances where variety is *not pleasing*."[18]

By the spring of 1892 Rattenbury had become convinced that there was nothing more his uncle could teach him. He was chronically ambitious and sure of his own abilities. Just slightly under six feet tall, he carried himself well, his erect bearing a clue to his belief in his own importance and his red hair hinting of an inner impatience to get on with the job of realizing his potential. He knew that the firm of Mawson and Hudson was going nowhere and he no doubt chafed under the tutelage and advice of his bachelor uncle. He was certainly shrewd enough to have correctly assessed the reasons for the early success of Lockwood and Mawson. He was sure that he was at least as architecturally talented as Lockwood had been. All that was left was for him to find the right place for his time. He could certainly eliminate Bradford. What he hoped to find was a town such as Bradford had been some thirty years before — new and growing, anxious to erect substantial buildings as evidence of its prosperity. He doubted if he could find such a city in all England which was beginning to draw a more relaxed breath after the hectic building boom which had accompanied the industry-spurred growth of the preceding decades. Encouraged to look further afield by the same early restlessness that had afflicted his father, in 1892 he set sail for Canada. But not just any part of Canada. He was bound quite purposefully for Vancouver, British Columbia.

2

A "B.C. Architect" and the Parliament Buildings
pleasure and pardonable pride

For most of the twenty-five years that had passed since 1867 when "Gassy" Jack Deighton had beached his canoe, his Indian wife and a case of rum at a tiny clearing in the rain forest bringing civilization to the shores of Burrard Inlet, any suggestion that Vancouver might one day become a great west coast seaport would have been greeted with hilarity. While the city of Victoria was bent on spreading over the southern tip of Vancouver Island and industriously establishing itself as the centre of business and commerce, the little settlement that grew up around "Gassy" Jack's saloon was a community without ambition or dreams of future glory. Given the unpromising name of Gastown,[1] it seemed content to remain a nondescript backwater, the home of a few mill workers and a motley company of sailors who had jumped ship and found safe haven at Deighton House. For eleven years Gastown dozed on but then with a treachery that long rankled Victorians, the Canadian Pacific Railway reneged on its commitment to make Victoria the western terminus of the transcontinental rail line, deciding instead to end the tracks at Burrard Inlet, and the little town shook itself awake and began to think about its future. Victorians were indignant when, at the suggestion of C.P.R. Vice-President Cornelius Van Horne, Gastown appropriated the name of their island and Victoria's businessmen sensed that the upstart town would soon compound that affront to local pride by stealing their city's commercial eminence.

In 1886 a major fire cleared the townsite of all but a few of the wooden frame buildings, many little more than shacks, that had sprung up in boom town fashion since the C.P.R.'s announcement. The building spree that followed was only slightly less exuberant as Vancouverites, sobered by the fire and finally aware of their city's potential, erected less combustible and more dignified buildings of brick and stone.

The Vancouver to which Rattenbury was attracted in 1892 had experienced six years of growing prosperity and unchecked optimism. The frontier shanty town had become a cosmopolitan city of 15,000 residents, a city billed in England as the "Constantinople of the West," a city of long streets, big blocks, handsome churches and elegant villas.[2] But it was also in the spring of 1892 a city on the brink of recession. Within a year, an economic depression in the United States would spread to British Columbia, the elegant mansions of "Blue Blood Alley" would be boarded up and all over the city land values would plummet. But in May when Rattenbury took rooms at Mrs. Morency's boarding house at 617 Richards, pleasantly situated in a quiet part of the city, only the most cautious suggested that the city might be already overbuilt and that progress and prosperity might not be endless after all.

Making himself known in a strange city presented no problem to Rattenbury who enjoyed the promotion of himself and his schemes as much as, if not more than, he enjoyed the practice of architecture. He called at the offices of the *Vancouver Daily World* and on July 5, 1892 a friendly article appeared on the pages of that paper.

Attention is directed to the advertisement of Mr. F. M. Rattenbury, architect, who has opened an office in the New Holland Block, Cordova St. He has been for ten years erecting all classes of buildings in conjunction with the well-known firm of Lockwood and Mawson — Bradford Town.

It was the first, but not the last, time that Rattenbury would consider it prudent to improve his reputation by claiming to have trained under Henry Francis Lockwood. Lockwood, who had died when Rattenbury was 11 years old and before that had practiced out of the firm's London office for seven years, enjoyed a wide reputation — a reputation from which Rattenbury was determined to benefit until he had established one of his own.

Just how many clients were attracted by Rattenbury's first foray into self-promotion via the newspapers is unknown, but soon after he arrived in the city he designed a house for Gustav Roedde on Barclay Street in the city's prestigious West End. And whether German-born Roedde was attracted to the architect by his puffed up reputation or by the common misspelling of his name as "Rattenberg," the building was a success, remembered many years later as a happy, comfortable house; the stairs winding up its many windowed tower, an exciting place to the Roedde children and grand-children.[3]

There are no records of Rattenbury's having designed any other buildings during his stay in Vancouver, but if he found that he had time to spare, he had no trouble in deciding how to fill it. He may have considered it a good omen when he noticed that the same page of the *Vancouver Daily World* that announced his presence in Vancouver carried a "Notice to Architects" announcing that a competition would be held for the design of new buildings to house the Legislative Assembly in Victoria.

Although it had only been fifty years since the first permanent European settlement had been established on Vancouver Island, the new legislative buildings would be the fourth in the series of buildings used to house government.

Meeting for the first time in 1856, the members of the House of Assembly had gathered around a dilapidated and picturesquely bulging[4] iron stove inside the Bachelors' Hall, a building constructed of squared logs within the walls of the Hudson's Bay Company fort. After several meetings in these spartan surroundings, the House had removed itself to a more noble building which also served as a jail and courthouse and settled in for a long stay. The discovery of gold on the Fraser River changed their plans.

During the summer of 1858 a swarm of 20,000 gold hungry prospectors and American merchants, wise to the ways of business after the California rush of '49, had transformed Victoria from a lonely Company outpost to a bustling city. While they pocketed the extravagant sums these foreigners were prepared to pay for their town lots, Victorians felt a certain uneasiness about this sudden influx of Americans with their republican ideas. The time seemed ripe for the construction of government buildings suitable to the maintenance of British law. Herman Otto Tiedemann was retained as architect and under his direction a group of most unusual buildings had begun to rise, across the harbour from the city, in the autumn of 1859.

Their construction had delighted William Alexander Smith, an eccentric Nova Scotian who had arrived in Victoria in the gold-mad year of 1858, changed his name to Amor De Cosmos, founded a newspaper, the *British Colonist*, and appointed himself editor. Nothing pleased De Cosmos more than an opportunity to rail in print at the follies of the colonial administration, and the new government buildings became the favourite target of his enthusiastic barbs. "No one competent to draw a plan or accept one would have hesitated one moment in rejecting the contemptible design which is now being carried into execution,"[5] he crowed in an editorial.

While some found their design to be Elizabethan and tasteful, De Cosmos saw them as something between a Dutch Toy and a Chinese Pagoda and condemned them as gingerbread contrivances. But whatever one thought of their design it had become apparent that some thirty years after their construction the "Birdcages" as everyone called them were no longer a suitable home for the government and its burgeoning bureaucracy. Clerks in the Colonial Secretary's office reported they could see through the walls and it was no surprise to anyone when in 1893 the Legislature found it necessary to adjourn for a week because it was impossible to keep the Legislative Hall at anything like a temperature at which a man could work.[6]

And then there was the question of the province's image. As the Victoria *Colonist* pointed out, "Mean and insignificant public buildings are outward and visible signs of a sordid, narrow-minded and uncultivated State or Province. Visitors are sure to judge the whole people by the buildings they erect for public uses. Those buildings ought to be handsome as well as commodious."[7] Premier Theodore Davie couldn't have agreed more. Under his leadership the Legislature passed the necessary monies and the Chief Commissioner of Lands and Works announced the competition to select the design of the new buildings. And Rattenbury, although only he would have considered it even remotely possible, was on his way to pulling off the most astounding architectural coup in the province's history — a feat due in no small part to his talent for self-promotion.

Two non-competing architects from eastern Canada, Curry from Ontario and Taylor from Quebec, had been chosen to judge the competition. They settled in to the homelike comforts of the Roccabella Guest House and began the prodigious task of selecting five preliminary winners from among the 67 sets of drawings the government had received. The judges were aware that the new legislative buildings should be symbolic as well as practical — they must be functional, of course, but they should also serve as a showpiece, an example of what British Columbia craftsmen working with local building materials could accomplish. It would be something of a set-back to provincial pride if none of the finalists in the architectural competition were from British Columbia. But Curry and Taylor's decision must be seen to be unbiassed and so all entrants had been asked to submit their designs identified only by a nom de plume.

Most of the competitors complied with the spirit of this rule showing a stunning lack of creativity in their choice of name. "Hopeful" and "Patience" were two uninspired and unhelpful choices. Some like "Utility and Dignity" were more ponderous than descriptive. One wit threw all caution to the winds and signed his drawings "Ta-ra-ra-boom-de-ay" convincing the judges that even he wasn't optimistic about his chance of winning.

Rattenbury gave his choice of nom de plume a great deal of thought. Guessing that both the government and the judges would be somewhat discomfitted if a local man was not among the finalists, he cast about for a name which while retaining his anonymity would give the contest judges a most welcome piece of information. His final choice left no room for doubt. "B.C. Architect" he signed himself and he must have been overjoyed and maybe even a little surprised when, on November 11, 1892, he received a letter telling him that he was one of the five finalists in the first phase of the competition.

As might have been predicted the local press found reason to be smugly proud. "British Columbia architects have to be especially congratulated in having taken two out of the five prizes out of the 67 sets submitted from all parts of North America. This speaks well of the skill of the profession in the Province,"[8] the Victoria *Colonist* bragged.

With the energy of a young man just four weeks past his twenty-fifth birthday, Rattenbury set to work enlarging and elaborating his drawings for the final phase of the competition. As the *Colonist* had noted two of the winning designs had been submitted by local architects, Rattenbury of Vancouver and Thomas Sorby of Victoria. The other finalists were Brown of Toronto, Garden of Chicago and Corner and Skillings of Boston and Seattle. Perhaps working on the theory that it was a shame to let a good opportunity go to waste and that it was foolish not to hedge his bets, Rattenbury identified his second set of drawings with a nom de plume which provided the useful information that their author was one of the British Columbians. "For Our Queen and Province" was certainly a title calculated to gently nudge the judges in his direction and it really needed to do little more for Rattenbury had submitted a fine set of drawings. While the judges deemed the designs of other competitors to be correct but somewhat commonplace, or picturesque ... but wanting dignity, Rattenbury's design variously described as "Renaissance Revival," "neo-classical" and "a blending ... of the Romanesque, Classic and Gothic," was pronounced by the judges to be very dignified and effective ... from all points of view.[9]

On March 15, 1893 he received a telegram from W. S. Gore, Deputy Chief Commissioner of Lands and Works, "Accept congratulations come to Victoria by tomorrow's boat if possible."

To Rattenbury his presence in the province's capital when the government announced his name as winning architect was not only possible — it was essential. He realized that the judges' decision might be questioned when it was discovered that the "B.C. Architect" who had submitted his design for his province was an unknown twenty-five-year-old Yorkshireman and the following day he was not only in Victoria but was also a resident of the Driard, the city's best hotel. And he was prepared to meet the press with a short history of his professional career guaranteed to consolidate his position. His credentials, as they were reported in newspapers in both Vancouver and Victoria, sounded so impressive that awkward questions were answered even before they had been framed.

When he began the profession of architecture he entered the office of his uncle, Richard Mawson — the firm being the well-known one of Lockwood and Mawson of Bradford, England. This firm was one of the seven chosen out of all England to compete for the great Law Courts in London, and they it was who built the grand Town Hall of Bradford and most of the other great public buildings of the town. They built the whole of the model town of Saltaire — churches, mills, universities and markets. On many of these Mr. Rattenbury worked, after having served his articles for six years, gaining great practical experience from them.[10]

The last statement was, quite simply, untrue. The contest to select the design of the Law Courts had been held in 1867. The construction of Saltaire had begun in 1850 and all the town's major buildings had been completed long before Rattenbury joined the firm. Likewise he had had nothing to do with the design of Bradford's town hall which had been officially opened in 1873 when Rattenbury was a child of six. But to Rattenbury it was at most a white lie born of the knowledge that while he possessed exceptional ability and talent his true experience sounded distressingly meagre. He could and did mention his design of the Cleckheaton Town Hall which had been displayed at the Royal Academy and his losing entry in the competition for the municipal buildings at Oxford which had been highly recommended by the judge but these two achievements alone would hardly have convinced the government that he could be entrusted with the construction of buildings for which they had voted what was then the enormous sum of $600,000.

The improved version of his professional career was accepted without question, the press noting with "pleasure and pardonable pride" that the winner was a British Columbian and execpt for a few disgruntled local architects, whose professional jealousy was to plague Rattenbury over the years, Victorians were simply relieved that they had succeeded in anchoring the province's capital in Victoria, and they no longer had to fear the agitation of vocal mainlanders.

Many residents of Victoria had come to suspect that the continued presence of the provincial government would prove essential to the economic survival of their city. As late as 1889 an observer had been able to state, quite truthfully, that Victoria was the largest and wealthiest city in the province.[11] That wealth had come from the city's bustling harbour, the home of the sealing and whaling fleets and a prime destination for coastal shipping, and from a strong manufacturing base. On the coast only San Francisco had an iron foundry larger than Victoria's Albion Iron Works. From his factory on the banks of James Bay, William Pendray shipped his soap as far east as Calgary and the 120,000 gallons of beer produced annually by Loewen and Erb's brewery slaked thirsts all over the province. Half a dozen factories manufactured cigars and another made the boxes to put them in. Four companies made carriages and wagons and five produced boots and shoes. With a sawmill, a planing mill, two book binderies, a meat packer, a vinegar factory, a corset maker and a flour mill, Victoria in 1889 gave every evidence of being a growing city of promising prospects and over the next two years more than a dozen new business blocks rose in the commercial district close by the harbour and the tram cars of the Electric Railway Company began to rattle through the town and out to the countryside of Oak Bay.

But by 1891 the picture had begun to change. The dominion census of that year revealed that Vancouver's population had equalled Victoria's and Victorians were forced to face the fact that Vancouver, as a mainland city and as the terminus of a transcontinental railway, enjoyed advantages which would make its commercial pre-eminence inevitable. By 1892, while Vancouver continued to boom, the pace of Victoria had already begun to slow. "I found in that quiet English town of beautiful streets quite a colony of old men doing nothing but talking, fishing, and loafing at the Club,"[12] wrote Rudyard Kipling. But Kipling, who seems to have spent most of his brief visit within the walls of the Union Club, was overstating the case. For Victoria was the home of the province's oldest and wealthiest families and their presence in the city, their grand homes set in sprawling park-like grounds, had given it a unique style, which combined with its mild climate and the natural beauty of its setting, would soon promote the growth of a new and prosperous industry. Atop the Fort Street hill surrounded by ten acres of terraced gardens was "Craigdarroch," the half million dollar Scottish baronial dream castle built by coal magnate Robert Dunsmuir. "Pentrelew," the Crease family's eighteen room Italian style mansion, "Gonzales," the Pemberton home facing the sea and set in 1,200 acres, "Hollybank," the Rithet home near Beacon Hill Park, "Cary Castle," the residence of the province's Lieutenant-Governors — these and other fine homes with their extravagant decoration, their studied elegance, their carefully laid out croquet lawns and tennis courts, suggested a life of ease punctuated by gay and glittering social events. They lent to the city an air of charm and grace and gave the impression that Victoria was a very desirable place in which to live — and, more than a few shrewd entrepreneurs thought, an equally desirable place to visit.

Since 1858, when the first brick hotel had been built to accommodate those passing through the city on the way to the gold fields, Victoria had taken pride in its hotels. By 1889 the city had been able to boast of more than a dozen hotels which enjoyed almost a world wide reputation for the excellence of their accommodations. But they had been built in the heart of the city, built for people who were travelling for business rather than solely for pleasure. In the early 1890's a new kind of hotel had begun to appear on the scene, one removed from the business district, sited to take full advantage of the scenery and designed to appeal especially to tourists. The "Dallas," on the waterfront near the city's outer wharf, faced south across the straits of Juan de Fuca and offered its clientele a breathtaking view of the Olympic Mountains. And the "Mount Baker" built at the end of the streetcar tracks on the beach at Oak Bay drew customers with the equally awe-inspiring sight of the snow-capped peak of the dormant volcano in Washington State.

By 1893, when Rattenbury closed his Vancouver office and moved to Victoria, the city's future had become clear. While industries slipped away to the mainland, prosperity would hinge on the growth of the provincial civil service and on the number of tourists that could be lured to the city. And Rattenbury would find that despite its quietness and the secondary role it was forced to play, Victoria suited him very well for in Victoria he was in continuing contact with the men who ran the government's Works department and with the men who were investing in the tourist industry and over the next thirty years these men would give him the commissions on which he based the most successful architectural practice in the province.

Rattenbury moved out of the Driard and into a boarding house on Menzies Street in the James Bay district only a few minutes' walk from the Birdcages and set to work preparing the specifications for the foundation of the Parliament Buildings.

The commission he had won was one of such complexity and symbolic importance that it would have been a sobering prospect for an experienced architect and it might be supposed that Rattenbury experienced more than a few sleepless nights when he considered the problems that would have to be faced in seeing a building of almost 600,000 square feet through to completion. But Rattenbury seemed immune from the anxiety of self-doubt. Instead he soon proved that as well as having sublime confidence in his ability, he was also quite recklessly ambitious.

The work on the foundation of the buildings had begun in the summer of 1893 and Rattenbury was preparing the detailed drawings and specifications for the second and largest part of the contract when he did something quite extraordinary considering the circumstances — he entered another competition.

Not to be outdone by the Canadian province to the north, the legislators of Washington State had voted one million dollars for the construction of new Capitol buildings to be erected in Olympia and in August of 1893 invited architects to enter the competition. Rattenbury was one of the 188 architects who accepted the invitation and submitted plans. How he thought he could have coped with two huge projects in two different jurisdictions with no experience in seeing any building nearly so large or complex through to completion is hard to fathom. But it seems he gave little thought to the problems he might encounter if he won the competition or to the fact that he might lose and that failure to win would dull the brilliance of his local success by suggesting that what was good enough for B.C. was second rate in Washington. It seemed that whether he won or lost Rattenbury stood to find himself in an unpleasant position — but events proved otherwise.

Shortly before the Washington Capitol Commission announced in April 1894 that Ernest Flagg of New York City had won the competition, a rumour which was attributed directly to Rattenbury began to circulate in Victoria. Rattenbury, the story went, had been contacted by the Commission and informed that his drawings had placed first. But when he had travelled to Olympia to meet with the Commissioners he had been greeted with the question, "Well, Mr. Rattenbury, if we give you first place what is there in it for us?"[13] Rattenbury had refused to bribe the Commissioners and lost the competition.

When the story reached Seattle and Olympia it was vehemently denied. Rattenbury was branded an unmitigated liar by the Commissioners. He had reached the very pinnacle of meanness and baseness, the Seattle press stormed. The story that the Commissioners were open to bribery amounted to nothing more than shameless abuse at the hands of a disgruntled architect.[14] For his part Rattenbury too denied the rumour. "The whole story is absurd,"[15] he said but then, should anyone take his denial too seriously, he was careful to add that he had been told by people in Victoria and Seattle that there was little use in sending in plans unless he was prepared to offer a consideration for their acceptance. Whether the Commissioners had attempted to line their own pockets or not, it was a nice exercise in face saving.

Any disappointment Rattenbury felt at having lost the competition must have been tempered by some feeling of relief for work on the Legislative Buildings was not progressing as smoothly as he might have hoped.

When the tenders for the second phase of construction had been opened, it was discovered that the lowest bid exceeded by more than $17,000 the amount allocated by the government for the completion of the entire project and to make matters worse it had been submitted by an American contractor from Tacoma. The next lowest bid had come from a Victoria man, Frederick Adams, and as Rattenbury hastened to assure the government, "Should it be desired to let the Contract to the local man, Mr. Adams, he would doubtless reduce his estimate considerably ... to conform to the other Tenders."[16]

Adams, a man in his fifties who had had considerable experience as a contractor in Ontario and Quebec before coming to Victoria, should have known better but he agreed to do just what Rattenbury suggested and won the contract. Bursting with pride he ordered new stationery proclaiming that he was "Contractor for the Parliament Buildings" and he must have felt that his reputation was made and his future secure. What he had not counted on was Rattenbury's tendency to refine and improve his original plans by designing on the spot as the work progressed. Nor could he have known that Rattenbury would disregard the fact that he had agreed to court financial disaster to bring in a tender which more closely matched the architect's estimates.

Two months into the contract Adams realized he was in trouble. Adams had gone along with the government's decision to use stone from two different quarries in the construction of the buildings. But when stone from the Koksilah quarry was delivered to the site, Rattenbury ordered the entire shipment rejected claiming that it was full of flaws and that the stability of the building would be imperilled by using it.[17] Although Adams had inspected the stone and found that only 27 out of 170 pieces were unsuitable, he dared not risk challenging the architect's decision for he had been warned by the government that he would be held responsible for unsound construction. The problem for Adams lay in the fact that the stone from the second quarry on Haddington Island was more expensive and so the substitution would add to the cost of the buildings. Adams had contracted to construct the buildings for a fixed price. Any increased expenditure would eat into his profits and eventually into his capital unless he received a note from the architect releasing him from his original contract price by stating that substitutions or additions not included in the contract had added to the cost of the building. Had Adams received such a paper regarding the Haddington Island stone his problems would have been solved. But Rattenbury was most reluctant to give him the written order he had requested because the true reason for his rejecting the stone from Koksilah was becoming all too apparent and he did not want to admit that a mistake of his was adding to the cost of a building already threatening to go considerably over budget.

Rattenbury had visited the Koksilah quarry and approved the stone before Adams had contracted to use it, but when the stone had been delivered to the building site he had seen at once that it was a much darker shade of grey than he had envisioned, so dark that even if used only on the sunny southern elevation it would not blend in with the lighter stone from Haddington Island. He had rejected the stone because of colour, not because of quality and his claim that the stone was flawed had become immediately suspect when John Teague, an architect who had practiced in the city for twenty years, decided to use the rejected stone from Koksilah which still lay in piles around the site for his addition to the Jubilee Hospital. Rattenbury was unwilling to admit that an aesthetic misjudgment of his was costing the government extra so Adams went without his paper, hoping that he could recoup his increased expenditure by cutting costs elsewhere. But rather than saving on other facets of the buildings' construction, Adams found his costs mounting there too as Rattenbury continued to insist on making changes to the original plans.

Adams, becoming quite desperate, insisted that Rattenbury give him a written order for the extra work and when the architect refused, saying he would not do any such thing, he threatened to go to the Attorney-General and request an investigation into the conduct of the contract. That he had badly underestimated his adversary became obvious to him a few days later when he received a letter from the Attorney-General. Rattenbury, outmanoeuvring him, had called at the Attorney-General's office himself and complained to him that Adams had "in a manner offensive to him, disputed his authority in matters coming within his jurisdiction."[18] The Attorney-General was not pleased. "I trust that he will not have cause in the future to complain of offensive references to his position,"[19] he chided Adams.

Adams now took his case to the Chief Commissioner of Lands and Works. He had not disputed the architect's authority, he said. Neither had he been offensive to him. But Haddington stone was costing 50 per cent more than stone from Koksilah and the stonework on the south side of the building was costing more than double due to changes Rattenbury had made to the original plans.

25

Rattenbury lost no time in giving the Chief Commissioner his version of the controversy. "I can assure you," he said, "that Mr. Adams has no real cause for complaint." In tones of pained patience he continued, "Mr. Adams alleges I refused to give him an order for a certain comparatively small alteration . . . I told Mr. Adams I would at once measure and value this work and give him an order — but Mr. Adams informed me that he would accept no valuation of mine for the work — and then broke into a storm of abuse directed against my authority and even the Government's."

Rattenbury dismissed Adams' complaint that the Haddington stone was proving to be even more expensive than he had anticipated. "This, even if true, which I doubt — is Mr. Adams' own lookout — Surely Mr. Adams does not suppose a Committee is going to investigate into the causes and results of his own lack of business knowledge."

Ending with a veiled threat, Rattenbury suggested to the Chief Commissioner the only course of action he felt appropriate. ". . . unless Mr. Adams is given peremptorily to understand that he is subject to my authority and that no attention will be paid to his complaints against myself . . . I cannot see how the work can proceed."[20]

And taking Rattenbury's advice the Chief Commissioner did adopt a peremptory tone when he wrote to Adams telling him exactly where he stood. The architect's decisions were final, he wrote, and his orders must be obeyed. In addition he must be treated with courtesy. Unless Adams could prove that Rattenbury was guilty of misconduct "it will be useless for you to prolong the complaint, as contempt of the Architect's authority will not be tolerated."[21]

Adams should have realized that he was finished but he hung on hoping he could salvage his reputation and preserve his solvency. The final blow came when he submitted for Rattenbury's approval an accounting of what was owing to him for work already completed on the buildings. Rattenbury refused to sign it, insisting that Adams had already been paid in full and maintaining that, rather than payment due, Adams was asking for an advance or a loan.

"If we advance Mr. Adams money beyond what is earned where are these advances to end?",[22] he wondered to the Chief Commissioner.

Adams had exhausted his capital and his credit had run dry. He was, as he put it to the Chief Commissioner, "in the unpleasant position of not being able to pay my weekly wages."[23] He had no choice but to give up the contract.

Rattenbury felt the controversy over, the issue closed. But to Adams the dispute was far from settled. And the government, although they had consistently defended their architect to Adams, suspected that the contractor had not been dealt with altogether fairly. John Turner, who became premier in 1895, later remembered, "It was evident that the architect was very anxious to keep down expenses to the lowest point. He had boasted that there would be no extras and he was evidently trying to keep to that statement." And as for the differences that existed between Rattenbury's and Adams' valuations of the work completed, "The government was not very confident of the architect's figures," Turner said, "for they had found very serious clerical errors in the figures sent in by the architect."

The government had arranged several meetings between Rattenbury and Adams in an attempt to reach an agreement but some of these meetings were "quite hostile" and both men had become "exceedingly excited neither willing to admit the statement of his opponent."[24] And Rattenbury had hardly endeared himself to the government when he submitted a bill for $3,000 for attending these meetings.

Adams was not going to let the matter drop. He intended to remain a persistent thorn in the architect's side, pestering both Rattenbury and the government until he was vindicated. But then a tragic accident removed him from the scene. On the night of March 22, 1895 three months after he had given up the contract, Adams sailed out of Victoria aboard the little forty-nine ton steamer *Velos* bound for Haddington Island. Caught by a southeast gale an hour after leaving port, the *Velos* refused to answer to her helm, was struck broadside by a heavy sea and thrown onto a ledge of rock near Trial Island. Adams and four members of the steamer's crew were drowned. The day after his death a chilling discovery was made — the afternoon of the day he sailed, Adams, perhaps as the result of some strange premonition, had written his will.

Eighteen months after Adams' death the stonework, under the direction of a new contractor, was completed and to mark the occasion the government treated the workmen to a celebratory dinner at the Mount Baker Hotel. Amid the general bonhomie cries went up

27

for the architect and Rattenbury toasted the assembly saying, "The pleasantest part of this work has been that it has gone through with such good feeling that there is not a man employed on it that I cannot tonight shake hands with."[25] A statement that no doubt rung true since he could scarcely shake hands with Adams.

3

Rattenbury versus the Chief Commissioner
I beg to remind you . . .

Commissioner of Lands and Works George Bohun Martin joined in the applause that greeted Rattenbury's friendly remarks at the Mount Baker Hotel but he might not have felt so inclined to cheer had the dinner been held a year later for by then he had found himself cast in the role of the architect's adversary and had learned that it could be an aggravating experience. So aggravating that in 1898 at the age of 57 Martin would resign from public life.

A successful cattleman from the South Thompson district first elected to the legislature in 1882, he had had little practical experience to equip him to handle the problems which would arise in the Works section of his ministry. Justifiably modest about his unspectacular political career, Martin who had served as a midshipman in the navy during the Crimean War, remained proud of his family's military tradition and somewhat wistful that he had been the only son to break with that tradition. His fondest memory was of pacing the decks of the *Victory* with his father, Flag Captain G. Bohun Martin, and his grandfather, Admiral Sir Thomas Briggs, and his real interest lay not in politics or the parliament buildings but in Victoria's still busy harbour.*

Martin, as a member of the legislature, had voted against the construction of the new government buildings. And Rattenbury bore this fact in mind as he prepared to do battle over the parliament buildings' marble — a battle in which, Rattenbury made sure, Martin would remain unaware that he had been engaged.

In 1893, when even the lowest tender submitted for the second phase of construction had proven to be much higher than he had estimated, Rattenbury had suggested to the government that $44,000

---

* Martin died in 1933 at the age of ninety-one. "He refused to go to the hospital," the *Colonist* reported, "insisting that he be allowed to remain in his home, overlooking the sea he loved so well." *Colonist*, August 30, 1933.

worth of marble might be omitted "without injuring the ... appearance of the building."[1] To the former Chief Commissioner Forbes G. Vernon and his deputy this had seemed an eminently sensible suggestion and they must have felt gratified that their architect had shown that he was willing to compromise his original artistic decisions in the cause of budgetary responsibility.

But Rattenbury had had no intention of omitting the marble from the completed building. Biding his time, waiting for two years until November of 1895 when the much-admired magnificent pile was rising grandly above the shores of James Bay and a general election had resulted in the appointment of a new Chief Commissioner, he reintroduced the subject of the marble in a letter to Chief Commissioner Martin.

I have ventured to place in the Executive Council Room, the samples of marble and stained glass which I have received. So beautiful are these in themselves, and so much time and money has been expended by the firms sending these samples that I trust you will at least examine them before coming to an irrevocable decision.

The Marble is so urgent a matter, and the omission of it would be so serious an injury to the building, that I trust you will reconsider this matter.

The Legislative Hall is the most important feature in the Interior of the building and is the leading "Motif" of the whole design. The exterior suggesting and emphasizing this feature. The Grand Entrance has been made rich and ornate — as an appropriate entrance — through this you pass into the great Domical Hall surmounted by the Dome — then onwards to the Legislative Hall.

The grandeur of the whole scheme would be absolutely ruined should the culminating feature "the Legislative Hall" be poor and commonplace, and it would be so if the Marble is omitted, for the whole character of the Hall depends entirely on the rich and massive marble columns and we cannot in any adequate way replace these with any cheaper imitation material. No future expenditure, however large, could in any way compensate for the omission — and the amount, in comparison to the cost and character of the buildings, is comparatively small, considering the marvellous improvement it would effect.[2]

Members of the government, perhaps unaware that Rattenbury had assured their predecessors in 1893 that the same marble could be omitted without injury to the appearance of the building, had viewed the samples and capitulated — just as Rattenbury had guessed they would.

By 1897 Rattenbury had been hovering over the construction of the buildings for four years and his patience had worn thin. With the buildings only a few months away from completion, he had neither the time nor the self-control to humour the Chief Commissioner or to travel circuitous routes to get his own way. When in the spring of 1897 Rattenbury was informed by Chief Commissioner Martin that the government had decided to use the East Block, designed to house the Land Registry Office, as a Museum and place the laboratories of the Mining Bureau in the basement, Rattenbury wasted no time in letting Martin know what he thought of politicians who dabbled in design.

"I firmly believe," he wrote to Martin, "that to carry out the instructions I have received from you in regard to these alterations will result in an extremely inconvenient, unsanitary, and evil-smelling arrangement, bad at any time, but almost ludicrous when occuring [sic] in a new and large building of the costly character of the New Parliament Buildings."

He was convinced, he told Martin, that "these arrangements will receive the universal condemnation and ridicule which they will merit.

"I speak strongly, because I feel strongly in this matter, and I must clear myself from all appearance of concurring in the suggested arrangement, for should I do so my reputation as an Architect will inevitably suffer."

Should Martin refuse to accept his advice "the responsibility (of what I consider will be spoiling the buildings) will rest on you,"[3] he warned.

Martin responded coolly, telling Rattenbury that he saw no reason to alter his decision as regards to the location of the Museum but he would reconsider siting the Department of Mines below it.

This did little to appease the architect and he answered with a letter of such passionate indignation that the Executive Council meeting on May 19, 1897 decided that the most charitable course would be to permit him to withdraw his "highly intemperate" letter as it had been intimated he wished to do.[4]

But if Rattenbury had wished to reconsider his intemperate language of May, by September he was again in high dudgeon when he discovered that the fittings of the Museum he had been asked to design had not only been designed without his knowledge but had also already been ordered without his approval.

Furious, he threw off a stinging letter to Martin, a letter alive with the impatient dashes with which he habitually littered his writing and which seemed to increase with his level of exasperation.

As Architect of the Parliament Buildings — pardon me for reminding you — that the design of all work that enters into the buildings, must pass through my hands — *so long as I am in charge and responsible for the work.*

After I have delivered up the buildings to you, as absolutely completed according to existing Contracts — you may introduce any materials or workmanship you may deem fit — but I strongly object to receiving the credit for workmanship that I have never even seen —

Should it be, Sir, that you decide that my professional advice & recommendations are not worthy of confidence —

Believe me — much as I would regret, to sever my connection with the Parliament Buildings especially after having for so many years — exerted every faculty — and made such painstaking endeavours — to carry out the works to as perfect and satisfactory a conclusion as possible — Still — I am ready to resign my position as Architect of the Buildings a position no longer tolerable, if not accompanied by confidence — and so afford you the opportunity of obtaining other professional advice and assistance — in which you could place confidence.[5]

Rattenbury knew that his reputation as an architect depended on the favourable critical acceptance of the Parliament Buildings and while the changes approved by Martin might not be drastic, they were highly visible. Convinced that Martin would ruin the buildings, Rattenbury, always quick to anger, had reacted with sputtering indignation. But when his blood had cooled, he realized that Martin's actions had been prompted not so much by an irresistible urge to improve on the original design but rather by a new-found determination to assert his authority. Rattenbury, with self-assured arrogance, had all but taken over the Department of Lands and Works and Martin, perhaps feeling rather sheepish, had decided that it was time for him to regain control now that the buildings were near completion and he could safely risk precipitating the architect's resignation. The more Rattenbury protested and the more insistently he demanded the right to exercise artistic control, the more determined Martin became to put him in his place. Rattenbury would have to curb his impatience and control his temper if he hoped to regain the upper hand.

A few weeks later when he received a letter from W. S. Gore, Martin's deputy, informing him that the Superintendent of Education was unhappy about the architect's intention to remove a partition wall in his office, Rattenbury faced the new confrontation with uncharacteristic composure.

Gore described himself as being somewhat surprised to learn of these changes. "I have not heard you mention the matter," Gore wrote, "and I must request you to call at my office and show me what you propose doing before you take any steps in the matter."

"I beg to remind you," Gore continued, "that as the professional deputy head of the Department I expect you to consult me on any material changes in connection with the building. . . ."[6]

Rattenbury's answer was prompt, politely hostile, and imperiously detached.

"In response to your rather peremptory demand that I should call at your office and show you what I propose doing before I take any steps in the matter — I have to inform you that I have already let the contract for this work."

Rattenbury, who understood well the psychological advantage of engaging in a battle of wills on his home ground continued, "Should you desire any information on this matter I shall be happy to make an appointment with you at my office. . . ."

In the meantime he requested that Gore "be good enough not to issue any instructions in the Buildings . . . as such instructions confuse and lead to endless trouble.

"As regards your desire that I should consult you in respect to every small change rendered necessary in my opinion to insure the due and satisfactory completion of the Parliament Buildings, I am afraid were I to do so I should take up more of your time than you could spare. I have been accustomed therefore to rely upon my own judgement and I think it wiser to do so as I have found that non-professional interference in technical work produces costly and disastrous results."[7]

This time it was Gore's turn to be vexed. Although he might not be an architect, Gore who had studied civil engineering and had served as the Surveyor General of British Columbia before becoming Deputy Commissioner, would hardly have considered himself as a non-professional. He wrote to Martin, enclosing his original letter and Rattenbury's reply which, he complained, "is not only framed in language discourteous to me but sets at defiance the authority of the Department in connection with the expenditure of public money on the Parliament Buildings."[8]

Martin apparently felt that the only course left to him was to take direct action. Howell, a government employee who was serving as Rattenbury's Clerk of Works and who had been taking his orders directly from the architect, was called to the Chief Commissioner's office and told to ignore Rattenbury's instructions regarding the removal of the wall.

If Martin had expected an explosion when Rattenbury discovered what had taken place, he must have been rather nonplussed by the mildness of the architect's response:

> I understand from Mr. Howell, that he was imperatively ordered by you ... to make certain alterations in the Education Dept according to your Instructions — Knowing that you were acting without professional advice — and convinced that you were making a serious blunder — I had previously instructed Mr. Howell not to make any change in the Contract work except with my sanction — As Mr. Howell — in my agreement with the Government — is expressly stated to be under my orders — I was very much surprised to hear of the Government giving orders to him direct — I consequently asked Mr. Howell to produce them — He informs me however — that altho the work has been carried out — that you refuse to issue the order to him in writing —
>
> In addition to the above matter — the Government on previous occassion [sic] have insisted — in spite of my advice & remonstrations — in making several very serious changes in the arrangement of the Parliament Buildings — which changes will eventually entail costly expenditures.
>
> I feel it therefore due to myself — that the responsibility of these changes shall rest upon the proper shoulders — at such times — when all matters — pertaining to the Parliament Buildings are brought before the Legislature.[9]

Martin, it seems, was about to be hoist on his own petard. It was November 1897, less than three months away from the buildings' official opening. So little work was left to do that Rattenbury now had no cause to concern himself with the possibility of Martin's further interference in design matters. It seems likely that Rattenbury, in order to estimate the total amount of commission due him, had begun to study his accounts and had calculated that the actual cost of the completed buildings would be close to one million dollars. By insisting on changes Martin would now have to share with Rattenbury any blame that might be attached to the expenditure of almost $400,000 over the amount voted by the Legislature and by refusing to give a written order for those changes he had confused the issue by making it difficult for any future investigation to ascertain just who had altered the original plans.

Martin, finally appreciating the problems he had created for himself flew, rather belatedly, into action.

On December 3, 1897 he wrote to the architect informing him that he would refuse to pay the contractor for any work done that had not first been sanctioned by the Works Department. And as Rattenbury soon discovered when he submitted a personal account, he had decided to hold back any further payments to the architect for services rendered.

Although irritated by this turn of events, Rattenbury seems to have enjoyed witnessing Martin's rather frantic attempts to assume control. When he learned that the contractor had been ordered by Martin to stop work on a sidewalk until he had received a written order from the Department, Rattenbury couldn't resist the temptation to needle the Chief Commissioner.

"As regards this sidewalk," he wrote, "as a matter of fact — it was ordered by me — at the request of yourself and Mr. Turner (the Premier) — of course — However — if you desire me not to take any instruction from you — unless in writing — I am quite prepared not to do so — But if you will permit me to remind you — that on a previous ocassion [sic] — on which you issued orders — which you insisted should be carried out — You refused to give those orders in writing — and I wrote to you about the matter . . . with no avail." And on two separate occasions, Martin had named two different individuals from whom Rattenbury should seek final approval before proceeding with any work.

"There certainly seems to be a little confusion in these various mandates," Rattenbury sighed.[10]

It is not too difficult to guess what Martin's reaction to this letter might have been, but publicly he had no choice but to grit his teeth and feign equanimity, for while Rattenbury might scorn his authority and try his patience, even he had to admit that the architect had produced buildings which did the government proud.

Just how he had managed to do it is hard to explain. There had been little in his early training to equip him for a project of the magnitude and complexity of the Legislative Buildings. And the buildings were designed in a style with which Rattenbury was not really enamoured, a style which he seldom used again. After the Legislative Buildings almost every major building that he designed was a variation on French château architecture, a style with which he never tired of experimenting.

A persistent and tantalizing rumour insists that the Legislative Buildings were inspired by the palace of an Indian prince and a variation of this story has it that they are a direct copy of that building. Like other long lasting rumours this one probably contains a grain of truth but it is not necessary to look to India or an Indian prince for the possible genesis of the story. When Lockwood and Mawson entered the competition for the design of Bradford's Town Hall they submitted two designs. Their gothic design won the contest but both architects admitted that they preferred the second design which they described as classical. It is possible then that Rattenbury's design for the Legislative Buildings, which he himself described as free classical, was an adaptation of Lockwood's losing design for the Bradford Town Hall. Richard Mawson felt that the firm of Mawson and Hudson should have received a percentage of the fees Rattenbury collected for the design of the buildings and his refusal to pay resulted in strained relations that lasted for many years. But whether this was because Rattenbury had used a design belonging to the firm or whether it was because Mawson felt it only fair that Rattenbury should share part of his first large commission in payment for the training he had received, is unknown.

Whatever the case, the Parliament Buildings were a stunning achievement.

Just as the government had hoped they were seen as "an imposing monument to the architectural skill, natural resources and commendable enterprise of this most western Canadian province."

The Victoria *Colonist* was decidedly enthusiastic. "The beauty of the structure calls forth the admiration of everyone who has seen it, while the perfection of the work and the thoroughness in which the details have been carried out is a surprise to visitors. In general design and in choice of the stone for the buildings the good taste and judgement displayed has been decidedly happy, the result being a harmonious picture delightful to the eye."

Obviously impressed by the buildings' size as much as their appearance, the *Colonist* informed its readers that the buildings covered an area of more than an acre. "The front of the building including the wings is 500 and the central building is 200 feet deep. To the top of the gilded figure of Captain Vancouver which surmounts the dome is a distance of 165 feet ... if the outside walls were all placed in a straight line they would extend half a mile in length."

The completed buildings proved, the *Colonist* said, that the choice of Mr. Rattenbury as architect had been a wise one.

Only later, after the buildings had opened, would it be discovered that Rattenbury's design had been guilty of singular faults and omissions.

Soon after they moved into their new meeting place it became evident to the Members of the Legislative Assembly that while the new hall might be grand and imposing it was also a room in which it was very difficult for them to hear one another. Some resourceful soul suggested that the bad acoustic properties of the hall might be corrected by hanging salmon net from the ceiling on a framework of steel wires and the members noted with some relief that this humble addition resulted in a marked improvement.[12]

Strangely, the members of the press, whom Rattenbury would assiduously court throughout his career, had been treated in a rather offhanded way in his original plans. Around the upper level of the Legislative Hall, Rattenbury's plans called for three spectators' galleries for the public, ladies and reporters. It seemed that Rattenbury, if he had considered the matter at all, felt that reporters were perfectly capable of taking notes with their papers balanced on their knees. Reporters who covered the first session in 1898 grumbled loudly and were far from mollified when at the next session they were seated on the floor of the house behind the legislators. The situation was corrected in 1900 when the Speaker's Throne was moved forward to allow the construction of the press' own gallery which reporters found to be fairly acceptable except for several glaring errors such as the provision of sloping desks and stationary seats "which can never be satisfactory to people doing much writing."

Apparently Lieutenant-Governors were not so likely to be vocal about their complaints and it was not until 1913, fifteen years after the buildings were opened, that it was brought to the government's attention that another Rattenbury omission was greatly inconveniencing the Lieutenant-Governor and his guests. To entertain visiting dignitaries and to play host at other social functions more properly held at the Legislative Buildings than at his official residence, the

Lieutenant-Governor had been provided with a suite of rooms on the third floor which offered a fine view of the harbour, the city and the Sooke hills. What they didn't have, according to a memo from a most sympathetic and understanding caretaker, was anything in the way of washroom facilities. "As the rooms now occupied by the Lieutenant-Governor are liable to always remain such," he wrote, "I would respectfully draw your attention to the entire absence of anything in the shape of Lavatory accommodation for either Ladies or Gentlemen, it has been found very akward [sic] at times when Entertainments were in progress we are compelled to furnish the crudest kind of accommodation for the Ladies and Gentlemen have a long way to travel before reaching a Lavatory, which on such occasions are always crowded."[13]

As opening day approached, these deficiencies, if they had been known, would have been dismissed as irrelevancies for the whole province was agog at the grandeur of the new government buildings.

Seven thousand invitations described as being ornate in the extreme had been issued and as people began to flood into Victoria filling every available hotel room a plea went out to Victorians to open their homes to accommodate the visitors. The official opening of the buildings had been timed to coincide with the opening of the legislative session of 1898 but, as the *Colonist* promised its readers, elaborate preparations had been made and the ceremonies would be far more imposing than anything hitherto seen and 4,000 people clamoured for one of the 650 tickets which would permit them to occupy a seat in the house.

On opening day, February 10, 1898 the sun shone, albeit intermittently, military bands played, crowds cheered, "the brave new flag of Canada fluttered from the giant flagpole" and the government closed the schools and presented each happy youngster with a picture of the new Parliament Buildings.

Inside the Legislative Hall the cream of provincial society, vying for breathing space yet unwilling to sacrifice any part of the proceedings to personal comfort, listened to inspiring patriotic anthems sung by the Arion Choir, to prayers offered by the bishops of the church and to the reading, by the Lieutenant-Governor, of a Speech from the Throne of welcome brevity.

Celebrations continued into the night. While a display of fireworks brightened the night sky, Lieutenant-Governor McInnes hosted a grand dinner at Government House. Inside the new buildings the band of the Fifth Regiment entertained the crowds that had accepted the government's invitation to come and explore the buildings and to peruse the collections of special historical interest displayed in various government departments.

It had been an exciting, gala day but as the *Colonist* put it "one factor appeared wanting to satisfy the public sense of the fitness of things" — the architect had not been present to accept the honours of his authorship.

Neither shyness nor humility had dictated Rattenbury's absence. Nor was he a magnanimous soul likely to modestly step aside so that his assistants could receive the praise and congratulations. Only one thing could have prompted his absence that day. He had, quite simply, more important things to do.

4

Klondike
the air is so exhilarating

On July 17, 1897 the steamer *Portland* sailing out of St. Michael, Alaska docked at Seattle and off-loaded sixty-eight prospectors and two tons of gold and the stampede to the Klondike was on! For years tales of the gold that was to be found along northern rivers had filtered down to the south. But the rumours had been so vague that only seasoned prospectors, men who felt at home with Yukon loneliness, had drifted about the territory studying gravelly river banks for the tell-tale glint of yellow. Now, suddenly, everyone knew that the stories had been true. There was proof — two tons of it — on the docks at Seattle. As the electrifying news spread up and down the coast, across the continent and around the world, thousands of men and women prepared to take part in what would become the greatest gold rush in history.

Ho for the Klondike! was the cry that rang out as west coast cities leapt joyously into competition each claiming to be the best jumping off place for the northern goldfields. While San Francisco and Seattle both proclaimed that they were "The Gateway to the Klondike," Victoria enjoyed a distinct advantage over the American cities. As the B.C. Board of Trade pointed out in a widely circulated pamphlet, Victoria was the gateway to "The quickest route, The nearest route, The safest route, The cheapest route," and most important of all, "The Duty Saving Route."

The goldfields were in Canada and Canadian law required that each prospector entering the territory bring with him enough supplies to make him self-sufficient for a year. Prospectors could avoid import duties if they purchased their supplies in a Canadian city and soon Victoria's Johnson and Yates Streets became clogged with piles of carefully packed supplies ready to be hauled down to the docks for loading aboard a Klondike-bound steamer.

Tappan Adney, a correspondent for *Harper's Illustrated Weekly*, observed that as early as August the streets of Victoria were thronged with strange men.

They are buying horses, and watching men who in front of stores explain the "diamond hitch"; they are buying thick warm woolens; belts that go round the waist, with flaps that button down over little compartments; little bags of buckskin, with gathering-strings at the top; heavy iron shod shoes ... and moccasins of moose hide ...

During the winter of 1897 Klondike gold and the business it could attract to the city became Victoria's preoccupation.

Victoria sells mittens and hats and coats only for Klondike. Flour and bacon, tea and coffee, are sold only for Klondike. Shoes and saddles and boats, shovels and sacks — everything for Klondike![1]

It seemed as though everyone wanted to get in on the act. "Don't go to the Klondike without an Albion stove," the Albion Iron Works warned and introduced three new portable models. Thomas Earle, "Wholesale Grocer," became Thomas Earle, "Klondike Outfitter" and only the most foolhardy would have dared venture north without first stopping at Thomas Shotbolt's drugstore to pick up a supply of Vasoline after reading that "It cures Coughs, Sore throats, Cuts, Burns, Frostbite. It is the best Lubricant for Metal Implements. It softens and preserves leather."

Some Victorians were content to remain in town, making their fortune by supplying prospectors. But for others this wasn't enough. For a time they struggled to control their growing excitement, but in the end they gave in to feelings that the world and opportunity were passing them by. Like the proprietor of the San Francisco House who announced in December 1897 that his large and well assorted stock of Gentlemens Furnishings would be absolutely sold at cost as he was leaving for the Klondike in January, they sold their businesses or quit their jobs, bought their miner's licence at the Customs' House on Wharf Street and boarded the first boat bound for Skagway or Dyea.

Rattenbury's seething impatience to be part of the adventure had added to his choler during the autumn months of 1897 and his threat to resign as architect of the Parliament Buildings had not been altogether empty. It was impossible for anyone with even the slightest imagination or adventurous spirit to avoid being caught up in the excitement and it was worse for Rattenbury who had hit upon a scheme for making his fortune — if only he could find the time to organize and promote the enterprise.

Recalling this period some years later, Rattenbury made what was for an architect a rather strange boast. During the winter of 1897, Rattenbury said, he had purchased some sixty head of cattle which after a perilous expedition had arrived in Dawson City in the Yukon just in time to prevent the residents from starving. Altruistic though it may sound, it was a venture motivated almost solely by profit for in Dawson that hungry winter cattle brought as much as a thousand dollars a head. It was a shrewd but rather improbable investment for him to have made since he had had no past experience in shipping cattle and while Rattenbury had a fertile imagination, a busy brain his friends said, it seems unlikely that the idea would have occurred to him if he had not met Pat Burns, a man who would play an important role in his career over the next few years.

A short plump little man with an amused twinkle in his eyes, Burns, through a combination of good luck, good humour, imagination and honesty, was already well on his way to earning his reputation as a man who became a millionaire without losing a friend. Born into an Irish Catholic family in Ontario in 1856, at twenty-two Burns had come west to homestead at Minnedosa some 150 miles outside Winnipeg. An unenthusiastic farmer, he soon set up a freight business, hauling supplies from Winnipeg to Minnedosa and trailing cattle back to the city. In 1885 he won the contract to supply fresh meat to railway workers constructing a line from Regina to Prince Albert. In 1890 he turned up in Calgary supplying workers on the new line being built between that city and Edmonton and a few years later he followed development into the interior of British Columbia establishing his headquarters in Nelson and shipping fresh meat to Rossland, Kaslo, Greenwood and other towns in the Kootenays.

During this time Rattenbury, too, was in the Kootenays working for a new client, the Bank of Montreal. In 1896 he had won a competition sponsored by the bank for the design of their head office in Victoria. The building, reminiscent of a French château, had pleased the company so well that they had asked Rattenbury to design buildings for their planned expansion into the interior of the province.

It seems likely that in some Kootenay town, probably Nelson or Rossland, Rattenbury and Burns' paths had crossed and each had recognized the other as a man with an eye to the main chance. And in 1897 the main chance was the Klondike.

From past experience Burns knew that he would find a ready market for his cattle in Dawson City. On August 4th, just two weeks after the *Portland*'s arrival signalled the beginning of the gold rush, Burns purchased eighty-five head of cattle in Alberta and shipped them to Vancouver where they were loaded aboard a steamer bound for Skagway. They crossed the White Pass in the last days of August and were driven overland to the Yukon River where they were slaughtered, tied on to rafts and floated down the river to Dawson arriving there on November 4th.

Encouraged by Burns, Rattenbury probably invested in this venture and his boast years later that he had saved the inhabitants of Dawson from starving was very near the truth for as early as October of 1897 it was reported that the stores had nothing to sell and a famine was predicted by early spring. With beef selling at $1.25 a pound healthy profits would have been absolutely guaranteed if it had not been for the losses faced on the last leg of the journey. The Yukon River could be unpredictable and a hurriedly constructed raft piled high with quarters of beef was not the easiest craft to handle. More than one of Burns' makeshift scows had lost their cargo of meat in the icy waters when they had been caught by the swift current, dragged into the wrong part of the river and dashed to pieces on the rocks. What was needed was a reliable system of water transportation, one which could guarantee the safe arrival of an entire herd of live cattle at Dawson. Knowing that if he could devise such a system he would be assured of large contracts from the P. Burns Company, Rattenbury set his busy brain to work on the problem.

For cattle and for men, the safest and most direct route to the Klondike began aboard a steamer sailing out of Vancouver or Victoria for the Lynn Canal and the Alaskan ports of Skagway or Dyea. From there the trail led through the coastal mountains over the White or Chilkoot passes to Lake Bennett and the headwaters of the Yukon River. From Bennett, the rest of the journey could be made by water — across Lake Bennett, known for its cold winds, across warmer Tagish Lake and the shallow waters of Marsh Lake to Miles Canyon where the river narrowed and boiled through sheer rock walls, over the White Horse Rapids and on to Lake LaBarge, Thirty Mile River and the Five Finger Rapids, where 250 miles upriver from Dawson, the waters flowed into the main stream of the Yukon River.

What was needed, Rattenbury decided, was a fleet of sturdy river boats, large enough to shoot the rapids but with a shallow draft to enable them to ply the boggy waters of Marsh Lake. They could be built in Vancouver or Victoria, knocked down and carried over the White Pass and re-assembled at Lake Bennett.

The honour of being present at the opening of his Parliament Buildings had paled beside the excitement of establishing this business and the anxiety that some other entrepreneur might have had the same idea. A week before the great ceremony took place Rattenbury left Victoria for London hoping that he could convince British capitalists to invest in his "Lake Bennett and Klondike Navigation Company."

In London it seems his salesmanship failed him, but by the spring of 1898 the construction of his first steamer, backed at least in part by local capital, was well underway. Rather than build a complete boat in Vancouver, parts and equipment had been packed in to Lake Bennett where, in some secrecy, the company established a mill a few miles along the shore from Bennett where thousands of Klondikers were encamped by the lake, building an oddly assorted fleet of rafts, canoes, skiffs and kayaks as they waited for spring melt.

When Pat Burns, as good as his word, announced in May that he and Rattenbury had signed a contract for more than forty thousand dollars to ship his cattle to Dawson, the success of the venture seemed assured. But Rattenbury was not satisfied. As manager of the Lake Bennett and Klondike Navigation Company he was determined to tap every possible source of profit. His steamers were fitted out for passengers as well as cargo but he knew that he would not find customers among the desperate, driven men who had spent their savings on supplies and arrived on the shores of Lake Bennett penniless. Instead he would have to sell his steamers' service to businessmen and monied adventurers — just the people who might be discouraged from venturing north by the stories of horrible hardships endured the previous winter.

The way in to Bennett lay over the White and Chilkoot passes. The White Pass was lower and wider but the journey was some ten miles longer than the trail over the Chilkoot. At the summit of both passes the North West Mounted Police waited, ready to turn back anyone who had not brought with them the ton of supplies calculated to make them self-sufficient for a year. For well-heeled Klondikers this presented no problem. They simply paid for their supplies to be packed in over the White Pass while they walked the Chilkoot unburdened and without too much difficulty. Thousands who couldn't afford this luxury went through hell upon earth and by the spring of '98 tales of the suffering they had endured had made the Chilkoot synonymous with inhuman toil, defeat and death.

From Dyea to Lake Bennett over the Chilkoot was a distance of only thirty-five miles and on thousands of mass produced Klondike maps it seemed to represent nothing more than a good, stiff hike. The first thirteen miles, from Dyea to Sheep Camp seemed easy enough, especially in winter when the trail led up a frozen creek bed. At Sheep Camp a stampeder cached his first load and returned to Dyea for the second, shuttling back and forth between the two some thirty-five to forty times until by the time he had packed all his supplies into Sheep Camp he had travelled over seven hundred miles, half of them staggering under the weight of a sixty to eighty pound pack. The next four miles gave him a real taste of what was to come. The trail rose steadily upward until a mile from the Scales, the stopping-off place at the base of the pass, the incline became a steady twenty-five degrees. Stumbling and cursing, with straining muscles and aching backs, stampeders trudged up that last mile and then, at the Scales, they had their first look at the summit. Many went no further. They sold their gear for whatever it would bring and returned home — for the trail over the pass seemed to lead straight up. Twelve hundred steps, the "Golden Stairs," had been hacked into the frozen snow and over the pass struggled an endless line of men, each burdened with a heavy pack. Locked in step, they plodded up the thirty-five degree incline toward the notch high in the towering wall of blinding white snow that marked the summit of the pass. Bad enough to have to cross the Chilkoot once, it required almost inhuman fortitude to face crossing and recrossing it, over and over again. A man who had crossed the Chilkoot was a man who had proved his mettle, a man who had passed a supreme test of his body and spirit. And when he finally reached Bennett he was anxious to talk, eager to compare stories with other stampeders who had crossed their Chilkoot too. Reading these stories in outside newspapers, many people began to wonder if even a fortune in gold was worth the risk. Then

45

in April of '98 even more alarming news reached Victoria. A spring blizzard followed by a warm spell had brought an avalanche thundering down into the pass. Hundreds had been buried, more than sixty killed and it was suspected that still more bodies were trapped beneath the snow.

Rattenbury knew that while some would be undaunted by this latest news, other less intrepid adventurers would decide against venturing north unless, of course, they could be encouraged by a firsthand account of a journey over the Chilkoot by someone who would not seek to dramatize himself with stories of danger faced and hardship endured. Being able to think of no one who fitted that description better than himself, Rattenbury decided to walk the route in the summer of '98 and to underline the fact that he viewed the journey as little more than a pleasant jaunt he took with him his bride, Florence Eleanor Nunn, who surely must have been one of only a few women to find herself honeymooning in a tent at Sheep Camp surrounded by dirty, dog-tired men and the stench of rotting horses appearing from beneath the melting snows.

But then Florrie at twenty-seven was a mature and not particularly attractive bride who might have counted herself lucky to have married any man at all, much less a handsome, ambitious man of some wealth and great promise.

They were married in a very quiet ceremony on Saturday evening June 18, 1898 exchanging their vows in the presence of a few friends at Christ Church Cathedral, Florrie proudly wearing a handsome crescent of diamonds presented to her by the groom and carrying a bouquet of white roses and stephanotis, a gift of Rattenbury's older brother, John,[2] now a sea captain who had come to Victoria to attend the wedding and to travel north with the couple to inspect his brother's fleet of steamers.

The next morning the party sailed for Vancouver to begin their journey to Dyea and the Chilkoot Pass. It was, of course, more business trip than honeymoon and a week after their marriage Rattenbury took time out to write a letter, which duly found its way onto the pages of the *Colonist*, in which he described their crossing of the Chilkoot Pass in terms that would have encouraged even the faintest heart.

"There were really no difficulties on the trail," he wrote. "We simply strolled along and actually did not know that we had come to the dreaded part of the Pass until we were told that we were at the summit. You can judge by this how ridiculous and exaggerated the accounts we have read of it must have been."

Florrie, he reported, had declared that she had often found the walk to Oak Bay and back more tiring and as for himself, well, ". . . really the air is so exhilarating that I myself did not feel the slightest fatigue."[3]

Martha Louise Black, a truly redoubtable woman, who would later deliver her baby alone in a Dawson cabin, become manager of a Dawson sawmill and win election to the federal parliament, crossed the pass two weeks later and described her experiences somewhat differently.

"I was straining every nerve, every ounce of physical endurance in that upward climb," she wrote. "There were moments when, with sweating forehead, pounding heart, and panting breath I felt I could go no farther.

"— stumbling — staggering — crawling — God pity me!

"Another breath! Another step — God give me strength. How far away that summit! Can I ever make it?"[4]

". . . the scenery is so interesting," Rattenbury wrote, "that if people only knew how insignificant the trip was, they would run up here for a day or two, just for the fun of it."

There were some nasty places on the trail, he admitted and it was hard to imagine horses picking their way along the boulder strewn path. "But when walking these places present no difficulties, but are simply good fun . . ."

For the less easily convinced Rattenbury provided an explanation for previous accounts which had stressed the rigours of the journey. "I fancy the descriptions of the hardships and terrors of the trail must have been written at so much a line."

Employees of the Lake Bennett and Klondike Navigation Company had made careful preparations for Rattenbury's visit and when his party walked into Bennett on the evening of June 25th they found everything in readiness for their arrival. Five tents, "capitally arranged" with terraces in front, had been pitched on the shores of Lake Bennett and after a good dinner in the dining tent and "a hearty laugh over the insurmountable perils we had overcome," Rattenbury listened with satisfaction to the news that his company promised to be at least as successful as he had hoped.

Their first vessel the *Ora* had created quite a sensation when she had steamed unannounced and at full speed up to Bennett from their mill camp. As well as being a great surprise to everyone, the company's steamers were looked upon as splendid craft, the topic of conversation from Bennett to Juneau. In testament to their reliability and the speed with which they could complete the journey from Bennett to Dawson they had been entrusted with the mail and, even more impressively, with the supplies for the Mounted Police.

If the trip left something to be desired as a honeymoon, it did provide Florrie with one sentimental moment. Rattenbury had decided to name two of his steamers after his wife using the short and familiar version of her given names Florence Eleanor. The *Flora* had been launched sometime earlier but Florrie was there to christen the latest addition to the fleet the *Nora* and then climb aboard her for the trip to Dawson.

The *Nora* steamed through Bennett, Tagish and Marsh Lakes at a steady nine and a half knots arriving at the entrance to Miles Canyon eleven hours after leaving Bennett. Although the *Ora* and *Flora* had managed to get through the canyon safely, shooting the White Horse Rapids, Rattenbury said, without so much as removing even a scrap of paint from their bottoms, the passage through the treacherous waters was both difficult and dangerous and, thanks to another enterprising Victorian, Norman Macauley, no longer necessary. As she neared the mouth of the canyon the *Nora* pulled into shore where passengers, baggage and freight were transferred to Macauley's horse-drawn tramcars which ran on wooden rails parallel to the river. Below the rapids, they boarded the *Ora* and two and a half days later arrived at Dawson.

Staying in Dawson for two weeks, Rattenbury collared anyone who had a moment to spare and a story to tell, eager to pick up any scrap of information that might help him to plot his company's future. Everything he saw and heard seemed to indicate that the Yukon was on the verge of unprecedented growth and development. That summer of '98 Dawson was reputed to be the largest city west of Chicago and north of San Francisco. Upwards of forty thousand people were milling about in its streets, town lots were changing hands for as much as five thousand dollars a front foot and merchants were finding plenty of customers ready to pay even the most exorbitant prices for anything from nails to French champagne. All the way down from Bennett Rattenbury had observed iron-stained rock and his opinion that the area was well mineralized had been confirmed when he learned from Captain Rant, the B.C. Gold Commissioner, that valuable quartz discoveries had been made at Tagish, one claim alone being worth an estimated $150,000. Already experimental oats and vegetables had been sown in the warmer regions around Marsh and Tagish Lakes and the agricultural possibilities of this area were thought to be very promising. With the booming city of Dawson, hungry for fresh vegetables, only three days down river, the profits for farmers, and for the riverboats which would carry their produce to market, could be nothing short of enormous.

He left Dawson in July, his mind racing as he considered a variety of schemes which would allow him to capitalize on northern expansion. With evangelistic zeal be began expounding on his vision of the Yukon's future the moment he stepped off the boat in Victoria. After taking care to let it be known that he carried with him twenty thousand dollars in gold, he hammered away at his constant theme that life in the north was not as rigorous as people had been led to believe. Reproaching a reporter he said, "... the very fellows you have been warning and advising and trying to frighten with stories of hardship, the class known as 'tenderfeet', are the very beggars who stand the hardships best. Your old-time prospector is always growling and grumbling at the country, but the undismayed tenderfoot takes the whole thing as a joke and continues to laugh at the hardships."

He praised the scenery. The journey up the coast to Dyea was a "most delightful four days voyage ... the countless small islands rising out of the sea, and the icebergs and glaciers being picturesque in the extreme, with an Italian sky overhead and a deep blue sea." Lake Bennett might be cursed with cold winds but soon one reached the Tagish, the garden valley of the Yukon, and here the country was "park-like, with grass meadows beautifully adorned with brilliant tinted wild flowers innumerable."

He dismissed the competition. "... the two rival steamboat lines on the lake ... each own a little wretched 50-foot boat, and one of these recently got wrecked on the rapids, and yet they are accepting contracts for freight and passengers, demanding payment in advance and guaranteeing to land the men and belongings at Dawson by their lines. Many unfortunates have thus got stranded half-way on the journey, and they simply have no means of redress. It is deplorable." He ran things quite differently, Rattenbury said. His company did not ask for payment until freighted goods had arrived at their destination.

Others shared his conviction that steady and orderly development would follow on the heels of the gold rush. Already construction had begun on a railway which would push its way through the mountains from Skagway to Bennett over the White Pass. Requiring a huge investment, the railway represented great confidence in the future of the Yukon. In some places the roadbed had been blasted out of solid rock and in others the tracks had to cross deep ravines. ". . . the whole work," Rattenbury said, "is of the most permanent and durable character."[5]

What Rattenbury didn't realize was that the gold rush was coming to an end with the same abruptness that had marked its beginning. The same psychology that had led to the boom, would soon lead, just as inevitably, to a bust. One hundred thousand people had streamed into the Yukon. All but a few had arrived too late. At Dawson they soon discovered that the promising claims had already been taken, staked before the gold rush had really begun. Stunned at first by the realization that they had come so far for nothing, they had wandered about in the streets of Dawson without quite knowing what to do next. A few stayed in the town finding jobs or opening businesses, others pursued vague rumours of rich new strikes, but as winter approached with its prospects of dark cold days and soaring prices, most admitted defeat and prepared to return home.

Without knowing it Rattenbury had visited the north just as the flood of gold hungry men and women to the Yukon was peaking. By the time the tide had turned and the signs that the rush was over had become unmistakable, he was back in Victoria preaching the gospel of the soundness of northern investment with an enthusiasm which proved to be unfortunately infectious.

On August 19th, two weeks after his return to Victoria he announced that he had formed a new company, the Arctic Express Company, backed with a capital of $100,000 which, Rattenbury said, he had raised in Victoria in only two days. To overcome the problem of Dawson's isolation once the rivers and lakes froze, immobilizing the river boats, the company would build a string of relay stations, log houses spaced thirty miles apart all the way from Dawson to Skagway. An agent of the company would be posted at each station ready to provide every comfort and convenience for the traveller; a warm shelter, a comfortable bed, and good food. Once the line was completed a man wanting to leave Dawson during the winter would no longer find it necessary to make the journey encumbered with a tent and bedding, a stove and all his food. Instead he could leave Dawson empty-handed, "carrying nothing with him save the clothes he stands in," knowing that after each day's walk he would find an Arctic Express Company station ready to see to his every need.

As well as providing wayside stations for travellers, the company proposed to set up a reliable and efficient express service, purchasing hundreds of sled dogs to carry the mail, newspapers and packages between Dawson and the coast. A businessman would no longer have to spend an anxious winter wondering how his investments on the "inside" were faring, Rattenbury said.

Already the company had secured an eighty thousand dollar yearly contract to carry the U.S. mail, supplies and equipment were on their way north and construction of the relay stations would soon begin. The opportunities for profitable business, Rattenbury reported, appear to be practically limitless.

But by October the Arctic Express Company was in trouble. Ice had formed on the rivers and lakes and the steamers were "snugly stored away for their winter rest"; the shelters were built and fully provisioned; the company's agents were poised to greet the first traveller; a "small army of Manitoba dogs" waited to be strapped into harness, but still the Yukon remained cut off from the outside world. Except for a few hurrying dashes there had been no snow. Until it came no sleds could move and men postponed setting out on the six hundred mile trek, knowing that a thick blanket of snow would make the trail more easily passable. The success of Rattenbury's system of relay stations, promoted as being "second in extent and completeness to none in the world, not even excepting the famous Siberian relay," depended on careful and constant organization. As the days passed with no Skagway bound travellers to provide the necessary incentive to maintain that efficient organization, the system began to fall into disarray.

The mail did go through, but no thanks to the Arctic Express Company. Rattenbury's contract called for the delivery of mail in Dawson every two weeks, but as Lieutenant-Corporal Sam Steele of the North West Mounted Police observed, ". . . there was no sign of the contractor or his men" and "no mails came through unless we undertook to bring them."[6] Rather than leave the inhabitants of Dawson cut off for another winter Steele and his men assumed the responsibility for carrying the mail. Corporal Richardson walked the route from Skagway to Dawson, recording a description of the trail and blazing trees as he went, covering the six hundred miles in just twelve days. Police detachments were already in position up and down the Yukon River at posts thirty miles apart. Men and dogs would be relieved at each post, Steele decided, and the mail was to be kept going and coming day and night. The first mail left Dawson on December 1 and soon a brisk competition sprang up among the men, each trying to cover his thirty mile stretch in the fastest possible time, the record going to a constable who covered the distance in four and a half hours, running behind his dog team all the way.

The Arctic Express Company did make an attempt to live up to its contract. On December 8 an agent for the company set out from Dawson but he reached no further than the Mounted Police station at Stewart River, seventy miles upstream from Dawson, where he gave up and handed the mail over to a police corporal who sent it on with one of his own dog trains. As Steele dryly noted, "All attempts made by others during the winter to send out mails were failures."

Failures too were the Arctic Express Company way stations. Anyone leaving Dawson that winter was more likely to be heading in the opposite direction — north toward the rumoured new strike at Nome. Government officials who travelled between Skagway and Dawson were provided with free food and lodgings by the police and sometimes even hitched a ride with one of their dog trains. Others leaving Dawson for the outside found that in return for an hour's work chopping wood they would receive a night's bed and board with each police detachment along the route. With an elite company of superbly conditioned and strictly disciplined men, who benefited from a very special esprit de corps, ready to leap into the breach when his company showed the first sign of faltering, Rattenbury was given no second chance.

The Lake Bennett and Klondike Navigation Company still promised success and when the ice broke up in May the following spring, the *Flora* was one of the first river boats to reach Dawson, triumphantly depositing thirty sacks of mail on the city's docks. But few booked passage aboard her for the return voyage to Bennett. The insubstantial rumours of the winter before had now taken form. There was gold at Nome, gold waiting to be scooped up from the sand of the beach! Eight thousand clamoured for a space aboard steamers bound for the mouth of the river and the port of St. Michael on the Bering Sea. By the end of the summer more than half of Dawson's population had left the city forever.

Rattenbury, warned by the failure of the Arctic Express Company, turned his back on the Klondike before this final disaster scuttled his steamers. But he could hardly admit that he was scrambling to divest himself of his northern interests and still hope to retain his reputation as an enterprising and canny businessman. The previous summer he had described his design work as a leisure time activity but now in April of 1899 he calmly announced that he was so busy with his architectural career that he had been forced to sever his connection with the Lake Bennett and Klondike Navigation Company. "Ratz," as people had come to call him, had invested his own money in the Arctic Express Company and his "busyness" with architecture was prompted by necessity rather than by a reawakening of the urge to create. But fortunately for Rattenbury his reputation as the province's premier architect, won for him by his design of the Parliament Buildings, stood him in good stead and soon he was at work on so many different commissions that what had been, in the spring, a face-saving excuse had become, by December, an accurate description of the facts.

5

Cary Castle
a personal and malicious attack

By the winter of 1899, Pat Burns alone had given Ratz enough work
to occupy the full attention of any architect. Burns, who had made
a fortune following the trail of western expansion ready to fill the
need for fresh meat almost as soon as it arose, was no longer content
to act only as a middle-man, buying beef from ranchers and selling
it to retailers. Perhaps savouring his title of Klondike Cattle King,
he had decided to become the ruler of a kingdom, in fact as well as
by repute. Raising beef on his own ranches, slaughtering and deliver-
ing it to his own string of butcher shops, he would control the business from beginning to end. He purchased vast acreages of range
land in Alberta, closed down his Nelson office, moved his headquarters to Calgary and asked Rattenbury to design the cold storage
warehouses and other buildings required to house his expanded
operations. And perhaps as an inducement for Eileen Ellis of Pentic-
ton, whom he married two years later, he also commissioned the
architect to design for him a grand and impressive residence to be
erected in Calgary. Built of sandstone quarried near the site, as were
most other buildings in the "Sandstone City," it was the largest residential building Rattenbury had ever been asked to design. An
eighteen room mansion boasting ten bedrooms and the almost un-
heard of luxury of four bathrooms, Burns' home set him back
$32,000, some $7,000 more than Rattenbury had estimated. A mixture of French château and Irish castle, it was completed in 1901,
just in time to receive Burns and his new bride.

In addition to all the work he was doing for Pat Burns, Rattenbury had, in the autumn of 1899, more than a score of other buildings in various stages of construction; offices for the Bank of Montreal in Rossland, New Westminster and Nelson; hotels at Greenwood and Rossland; office blocks in Vancouver and New Westminster; a residence at Deer Park on the Lower Arrow Lake; and

two residences in Victoria, one of them his own home on the water-front in Oak Bay. Even for a man who thrived on an almost manic level of activity, Ratz should have been content. But he had set his sights on yet another commission — one that threatened to elude him and one that he was prepared to go to almost any lengths to win.

In the spring of 1899, Cary Castle, the official residence of B.C.'s Lieutenant-Governor, had been destroyed by fire. An eccentric building with an equally eccentric history, Cary Castle was a familiar Victoria landmark, a well-loved oddity, and a very special building would be required to replace it.

It had been built as the home of the first Attorney-General of the colony of British Columbia, George Hunter Cary. Cary was more than just a little mad and his credentials were questionable, but well-placed relatives in England had recognized in the post of Attorney-General in a far flung colony a god-sent opportunity to remove a potential embarrassment from the bosom of his family and pressed for his appointment. So in 1859 Cary had arrived in Victoria, armed with "six law books, a carpet bag and a tooth brush," in search of colonial experience and alert to the possibilities of pickings unknown.

Cary dreamt of building a castle and when certain mining speculations seemed about to pay off he began to scour Victoria looking for a perfect site. When he stood on a bleak, windswept, rocky hill at the top of Belcher Road, he knew that he had found it. In the best tradition of castle-building, the location allowed for a commanding view, not just of the growing settlement of Victoria, but also out across the Straits of Juan de Fuca to the towering peaks of the Olympic Peninsula.

Designed by Fred Walter Green who later found his true calling as a city engineer, Cary's medieval fantasy had slowly begun to rise, "a queer architectural intrusion of the wild landscape," but after the completion of one wing and a tower, three stories high topped with battlement-like crenellations, Cary, discovering that he had over-estimated the returns from his investments and underestimated the costs of castle building, had been forced to face reality and compromise his dream. Rather than completing the building according to the original plans, he could only afford to add a squat one storey wing with matching crenellations and featuring a most unlikely bay window to take advantage of the view.

Cary was not to be king of his abbreviated castle for long. He had been accused of handling cases in a hot impulsive wayward manner and by 1864 his mental condition had deteriorated to such an extent that friends urged him to resign. Cary sold his castle and returned to England where he died in 1866 of an "overworked brain and a weak constitution" at the age of thirty-five.

In 1864 when Arthur Kennedy arrived to assume the post of Governor, he had been encouraged by the enthusiasm of his welcome, but he soon found that while the people might be prepared to accept him, they weren't about to house him. During James Douglas' tenure as Governor, Government House had been Douglas' own home adjacent to the legislative buildings. But Douglas was still in residence and the House of Assembly had been of the opinion that Kennedy or the British Parliament should be responsible for providing an official residence. For a while Kennedy bided his time, but finally growing tired of rented accommodations, he had purchased Cary Castle.

Architects Wright and Saunders set to work replacing the old crenellated roof with a Gothic roof broken by finialed dormer windows. The exterior walls were shingled or plastered to keep out the weather and the *Colonist* voiced popular opinion when it stated, "From the southern elevation the improvements to the old building appear to the best advantage, none of the old castle being visible except the tower."

Having finally voted funds for the provision of an official residence and faced with a fait accompli, the Assembly purchased Cary Castle and for more than thirty years the official representatives of the British Throne were housed in a medieval-cum-gothic castle, "an unsightly pile of buildings on the summit of a great rock . . . exposed to every wind that blows."

Kennedy's personal philosophy was that "It is better to be decidedly wrong than undecidedly right." Many Governors and Lieutenant-Governors would come to be of the opinion that in the case of Cary Castle, Kennedy had been most decidedly wrong. For Cary Castle was damp, draughty and bone-chillingly cold. Fires burning in every room did little to counteract the icy wind that found its way through the cracks in the walls. On at least one occasion the annual ball was advanced to October so it wouldn't be too cold and the ladies wouldn't catch pneumonia.

Governors and later Lieutenant-Governors grumbled and complained and balked at moving in. But one royal visitor housed at Cary Castle while its official occupants willingly vacated to the warmth and comfort of a local hotel had found the castle strangely agreeable. "This place is half way between Heaven and Balmoral,"[1] Princess Louise wrote to her mother Queen Victoria.

With its cold draughts and steeply banked fireplaces Cary Castle had displayed an alarming, if not surprising, penchant for catching fire. Lieutenant-Governor McInnis, a dour Nova Scotia-born doctor who took up residence in the castle in 1897, must have been particularly susceptible to the cold. More than half the fires at the castle occurred during his tenancy, and it was he who had been awakened from his sleep on the morning of May 18, 1899 and escaped from the house with no more than the clothes on his back as sparks from an overworked chimney ignited the roof and the wind from the sea fanned the smouldering embers into a roaring blaze.

The government moved McInnes into Mrs. Green's elegant home "Gyppeswyk" on nearby Moss Street and then became hesitant and indecisive, unwilling to commit itself to the unexpected expense of a new Government House.

Rattenbury was not the only architect who waited impatiently for the government to reach a decision. The new Cary Castle, and no one ever suggested that it could be called anything else, would have to be a very special building, recalling the traditions of the old but on a grander scale. As the home of the Lieutenant-Governor and the home-away-from-home of visiting royalty, it was expected to be the most imposing residential building in the province. To architects it was a coveted commission. After a year passed with no official government announcement, Ratz felt he could wait no longer.

In June 1900, shortly after assuming the office of premier, James Dunsmuir had appointed as his minister of lands and works Wilmer Cleveland Wells, the sixty-year-old owner of a sawmill on the Kicking Horse River who had first been elected to the legislature in 1898. On August 27, after allowing Wells a scant two months to settle into office, Rattenbury wrote two letters to the new Chief Commissioner.

Although more than two years had passed since the completion of the Parliament Buildings, Rattenbury was still at odds with the government over the amount of commission due to him. His commission was based on a percentage of the buildings' final cost and the government continued to pore over accounts, work orders and memos determined to ensure that the architect would not profit from increased expenditures caused by his own mistakes or by extras he had ordered without government approval. While Rattenbury was not prepared to give up his claims against the government, he understood that, if he hoped to win another important government contract, it would be politic to remove himself somewhat from the unpleasantness engendered by direct confrontation. This he accomplished in his first letter to Wells. Written in his handwriting but signed by his wife Florrie, it read,

I hereby notify you that Francis M. Rattenbury of Victoria, B.C. has assigned to me, all his claims against the Government of British Columbia, for services rendered as Architect on the Parliament Buildings of British Columbia at Victoria B.C.

Having settled that matter to his satisfaction, he wrote a second letter to the Chief Commissioner in which he made a direct appeal to be engaged as architect of Government House.

Unless you have already made other arrangements I should be very happy to lay before you, for your consideration some designs for the rebuilding of Government House —
At sundry times during the past year, I have prepared designs suitable for the exquisite site on which the building will be erected. And I have, I think, evolved a plan which would result in a picturesque and stately residence suitable for the purposes for which it will be used.
It is such a charming subject for an Architect to design that, should you entrust me with the work, I can assure you, I should spare no pains to render the building a credit to the Government and to myself.
If the Government desired, I would prepare a full set of plans specifications and full size details of every part, and the Government could engage another architect to carry out the work from the plans — as I myself am desirous of travelling abroad this winter.

Rattenbury, who owed his reputation to the winning of one competition warned Wells about the dangers of holding another.

I have heard it rumoured that there may be a Competition for this particular Government work. I sincerely hope, however, that you will not so decide, for I do not think it is a class of building suitable for competition and I think all other architects will agree with me on this.
The charm of a Residence, as you are aware, lies in its harmony with the surroundings, and in broad and picturesque groupings and choice of materials — qualities not particularly observable in geometric drawings

In a competition a more showy and ornate elevation on paper would most likely be sent in — which whilst more attractive on paper, would in execution look commonplace and tawdry —

He ended by offering his services in a manner calculated to completely disarm the Chief Commissioner by demonstrating that he sought to gain no personal or professional advantage.

Should the Government however decide on a Competition, I should be most happy, not being a Competitor, to render any assistance I may be able, in getting out the particulars or in assisting at the selection of a design. Should you desire me to do so.[2]

But Rattenbury's was not the only letter the Chief Commissioner received. Thomas Hooper, an architect who since his arrival in Victoria in 1890 had built for himself a considerable reputation, had learned of Rattenbury's letter and the following day he wrote to Wells on his own behalf. "I have the honour to make application to you to be retained as Architect for the proposed new Government House,"[3] he wrote and then listed four prominent citizens, who also happened to be members of the Provincial Parliament, who would bear witness to his abilities. Quite understandably Wells decided to hold a competition.

The "Notice to Architects" released on October 31, 1900 made it clear that the government did not intend to provide the Lieutenant-Governor with lavish accommodations. The building was to be plain though dignified, built of wood on a stone foundation and the entire cost was not to exceed fifty thousand dollars. Entrants were to use a nom de plume and two non-competing architects would judge the competition which was to close on December 22.

The matter seemed settled when on January 16, 1901 the judges, local architects W. Ridgeway-Wilson and J. C. Keith, announced their decision. The winners were Byrens and Tait of Vancouver. Since the *Colonist* found their design to be imposing, dignified and most picturesque, and considering that Byrens and Tait estimated that it could be constructed for four thousand dollars less than the sum budgeted by the government, Wells was quite unprepared for the storm of protest that broke about his head.

The *Colonist* received a flood of angry letters to the editor and if Rattenbury was not the author of one or more of them there can be little doubt that he agreed wholeheartedly with the sympathies expressed. The government had stipulated that the ground floor plans should be so arranged that all the rooms, or as many as possible, be thrown open en suite with the ballroom. This condition was conspicuous by its absence, "Architect" grumbled in a letter dated January 18. "Fair Play" agreed. Any person could see at a glance that only three entrants had complied with the government's specifications and the Byrens and Tait design was not among them, he wrote. Adding his voice to the chorus, "A Citizen" heaped abuse on the judges, claiming that they had not judged according to the conditions given. The winning design would cost closer to seventy-five thousand dollars, he maintained. And it had been drawn on a larger scale than that called for by the government and the details of the interior and exterior were incomplete. He went on to question the judges' honesty as well as their competence saying that the plans should have been judged by experts from outside the province "who do not know the different styles of drawing of the local men."

Finding himself in somewhat of a quandary, Wells turned to Rattenbury who had been waiting patiently in the wings anxious to play his promised role of disinterested advisor. Would he meet with Byrens and Tait, Wells asked, and study their design to determine if the charges made against it were valid.

On August 14, 1901 Rattenbury wrote to Wells reporting on the meeting he had had with the two architects. He had gone over the plans with them and together they had calculated the area of the building and found that it would contain some 935,000 cubic feet. At a cost of eight cents per cubic foot the building would cost seventy-five thousand dollars to construct. Byrens and Tait would have to go back to the draughting table for as Ratz carefully pointed out "the changes to be made to come within the Government estimate of $50,000 will have to be radical." But, he hastened to assure Wells, the government should not think that their original budget had been impractical. "I think there should be no difficulty in building a very good and suitable residence for the sum of $50,000,"[4] he wrote.

When Byrens and Tait received a copy of Rattenbury's letter they sensed, quite correctly, that he was out to trump their ace. They did not agree with Rattenbury's estimate of cost, they protested to Wells, and they questioned the accuracy of arriving at the cost of a building based on its cubic content. But their protests were to no avail. Wells, quailing at the very thought of approving a design that might cost $25,000 more than the sum set aside by the government, awarded them the $250 prize for placing first in the competition and began to look elsewhere for a design that could be built for a more modest price.

Again Byrens and Tait wrote to the Chief Commissioner charging that Rattenbury's estimate was deliberately misleading. On September 11, when he responded to these charges Ratz assured the Chief Commissioner that in rejecting their plans he had made the right decision.

"As a matter of fact," he wrote, "I measured the cubical contents of the building in conjunction with Mr. Sait (as he consistently referred to Tait) and we did agree that it would not be possible to erect a suitable building for less than 8 cents per foot.

"As regards the accuracy of arriving at an Estimate of Cost of a building by cubing it, and then pricing it out proportionately with other buildings of a similar character, I may say that I have used this system for many years, and found it to work out almost invariably with the contract price."

He had really gone out of his way to be fair to the architects. After all a recently erected Victoria home had cost fifteen cents per cubic foot. That house had "a good deal of hardwood panelling on the ground floor, and whilst I understand that Messrs. Byrens and Sait had specified similar work in their Design, I only estimated in my Report to you for a simply finished Interior executed mainly in Cedar.

"I should very much regret that Messrs. Byrens and Sait should suppose, that my very moderate report to you, should have been written with any intention of prejudicing them. It seemed to me a moderate statement of facts."[5]

Rattenbury could afford to be patient and reasonable. Five days before he wrote this letter, the government had invited contractors to submit sealed tenders for the construction of Government House and it seems more than likely that the plans they studied in order to estimate their costs were Rattenbury's.

After deciding against using the Byrens and Tait plans, Wells had asked Rattenbury to design the building. But Ratz had demurred, pointing out to Wells, who seems to have been politically naive as well as quite spectacularly malleable, that both he and Wells would be open to criticism if he were given the commission after having scrutinized and evaluated the plans of the winning architects. There was, however, a much more acceptable solution. He would agree to serve as supervising architect, if another architect were named as the designer. Perhaps Samuel Maclure might be interested. Maclure was indeed interested. An architect who excelled in residential design, he had already built several large homes for members of Victoria's aristocracy. A commission like Cary Castle would go a long way to solidifying his position as the city's most sought after domestic architect. For an equal share of the commission, he agreed to work with Rattenbury on the building.

Maclure may have provided the designs for the building, but as only three weeks passed from the time Rattenbury was first asked to study the Byrens and Tait plans until tenders, based on the new plans, were called there had been scant time for an architect to draw new plans complete with specifications, especially an architect who showed such painstaking attention to detail as Maclure was wont to do. It seems more likely that the two architects agreed to share the design work, Rattenbury using the plan he had described the year before as one which would result in a picturesque and stately residence for the exterior and Maclure assuming the responsibility for the interior.

It happened that during the early stages of the building's construction Maclure fell ill and while Rattenbury may have been secretly delighted that this turn of events gave him the full control he had always wanted, later it would be Maclure who would be grateful that poor health had removed him from the scene.

When the new Cary Castle was ready to receive its official occupant in August of 1903, Rattenbury was given sole credit for its design. As he had predicted, it was both picturesque and stately. Its *porte cochère* and centre block were of rough stone recalling the old castle and so there could be no mistake as to the building's antecedents, Rattenbury had added a fat round tower, built of wood and shingled but topped with the same battlement-like crenellations that had adorned Cary's tower. Then he had crowned the building with the closed-in gables which were becoming an unmistakable Rattenbury stamp, the same château-like gables that adorned Pat Burns' Calgary home and which he would later use on the additions to his own home in Oak Bay. Describing the building as "baronial English," the *Colonist* deemed it to be one of Mr. Rattenbury's happiest creations, a building which appeared both imposing and noble while at the same time retaining a look of cosiness and comfort.

Through a nice combination of tactics and luck Ratz had achieved his ends. He was now architect of the two most important government buildings to be built in British Columbia during his lifetime. But trouble was brewing and he was to find his reputation tarnished by charges of incompetence, dishonesty and downright thievery, charges that might have remained unspoken if it had not been for the resentment caused by his arrogance and the jealousy engendered by his success.

George Jeeves who as Clerk of the Works had the responsibility of supervising the supervising architect on the government's behalf had become concerned about the number of extras Rattenbury was ordering for the interior of Cary Castle. He felt that the plans that had been approved by the Chief Commissioner should be followed more closely and he was disturbed by Rattenbury's habit of making changes in the design as the work progressed. Ratz, who felt he was a law unto himself when it came to government contracts, resented Jeeves' poking about the building asking bothersome questions and he told the contractor to ignore him. This advice the contractor followed, for when Jeeves asked why a window which had been shown on the original plans did not appear in the almost completed building he was told to "go to h . . . and find out."

After inspecting the building shortly before the Lieutenant-Governor was due to move in, Jeeves, who admitted that he didn't care for Rattenbury any more than Rattenbury cared for him, had written to the architect protesting that the interior finishing of the castle was "the worst piece of work I ever saw." And when the contractor's bill came in at $30,000 over the contract price, the preservation of his own reputation became Jeeves' prime concern. When the new premier, Richard McBride, asked him what he knew about the extra work done at Cary Castle, he replied, "practically nothing" and asked that an investigative committee be appointed "as I desire to protect my Reputation as an Honest Citizen."

Faced with contractor Richard Drake's bill for $75,000 for a building which he had contracted to build for under $45,000, McBride felt it wise to grant Jeeves' request and he appointed a three-man board of arbitration to decide how much the contractor deserved to be paid. Unfortunately for Rattenbury, the board included two Victoria architects, Thomas Hooper and A. Maxwell Muir, whom he described as professional and personal opponents, and they had in mind an inquiry of a much broader scope than that considered by McBride.

It may have been impossible for Rattenbury to receive a completely fair and unbiased hearing from any board that included local architects. During the ten years he had spent in Victoria, he had built up the largest practice in the city. Many of his fellow professionals were jealous of his success not only because he possessed an almost uncanny ability to win commissions, but also because so few commissions, however insignificant, escaped his attention. In 1900 he had been awarded the work of designing a home for the Royal Jubilee Hospital's resident medical officer. Rattenbury had designed and supervised the construction of the building but had graciously declined to accept the commission of $127.57 — an act of generosity which may have endeared him to the hospital board but not to the city's architects many of whom were hungry for work.

It could be very frustrating to compete with Rattenbury and there were few Victoria architects who did not take some comfort from their suspicion that superior tactics rather than superior talent accounted for his success. And yet at the same time they resented his competence. Even Sam Maclure, whose residential practice was secure and who saved his spleen for contractors guilty of shoddy workmanship, experienced some pangs of envy when he saw the lightning speed with which Rattenbury could complete drawings. Others, more threatened than Maclure, found that Rattenbury, who seldom felt the need to hire assistants, was greedy rather than gifted and they complained about his unwillingness to share his good fortune with others by spreading the work around.

Outclassed by Rattenbury for reasons they felt had very little to do with talent, most Victoria architects harboured varying degrees of ill-will toward him but Hooper and Maxwell Muir were two of those who had felt sufficiently aggrieved to attack him publicly.

Thomas Hooper, a man as ambitious and intemperate as Rattenbury, had more than one axe to grind. A native of Devonshire, Hooper had worked as a joiner in Ontario before moving to Winnipeg in 1878 where he had become an architect and a contractor. He had arrived in Vancouver shortly after the great fire of 1886 and four years later at the age of thirty-three he had moved to Victoria where he enjoyed a wide and varied architectural practice. Hooper had asked to be retained as architect for Government House but had found himself outmanoeuvred by Rattenbury. And Rattenbury had beaten him out of another commission in a way Hooper found highly suspicious.

In June of 1901 the City of Victoria had announced a competition for the design of a new high school building. Entrants were to submit their plans anonymously together with an envelope containing their name. The plans and the envelopes would be marked with corresponding numbers as they were received. After the winning design was selected, the envelope carrying the same number would be opened and the winning architect identified. The School Board's decision was announced on August 16. Rattenbury had won the contest, Thomas Hooper had placed third. Four days later the *Colonist* reported that quite a controversy had arisen over the selection of Rattenbury's plans, adding that "some of the unsuccessful architects have gone so far as to make charges against the trustees."

It was rumoured that certain members of the School Board had decided in advance to give the contract to Rattenbury, that they had ignored the advice of an assessor who had recommended the selection of another set of plans, and that the final choice of a design had been made only after the plans had been identified. And Rattenbury with a notable lack of discretion had lent credence to these charges when, the day after winning the contest, he called for tenders for the construction of the building, having with either reckless confidence or guilty foreknowledge, taken the time to produce detailed drawings and the list of specifications in advance of the official announcement.

The School Board Chairman's vehement denial of these charges confirmed Hooper's suspicions. The fact that he had "waxed thus indignant" suggested to him, Hooper said, that all was not "square and above-board." A. Maxwell Muir had been even more to the point. "I think," he wrote to the editor of the *Colonist*, "that my plans should have placed first."

Muir, who had begun his career in his native Glasgow and who had worked in John Teague's office until 1891 when he had established his own practice, had been just as direct but much more impassioned when, two years later, he locked horns with Rattenbury over the question of the design of the Carnegie Library.

In March 1902 Andrew Carnegie had offered to give the city $50,000 for the purpose of erecting a public library and for the next twelve months an embattled city council had found itself at the centre of a heated debate. Was it proper, some Victorians asked themselves, for a Canadian city to accept the gift of an American millionaire? And was his money tainted because, as some said, he had made his fortune by the exploitation of human labour? And if the city did accept his offer where should the building be sited? On Government Street opposite the Post Office? On Cathedral hill? On Fort or Yates streets? Two plebiscites were necessary before it was finally decided on April 3, 1903 that the city would take Carnegie's money and that the building would be located at the corner of Blanshard and Yates. Weary of the whole subject of the library, the aldermen welcomed a petition signed by local architects Hooper, Watkins, Muir, Keith and Maclure praying that one of their number be appointed to prepare plans. Relieved that this issue could be resolved amiably and expeditiously, Council voted to select an architect by secret ballot. But the aldermen were soon disabused of the notion that they might avoid bickering and contention by following the advice of the city's established architects. At a council meeting on April 20th a letter from Rattenbury was read into the record and the aldermen were thrown "all in a heap."

Gentlemen,

I regret to learn that you propose obtaining designs for the Carnegie library by appointing an architect by secret ballot, opening the way to favoritism, in place of having a competition: giving a fair field to all and no favor.

In a competition each man has a chance of showing the best building he can design. In the ballot system only one man has this chance, and the city does not know what kind of building they are to have, whereas in a competition they do.

In order that the aldermen may select the most competent man to erect this building, it must be assumed that the aldermen are competent themselves to judge the professional abilities of the several architects of the city: but are they?

I cannot see how you can be any more qualified to give an authorative decision on this point than I am to judge of the professional attainments of musicians, and I should think myself impertinent if I attempted to do so.

I certainly must decline to allow my name to be balloted for in any such manner.

It is generally supposed also that the amount of canvassing that has been going on, and I think you must have all been canvassed, must thwart your judgement. In fact, I have heard it said that several aldermen have already pledged themselves, and had done so before this system of secret balloting was adopted.

Sir Titus Salt's mill at Saltaire designed by Lockwood and Mawson in 1850.
BRADFORD METROPOLITAN LIBRARIES

Bradford Town Hall designed by Lockwood and Mawson and officially opened in 1873. BRADFORD METRO-POLITAN LIBRARIES

Cleckheaton Town Hall designed by Rattenbury in 1887 and exhibited by the Royal Academy in 1891.
D. REKSTEN

Rattenbury's sketch for the B.C. Parliament Buildings. PABC

Autumn 1893. In a field near the site, stonemasons square blocks of granite for the Buildings' east wall. PABC

Since the government could hardly be left homeless for five years while construction progressed, the new buildings were sited between and around the old Birdcages. PABC

Official opening ceremonies February 10, 1898. The only dignitary conspicuous by his absence was the architect. L. MCCANN AND MARY BURTON

The completed buildings after the removal of the Birdcages. The photographer, perhaps Rattenbury himself, has taken care to capture the view shown on the architect's competition sketch. L. MCCANN AND MARY BURTON

Florence Eleanor Nunn on her wedding day, June 18, 1898. PABC

The *Ora* lining up the Five Finger Rapids. She shot the rapids, Rattenbury reported, without so much as removing even a scrap of paint from her bottom. PABC

Florrie christened the *Nora* and then climbed aboard her for the trip to Dawson. PABC

Pat Burns' Calgary home designed by Rattenbury in 1899. GLENBOW-ALBERTA
INSTITUTE

Cary Castle, B.C.'s Government House. A well-loved oddity it was destroyed by
fire in 1899. PABC

The kitchen of Rattenbury's home, lined from floor to ceiling with marble. L. CARROLL

Completed in 1903, Rattenbury's Cary Castle was reminiscent of the old but on a grander scale. A Board of Arbitration found that "striking irregularities" had prevailed throughout the course of the contract. PABC

A special English grate, easily recognizable as a mate to those at Cary Castle, graced the fireplace of Rattenbury's dining room. L. MCCANN AND MARY BURTON

"Iechineel," Rattenbury's home on the beach at Oak Bay c. 1900. A country cottage of rough stone and dark stained shingles, it was very much in keeping with Oak Bay's rural character. PABC

The Rattenbury designed Rockland Avenue home of Lyman Poore Duff. PABC

Rattenbury's "addition" to Mount Stephen House. The first gable on the far left is the original hotel. PABC

A PALACE FOR THE PUBLIC.

The New Hotel Vancouver will be Equal to Any in Canada.

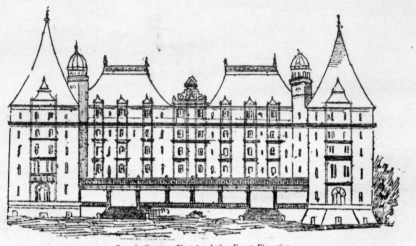

Rough Outline Sketch of the Front Elevation.

Rattenbury's preliminary sketch for the reconstruction of the Hotel Vancouver.
VANCOUVER PROVINCE, FEBRUARY 19, 1901

HOTEL DALLAS.

The "Dallas" near Victoria's Outer Wharf, remodelled by Rattenbury in 1902 and bankrupted a few years later by the success of the Empress.
DAILY COLONIST, MAY 4, 1902

SKETCH FOR PROPOSED C.P.R. HOTEL, JAMES BAY CAUSEWAY.

Rattenbury's sketch of the Inner Harbour with the Empress sitting grandly atop the reclaimed mud flats. The Parliament Buildings are on the right and the proposed Carnegie Library is on the left. DAILY COLONIST, MAY 23, 1903

Rattenbury's Empress rising grandly above the Causeway. A banner proclaims that the plate glass was supplied by the Melrose Company Ltd. but doesn't mention that Ratz was one of the company's directors. PABC

The Oak Bay Hotel designed by Rattenbury for his friend John Virtue in 1904.
PABC

The Nelson courthouse designed in 1906. PABC

Rattenbury found the continuing urge to improve his home well nigh irresistible and by 1912 the beachside cottage had become a waterfront mansion. PABC

The Victoria High School, designed by Rattenbury in 1901 and described as a "barn-like structure" by school trustee Dr. Hall. PABC

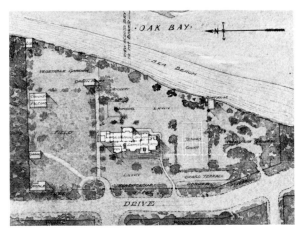

Rattenbury's plans for the grounds of "Iechineel."
L. MCCANN AND MARY BURTON

Prince Rupert c. 1910. The city, Charles Melville Hayes declared, was foreordained to be a western metropolis. The large frame building in the centre of the picture is the Grand Trunk Pacific's first hotel designed by Rattenbury in 1906. PABC

The aldermen should know that all the finest buildings of modern times have been erected by competition, and whilst it is possible to get unsatisfactory results, it is generally owing to unfair conditions, or poor judgement in choosing an assessor, or some such cause. There is no reason why these conditions cannot be satisfactory if a little care is exercised.

But if there are to be no competitions in Victoria, and as we are always debarred from competing for civic buildings in Vancouver or elsewhere (owing to being non-resident) what inducement is there to practice in Victoria?

There is very little private practice here. Personally I have not made office rent in Victoria, out of my private practice in the last ten years, except for competition work. At the same time I have a large practice outside the city, for which I purchase supplies and men are employed here to the extent of many thousands of dollars a year. If it becomes so much more advantageous to open an office in Vancouver this business naturally follows.

I am not advancing all this as any reason for entrusting the Carnegie library to me. I don't care tuppence about it, but you are adopting a principle which will cause trouble all the time.[6]

If his letter had been enough to throw Council in a heap, its effect on the city's architectural community must have been awe-inspiring. For, although Rattenbury may not have been aware of it, the contents of his letter to the Chief Commissioner in which he had advised against holding a competition for the design of Government House were well known.* What wasn't understood was how he had come to be given that particular work but, as in the case of the high school, the feeling was that all had not been square and above-board.

It was all more than Maxwell Muir could take. His career spanned twenty-five years but compared to Rattenbury, his success had been modest. As Muir himself said, "Mr. Rattenbury has been more fortunate in his efforts than any other man, perhaps in this country."

* As a correspondent to the *Colonist* who chose to hide behind the pen name "Ratepayer" put it ". . . how does this argument of Mr. Rattenbury coincide with the previous opinion of his given to the provincial government a little over two years ago. At that time Mr. Rattenbury strongly urged the government to discard competitive plans, and appoint an architect to carry out the work of building a new Government House. Notwithstanding this advice, a competition took place and Mr. Rattenbury did not compete, but nevertheless we find that subsequently Mr. Rattenbury got the work and is today, as architect, superintending the operations of the contractor." *Daily Colonist*, April 26, 1903.

In an unguarded letter to Council, Muir gave full reign to his hostility and bitterness. Particularly incensed by Ratz' claim that he had not done enough local work to pay his office expenses, Muir wrote, "(Rattenbury) has done more local work in this city during the last ten years than any other man." What more did he want, Muir demanded. Especially since he employed no assistants and spent no more money in the city than he could possibly avoid.

"... he declares he does not care 'tuppence' for the library," Muir sputtered. "Why then does he worry himself so much about it as to write? The truth is, he is anxious for the almighty dollar, aye, more so than many of his professional brethren, who if they had made as much by a fortuitous set of circumstances, rather than by pre-eminent ability, would have retired long ago and left the field to others less fortunate."[7]

Muir must have come to regret that he had so openly identified himself as one of those less fortunate who couldn't hope to compete with Rattenbury. Especially since the aldermen proved the extent of Ratz' influence over them by reversing their earlier decision and voting in favour of holding a competition.

"... it appears to me," grumbled architect Edward Mallandane, "it was the intention of Council to select Mr. Rattenbury by ballot, and now they hope to get him by sidewind."[8] And, as illogical as that charge might be, it was the commonly held belief.

Rattenbury, perhaps welcoming the opportunity to prove his adversaries wrong, did not enter the competition. On June 18, 1903 it was announced that Thomas Hooper's plans had won first prize. But if either Hooper or Muir felt any satisfaction at seeing Ratz beaten out of a commission it proved to be short lived.

A new wing was to be added to the Jubilee Hospital and both Hooper and Muir submitted plans for the hospital board's consideration. Rejecting Hooper's design because it included wider corridors and fewer rooms, the board's building committee had given Muir to understand that his plans would be accepted. But on July 24th at a meeting of the full board it was decided that because Rattenbury had previously sketched designs for an addition that had not been built, the work should be given to him.

Rattenbury would hardly have expected sympathy from these two architects, now members of the board of arbitration, but he was completely unprepared for the damning accusations they made against him in their final report.

Attached to their award,[9] which gave the contractor $19,500 of the $29,000 he had claimed, was a memorandum in which the arbitrators stated that their investigation had been greatly handicapped by the striking irregularities that had prevailed throughout the whole of the contract. In particular they cited the looseness and evident carelessness shown in conducting the work, the lack of proper and effective means of checking the work, the remarkable number of changes, and changes upon changes, made from time to time by the architect, evidencing a want of proper pre-consideration of the drawings, specifications and contract, and involving much unnecessary labour on the part of the contractor. The imperfect plans and skimpy specifications had produced a chaotic condition throughout construction. "The want of proper precaution in ordering extra work, the informal, rapid and casual way in issuing instruction without due care in keeping records of same . . . has produced a great deal of misunderstanding."

That much would have been enough to drive Rattenbury into a rage for without mincing words the arbitrators had charged him with incompetence both as a designer and as a supervising architect. But the arbitrators continued. Calling it a reprehensible practice, they condemned Rattenbury for interfering with the proper functions of the contractor by ordering and buying materials in his own name. ". . . some hundreds of dollars have been paid out on the architect's orders for goods purchased by himself, the invoices for which we have not been able to see, but from evidence given by various witnesses all the goods charged to and paid for by the Government have not been used in the building . . ."

The arbitrators provided specific examples. Marble specified for use in the banqueting room had been ordered by the architect and paid for by the government, but did not appear in the completed building. And they had also discovered that "while ten English grates have been paid for, only nine have been used, and in lieu of the missing grate, a very much cheaper American grate has been used."

And, the arbitrators suggested, Rattenbury had ordered goods in his own name so that he, rather than the contractor, would receive the kick-backs, euphemistically called commissions, which dealers customarily paid to contractors who placed large orders.

Ratz' fury was evident in the blistering letter he wrote to the Chief Commissioner after having read the award. The memorandum attached to the award was a

... personal and malicious attack upon myself in which the Arbitrators ... have exhausted every source of invective and innuendo at their command to destroy my character as a professional man, both as to my ability, my trustworthyness, and my probity.

The whole of the charges made against me, are gratuitous on their part, and they have been made, *without letting me have the slightest knowledge that they proposed to make such charges and without affording me the slightest opportunity of meeting them.*

I emphatically deny the charges made, and on my part, claim, that they are slanders, maliciously and knowingly made by the Arbitrators, for the purpose of discrediting me, in the eyes of the Government and the people of British Columbia.

It was bad enough that the arbitrators had made the charges, but what was worse was that when the award was tabled in the Legislature, the charges would become public. "The whole will appear when called for in the House, as a verdict against me, arrived at under oath, by impartial and unprejudiced Arbitrators," Rattenbury wrote. Even if the charges were disproved his reputation would be injured beyond recovery and his professional career would be ended.

Hooper and Maxwell Muir had used their "temporary position" as arbitrators to "wreak their private malice upon me," Rattenbury said and he suggested that the government not accept the award until the charges against him had been deleted.[10]

It seems as if the Chief Commissioner, as anxious to avoid a public disclosure of the charges as was Rattenbury, agreed to this proposal, but on January 20, 1904 a petition from Hooper and Maxwell Muir asking for an investigation into all matters relating to the construction of Government House was presented to the Legislature. A select committee was appointed and two weeks later a very public hearing began.

Rattenbury was in a very awkward position. That the building had cost almost double the original estimate was not surprising. Rattenbury himself maintained that it was impossible to erect a building of an artistic nature without making changes and additions as the work progressed. And on Moss Street, just a few minutes' walk away from the site of Cary Castle, lived the new Lieutenant-Governor, Sir Henri de Joly Lotbiniere, a cultured French-Canadian gentleman, who took a most proprietory interest in the house being built for him. Sir Henri had definite ideas about the class of residence suitable for a Lieutenant-Governor and Ratz had been only too happy to oblige him, agreeing among other things to substitute oak panelling for the simple plaster finish planned for the dining room.[11]

But much more serious were the charges that Rattenbury had ordered materials in his own name so that he could pocket the dealers' commissions and also so that he could disguise the fact that materials ordered for Cary Castle and paid for by the government, had been redirected. In their memorandum Hooper and Maxwell Muir had simply stated that some of the marble and an English grate did not appear in the completed building. But anyone who had visited Ratz' home knew that a very unusual grate, easily recognizable as a mate to those at Cary Castle, graced the fireplace in his dining room and that the kitchen of his home contained such an extravagant amount of marble that it remained as cool as a mausoleum, no matter how warm the day or how hot the stove — sheets of marble over an inch thick lined the walls from floor to ceiling, marble covered the counter tops, slabs of marble served as shelves in the pantry, even the back hall leading to the servants' entrance was rich with finely polished marble.

With his accounts in their usual jumbled state, Ratz knew it would be difficult, if not well nigh impossible, to provide the evidence necessary to clear his name. When he learned that Hooper and Maxwell Muir had petitioned the Legislature requesting an investigation, he decided to counter-attack and he engaged Lyman Poore Duff to carry his colours into battle. Duff, for whom Rattenbury had designed a home on Rockland Avenue, was the city's best legal mind. Born in Ontario in 1865, Duff had been appointed Queen's Counsel at the age of thirty-four and in 1904, shortly after having acted as Rattenbury's counsel at the select committee hearings, he would be named a judge of the British Columbia Supreme Court.

Duff informed the arbitrators that his client intended to use any statements they might make to the committee as the basis for launching a legal action charging them with slander. Upon receiving this news Maxwell Muir and Dalton, the Vancouver architect who had served as the third member of the board of arbitration, faded discreetly into the background, refusing to testify and leaving only Thomas Hooper to defend the charges they had made against Rattenbury.[12]

Hooper, anxious to avoid making statements that might be actionable but at the same time determined to make the charges against Rattenbury stick, was irritable and unco-operative on the stand. He took serious objection to being sworn, claiming that the memorandum attached to the award was privileged and that he should not now be called to defend his statements as if he were in court.

He objected to the presence of lawyers — he was being bulldozed, Hooper angrily maintained.

Deputy Attorney-General McLean, who was appearing for the Department of Lands and Works and for whom Rattenbury had also designed a house, got very little information out of Hooper. Hooper, who had made it clear that he was giving evidence under protest, stated that it was absurd for McLean to expect him to remember every little detail of all the plans, accounts and invoices he had studied. And later when McLean tried to get clarification of some of Hooper's cautious and roundabout statements, Hooper responded that he must be very dense if he didn't already understand the answers he had given.

When it was his turn to quiz the witness, Duff began by questioning Hooper's own professional integrity. What about the stained glass for the Methodist Church, Duff asked, referring to a building Hooper had designed shortly after his arrival in Victoria. Had Hooper ordered the stained glass himself? Yes, Hooper said, but only after receiving the consent of the contractor. And what about the stonework for the same church, Duff asked. Wasn't it true that Hooper had given that work to his brother? Yes, Hooper bristled, but there was no parallel between his case and Rattenbury's because he had always acted with the consent of the contractor while Rattenbury had not.

Did he have a poor opinion of Mr. Rattenbury as an architect, Duff wondered and Hooper answered, No, as an architect Rattenbury was all right but he was a poor businessman for his client.

Do you think it proper, Duff asked, for contractors to purchase goods at a ten per cent discount but charge a client the full invoice price?

Yes, Hooper replied, he thought that was proper.

Well, Duff said, Mr. Rattenbury thought it was not!

He didn't care what Rattenbury thought, Hooper retorted.

Did he now think or had he ever suggested that Rattenbury had benefited himself improperly through the work on Government

House, Duff queried. "I know nothing about that," Hooper hedged. "I don't know if he did or not."

But it soon became clear that the rumours that Rattenbury had misused government funds had originated with Hooper. Gamble, an engineer with the Department of Lands and Works, had an interesting story to tell. "The question of the marble was brought up," he testified, "and in discussing it with Mr. Hooper that gentleman said something about Mr. Rattenbury having it in his own house. I then said, 'You mean in plain words that Mr. Rattenbury is a thief?' and he agreed with me by nodding his head."

Compared to the cantankerous Thomas Hooper, Rattenbury appeared coolly logical and patiently reasonable on the stand. There might be "a few clerical errors" in his accounts, Ratz admitted but there were positively no architectural errors in the building. He had made some minor alterations and a few little changes had been suggested by the Lieutenant-Governor, but he had always consulted with the Chief Commissioner before proceeding with these changes, Rattenbury assured the committee. He had ordered goods in his own name but he had always made it clear that he was acting in his professional capacity naming the building for which they were intended when placing the order and he had always deducted any commissions paid by dealers before submitting the bills to the government. In fact he had on one occasion written a stinging letter to an English firm upbraiding them for having credited him with a commission amounting to $140. He had deducted that amount from the invoice he sent to the government, Ratz said, and as a result was still out the $140 since the company had not yet sent the money.

Rattenbury had a ready answer to the question of the missing grate. The ten English grates that had been ordered were suitable only for burning coal. A larger grate was needed for the smoking room if the gentlemen were to enjoy a crackling wood fire and so an exchange had been made for a larger American grate. He had then decided to use the smaller grate in his own home and by mistake the supplier had billed the government. But, Rattenbury insisted, he had ordered the dealer to correct the mistake as soon as he had noticed it.

As for the missing marble, he agreed that marble delivered to Cary Castle had been sent elsewhere. A case of marble had arrived at Government House but when he had opened it, Ratz said, he had discovered that it was marble he had ordered for his own home.

He had $500,000 worth of buildings going on under his supervision and it was quite possible for some things to be sent to the wrong site.

Although Rattenbury's answers to the charges made against him had sounded reasonable, the committee members were not satisfied. They had read the memorandum, they had heard the evidence of Hooper, Rattenbury and officials from the Department of Lands and Works, but as yet no one had produced any documents to support his version of the facts. The hearing had gone on for two weeks, much longer than they had expected and now the legislature was due to prorogue. They toyed with the idea of continuing their investigation but in the end they decided to present their findings to the legislature before the end of the session. Their dissatisfaction was evident in the wording of their report, which, while it cleared Rattenbury of the charges made against him, carefully left some room for doubt by hinting that their decision might have been different had they been allowed more time to investigate.

... the Committee is convinced that Mr. F. M. Rattenbury, as Supervising Architect, thoroughly protected the interests of the Province, and that in all matters brought to its notice his conduct throughout has been honourable and satisfactory.

Your Committee further beg to report that, owing to the premature ending of its labours, it feels it is not justified on commenting further on the evidence produced.[13]

The Committee's verdict could be taken to mean not proven rather than not guilty but for Rattenbury it was vindication enough. People would take the charges against him only as seriously as they took his chief accuser, Thomas Hooper, and soon a story would be abroad that seemed to suggest that Hooper himself was not above a little petty larceny at public expense.

For his services as an arbitrator, Hooper had billed the government $1,400. But an inquiry by the Attorney-General uncovered the fact that of the fifty-six separate sessions he claimed to have attended, twenty-three had been afternoon meetings, separated from the morning sessions only by lunch. Hooper, it turned out, had billed the government $545 more than the amount to which he was entitled by the terms of the Arbitration Act. He may have made an honest mistake, simply misinterpreting the terms of the Act. But nevertheless his padded expense account did tend to make him seem rather ridiculous especially since he had appeared so morally indignant and professionally outraged at Ratz' alleged wrongdoing.

Rattenbury had emerged from the Government House hearings virtually unscathed — but it had been a very near thing. Although Hooper's charges had no discernible effect on his reputation or career, Rattenbury's dislike of the other architect remained intense. Still harbouring a grudge two years later, he proved that he was quite prepared to appear small-minded and petty if that was the price of showing his contempt for Hooper. For five years Rattenbury had acted in a casual way as the Jubilee Hospital's consulting architect. In addition to the doctor's residence he had done a number of minor jobs for the hospital board without charging his normal fees counting the gratitude he received and the increased status he enjoyed payment enough. In May 1905 the board asked Hooper to prepare plans for a children's ward — a not unreasonable decision since Rattenbury was planning an extended trip to England at the time. An infuriated Rattenbury immediately placed before the board a bill for $348 for past services rendered — an action correctly interpreted by one board member who stated that he was convinced that Rattenbury would not have said a word if any other than "that certain architect" had been employed.

Hooper's charges of incompetence and dishonesty could not have come at a worse time, for during the years 1903 and 1904 the most important non-governmental client Rattenbury had yet to attract was trading on both his reputation for architectural brilliance and his good name in the community to wring significant concessions out of the City of Victoria. If either his professional ability or his personal honesty had remained in doubt he might well have lost the opportunity to design the building which many see as his best architectural work — the Empress Hotel.

6

Sir Thomas Shaughnessy and the Empress Hotel
to the last tittle and jot

"No," said C.P.R. president Sir Thomas Shaughnessy, "the company has no intention of building a tourist hotel in Victoria."

A story had appeared in an eastern newspaper stating that construction would begin at an early date. But that story was nothing but a rumour, Sir Thomas said, the company was not even contemplating such a move.

The members of the Board of Trade's hotel committee set up to discover what plans the C.P.R. had in store for the city, were stunned. After all, two events had occurred earlier that same year that seemed to indicate that the company would take a lively interest in Victoria's future.

In January 1901 the C.P.R. had purchased the Canadian Pacific Navigation Company and its fourteen somewhat elderly vessels. The C.P.R. intended to update the fleet, Victorians were assured, and particular attention would be paid to be Victoria-Vancouver run.

Then in February it had been announced that after a very keen competition with some of the leading architects in New York, Montreal and Toronto, Victoria's most celebrated architect, Francis Mawson Rattenbury, had been selected to prepare plans for the enlargement of the C.P.R. hotel in Vancouver.

In choosing Rattenbury as their western division architect, the C.P.R. couldn't have done better. In fact the wonder is that they bothered to hold a competition at all. He was practiced in that company symbol, the château style of architecture. He enjoyed an unparalleled reputation in the west for his design of the Legislative Buildings. And, perhaps most importantly, he brought a certain missionary zeal to the promotion of his projects — a quality that would become invaluable later on — for despite Sir Thomas' denials, it seems likely that at an early date the company had decided to build an hotel, but had decided to delay any official announcement until they had winkled the best possible concessions out of the City of Victoria.

Built fifteen years before in Vancouver and the Rockies, the C.P.R.'s western hotels had already proved to the company just how lucrative the tourist trade could be. Although it had already been extended once before in 1892, the Hotel Vancouver had become badly overcrowded and distinctly humble compared to the C.P.R.'s eastern hotels. Following Rattenbury's plans an entire new wing would be added. And as for the existing building, "The idea is," Ratz said, "to rebuild everything except the present dining room." The completed hotel would contain some 250 bedrooms, fitted with all the latest and most approved conveniences. The entire project would cost between $400,000 and $500,000, Ratz predicted and winning a few more points for the C.P.R. in Vancouver he repeated the company's promise that "the work shall as far as possible be placed in the hands of local firms."

"When reconstructed, the Hotel Vancouver will have few rivals in Canada," he enthused. "The Windsor in Montreal will be somewhat larger; the Frontenac at Quebec will be about the same size — and these are the only ones that are really in the same class."[1]

Also in need of improvement were the company's hotels in the Rockies. The C.P.R. had discovered "a number of very scenic picturesque effects" in the vicinity of Field and tiny Mount Stephen House wouldn't begin to be able to accommodate all the tourists who would pour off the trains once the company had cut roads through to the various points of attraction such as the large glacier and the waterfall 1,200 feet high. Under Rattenbury's direction the little Swiss chalet was transformed into a large, but suitably rustic, hotel of fifty rooms, a huge rambling shingled building which combined chalet, château and tudor styles and stood just a few paces away from the tracks dwarfing the little log railway station.

The owners of Victoria's Hotel Dallas, encouraged by the C.P.R.'s promise to improve the passenger service between Vancouver and Victoria and impressed by the company's obvious confidence in the future of the hotel industry in Vancouver, decided to take a leaf from the C.P.R.'s book by commissioning Rattenbury to remodel their hotel on the waterfront near the city's Outer Wharves. After being closed for some months undergoing a most complete refitting and furnishing from top to bottom, the Hotel Dallas re-opened in May 1902. With its magnificent view of the Straits and Olympics, its seventy "tastefully arranged bedrooms, its capacious balconies, its public rooms fitted up in the highest style of the art" and its kitchens which had become "culinary apartments," the Dallas could expect to remain one of the most attractive and favourite resorts on the Pacific Coast. It was after all Victoria's only seaside hotel, and as far as Mr. and Mrs. Patterson, the Dallas' proprietors could tell, it was re-opening for business under very favourable conditions. What they didn't know, was that after he had indulged in an appropriate period of flirtatious hesitation Sir Thomas Shaughnessy was quite prepared to let himself be seduced by the persistent wooing of the Board of Trade's hotel committee.

In June 1902 a month after the Dallas re-opened Shaughnessy arrived in Victoria on his annual cross-country tour of inspection. Welcoming this opportunity to press their suit in person, the members of the committee accompanied by Mayor Hayward, "waited on" Sir Thomas and pointed out all the advantages Victoria offered as the location for a first class tourist hotel. As a site they suggested the gardens of James Douglas' former residence. Close by the Parliament Buildings and enjoying an historical association with the "Father of British Columbia," the gardens represented Victoria's most prominent and prestigious site.

The committee noted that at first Sir Thomas appeared to be averse to the proposal but ultimately he admitted to having been impressed by their arguments.

"It may be taken for a matter of almost absolute certainty," the Board of Trade assured City Council, "that the new C.P.R. hotel will be erected on the property of the Douglas estate . . . an ideal site for such a building."[2]

"It is a matter of common knowledge," the *Colonist* reported, "that the C.P.R. has had a bond on the Douglas property for some time."

Everyone agreed that the Douglas estate was an excellent site. "While handy to the city, and commanding a splendid view of the harbour and its environs, it is close to all points of interest — the Parliament Buildings, Beacon Hill park, the Beach drives, etc." The C.P.R. could do no better. Or then again maybe it could. It was not beyond the bounds of probability, an unidentified informant told the *Colonist*, that the C.P.R. might prefer to build on the reclaimed land behind the newly built Causeway.

Until 1901 the city had been divided by James Bay, a narrow protected inlet which dwindled into a tidal mud flat extending well inland and separating the James Bay residential area and the legislative precinct from the downtown business district and the harbour. In 1859 a bridge had been built across the inlet connecting Government Street with Birdcage Walk and shortening the journey between the two parts of town. Over the years the mud flats had become a stinking tidal garbage dump, rank with rotting seaweed, the occasional dead horse, the effluvia from the Pendray Soap Factory and anything else passing citizens happened to throw into the water. In 1901 the City held a plebiscite asking voters to approve the expenditure of their tax dollars to replace the rickety old bridge with a causeway which would cut the mud flats off from the sea and allow them to be filled in. Appalled by the *Colonist*'s description of the mud flats as an unsightly cesspool and the bridge as a tottering structure and alarmed when the provincial medical health officer termed the flats an absolute menace to health, the voters approved the by-law, little guessing that the reclaimed land would become the most desirable and the most valuable piece of real estate in the city.

After several months passed with no further word from Sir Thomas, a more influential hotel committee was formed comprised of representatives from the Board of Trade, the Tourist Association and City Council. This committee, charged with preparing definite proposals to put before Shaughnessy on his next visit to the city, came up with three alternative suggestions. If the C.P.R. agreed to build on Douglas' garden the City, with ratepayer approval, would exempt the company from taxation for a period of twenty-five years and in addition would, at its own expense, lay out the reclaimed James Bay flats as pleasure grounds and gardens. If the company decided instead to purchase and enlarge the existing Driard Hotel the same exemptions would apply. Then, almost as an afterthought, the committee added a third proposal. If the company should happen to prefer to build on the reclaimed land behind the Causeway, a site which was after all according to the Mayor, practically valueless, then the city would make the C.P.R. a gift of the land, free of cost.

The committee put the sweetened pot on the back of the stove until May 1903 when Shaughnessy once again paid his annual visit to the city. Arriving at the appointed hour, the committee met with Sir Thomas in the parlour of the Driard and received a most distressing piece of news.

"Now, I understand you gentlemen want to talk to me about a hotel," Sir Thomas said, getting right to the point. "I want to say that our company is very much adverse to going any further into the hotel business."[3]

But, the committee protested, a tourist hotel in the city would prove to be a very profitable venture.

"Well, as I have said before," Sir Thomas reminded the despondent committee, "we do not want to go into the hotel business. In addition to it locking up a great amount of capital . . . it entails a good deal of permanent expense, and the success of it otherwise rests upon our being able to secure an efficient manager and staff which is often extremely difficult. Consequently such an undertaking is a continual source of trouble."

"At the same time," Sir Thomas continued and the committee's spirits began to rise, "provided I was prepared to recommend to our company the erection of such a hotel, what co-operation could we expect on the part of the citizens?"

What the C.P.R. could expect, the committee assured Shaughnessy, was the acceptance of one of the proposals that had been worked out over the last few months and they carefully explained the advantages of each. After studying the three alternatives, Shaughnessy suggested a fourth.

"If the city will supply the site," he said, "and exempt us from taxation and give us free water for 20 years, we will build a hotel to cost not less than $300,000."

Elated, the members of the committee thanked Shaughnessy for making a distinct offer. But the Mayor did have one reservation. If the City donated the site it might be difficult to win voter approval for a tax exemption lasting twenty years, he warned.

"Well, that is my proposition," Shaughnessy said, "if you care to accept it all right, but if not, you can make one, but bear in mind that the company is not anxious to go into the hotel business."

The committee scurried to City Hall to get a copy of the plans of the James Bay flats, the piece of city owned land they felt most likely to meet with Sir Thomas' approval and taking the plans to Rattenbury, they asked him to sketch in the ground floor of an hotel to prove to Shaughnessy that they were offering him a suitable site.

The following evening, armed with Rattenbury's sketches which showed much more than they had asked for, they called on Shaughnessy and showing him the plans, asked if the four and a half acres they proposed to give the company would be satisfactory to him. Indeed, the land did seem to satisfy Sir Thomas. In fact only one thing concerned him. The plan sketched by Rattenbury was for a five storey hotel of 150 bedrooms. That, said Sir Thomas, would not be large enough! He preferred one of not less than 250 rooms.

"If we build a hotel it must be a good one and adequate to our needs," Shaughnessy informed the members of the committee who didn't stop to think that this was a rather odd thing for Sir Thomas to say since, for the last two years, he had consistently maintained that it was not in the company's best interest to build any hotel in the city at all.

Even stranger was the illustration run by the *Colonist* the following day when the paper broke the story of Shaughnessy's distinct offer. Identified as a sketch "made some time ago" by Rattenbury, it showed a truly monumental Inner Harbour. On the right were the Parliament Buildings, and beside them on the site of Douglas' garden was a building identified as a college. On the left was the already built Post Office and beside that the Carnegie Library. And there, in the middle, atop the reclaimed mud flats, sat the C.P.R. tourist hotel, the magnificent centrepiece, the pivotal point around which Rattenbury's whole grand Inner Harbour scheme revolved.

Surprisingly the sketch raised nary an eyebrow although it had obviously been drawn at least two months earlier, at a time when the committee still considered the Douglas gardens to be the chosen site. After a year of argument and discussion, it had been decided on April 3, 1903 to site the Carnegie Library on Yates Street. But Rattenbury's sketch clearly showed the library at the corner of Government and Humboldt Streets. He had sketched the Inner Harbour plan showing the tourist hotel sitting elegantly on the mud flats two months before the committee had first suggested the site to the C.P.R.

Perhaps Rattenbury had, at the committee's request, sketched plans for each of the three sites proposed to Shaughnessy. Or perhaps the prominent Victorians who served on the committee and City Council had promised the reclaimed land to the company well in advance of any official announcement and had been carefully preparing voters for the city's final offer to the C.P.R. But more likely, like the ordinary citizens who later approved the by-law granting concessions to the company, they too had been manipulated by the

C.P.R. with Rattenbury, Shaughnessy and Captain Troup, manager of the company's coastal steamers, pulling the strings.

Despite the C.P.R. president's apparent disinterest, it seems highly probable that the company had decided to build an hotel at the time they acquired the Canadian Pacific Navigation Company's fleet in 1901. Shaughnessy, had he not recommended the construction of a tourist hotel in Victoria, would have been reversing a company policy which had proved to be highly successful since 1886 when the first tourist hotels in the Rockies had been built.

The C.P.R. had already invested over $700,000 in its coastal fleet, when in February 1902, Captain Troup announced that the company had commissioned the construction of a ship designed to be the fastest and most luxurious vessel in service on the coast and intended for use on the Vancouver-Victoria run. From the beginning Troup had had no doubts that Victoria had the potential of becoming a tourist mecca, attracting the extremely wealthy class of people who were then travelling about the continent in search of the warm climate, the scenic drives and the picturesque waterfront that the city offered. All that Victoria lacked was the truly first class accommodation to which such people were accustomed. With its vast resources and its experience in running grand hotels in Montreal and Quebec City, the C.P.R. was certainly capable of correcting that deficiency.

Rattenbury would have been content with neither a reconstructed Driard Hotel nor a new structure on the Douglas gardens. An architect who could never be accused of thinking small, he had envisioned not just a château-style hotel but a whole harbourscape, a picturesque waterfront ringed with impressive structures, and dominated by buildings he had designed. Sited on the reclaimed land the hotel rising imposingly above the causeway would grasp the attention of passengers lining the rails of steamers sailing into the harbour. The first building seen after rounding Laurel Point, it would become etched on a visitor's memory as the building which, above all others, he identified with Victoria.[4] Such a concept would have appealed to Shaughnessy as much as it did to Rattenbury and there can be little doubt that they decided together that only this spectacular site would do. Of course to have admitted such a thing at the outset would have meant that the C.P.R. might have had to be content with only a gift of the land. By coyly feigning indifference to the very idea of an hotel, the C.P.R. could expect to be showered with civic favours. Victoria was desperately eager to be made a C.P.R. town.

"Take the case of Quebec," Alderman Rickaby intoned. "Ten years ago that city was practically dead, but today it is one of the finest and most prosperous cities in the Dominion. The whole character of the city has been changed by the influence of the C.P.R. hotel there. Tourists and visitors are attracted from all portions of the globe and the fine service furnished, coupled with the historic interest in the environment has caused the fame of Quebec to be known everywhere. The car service is as good as any in the Dominion, and the streets are beautifully paved and clean. Not only the C.P.R., but every other hotel in the city is crowded and business is in the very best shape."[5]

So excited were Victorians, so grateful were they that the C.P.R. had been persuaded into bestowing such great benefits on their city, that it was almost impossible to find anyone who opposed the by-law granting concessions to the company. The ballots, counted on September 16, 1903 showed that while only eighty-five voters had any serious reservations, 1,810 had heartily supported the by-law. The C.P.R. would be given the reclaimed land but the city had driven a hard bargain regarding the other concessions and the company would be provided with free water and tax exempt status for only fifteen years — five years less than the twenty they had originally demanded. However the city did guarantee to complete the land fill, to build good roads and sidewalks around the property, and to prevent the construction of any "bad" buildings near the site.

Sir Thomas announced that he was pleased with the results of the vote and promised Victorians that construction would begin at an early date. By December 1903 Rattenbury's plans were ready.

The company would build a substantial seven storey building, "a picturesque castle effect of the French Renaissance school of architecture . . . suggestive of the much-admired Château Frontenac." For skeptical Victorians who pictured so large a stone building sinking majestically out of sight down and down through many layers of fill, Ratz added the assurance that an eminent experienced engineer would be employed to solve the problems of the hotel's foundation. While the foundation was being laid, Rattenbury said, he would prepare the detailed working drawings so that construction could proceed without delay. With its many elaborate features, the hotel itself would become a tourist attraction. Its "Old English style" entrance hall which would be furnished and designed without regard to cost, its large glass roofed palm garden decorated Chinese style in red and gold, its massive dining room which would be nobly and elaborately decorated and would feature "nothing quaint," its oval shaped ladies' salon decorated in the "Marie Antoinette style," and its oak panelled reading room and library with Inglenook fireplaces would lure visitors to the city and charm them into a long stay. To Victorians it all sounded quite exotic and should there be any final doubters, C.P.R. president Sir Thomas Shaughnessy promised that the company would turn the old mud flats into "the beauty spot of Canada." A promise not to be taken lightly according to Rattenbury who said that Sir Thomas intended to fulfill his commitments to the city "to the last tittle and jot."

But to make a beauty spot out of a mud flat took longer than Ratz or the C.P.R. had predicted. An hotel of the size of the one designed by Rattenbury could not be properly centred on the causeway using only the land the company had received from the city and rather than see the hotel squeezed over to the right the C.P.R. had decided to delay construction while they quietly purchased land along Humboldt Street. By June 1904 they had managed to buy out all the property owners except one. He owned a key lot at the southeast corner of Government and Humboldt Streets and he refused to sell. Dismayed at the prospect of one recalcitrant landowner delaying the construction of the long awaited tourist hotel, the City Council decided to expedite the negotiations by adopting the simple course of expropriating the property. Now the C.P.R. was ready to proceed — provided of course the voters would agree to extend the company's tax exempt status to the newly-acquired land along Humboldt Street. Once again ratepayers went to the polls and once again they overwhelmingly approved the granting of concessions to the C.P.R. But the ballots, counted on July 7, 1904, showed that this time the turnout had been much lower. Interest in the much-vaunted tourist hotel was flagging.

By the time construction was finally underway in August 1905, the C.P.R. hotel which had caused such excitement had become a subject viewed with distinct ennui by all those who weren't still grumbling about the delays. It was time for him to pique public interest, Ratz decided.

For years the building had been known simply as the "C.P.R. hotel" or the "tourist hotel." Now, although the company may well have already decided that only the "Empress" would do, evoking as it did the great days of the British Raj when Queen Victoria had been named Empress of India and more practically identifying the hotel with the same company that ran the Empress line of sleek steamers sailing between the west coast and the Orient, Rattenbury suggested that it might be a good idea to hold a public competition to select a name for the hotel and he mused aloud to a handy reporter from the *Colonist* about possible choices.[6]

The question of a name for the hotel was one that "bristles with difficulties," Rattenbury said dangling the carrot in front of the donkey.

There are so many considerations to be borne in mind. [It must be a name both dignified and attractive and it should also have some historical associations.]

"The Hotel Van Horne" is good, but it has been snapped up by Winnipeg. "The Douglas Arms" would have the desired heraldic advantage, but otherwise is the sort of name adopted by places of lesser consequence.

It would be a good idea to get His Majesty King Edward to plant an oak for us, having it shipped out for replanting and name the hotel "The Royal Oak" but that again has its objections, and through constant use has become hackneyed and lost something of its dignity.

"The San Juan de Fuca" has been suggested, but is rather too much of a mouthful, besides having other euphonic objections.

Another suggestion had been "The Camosun" and while Rattenbury admitted that the name did have local colour he felt the reference was obscure and little known and would hardly serve the purpose.

The decision would have to be made soon, Ratz warned, for the hotel would be completed by the following summer.

If all Victoria wasn't talking about the C.P.R. hotel now, it certainly wasn't Rattenbury's fault.

But by November 1906, fourteen months after Rattenbury's optimistic prediction, the hotel had still not opened its doors and the Tourist Association, doubting that it would be ready to receive guests by the following summer, wondered where the visitors attracted by their 135,000 judiciously circulated pamphlets would stay.

"It is high time something be done," Rattenbury said with some disgust, placing the blame for the delay firmly on the city. The agreement between the C.P.R. and the city clearly stated that preparing the grounds for landscaping was a civic responsibility, but as yet the land was still seven feet lower than the necessary level.

The company planned to lay out tennis lawns, pleasure grounds and rockeries, Rattenbury said, "but it is useless to talk of all that until there is some sign of the first preliminary measures being taken by the city to fulfill their part of the contract. Then will be time enough to talk about the completion of ours."[7]

Had he been produced from a company mold, Rattenbury could not have been a more fitting representative of the C.P.R.'s interests on the west coast. And, in his turn, he had exerted a powerful influence over the company's public image. In the space of a few years he had designed an almost new Hotel Vancouver, he had been charged with the interior decoration of the company's luxurious steamer, the *Princess Victoria*, he had designed and supervised the construction of the Empress Hotel. As well as his addition to Mount Stephen House at Field, he had been asked to prepare plans for the enlargement of the Banff Springs Hotel. Soon tourists, journeying from Calgary to Vancouver Island, would travel the entire route stopping off in Rattenbury-designed hotels and sailing to the island on a Rattenbury-decorated ship.

It was astounding news then when Rattenbury announced on December 4, 1906 that he had severed his connection with the C.P.R. The company's head architect, Walter S. Painter, had ordered changes made in the arrangement of rooms on the first floor of the Empress. Rather than agree to the changes, Ratz had chosen to resign, claiming he was much too busy to make the trip to Montreal to discuss the matter with Painter. The relatively minor changes ordered by Painter would not in themselves have been enough to precipitate Rattenbury's resignation. What had really irritated him was that the suggestion to make them had come from the office of the Superintendent of Hotels, Hayter Reed, whose wife had been chosen to take charge of the interior decoration of the hotel. Mrs. Reed's interiors, with their positively lavish use of wicker, were certainly not what Ratz had had in mind for the Empress — hardly Marie Antoinette or Old English. He had issued the C.P.R. with an ultimatum — either follow his advice on design matters or accept his resignation. The C.P.R. had chosen to support Mrs. Reed — a decision due, at least in part, to the company's growing displeasure with their western division architect caused by his involvement with a competing railway line, the Grand Trunk Pacific.

In November 1902, Charles Melville Hays, second vice-president and general manager of Canada's oldest railroad, the Grand Trunk, had announced that his company intended to build a transcontinental railway with a terminus on the North Pacific Coast. Operating under a separate charter, the Grand Trunk Pacific would inject new life into the moribund parent company by giving it access to the west coast and the lucrative Oriental trade.

Like Van Horne and Shaughnessy, the two men most responsible for the success of the C.P.R., Hays was an American, born in Rock Island, Illinois in 1856. After spending more than twenty-five years in the employ of American railroad companies, Hays, whose forceful personality and innovative ideas had saved several lines from bankruptcy, had accepted the position offered to him by the Grand Trunk and had immediately begun planning the transcontinental rail line which would undo the monopoly the C.P.R. had enjoyed for almost twenty years.

Whatever the C.P.R. did well, Hays decided, the Grand Trunk Pacific would do better. The new line would be of the most modern and up-to-date character, he promised. Bridges would be built of steel rather than wood. The tracks would be carefully laid out to avoid steep grades and sharp curves and ample station facilities would be built to handle passengers and freight. Benefiting from technological advances, the Grand Trunk Pacific would offer passengers the safest and most comfortable ride available on any railroad on the continent.

But as Hays made clear, he had plans for more than just a railroad. "Having reached the Pacific Coast," he said, "the company will undertake to establish a line of steamships to run to China, Japan and the Orient."[8] Ships, Hays might have added, which would offer direct competition to the C.P.R.'s Empress fleet and which would have the advantage of sailing out of a port five hundred miles closer to the docks of Hong Kong and Yokohama.

The Grand Trunk Pacific had selected as its western terminus a location suggested to the C.P.R. by Sanford Fleming in 1877. Taking a much more northerly course than that finally selected by the C.P.R., the tracks would pass through central British Columbia following the Nechako, Endako and Bulkley rivers emerging on the Pacific at the mouth of the Skeena, where the terminal city would be built on a lonely lump of rock and muskeg known as Kaien Island. Kaien, which meant "foam which floats upon water," was hardly a name that rang with promise and in 1905 Hays had announced that a nation-wide competition would be held to select a more appropriate one. For a prize of $250, contestants were asked to come up with a name which had some British Columbian significance and contained fewer than ten letters and no more than three syllables. The contest had the desired effect keeping the G.T.P. in the public eye and attracting 12,000 entrants, some of whom may have been rather distressed when they learned that the prize had gone to the niece of Manitoba's Lieutenant-Governor, Miss Eleanor MacDonald, who had ignored most of the rules, but in suggesting Prince Rupert had apparently come up with a name which sounded just the right note of noble adventure and profitable investment — although just what B.C. connections were enjoyed by the Governor of the "Company of Adventurers of England trading into Hudson's Bay," only the Grand Trunk Pacific knew.

Hays foresaw a day when Prince Rupert would become the Venice of the north, a glittering and elegant city of wide boulevards and magnificent buildings. And it seems that from the beginning Rattenbury had shared his dream. On November 6, 1906 just four weeks before he resigned from the C.P.R., Rattenbury had announced that he had completed plans for a G.T.P. hotel to be erected in Prince Rupert. A handsome frame structure costing between $40,-000 and $50,000, it was only the beginning, meant to be used only temporarily until the day when the rail line was nearing completion and a truly grand hotel would be built.

And in 1903, Ratz had purchased eleven thousand carefully selected acres in the Nechako Valley — a full five years before the G.T.P. publicly announced that the tracks would be definitely located through the area. Ratz was certainly blessed with enviable prescience. Or, perhaps more likely, he had received some friendly advice from G.T.P. personnel.

In 1899 he had designed a home on Rockland Avenue for Ernest Victor Bodwell. One of the most prominent lawyers in the province, Bodwell had been appointed by the G.T.P. to act as their agent in the rather indirect purchase, through an American investor Peter Larsen, of ten thousand acres of crown land on Kaien Island and the mainland. Bodwell was certainly in a position to make more than an educated guess about the route the railroad would take through British Columbia and he may well have advised Rattenbury that land along the Nechako River would prove to be a very sound investment.

As well as offering him a chance to dabble in land speculation, Rattenbury's involvement with the G.T.P. would also present him with, what was for an architect, a once in a lifetime opportunity to let loose his imagination and exercise his talents on a spectacularly grand scale. But that was in the future, when the line was nearing completion, and in the meantime Rattenbury would have to endure some hard times and some particularly bitter disappointments.

7

His Reputation Begins to Dull
somewhat disappointed

"A good New Year to you," William Oliver, a lawyer who would later become the first Reeve of Oak Bay, wrote to a friend on January 4, 1906. "We missed you at the national annual sacrament. The usual archangels were there — Pike Holland Hamfields McGregor Irvine Rattenbury Newton. Irvine broke one of my wifes best drawing room chairs, and Rattenbury's dress coat which was bought for the occasion was hanging in rags as he left. It was a very successful celebration and as my wife and family are still in the old country no one was disturbed. I was surprised to find so much spirit of abandon still lurking in lads from 38 to 55."[1]

The year the lads had greeted with such abandon proved to be a most satisfactory one for Rattenbury. In January, he toured northern Alberta with David Ker of the Victoria based Brackman-Ker milling company. Ker, who had travelled to the area to select sites for his company's wheat elevators, and Rattenbury, who remained alert to whatever possibilities for sound investment might present themselves, had been so overcome by the booming city of Edmonton that within twenty-four hours of their arrival they purchased a lot on Jasper Avenue. The sale was a high water mark in the price of realty on Jasper Avenue, the *Edmonton Daily Bulletin* reported, adding that the deal was one of the quickest that had been consumated in Edmonton for some time.

Rattenbury's share of the $30,000 required to buy the property was proof not only of a healthy bank account but also of an unbridled confidence in the success of the Grand Trunk Pacific. Edmonton was already growing apace. Its population, estimated at fourteen thousand people, was increasing at thirty per cent a year as settlers flocked to the city and the surrounding rich farmland from Eastern Canada, the United States and Europe. One transcontinental rail line, the C.N.R., had reached Edmonton the year before but as yet, Rattenbury was convinced, the city was only on the brink of the fantastic growth and development which would follow once the G.T.P. arrived on the scene.

Exhilarated by the thought that he had been one of the first to recognize the potential of the city, Rattenbury became an energetic Edmonton booster. Returning to Victoria in February he painted a glowing picture of "Sunny Alberta." For Edmonton in particular he predicted a splendid future.

"Do you know that you can get coal in Edmonton at the present time for a dollar and a half a ton?" he asked a *Times* reporter. "Think of that, and what we are paying for it on the coast here,* and remembering that the fields are scarcely opened up, and you may perhaps obtain some idea of its possibilities." And not only that, but the surrounding countryside was "very pretty" and the climate "excellent."[2]

While in Edmonton, Rattenbury had purchased another piece of property and the sense of relief he experienced at finally having the deed to Mary Tod Island in his pocket had added to the cheerful optimism that had been so evident on his return to Victoria. The tiny island of about five acres which lay just a few hundred yards off the beach in front of Rattenbury's home and John Virtue's Oak Bay Hotel, which Rattenbury had designed in 1904,[3] had come into the possession of one St. Clair Blackett who resided in Edmonton. For several years Ratz and Virtue had shared the nagging worry that someone might build a house, or even worse a fish packing plant, on the island spoiling the uncluttered view they both enjoyed. But happily, Ratz had induced Blackett to sell and the following summer the gorse and broom which he had planted in his greenhouse in preparation for just this event would make the "rather bleak bit of rock a thing of beauty and an object of attraction."[4]

Other Oak Bay concerns were to occupy a great deal of Rattenbury's attention that year. In 1862 when Victoria was incorporated as a city, little thought had been given to including Oak Bay within the civic boundaries. Lying along the southeast shore of the island, three miles from the centre of the city, Oak Bay was considered to be remote and with its 2,500 acres divided among only five landowners, sparsely settled. The Hudson's Bay Company's 1,000 acre Uplands Farm sprawled over the high ground to the north. South

* $8.00 a ton.

of the Company land was John Tod's 400 acre farm and, except for smaller holdings farmed by the Ross and McNeil families, the rest of Oak Bay was part of J. D. Pemberton's vast estate. In the 1880's following John Tod's death, small parcels of his land were sold and a few houses began to appear scattered along Cadboro Bay Road, the narrow country lane which ran from Tod's farmhouse down to the city. But it was not until the 1890's that Oak Bay came to be regarded as a desirable place to live by more than a handful of people.

Victoria housewives, especially those who lived near the harbour or the business district, had come to dread the hot summer months, when the noise of the city rumbled and clattered through windows thrown open to catch the breeze and the sooty smoke from ships and waterfront industries combined with the dust from unpaved streets to settle in a grimy film over furniture and draperies. Oak Bay with its rural peace, its clear air and its sheltered beaches became home to a growing number of summer people as families deserted the city and spent the season in wooden-floored tents and little cottages strung along the beach.

Witnessing this annual exodus, Beaumont Boggs calculated that fortunes might be made by capitalizing on Oak Bay's appeal. Boggs and a group of fellow Victoria realtors pooled their resources to buy a large tract of land on the shores of the bay. Some of the land they intended to subdivide and sell under contracts carefully drawn to insure the erection of only the finest class of residence. A few acres along the waterfront they set aside as the site of a handsome hotel, with lawn-tennis and pleasure grounds attached, and Boggs threw himself into the promotion of the scheme.

It is certainly fair to say that no more picturesque location could be found. The land itself, interspersed with moss-grown rocks and oak trees, is at once a delightful pleasure resort; while the sandy pebbled beach furnishes a recreation ground for children. The water itself is warm and furnishes splendid bathing; while from the jutting banks of rocks, stretching out here and there, the fisherman seldom returns empty handed. The bay is simply superb, with its placid waters naturally protected by the islands to be seen in every direction, and here the troller will find plenty of salmon or the huntsman water fowl; while in the woods, a quarter of a mile back from the shores the pheasant and grouse are numerous.[5]

And all this, Boggs enthused, was to be found an easy drive from Victoria. Before they had committed themselves to buying the land, the members of Boggs' syndicate had reached an agreement with the Electric Railway Company to extend its Fort Street line out to the water's edge and soon Oak Bay's countryside became easily accessible as well as highly desirable.

Built in 1891, the hotel, designed by architects Teague and Muir and christened the Mount Baker, proved to be an instant success. Managed by John Virtue, who had been lured away from the C.P.R.'s Hotel Vancouver, it became famous on three continents as a popular stopping off place for English residents of the Orient who passed through Victoria on their way to and from the Old Country. And so great were Virtue's innkeeping abilities that it became fashionable for Victorians to hold banquets and balls at the Mount Baker in spite of the fact that these festivities had to end at an unfashionably early hour so that the celebrants could catch the last streetcar home.

Not wanting to rely solely on the hotel's patrons for customers, the streetcar company developed a sportsfield at the end of the Oak Bay line with space provided for soccer and rugby games as well as track and field competitions. And after the Victoria Golf Club laid out its course on part of the Pemberton estate, Oak Bay could boast of offering the best there was in the way of elegant indoor entertainment and vigorous outdoor recreation.

Gradually people came to think of Oak Bay as more than just a summer resort. In 1899 Rattenbury began building his home on five waterfront acres along the beach from the Mount Baker Hotel. And among those who joined him as early residents were two men who were to become his friends and who would share his interest in the political life of Oak Bay, William Oliver and James Herrick McGregor.

William Oliver had come to Oak Bay to be near the golf course. A lawyer and one-time partner of Lyman Duff, he glowed with the good humour of a man who, despite his prominence in the legal community, refused to take himself altogether seriously.

James Herrick McGregor was a partner in one of the province's largest firms of land surveyors. A cheerful outgoing man who shared with Rattenbury an early and abiding affection for the automobile and who revelled in the hectic races staged by fellow enthusiasts, he also enjoyed solitude and the opportunity to let his mind wander over a wide range of topics. He was an actor, a poet and a philosopher — equally at home spouting Robert Burns' poetry with an exuberance which led people to believe he had been born in Scotland rather than Montreal, regaling the patrons of the Boomerang Saloon with tall stories of his travels throughout the province or composing poetry and essays which combined "pearls of wisdom, bits of philosophy, religion and humour."[6]

By 1906 over one hundred families resided in Oak Bay and to many of them it had become apparent that living in an essentially rural unorganized community had certain drawbacks. To travel on the narrow, rutted roads meant being choked by summer dust or mired in winter mud. Wandering cows grazed through gardens trampling flowers that had managed to survive despite the competition from thistles and other weeds blown from farmers' fields. With no sewage system, Oak Bay's open roadside ditches had developed a distinctive aroma which became particularly disagreeable when combined with the stench from the large piggeries which operated on part of the former Tod farm.

Rattenbury, Oliver, McGregor and other permanent residents including Sam Maclure, who had built his house on the waterfront between the hotel and Rattenbury's home, formed the Oak Bay Improvements Association and after an unsuccessful attempt to convince Victoria to extend its boundaries to include Oak Bay, they petitioned the Provincial Secretary for the right to form a separate municipality. And on July 2, 1906 the Letters Patent were signed creating the "Corporation of the District of Oak Bay." At a meeting of the Improvements Association chaired by McGregor and held "to discuss some unanimous acting with the object of preventing, if possible, the expense and annoyance of an election," William Oliver was appointed Reeve and Rattenbury agreed to serve as one of four Councillors.

One issue which loomed large for Oak Bay's first council was the matter of the municipal seal. At the first council meeting held on July 14, Rattenbury was given full power to act and in due course he produced the design which over the years many people have found somewhat puzzling — for unlike other civic crests, which tend to run to lions, unicorns and matronly angels, the seal of B.C.'s most English municipality carries the likeness of an American mountain. Rattenbury simply gazed out of his window and sketched what he saw — Mount Baker towering above the waters of the straits with a sailboat gently heeled over in the foreground.

But more than local politics was keeping Rattenbury busy in 1906. An architect who had seldom lacked domestic commissions he found that since the completion of Cary Castle his services were even more in demand and during that summer and fall he designed homes for several prominent Victorians, including County Court Judge Peter Secord Lampman. And in addition the provincial government asked him to design two new courthouses, one for Vancouver and the other for Nelson. The Vancouver courthouse, expected to cost $150,000 and described as being classic in design, would "take second place only to the parliament buildings among the large public structures in British Columbia." The Nelson courthouse would not be as massive as that at Vancouver, Rattenbury's plans calling for "a more elaborate form of architecture, beauty instead of imposing grandeur being sought."

By the end of 1906 Rattenbury's influence was felt throughout the province — from Victoria where the Parliament Buildings and Empress Hotel gave a monumental importance to the Inner Harbour, to Vancouver where the C.P.R. hotel and the courthouse defined the heart of the city, to Prince Rupert where the G.T.P. hotel would soon stand as a symbol of the railway's intention to create a magnificent metropolis, and to Nelson and Rossland and other Interior towns where his buildings had become landmarks signifying permanence and confidence in the future. In the fourteen years that had passed since his arrival in British Columbia, his architectural reputation had never been higher. Throughout those years he had managed to win, by one method or another, almost every important commission that he had chosen to pursue. Now he was invariably described by the press as the well-known architect or the celebrated architect. His artistic abilities appeared to be unchallengeable, his position so secure that his continued success was unquestionable. But then quite suddenly and without warning everything changed.

It all began in December 1906, when the C.P.R. surprised him by accepting his resignation. Then on January 3, 1907 he was sent reeling by a very pointed and equally public attack on his ability as an architect.

The Victoria High School, which he had designed six years earlier, had become severely overcrowded and School Trustee Jay had

95

spoken to him about preparing plans and estimates for an addition. Rattenbury had graciously offered to prepare the plans free of charge and had probably thought no more about it. But when Jay suggested, at the School Board's first meeting of the new year, that Rattenbury be asked to prepare the plans, he found himself set upon by one of his fellow board members, Dr. Ernest Hall.

Born in 1861 in Milton, Ontario, into one of the area's oldest families, Ernest Hall had been graduated from the Royal College of Physicians in Edinburgh and for the last eighteen years had practiced his profession in British Columbia. Dr. Hall was nothing if not outspoken. He objected to having the plans prepared by Rattenbury, he fumed.

"The barn-like structure known as the Victoria High School is a specimen of that gentleman's work," Dr. Hall stormed as the other board members fought to retain their composure, "and I don't want any more of his work on the school."

Several trustees disagreed with Dr. Hall. The building was at least serviceable, they opined, and they voted in favour of asking Rattenbury to prepare the drawings and estimates for the addition.

Dr. Hall's remarks might have received little attention and been soon forgotten if Ratz had not been so sensitive to criticism. Quivering with rage, he penned a vitriolic condemnation of Dr. Hall — a long rambling letter in which the height of his passion was matched only by the length of his sentences.

For Dr. Ernest Hall's private opinion as to the merits of any architectural work of mine I have the same contempt as I have for Dr. Hall himself, but I do not propose to allow Dr. Ernest Hall to prostitute his official position as school trustee to the purpose of attacking my professional ability . . .

Some years ago, Ratz recalled, Dr. Hall had written an abusive letter to the *Times* criticizing the design of the High School but he had published it anonymously which, Ratz continued, was characteristic.

Now, acting as a school trustee and posing as an authority, he repeats his abuse — practically saying that he does not consider I have the ability to build an extension to a school. It is too much, I suppose, to expect Dr. Ernest Hall to know what fair criticism is or what is or is not decent and honourable as between professional men.

... the man who could voluntarily get up before the Women's Council as he did lately and deliver an abominable lecture, which I think he entitled "Lifting the Lid Off Hell" in which ... he made atrocious statements reflecting grossly on the men of Victoria, which statements are without any question absolutely untrue and for which he ought to be kicked individually and collectively by every man in Victoria — must have gall enough for anything.

Dr. Hall, credited with being the first to advocate the instruction of both sexes on the subject of venereal diseases, sex problems, etc., would at the slightest provocation rise to his feet and deliver a version of his all purpose lecture entitled "The Relation of Intemperance to Public Life and the Relation of Social Disease to Society." But, although Dr. Hall enjoyed the respect of the most able and successful physicians in the province, Rattenbury was convinced that only self-promotion had prompted his lecture to the women's group.

These statements certainly obtained and were intended to obtain for Dr. Ernest Hall a considerable amount of cheap advertising. Any quack can, however, obtain similar advertising but he generally has to pay for it, whilst Dr. Hall obtained his for nothing.

Such a man, however ignorant he is, may and generally has the cheek, to think that he can offensively criticize anybody or anything. But he certainly, then, cannot reasonably object to others criticizing him. He cannot object to my saying that I consider him a pretty mean specimen of a man, and by no means a credit to his profession. For my own part, I would think, were I to entrust myself to his medical care, I should either be qualified for New Westminster [site of the provincial asylum for the insane] or was desirous of quickly terminating my existence.[7]

It was a particularly nasty, petty exchange and it did not bode well for the following year. And it probably prompted Rattenbury to announce, three weeks later, that he had decided to enter a federal competition being held to select the design for a building to house the Supreme Court in Ottawa. Throughout his career Rattenbury seemed able to find a friendly reporter waiting at his elbow whenever he needed one and this simple announcement was treated as a momentous piece of news.

The competition is open to the world, and will be participated in by the best architects of England, the United States and Canada. That Victoria should be able to boast an architect capable of taking part in the competition with such men is a matter of no small credit to the city.

Even should Mr. Rattenbury be unsuccessful in obtaining first place, the fact that Victoria should be represented in the competition at all will serve to bring the city before the attention of the people of the East, while, should his plans be accepted — and Mr. Rattenbury's friends are sure that for the designing of public buildings there are few in America who can surpass him — this advertisement would be one of the best that it would be possible to secure for this city.[8]

So much for Dr. Hall's architectural opinions.

It could be a risky business, this announcing that a bird was in the bush before it was to hand, but luckily for Ratz when the federal government decided to award first prize to E. S. Maxwell of Montreal, the newspapers remained discreetly silent.

It had proved to be so successful an exercise in reputation building that he didn't hesitate to use it again when in August 1907 he was invited to enter another contest — one that he was sure he would win.

For the past two years, since Saskatchewan had entered Confederation and Regina had been selected as the provincial capital, Premier Walter Scott had been puzzling over how best to select an architect to design the province's legislative buildings.

On the morning of September 5, 1906 Scott who was visiting the west coast had met with Rattenbury in Victoria. They had discussed Scott's plans to erect new government buildings and Rattenbury had warned the premier of the dangers of holding a competition. It would be much safer, Ratz had said, to give the work to an architect with an established reputation, namely himself. Scott had hedged. If he decided against holding a competition it might be best to give the commission to a local architect he had said. But Rattenbury was not to be put off that easily. That same afternoon he had written a lengthy letter to the premier in which he had adopted the same tone of disarming helpfulness that he had used six years earlier when he had written to the Chief Commissioner of Lands and Works asking to be retained as architect of B.C.'s Government House.*

* And it should be noted completely reversing his expressed opinions regarding the Carnegie Library.

Victoria B.C.

Sept 5th 1906

re PARLIAMENT BUILDINGS

SASKATCHEWAN

Hon Walter Scott

Dear Sir

In our conversation of this morning, as to the best method to adopt to ensure the new Parliament Buildings being a success.

You rightly pointed out, how desirable it would be, that the Architect entrusted with this work, should be on the ground, so that he could study the building on the site, and also the materials to be used

A weak point in a Competition would be, that it would only be in rare cases that an Architect in practice could arrange to leave his practice and establish himself in the locality,

In case the great honor of designing your new Parliament Buildings were entrusted to me, I am so situated at the present time, owing to the various large buildings that I am now erecting all being close to completion at the same time.

That I could and would be delighted to come and live in Saskatchewan and study the conditions on the ground, and make the Plans and Models of the building there, and in consultation with you and your Ministers.

I am sure that we could erect Buildings that would utilize the site to obtain a magnificent result, and that the Parliament Buildings both in arrangement and in Design would be worthy of the great future of the Province.

It would be a source of great pride and pleasure to me to be associated in the erection of a Building having such great possibilities to attain a beautiful result

And I would be most happy to make you Sketch Designs on the ground as before suggested, and if I did not achieve as successful a solution of the problem, as you thought possible,

I would not make any charge whatever, and you would be left open to then have a Competition if you deemed it advisable,

I think however that from the experience that I have had in similar works and the Study and labor that I would give to this work, that I need not fear that such action would be found necessary,

I have the honor to be

Yours obediently

F. M. Rattenbury

Architect.[9]

99

Scott found that his presence was urgently required in Regina and he did not respond to Rattenbury's offer for almost two months.

"While my personal view is pretty strongly in favour of putting the work directly in the hands of an architect of acknowledged standing," Scott had written, "I found that the competition method, especially in regard to a public building, appealed to some of my colleagues with force."[10]

They had decided to hold a limited competition in which Rattenbury and four or five other architects would be invited to enter.

"I shall be most happy to submit Designs in Competition for your proposed Parliament Buildings," Rattenbury had answered "and shall do my best to win."[11]

The following year when he and architects from Regina, Montreal, Toronto, New York and London, England were officially invited to enter the competition, Rattenbury lost no time in informing the Victoria newspapers, and as with the federal competition the resulting article bolstered an architectural reputation that had begun to show some signs of sagging. "F. M. Rattenbury Asked for Designs for Saskatchewan Capital," the *Colonist* headlined the story suggesting to the casual reader that he had already won the contract.

Rattenbury himself may have been lulled into believing that the competition was a mere formality. All contestants had agreed to two assessors or judges — Percy Nobbs, a professor of architecture at McGill University, and Bertram Goodhue, an architect from New York City. But then Scott had written to the competitors asking them if they had any objection to his joining the panel as a third judge. Rattenbury, for one, had no objections. The previous year Scott had written that he had been in favour of giving the contract to an architect of acknowledged standing and Ratz was confident that Scott had been referring to him. He would be most gratified if Scott could see his way clear to act with the other assessors, he wrote to the premier.

"I think it would be a very wise step. For conscientious as Architectural Assessors may be, they are often inclined to lay undue weight on a clever piece of drawing, with the result that whilst the building may be original, it is often not pleasing, and not what you would have desired."[12]

During the previous month, September of 1907, Scott, an angular gaunt faced man whose health was far from robust, had suffered a serious illness and perhaps a recurrence of that illness led him to reconsider his decision to serve as one of the judges. A third assessor was appointed, but he was Frank Day, retiring president of the American Institute of Architects. And Rattenbury was feeling distinctly ungracious when, on November 15, 1907, he received a telegram from Scott asking if he would agree to an extension of fourteen days as requested by some of the competitors.

"My plans completed, so extension of no use to me," Ratz wired back.

The winner was announced on December 21, 1907 and although Ratz would admit to being only somewhat disappointed, it must have been a crushing blow to learn that the winner was E. S. Maxwell, the same architect to whom he had lost the federal competition.

8

Reeve of Oak Bay
to save the golf links

Over the next few years Rattenbury designed no buildings of any consequence — unless he chose to remain unusually quiet about them. With no important commissions tying him down he took the opportunity to indulge his passion for travel. As well as criss-crossing the country several times when he was employed by the C.P.R., he had, since his arrival in British Columbia in 1892, returned to England at least twice — in 1898 to interest investors in the Lake Bennett and Klondike Navigation Company and in 1905 when he had visited London and New York to study the improved modern system of hotel construction.

Not by any means an aimless sightseer, wherever he went he remained alert, actively seeking out new ideas and quick to see how those ideas could be applied to Victoria.

"Two things especially forced themselves on my mind," Rattenbury had reported in 1905 when he returned from his trip to London and New York. "One was that since the motor car as an institution has come to stay, it is obvious that with even the finest system of roads . . . motor travelling is and will continue to be objectionable to everybody, except the occupants of the motor, by reason of the dreadful dust they raise."

While in London he had observed an experimental road paving program with great interest. "What they are doing," he had said, "is to lay on top of the ordinary macadam a layer about six inches thick of a composition made of broken rock, gravel, asphalt and, I understand, some patented mixture." The hoped for result was, he continued, "a pavement at once elastic, practically dustless, fairly noiseless and durable.

"This operation must commend itself to us in Victoria since something of the same nature will certainly require to be done here in the near future."

Something else that had struck him, Rattenbury had said, sounding very much like an architect trying to talk himself into a commission, was the design and the popularity of the modern exhibition buildings to be found in many American cities. Since the city was considering a proposal to build a winter garden, he had been careful to study similar buildings on his travels and had found them to be "palaces of delight for the public."

"Coney Island, for instance, burnt and rebuilt in a palatial manner, remains as a permanent place of amusement and fairyland of light and beauty, and not for the original rough population of Coney Island is this metamorphosis achieved, but for the joy and delectation of New York's working thousands generally. The buildings are practically palaces and are as cheering and attractive as it is possible to make them."[1]

For Rattenbury travel was therapeutic — not because he found it relaxing but because it stimulated and excited him. A man with a fiery temper and burning energy he was only really content when his life was a whirl of feverish activity. When he had no artistic battles to fight, when he had no new ideas or no promising investments to promote, he slipped easily into a state of grim depression. Despondent over the loss of the Regina competition, he decided early in 1908 to take an extended European holiday. Three years before he had been forced to cancel his intended visit to the Continent because of the excessive July heat across the channel. Now he left Victoria in March and taking advantage of the milder spring weather he spent a full three months abroad. He visited Paris and motored around Southern France and then continued south to Florence, Rome, Naples and Pompeii, then turning north he visited Venice and toured the Italian lake district making a special side trip to Lucerne, a city which he felt was in many ways similar to Victoria.

He returned to Victoria in June in what was for him a happy state of impatience and enthusiasm. He had been impressed by what he had seen and he was quick to share the lessons he had learned. And he was driven by a sense of urgency. Victoria's officialdom must follow his advice now — before it was too late.

He was convinced that Victoria's economic future depended on its success as a tourist city. In a tourist city it was especially important, he said, to confine industry to specified areas.

"There has been a piece of beautifying carried out on the causeway," he said referring to the Empress Hotel and its grounds, "and nothing in the way of factories along the James Bay waterfront should be allowed to mar that. The smoke from tall chimneys in that section would be driven over various residential parts, and should not be allowed."

He felt strongly that the height of buildings should be controlled. Lucerne, he said, was strictly a tourist city and everything was made to conform to the idea that it was such.

"A great hotel there of about 6 or 7 stories in height had sought to build 3 or 4 stories higher, but the authorities stepped in and disallowed it, as it would mar the beauty of the place. There was no question raised there as to the power of the municipality to control the situation."

There should also be some civic control over the design of buildings, he argued. In London the city had "an architect of the highest standing in the profession, who exercised, under authority from the council the right to pass on all buildings put up. There the front of a hotel was altered by him because it did not comply with the general scheme of the surroundings as he saw it."[2]

Ratz had always been sensitive to the need to preserve trees. Eleven years earlier, in 1897, he had been aghast when overzealous landscaping had led to the felling of trees around the Parliament Buildings. ". . . it makes me heartsick to see each tree as it falls to the ground," he had written.

"It is so rarely that an architect is fortunate enough to have the opportunity of erecting a large building amongst the delicate tracery of woodland scenery. And the peeps of high masses of stone masonry through the trees gives so distinctive a charm so different to what one would ordinarily see, that words fail to express my grief at seeing that charm disappear. . . . The old axion is a good one, to think twenty times before you cut down any tree."[3]

He had been pleasantly surprised to learn that in Lucerne the civic authorities agreed with him. There the course of a street had been altered to save a tree. "Imagine a Victoria council doing that," he exclaimed.

He had also come to recognize the importance of setting aside land for parks and playgrounds in rapidly developing cities. In Chicago, he said, determined efforts were now being made to institute a system of parks. "The land is being repurchased at enormous cost, whereas with proper precautions years ago it might have been reserved without an outlay."

He cited Vancouver as an example of a city which had rapidly reached metropolitan proportions only to feel the effects of this grave oversight.

"Already people there who have been almost feverishly engaged in building and expanding in a material way, realize that they have no open spaces in the centre of their city and are agitating to have the provincial government convey the old court house square, now of enormous value, to them for that purpose."

Ratz felt that the government "should insist that all townsite plans should pass a board or bureau, whose duty it would be first, to reserve these open spaces and second, see that the deadly straight street with its deadly rows of uniform buildings, should be prevented, and instead some artistic taste brought to bear in the treatment of streets and buildings."[4]

Rattenbury's ideas must have sounded wildly radical to the members of Victoria's city council. Progress was synonymous with development and might not development be slowed if controls were exercised? And if a man owned a piece of property didn't he have the right to build whatever he wanted on it whether it was a factory or a housing subdivision laid out in the economical grid system? And wasn't Victoria's future as a tourist city guaranteed now that the Empress had finally opened its doors and become the subject of the C.P.R.'s world-wide promotional campaigns?

If they had paused to consider the source of these new ideas they might have reacted differently. Rattenbury was after all something of a land speculator himself and as an architect he had consistently defended his right to exercise full artistic control. He would not have pleaded for governmental control of development unless he felt it was absolutely necessary.

The City of Victoria ignored him. Over the years industries along the waterfront expanded. A paint factory was established on Laurel Point and huge oil storage tanks were sited across the harbour from the Empress Hotel. With no design controls, architects adopted the stark unadorned new styles which might look well in other cities but seemed to be strangely at odds with the city's quaint character and old world charm which the tourist brochures continued to describe with such conviction.

Almost seventy years would pass until it would suddenly occur to Victorians that Rattenbury had been right. Only then, when the flow of tourists had dwindled to a trickle, would businessmen-politicians begin to see the necessity of controlling the design of new construction. And only then would a program be launched to reclaim the industry-scarred land around the Inner Harbour.

But Rattenbury did see his theories put into practice — in his home municipality of Oak Bay and especially in that part of Oak Bay known as the Uplands. The Uplands, although it lay within the municipal boundary, was set up as a distinct entity, subject to bylaws which did not apply to the rest of Oak Bay and from the beginning the exclusive subdivision built on more than four hundred acres which had been part of the old Uplands Farm, benefited from long range planning and strict controls. Laid out by landscape architect Frederick Law Olmstead, Jr., whose father was credited with being America's first landscape architect and town planner, roads in the Uplands flowed gracefully, winding and curving as they followed the natural rise and fall of the land. Only residential buildings were allowed and those buildings were required to meet rigid quality standards, not the least of which regulated design. Houses could be built in whatever style the owner preferred, but they must be unobtrusive, blending with the landscape in keeping with the character of a garden community. The Uplands Company didn't have to look far for an architect whose ideas dovetailed with their own and, as the early development of the Uplands proved, their decision to appoint Rattenbury as their advisory architect was a wise one.

But Rattenbury's influence was felt not just in the Uplands, but throughout the whole municipality. From 1906-1908 he served as a member of Oak Bay council and at his urging a special committee, which became known as the Beauty Committee, was set up "to keep watch and ward over the decorative effect produced by trees planted on boulevards and sidewalks." As the *Times* noted, "The protection of the trees in the municipality of Oak Bay is a perennial question much as it is in the City of Victoria, only that the Oak Bay council seems more anxious to protect than are the aldermen of the city."

In January 1913 Rattenbury announced that he had yielded to the expressed wishes of a host of friends, and had consented to stand for the Reeveship. He was running to save the golf links, he said. The continued existence of Oak Bay's magnificent waterfront golf course was threatened by rising municipal taxation. At that time only land was assessed for tax purposes and if some members of Oak Bay Council had their way the golf course's hundred acres would be assessed at the same rate as land used for housing. The owners of the land, the Gonzales Point Land Company, were bound by an agreement, made at the time of purchase, which fixed the rental charged to the golf club at a maximum of $3,000. If the assessment were to go beyond the amount of rents collected, the Gonzales Point Land Company would subdivide the property. Ratz had decided to run to prevent the subdivision of the golf course but once involved in the campaign he made it clear that it was not the only issue that concerned him.

For Victoria 1912 had been a boom year and the optimism that had prompted the city's growth had had its effect on Oak Bay. Victoria realtors had predicted that the population of the city would soon reach 100,000 and for a time it had looked as if they might be right. In the Fairfield district the swampy fields where children had skated the winter before had become the site of solid Edwardian middle-class houses. On Douglas Street the Hudson's Bay Company had begun construction of the city's largest, most up to date department store. Plans had been announced for a ten-storey skyscraper on Johnson Street. And the first of Victoria's famed cluster lights, known as "Morley's Folly" after the mayor who had campaigned for their installation, had appeared on downtown streets.

In Oak Bay a new municipal hall had opened at the corner of Hampshire and Oak Bay Avenue. Property in the Uplands had been offered for sale and the McNeil farm and part of the Pemberton holdings had been subdivided into small residential lots.

Rattenbury, who carried with him a mental picture of Saltaire, the community designed by Lockwood and Mawson, as an example of what could be accomplished if thoughtful planning preceeded growth, hoped that Oak Bay could avoid the unhappy results of rapid urbanization he had seen in other cities. His platform, as defined in an open letter to the electors, established what has become a tradition in Oak Bay for since his day few municipal elections have been fought in which the preservation of the urban environment has not been the central issue.

I think that the Oak Bay district is one of the most lovely residential areas that I have ever seen, and it is my desire to retain this beauty as far as possible, and the hope that I can help to do so is my only reason for being a candidate at the coming election for Reeve.

One of the leading thoroughfares to Oak Bay is Oak Bay Avenue. There seems to be a tendency at present to erect along this avenue very ugly and cheap looking shacks rented as stores. I think this is ill-advised

107

and will depreciate the values of the property, not only in the avenue itself but in Oak Bay generally. I am of the opinion that regulations should be passed to prevent this, for with very little extra expense these buildings could be made attractive in appearance, and this should be insisted upon.

The beautiful beach drive through the golf links and along Shoal Bay has been the favorite walk and drive in Victoria for years, and there are few drives in the world more beautiful and with such rich and glorious scenery.

To force the links into the ordinary, though perhaps lucrative, building subdivision, — destroying this lovely drive — would be a calamity to Oak Bay and to Victoria, and every effort should be made to avoid this occurring.

Rattenbury was determined to make his appeal as broadly based as possible. "We do not have very many working men in Oak Bay," he wrote, "but I certainly think that in all municipal works, preference should be given to the ratepayers and inhabitants of Oak Bay." And there was one particular municipal work uppermost in his mind. "I think the time has come to build permanent roads," he said. "The old macadam roads will no longer sustain the heavy traffic of today, and any money spent on them seems to be absolutely wasted."

But more than anything else he was concerned about the effects of rapid, unplanned growth which, he was convinced, would erode the residential quality of Oak Bay.

The subdividing of property into comparatively small lots is proceeding so quickly that it is easy to foresee the time when the youngsters will have nowhere to play but in the streets. Open spaces where they can play games should, and must, be obtained immediately.

In regard to taxation, the leading principle to be followed should be that as far as possible all those who pay taxes should receive an adequate return. I personally think that in a residential district it is a question whether the exemption of taxation of all buildings is in accordance with this principle. To my mind it would appear that the taxation of gardens for the support of buildings providing fire protection, police, lighting and schools for the buildings means that inevitably gardens will disappear and close building ensue.[5]

Rattenbury and the slate of aldermanic candidates who supported his views received the backing of a group of prominent Oak Bay residents, which included such men as William Oliver, the ex-Reeve, and John J. Shallcross, a wealthy insurance agent and importer whose Maclure-designed house was set in a five acre Oak Bay estate. Oliver, Shallcross and the other members of the group campaigned for their chosen candidates by placing in the *Times* and *Colonist* large advertisements which seemed to suggest that it was not considered gentlemanly to ask a candidate just where he stood on any particular issue.

We have not asked these gentlemen to pledge themselves to any special policy nor have we asked them to express an opinion on municipal affairs.

We support them simply because we consider them reliable businessmen who may be trusted to manage the affairs of the municipality in a competent and fairminded manner. As such we ask you to vote for them.[6]

If Rattenbury had committed a minor gaucherie by publicly stating his policies, he at least forced the hand of his opponent William Henderson. Henderson, who had the honour of being Oak Bay's first elected reeve, was a seventy-six-year-old architect who had for many years been employed by the federal government. He was running, he said, at the urgent request of a large and influential body of ratepayers.

"I am entirely dissatisfied with the manner in which the affairs of the municipality have been conducted during the past year," he said, taking aim at Oliver, who had served as Reeve in 1912 and whose devotion to the game of golf bordered on conflict of interest. While many property owners had seen their assessments tripled, the golf course continued to be assessed at a very low rate. He didn't want to see the golf course driven out of business, Henderson said, but it was only fair that that property assume a more reasonable share of the tax burden.[7]

The keenest election in years was held on January 18, 1913, the intense interest resulting in one of the largest turnouts in Oak Bay's history. J. Herrick McGregor and the other candidates who had allied themselves with Rattenbury won handily. But Rattenbury himself squeaked in with a majority of only twenty-four votes. Nevertheless he soon proved that despite his slim majority he intended to put his ideas into practice, when in the first months of his reeveship he arranged for the purchase of three and a half acres of land along Willows beach. Children needed open spaces, he had said.

It may well be that given the opportunity he would have initiated bylaws regulating lot size and controlling the design of buildings, but early in his term in office Victoria's speculative bubble burst and the shock waves were felt throughout Oak Bay. Lots went unsold and as development pressure eased, the incentive to institute controls was lost. With the golf course no longer threatened, a change in the method of assessment became an unpalatable prospect, particularly as it became apparent that some Oak Bay residents would be unable to pay their current taxes. And the area's roads continued to be a problem as municipal bonds, meant to finance Rattenbury's extensive road paving program, went unsold.

Rattenbury could hardly have chosen a less auspicious time to serve as Reeve and by the end of 1913 he must have felt discouraged and somewhat dejected. But the realization that he had been able to accomplish so little was only a minor disappointment compared to what the next few years would bring.

9

A Bankrupt Railroad and a Failing Marriage

In 1898, Chief Commissioner of Lands and Works, George Martin, was reputed to have said of the Parliament Buildings, "Never, in 500 years, will the government have enough employees to fill this vast building." But by 1911 the work of the government had expanded to fill every available nook and cranny. Rather than hold a competition, the government decided to ask Rattenbury to design the additions which would nearly double the size of the original buildings. From the time he submitted the first designs, which the government rejected, until he testified at the hearings which seemed to wind up most large government contracts, the east and west wings and the south wing, housing the glass-domed provincial library, would keep Rattenbury busy on and off for the next five years. But they were far from being important enough to occupy his full attention, for although he would have been enraged had any other architect been employed on the Parliament Buildings, his work for the government ranked only second to the commission he had been given by the Grand Trunk Pacific Railway.

By 1911 construction of the line was far from complete, in fact three years would pass before the first transcontinental train steamed into Prince Rupert. But while progress seemed slow the ultimate success of the railroad remained unquestioned, mainly due to the skills of Charles Melville Hays, an aggressive and imaginative promoter.

Prince Rupert had a special place in Hays' affections. Only he could have looked fondly on the bare rocks, the water-logged ground and the raw tree stumps that marked the townsite in 1906 and declare that Prince Rupert was foreordained to be a western metropolis. Expert surveyors were at work planning the streets and parks, the G.T.P. reported in that same year, and American landscape architects would be employed to ensure that Prince Rupert became "the most perfectly laid out and most beautiful city in the Dominion . . . the Washington of Canada."

So convincing was Hays that in May 1909, when the first town lots were auctioned in Vancouver, very spirited bidding from 1,500 eager purchasers pushed prices up to as much as $8,000 for a single lot.

G.T.P. literature promoted the growing town with glowing pride and rosy optimism.

To this new port will come the ships of the Seven Seas. Ships of the East, laden with silk and rice will soon be riding at anchor in this splendid harbor, to sail away laden with lumber; . . . ships from the shore of far-off continents, trading through the new and picturesque port of Prince Rupert . . .[1]

New it certainly was, and some may have found it picturesque in a rough frontier sort of way — but with an annual rainfall of almost one hundred inches it was, above all else, muddy. And by 1909 the 3,000 residents found it advisable to take to the intricate system of boardwalks if they wished to avoid being mired in the ooze. But to Charles Melville Hays the streets were lined with gold. His optimism never wavered.

The town was incorporated the following year, and Hays to avoid heavy municipal taxation and to gain other concessions for the G.T.P., agreed to build a large modern hotel. The work of designing that hotel he gave to Rattenbury.

Ratz later said that it was not until 1911 that he had been appointed architect for the Grand Trunk Pacific. But it seems that at a much earlier date, perhaps at the time he designed the original frame hotel for Prince Rupert, Hays had given him to understand that he would receive this commission. On his grand European tour of 1908, Rattenbury had "visited every hotel of standing possible in the hope of gaining future knowledge in that line of architecture to be used by him in the future." Since he was at that time no longer working for the C.P.R., it seems likely that Rattenbury was intending to apply this knowledge to the G.T.P. hotels and the buildings he designed for the rail line certainly evidenced a great deal of thought and careful consideration.

As designed by Rattenbury the G.T.P. hotel at Prince Rupert would be part of a great transportation complex. At the water's edge would be a long covered dock dominated by two sixty foot high cupola-topped towers. Passengers disembarking from a G.T.P. steamer would be enveloped in luxury the moment they stepped ashore. Just behind the steamship terminal, where the tracks of the Grand Trunk Pacific hugged the shore, would be a deluxe railway station carefully designed to impress passengers alighting from G.T.P. trains with its splendor. And whether a tourist arrived by boat or train he would find himself at the doorstep of the most imposing château style hotel ever designed for the west. Located on a slight rise above the steamship terminal and railway station, the hotel, with its 450 bedrooms and its dining room capable of seating 265 people, was expected to cost as much as two million dollars to construct. Twice as tall as the Empress, it would reign supreme over a garden city of formal parks, wide tree-lined boulevards and gently curving residential by-ways envisioned by the landscape architects.

But it was not only for Prince Rupert that Rattenbury was asked to design hotels. Keeping a watchful eye on the C.P.R., Hays must have noted with interest that the Banff Springs Hotel was becoming almost too popular. During the summer of 1910 the hotel had often been booked to capacity and an overflow of four hundred people had been bedded down in sleeping cars near the Banff station. The following season had been even more hectic with 22,000 persons registering at the hotel during the summer of 1911.

Taking the Yellowhead Pass through the Rockies, the Grand Trunk Pacific passed through spectacularly beautiful country. As eager to capitalize on the scenery as the C.P.R. had been, the G.T.P. commissioned Rattenbury to design a string of resort hotels sited to take advantage of the best the mountains had to offer. Three locations were selected; at Jasper by the shores of Lac Beauvert; at Miette, where hot springs offered the same therapeutic benefits that drew tourists to Banff; and at the base of Mount Robson, the tallest peak in the Canadian Rockies.

The Mount Robson hotel conceived by Rattenbury was the most sensitively designed of all the mountain hotels. Compared to fortress-like structures such as the Banff Springs Hotel, the Mount Robson appeared light and airy, almost delicate. Six wings decorated with Dutch gables radiated out from a château style centre block and the irregular roofline, broken by slender randomly spaced towers, echoed the peaks and valleys of the surrounding mountains. Set in formally landscaped gardens with circular drives and curving walkways, Rattenbury's Hotel Mount Robson would epitomize Edwardian elegance.

As well as planning a promotional campaign appealing to tourists, the G.T.P. intended to entice settlers aboard their trains by extolling the virtues of the rich farmlands the line would open for colonization. And, as it happened, much of that land belonged to Rattenbury. In 1908, a few days after the G.T.P. had stated that the line would definitely be constructed through the area, Rattenbury had announced that he had sold his Nechako Valley holdings to Trafford Huteson, an Englishman recently arrived in Seattle, who in turn intended to promote the sale of parcels of the land to bona fide farmers. The $100,000 Ratz claimed to have received for his 11,000 acres must have gone a long way to financing his travels. But he had, by no means, sold all of his land. He still retained some 50,000 acres in the Bulkley Valley and through his company, Rattenbury Lands Ltd., he intended to oversee the colonization of this land himself. He was an empire builder, he bragged to his friends.

He could foresee a day in the not too distant future when his influence would be felt from the Rockies to the Coast. All G.T.P. buildings would have been designed by him — from the most rustic mountain railway station to the magnificent hotel at Prince Rupert. Settlers pouring off G.T.P. trains would collect their baggage at a Rattenbury-designed station and then spread over the countryside to begin farming thousands of acres on which Rattenbury would hold the mortgage. The $100,000 he had collected in 1908 would be a paltry sum compared to the money he could expect to make once the railroad was completed. When that day came his land holdings would bring him great personal wealth and the Grand Trunk Pacific hotels would become monuments to his genius, the buildings that would mark the high point of a brilliant architectural career.

But then disaster struck, a disaster from which Ratz and the Grand Trunk Pacific never really recovered. In the spring of 1912 Hays travelled to England to promote the company and to gain the approval of its British shareholders for his latest plans which included a contract with a Pittsburgh syndicate for the export of coal via the Grand Trunk Pacific and Prince Rupert. Returning from England with all his visionary plans in his head and the signed contracts in his pocket, Hays went down with the *Titanic*.

He was replaced by E. J. Chamberlain, a more cautious man who shared neither Hays' determined optimism nor his enthusiasm for the potential of Prince Rupert.

If Hays' death was a major blow to the G.T.P. the coup de grâce came two years later. The tracks had finally been completed and the first train rolled into Prince Rupert on April 8, 1914. Regular service was scheduled to start in September and the company had launched an extensive advertising campaign designed to appeal to both tourists and settlers.

Trains of the Grand Trunk Pacific will traverse some of the finest scenery to be found on the American continent, across wild and fertile fields, by the banks of mighty rivers of the North, through deep dark canyons where in midsummer from beneath the north windows of westbound trains will come the sweet fragrance of wild roses while from the south windows the traveller can look out on a glittering glacier whose cloud shroud trails to the margin of the mountains — this is the trail the railroad follows on its shortcut across Canada.[2]

Just how many settlers might have been attracted to the fertile fields, or how many romantic tourists lured aboard the Grand Trunk Pacific by the promise of wild roses and glittering glaciers, will never be known for on August 4, 1914 Britain declared war on Germany and the Grand Trunk Pacific was finished before it had even begun.

Since few tourists could be expected during the war years, work on the G.T.P.'s mountain hotels was postponed indefinitely. And, although the railway did make a desultory start on the hotel at Prince Rupert, digging the foundation and ordering some building materials, it, like the resort hotels was never built for by the time the war finally ended the Grand Trunk Pacific was bankrupt.

The hoped-for colonists did not materialize. What settlers there were left the land to serve in the army or work in factories. "All the money I earned in building the Parliament Buildings, the Empress Hotel and numbers of other buildings, I invested in buying lands,"[3] Ratz said. And now, rather than a profitable investment those lands had become a burden, tens of thousands of undeveloped acres on which he would have to pay taxes and from which he could expect no return. He hung on to his land holdings, not through any sense of optimism but simply because there were no buyers and other than forfeit the land to the Crown there was nothing else for him to do.

He had been engrossed in his architectural work for the Grand Trunk Pacific for at least three years, doodling rough sketches on odd bits of paper, experimenting with designs and finally preparing presentation drawings. Now he rolled up all his plans and sketches and put them away in his attic where they remained out of sight but no doubt very much on his mind. His grand architectural dream had become a nightmare that would haunt him for the rest of his life.

In 1911 he had served as President of the Architectural Association, but now he let his membership lapse and although he was later credited with designing several buildings in Victoria during the twenties, he never again entered actively into the practice of architecture.

Ratz had invested everything — his reputation, his hopes and his money in the railroad's future. The failure of the Grand Trunk Pacific was a professional and personal disaster. He would never again exhibit quite the same brash, energetic confidence, but he did survive the blow — only because he seems to have anticipated it.

Rattenbury, perhaps more than anyone else, would have realized early what Hays' death could mean to the success of the G.T.P. He was enough of a promoter himself to know that opportunities must be seized by men of vision who revelled in the taking of risks. Caution and faint hearts did not build empires in central British Columbia or anywhere else. When Hays was replaced as G.T.P. president, Ratz may have begun to feel less sure of the ultimate success of the rail line. There is one small hint that he may have sensed that the Parliament Buildings, rather than the string of elegant and sensitively designed railway hotels, would come to be the body of work on which his architectural reputation would depend.

The cornerstone for the foundation of the Provincial Library was laid on September 28, 1912, five months after Hays' death. To the original plans he had submitted the year before, Rattenbury had made several changes and one rather significant addition. Set in niches, high on the Library's exterior walls were statues — not of the thirty-five English monarchs that had adorned Henry Francis Lockwood's Bradford Town Hall, but of the men who had shaped the history of British Columbia, such men as Captains Cook and Vancouver, Dr. John Helmcken and Sir Matthew Baillie Begbie. Lockwood, an architect whose talent Rattenbury greatly admired, had designed many buildings, but Bradford's Town Hall was regarded by many as his magnum opus, the one building felt to mark the pinnacle of his career. And so it may be that the Library's statues, gazing grandly out over the city from their high niches, were intended by Rattenbury to be a symbolic postscript to an architectural talent that would now never be fully realized. Some twenty years before he had designed a building, probably based on an original Lockwood design, and now that building would remain his master work, his most significant contribution to the architectural heritage of British Columbia.

Rattenbury's interpretation of Hays' death as a warning, an omen foreshadowing the demise of the railroad, was due at least in part to the fact that his personal life was so joyless that he was predisposed toward pessimism. In 1912 he was forty-five, his red hair thinning and touched with grey, middle-aged but still vigorous and handsome. Slender and straight, a dominating forceful man whose sensitive aesthetic eyes belied his irascibility and impatience. He enjoyed good health, he was prosperous and successful. He should have been happy and content. But instead he was resentful and despondent, for before him stretched years of marriage to a woman for whom he had developed an intense dislike.

From the start Florrie had seemed an odd choice for a man of Rattenbury's stature in the community. Ratz was capable of controlling his passions and acting in a calculating and logical way when the situation demanded it. A man with a healthy sense of his own worth, the major factor in his life was his towering ambition and he might have been expected to choose as a wife the daughter of one of the city's monied families, a woman who enjoyed some connection to Victoria's aristocracy. But Florrie brought her husband neither wealth nor position. Her father, Captain George Elphinstone Nunn, had served with the British Army in India for several years before news of the Fraser River gold rush attracted him to British Columbia's west coast. In 1862 he had sailed into Victoria's harbour with his wife, older children and parrot in tow to find that while the gold excitement had abated, the free port of Victoria was thriving. He signed on as an officer on one of the coastal vessels sailing between Victoria and San Francisco, leaving his wife in Victoria to raise their growing brood of children. Some fifteen years later, when she learned of Captain Nunn's death in San Francisco, Florrie's mother, apparently having had quite enough of the joys of single parenthood, packed her bags and left town moving to Portland,

Oregon to live with one of her older daughters who had married rather well. Her younger children, Charles born in 1874 and Florrie some three years earlier, she left with friends in Victoria. Charles was raised on a farm in Saanich and Florrie was left in the care of Eleanor Howard who had been widowed, as she put it, by the appearance in Victoria of her husband's first wife and who supported herself by running a genteel boarding house on Rae Street near the city's business district.[4] Florrie had no money, no family and to the city's elite her origins were distinctly humble. Rattenbury had not improved his position or his prospects by marrying her.

But neither was Florrie the type of woman who inspired men to reckless, headlong, pursuit. She was stocky and rather plain, a short little woman with a large nose and stubborn jaw. Her pale blue eyes were her most prominent feature, but even her friends admitted that they were perhaps too prominent — frog-like, they described them. A shy retiring girl, gifted with a patient serenity, Florrie was recognized by many people as the kindest, sweetest person they had ever met. And perhaps that's the way Ratz felt about her too for his relationship with her seems to have been marked by growing familiarity rather than fiery passion.

When he first arrived in Victoria in 1893 marriage had been far from his mind. An architect caught up in the largest and most complex commission of his career, he had little time for social calls, but it happened that the one man whose company Ratz did seek out lived at the Rae Street house. An Irishman who had resigned his commission in the Royal Engineers to settle in the Yale district and to engage in mining and in raising imported blooded cattle, Forbes G. Vernon had been elected to the provincial legislature in 1874. He had served several terms as Chief Commissioner of Lands and Works and, although he would resign to become the province's agent-general in London in 1894, he still held that important cabinet post during the time the decision to build new legislative buildings had been reached and Rattenbury had been selected as their architect.

Vernon, who found the old Birdcages as cramped and inconvenient as did many other members of the government, directed much of the work of his department from Mrs. Howard's boarding house and Rattenbury was a frequent visitor, meeting with Vernon to discuss working drawings, estimates for the buildings' foundation and the time-table for the first phase of construction.

If, as seems likely, Ratz had met Florrie shortly after his arrival in Victoria his courtship of the girl was quite unchivalrously unhurried. They were married on June 18, 1898 in a quiet evening ceremony at Christ Church Cathedral. After their return from the Klondike from what must have been for Florrie a romantic adventure despite its hardships, they took up residence in "Hochelaga," the elegant Rockland Avenue home Ratz had rented from A. J. C. Gellately, the manager of the Victoria branch of the Bank of Montreal. And there on January 14, 1899 their first child, a son, was born.

The boy, christened Francis Burgoyne Rattenbury, was born with clubfeet, so badly deformed that it seemed unlikely that he would ever be able to walk. Florrie had reacted with predictable maternal concern, smothering him with attention, and later, when he was older, taking him many times to San Francisco where she hoped more sophisticated medical attention might straighten his twisted feet.

Frank was in awe of his father, soberly repeating Ratz' most outlandish boasts to anyone who would listen. On one occasion Ratz, an avid motorist, had purchased a sleek, black electric car. His father said it was a black pearl, Frank informed his friends, and black pearls were the most expensive.

Their second child, a daughter, born on May 11, 1904 and named Mary after Rattenbury's mother, grew into a lovely girl, tall with her father's erect carriage and his sensitive eyes. But Mary was a nervous, highly strung child who developed an emotionally rooted speech impediment as she sensed the tensions and growing hostility that existed between her parents.

At first Ratz and Florrie had seemed happy enough. He had designed for them a picturesque home of rough stone and dark stained shingles on the beach in Oak Bay and there Florrie had been content. The city's fashionable Rockland Avenue had not been her milieu for she lacked the confidence or practised grace that might have allowed her to ease herself gradually into Victoria's social scene. Wealthy matrons did not overlook the fact that she was the adopted daughter of a boarding house keeper or that her brother Charles was nothing more than a waiter at the Globe Restaurant. But in Oak Bay Florrie could avoid the stigma of not being accepted. At the time Rattenbury built their house there were few other permanent residents along the beach. There were summer people, like the Helmckens, who deserted the city as the warm weather came and for two or three months of every year lived in their little cottages dotted along the waterfront of Oak Bay. With these people, relaxed by beach-side casualness, Florrie could feel comfortable and each year she and Ratz entertained at a summer garden party at which Florrie, who treasured the flowers in her seaside garden and who took more pride in a clever floral arrangement than in the grand table on which it was placed, could feel secure under the oaks heavy with hanging flower baskets as her guests were easily distracted with games of tennis and croquet.

Ratz surrounded Florrie with the accoutrements of wealth and position; exquisite jewels of such high quality that they achieved a fame of their own; expensive, finely crafted furniture; and as many as six servants — a cook, gardeners, a chauffeur, maids and a governess for the children. But despite it all Florrie remained a simple soul, kind, motherly, increasingly stout and, above all else, dull. Rattenbury moved easily among the lawyers, politicians and businessmen who were forming Victoria's new aristocracy and he may have resented the fact that Florrie could not do the same. And Florrie had become more prim than the most proper society matron. She avoided their nearest neighbours because she was convinced that Mrs. Bowker Senior, born Mary Tod, had been part Indian. She had an unbending code of what she considered correct deportment for her children's playmates. On one occasion Frank's friend, Tom Floyd, had been sailing high on the garden swing when he had called out to a boy who had come dangerously close, "Watch out or I'll bloody your nose." To his amazement Tom had been promptly banished by Florrie who had been incensed by his bad language.

For a time Ratz and Florrie had been able to conceal the growing antipathy they felt for each other. Kyrle Symons, headmaster of Frank's school, seems to have noticed nothing amiss in January of 1912 when he and his wife accepted an invitation to have tea with the Rattenburys. In fact if anything impressed Symons as being out of the ordinary it was Rattenbury's casual generosity. To attend "Symons' School" in those days amounted to having private tutoring. The school with a total enrollment of only six boys was conducted in Symons' rented home on Esquimalt Road. Proud of his school's academic program, Symons had to admit that the rocky sloping lot on which the house stood did not encourage the kind of games one usually associated with the playing fields of Eton. One day as he stood on the verandah of his house Symons had watched the boys at play.

"One of them," he told Rattenbury, "was on all fours and being led along by the others with a rope around his neck — stopping at intervals to crop a bit of grass. They were all farmers and he was a cow being taken out to pasture."

"Look here, Symons," Rattenbury said, "go round and find some level ground, build a house for yourself and a school on it. I'll pay for it and you can repay me in so many years."[5]

Symons, aware that Rattenbury had a reputation for being close, had been surprised by this offer but taking him at his word he ran up a bill for over $5,000 which Ratz apparently paid without complaint.[6]

Gradually the animosity between Ratz and Florrie had grown until finally they had stopped speaking to one another, communicating only through Mary who carried messages between the two. Ratz' room became a separate apartment in which he dined in solitude while the rest of the family sat around the dining room table below. He became a hermit in his own house avoiding Florrie and "Grannie" Howard who had moved into their home after giving up her Rae Street boarding house and whose perpetually clacking knitting needles and staunch loyalty to Florrie Ratz found particularly irritating. Never an abstemious man, he was known as a jolly good fellow, a rowdy participant in the not-so-gentlemanly revels which took place at Victoria's Union Club. But now his drinking habits changed. Each night, alone in his room, he steadily consumed the better part of a bottle of whisky as he brooded over the shambles his personal life had become and worried about the future of the Grand Trunk Pacific, the grand scheme in which he had invested so much money and so much hope.

In the winter of 1913 as his term as Reeve of Oak Bay neared its end, he decided to shake himself out of his depression by taking a trip, an around-the-world cruise with the only person of whom he was genuinely fond, his daughter Mary. For a time Mary had attended St. Margaret's School where, having been gifted with her father's artistic ability, she had won many drawing prizes but as the estrangement between her parents had deepened, Mary's "nerves" had become worse and she had dropped out of school to be taught at home by a private tutor. Now, Ratz instructed her teacher to concentrate on history and geography so that Mary would be better able

121

to appreciate the many countries they would visit and Mary began to look forward to the unexpected treat of an extended holiday with her father. She knew that he doted on her, "spoiled her rotten" her friends said, and she responded with feelings of deep affection for him. Alone with her father, away from the domestic strife at home, she could expect to be relaxed and happy, fussed over and catered to, and she would also have a chance to visit her brother Frank who was at school in England.

Frank had been sent to Wyllie's School at Hampstead Heath outside London. Wyllie's offered "special tuition . . . for boys to whom Preparatory or Public Schools may not be suitable." His son was being trained for the diplomatic corps, Rattenbury said.

By July of 1914 Mary's wardrobe had been chosen, their tickets bought and their schedule finalized when Mary suddenly changed her mind. She loved both her mother and "Grannie" Howard. To go away with her father, whose dislike of the two woman was unconcealed, Mary suddenly saw as treacherous disloyalty and she decided to remain at home.

Ratz, sorely disappointed and no doubt blaming Florrie for Mary's change of heart, set out alone. He arrived in England in August and Frank travelled up to London to meet him. The two were together dining in a London hotel when the orchestra leader interrupted the dinner music to announce that Britain had declared war on Germany and to break into a stirring rendition of "God Save the King."

Accompanied by Frank, Rattenbury returned home to Victoria, to a town that was very different from the one he had left. The Willows race track had been transformed into an army camp; the temporary billet of over a thousand volunteers who waited to be shipped overseas. Uniformed men were everywhere; digging trenches at Clover Point and the Willows, polishing their marching skills along city streets, taking part in patriotic rallies and on one wild night, when news of the *Lusitania*'s sinking sparked anti-German rioting, patrolling downtown streets and mounting guard outside the grounds of Government House.

Frank recalls that Rattenbury tried to enlist but that he was turned down because, at forty-six, he was considered too old. James Herrick McGregor, two years his junior, was more successful. In September 1914 McGregor resigned from the presidency of the Union Club and from his seat on Oak Bay council[7] and enlisted in the 50th Gordon Highlanders. Seven months later, serving in France as a captain and paymaster of the 16th Canadian Scottish battalion, he was shot down as he "strolled along with a cane under his arm, seemingly unaware that a war was being fought around him."[8]

There was no getting away from the war and the effect it had on Victoria. It seemed as if almost every day the *Colonist* carried the sad news received by a Victoria family that a son or brother was wounded or missing in action. Throughout the city houses stood empty, their owners somewhere in France. "For Rent" signs became permanent fixtures on the office blocks built during the boom years before 1913. As businesses folded and men were thrown out of work, some families were reduced to such desperate straits that in Oak Bay municipal employees were put to work growing potatoes and beans in vacant lots and in Willows Park to feed them.

Although they may not have actually gone hungry, the city's architects were faced with some lean years. Even a man as sought after as Sam Maclure found that there was little work to do and closing his business office, he worked out of his home on Beach Drive. Rattenbury, thanks to the work he had been given by the provincial government fared better than most. His additions to the Parliament Buildings which cost over two million dollars netted him tens of thousands in commission — more than enough to see him through the war years. But nevertheless those were years of debilitating inactivity for Ratz. When the war everyone had thought would last for only a few months finally ended, he was past fifty and the years of enforced idleness had taken their toll. He had become fleshy, his features blurred and coarsened by the whisky upon which he was becoming increasingly dependent. In 1919 when the Grand Trunk Pacific declared bankruptcy and was taken over by the Canadian National Railway any faint hope he may have had that his hotels might yet be built was dashed. The western terminus of the C.N.R. was Vancouver and instead of a bustling city at the western end of a transcontinental rail line, Prince Rupert became an almost forgotten town at the end of a not very profitable branch line. And in the twenties when the C.N.R. built a resort hotel at Jasper, it was a cautiously modest shingled building, quite unlike anything Rattenbury had designed for the Grand Trunk Pacific during the headily optimistic pre-war years. Now he knew for a certainty that he would be remembered for the Parliament Buildings and he also knew that it was common gossip in Victoria that he had stolen their design. The irony of it all added to his grim despondency. He became increasingly bad tempered. The children of the neighbourbood called him "Old Ratz" and, agreeing that he was not a nice man, did their best to keep out of his way. His mood had darkened when he heard that William Oliver had dropped dead of an apparent heart attack while holidaying at his summer home on Cowichan Lake. Oliver had been a friend. And now he was dead at fifty-three — exactly the same age as Rattenbury.

In 1920 as Victoria began to stir with post-war prosperity Rattenbury chose not to re-open his architectural office. He was weary of his architectural practice and soured on life. He seemed content to live off the commission he had received for the additions to the Parliament Buildings while he tried to promote the sale of his land holdings in the Bulkley Valley. But then, in 1921, the Victoria Chamber of Commerce approached him with an idea that soon re-kindled his interest in architecture on the grand scale and brought back some of his old vitality.

In 1912 the Chamber of Commerce had backed a by-law which would have increased municipal taxation to pay for a civic swimming pool and although at the time Victoria was enjoying widespread prosperity the voters had soundly defeated the referendum. In 1921 the Chamber re-introduced the idea and sensing that the taxpayers' former reluctance may have been due at least in part to the crude design which had been used to promote the scheme, they turned to Rattenbury knowing that if they could pique his interest he would produce plans for an exciting building and would also promote the scheme aggressively and skilfully.

For years, ever since he had been so impressed by the palaces of delight for the public he had seen at Coney Island, Ratz had hoped to see something of the sort built in Victoria. The opportunity to design such a building was perhaps the only thing that could have brought him back to his drafting table. Hc produced sketches of a building which must have stunned even the Chamber of Commerce with its magnificence. The Chamber had asked for a swimming pool. Rattenbury gave them an Amusement Centre. Covering an area of over 100,000 square feet, the building contained not one but three heated sea-water swimming pools. Towers at each corner would fly bright and festive banners and the whole complex, which would include ballrooms, picture galleries and shops, would be topped by a greenhouse roof of glass and steel. By day sunshine would sparkle on the water of the pools and play on the leaves of the lush tropical garden planned for the wide promenade above the pools. By night, the centre would become an exotic fantasy world. Coloured lights on the floors of the pools would glisten in a glorious rainbow effect through the water and a fountain of water shooting forty feet into the air would be specially lit to give it the appearance of a living stream of fire. The building would become a magical garden, a wonder palace.

Reluctant to seek taxpayer support too soon, the Chamber began to cautiously test the waters by canvassing other businessmen and Rattenbury in the meantime asked another architect, Percy Leonard James, if he would be interested in doing the actual work of producing working drawings and supervising construction should the Amusement Centre he had designed ever be built.

Designing the Amusement Centre and the prospect of promoting it to the voters, had made of Rattenbury a new man. Almost. Still gnawing away at him were the bitter feelings of disappointment and regret he had experienced over the last few years. While this current project had stimulated and excited him, he lacked the energy or the desire to re-open his architectural practice. James, an architect in active practice who had had experience in the construction of swimming pools in England before settling in Victoria in 1909, readily agreed to do the more detailed, time consuming work in return for a share of the commission. Over the next two years, while the Chamber dithered about the advisability of launching a full scale campaign to win support for a new money by-law, the two, Rattenbury and James, decided to extend their unofficial partnership to include other buildings as well. Clients, attracted to Rattenbury by his still prominent name got little more than that. Ratz would make the original contact and produce the first rough sketches, but all the rest of the work was left to James. The finished product might owe more to James than Rattenbury but Rattenbury's name appeared on the drawings and an owner could say that his home had been designed by the architect of the Parliament Buildings and Government House, a boast considered by some to be well worth paying for.

By 1923 the Chamber of Commerce had reluctantly admitted defeat. No matter how grand the scheme, or how prominent the architect, a new swimming pool by-law had little chance of passing. Then Victoria's "old friend," the Canadian Pacific Railway, came up with a suggestion that bowled the Chamber over with its generosity. The concessions the company had enjoyed for fifteen years, since the completion of the Empress Hotel in 1908, had expired. Now, the C.P.R. said, they were prepared to build an Amusement Centre, costing not less than $200,000 provided that the city leased them the site for one dollar a year; exempted the building from taxation for twenty years; provided free water for the swimming pool for twenty years; and froze the current taxes paid by the Empress for the same period.

In return for a $200,000 Amusement Centre which would be open to the public at popular prices and the profits of which would be kept by the C.P.R., the company would receive new concessions amounting to some $750,000. But as the special Amusement Centre committee set up by the Chamber pointed out to Victoria taxpayers, it wouldn't actually cost the city anything.

As the Committee got into high gear Rattenbury's sketches appeared everywhere; on thousands of handbills printed by local newspapers, on the screens of Victoria's motion picture cinemas, in shop windows all over town. And Rattenbury appeared everywhere — speaking to the Music Society, the Rotarians, the Alpine Garden Society — extolling the virtues of his Amusement Centre.

The referendum, held on December 29, 1923, passed with an overwhelming majority of 2,909 to 352. That evening a celebratory banquet was held in the Empress Hotel and Rattenbury was the man of the hour, fêted for his contribution as architect and promoter.

After the dinner, flushed with success and bouyant with praise he drifted into the Empress' lounge to enjoy an after dinner cigar with his admirers and there he met Alma Pakenham and his life was never the same again.

10

Alma
Which Mrs. Rattenbury?

Alma Victoria Clarke Dolling Pakenham was beautiful. She had a lovely oval face, deep hauntingly sad eyes and full lips which easily settled into a pout, at once fashionable and sensuous. A modern woman, quite uninhibited by any lingering code of Victorian morality, she was a flapper, gay and adventurous, a woman who drank cocktails and smoked cigarettes in public. She wore the shapeless clothes dictated by fashion and her hair was bobbed, cropped almost to her ears. But on Alma, the clothes, despite their boyish cut, revealed the soft round figure of a woman and her dark blonde hair escaping the bonds of her headband curled playfully around her face. She was funloving, warm, generous and kind. But she was also a creature ruled by her emotions, a person totally lacking in empathy, unable to understand how anyone could take offense to, or be hurt by, anything she did.

She had learned early that the world revolved around her. Born in 1895 or 1896, she was the daughter of Walter and Elizabeth Clarke of Kamloops, B.C., a community of some 1,500 which had grown up around the C.P.R. station and served as a supply centre for the ranching district. Walter William Clarke was co-owner of the *Kamloops Standard*, a weekly newspaper that he somehow managed to publish every Thursday, despite the fact that he had the triple task of managing the paper's business affairs, writing the news, and then printing it on the press in his home on Victoria Street. Alma's mother, herself an able musician, had been quick to recognize in her daughter the glimmerings of a precocious musical talent, a talent that she, as a teacher of piano and violin, felt a special responsibility to develop and nurture. It was not long before she became convinced that Alma was nothing less than a child prodigy and Alma learned early to enjoy and to need the approval and praise that a good performance could win for her. But Alma did not become a withdrawn, lonely child-genius. She was born with an outgoing, bouncy vivacity that overcame the long, solitary hours of practice. Her teacher at St. Ann's School remembered her as a well-adjusted child, "brilliantly clever . . . a vivid little thing full of happiness and music, with a special attraction of her own."[1]

By 1902 Clarke had given up Kamloops and the *Standard* to become a travelling journalist and for the next twelve years the family moved so often that only fleeting glimpses of Alma remain. In 1902 they were in Toronto where, Raymond Massey recalls, Alma was enrolled in his class at Havergal School.[2] The following year the family was in Victoria and as a result of her mother's careful coaching Alma was making a name for herself in the city's musical circles, the ladies quite taken with the little girl with the blonde curls, "a tiny little thing whose feet could barely reach the pedals."[3]

Alma would later blame her lack of emotional control on the strain of these early performances. But with the strain came applause and acceptance. She was pampered and spoiled, patted on the head and told that she was pretty and clever and talented and she learned that tantrums could be excused as artistic temperament and that she had a special sparkle that made people want to make a fuss of her and to make allowances for her.

Before long the family was on the move again, returning to Toronto, where, when she was seventeen or eighteen, Alma gave the performance which she would remember as the highlight of her public career. At a concert given by the Toronto Symphony Orchestra she played two different concertos — one on the piano, the other on the violin.

Then it was back to the west coast, to Vancouver where her father had taken a job with a local newspaper, the *Sun*. And it was in Vancouver that Alma met and married her first husband, Caledon Robert Radclyffe Dolling. Dolling was a younger son, educated at Tonbridge School in preparation for Sandhurst and the Indian Army but poor eyesight had ended his hopes of a military career and he had left England for British Columbia lured west by the C.P.R.'s breathless accounts of the province's booming economy and unparalleled opportunities.

Arriving in Vancouver in 1910, a year that saw the city's population growing at the rate of 1,000 a month, Dolling had opened a real estate agency in partnership with Robert Stark and the following year was advertising himself as a specialist in Port Mann and New Westminster properties.

He and Alma were married in the spring of 1914. In August, three days after the declaration of war, Dolling offered his services, and his eyesight having improved relative to the worsening situation, he was given a commission and sent to Prince Rupert as second in command of the garrison there. Alma travelled north with him and the young couple immediately gained the friendship of everyone in the station. Dolling organized boxing and football matches and Alma's brilliant piano playing was particularly appreciated.[4] Some months later Dolling was gazetted to the 2nd Battalion Welsh Fusiliers and sent to France. And Alma followed him to England taking a job at Whitehall so that she could be with him when he was sent to London on leave.

In February 1916 he was wounded and received the Military Cross. He was wounded again in April and invalided back to England but he had returned to his regiment by July, in time to fight in the battle of the Somme. And then Alma received word that on the night of August 20, 1916, 2nd Lieutenant and Temporary Captain Caledon Dolling had been blown apart by a shell during the battle of Mametz Wood.

"You have the whole regiment's sympathy," his commanding officer wrote. "They are all fond of him and relied on him and trusted his leadership. . . . He was such a man and had no fear and loved his work . . . I have lost a brilliant company commander and a friend."[5]

Alma left her job at Whitehall and joined a women's ambulance corps hoping that she would be sent to France where she intended to search for her husband's grave. Instead she found herself in Salonika working as a field ambulance orderly and it was later said of her that she displayed remarkable aptitude in her work, so much so that she received a decoration from the French government.[6]

With the end of hostilities Alma returned to London and there she met her second husband, Thomas Compton Pakenham, nephew of the renowned Admiral Pakenham, and a hero in his own right having won a Military Cross for his exploits as an officer in the Coldstream Guards. The problem of Pakenham's five-year-old marriage to Phyllis Price was overcome by a divorce in which it seems likely Alma was named co-respondent. She and Pakenham were married in 1921 and almost immediately afterwards left England for New

York where Pakenham had been offered a position at an American university. Their son Christopher was born on July 8, 1921 but their marriage proved to be a disaster. By 1923 Alma's mother, distressed by the letters she was receiving from her daughter, travelled to the east and brought Alma and Christopher back to Vancouver with her. Alma took up her music once again and she was so well remembered that soon she was being invited to give concerts in Vancouver and Victoria. The night that the banquet to celebrate the success of the Amusement Centre by-law was held she had been in the lounge of the Empress, relaxing after having played at an evening recital.

"I had been playing in Victoria," Alma wrote to a friend, "and on returning to the hotel I sat yarning for a while with K. in the lounge. From the banqueting hall came the sounds of revelry and singing. Those men whoever they were did put some real enthusiasm into 'For he's a jolly good fellow'. You know how raucous this can sound. This was quite different. So much so that we guessed that every word was meant.

"K. suggested that we should try to get a peep into the room, which we did, and to K.'s amazement he found that the honoured guest, the man who had inspired this outburst, was an acquaintance.

"Soon after we had gone back to our places in the lounge the banquet ended, and some of the men strolled in to finish cigars and pipes. K. introduced me to his acquaintance, and so it was that I first met my Ratz.

"The memory of that singing had gone to my head, and though I had resolved, as you know, never to marry again, but to devote myself to my music, that song seemed to make all the difference. . . . Well, my dear, if I don't love him, I simply don't know what love is."[7]

Of course it had been more than the heartfelt song that had interested Alma. Alma, who had never met Ratz before, could not know how drastically his appearance had altered, could not guess that he was barely recognizable as the same man who had served ten years earlier as the Reeve of Oak Bay. She saw only the tall elegantly dressed man who stood before her, flushed with success and exuding confidence as he accepted the praise and gratitude of the city's most prominent citizens. He had designed the very hotel in which they met and from almost any window she could look out and see the outline of his Parliament Buildings, still unmatched as the best known and most important architectural work in the city and the province. Alma was impressed.

Just how or when they agreed to meet again is unknown but early in 1924 Alma moved to Victoria, settling for a time with an aunt who lived on Dallas Road until a house was found for her in James Bay near Beacon Hill Park. She would support herself and her small son by giving piano lessons, Alma bravely declared. And the ladies of the community welcomed her with open arms — unaware that the little house on Niagara Street had become the place of discreet meetings between Alma and the still married Rattenbury. When the Bullens decided to hold a dinner party to celebrate the move into their new Rockland area home, Rattenbury as architect of the house was an honoured guest and "because he loved music so," Alma was invited too. No one was surprised when Ratz attended the party alone for he and Florrie had not appeared together in public for years but they might have been scandalized had they known that by pretending that they had not met until that night Ratz and Alma were acting out a deliciously exciting charade.

Mrs. Maclure who with her architect husband Sam was the leader of the city's artistic and musical community had been quick to make Alma feel at home. She invited Alma and her little boy to afternoon tea and the Maclure daughters, who counted their mother a strict disciplinarian, wondered at her patience as they watched Christopher, or "Toffy" as Alma called him, dismember their parlour. First Toffy began with the cushions, removing them one one by one until they made a satisfying heap in the middle of the floor. Then he started on the ornaments, placing them precariously on top of the cushions.

"Mummy doesn't want you to do that, Toffy," Alma protested ineffectually, remaining seated in her chair and Toffy, ignoring her continued. Mrs. Maclure held her tongue until Toffy climbed upon a cushionless chair and reached for the pictures hanging on the wall.

"Don't let him get at the pictures," Mrs. Maclure warned with angry finality. "They might fall and hurt him."[8]

But Alma and Toffy were forgiven this breach of etiquette and invited to return for Mrs. Maclure, like many others, found that Alma, who as a girl had shown such promise and as a woman had experienced such tragedy, was not an easy person to deny.

A few weeks later Mrs. Maclure heard that Alma had not been well and feeling sorry for her she began taking soups and hampers of food to the Niagara Street house. At least the poor girl wouldn't have to worry about cooking, Mrs. Maclure thought. Then one day she received a call from a friend, a singer who happened to live across the street from Alma. Shortly after Mrs. Maclure's last visit, the woman reported, she had seen Alma and Rattenbury leaving the house. They had strolled to Beacon Hill Park and there had picnicked happily on the contents of Mrs. Maclure's thoughtfully prepared hamper.

Mrs. Maclure was furious. She telephoned Alma and confronted her with the story. Alma denied nothing.

"People have been saying things about you," Mrs. Maclure told Alma, "and now I can see that they were right."[9]

Alma didn't care. Those same people would be begging to come to her house one day, she retorted and it was obviously what she believed. In the past people had always been forgiving and understanding. She had always been fussed and spoiled, always able to get her own way. Why should anything be different now, especially since Rattenbury's position in the community seemed unassailable.

And Ratz must have felt the same way. Florrie had been all but ignored by Victorian society. A stout little woman who kept to herself pottering about in her garden, she was never invited to the winter dinner parties or summer picnics at which Victoria's wealthy residents met to listen to good music, to gossip about the latest scandal, to play energetic games of tennis and sedate games of croquet, and to discuss the merits of investing in developing industries. But Ratz was a frequent guest. On the piano, he was a gifted amateur. On the tennis courts, he played with the skill that comes of hating to lose. He was a member of the Yacht Club and when he wasn't sailing he was sketching boats. Yawls and ketches with the wind in their sails appeared on the presentation drawings of every building he designed which happened to be sited by a body of water. He was a smart businessman who carefully set aside part of his income for safe investments including shares in an Alberta brewery and in a local painting and decorating firm.

He knew that people had wondered over the years why he had married Florrie and he was sure that while a divorce might cause tongues to wag, his decision to leave his wife would be understood and accepted. At first he had tried, quietly and privately, to convince Florrie to consent to a divorce while he kept his affair with Alma hidden. But now that Mrs. Maclure had uncovered their secret and there was no longer any need for discretion, he became blatant. He acquired a prominent box in the theatre and clad in a newly purchased opera cape swept in with Alma on his arm, flaunting their relationship.

He seemed set on inviting censure and Sam Maclure who had known Rattenbury for almost thirty years was at a loss to explain his behaviour.

"The man's bewitched," he said shaking his head.[10]

And there were those who went further, who could not believe that feminine charms alone accounted for Alma's sorcery. They said she was addicted to drugs and hinted that Rattenbury had become a changed man under their influence.

Probably no one will ever know for a certainty if this was the case. Alma may well have developed a drug dependency during the years she spent with the ambulance corps during the war. In battlefield hospitals both morphia and cocaine were used as anaesthetics and while morphia was known to be addictive, the properties of cocaine were not clearly understood. But cocaine was known to increase vitality and the capacity to work and since it was generally regarded as a harmless drug Alma may have begun to use it to keep her going for long hours of unaccustomed hardship and labour. And cocaine was also known to produce exhilaration and lasting euphoria, both commodities in short supply amid the ugliness and stench of war. Other Victoria girls, serving as nurses or drivers during the war, had returned home with an addiction to morphia or a dependency on cocaine, but most surrounded by the soothing presence of family and friends in peaceful post-war Victoria had overcome their drug habit. Perhaps Alma had not — for Alma certainly had an addictive personality. Self-denial was alien to her. One drink, more often than not, led to two or three more. She was a chain smoker who found it difficult to finish a meal without pausing between courses to smoke a cigarette. Rattenbury's children, Frank and Mary, who were twenty and twenty-five at the time *l'affaire Rattenbury* became the talk of Victoria, remain convinced and take some comfort from their conviction that "dope" played a role in their father's entrapment and they may be right. Cocaine may have brought back his youthful virility and may have induced in him a state of excitement and euphoria that encouraged his recklessly indiscreet behaviour.

But Rattenbury's behaviour can be easily understood without accepting the rumours that Alma had seduced him by introducing him to stimulating drugs. When they met he was fifty-six years old and beginning to feel his age. For twenty-six years he had been married to a woman for whom he now felt only an intense dislike. For the last ten years he had been weighed down by the conviction that his artistic career was at an end. Coincidentally with his meeting Alma, he had been given the opportunity to design the Amusement Centre, or Crystal Garden as it had come to be known, the building which would become the social heart of the city, winning the affections of Victorians as no other building ever could and in the campaign to win approval of the voters for its construction he had proved himself to be an hypnotically persuasive promoter. That alone could have brought back some of his driving energy. And how his manly pride must have been aroused by the discovery that a beautiful woman, a gay, giddy, vivacious and talented young woman, thirty years his junior, was in love with him.

Common sense might have suggested to him that he keep Alma as a mistress preserving his reputation by maintaining a façade of respectability. But his passion for her was so great that he was past discretion, past caring, or so he thought, about Victoria's opinion of him. Florrie — stubborn, dull, matronly Florrie — was the obstacle to his happiness. He must rid himself of her.

But Florrie remained adamant. She would not divorce him. And so Ratz embarked on a course of action that would result in his complete ostracism by even his oldest friends and associates. As everyone said, it wasn't so much what he did, as the way that he did it.

He decided to harass the seemingly immovable Florrie. He moved out of the house, the house called "Iechineel" which meant, Ratz had once said, "a place where a good thing happened," and sent moving vans to remove the better pieces of furniture. But as the movers carried one piece out the front door, Florrie with the help of her Chinese servant, Wee, moved another into the maid's room, the one room in the house for which only Florrie had the key. Between them they managed to squirrel away the most valuable pieces of furniture and Florrie took particular pleasure in noting that part of their hoard included Rattenbury's stock of imported champagne.[11]

Ratz retaliated by laying siege to the house, ordering the light and heat turned off and Florrie, fortified by the food hampers she now received from Mrs. Maclure, took him to court filing a successful injunction against him on July 28, 1924 for a declaration of the plaintiff's right to reside in the house of her husband.

Disgusted by this turn of events, Rattenbury left Victoria for two months, taking, it was rumoured, a Mediterranean cruise with Alma. On his return, in a desperate attempt to finally be free of the woman, he devised a particularly mean scheme. He began bringing Alma to the house entertaining her in the parlour and forcing Florrie to retire to one of the upstairs rooms, where she took to her bed, the throbbing indignation and resentment she felt affecting her heart that she had already strained by years of overweight.

One night Florrie was lying in her bed, listening with a combination of anger and fear to Alma gaily playing the piano and to the sound of her own wildly beating heart. Mary concerned at seeing her mother so agitated had gone downstairs and asked her father and Alma to please be quiet as her mother was upset and unable to sleep. Alma responded by playing a thumpingly loud rendition of the funeral march, its heavy chords resounding through the house and filling the room in which Florrie lay.[12]

Perhaps the events of that night finally convinced Florrie that she would not know a moment's peace until she agreed to a divorce for soon after she and Mary moved out of "Iechineel" into a house on Fort Street and she resignedly began divorce proceedings against her husband.

But although the divorce was granted on January 28, 1925 Rattenbury would discover that until her death he would never be quite free of Florrie. In addition to an alimony payment of $225 a month he had agreed to provide her with a house of her own. Real estate agent Chartres Pemberton took Florrie about town showing her several sites on which her house might be built. But none of them would do, for as Pemberton discovered there was one rather special criterion which the site would have to meet. The place where she built must have a good view of her husband's house. "She was very definite about that," Pemberton remembered. She finally selected a lot just off Oak Bay Avenue at the top of Prospect Place. And there she sat, in her little Maclure-designed bungalow, a silent watchful presence on the rocky hill above "Iechineel."

Just when or where Rattenbury and Alma were married remains something of a mystery. But it does seem that once legally free of Florrie, Rattenbury found his desire to remarry cooling. Records show that they were not married in British Columbia and yet Ratz remained in Victoria until at least June of 1925, six months after his divorce became final. And it was during this period that he came to realize just how much his scandalous personal conduct would affect his professional life.

In May 1925 architect Percy Leonard James, perhaps emboldened by the general disfavour with which Rattenbury had come to be viewed, wrote to Ratz claiming that he had done the lion's share of the work on the Crystal Garden and demanding a greater share of the commission. Rattenbury's reply had been nothing less than insulting. Except for minor details the completed building had been constructed according to his original design, he informed James. James could have turned down the work, he continued, in which case he would have hired a draughtsman to do the job. He had really done James a favour. ". . . you were not only satisfied with the terms — but very pleased to get the work — ."[13]

What had begun as a business disagreement became a personal feud. Now James not only wanted a greater share of the commission but he also felt that all of the credit for the building's design should go to him and he found no shortage of people who would champion him in a dispute with Rattenbury. "Stick to your guns," they told him, relishing the prospects of seeing Rattenbury put in his place.

Rattenbury took his case to the press. The Crystal Garden had been "designed and sketched out by me," he wrote in a letter to the editor and any statements to the contrary were very erroneous.[14] Then he called on Basil Gardom, the C.P.R.'s Superintendent of Construction, sure that the company would support his claim of being sole architect of the Crystal, since they had hired him as architect in the first place. But Gardom had been only too happy to stand by James. "Rattenbury came to my room like a lion," he reported to James, "but left in quite a decent frame of mind and I am sure the truth of what I told him was brought home to him . . ."[15]

Rattenbury now realized that as well as a social outcast he had become, almost overnight, a professional pariah. It seems that for a time he and Alma left Victoria, Ratz to avoid further humiliation and both of them hoping that their absence would cause the scandal to die down. It may be that they were married during this extended trip, for on their return in the spring of 1927 Alma was calling herself Mrs. Rattenbury and was anxious to be re-admitted to the city's cultural community. She telephoned Mrs. Maclure. "Mrs. Rattenbury speaking," she introduced herself. "Which Mrs. Rattenbury?" Mrs. Maclure demanded and upon being told, informed her caller that she knew only one Mrs. Rattenbury — the Mrs. Rattenbury of Prospect Place.[16]

Ratz fared no better. He continued to be avoided on the street, cold shouldered in the Union Club and shunned by former clients and business associates. A man who was short tempered, blunt and almost unscrupulously ambitious, he had never been an easy person to like but he had been accepted because he was wealthy and, while he had concealed many of his professional failures, his successes had been well-publicized and were undeniably brilliant. He had been seen as an important man, a genius many people said. He had relied on his reputation as an architect and as a prominent citizen to attract commissions but now his name had become an undesirable commodity and his reputation as an architect counted for nothing. Now people found just how very easy it was to despise him. To divorce and re-marry was bad enough but to have left his wife for Alma who was seen as an immoral woman, "a man-eating tigress," was quite beyond the pale.

The birth of their son John on December 27, 1928 did nothing to soothe the community's outraged morals. And Alma, as she pushed the baby carriage along Oak Bay streets, would find that her friendly smile and warm hello would not receive so much as an answering nod from people who had once welcomed her into their homes. Alma's relatives and a few of her friends remained loyal but Rattenbury's ostracism by his former associates was complete as people who had once never given Florrie a second thought now saw her as the victim of a "harlot's" attempt to improve her social position.

On October 13, 1929 Florrie died and Alma in an act of quite incredible insensitivity called on Mary to offer her sympathy. Alma may have felt genuinely sorry for Mary. In anything that did not relate directly to her own happiness she could be kind, open-hearted and disarmingly generous. More than one visitor to her home had been rather disconcerted when their admiration of some object would be answered by Alma's urging them to take it. "If you like it, it's yours," she would say, admitting later that it might not make much sense but that was her disposition. She sincerely believed that she would never knowingly hurt anyone, apparently the victim of a most convenient mental block when it came to other men's wives. She would have found it hard to believe that Mary would harbour any negative feelings toward her and she may have felt that they would fall into each other's arms, let by-gones be by-gones, and become friends.

But self-interest rather than sympathy may have prompted her visit. With Florrie dead, Mary might welcome the offer of friendship. If Mary was prepared to forgive and forget, if she was prepared to accept Alma as her father's wife now that her mother was dead . . . the community as a whole might gradually follow suit.

Whatever the case she had seriously misjudged the depth of Mary's feelings. Still harbouring feelings of bitter hatred and resentment some fifty years later, she was on that day in no mood to forgive and she refused to talk to Alma, saying afterwards that Alma had been "high on dope" at the time of her visit.[17]

Mary's angry dismissal of Alma was the final wedge between Rattenbury and his daughter. Realizing that there could never be a reconciliation and without it he and Alma would remain *persona non grata*, he decided to leave Victoria. But not before he changed his will. In a new will, dated December 18, 1929 he disinherited both Mary and his son Frank. His entire estate would go to Alma, Christopher and John. Only Ratz knew just how empty a gesture it was.[18]

Soon afterwards, they left Victoria for good. Only Frank appeared at the dock to see them off. It was an humiliating departure and particularly so if Frank's recollections are correct. "Alma was in a stupor," he reported, adding darkly, "booze, I suppose, or something else."[19]

Part II

ALMA: England 1930-35

11

Bournemouth

Oh poor Ratz. What has happened?

Nothing more was heard of them until September of 1930 when a small item appeared in the local newspapers. Mr. and Mrs. Francis Mawson Rattenbury, it was reported, had visited Okehampton for the purpose of having their son John baptized in the parish church.

It would seem that Rattenbury, having acted on his decision to leave Victoria, had begun to feel rootless and strangely anonymous away from the symbols of his success and the reminders of the man he had once been. For Okehampton was not just any town. It is in that ancient village in the gently rolling hills of west Devon that the first records of the Rattenbury family appear. During the seventeenth century the family had risen to a position of considerable importance in the town, the most prominent member being one John Rattenbury who was remembered as "one of the principal burgesses . . . having been town clark and steward of the borough for above thirty years and four tymes mayor, a great preserver of the Records and priviledges belonging to the town." For many years mayors of Okehampton had proudly worn "a little silver seale, having Okehampton town arms engraved thereon, tyed with a black ribbon" which John Rattenbury had presented to the mayor in 1654.[1]

But if Rattenbury had hoped that this pilgrimage to Okehampton would lead him to discover a proud sense of his family's history and to help him recapture feelings of personal importance, he must have been disappointed for Okehampton had become a depressing backwater, "an ugly, dirty and stupid town" and the little silver seal which his ancestor had presented to the town so many years before, had been lost.

Another hint that Ratz was finding it difficult to put his old life in Victoria behind him was his decision to settle in Bournemouth. If he had searched the wide world over he could not have found a place more like Victoria. Both cities look south over the sea. The gulls, the cliffs, the pine scented, ozone-laden air were the same. Even the people were the same — for Bournemouth, a young city by English standards, had become a retirement centre to which well-to-do colonials flocked to enjoy a life of ease. And Bournemouth must have been Rattenbury's choice for it would not have been Alma's. Alma would have opted for London with its theatres and shops and its promise of parties and concerts. Still in her thirties she was energetic and talented with lingering musical ambitions. But she was also compliant. She had an easy unquestioning willingness to take whatever fate placed in her path whether it was another woman's husband or premature retirement. And so they settled in Villa Madeira, a cottage on Manor Road a few paces away from the East Cliff and there amid constant reminders of Victoria Ratz discovered too late just how important his former prominence had been to his self esteem.

In Victoria he had been such a well-known figure, a man who had played so significant a role in the developing province, that his home was included on the tourist circuit. He had often listened with amusement and no small amount of pride to the drivers of the tour buses that crawled past "Iechineel" every day in the summer informing their passengers that this is the home of Francis Mawson Rattenbury. And as they rattled off the highlights of his career tourists would crane their necks hoping to catch a glimpse of the renowned architect.

But in Bournemouth he became just another retired colonial with a few interesting stories to tell. No one remembered the brash young man with dark red hair and clipped moustache whose ambition had left an indelible mark on a capital city and whose imaginative schemes might have changed the course of a province's history. Instead they saw only a tired man, a man past sixty and showing his years, a man becoming increasingly deaf, his features puffy and blurred by heavy drinking and an elderly man in the slightly ridiculous position of having encumbered himself with an infant son.

He was certainly no longer the man with whom Alma had pictured herself madly in love. Alma would later recall that since the birth of their son she and Ratz had ceased to have sexual relations. His advancing years in combination with the whisky he drank had, it seems, rendered him impotent. Alma had become little more than a loving companion. She saw to his needs, humoured him, drank with him and tried to jolly him out of his increasing bouts of depression. Other than Dr. O'Donnell, Alma's physician, whose calls to the house were too frequent to be entirely professional, they had few friends or visitors. As Ratz became more solitary and introspective, sinking deeper and deeper into a state of near constant gloom, Alma tried to coax him into a lighter mood by suggesting interesting outings. In September of 1932 she persuaded him to accompany her to visit a phrenologist, who after examining her head, declared that she "was a woman of small brains, with weak will, no grit, no backbone . . . one of those people who when they come under influence, give way to temptation very easily," an unsound woman who must guard against emotional excitement. Oh yes, Alma said, he was quite correct and Rattenbury found that he too had no cause to quarrel with the man's assessment of his wife.[2]

What Ratz needed to cheer him was work — a building to design or a scheme to promote — but although he occasionally managed to pull himself together and design a few speculative apartment blocks, the plans came to nothing. He had never been able to cope with idleness and now to enforced leisure was added a new anxiety; he was very nearly broke. Although Alma still considered him well off, Rattenbury knew better. His land holdings in British Columbia had become almost worthless. Before leaving Victoria he had challenged the government's right to levy heavy taxes on unimproved land. He was not a land speculator, he claimed, he had done everything humanly possible to encourage the colonization of his holdings. He had taken his case all the way to the Supreme Court of Canada, but the Court had upheld the government leaving Rattenbury with not only an enormous tax bill but large legal fees as well. Some of his land had been settled but he held the mortgages and as the real value of the land fell below the face value of the mortgage many farmers had stopped making payments. Casting about for some way of increasing his income, he had hit upon the idea of turning his beachside home in Oak Bay into an inn. "St. George and the Dragon," he had decided to call it and hoped to turn at least a small profit from the venture but his plans had been turned aside by the successful lobbying of irate Oak Bay ratepayers who bombarded the local council with their protests, furious at the thought of an absent Rattenbury proposing a scheme that might destroy the character of the neighbourhood he had once so staunchly defended.

During those years they spent in Bournemouth, living in the same house, if not actually together in the accepted sense of the phrase, Alma seems to have been strangely content. Deeply attached to her children she was a devoted mother who often visited Christopher at his boarding school and eagerly anticipated his visits home during the holidays and who spent hours of every day playing with John before tucking him into his little bed in the corner of her room. Although she no longer gave public concerts, music still played an important part in her life. Under the name of "Lozanne" she had turned to composing popular, dreamily sentimental ballads of good enough quality to win the collaboration of well-known lyricists and to be recorded by vocalists such as Frank Titterton, a tenor who set feminine hearts aflutter. Several times a year she visited her music publishers in London where she was still remembered as many as forty years later as a pianist who was so expert that she could make even a poor composition sound good. But perhaps more than her children and her music Alma's happiness depended on Irene Riggs. Irene, the daughter of a local gravedigger, had spent several years in service before coming to work for Alma as a companion help. Some ten years younger than Alma, she had been flattered by the friendship which grew up between them, touched by Alma's generosity and grateful for the opportunities to accompany Alma on her occasional trips away from Bournemouth. They became more like sisters than mistress and maid and Irene was careful never to abuse her position, never to betray a confidence.

It was Irene who sat with Alma through the long nights when, either as a result of the tensions created by her unfulfilled sexual needs or, as it would be hinted later, as the result of taking cocaine, she exploded in bursts of frenetic energy. These bouts usually began after Alma had consumed more than her customary number of pre-dinner cocktails. With John safely asleep upstairs and Ratz lying more unconscious than asleep in his own room, Alma would begin to pace frantically about the house, wringing her hands, a stream of words pouring from her lips, pausing in her ramblings only to refill her glass. Irene would keep vigil with her during the night, comforting and consoling, until, hours later, Alma exhausted and spent, would allow Irene to lead her to bed.

As the years passed Rattenbury became more and more preoccupied with his dwindling finances. Brooding about the dead end into which he had directed his life, he began to talk about committing suicide. Alma would try to cheer him up, try to brighten his dark moods with gay chatter and friendly attentiveness. But one July night in 1934 her patience wore thin.

Ratz in a particularly black mood that day again stated his intention to end his life.

"Why don't you do it then?" she impatiently demanded.[3]

Ratz with a sudden surge of desperate fury struck her in the face blackening her eye and stormed out of the house apparently bent on hurling himself off the East Cliff. Dr. O'Donnell arrived at midnight, gave Alma a quarter grain of morphia to calm her and in response to her tearful pleadings left with Irene to search for Ratz who wandered into the house sometime later, cooled down, sobered up and somewhat abashed at Alma's hysterical reaction to his suicide threats.

Life at Villa Madeira might have gone on, its routine broken by occasional scenes if Alma had not taken a lover. A warm, open-hearted woman she had been deprived of normal sexual relations with her husband for almost six years. For several years she had suffered from smouldering tuberculosis and was prone to the increased sexual desires often afflicting victims of this disease. And yet Alma with an incurious, distracted husband and many opportunities when she travelled to London to visit her music publishers did not seek out a lover. She waited until fate presented a man on her doorstep under the most unlikely circumstances.

On September 23, 1934 the following advertisement appeared in the *Bournemouth Daily Echo* under "Situations Vacant":

> Daily willing lad, 14-18, for housework:
> Scout-trained preferred. Apply between
> 11-12, 8-9, 5 Manor-road. Bournemouth.

One of the applicants was Bert Parsons who remembers being interviewed by a woman with beautiful blonde hair and a gorgeous figure who reminded him of Madeleine Carroll. He was distressed when he learned that driving would be part of his duties, and he had to admit reluctantly that he didn't know how to drive a car.

"We'll soon teach you," Alma smilingly assured him. "The job is yours if you want it."

Bert went to talk it over with his older sister, who advised him not to take the position, concerned that it seemed a bit too good to be true.[4]

There was at least one other applicant and having none of Bert's misgivings he accepted the job. George Percy Stoner was short and stocky with slightly bowed legs. He was far from handsome but he did have an open honest face with a boyishly appealing charm.

The son of George and Olive Stoner, he was an only child born while his father served with the Machine Gun Corps during the war. After the war his father had found it necessary to travel about the country in search of work and rather than take the boy along his parents had settled him with his grandmother who lived in the working class suburb of Ensbury Park some three miles from the fashionable cliffside residences of well-to-do Bournemouth.

As a child Stoner had "something the matter with his legs" and did not learn to walk until after his third birthday. His grandmother found him "an extraordinarily good boy" but even she had to admit that he was "very, very backward."

He grew up shy and solitary with no companions of his own age. "He never wanted to go out on the road and play with other children; he always wanted to stay in and mess about with his old bicycle or making things up to try and get electricity." The few friends he had were "rather younger than himself, and he was a champion boy for those boys, because if they were oppressed at all he would help them out."

A weak child subject to fainting fits, he had very little schooling. His rather admitted that he "did not seem to be very brilliant in mind at lessons" and was vague about the number of years he had spent at school.

For a time he worked with his father as a carpenter's helper and a few weeks before applying for the position at Villa Madeira he had worked for a local motor firm.

He seemed admirably suited for the job Alma offered him and began work right away counting himself fortunate at finding a position which so well suited his meagre talents. His duties were certainly not onerous. Each day he would drive John to and from school, chauffeur Alma and Irene about town on shopping excursions and then spend the rest of the day doing odd jobs around the house, returning to his grandmother's home for the night.

He was shy, not very bright, totally unsophisticated and at seventeen young enough to be Alma's son, but the mere fact of his daily physical presence about the house was too much for Alma and she seduced him. By November he was installed in the spare bedroom and had become Alma's lover-in-residence. And Alma, sentimental and romantic, convinced herself that she was in love with him.

He became part of the household. Seeing him lounging about the house, smoking a relaxed cigarette in the drawing room or companionably playing cards with Ratz, many callers to the house took him for a visiting relative rather than hired help.

Alma did not see the potential for trouble in their relationship. She had been able to control her unusual friendship with Irene whom she could address as "Darling," trust with intimate confidences and still impatiently reprimand if household chores were not performed satisfactorily. Rather than resenting the fact that she was treated as a friend but still expected to perform as a servant, Irene had become a loyal ally. Alma may have thought the same thing was possible with Stoner and for a while it was.

But Stoner like Alma had fallen in love. And by Christmastime the pressures of his dual relationship with Alma were beginning to tell and his grandmother worriedly noticed that on his visits to her home he appeared pale and withdrawn. A boy who no one could ever remember having been seen with a girl, he was now the lover of an experienced woman whose charms had attracted three husbands. Overwhelmed by new sensations, he was preoccupied with Alma and found it difficult to accept the transition from passionate lover in the bedroom to servant in the parlour.

At first he reacted with boyish simplicity. He must impress Alma, make her understand that his feelings were something to be reckoned with. He took to carrying a dagger about with him, a swaggering imitation of the dashing movie heroes of the day. He also tried melodrama, telling Alma that there was something queer about his brain, for which he had to take a mysterious medicine. This had the desired effect and for a time Alma, both interested and alarmed, quizzed him about it, but then deciding he was really quite normal she let the subject drop.

Stoner was driven wild by the possibility that Alma might lose interest in him. He was jealous of her small attentions to Ratz and reacted passionately to any suggestion that he and Alma should sever their relationship. On several occasions Alma, needing reassurance, had worried aloud to Stoner about the difference in their ages and suggested that it might be better if Stoner found a younger woman. The violence he showed on these occasions both dismayed and pleased her. And she took secret pride in this proof of the depth of his feelings for her. But on at least one occasion she went too far.

The argument had begun in the usual way, Alma suggesting that their affair end. Stoner responded angrily and a noisy altercation raged back and forth between their two bedrooms. Then Stoner dropped a bombshell. He was addicted to drugs he told her. He used them regularly and was going to London the next morning to make a purchase. Alma, who by this time seems to have developed a profound aversion to anything she considered dope, had responded with passion and finally the screaming and shouting had risen to such a pitch that Irene had run into Stoner's bedroom and found them there, Stoner with his hands around Alma's throat seemingly about to strangle her.

Alma should have been worried that his love for her could bring out such violence in a normally quiet, shy boy. But she continued to put it down to play acting, to attempts for effect, sure of her ability to placate him and smooth things over. Given to a certain theatricality in her own behaviour, she remained insensitive to Stoner's true feelings and saw no potential for trouble when she suggested the trip to London which would ultimately precipitate two deaths.

In March of 1935 Alma once again found herself overdrawn at the bank. She knew that if she told Ratz he would be annoyed and lecture her about her extravagance. She considered him mean with money, sure that he was still well-off despite his brooding worry about his finances. Rather than asking him often for small amounts, she had adopted the technique of three or four times a year fabricating some excuse to ask for a large sum which would see her through several months. This time using her chronic chest problems as an excuse she told him that she needed £250 for an operation to be performed in London.

With Stoner driving, she set out on the morning of Wednesday, March 20. Arriving at the Royal Palace Hotel in Kensington that afternoon they signed the register as "Mrs. Rattenbury and brother" and were given rooms across the hall from each other. They stayed on in London until Friday evening and for Stoner those three days became a strangely real fantasy. With no cruel reminders that he was simply a chauffeur, Stoner became a gay man about town, squiring Alma to dinner and the theatre. And Alma made sure he looked the part. Soon after their arrival she led him to Harrod's where under her direction Stoner was outfitted from head to toe. It was Alma's nature to be generous but that day she really outdid herself. At the end of their shopping spree Stoner was the proud new owner of three shirts, three ties, one dozen linen and two silk handkerchiefs, three pairs of socks, two pairs of gloves, two suits of underwear, two pairs of shoes, two suits and three pairs of *crêpe de Chine* pyjamas. In the space of one afternoon she had lavished him with gifts totaling £40 14s. 6d. — an amount that Stoner could not have matched had he worked for nine months and saved every penny he earned.

In London away from Irene and Ratz and Villa Madeira it was easy for them to fool themselves, to pretend they were quite different people in quite different circumstances. Their self-delusion was so great that Alma could quite seriously appear grateful and touched when Stoner presented her with a diamond ring which she had given him the money to buy.

For Alma their sojourn in London was no more than a pleasant and delightful interlude and she could quite easily put the charade behind her when they returned to Bournemouth expecting Stoner to do the same.

They returned to Villa Madeira late Friday night and as usual by this time of day Ratz was feeling extremely mellow, so mellow in fact that he didn't think to inquire about her operation.

Saturday was a restful routine day, Stoner driving Alma and John to watch a cricket match in which Christopher was playing and it seemed as if Stoner might be able to slide easily back into his role as hired help.

But Sunday found Ratz particularly depressed, sunk in what Alma called the blues. Hoping to cheer him up she coaxed him to accompany her and John on an outing to visit their puppies being boarded at a nearby kennel and a resentful Stoner was required to drive while Rattenbury took his place beside his wife.

Sunday was Irene's half day and after she left for the afternoon it was Stoner's job to serve afternoon tea to Alma and Ratz. As usual they took their tea in Alma's bedroom sitting by the French doors which opened onto the tiny balcony overlooking the garden.

Ratz was morbid and gloomy. Money was particularly tight and he was having difficulty financing a block of flats which he had designed and hoped to build. And to make matters worse he had spent the weekend reading a singularly depressing book. It was called *Stay of Execution* and in it Ratz had found Stephen Clarke, a character with whom he could immediately identify.

Stephen is bent on suicide. He has thought it all out coldly and logically. At one time a man of driving ambition and lusty appetites, now, at forty-five he feels worn out and useless, filled with revulsion at the prospects of old age. He is sitting in his Chelsea flat, a revolver in his mouth, his hand on the trigger, when he is interrupted by the arrival of a friend who persuades him to give life another chance, to put off his suicide for a month and think things over. Stephen grudgingly agrees. During his thirty day reprieve he meets Cecily, a young girl who is fascinated by his world weariness and fancies herself in love with him.

Ratz had read on wallowing in depression and despair along with Stephen until he came to page 296. The sharp stab of recognition was so intense that he marked the page and rather pointedly read it to Alma at tea that Sunday afternoon.

Cecily has declared her love for Stephen and begged him to marry her and Stephen tries to convince her that it won't work.

"What sort of person do you think would stand you?" she asked.

"Oh — some elderly frump, who couldn't get anything else. A staid motherly soul, who'd treat me like a child . . ."

"You don't think marriages between young girls and — and men a good deal older than themselves are possible?"

"They're possible all right. For some reason elderly men have a peculiar attraction for young girls. That may be due, nowadays, to the quality of young men of the day; but I don't think it is. It's always been so. And — the old men like to marry young girls; and after a bit it's hell for both."

"Why?"

"Because it's naturally annoying to a young girl to see her husband mouldering while she still feels frisky. To see the bare patch on the back of his head growing bigger and shinier. To have the shock, one day, of coming across most of his teeth grinning at her out of a glass of water. And there are other things, besides."

"What things?"

"Well — if you will have me enter into physiological details — a woman, let's put it, always wants more than a man. And when a man's a good deal older, she wants a good deal more than him. A good deal more than he can give her. It takes all his time for a young man to keep pace with a young girl. And an old man hasn't a chance of doing it. And then — she usually goes somewhere else to make up the deficiency."[5]

Alma was stunned. She had decided long ago that Rattenbury either didn't know or didn't care about her affair with Stoner. He was becoming quite deaf and he consumed enough whisky to guarantee that he slept soundly and in addition his room was on the ground floor. There was a chance that he had simply never heard what was going on upstairs. But if he had known, he had never given any indication that he cared, even when Alma some months before in an attempt to ease her conscience had alluded to her relationship with Stoner by telling Ratz that she intended to live her own life.

Now she knew that at the very least he suspected that Stoner had become her lover and that he not only cared, but cared very deeply. Just how Alma reacted to this news is unknown. But it is certain that the bedroom door usually held ajar was closed that afternoon and that Stoner who had heard snatches of the conversation was convinced that Alma had made love to her husband. Later Stoner's belief that Ratz and Alma had had intercourse would be explained as an hallucination induced by cocaine and Alma herself would recoil from the very suggestion that she might have performed as a wife that afternoon. But it does seem likely that she and Rattenbury had enjoyed some form of marital intimacy. Rattenbury might often talk of suicide but he had never taken any deliberate steps to end his life. Alma may not have been the brightest woman in England but she certainly had enough sense to realize that rather than establishing a further reason for suicide he had been asking for reassurance, begging to be shown that she still considered him a man. Alma did not want Rattenbury to die, hated to see him so depressed but, at the same time, she knew that she would never be able to bring herself to give up Stoner. Faced with this crisis, the most natural thing for her to have done was to quietly close the bedroom door and then kiss and caress her husband, perhaps even arousing some of his long lost passion. Whatever she did or said she appeared downstairs later that afternoon cheerful and unruffled, sure that she had nothing to fear from the revelations Ratz had made that quiet Sunday afternoon. She had managed to pull him out of his despondency and had encouraged him to take a practical approach to his business woes. Why not visit Mr. Jenks, she had said. Jenks, a business acquaintance of Rattenbury's, might be persuaded to provide the capital to get his apartment building scheme off the ground. He lived in a large manor house surrounded by pleasant grounds near Bridport, a quiet little town some two hours' drive from Bournemouth best known as the Port Brede of Hardy's novels. There was no need to travel back and forth in one day, Alma coaxed, they could combine business with pleasure and stay overnight at the manor. Rattenbury agreed and seems to have been somewhat cheered by the prospects of their visit's success.

After tea, with Ratz comfortably ensconced in his armchair, a drink in his hand, Alma called Jenks on the phone and gaily made arrangements for their visit the following day. Stoner overheard the conversation. As soon as she replaced the receiver he grabbed her, thrust what she took to be a revolver in her face and in a rage vowed he would kill her if she went to Bridport. He either knew or guessed that their secret was out and he was convinced that Alma in order to placate Ratz had made love to him that afternoon. He was terrified that he might soon be told by Rattenbury to leave the house. The trip to Bridport, where he was sure that Ratz and Alma would share a room, he saw as the beginning of a new relationship between Alma and her husband.

Alma managed to keep her head. He was a fool, she told him, of course she had not slept with Ratz and there would be no need for them to share a bedroom in such a large house as Mr. Jenks'. Gradually Stoner calmed down and after Alma agreed to two childishly simple promises, that she would never again close the bedroom door when she was alone with Ratz and that if they did go to Bridport she would not expect Stoner to drive, he appeared to have relented and Alma once again felt that she was in control of the situation.

Stoner left with the car to visit his grandmother, and Alma, sure that she had soothed his anger and anxiety, relaxed playing cards with Ratz until 9:30 when she went upstairs to pack.

Irene returned to Villa Madeira some 45 minutes later and as it seemed the rest of the household had retired she went directly to her room, but then feeling hungry, she decided to go back downstairs to the kitchen to make herself something to eat. As she walked along the lower hall she heard the sound of unusually heavy breathing and she stopped, a strange sense of unease which she would later describe as a premonition that something was wrong creeping over her. She listened outside Ratz' bedroom and then carefully opening the door, she reached inside, turned on the light and peered into the room. The bed had not been disturbed. She concluded that he had fallen asleep in the drawing room chair and slumped into an awkward position was beginning to snore. Although she felt relieved the experience had unnerved her and driven the thought of food from her head and she returned to her room without going to the kitchen. A few minutes later as she walked along the landing to the bathroom, she found Stoner dressed in pyjamas, leaning over the railing looking down into the hall below.

"What's the matter?" she asked and Stoner replied, "Nothing, I was looking to see if the lights were out."

Moments after she had returned to her room she was joined by Alma who sat on her bed and chatted happily about the planned excursion to Bridport. She had had a bit of a rumpus with Stoner, she said, but now it had blown over. She wasn't sure whether Stoner would be driving them to Bridport, but she was convinced that she would be able to fix it all right.

After Alma's visit Irene settled herself into bed and was on the edge of sleep when she heard the sound of someone rushing down the stairs followed minutes later by Alma screaming hysterically "Irene! Irene!"

Alma had been in bed with Stoner when their whispered conversation had been interrupted by a loud groan from below, a groan that had brought her leaping out of bed and flying barefoot down the stairs. She had found Ratz slumped in his chair and at first she thought he was asleep, but then she saw that his right eye was purple and swollen and his hair was matted with blood. There was blood on the chair, blood in a pool on the carpet. She had snatched up Ratz' unfinished whisky, gulped it down, retched, and fought to keep down a second mouthful. Somewhat steadied she had begun her feeble attempts to make Ratz all right. Picking up his false teeth which had flown out with the force of the blow, she had tried to get them back in his mouth thinking that if only he had his teeth he would be able to talk to her and tell her what had happened. And then suddenly appalled by her actions she had backed away from the chair and screamed for Irene.

She told Irene to phone for the doctor and then together they called for Stoner and between the three of them managed to carry Ratz to his bed. Stoner was dispatched to collect the doctor and while Irene tried to get Ratz undressed, Alma, another drink in her hand hovered over her husband moaning, "Oh poor Ratz. What has happened?"

Dr. O'Donnell arrived at the house just before midnight and found Ratz unconscious, his head bathed in blood, his breathing laboured and his pulse slow and irregular. Ratz' condition was serious and realizing he needed help, O'Donnell telephoned for a local surgeon, Mr. Rooke, and while he waited for Rooke to arrive he turned his attention to Alma who was already in his opinion inclined to be intoxicated. Thinking that perhaps Ratz had fallen and hit his head on the piano or some other heavy piece of furniture, he asked Alma what had happened, but she evaded his question.

"Look at him, look at the blood," she wailed. "Somebody has finished him."

Alma, still relatively sober, hoped that she could fix the blame on an unknown intruder, a mysterious somebody. But as O'Donnell questioned her further a new possibility struck her. Perhaps she could convince the doctor that Rattenbury had taken his own life. He had been reading a book about suicide, she said, here it was on the piano. She thrust the book at O'Donnell urging him to read it, but the doctor impatiently told her to put it away and returned to his patient.

Mr. Rooke arrived shortly after midnight and almost immediately decided to remove Rattenbury to a nursing home. Not only was he badly wounded, but a proper examination was made impossible by Alma who was making a nuisance of herself by her stumbling and clumsy attempts to minister to her husband.

"If you want to kill him you are going the right way to do it," Rooke reprimanded her. "Do let me near him and attend to him."

An ambulance carried Ratz to the Strathallen Nursing Home and there Rooke, after making a careful examination, concluded that his injuries had not been accidental but were the result of three separate blows to the head delivered by a blunt instrument. He called the police.

Constable Bagwell arrived at Villa Madeira at about 2:00 o'clock that morning. He questioned Alma about her husband's injuries and she made the first of a series of statements, each recorded by the police, which would lead her to the Old Bailey..

"At about 9 p.m. I was playing cards with my husband in the drawing room and I went to bed," she told Bagwell. "At 10:30 I heard a yell. I came downstairs and went into the drawing room and saw my husband sitting in the chair. I then sent for Dr. O'Donnell. He was then taken away." Alma was still clinging to the hope that she could place the blame on a stranger to the household.

Shortly afterwards a second policeman arrived at the house. Inspector Mills found Alma very excited and although it was apparent to him that she had been drinking he too questioned her about her husband's injuries. She repeated the same statement she had made to Bagwell only this time it had not been a yell but the sound of someone groaning that had brought her downstairs.

154

Mills pointed to the French doors opening off the drawing room into the garden. "Were these windows open when you came down?" he asked.

Without pausing to think Alma answered, "No, it was shut and locked." And then in one of her last moments of clarity she realized her mistake. If she had said, yes they were standing open, she might still have had a chance of convincing the police that a burglar had come in by these doors, awakened Rattenbury and panicked by discovery had delivered the blows to silence him and then fled before Alma entered the room. Now she realized that the police would certainly suspect someone in the house and as the minutes passed a new thought lodged itself in her whirling brain. She saw herself as the only alternative to Stoner. She must accept the blame.

Inspector Mills had gone to the nursing home leaving Bagwell behind at Villa Madeira, when fortified by several more whiskies, Alma approached the constable and said, according to Bagwell's later testimony, "I know who done it." Bagwell cautioned her and Alma continued, "I did it with a mallet." Why, Bagwell asked. "Ratz has lived too long." Where was the mallet, Bagwell wanted to know and Alma answered, "It is hidden." There came a dim realization of the enormity of the crime to which she was confessing and Alma's resolve weakened. "No, my lover did it," she blurted out and then recoiling from this accusation she tried to buy the constable's silence. "I would like to give you £10," she declared, but then perhaps seeing from Bagwell's reaction that that approach wouldn't work she gave up saying, "No, I won't bribe you."

The next hour was a difficult one for Bagwell. Alma was becoming very drunk. Perhaps to console herself she had put a recording of one of her songs on the record player and as the sentimental strains of "Dark Haired Marie" filled the house a new idea had occurred to her.

> Are you waiting in your garden
> By the deep wide azure sea?
> Are you waiting for your loveship,
> Dark haired Marie?
>
> I shall come to claim you someday,
> In my arms at last you'll be,
> I shall kiss your lips and love you,
> Dark haired Marie[6]

. . . the tenor sang and Alma began to think of romance. In the past her charms applied at the right time had always smoothed things over for her. She need only win Bagwell over and everything would be all right again. She began to relentlessly pursue the constable about the house, fawning over him, trying to kiss him. And Bagwell finding it impossible to discourage her finally stepped outside. Determined to follow him, Alma rushed to the door and would have trailed him into the garden if Irene had not caught hold of her, forced her into a chair and then sat on top of her in a desperate attempt to calm her down. Luckily for Bagwell he encountered a policeman walking his beat and in the company of this constable he felt it was safe to re-enter the house.

At 3:30 a.m. Inspector Mills returned to Villa Madeira and informing Alma that her husband was in critical condition, he cautioned her, warning her that anything she said would be taken down and used as evidence. Alma then made a rambling, disjointed statement in which she accepted full blame for the attack. "I did it," she said. "He gave me the book. He has lived too long. He said, 'Dear, dear.' I will tell you in the morning where the mallet is. Have you told the Coroner yet? I shall make a better job of it next time. Irene does not know. I made a proper muddle of it. I thought I was strong enough."

Some ten minutes later Dr. O'Donnell returned to the house accompanied by Stoner who had spent the last few hours peacefully asleep in the car outside the nursing home waiting for the doctor. O'Donnell was astounded at the scene that greeted him at Villa Madeira. Lights were blazing from every room in the house. Two other constables had joined Mills and Bagwell and Alma was on her feet staggering from one to the other, clinging to them, trying to wrap her arms around them, talking excitedly over the din of the record player. O'Donnell took her upstairs to her room and gave her a half grain of morphia, hoping to quieten her.

As morphia joined the alcohol in her spinning head, Alma suddenly saw a fourth alternative. Ratz had been wounded not by a burglar, not by Stoner and not by herself, but by someone who she knew detested her and who remained incurably bitter about Ratz' second marriage — his eldest son. This sudden inspiration drove Alma from her room and down the stairs to Inspector Mills.

"I know who did it — his son," she said to the Inspector.

"How old is he?" Mills asked thinking the only Rattenbury son was six years old tucked in bed upstairs.

"Thirty-two," Alma answered and then for a moment reason returned and seeing it was no use she added, "but he is not here."

Mills and O'Donnell half carried Alma back to her room and she was left to sleep, but not for long.

At 4:30 Detective Inspector Carter arrived at Villa Madeira and after making an inspection of the house and grounds he took up a position in Alma's room. He was there when she awakened from drugged sleep at six o'clock. He ordered coffee for her and while she bathed under the supervision of a police matron, he questioned Stoner. He had gone to bed just after eight o'clock the night before, Stoner said. He had been aroused at 10:30 by Alma's shouting for him to come down. Alma had been screaming and crying. He had asked her "How did this happen?" and Alma had answered that she didn't know. He had never seen a mallet on the premises before and he had heard no sounds of a quarrel before he had been called.

Satisfied with Stoner's version of the events of that night Carter returned to Alma's bedroom. She was dressed and appeared to be rational and able to understand him. Shortly after eight o'clock he charged her with the wounding of her husband. "At about 9 p.m. I was playing cards with my husband," Alma said, "when he dared me to kill him as he wanted to die. I picked up the mallet. He then said, 'You have not guts enough to do it.' I then hit him with the mallet. I hid the mallet outside the house. I would have shot him if I had a gun." Written down by Carter and read and signed by Alma, it was the most damaging statement she had made that night.

Alma was taken to the Bournemouth Police Station where the charge against her was repeated and so there could be no mistake she answered the charge with the words, "That is right. I did it deliberately and would do it again." And it seemed that she had sealed her fate.

In the days following Alma's arrest an edgy truce existed between Irene and Stoner both of whom remained in residence at Villa Madeira. On Tuesday they were together in Rattenbury's car, perhaps going to collect Irene's mother who had agreed to move in with her for the time being. Stoner chose a route which led past his grandmother's house, pointed it out to her and, with the braggadocio of a small boy who has escaped punishment for some minor misde-

157

meanor, proudly informed her that that was where he had borrowed the mallet.

Irene had no reason to doubt him. She had been convinced that Alma could never have delivered the blows to her husband's head. But to be absolutely sure that she was not misinterpreting an empty boast for an admission of guilt, she asked him, "Won't your fingerprints be on the mallet?"

"No," Stoner replied. "I wore gloves."

Irene was in a terrible quandary. Alma was in prison charged with wounding her husband but so far her relationship with Stoner had remained a secret, a secret which Alma had trusted Irene to keep. If the police were to direct their attention to Stoner, all the details of Alma's adultery would become public. Until she saw Alma, Irene decided, she must keep her conversation with Stoner to herself.

The following day, Wednesday, March 27, was Irene's usual evening off. Although not a Catholic, she had visited a priest not so much to ask advice but to confide in someone on whose silence she could rely. When she returned to Villa Madeira, her mother met her at the door and told her that Stoner was very drunk. He had been brought back to the house by a taxi driver who had found him wandering up and down the road and now he wanted to speak to Irene. Stoner, who Irene found to be in a very peculiar state, told her that the following morning he was going to travel to London to visit Alma. He was determined, he said, to give himself up.

Stoner had received a letter from Alma that day and perhaps for the first time understood the seriousness of her situation. In the letter sent from Holloway Prison Alma had written.

I am trying to have the lawyer's letter I received to-day sent to you, darling, so that you can make arrangements to come up with him, or make arrangements yourself with the governor. But I must see you darling. Please write to me. This is the third letter I have written. Hope you receive this. I hardly know how to write now. Let me know how Ratz is getting along. No more now. God bless you. My love be with you always.

Lozanne

Have you talked with Dr. O'Donnell about how Ratz is? Goodness there is so much I want to know. Please tell Irene to give you a few bobbing pins for my hair. I think they would be allowed.

The next morning Stoner got up early and caught the train to London. While he was gone Dr. O'Donnell arrived at the house. Rattenbury had died that morning without regaining consciousness, he told Irene. Alma would now be charged with murder.

Irene phoned the police and when Stoner stepped off the train from London, Detective Inspector Carter was waiting for him. Charged with the murder of Francis Mawson Rattenbury, Stoner responded simply, "I understand."

12

The Old Bailey

On May 27, 1935 Alma and Stoner were brought to trial in the Old Bailey. The case against them seemed one of classic simplicity. To the Crown the motive for murder was clear: "The relationship between Mrs. Rattenbury and Stoner had ceased to be that of the wife of the employer and the man employed but had become an adulterous intercourse and Mr. Rattenbury stood in the way of their indulgence of this guilty passion."[1]

Alma had first become the object of police suspicions as the result of the statements she had made during the hours after the discovery of Rattenbury's injuries and now, although she had repudiated her confessions saying that she had been drunk and drugged and that she hadn't known what she was saying, her own words recorded by the police remained the strongest evidence against her.

Stoner's situation was quite different. The Crown would produce expert testimony which would prove that the murder weapon had been a heavy wooden mallet belonging to Stoner's grandmother and witnesses would testify that Stoner had borrowed the mallet on the evening of the attack. And Stoner, too, had confessed to the crime. But unlike Alma, he had confessed not to wounding but to murder. The day after Rattenbury's death Stoner had been sitting with Detective Constable Gates in a detention room waiting for his appearance in police court when he had turned conversationally to Gates. "You know Mrs. Rattenbury, don't you?" he asked. Gates had answered that he did and Stoner had continued, "Do you know Mrs. Rattenbury had nothing to do with this?" Gates cautioned him and Stoner had stated simply and matter-of-factly, "When I did the job, I believed he was asleep. I hit him and then came upstairs and told Mrs. Rattenbury. She rushed down then. You see, I watched through the French windows and saw her kiss him goodnight, then leave the room. I waited and crept in through the French window which was unlocked. I think he must have been asleep when I hit him, still it ain't much use saying anything. I don't suppose they will let her out yet. You know there should be a doctor with her when they tell her I am arrested, because she will go out of her mind."

Another telling piece of evidence against Stoner was a letter Alma had written to Irene from Holloway Prison on April 18th.

Darling,

Was glad to see you looking so nice, also your M. and F. I wrote you dozens of letters in my mind last night, and have nothing but an empty box on top this morning. Will you hand to Mrs Greig [wardress] to give me before I go to Court a pair of tweezers, Yvettes' rouge, things to do my nails with, and liquid polish, light colour. I think the perfume in small bottles will last longer, also that gray or fawn pair of slippers (same colour you were wearing), in case the brown suede are not O.K. and I can best in that case change over. The brown shoes with laces would be best. You might tell Mrs Greig how much I appreciate her kindness, which has been most considerate. Oh darling, I hardly know how to write. My mind is frozen. When Manning [her Bournemouth solicitor] advised me to write about nothing but clothes &c., it almost made one smile. I can hardly concentrate on even them. I think my macintosh would help. Also that red woolen dress the skirt needs a hook on or something, and if I haven't a red belt; you might get a wide one. Oh Lord, and tomorrow Good Friday and I dare not think of the children. I even pretend I haven't any here. If one thought for five minutes they'd go mad. I saw nothing in the papers yesterday except what was cut out; I seem to see nothing but the missing parts. Darling, will one ever be happy again? Friday will be like Sunday here. Of all the days in the week Sunday is the worst. I have to control my mind like the devil to not think of little John. Yes, take him out on Sundays, darling. C. [probably her other son Christopher] was awfully pleased to hear from you. I cannot understand my M. not doing anything, can you? Messages of love are not much use to me now, when I wanted her help with Long &c. However, if I feel awfully sad, being separated in such a ghastly way from everything one loves, S's feelings must take some weighing up, but he'll be the same and not allow himself to think. Should think his remorse at what he's brought down on my head, the children's &c. — smashed lives — would drive him a raving lunatic — a frightful responsibility to hold in one persons hands. God deliver me from such a hellish responsibility. I couldn't have courage to bear that pain; my own is enough in a hundred lifetimes as it is. Two times have found my feelings very hard and bitter — Oh, my God, appallingly so — but have managed to drown these feelings and get one's heart soft again. Darling, God bless you, bless us all and get us out of this nightmare. My love to your M. and F. My love be with you always.

Lozanne

There was little doubt in anyone's mind that the "S" referred to by Alma in her letter was Stoner and the implication was clear, Alma held him responsible for the attack on Rattenbury.

"How do you plead?" Alma was asked and standing in the dock she answered softly, almost inaudibly, "Not guilty." Her confessions, her defence would claim, had been hysterical, irrational ramblings produced by a mind sodden with whisky and confused by morphia.

Although Stoner did not deny the veracity of the statement he had made to Constable Gates, he too answered, "Not guilty," to the charge. He was addicted to cocaine, he would claim. He had been under its influence at the time he had attacked Rattenbury and the drug had rendered him incapable of forming the intent to kill. He was suffering from a disease of the mind and was guilty, but insane.

In England, as in Victoria, interest in the case was intense. Some twelve hours before the trial was due to commence a line of people had begun to form along the pavement outside the entrance to the Old Bailey. The next morning late-comers had gladly parted with a few pounds in exchange for a place in the queue and the chance of being admitted to the spectators' gallery. Most of the curiosity was directed toward Alma and for the press and the public the highlight of the trial came on the third day when Alma was called to the stand to testify in her own defence.

"She walked slowly across the well of the court followed by a wardress," observed a *Daily Mirror* reporter, "and took the oath in a low voice." Mr. T. J. O'Connor, K.C., Alma's counsel, asked her to "help us all by speaking up" and Alma answered his questions clearly and with quite remarkable composure. O'Connor gently led her through the details of her personal history; she had been married to Rattenbury for seven or eight years; she had been married twice before, her first husband had been killed in the war and she had divorced her second; from her second marriage she had a thirteen-year-old son Christopher who was away at school and she had another son who would be six and a half in June, a child of her marriage to Rattenbury.

"Since the birth of that child, did you and Mr. Rattenbury live together as man and wife?" O'Connor asked.

"No."

"Did you occupy separate rooms?"

"Yes."

"On what terms were you with your husband?"

"Quite friendly."

"No marital intimacy, but you were friendly?"

"Absolutely."

"Was your married life happy?"

"Like that." Alma gestured with her hands, implying that it was no better and no worse than many other marriages.

"We were told about a quarrel. Were quarrels between you and he frequent or not?"

"Not very frequent."

"Were they severe when they occurred, or were they just trifling quarrels?"

"It all depended on whether Mr. Rattenbury got into a temper or not," Alma said. "Sometimes he did." Then O'Connor led her through an account of the night in July when Rattenbury had blackened her eye. "He was queer, morbid," Alma said, "and there was the usual talk of committing suicide, so I asked him, seeing that he was always frightening me that he was going to commit suicide, why did he not do it for a change?" Rattenbury had lost his temper and hit her, Alma said.

The prosecution alleged that Alma had obtained money from her husband for the sole purpose of financing the "orgy" at the Royal Palace Hotel, while Alma claimed that she had needed the money to balance her overdrawn account and that having concocted a story she and Stoner had had to travel to London, her absence being necessary to support her story that she was having an operation.

"What were the relations between you and your husband as regards money?" O'Connor asked her. "Was he free with money?"

"Very close — well, not very generous."

"Used you to have to say things of which you are ashamed in order to get money from him?"

"All my married life, yes."

"Tell him lies?"

"Yes; it saved rows." O'Connor would return to this subject later. Now he began to quiz Alma about her relations with Stoner.

Stoner had been employed as a chauffeur in September of 1934,

Alma testified. She had become his mistress two months later, before he had come to live at Villa Madeira.

"Just taking it quite generally, from that time until your husband's death did relations take place between you and Stoner regularly?"

"Yes."

"In his room or yours, or in both?"

"Yes."

"One or the other. What attitude did your husband take towards this, if he knew it?"

"None whatsoever."

"Did he know of it?"

"He must have known because he told me to live my own life quite a few years ago."

"As I understand it, there was no occasion on which you told him about Stoner, but your husband knew about it."

"No, I told him that I had taken him at his word and was living my own life."

"Oh, you told him that did you? Can you tell me when that was?"

"No, I would say it was somewhere round about Christmas that I told him." Alma was not being completely honest. She was telling the truth when she stated that she was reasonably sure that Ratz had known about her affair with Stoner, but she had much more recent evidence that this was the case. She could not have heard Ratz reading that particular passage from *Stay of Execution* without being convinced that he knew about her relations with Stoner. But she could not let the jury know that this revelation had been so recent for had they known that Rattenbury had confronted Alma with her infidelity on the afternoon of the attack, the jury would certainly have interpreted it as a motive for murder.

O'Connor turned his attention to the Friday night before the murder, the night Alma and Stoner had returned from London.

Had her husband asked her anything about the operation she was supposed to have had in London, O'Connor wondered.

"No," Alma said, "he was always jolly late at night," and O'Connor established that jolly was a euphemism Alma often used for drunk.

The weekend had been unremarkable, the same as many previous weekends, except that Ratz was particularly depressed.

"Did you say anything to try and cheer him up?" O'Connor asked.

"Yes, I was very nice to him to try and make the 'blues' go. He had the 'blues'." She had persuaded him to come for a drive on Sunday but that hadn't improved his mood and he had remained very depressed. They had had tea together in her room, Alma testified, Stoner had served them, the usual practice when Irene was out. O'Connor questioned her about the door to her room and Alma said she thought that for at least some of the time the door had been closed.

"The normal thing was the door to your room should not have been closed?" O'Connor asked.

"Exactly," Alma said.

O'Connor returned to her husband's mood. He had been reading a book, Alma said, about a person who committed suicide. He said he admired a person who finished himself off before he became old and doddering. He was obviously depressed and gloomy, O'Connor observed. "Now what did you do to cheer him up?" Alma replied that she had suggested many things, among them a trip to London, finally getting him to agree to a trip to Bridport to visit a business friend, Mr. Jenks.

She had telephoned Jenks sometime between 6:30 and 7:00 and while she was telephoning Stoner had come into the room. He had what looked like a revolver in his hand. Stoner was very angry, Alma said. "He said he would kill me if I went to Bridport."

Rattenbury had been in the next room. "Could you go on talking without being overheard by your husband?" O'Connor wondered.

"Yes, practically. One could have, because Mr. Rattenbury did not really take very much notice."

Stoner had accused her of having relations with her husband behind the closed bedroom door, Alma said. She had assured him that she had not. "He was very annoyed at my going to Bridport. We had quite an unpleasant time about it, but afterwards I thought it was all right."

"Did he say why he did not want you to go to Bridport with Mr. Rattenbury?" O'Connor asked.

"He was very jealous of Mr. Rattenbury — unnecessarily so."

Stoner thought, Alma said, that she and her husband would have to share a bedroom at Mr. Jenks' home. She assured him that they would not and she felt that he had believed her and calmed down.

After this scene with Stoner she had gone into the drawing room and chatted with Ratz. "I talked about how nice it was we were going to Bridport the next day, and I still tried to make him 'jolly', you know, and drive away the 'blues'."

She had put John to bed sometime between 7:30 and 7:45, Alma said. Then she had played cards and talked to Ratz who was quite "jolly" by then. At 9:30 she had let the dog, Dinah, out by the French doors and gone upstairs to prepare for bed. She had gone along the upstairs hall to the bathroom and when she returned to her bedroom some five minutes later Dinah was there.

She had closed her bedroom door, she said, and begun to make preparations for the trip. Shortly after ten o'clock she had visited Irene to tell her about the plans for the next day. Then she had returned to her room and sometime later, she really had no idea how much time had elapsed, Stoner whom she had been expecting had come into her room in his pyjamas and got into bed with her.

She noticed that he was a little queer.

"How long had he been in bed before you noticed what you are just going to describe?"

"Almost right away."

"What was it? Tell your own story Mrs. Rattenbury. I do not want to lead you at all on this."

"Well, he seemed agitated, and I said, 'What is the matter, darling?' and he said he was in trouble, and could not tell me what it was, and I said, 'Oh, you must tell me,' and we went back and forth like that for two or three minutes, and he said no, that I could not bear it. I thought he was in trouble outside, you know — his mother or like that — and then I said I was strong enough to bear anything and he told me that I was not going to Bridport the next day as he had hurt Ratz. It did not penetrate my head what he did say to me at all until I heard Ratz groan, and then my brain became alive and I jumped out of bed."

"Did Stoner say anything about how he had done it?" O'Connor asked.

"He said he had hit him over the head with a mallet."

"Anything more about the mallet?"

"That he had hidden it outside."

She had rushed down to the drawing room, Alma said, and found Ratz sitting in his chair. "I tried to rub his hands; they were cold. I tried to take his pulse, and I shook him to try and make him speak."

"Did you call for help?"

"Not right away. I tried to speak to him, and then I saw this blood, and I went round the table and I trod on his false teeth, and that made me hysterical, and I yelled — I cannot remember, only vaguely. I took a drink of whisky to stop myself being sick."

"Was that the only drink of whisky you had?"

"No, I took one drink of whisky neat, and I was sick, and then I remember pouring out another one. I cannot remember drinking the next one; I tried to become insensible, to block out the picture." And according to Alma's version of events she had been successful for she claimed to remember nothing more about what had taken place that night.

"Mrs. Rattenbury," O'Connor asked, "did you yourself murder your husband?"

"Oh, no."

"Did you take any part whatsoever in planning it?"

"No."

"Did you know a thing about it till Stoner spoke to you in your bed?"

"I would have prevented it if I had known half — a quarter of a minute before, naturally."

O'Connor was finished for the time being and he turned the questioning over to Mr. J. D. Casswell, Stoner's counsel. It was not necessary for Stoner's defence for Casswell to shift the blame to Alma and before he began to question her he assured her that he was not suggesting that she had had anything to do with the attack nor was he implying that she had incited Stoner or that she had had any advance knowledge of Stoner's intentions. What he was going to suggest, and this he did not tell Alma, was that Stoner was a seduced innocent, the victim of the practiced charms of an older woman, who had used the lad unfairly to relieve her loneliness and boredom.

He asked her about her relationship with Stoner. Had she suggested their living together, he wanted to know. No, Alma replied, she thought that the idea had been mutual. Casswell found this hard to believe.

"Mutual? Because you see, he was in a position of a servant was he not?"

"Yes."

"And quite a young man?"

167

"Yes," Alma replied and the jury must have thought it unlikely that Stoner would have suggested the liaison without a good deal of encouragement.

"Did you think it might have had a deleterious effect on him?"

"No," Alma answered, "I would never have started it if I had."

Had she told Stoner that she and her husband were not living together as man and wife, Casswell asked and Alma responded, "It was obvious to anyone living there; they would know it."

"He would know it?"

"Naturally."

"Did you tell him you were looking for sympathy?" Casswell asked.

"No, most decidedly not," Alma said firmly.

"You were looking for that from someone?"

"No, I certainly was not." Casswell was painting an unattractive picture of her and Alma answered his questions indignantly.

Casswell turned to the subject of drugs, asking Alma if she herself had ever taken drugs. "No, absolutely not," Alma replied and in this she may have been less than truthful, but Casswell unaware of the dark rumours of her drug-taking that circulated in Victoria, lacked the information which might have allowed him to pin her down with a more specific question.

"Are you quite sure of that?" he pressed.

"Absolutely."

"From time to time we have heard that you used to get very excited at times and then get drowsy afterwards?" Casswell said implying that this sounded like the results of drug taking to him.

But Alma had a ready answer, "Well all my life with Mr. Rattenbury was so what we call montonous that at times I used to take too many cocktails to liven up one's spirits — take them to excess, say, or wine." Stoner did not drink with her, she said, in fact he was upset about her drinking and she stopped taking cocktails after he came. Casswell hardly wanted to discover that Stoner had been a good influence on Alma, he was after all attempting to show that she had been a bad influence on him. He quickly changed the subject, quizzing her about Stoner's claim that he was addicted to drugs.

She had gone to see Dr. O'Donnell in February, Alma said, because she had become very alarmed about Stoner's violent behaviour. Stoner had said he had to go to London that morning to get his drug. "I begged him not to go, but he had to go, and when

Rattenbury's sketch of the impressive transportation complex and towering château style hotel which the Grand Trunk Pacific planned to build in Prince Rupert. PABC

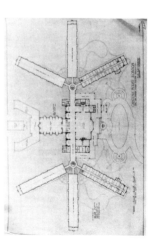

As designed by Rattenbury the G.T.P.'s hotel at Mount Robson would epitomize Edwardian elegance. PABC

Rattenbury c. 1913, Reeve of Oak Bay.   MUNICIPALITY OF OAK BAY

Alma Victoria Clarke Dolling Pakenham taken at about the time she first met Ratz.

Mrs. Florence Eleanor Rattenbury

Francis Mawson Rattenbury c. 1924. He was barely recognizable as the man who had served as Reeve of Oak Bay. VCA

Alma and Ratz with John on the beach at Bournemouth. DAILY COLONIST, APRIL 25, 1935

"Villa Madeira," 5 Manor Road, Bournemouth. An unlikely setting for murder. D. REKSTEN

George Percy Stoner. He was eighteen, shy,
not very bright and totally unsophisticated.

Marked only by a stunted hydrangea, Rattenbury's grave at
Wimbourne Road Cemetery, Bournemouth. D. REKSTEN

he went I was so upset — it was dreadful — I telephoned to Dr. O'Donnell to explain everything to him and said could he help this boy."

"Now had you any doubt that that boy at that time had such a craving that he went to London and nothing you said would stop him?" Casswell asked, sure that Alma's answer would support Stoner's defence. But she replied, "To be perfectly candid, I was not certain then, and I am not certain now. I cannot answer that and say yes or no. I do not know." The doctor had reported back to her that Stoner claimed to be addicted to cocaine. "Did you do anything more about it?" Casswell asked her.

"No," Alma said, "because Stoner was better from then onwards, and he said he could not get the drug, and I did not want to agitate him in case he was longing for it, we just went on smoothly, and I never brought the subject up again. He said he had stopped it from then onwards, and, well, everything was all right. I thought he had."

Justice Humphreys was curious about something, something that had not yet been answered to his satisfaction. "Did you know his age when he came to you?" he inquired from the bench and Alma replied that she had thought he was older. Stoner had told her that he was twenty-two. When had she learned that his real age was eighteen, the judge asked. On his birthday, Alma said, on November 19. And Casswell missed an important point in Stoner's defence for Alma was not being entirely honest. She had earlier testified that their affair had begun on the 22nd of November so she had known Stoner's true age when their sexual relationship began.

When Mr. R. P. Croom-Johnson, K.C., began the prosecution's cross-examination he knew that Alma's testimony had damaged the Crown's case against her. True, Alma had admitted that on many occasions she had lied to her husband, that on occasion she drank too much and that she had welcomed a sexual relationship with a boy young enough to be her son. But Croom-Johnson was aware that none of this had seemed so scandalous or reprehensible when Alma spoke about it quietly and openly. Wearing a dress of navy blue silk with a fur cape about her shoulders and speaking in her rich low voice, she had appeared as dignified as it were possible for a woman to do under the circumstances and Croom-Johnson knew that she had impressed the jury.

He questioned her about the state of her husband's finances. Wasn't her husband retired and living largely, if not wholly, on his means, he asked her. And Alma said, yes, but she understood he was very well off. Had the question of money between you and your husband been a matter about which you had differences of opinion in the past, Croom-Johnson wondered. "Oh, yes," Alma said.

"Am I putting it fairly when I suggest that you were in the habit of deceiving your husband in order to get what you regarded as sufficient money for your needs?"

"Absolutely," Alma replied with disconcerting directness.

Did she know that her husband's securities had fallen considerably in value, he asked.

"No. He was always talking like that; so it was the case of the lamb crying wolf; if it was so one would not have believed him."

Alma was distinctly vague about the state of her husband's finances and Croom-Johnson had no better luck when he questioned her about her own. How much money did her husband give her in the course of a year, he inquired. "Oh, I really could not tell you that," Alma replied sounding surprised that anyone could seriously ask her such a question.

"Considerable sums in the course of a year?" Croom-Johnson persisted. And again Alma could not answer.

"Hundreds?"

"I suppose so," Alma helpfully agreed.

Croom-Johnson tried another tack. Out of her household account she had paid the servants' wages. Yes, Alma agreed, all the household expenses and all the clothing for her husband and the children and their schooling. "It was too much; that is why I was always overdrawn."

"About how much a year did he give you?" Croom-Johnson asked. And Alma remembered now that it was about fifty pounds a month but she was always overdrawn and had to ask for more.

"Fifty pounds a month would be about six hundred pounds a year," Croom-Johnson said.

"I see," Alma said with interest as if it was a new piece of information for her. With the additional money she had asked for that would be something over one thousand pounds a year, Croom-Johnson prompted. "Yes, I daresay," Alma answered offhandedly. The prosecution's suggestion that Alma had asked for £250 for the purposes of financing the "orgy" in London, had been badly undermined by Alma's answers which must have proved to the jury that finances were not her forte and that her reason for asking for the money was simply to balance her household accounts.

Croom-Johnson dropped the subject and began to quiz her about her intimacy with Stoner, knowing that he could bring out facts which would shock the jury and might lead them to believe that she was capable of anything.

"You have told us that on Sunday night Stoner came into your bedroom and got into bed with you?"

"Yes."

"Was that something that happened frequently?"

"Oh, always."

"Always? Were you fond of your little boy John?"

"I love both my children."

"Were you fond of John."

"Naturally."

"Did John sleep in the same room?"

"Yes, but in another bed at the other side of the room," Alma said as she caught the drift of Croom-Johnson's questions.

"It is not a very large room?"

"No, but little John was always asleep."

"Are you suggesting to the members of the jury that you, a mother fond of her little boy of six, were permitting this man to come into this bedroom with you, in the same room where your little innocent child was asleep?"

"I did not consider that was dreadful; I did not consider it an intrigue with Stoner," Alma protested weakly. Alma stood convicted of a complete lack of taste. The only thing that could be said in her favour was that John did indeed seem to be a sound sleeper. In no witness's version of the events of the night of March 24th, when the house was full of policemen wandering in and out of the bedroom, is there any mention of John who seems to have slept through the whole thing.

Croom-Johnson next turned to Alma's alleged loss of memory. She remembered calling for Irene, Alma said. She remembered pouring herself a glass of whisky and being sick. But after that nothing. "Are you telling the members of the jury that from the time practically that you were sick and poured yourself a glass of whisky your memory does not serve you at all?" he challenged her.

She remembered, she said, placing a towel around her husband's head. She remembered rubbing his cold hands, she remembered trying to get his false teeth back in so that he could talk to her and tell her what had happened. And that was all, except for little John's face at the door the next day when she was being taken away.

"Do you recollect Dr. O'Donnell coming?"

"I cannot," Alma said and although Alma admitted that the doctor was a person whose presence should have soothed her rather than excited her, she insisted that she had tried to remember but it was all a complete blank. Strangely, Croom-Johnson did not refer to a statement she had given on the 28th of March in which she said she remembered both Dr. O'Donnell and Mr. Rooke arriving, Mr. Rooke telling her to keep out of the way, and later Dr. O'Donnell returning to the house and giving her something to make her sleep. Apparently Alma's loss of memory was most conveniently retrogressive.

In spite of repeated attempts by Croom-Johnson to trap her into an admission that she remembered more than she had previously testified, she remained consistent. She remembered none of the policemen, none of the statements attributed to her. Shown her signature in the notebook in which Carter had recorded her statement, she shook her head, she couldn't remember, "It's all double-dutch to me."

In his re-examination of the witness, O'Connor, Alma's counsel returned to the subject of Alma's confessions. In previous testimony a parade of police witnesses had clung to the official version of events. Yes, they had admitted, Alma had been drinking but she had not been drunk, at least not incapably drunk. Inspector Carter had assured the jury that when he had taken a statement from Alma on the morning after the attack she had appeared normal and had spoken clearly and deliberately. In Alma's favour was the testimony of Dr. O'Donnell who had stated that in his opinion Alma had been very intoxicated and had not been in a fit condition to make any statements. But Dr. O'Donnell was one witness who had not impressed the jury favourably. He had admitted that in response to Alma's entreaties he had asked Stoner what drugs, if any, he was in the habit of using and upon being told by Stoner that he was addicted to cocaine he had simply advised him that cocaine was a dangerous drug and left it at that. He had made no attempt to discover how much of the substance Stoner used or where he purchased it. His inaction in the face of what he admitted could be a serious medical problem cast a pall of doubt over his competency and his reliability as a witness.

That Alma had said she had delivered the blows that killed Rattenbury could not be denied. Whether or not she had been mentally competent when she confessed to the crime remained in doubt. O'Connor knew that even if they accepted his assertion that Alma had been hopelessly drunk when she had said "I did it" the jurors would ask themselves why she would confess to such an act without being guilty of at least complicity. Now he hoped to provide the answer — Alma had confessed to protect Stoner.

"When Stoner told you this story, what did you desire to do as regards to Stoner?" he asked.

"I thought he was frightened at what he had done because he had hurt Mr. Rattenbury. I think he just sort of thought he had hurt him bad enough to stop him going to Bridport, and when I said, 'I will go and see him', then he said, 'No you must not.' He said, 'The sight will upset you' and I thought all I had to do was to fix Ratz up and that would make him all right."

"When you saw your husband, did you make any decision as to what you were going to do regarding Stoner?"

"No, he was worse than what I anticipated." Alma was missing the point. The answer O'Connor wanted was that she had decided to protect Stoner, for only this explanation would satisfy the jury that her drunken confessions had not been prompted by guilt.

"Did you decide to do anything as regards Stoner?" he asked again, but still Alma did not see what he was getting at. "No, my mind went — awful, dreadful," she said.

O'Connor adopted a new tactic, attempting to prove that the statements Alma had made were in themselves full of irrational sentences. Yes, Alma said, she had played cards with her husband that night, the first part of her confession was true.

" 'He dared me to kill him as he wanted to die'." O'Connor read. "Had he ever dared you to kill him?" and Alma answered that Ratz had often mentioned suicide. "Did he dare you to kill him?" O'Connor persisted. "No, not to my knowledge," Alma said, "except that he had talked of suicide and the gas oven and things like that; that would be a dare. That is why I had that quarrel that night. I was getting fed up."

"Very well," O'Connor said and he must have cursed his client's obtuseness for instead of simply declaring her statements to be ridicu-

173

lous Alma seemed determined to make sense out of them. " 'I picked up the mallet'," he said reading the next sentence in Alma's signed statement. "Do you have mallets lying about in the drawing room?"

"I could not have picked it up; it would have been an impossibility to pick up a mallet that was not there." Alma was finally on the right track.

O'Connor continued reading Alma's statement, "He then said, 'You have not guts enough to do it'. I then hit him with the mallet" and asked, "Did you hear the police sergeant say there was no sign of a struggle on the part of Mr. Rattenbury?"

"Yes," Alma said, she had heard that the blow was struck from behind.

O'Connor turned to other absurdities which had appeared in some of the other statements Alma had made that night. In one she had accused Rattenbury's son. And Alma said that she had known him to be in Canada on the night of the attack. Inspector Mills had testified that Alma had asked him if he had told the coroner about Ratz' injuries. "Did you imagine that these important officials were available at half past three in the morning," O'Connor asked and Alma answered, "No, it is too absurd." Constable Bagwell claimed that Alma had attempted to bribe him. "Has it ever crossed your mind that you might get off on a charge of unlawfully wounding by giving the police ten pounds?" "No," Alma said, "it is all absurd," and O'Connor hoped that the jury would agree with her.

Stoner's defence was not well served by the expert medical witnesses called to the stand by Casswell.

Dr. Lionel Weatherly, who said he had been a medical man for sixty-two years, listed a string of impressive credentials which included past-presidency of the Society of Mental and Nervous Diseases. Dr. Weatherly had examined Stoner ten days after his arrest. He had noted that Stoner's pupils were dilated and did not react to light and such physical symptoms were undoubtedly consistent with the taking of cocaine, he said. And Stoner had described fairly, feasibly and accurately the effects of taking a dose of cocaine and had described an unusual hallucination — the sensation of a rash under the skin, a rash that seemed to move about — that was, in the doctor's opinion a definite symptom of cocaine.

Cocaine might affect the emotions and trigger an insane suspicious jealousy, he said. Addicts experienced very definite delusions of persecution which explained Stoner's carrying a dagger about with him,

Dr. Weatherley testified. According to the doctor, Stoner's belief that Alma and Rattenbury had had intercourse behind the closed bedroom door was entirely an hallucination of hearing.

Stoner's behaviour on the night of the attack, his sudden and violent reaction to the proposed trip to Bridport, his waving a revolver in Alma's face and his threatening to kill her were consistent, the doctor maintained, with his having taken a dose of cocaine that afternoon.

And Mr. Justice Humphreys inquired from the bench, "Are they also consistent with his being very angry and very jealous of his mistress?" To which Dr. Weatherly who was several more years removed from the passions of youth than was Justice Humphreys answered firmly, "I doubt it."

Dr. Weatherly was in his eighties, an elderly gentleman who was enjoying the spotlight. In all his years as a doctor he had treated only three cases of cocaine addiction. And after Crown counsel's careful interrogation, it became clear that in his excitement at having been presented with what appeared to be a classic case of cocaineism he had allowed his judgment to become impaired and had accepted Stoner's story with unprofessional alacrity.

Dr. Robert Gillespie, who followed him to the witness box, was more cautious than Dr. Weatherly had been. It was extremely difficult to tell whether a person was an addict, he said. Rather than physical symptoms, one looked for sudden mood changes, elation coupled with mental and physical activity followed by lethargy and depression. In extreme cases an addict might lose weight and begin to hallucinate. Although he too testified that Stoner's actions had been consistent with the taking of cocaine, Dr. Gillespie admitted that they might just as well have been the result of passionate jealousy.

In defending Stoner, Casswell must have known he was faced with an almost impossible task. The jury, if they were typical of the general public, felt more sympathy for Stoner than they did for Alma. But Alma had taken the stand and although she may have been reluctant to do so, she had thrown the blame on Stoner. She had impressed the jury. Stoner did not testify. His defence depended entirely on Casswell's ability to convince the jury that his client had been driven near madness by cocaine. It was a feeble defence and Casswell must have had little hope of winning an acquittal.

Stoner had described the cocaine he had taken as being brownish in colour with darker flecks and even his staunchest defender, Dr. Weatherly, had been forced to admit that cocaine, evenly grossly adulterated cocaine, was pure, snowy white. The sensation Stoner had described as a moving rash under the skin was a not unknown symptom of prolonged and intensive cocaine use. Usually described as the feeling that insects were crawling about under the skin, this sensation drove those afflicted to pull and tear at their skin opening running sores all over their bodies in their efforts to remove the cocaine bug. Stoner's description of this hallucination may have been original but no evidence was introduced to show that he had ever exhibited any of these characteristic lesions. And, the jury must have asked themselves, how could Stoner on his salary of £4 a month have supported an expensive habit.

The jurors reached their verdict with little dissension or debate. Recessing for only forty-seven minutes they filed back to their places and Stoner and Alma listened tense and immobile as the Clerk of the Court asked, "Do you find the prisoner, Alma Victoria Rattenbury, guilty or not guilty of murder?"

"Not guilty." Alma heard the verdict with composure giving no outward sign of emotion.

"Do you find the prisoner George Percy Stoner, guilty or not guilty of murder?"

"Guilty," the foreman said, "but we should like to add a rider to that, we recommend him to mercy." Alma staggered and seemed about to collapse. Those sitting near the dock thought they heard a choked "Oh, no!" before she was helped from the dock and supported out of the courtroom by a wardress.

Stoner moved to the centre of the dock and heard the judge deliver formal sentence of death. It was Friday, May 31st.

13

Suicide and Reprieve

At 8:30 on the evening of June 4th William Mitchell was walking along a lonely path near the outskirts of Christchurch, a town lying on the coast a few miles east of Bournemouth. Employed by a local dairyman, he was distracted from his task of rounding up stray heifers by the sight of a woman sitting alone on the riverbank near the arched railway bridge which carried the London to Bournemouth train over the River Avon.

It was unusual to see anyone in this remote spot which could only be reached with some difficulty either by crossing a swampy meadow, clambering up the steep railway embankment and following the tracks across the bridge to the other side, or by walking through several hundred yards of wet marshland thick with reeds and rushes. His curiosity aroused, Mitchell made his way up the embankment to the tracks, intending to cross the bridge to get a better look at the woman who sat quite still and alone smoking a cigarette amid the wild irises and buttercups of the riverbank.

As he approached he saw her stand and shed a short fur coat. His interest turning to astonishment he watched as she strode, her arms swinging purposefully, to the water's edge. She seemed to bend into a crouching position and then topple into the water.

Now really alarmed, Mitchell ran to the spot and wading into the water tried to catch hold of the woman's feet. But she had floated out too far and Mitchell who was unable to swim couldn't reach her. He threw himself up the bank and grabbing the woman's coat swung it out to her.

"Catch hold of this," he yelled but the woman did not respond. Instead she seemed to thrust herself backwards and Mitchell saw with mounting horror that the water around her body was red.

He raced for help. Arriving at the nearest cottage he told its occupant, James Penney, about what he had seen and while Penney hurried to the scene, Mitchell made for the police station on a borrowed bicycle.

By the time the police arrived, Penney had succeeded in getting the woman ashore. She was dead, her left breast lacerated by ugly knife wounds. The police examined her few belongings left behind on the riverbank; a tin of cigarettes, a hat and a fur coat, a fountain pen, a brown paper bag containing an empty dagger sheath and a handbag. Rummaging through her purse hoping for some clue as to her identity, they found a strange assortment of scribbled letters. One dated June 3rd read:

If only I thought it would help Stoner I would stay on, but it has been pointed out to me all too vividly I cannot help him. That is my death sentence.

The other letters were written on June 4th.

I want to make it perfectly clear that no one is responsible for what action I may take regarding my life.

I quite made up my mind at Holloway to finish things should Stoner ... and it would only be a matter of time and opportunity.

Every night and minute is only prolonging the appalling agony of my mind.

Eight o'clock. After so much walking I have got here. Oh, to see the swans and spring flowers.

And how singular I should have chosen the spot Stoner said he nearly jumped out of the train once at.

It was not intentional my coming here. I tossed a coin, like Stoner always did, and it came down Christchurch.

It is beautiful here. What a lovely world we are in. It must be easier to be hanged than to have to do the job oneself, especially in these circumstances of being watched all the while. Pray God nothing stops me tonight.

I tried this morning to throw myself under a train at Oxford Circus. Too many people about. Then a bus. Still too many people about. One must be bold to do a thing like this.

It is beautiful here and I am alone. Thank God for peace at last.[1]

The dead woman was Alma Victoria Rattenbury. They placed her body on a stretcher, carried it across the bridge and over the fields to a waiting ambulance at Stony Lane and then as Alma's body was whisked away to the mortuary at Fair Mile House, the police prepared to begin their investigation into her last five days.

The public's last glimpse of Alma had been on Friday, May 31st when she had been ushered out of the Old Bailey by the barrister's entrance to avoid the crowds gathered outside the main entrance hoping to catch sight of her.

Dixie Dean, a young photographer with the *Daily Mirror*, guessing she would take this route, pursued her to the door of the taxi waiting to speed her away to a nursing home. Dean, who would have been content with a picture, couldn't believe his good fortune when Alma invited him to accompany her. Together they rode to a nursing home in Cleveland Gardens, Bayswater, where Dixie had another surprise.

Would he wait while she got herself settled and then come up to her room, Alma asked.

Dean readily agreed and later found himself the rather embarrassed witness to Alma's sorrow as she sat propped up in bed holding a picture of Stoner, bewailing the fate of her "darling boy" and asking Dean to photograph her as she lovingly kissed the portrait she held in her hand.[2]

Bordering on hysteria, Alma had been in no state to answer Dean's questions and the next day, Saturday, June 1st she seemed little improved.

On Saturday she had had at least two visitors; Ratz' nephew Keith Jones who had remained loyally concerned throughout the trial and who had arranged for an acquaintance of his, a Dr. Bathurst of Harley Street, to care for her and Irene Riggs who had arrived with an armful of pink roses. To Irene Alma had spoken of her intention to commit suicide and had begun planning her funeral telling Irene she wanted to be buried in a pink coffin wearing a pink nightgown. As Alma might have guessed Irene had become greatly distressed and finally the matron of the nursing home had thought it wise to put an end to their tearful meeting.

Alma spent her moments alone reading newspaper accounts of the trial, re-living her testimony over and over again, worrying over each answer she had given. She thought of no one else but Stoner and the evidence she had given against him. She wrote to him at Pentonville Prison and then read the following day that he had been moved to another prison. Grief stricken, sure that he would not receive her letter, she begged the matron to telephone the prison. But by the time she learned that Stoner was still being held at Pentonville, she had decided that a letter wasn't enough. She had to see him. She begged the doctor and the matron to help her saying, "If I had just one word with him, even if I just had one look at his face again, he would understand. I must see him once again ... Can't something be done?"[3]

Dr. Bathurst, fearing for her sanity, petitioned the governor of the prison asking that Alma be allowed to see Stoner. He received a "most charming and sympathetic letter" in reply, but it arrived too late. By the time the visit had been arranged Alma was dead.

On the morning of Monday, June 3rd the matron had noticed a change in Alma and feeling the time was ripe she suggested her standard remedy for feminine depression, a full beauty treatment. As she had suspected, it worked wonders. A hairdresser had waved Alma's hair and a manicurist had come to do her hands. Her face had been carefully made up and the matron had been gratified to note that Alma was like a new woman.

That afternoon Alma had written to her Bournemouth solicitor, Lewis Manning, instructing him to spare no expense in an effort to win an appeal or a reprieve for Stoner. Money was no object she assured him, convinced that her notoriety would bring her songs at least a brief burst of popularity.

"Now is the time for the rest of my songs to be published; they'll sell like hot cakes now," she said, showing she had gained a nicely cynical hold on reality.

Dr. Bathurst, who visited Alma daily, had also noticed a definite improvement when he called at the nursing home at 5 o'clock that same afternoon. To him she had seemed to be infinitely better. Whereas before she had been highly nervous and hysterical, that afternoon she had spoken to him quite calmly and seemed to have regained full control of herself. She had not objected when he told her that he wanted her to stay in the nursing home at least a month. She seemed anxious to recover her health and had spoken at length about her future plans which centred obsessively on how best she could help Stoner.

Dr. Bathurst had left that afternoon feeling, for the first time, optimistic about Alma's chances for recovery. He had been astounded when he received an excited telephone call from the matron late that same night telling him that Alma had left the nursing home. Totally mystified, he was sure that something must have happened to make Alma change her plans and as it turned out he was quite right.

In the first days after the trial Alma had spoken wildly of suicide. She had appeared so distraught and hysterical that no one had been hopeful that she would ever regain the ability to face the future rationally. But in the soothing atmosphere of the nursing home, fussed over by a solicitous matron, she had managed to calm herself and as her mind cleared she had realized that the best way of relieving her feelings of guilt for having testified against him was to devote herself to procuring Stoner's freedom. When she had spoken to the doctor that afternoon she had been sure that she would be able to help him and she had begun to view the future with optimism. But later that same day she had written, "If only I thought it would help Stoner I would stay on, but it has been pointed out to me all too vividly that I cannot help him."

Later that evening, after the doctor had returned home well satisfied with Alma's progress, she had had another visitor and there can be little doubt that this was the person who pointed out so vividly that there was nothing Alma could do to save Stoner.

Known only to the matron as a friend of Mrs. Rattenbury's, the woman had sat talking for several hours. At about 9:30 the matron remembered that the evening post had arrived and sorting through it found several letters for Alma. She had taken them up to her room and had been surprised to find Alma and her friend still engaged in what seemed to be a very serious conversation.

About a half an hour later the woman had come downstairs and said, "She's going."

Hardly able to take this in the matron had replied, "No she's not. She can't be. She's going to sleep for the night."

"She's going and no one can stop her," the woman said.

The matron remonstrated. Alma was in a very delicate state of health. It would be foolish, if not dangerous, for her to go.

Alma's mind was made up and nothing would stop her, the woman said. She realized that she was taking a terrible responsibility, she continued, but she would arrange for a nurse to be with Alma at all times. She had been vague about where she and Alma planned to go, saying only that perhaps they would take a flat together, or failing that take a room at an hotel.

The matron pronounced the plan ridiculous and went upstairs to talk to Alma. She found her out of bed, dressed, her packing almost finished. She tried to reason with her. It was late, too late to try to find a flat, too late to easily find an hotel room.

"Just go back to bed tonight and have a long sleep," she coaxed. "You'll feel much better in the morning. Then you can move in comfort."⁵

But Alma, her mind made up, had been adamant, crossly pointing out that no one could keep her there against her will.

Moments later Alma and the woman had driven away from the nursing home in a private car. They were not together for long. Later that night, when Alma arrived at the door of the Elizabeth Fullcher nursing home on Devonshire road she was alone.

At about 2:30 the next afternoon, she had borrowed £2 from one of the nurses saying that she was going out for a while and promising to return by nine o'clock that night. Instead she had used the money to buy a knife, caught a train to the south coast and stabbed herself to death in a lonely spot on the banks of the Avon.

At the coroner's inquest into her death held in Christchurch on the 7th of June, Dr. Geoffrey Jones related the results of his post mortem examination. He had discovered six stab wounds in the left breast. Five had been large wounds passing inwards and downwards between the ribs. Judging by the shape and direction of the wounds, the doctor concluded that they had been self-inflicted by a sharp instrument held in the right hand. The heart had been punctured three times. Death had been almost instantaneous, in fact Alma had probably died before entering the water.

No attempt was made to identify the woman who had called on Alma the night before her death nor was Mrs. Maude McClellan, the matron of the Elizabeth Fullcher nursing home, asked if prior arrangements had been made for Alma's admittance.

Calling Alma's suicide notes neurotic statements the coroner read them into the record and then announced his verdict. "The deceased not being of sound mind did kill herself."

Alma was buried in the Wimbourne Road cemetery in Bournemouth just a few steps away from the unmarked grave of her husband, Francis Mawson Rattenbury.

Long before the funeral was due to take place hundreds of people gathered at the cemetery where they chatted contentedly, leaning against headstones as they waited for the arrival of Alma's coffin. When the funeral began the crowd, by then numbering over three thousand, surged toward the chapel eager to be admitted to the service. Alma's burial had to be delayed while the handful of mourners waited for the arrival of the Bournemouth police who had been called in to clear a path through the mob from the chapel to the gravesite.

Reverend Freeman of St. Peter's church in Bournemouth who conducted the service was disgusted by the behaviour he witnessed that day. He found the crowd of curiosity seekers to be entirely without restraint.

"It would have made me happier," he said, "if there had been some show of respect or sorrow, but it was a gathering without devotion and without sympathy, and only moved apparently by morbid curiosity."[6]

Curious sightseers pushed and jostled each other trying to get a better look and Irene Riggs, supported by her father, sobbed uncontrollably as Alma's coffin was slowly lowered into the grave lined with her favourite pink and mauve flowers.

Going almost unnoticed as he mingled among the crowd was a quiet little man collecting signatures on a petition form. He was campaigning for the reprieve of George Percy Stoner.

The campaign for Stoner's reprieve had begun only hours after Justice Humphreys had passed sentence of death. With Stoner's execution scheduled for June 18th, the members of the small committee headed by F. W. Thistleton, a Bournemouth accountant, had known that they had little time to lose. They sought a commutation of the death sentence to one of life imprisonment bringing with it the possibility that Stoner might sometime in the future be released. Their appeal for clemency was based on nine points which included every possible argument the committee could muster to support their plea for mercy.

George Percy Stoner is a boy.
He was subjected to undue influence.
He was a victim of drugs.
He was probably under their influence when the crime was committed.
He showed by his behaviour at the trial that he was capable of better things.
His execution, while strictly legal, benefits the community in no respect.
He might, if reprieved, turn out to be a successful member of society, and be an asset to the state.
He was temporarily insane when the crime was committed, though not legally so.
He might have been the son of any of us.[7]

The Committee had ordered the printing of 2,000 petition forms, enough for 144,000 signatures, and was preparing for a door-to-door canvas of the Bournemouth area when newspapers, their grim headlines reading "Mrs. Rattenbury Found Dead," hit the streets. Overnight a local campaign became a national *cause célèbre*.

Alma's suicide was a bonanza to the national press. Reporters recounted with relish the events of the trial long after interest in the case would normally have waned. Sifting through the details of her early life, they created of her an artistic and tragic heroine; a brilliant and talented musician and composer whose first love was her art; a gay young wife plunged into heartbreaking widowhood by the untimely death of her gallant officer-husband on the battlefields of France; a bereaved young widow searching for her husband's grave while serving with devotion and dedication as a war nurse. One article which appeared in the *Daily Mirror* surrounded by a heavy black border was particularly maudlin.

Alma had been driven to suicide by utter hopelessness convinced that nothing she could do would help Stoner. If it had occurred to her that her death might save him, she would not have slipped away to an isolated spot where her body might not have been found for days. Now sympathy felt for her was directed to Stoner. No longer held back by the unpalatable prospect of a freed Stoner rushing into the arms of his waiting mistress, volunteers flocked to Thistleton's office. The Mayor of Bournemouth publicly signed the petition as did several aldermen. From Westminster the Member of Parliament for East Dorset, G. R. Hall Caine, recognizing a popular cause when he saw one, pledged his support and offered to deliver the petition to the Home Secretary personally. Bournemouth clergymen announced from their pulpits that petition forms would be posted in their churches and encouraged their parishioners to sign. Throughout the city shopkeepers tacked the petition on their doors, among them Mrs. Maude Price, the owner of Villa Madeira, who prominently displayed a form outside her tobacconist's shop on the Old Christchurch road.

Hundreds of vacationers, who had come to enjoy the sun and sand of Bournemouth during the spring Bank Holiday, patiently queued at the temporary booths erected along the seafront waiting to add their names to the petition. One young man who had spent all his holiday Monday on the Bournemouth Pier collecting over 1,000 signatures typified the heady dedication of all the volunteers when

FUNNY STORY FOR TO-DAY!

So they are burying Mrs. Rattenbury to-day.
I was in a lift when I heard she'd killed herself. The liftman told me and laughed. His laughing shocked me.

I can see most jokes, but this one got by me. I couldn't get that last journey of hers out of my head — the journey down to the Sunny South Coast.

* * *

The cruel, monstrous apparatus of publicity had done its best.

The poor, half-crazed woman (are you smiling?) wanted to get away from it all.

The only point was, that there wasn't anywhere to get away to (the liftman would have laughed at this).

Well, as you know, she got to Bournemouth all right. God knows what happened there.

Then on to Christchurch.

At this stage a knife comes into the picture.

"A long thin knife," says one paper; "a stiletto," "a dagger," "a bread knife," "a sort of bowie knife" — the horrible, gloating chorus is a bit out of harmony. (Funny story, eh?)

* * *

Then out into the quiet fields.

Now she sits and the pathetic last letters are scrawled down. Is she thinking of Stoner? — What is he doing? How are they treating him?

What'll he say when he hears of this . . .

* * *

You know the rest.

The clumsy stabbing, and the attempted drowning just to make sure.

Make sure of what?

To make sure of getting away, not from the law that says she's an innocent woman, but from you and me. And millions like us.

* * *

And, of course, from the liftman who laughed.

he said at the end of a long day, "I am aching all over but it is in a good cause."

The committee worked late every night answering inquiries from all parts of the country. From Liverpool an Alderman Walker called asking for 100 petition forms. From Brighton, from Swansea, from London, from Manchester came a flood of telephone calls and telegrams asking for all the forms the committee could spare. From Weymouth a writer called the committee pledging to collect 5,000 signatures in his area and from Altrincham the secretary of a political club called asking for forms and voicing the common opinion when he told the committee, "I am convinced the lad was led astray."

On June 11, a week before Stoner's execution was scheduled to take place, E. W. Marshall Harvey, Stoner's Bournemouth solicitor lodged a notice of appeal on his behalf. Although heartened by this news, the volunteers thought it best to be prudent and proceed according to their original schedule.

Shortly before 11 o'clock on the morning of June 14 a car drew up outside the Home Office. Out stepped three men; two members of Parliament, Hall Caine and Sir Henry Page Croft and the campaign organizer, F. W. Thistleton. They struggled up the steps carrying four brown paper packages each labelled "Stoner Petition." Sir John Simon, the Home Secretary, was discreetly absent enjoying a "brief respite from his official duties." And so the three presented the petition to his private secretary and left telling the press that the signatures numbered over 305,000.

And more petitions were arriving by the hour. Thirteen thousand signatures had arrived by morning post and the committee was still receiving requests for petition forms. Late the night before an elderly woman had travelled to Bournemouth from her home in London hoping to deliver her petition forms before the deadline. A schoolboy had arrived at Thistleton's office that morning with 173 signatures he had collected himself.

The pressure on the Home Secretary was mounting daily and he cannot have been sorry that he could delay any decision until after the hearing of Stoner's appeal.

*   *   *

Midsummer's Day brought with it clear bright skies and the highest temperatures of the year. In Bournemouth where the mercury hovered near 90 degrees holiday makers sought relief from the heat, lolling idly at the water's edge or sipping iced drinks beneath the wide trees of the pleasure grounds. Some stoical Bournemouth businessmen went about in stiff collars and bowler hats, but most loosened their ties, shed their jackets and then their vests as the temperature continued to climb.

In London people grumbled through the hottest day recorded since 1878. The sun blazed down on Mrs. Violet Van der Elst and her little band of sandwichmen as they gathered outside the Court of Criminal Appeal to continue their fight against capital punishment. "STONER MUST BE REPRIEVED," "STOP THE LAW KILLING THIS BOY," "STOP ILLEGAL KILLING," "END CAPITAL PUNISHMENT" their placards read as they paraded up and down outside the court where Stoner's application for a new trial would be heard.

Despite the stuffy heat of the courtroom, Stoner's face was white with tension as he took his place in the dock accompanied by three warders. He wore his only good clothes, the grey suit which Alma had bought for him at Harrod's and which he had worn throughout the trial. Not daring to look at the three judges, he let his eyes wander about the courtroom. He seemed to be searching for a familiar face among the throng of spectators fidgeting uncomfortably in the oppressive heat of the public gallery.

Calling Rattenbury's murder a clumsy crime, Casswell who had defended Stoner at the Old Bailey began his arguments. Carefully and slowly he detailed the evidence presented at the trial. Not even the smallest detail escaped his attention as he plodded on. Twice he was interrupted by the Lord Chief Justice who asked with sweaty impatience, "What is the proposition in law that you are putting forward? It may be my fault but I do not understand the relevancy of these observations."

Casswell answered that the point he was trying to make was there ought to have been separate trials, that joint trials had presented a serious possibility of a miscarriage of justice. And then inexorably he returned to a blow by blow account of the evidence presented at the Old Bailey.

Finally an exasperated Chief Justice interrupted again.

"Does it appear to you that all this is so interesting that it is our duty to hear it twice?"

And Casswell apologized. He was not aware that the justices were familiar with the evidence, he said.

To which the Chief Justice replied with no small amount of sarcasm, "We have spent a pleasant weekend, you know, reading this sort of thing. Please remember we know the evidence on this case."

Casswell, finally taking the hint, made an effort to summarize. He repeated his contention that separate trials should have been granted. Stoner had not known, Casswell said, that Alma would take the stand and throw the blame on him. He had been unwilling to testify as he had not wanted to implicate Alma. If separate trials had been held, Alma would have been tried first as her name appeared first on the indictment. Then Stoner at his own trial would have felt free to tell his side of the story knowing that nothing he said could harm Alma.

After a short consultation, the Lord Chief Justice put forward the court's point of view. The defence had not argued that there had been insufficient evidence to convict Stoner. Stoner's appeal had been based solely on the contention that separate trials should have been ordered. The court was being asked to believe that Justice Humphreys with all the evidence before him had erred in his decision to let joint trials proceed and "Anyone who would believe that would believe anything," the Chief Justice scolded.

He found Stoner's request to testify now that Mrs. Rattenbury was dead "almost sinister" and he refused Stoner's application to take the stand and "swear what he would not swear, and was not prepared to swear while she was alive."

Calling the case sordid and squalid, the Chief Justice concluded, "The fact, if it be a fact, that a lad of good character was corrupted by an abandoned woman old enough to be his mother raises no question of law that can be employed as a ground of appeal. The court has neither the power, nor the inclination, to alter the law as regard to that. The case is dismissed."[8]

Stoner pale and dazed remained standing in the dock seemingly unaware that his appeal was over until a warder touched him on the shoulder and led him through the curtained doorway behind the dock to the stairway leading to the cells below.

Now his only hope lay with Sir John Simon. The jury in finding Stoner guilty had recommended mercy. The Home Office had received nearly 350,000 signatures pleading for Stoner's reprieve. There was really little question as to what the Home Secretary's decision would be.

On Tuesday, June 25, three months and one day since the murder of Francis Mawson Rattenbury, he announced his decision. Stoner would not hang, his sentence was commuted to one of penal servitude for life.

Notes

CHAPTER ONE

1 Reverend Gervase Smith, D.D. "Memorial Sketch" *The John Rattenbury Memorials*, (ed.) Reverend H. Owen Rattenbury, T. Woolmer, London, 1884.

2 *Ibid.*

3 *Ibid.*

4 Reverend H. Owen Rattenbury, *op. cit.*

5 Obituary Notice, *Minutes of Conference 1904*, Wesleyan Methodist Book-Room, London, 1904.

6 Reverend H. Owen Rattenbury, *op. cit.*

7 John Rattenbury, *Memoirs of a Smuggler, compiled from his Diary and Journal: containing the principal events in the life of John Rattenbury, of Beer, Devonshire; Commonly called "The Rob Roy of the West,"* J. Harvey, London, 1837.

8 Later generations took a kinder view. Recalling this incident Harold Rattenbury (Mary Owen's grandson) adds ". . . it was long years before other copies of his diary became our proud possession again. Whether he was a direct ancestor or not may perhaps be left in doubt. We never wanted to check the matter up; but we certainly claimed him as our own." Harold B. Rattenbury, *China-Burma Vagabond*, Fred. Muller Ltd., London, 1946.

9 Saltaire, today, remains a model of a planned community. Although the suburbs of Bradford have crept up to and encircled Saltaire, the town planned by Lockwood and Mawson retains its distinct identity.

10 W. E. Forster, M.P., cited by A. H. Robinson, "Lockwood and Mawson. The story of a Great Partnership," *Bradford Bystander*, November 1971.

11 *Yorkshire Daily Observer*, December 12, 1904.

12 *Ibid.*

13 *Bradford Daily Telegraph*, December 10, 1904.

14 *The Architect*, January 17, 1890.

15 *The Architect*, May 8, 1891.

16 *The British Architect*, April 29, 1892.

17 *Daily Colonist*, March 17, 1893.

18 *The British Architect*, April 29, 1892.

CHAPTER TWO

1 Gastown's official name was Granville.

2 Douglas Sladen, On the Cars and Off ..., London, 1895 and W. G. Blaikie, Summer Suns in the Far West, London 1890, cited by Margaret Ormsby, *British Columbia: A History*, Macmillan, 1958.

3 Vancouver *Province*, May 3, 1975.

4 J. S. Helmcken, *Daily Colonist*, January 1, 1891.

5 *British Colonist*, July 20, 1859.

6 Dorothy Blakey Smith, *The Parliament Buildings: A Postscript to Parkinson*, May 1962, mss. (PABC).

7 *Daily Colonist*, March 16, 1893.

8 *Daily Colonist*, November 8, 1892.

9 Judges' Report (PABC).

10 *Vancouver Daily World*, March 18, 1893.

11 "Victoria the Capital City of British Columbia," The West Shore, Portland, June 1889 reprinted in *Victoria Historical Review*, Victoria Celebrations Society, 1962.

12 Rudyard Kipling, *From Sea to Sea and Other Sketches*, (copyright 1899, 1907) Mandalay Edition, Doubleday, 1927.

13 *Daily Colonist*, March 18, 1894.

14 *Seattle Post-Intelligencer*, March 14, 1894.

15 *Daily Colonist*, March 18, 1894.

16 F. M. Rattenbury, Report Upon Tenders for New Parliament Buildings, December 1, 1893 (PABC).

17 F. M. Rattenbury, notes assembled to defend his rejection of Koksilah stone, November 1894 (PABC).

18 Theodore Davie (Attorney General) to Adams, November 22, 1894 (PABC)

19 *Ibid.*

20 F. M. Rattenbury to G. B. Martin (C.C. of L. and W.) November 22, 1894 (PABC).

21 G. B. Martin to Adams, November 27, 1894 (PABC).

22 F. M. Rattenbury to G. B. Martin, December 3, 1894 (PABC).

23 Adams to G. B. Martin, December 10, 1894 (PABC).

24 *Daily Colonist*, October 11, 1898.

25 *Daily Colonist*, September 27, 1896.

CHAPTER THREE

1 F. M. Rattenbury, "Report upon Tenders ..., December 1, 1893 (PABC).

2 F. M. Rattenbury to G. B. Martin, November 13, 1895 (PABC).

3 F. M. Rattenbury to G. B. Martin, April 9, 1897 (PABC).

4 Extract from Minutes of meeting of Executive Council of May 19, 1897 (PABC).

5 F. M. Rattenbury to G. B. Martin September 19, 1897 (PABC).

6 W. S. Gore to F. M. Rattenbury, October 5, 1897 (PABC).

7 F. M. Rattenbury to W. S. Gore, October 5, 1897 (PABC).

8 W. S. Gore to G. B. Martin, October 7, 1897 (PABC).

9 F. M. Rattenbury to G. B. Martin, November 14, 1987 (PABC).

10 F. M. Rattenbury to G. B. Martin, December 26, 1897 (PABC).

11 *Daily Colonist*, February 10, 1898.

12 Although improved by the salmon net, the acoustic properties of the hall remained a problem, the members having "great difficulty" in hearing one another — prompting one member to suggest, "As the salmon net has not proved a success perhaps a fish trap might prove more effectual." *Daily Colonist*, May 1, 1903.

13 Rigan (Chief Caretaker) to J. E. Griffith (Public Works Engineer) May 27, 1913 (PABC).

CHAPTER FOUR

1 Edwin Tappan Adney, *The Klondike Stampede of 1897-1898*. Harper and Brothers, New York, 1900.

2 John Rattenbury's stay in B.C. and the Yukon was brief. His cousin, Methodist missionary Harold B. Rattenbury reports that he became "a steamship captain, running between Malaya and the China Coast. When I reached China in 1902 expecting to meet him, I was met by his widow instead, who took me to see his grave in the famous 'Happy Valley' in Hong Kong." Harold B. Rattenbury, *op. cit.*

3 F. M. Rattenbury to T. M. Potts, June 26, 1898 reprinted in the *Daily Colonist*, July 9, 1898.

4 Martha Louise Black, *My Ninety Years*, ed. Flo Whyard, Alaska Northwest Publishing Co., 1976.

5 From Skagway to Dawson. A Talk with Mr. T. [*sic.*] M. Rattenbury, *The Mining Record*, 1898.

6 Col. S. B. Steele, *Forty Years in Canada*. Dodd, Mead & Co., New York, 1915 (facsimilie edition Coles, Toronto, 1973).

CHAPTER FIVE

5 The fact that Princess Louise (wife of the Marquis of Lorne, Governor General of Canada) found the residence in any way heavenly seems to have been due to her husband's absence rather than any celestial pretensions enjoyed by Cary Castle. According to Elizabeth Longford (*Victoria R.I.*, London, 1964) "The Princess had suffered an appalling sleigh accident ... she was dragged by the hair for several minutes and lost one ear. To this shock the Queen attributed an aversion to her husband which had to be accepted as a sad but inescapable fact ..."

2 F. M. Rattenbury to W. C. Wells (C.C. of L. and W.) August 27, 1900 (PABC).

3 Thomas Hooper to W. C. Wells, August 28, 1900 (PABC).

4 F. M. Rattenbury to W. C. Wells, August 14, 1901 (PABC).

5 F. M. Rattenbury to W. C. Wells, September 11, 1901 (PABC).

6 *Daily Colonist*, April 21, 1903.

7 *Daily Colonist*, April 28, 1903. The day after Muir's letter was printed in full in the *Colonist* the following item appeared in the same paper. "To Build a Bungalow" "F. M. Rattenbury is calling for tenders up to Monday next for the erection of a bungalow residence on Belcher street." Muir's reaction to this piece of news was not recorded.

8 *Daily Colonist*, April 30, 1903.

9 Award in the matter of Drake vs. the Government of B.C., n.d. but probably December 1903 (PABC).

10 F. M. Rattenbury to R. Green (C.C. of L. and W.) December 17, 1903 (PABC).

11 At Sir Henri's suggestion Cary Castle was equipped with an unusual shower, a white marble enclosure with an array of pipes and taps which afforded a bather the luxury of being sprayed from all angles with temperature controlled jets of water. The design so impressed Rattenbury that he ordered a similar unit for his own home.

12 The hearing of the legislative committee were reported at length in the *Daily Colonist*, February 5-12, 1904.

13 Journals of the Legislative Assembly of the province of British Columbia, session 1903-1904.

CHAPTER SIX

1 Vancouver *Province*, February 19, 1901.

2 *Daily Colonist*, November 26, 1902.

3 *Daily Colonist*, May 23, 1903.

4 Rattenbury had calculated that an Inner Harbour completed according to his plans would have an immediate impact on every visitor no matter how well-travelled and blase he might be. And he was quite right. Rudyard Kipling visited Victoria for a second time shortly before the Empress was completed and later wrote, "There is a view, when the morning mists peel off the harbour where the steamers tie up, of the Houses of Parliament on one hand, and a huge hotel on the other, which as an example of cunningly-fitted-in waterfronts and facades is worth a very long journey." *op. cit.* A correspondent attached to the Prince of Wales' 1919 tour was equally impressed. "The bay goes squarely up to a promenade. Behind the stone balustrade is a great lawn, and beyond that ... is a finely decorated building, a fitted background to any romance, though it is actually an 'hotel deluxe' ... To the right is a rambling building, ornate and attractive, with low, decorated domes and outflung and rococo wings ... The whole of this square grouping of green grass and white buildings ... gives a glamorous air to the scene." W. Douglas Newton, *Westward with the Prince of Wales*, 1920.

5 *Daily Colonist*, May 23, 1903.

6 *Daily Colonist*, August 17, 1905.

7 *Daily Colonist*, November 3, 1906.

8 *Daily Colonist*, November 25, 1902.

CHAPTER SEVEN

1 Oliver to Newcombe, January 4, 1906 Newcombe Collection, (PABC).

2 *Victoria Times*, February 3, 1906.

3 Virtue's first hotel, the Mount Baker, had burned down two years earlier. The new hotel, known as the Oak Bay, designed by Rattenbury and erected in only 19 working days was later renamed the Old Charming Inn and survived until the 1960's when it was demolished to make way for an apartment building, the Rudyard Kipling.

4 Shortly after he purchased Mary Tod Island, Rattenbury agreed to lease it to Virtue for one dollar a year. When Virtue died 23 years later, in 1929, he had come to think of the island as his own and he bequeathed it to the municipality for use as a park. Rattenbury generously agreed to abide by Virtue's wishes.

5 *Victoria Illustrated*, 1891.

6 Margaret Williams, *Daily Colonist*, November 27, 1966.

7 *Victoria Times*, January 4, 1907.

8 *Daily Colonist*, January 24, 1907.

9 F. M. Rattenbury to W. Scott (Premier) September 5, 1906 (SAB).

10 Scott to Rattenbury November 1, 1906 (SAB).

11 Rattenbury to Scott November 5, 1906 (SAB).

12 Rattenbury to Scott October 31, 1907 (SAB).

13 Rattenburg [*sic*] to Scott November 15, 1907 (SAB).

CHAPTER EIGHT

1 *Daily Colonist*, August 8, 1905.

2 *Victoria Times*, June 10, 1908.

3 *Daily Colonist*, December 18, 1897.

4 *Victoria Times*, June 25, 1908.

5 *Daily Colonist*, January 14, 1913.

6 *Daily Colonist*, January 11, 1913.

7 *Daily Colonist*, January 11, 1913.

CHAPTER NINE

1 Cited by Phyllis Bowman, *Muskeg, Rocks and Rain*, 1973.

2 *Ibid.*

3 *Victoria Times*, February 22, 1918.

4 In the late 1880's Mrs. Baillie-Grohman stayed briefly at the Rae Street house while her husband visited the Kootenays to oversee his canal building scheme. "I could not very well stay at the Driard, as a good deal of drinking went on there in the evening," she wrote. ". . . we went for a short time to a little bungalow opposite the Cathedral, owned by a Mrs. Howard. She was a widow and a pretty daughter lived with her. They let rooms to bachelors. This place I found would not do very well either, as I felt the three or four men living there would rather have it to themselves." cited by J. K. Nesbitt, *Daily Colonist*, October 27, 1968.

5 Kyrle C. Symons, *That Amazing Institution*, n.d.

6 Ratz took a similar interest in his daughter's school, St. Margaret's. In 1911 he prepared plans for the new school buildings erected the following year on two acres of land at the corner of Fort and Fern streets.

7 Oak Bay Council refused to accept his resignation — suggesting instead that he take a three month leave of absence.

8 Colonel H. M. Urquart, History of the Sixteenth Battalion, cited Williams, *Daily Colonist*, November 27, 1966.

CHAPTER TEN

1 *Sunday Dispatch*, June 9, 1935.

2 Raymond Massey, *When I Was Young*, McClelland & Stewart, Toronto, 1976.

3 Miss C. Maclure, Interview, January 3, 1975.

4 *Sunday Dispatch*, June 9, 1935.

5 *Ibid.*

6 *Vancouver News Herald*, April 20, 1935.

7 *Daily Express*, June 6, 1935.

8 Miss C. Maclure.

9 Miss C. Maclure.

10 Miss C. Maclure.

11 Frank B. Rattenbury, Interview, August 1974.

12 Mrs. E. Burton (Mary Rattenbury), Interview, November 9, 1974.

13 F. M. Rattenbury to P. L. James, May 28, 1925 (PABC).

14 *Victoria Times*, June 11, 1925.

15 B. Gardom to P. L. James, June 11, 1925 (PABC).

16 Frank B. Rattenbury.

17 Mrs. E. Burton.

18 In 1935 the net value of his estate amounted to only $2,610.

19 *Vancouver Sun*, April 17, 1935.

CHAPTER ELEVEN

1 W. H. K. Wright, ed. *Some Account of the Barony and Town of Okehampton: Its Antiquities and Institutions. Including the Journals kept by Messrs. Rattenbury and Shebbeare, Gents. and Burgesses, from the 21, James I, to the death of William III*, Masland, 1889.

[2] *Sunday Dispatch*, June 9, 1935.

[3] F. Tennyson Jesse, ed. *Trial of Alma Victoria Rattenbury and George Percy Stoner*, Notable British Trials Series, William Hodge and Co. Ltd., London, 1935. (Unless otherwise indicated all other direct quotations in Chapter Eleven are taken from this transcript of the trial.)

[4] Bert Parsons, Interview, June 7, 1975.

[5] Eliot Crawshay-Williams, *Stay of Execution*, Jarrolds, London, 1933.

[6] *Dark-Haired Marie*, words by Edward Lockton, music by Lozanne Keith Prowse and Co. Ltd., London, 1932.

CHAPTER TWELVE

[1] F. Tennyson Jesse, *op. cit.* (All other direct quotations in Chapter Twelve are taken from this transcript of the trial).

CHAPTER THIRTEEN

[1] *The Western Morning News and Daily Gazette*, June 8, 1935.

[2] Dixie Dean, Interview, June 9, 1975.

[3] *Sunday Dispatch*, June 9, 1935.

[4] *Ibid.*

[5] *Ibid.*

[6] *Bournemouth Daily Echo*, June 10, 1935.

[7] *Bournemouth Daily Echo*, June 7, 1935.

[8] *Bournemouth Daily Echo*, June 24, 1935.

Bibliography

NEWSPAPERS

Bournemouth Daily Echo
Bradford Daily Telegraph
Daily Express
Daily Mirror
Sunday Dispatch
Western Morning News and Daily Gazette
Yorkshire Daily Observer

Vancouver Daily World
Vancouver News Herald
Vancouver *Province*
Vancouver Sun
Victoria *Daily Colonist*
Victoria Times

Seattle-Post Intelligencer

PERIODICALS

The Architect
The British Architect
The Illustrated London News

BOOKS AND PERIODICALS

Adney, Edwin Tappan. *The Klondike Stampede of 1897-1898.* Harper and Brothers, New York, 1900.

Berton, Pierre. *Klondike*. McClelland & Stewart, Toronto, 1963.

Bissley, Paul. *Early and Late Victorians. A History of the Union Club of British Columbia*. 1969.

Black, Martha Louise. *My Ninety Years*. ed. Flo Whyard. Alaska Northwest Publishing Co., Anchorage, 1976.

Bowman, Phyllis. *Muskeg, Rocks and Rain*, 1973.

Cotton, Peter. "The Stately Capitol," *RAIC Journal*, April 1958.

Curl, James Stevens. "A Victorian Model Town," *Country Life*, March 9, 1972.

Debrett's *Peerage*. London, Odhams, 1970.

Fieldhouse, Joseph. *Bradford*. Local History Series. London, 1972.

First Biennial Report of the State Capitol Commission of the State of Washington, December 31, 1894 (Washington State Library).

Hamilton, Walter J. *The Yukon Story*. Mitchell Press, 1967.

Jesse, F. Tennyson, ed. *Trial of Alma Victoria Rattenbury and George Percy Stoner*. Notable British Trials series. W. Hodge, London, 1935.

Kalman, Harold D. *The Railway Hotels and the Development of the Chateau Style in Canada*. University of Victoria Maltwood Museum Studies in Architectural History, 1968.

Large, R. G. *Prince Rupert — a Gateway to Alaska and the Pacific*. Mitchell Press, 1973.

Lower, J. A. "The Construction of the Grand Trunk Pacific Railway in British Columbia," *British Columbia Historical Quarterly*, July 1940.

Minute Book, Oak Bay Council Meetings, Oak Bay Municipal Hall.

Minutes of the Conference 1904, 1962 Wesleyan Methodist Book-Room, London.

Morgan, Murray. *One Man's Gold Rush*. J. J. Douglas Ltd., Vancouver, 1973.

Murdoch, George. *A History of the Municipality of Oak Bay from Prehistoric Times to the Present*. 1968. Oak Bay Municipal Hall (typescript).

Ormsby, Margaret. *British Columbia: A History*. Macmillan, 1958.

Public Schools Year Book, 1914.

Rattenbury, T. [*sic*] M., A Talk with. "From Skagway to Dawson." *The Mining Record*, 1898.

Rattenbury, Harold B. *China-Burma Vagabond*. Muller Ltd., 1946.

Rattenbury, H. Owen (Rev.), ed. *The John Rattenbury Memorials*, T. Woolmer, London, 1884.

Rattenbury, John. *Memoirs of a Smuggler, compiled from his Diary and Journals containing the principal events in the life of John Rattenbury, of Beer, Devonshire; commonly called the "Rob Roy of the West."* J. Harvey, London, 1837.

Robinson, Bart. *Banff Springs. The Story of a Hotel*. Summerthought, Banff, 1973.

Robinson, A. H. "Lockwood and Mawson. The Story of a Great Partnership," *Bradford Bystander*, September, November 1971.

Sampson, Mrs. Curtis. *Reminiscences of Bygone Days at Government House*. typescript (PABC).

Satterfield, Archie. *Chilkoot Pass. Then and Now*. Alaska Northwest Publishing Co., Anchorage, 1973.

Scholefield, E. O. S. and F. W. Howay. *British Columbia from earliest times to the present*. Vancouver, 1914.

Shiels, Bob. *Calgary*. The Calgary Herald, 1975.

Sproule, Albert F. *The Role of Patrick Burns in the Development of Western Canada*. M.A. Thesis, University of Alberta, 1962.

Steele, Colonel S. B. *Forty Years in Canada*. Dodd, Mead and Co., New York, 1915.

Symons, Kyrle. *That Amazing Institution*. 1948.

Victoria Historical Review, Victoria Celebrations Society, 1962.

Victoria Illustrated. The Colonist, 1891.

Wilson Edmund, ed. *Leeds Grammar School Admission Books 1820-1900*. Leeds, 1906.

Wright, W. H. K., ed. *Some Account of the Barony and Town of Okehampton, Its Antiquities and Institutions. Including the Journals kept by Messrs. Rattenbury and Shebbeare, Gents. and Burgesses, from the 21, James I, to the Death of William III*. Masland, 1889.

Index